THE

OFFICIAL
ANTIQUES
REVIEW 1997

THE LYLE OFFICIAL ANTIQUES ANTIQUES REVIEW 1997

A PERIGEE BOOK

Perigee Books
are published by
The Berkley Publishing Group
200 Madison Avenue
New York, New York 10016

ISBN: 0-399-52246-8
ISSN: 1089-1544

First Edition: December 1996

Cover design by Jack Ribik

Printed in the United States of America
2   3   4   5   6   7   8   9   10

This book is printed on acid-free paper
∞

INTRODUCTION

This year over 100,000 Antique Dealers and Collectors will make full and profitable use of their Lyle Antiques Price Guide. They know that only in this one volume will they find the widest possible variety of goods – illustrated, described and given a current market value to assist them to BUY RIGHT AND SELL RIGHT throughout the year of issue.

They know, too, that by building a collection of these immensely valuable volumes year by year, they will equip themselves with an unparalleled reference library of facts, figures and illustrations which, properly used, cannot fail to help them keep one step ahead of the market.

In its twenty seven years of publication, Lyle has gone from strength to strength and has become without doubt the pre-eminent book of reference for the antique trade throughout the world. Each of its fact filled pages is packed with precisely the kind of profitable information the professional Dealer needs – including descriptions, illustrations and values of thousands and thousands of individual items carefully selected to give a representative picture of the current market in antiques and collectables – and remember all values are prices actually paid, based on accurate sales records in the twelve months prior to publication from the best established and most highly respected auction houses and retail outlets in Europe and America.

This is THE book for the Professional Antiques Dealer. 'The Lyle Book' – we've even heard it called 'The Dealer's Bible'.

Compiled and published afresh each year, the Lyle Antiques Price Guide is the most comprehensive up-to-date antiques price guide available. THIS COULD BE YOUR WISEST INVESTMENT OF THE YEAR!

Anthony Curtis

The publishers wish to express their sincere thanks to the following for their involvement and assistance in the production of this volume.

ANTHONY CURTIS (Editor)

EELIN McIVOR (Sub Editor)

ANNETTE CURTIS (Editorial)

CATRIONA DAY (Art Production)

ANGIE DEMARCO (Art Production)

DONNA RUTHERFORD (Advertising)

SONIA KARAITIANA (Production)

PAULA KARAITIANA (Production)

CONTENTS

ACKNOWLEDGEMENTS

AB Stockholms Auktionsverk, Box 16256, 103 25 Stockholm, Sweden
Abbotts Auction Rooms, The Auction Rooms, Campsea Ash, Woodbridge, Suffolk
Academy Auctioneers, Northcote House, Northcote Avenue, Ealing, London W5 3UR
James Adam, 26 St Stephens Green, Dublin 2
Jean Claude Anaf, Lyon Brotteaux, 13 bis place Jules Ferry, 69456, Lyon, France
Anderson & Garland, Marlborough House, Marlborough Crescent, Newcastle upon Tyne NE1 4EE
Antique Collectors Club & Co. Ltd, 5 Church Street, Woodbridge, Suffolk IP12 1DS
The Auction Galleries, Mount Rd., Tweedmouth, Berwick on Tweed
Auction Team Köln, Postfach 50 11 68, D-5000 Köln 50 Germany
Auktionshaus Arnold, Bleichstr. 42, 6000 Frankfurt a/M, Germany
Barber's Auctions, Woking, Surrey
Bearnes, Rainbow, Avenue Road, Torquay TQ2 5TG
Biddle & Webb, Ladywood Middleway, Birmingham B16 0PP
Bigwood, The Old School, Tiddington, Stratford upon Avon
Black Horse Agencies, Locke & England, 18 Guy Street, Leamington Spa
Boardman Fine Art Auctioneers, Station Road Corner, Haverhill, Suffolk CB9 0EY
Bonhams, Montpelier Street, Knightsbridge, London SW7 1HH
Bonhams Chelsea, 65–69 Lots Road, London SW10 0RN
Bonhams West Country, Dowell Street, Honiton, Devon
Bosleys, 42 West Street, Marlow, Bucks SL7 1NB
Michael J. Bowman, 6 Haccombe House, Near Netherton, Newton Abbot, Devon
Bristol Auction Rooms, St John Place, Apsley Road, Clifton, Bristol BS8 2ST
British Antique Exporters, School Close, Queen Elizabeth Avenue, Burgess Hill, Sussex
Butterfield & Butterfield, 220 San Bruno Avenue, San Francisco CA 94103, USA
Butterfield & Butterfield, 7601 Sunset Boulevard, Los Angeles CA 90046, USA
Canterbury Auction Galleries, 40 Station Road West, Canterbury CT2 8AN
Central Motor Auctions, Barfield House, Britannia Road, Morley, Leeds, LS27 0HN
H.C. Chapman & Son, The Auction Mart, North Street, Scarborough.
Chapman Moore & Mugford, 8 High Street, Shaftesbury SP7 8JB
Cheffins Grain & Comins, 2 Clifton Road, Cambridge
Christie's (International) SA, 8 place de la Taconnerie, 1204 Genève, Switzerland
Christie's Monaco, S.A.M, Park Palace 98000 Monte Carlo, Monaco
Christie's Scotland, 164–166 Bath Street Glasgow G2 4TG
Christie's South Kensington Ltd., 85 Old Brompton Road, London SW7 3LD
Christie's, 8 King Street, London SW1Y 6QT
Christie's East, 219 East 67th Street, New York, NY 10021, USA
Christie's, 502 Park Avenue, New York, NY 10022, USA
Christie's, Cornelis Schuytstraat 57, 1071 JG Amsterdam, Netherlands
Christie's SA Roma, 114 Piazza Navona, 00186 Rome, Italy
Christie's Swire, 2804–6 Alexandra House, 16–20 Chater Road, Hong Kong
Christie's Australia Pty Ltd., 1 Darling Street, South Yarra, Victoria 3141, Australia
A J Cobern, The Grosvenor Sales Rooms, 93b Eastbank Street, Southport PR8 1DG
Cooper Hirst Auctions, The Granary Saleroom, Victoria Road, Chelmsford, Essex CM2 6LH
The Crested China Co., Station House, Driffield, E. Yorks YO25 7PY
Cundalls, The Cattle Market, 17 Market Square, Malton, N. Yorks
Clifford Dann, 20/21 High Street, Lewes, Sussex
Julian Dawson, Lewes Auction Rooms, 56 High Street, Lewes BN7 1XE
Dee & Atkinson & Harrison, The Exchange Saleroom, Driffield, Nth Humberside YO25 7LJ
Garth Denham & Assocs. Horsham Auction Galleries, Warnsham, Nr. Horsham, Sussex
Diamond Mills & Co., 117 Hamilton Road, Felixstowe, Suffolk
David Dockree Fine Art, The Redwood Suite, Clemence House, Mellor Road, Cheadle Hulme, Cheshire
William Doyle Galleries, 175 East 87th Street, New York, NY 10128, USA
Downer Ross, Charter House, 42 Avebury Boulevard, Central Milton Keynes MK9 2HS
Dreweatt Neate, Holloways, 49 Parsons Street, Banbury
Hy. Duke & Son, 40 South Street, Dorchester, Dorset
Du Mouchelles Art Galleries Co., 409 E. Jefferson Avenue, Detroit, Michigan 48226, USA

ANTIQUES REVIEW

Duncan Vincent, 1 Station Road, Pangbourne, Berks RG8 7AY
Sala de Artes y Subastas Durán, Serrano 12, 28001 Madrid, Spain
Eldred's, Box 796, E. Dennis, MA 02641, USA
R H Ellis & Sons, 44/46 High St., Worthing, BN11 1LL
Ewbanks, Burnt Common Auction Rooms, London Road, Send, Woking GU23 7LN
Fellows & Son, Augusta House, 19 Augusta Street, Hockley, Birmingham
Finarte, 20121 Milano, Piazzetta Bossi 4, Italy
John D Fleming & Co., The North Devon Auction Rooms, The Savory, South Molton, Devon
Peter Francis, 19 King Street, Carmarthen, Dyfed
Fraser Pinney's, 8290 Devonshire, Montreal, Quebec, Canada H4P 2PZ
Galerie Koller, Rämistr. 8, CH 8024 Zürich, Switzerland
Galerie Moderne, 3 rue du Parnasse, 1040 Bruxelles, Belgium
Geering & Colyer (Black Horse Agencies) Highgate, Hawkhurst, Kent
Glerum Auctioneers, Westeinde 12, 2512 HD's Gravenhage, Netherlands
The Goss and Crested China Co., 62 Murray Road, Horndean, Hants PO8 9JL
Graves Son & Pilcher, 71 Church Road, Hove, East Sussex, BN3 2GL
Greenslade Hunt, Magdalene House, Church Square, Taunton, Somerset, TA1 1SB
Halifax Property Services, 53 High Street, Tenterden, Kent
Halifax Property Services, 15 Cattle Market, Sandwich, Kent CT13 9AW
Hampton's Fine Art, 93 High Street, Godalming, Surrey
Hanseatisches Auktionshaus für Historica, Neuer Wall 57, 2000 Hamburg 36, Germany
William Hardie Ltd., 141 West Regent Street, Glasgow G2 2SG
Andrew Hartley Fine Arts, Victoria Hall, Little Lane, Ilkely
Hauswedell & Nolte, D-2000 Hamburg 13, Pöseldorfer Weg 1, Germany
Giles Haywood, The Auction House, St John's Road, Stourbridge, West Midlands, DY8 1EW
Muir Hewitt, Halifax Antiques Centre, Queens Road/Gibbet Street, Halifax HX1 4LR
Hobbs & Chambers, 'At the Sign of the Bell', Market Place, Cirencester, Glos
Hobbs Parker, Romney House, Ashford Market, Ashford, Kent
Holloways, 49 Parsons Street, Banbury OX16 8PF
Hotel de Ventes Horta, 390 Chaussée de Waterloo (Ma Campagne), 1060 Bruxelles, Belgium
Jacobs & Hunt, Lavant Street, Petersfield, Hants. GU33 3EF
P Herholdt Jensens Auktioner, Rundforbivej 188, 2850 Nerum, Denmark
Kennedy & Wolfenden, 218 Lisburn Rd, Belfast BT9 6GD
G A Key, Aylsham Saleroom, Palmers Lane, Aylsham, Norfolk, NR11 6EH
George Kidner, The Old School, The Square, Pennington, Lymington, Hants SO41 8GN
Kunsthaus am Museum, Drususgasse 1–5, 5000 Köln 1, Germany
Kunsthaus Lempertz, Neumarkt 3, 5000 Köln 1, Germany
Lambert & Foster (County Group), The Auction Sales Room, 102 High Street, Tenterden, Kent
W.H. Lane & Son, 64 Morrab Road, Penzance, Cornwall, TR18 2QT
Langlois Ltd., Westway Rooms, Don Street, St Helier, Channel Islands
Lawrence Butler Fine Art Salerooms, Marine Walk, Hythe, Kent, CT21 5AJ
Lawrence Fine Art, South Street, Crewkerne, Somerset TA18 8AB
Lawrence's Fine Art Auctioneers, Norfolk House, 80 High Street, Bletchingley, Surrey
David Lay, The Penzance Auction House, Alverton, Penzance, Cornwall TA18 4KE
Gordon Litherland, 26 Stapenhill Road, Burton on Trent
Lloyd International Auctions, 118 Putney Bridge Road, London SW15 2NQ
Brian Loomes, Calf Haugh Farm, Pateley Bridge, North Yorks
Lots Road Chelsea Auction Galleries, 71 Lots Road, Chelsea, London SW10 0RN
R K Lucas & Son, Tithe Exchange, 9 Victoria Place, Haverfordwest, SA61 2JX
Duncan McAlpine, Stateside Comics plc, 125 East Barnet Road, London EN4 8RF
McCartneys, Portcullis Salerooms, Ludlow, Shropshire
Christopher Matthews, 23 Mount Street, Harrogate HG2 8DG
John Maxwell, 133a Woodford Road, Wilmslow, Cheshire
May & Son, 18 Bridge Street, Andover, Hants
Morphets, 4–6 Albert Street, Harrogate, North Yorks HG1 1JL
Neales, The Nottingham Saleroom, 192 Mansfield Road, Nottingham NG1 3HU
D M Nesbit & Co, 7 Clarendon Road, Southsea, Hants PO5 2ED
John Nicholson, 1 Crossways Court, Fernhurst, Haslemere, Surrey GU27 3EP

ANTIQUES REVIEW

Onslow's, Metrostore, Townmead Road, London SW6 2RZ
Outhwaite & Litherland, Kingsley Galleries, Fontenoy Street, Liverpool, Merseyside L3 2BE
Phillips Manchester, Trinity House, 114 Northenden Road, Sale, Manchester M33 3HD
Phillips Son & Neale SA, 10 rue des Chaudronniers, 1204 Genève, Switzerland
Phillips West Two, 10 Salem Road, London W2 4BL
Phillips, 11 Bayle Parade, Folkestone, Kent CT20 1SQ
Phillips, 49 London Road, Sevenoaks, Kent TN13 1UU
Phillips, 65 George Street, Edinburgh EH2 2JL
Phillips, Blenstock House, 7 Blenheim Street, New Bond Street, London W1Y 0AS
Phillips Marylebone, Hayes Place, Lisson Grove, London NW1 6UA
Phillips, New House, 150 Christleton Road, Chester CH3 5TD
Andrew Pickford, 42 St Andrew Street, Hertford SG14 1JA
Pieces of Time, 1–7 Davies Mews, Unit 17–19, London W17 1AR
Pooley & Rogers, Regent Auction Rooms, Abbey Street, Penzance
Pretty & Ellis, Amersham Auction Rooms, Station Road, Amersham, Bucks
Harry Ray & Co, Lloyds Bank Chambers, Welshpool, Montgomery SY21 7RR
Peter M Raw, Thornfield, Hurdle Way, Compton Down, Winchester, Hants SC21 2AN
Rennie's, 1 Agincourt Street, Monmouth
Riddetts, 26 Richmond Hill, Bournemouth
Ritchie's, 429 Richmond Street East, Toronto, Canada M5A 1R1
Derek Roberts Antiques, 24–25 Shipbourne Road, Tonbridge, Kent TN10 3DN
Rogers de Rin, 79 Royal Hospital Road, London SW3 4HN
Russell, Baldwin & Bright, The Fine Art Saleroom, Ryelands Road, Leominster HR6 8JG
Rye Auction Galleries, Rock Channel, Rye, East Sussex
Schrager Auction Galleries, 2915 N Sherman Boulevard, PO Box 10390, Milwaukee WI 53210, USA
Selkirk's, 4166 Olive Street, St Louis, Missouri 63108, USA
Skinner Inc., Bolton Gallery, Route 117, Bolton MA, USA
Soccer Nostalgia, Albion Chambers, Birchington, Kent CT7 9DN
Sotheby's, 34–35 New Bond Street, London W1A 2AA
Sotheby's, 1334 York Avenue, New York NY 10021
Sotheby's, 112 George Street, Edinburgh EH2 2LH
Sotheby's, Summers Place, Billinghurst, West Sussex RH14 9AD
Sotheby's Monaco, BP 45, 98001 Monte Carlo
Southgate Auction Rooms, 55 High St, Southgate, London N14 6LD
Spink & Son Ltd, 5-7 King St., St James's, London SW1Y 6QS
Michael Stainer Ltd., St Andrews Auction Rooms, Wolverton Rd, Boscombe, Bournemouth BH7 6HT
Mike Stanton, 7 Rowood Drive, Solihull, West Midlands B92 9LT
Street Jewellery, 5 Runnymede Road, Ponteland, Northumbria NE20 9HE
Stride & Son, Southdown House, St John's St., Chichester, Sussex
G E Sworder & Son, 14 Cambridge Road, Stansted Mountfitche, Essex CM24 8BZ
Taviner's of Bristol, Prewett Street, Redcliffe, Bristol BS1 6PB
Tennants, Harmby Road, Leyburn, Yorkshire
Thomson Roddick & Laurie, 24 Lowther Street, Carlisle
Thomson Roddick & Laurie, 60 Whitesands, Dumfries
Timbleby & Shorland, 31 Gt Knollys St, Reading RG1 7HU
Truro Auction Centre, Calenick Street, Truro TR1 2SG
Venator & Hanstein, Cäcilienstr. 48, 5000 Köln 1, Germany
T Vennett Smith, 11 Nottingham Road, Gotham, Nottingham NG11 0HE
Duncan Vincent, 92 London Street, Reading RG1 4SJ
Wallis & Wallis, West Street Auction Galleries, West Street, Lewes, E. Sussex BN7 2NJ
Walter's, 1 Mint Lane, Lincoln LN1 1UD
Wells Cundall Nationwide Anglia, Staffordshire House, 27 Flowergate, Whitby YO21 3AX
Woltons, 6 Whiting Street, Bury St Edmunds, Suffolk IP33 1PB
Peter Wilson, Victoria Gallery, Market Street, Nantwich, Cheshire CW5 5DG
Wintertons Ltd., Lichfield Auction Centre, Fradley Park, Lichfield, Staffs WS13 8NF
Woltons, 6 Whiting Street, Bury St Edmunds, Suffolk IP33 1PB
Woolley & Wallis, The Castle Auction Mart, Salisbury, Wilts SP1 3SU
Worthing Auction Galleries, 31 Chatsworth Road, Worthing, W. Sussex BN11 1LY

ANTIQUES

REVIEW 1997

THE Lyle Antiques Price Guide is compiled and published with completely fresh information annually, enabling you to begin each new year with an up-to-date knowledge of the current trends, together with the verified values of antiques of all descriptions.

We have endeavored to obtain a balance between the more expensive collector's items and those which, although not in their true sense antiques, are handled daily by the antiques trade.

The illustrations and prices in the following sections have been arranged to make it easy for the reader to assess the period and value of all items with speed.

You will find illustrations for almost every category of antique and curio, together with a corresponding price collated during the last twelve months, from the auction rooms and retail outlets of the major trading countries.

When dealing with the more popular trade pieces, in some instances, a calculation of an average price has been estimated from the varying accounts researched.

As regards prices, when 'one of a pair' is given in the description the price quoted is for a pair and so that we can make maximum use of the available space it is generally considered that one illustration is sufficient.

It will be noted that in some descriptions taken directly from sales catalogues originating from many different countries, terms such as bureau, secretary and davenport are used in a broader sense than is customary, but in all cases the term used is self explanatory.

ADDING MACHINES

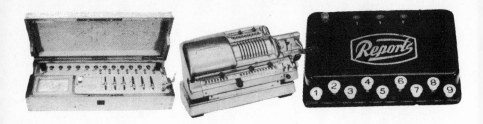

A Colmar Arithmomètre, the world's first mass-produced adding machine, in light oak case, circa 1885.
(Auction Team Köln)
$3,850

An East German Triomphator Model CRN2 barrel calculating machine, circa 1957.
(Auction Team Köln) $107

'Reports', a bakelite model of the German Adix version of a 9-key calculator, circa 1955.
(Auction Team Köln)
$154

An Anita Model 1011 classic electronic desk calculator by the Bell Punch Co., England, circa 1965.
(Auction Team Köln) $136

Consul, The Educated Monkey, a rare tinplate calculating toy by the Educational Toy Mfg Co Ltd. USA, in original box, circa 1918.
(Auction Team Köln) $462

American tinplate toy calculator Modern Math-Addition, by Wolverine, circa 1943.
(Auction Team Köln) $53

An Alpina four-function adding machine with table stand, 1961.
(Auction Team Köln) $733

The Spalding Adding Machine, an early calculator with 9 keys and 2-scales, with original invoice and contemporary letter, 1884.
(Auction Team Köln)
$5,783

A Resulta P7 7-place rapid calculator, circa 1930.
(Auction Team Köln) $91

A Belga polychrome enamel sign, 1953, 47 x 70 cm.
(Auction Team Köln) $122

A model of Nipper in painted papier-mâché, 11in. high.
(Christie's) $527

An HMV display record of ebonized blockboard, with plum label (B4368, Gracie Fields), 54in. diameter.
(Christie's) $562

A Coca Cola advertising clock, yellow varnished metal casing, white plexiglass and red lettering, with electric illumination, 27 x 36 cm.
(Auction Team Köln) $154

Mechanical display doll on wooden base, rolls eyes, indicates with hand, which is adapted to hold an advertising board, 65 cm. high.
(Auction Team Köln) $577

Tom Purvis, Austin Reed's of Regent Street, double crown, 76 x 51cm.
(Onslow's) $1,473

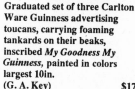

A Bibendum 5-color rubber Michelin Man advertising figure.
(Auction Team Köln) $15

Graduated set of three Carlton Ware Guinness advertising toucans, carrying foaming tankards on their beaks, inscribed *My Goodness My Guinness,* painted in colors largest 10in.
(G. A. Key) $174

A Swatch advertising display, with quartz watch, in working order, 60 cm. high.
(Auction Team Köln) $169

Alcyon Cycles, an original poster, color lithograph, linen backed, 25in. x 18in.
(Christie's) $158

Brentleigh ware plaster advertising plaque, modelled as black and white Scottie dogs, with raised inscription *Scotch 'Black and White' Whisky* to oval base, 9in. high.
(Peter Wilson) $62

George Foreman vs. Muhammad Ali poster, for the telecast at the Cinerama & Penthouse theaters, NYC.
(Butterfield & Butterfield) $345

After Marodon, La Française '1er Paris-Bordeaux', a good original poster for early cycles, full-color lithograph, linen, backed, French, circa 1903, 60in. x 43in.
(Christie's) $880

Clyde Beatty and Cole Bros. World's Largest Circus, depicting a white-clad clown and showgirl on a white horse, linen backed, 36 x 41in.
(Butterfield & Butterfield) $230

Ringling Bros. and Barnum & Bailey Circus, The Greatest Show on Earth, Maxwell Frederic Coplan, depicting a showgirl and a white horse, linen backed, 52 x 28in.
(Butterfield & Butterfield) $258

English painted touring sign, late 19th century, advertising Poulson's Tours of Russia and Trans-Siberian Railway, painted in gold, red and black, 47in. x 26$\frac{1}{2}$in.
(Skinner) $2,415

Huiles Renault, advertising oil crate, printed tin sides to wooden box, circa 1930, 20in. x 26in. x 13in.
(Christie's) $141

Aiglon Cycles, a good early original poster, color lithograph by Affiches Gaillard, linen-backed, circa 1910, 60in. x 44in.
(Christie's) $563

AERONAUTICAL ITEMS

Hull Aero Club Certificate No. H.1, issued to Miss Amy Johnson C.B.E. by National Flying Services Ltd., undated, signed *Mark Goulden*, Honorary Secretary.
(Christie's) $1,973

A laminated mahogany four bladed propeller, of unusually small size, the boss stamped *R.A.F. T 2985/479*, 54in. long.
(Christie's) $370

A rare marble desk piece, with polished calcite inkwell container, the lid incised in white with an illustration of LZ.129, the rim incised *Graf Zeppelin New York 1936*, 14⁵⁄₈in. wide.
(Christie's) $708

A rare Dinner menu signed *L Bleriot* with legend, The Hotel Cecil, September 15th 1909.
(Christie's) $495

Blackpool Aviation Week 1909, three china coffee cups decorated with an early biplane flying over Blackpool Tower, each 2¹⁄₂in. high.
(Christie's) $393

A W.W.II R.A.F. pattern transmitter T.1154, and the associated receiver T.1155, 16¹⁄₂in. wide.
(Christie's) $358

Handley-Page Hampden, a chromium plated model of this medium bomber with rotating three-blade propellers, 11in.
(Christie's) $168

A leather and canvas cushion with carrying handle, one side stamped in gilt *Presented to Miss Amy Johnson, C.B.E. by 1st Bn. A.I.F. Association, Sydney June 1930*, 13¹⁄₂in. x 18in.
(Christie's) $540

A cream canvas flying helmet, with 'Gosport' tube ear-phone attachments, and a pair of early 1930s flying goggles with canvas side fur rims.
(Christie's) $3,947

AERONAUTICAL ITEMS

An R.A.F. sector clock with fusee movement by T. W. Elliot Ltd., No. 18213, 1941, the white enameled dial with arabic numerals, 13½in. dial diameter.
(Christie's) **$717**

An early 20th century Russian barometer, with thermometer graduated in C and F with silvered ring dial, dial diameter 7³/8in.
(Christie's) **$339**

A cast bronze plaque, embossed with a male head and shoulders wearing jacket, and *Wilbur Wright A.D. 1908 Camp de Anvours*, 3³/8in.
(Christie's) **$502**

A W.W.II period U.S. Army Airforce leather flying jacket, the back painted in colors with head and shoulders of a lady, a facsimile copy of the Herald Tribune.
(Christie's) **$1,794**

An unusual four blade propeller, the laminated mahogany blades with brass tips, boss stamped *A.D. 552. R.H., 100 H.P. ANZANI, CURTISS. F.B. MALTAYARD, NO. 278*, 93in.
(Christie's) **$1,344**

Cameo brooch, decorated with head and shoulders of a young girl with diamond earring, said to be Col. Fitzmaurice's wife waving to the Bremen Junkers Plane arriving in New York, 2in. wide.
(Christie's) **$1,350**

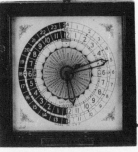

A pair of Second World War period German military pattern long range binoculars, probably by Zeiss, with tripod.
(Christie's) **$830**

A Sky Pilot World timepiece, paper dial with volvelle, inscribed with various cities and countries, case 15³/4in. square.
(Christie's) **$393**

A souvenir cigarette lighter, mounted on a model of Graf Zeppelin LZ-127, dated *1928*, flying over a stylized cloud base, 6in. long.
(Christie's) **$1,076**

AERONAUTICAL ITEMS

Aviator's Certificate No. 8662 (British Empire), issued to Miss Amy Johnson by the Federation Aeronautique International on 28 June 1929.
(Christie's) **$9,330**

A Blackburn Beverley control yoke, removed from XM–III; and a Bristol Centaurus piston and connecting rod.
(Christie's) **$149**

A rare porcelain coffee cup and saucer, from the Graf Zeppelin service, by Heinrich & Co., with the company logo and gilt border, 4½in. wide.
(Christie's) **$2,700**

 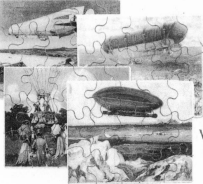 

An R.A.F. Sergeant's Mess mantle timepiece, with fusee movement, the silvered dial engraved with a pair of Royal Air Force wings, 18¾in. high.
(Christie's) **$413**

Jigsaw puzzles, a collection of four early 20th century puzzles depicting airship and ballooning scenes on board backing, 9½in. wide.
(Christie's) **$161**

Menu and Souvenir Program of the London Aerodrome, Hendon NW First Annual Dinner, Friday March 20th 1914, text, cartoons, sepia and color plates.
(Christie's) **$270**

An R.A.F. sector clock, with fusee movement by T. W. Elliot Ltd., No. 5548 1938, the white enameled dial with roman numerals, 13⅝in. dial diameter.
(Christie's) **$907**

Three Vietnam-war period squadron badges, one of silver and gold wire with colored silk inscribed *Vietnam*; another inscribed *101st* and another of the 76th fighter group.
(Christie's) **$161**

An enameled button hole badge, depicting aeroplanes flying round Blackpool Tower with border lettered *Blackpool Aviation Week October 1909*, ⅞in. diameter.
(Christie's) **$430**

A large alabaster figural group, Diana holding the dying Acteon after having shot him as a stag, 12in.
(Academy) $455

An alabaster bust of Joan of Arc, on shaped socle, 42.5cm.
(Bristol) $236

Italian alabaster bust of a shepherd girl, circa 1880, signed *A. Cippie*, the base carved with a frieze depicting a flock of sheep and shepherdess, 18in. high.
(Skinner) $862

An Italian alabaster figure of Rebecca at the well by ? Pugi, late 19th/early20th century, 25in. high.
(Christie's) $5,285

An Hispano-Flemish alabaster relief of the Entombment, late 16th/early 17th century, the Holy Kindred mourning and placing the limp figure of Christ on the sepulchre, $18^{1}/_{4}$ x $22^{3}/_{4}$in.
(Sotheby's) $7,475

Siren and dolphin, 1930s, alabaster, modeled as a naked nymph blowing a conch shell, supported by a stylized dolphin, 43.5cm.
(Sotheby's) $2,907

A parcel-gilt marble and alabaster bust of Beatrice, carved from a model by Besji, Italian, 19th century, signed *Prof. G. Besji* and inscribed *Beatrice*, 19in. high.
(Christie's) $2,760

A painted and molded composition bust portrait of George Washington, American, 20th century, height $23^{1}/_{4}$in.
(Sotheby's) $1,035

An Italian alabaster figure of Rebecca at the well by ? Pugi, late 19th century, seated on a rock, resting pensively on her urn, 23in. high.
(Christie's) $4,340

Acoma polychrome pottery jar, the flaring sides with connected stepped and fine-line diamond lozenges, checkered diamonds within, 12in. diameter.
(Butterfield & Butterfield)
$2,587

Kiowa beaded hide model cradleboard, consisting of a hide liner wrapped in trade cloth and fully beaded in a three color zoned pattern, 21in. long without fringe.
(Butterfield & Butterfield)
$6,900

Yokut polychrome basket, the large bowl with slightly curving and flaring sides, carrying two horizontal diamond bands, 16 1/2in. diameter.
(Butterfield & Butterfield)
$3,162

Mimbres black-on-white pictorial pottery bowl, depicting a long-legged water fowl with elongated sinuous neck, a fish dangling from its bill, 10in. diameter.
(Butterfield & Butterfield)
$4,600

Ojibwa beaded bandolier bag, fully beaded on the square pouch and wide strap in a naturalistic floral pattern, with multi-colored flowers and vines, 39in. long.
(Butterfield & Butterfield)
$1,265

Pima polychrome basketry olla, with wide shoulder, pinched neck and flaring rim, drawn in a large-scale pattern of outlined fretted bands, 12 1/4in. high.
(Butterfield & Butterfield)
$1,265

Hopi Kachina doll, standing tall, with one blossom ear and long snout, the face painted yellow, white and pale blue, 12 3/4in. high.
(Butterfield & Butterfield)
$862

Kiowa beaded hightop moccasins, with soft hide uppers and down-turned cuffs, a beaded geometric band on white about the ankle and lining the vertical flap, 9 1/4in. long.
(Butterfield & Butterfield)
$1,035

Anasazi shell necklace, consisting of a large number of double-lobed figure-eight white or purple shell beads, 17in. long.
(Butterfield & Butterfield)
$3,162

Zia polychrome pottery jar, with traditional arches framing a pair of roadrunners, 9½in. high.
(Butterfield & Butterfield)
$690

Cheyenne beaded moccasins, the allover translucent ground divided by narrow bands and set with four-pointed blossom motifs, 10¾in. long.
(Butterfield & Butterfield)
$517

Maidu tray, drawn with two concentric circles surrounded by a large multi-petalled rosette, 15in. diameter.
(Butterfield & Butterfield)
$517

Apache saddlebags and packsaddle, the bags of characteristic rectangular form, along with an A-frame saddle covered in cow-hide over bent branches and slats of yucca fibre.
(Butterfield & Butterfield)
$3,000

Navajo Two Gray Hills rug, with complex central medallion, showing connected stepped and hooked diamond lozenges, combs, terraced diamonds and other hooked motifs, 6ft. 2in. x 4ft. 10in.
(Butterfield & Butterfield)
$2,300

Apache dress, the two-piece garment consisting of heavily fringed bodice, concentric circles and stars painted in black and red on the front, skirt 33in.
(Butterfield & Butterfield)
$2,000

Pueblo ceremonial shield, the circular ornament showing multiple layers of paint, with striped bottom in mustard and yellow, 19in. diameter.
(Butterfield & Butterfield)
$2,875

Apache tray, the small dark center encircled by a narrow band giving on to zig-zags of connected triangles, 16¾in. diameter.
(Butterfield & Butterfield)
$977

Hopi polychrome pottery jar, Frog Woman, the white-slipped vessel painted in a panel style, showing various bird and feather motifs, 10½in. high.
(Butterfield & Butterfield)
$2,070

Apache basket, the flaring bowl sides woven in a pattern of complementary stepped diagonals, 12¼in. diameter. (Butterfield & Butterfield) $460

Sioux beaded moccasins, with outlined terraced design on the medium blue vamp, 9½in. long. (Butterfield & Butterfield) $517

Navajo concha belt, consisting of five oval scalloped silver conchas alternating with four butterfly spacers, 37in. long. (Butterfield & Butterfield) $1,035

Apache pictorial olla, woven with three horizontal zig-zag bands, small dog figures within the central band, 8½in. diameter. (Butterfield & Butterfield) $1,725

Large Navajo Germantown rug, the square weaving worked in a series of concentric solid color boxes, 9ft. x 9ft. approx. (Butterfield & Butterfield) $11,500

Apache pictorial olla, of jar form, decorated with a large-scale outlined diamond lattice, having dog motifs, 8¼in. diameter. (Butterfield & Butterfield) $1,725

Nez Percé cornhusk bag, decorated with both dyed cornhusks and colored yarns, one side with an arrangement of polychrome sawtooth diamonds, 13¾in. wide. (Butterfield & Butterfield) $805

Tlingit rattletop lidded basket, the straight sides woven with three bands of false embroidery, worked in diagonal checkered panels and fretted meanders, 7½in. diameter. (Butterfield & Butterfield) $2,185

Laguna/Acoma polychrome pottery jar, painted in a single elaborate design band of repeated and complementary feather and plant motifs, 10¼in. high. (Butterfield & Butterfield) $862

Rotomat, an amusement machine by Günther Wolff Automatenbau, Berlin, 1960. (Auction Team Köln) $169

A Chocolat Menier tin mechanical money bank for chocolate pieces, with dispenser and hinged roof, French, circa 1935. (Auction Team Köln) $137

An American Shooter chewing gum dispenser, scoring a goal dispenses gum, otherwise coin is returned, circa 1930. (Auction Team Köln) $516

A circa 1910 Stereo Viewer from Coney Island, New York, the 1 Cent viewer featuring The Many Worlds of Love, light oak case, stained glass windows, 70in. high. (Christie's East) $3,680

Automatic Skill Shooter, the first cast iron amusement machine by Robbins & Co. London, 1894. (Auction Team Köln) $20,430

A stereo coin operated film viewer, the Hollywood View-a-Scope, in decorative blue casing, for stereo film strips. (Auction Team Köln) $608

The Little Five Win pinball machine, circa 1935. (Auction Team Köln) $345

A table football games machine by René Pierre, of wooden construction with cast iron figures, French, 1935. (Auction Team Köln) $750

An IMO Battery Bomber amusement machine, German, 1937. (Auction Team Köln) $732

An Attic Black Figure eye cup, similarly decorated on both sides with a central figure of a standing cockerel, circa 450 B.C., 3¹/₂in. high.
(Bonhams) $3,744

An important early Roman mosaic glass footed cast deep 'pillar-molded' bowl, composed from sections of single canes with a cobalt blue background, late 1st century B.C. – early 1st century A.D., 4in. high.
(Bonhams) $343,200

A small Gnathian ware kylix on a ridged ring base decorated in added white with incisions, 2¹/₂in. high., Greek, South Italy, circa 4th century B.C.
(Bonhams) $455

A Roman limestone Sylvanus figure of a fertility male, lacking head and lower half of legs, anatomically altered in the 19th century, 25in. high.
(Butterfield & Butterfield) $3,737

A Cypriot limestone group of a maned horse and rider bearing a shield, Iron Age, circa 8th–6th centuries B.C., 4¹/₂in.
(Bonhams) $702

A Cypriot limestone male from a votive figure wearing a close-fitting conical cap, with archaic smile and pronounced ears, circa 6th-5th century B.C., 7in.
(Bonhams) $2,250

A marble relief fragment with a central winged Medusa head above a swag of thick garlands, Roman, Eastern Empire, circa 2nd century A.D., 15 x 17³/₄in.
(Bonhams) $975

An Old Kingdom wooden male head with a short layered wig and grooved eyes, 6th Dynasty–1st Intermediate Period, 2345–2040 B.C., 4in. high.
(Bonhams) $1,462

A Byzantine marble reliquary, 6th-8th century, of rectangular form, the ends carved with flared crosses, 4 x 7⁵/₈ x 4³/₄in.
(Christie's) $5,279

An Egyptian limestone male head wearing a bag wig, 25th Dynasty, after 600 B.C., 3in. high.
(Bonhams) $3,432

A Luristan bronze horse-bit, the openwork cheekpieces decorated with a central horned figure, 8th–7th B.C., 4^1/$_8$in. high.
(Bonhams) $1,326

A Palmyran ribbed pottery bag-shaped amphora with two small handles at the neck, 1st century B.C./A.D., 20in. high.
(Bonhams) $406

A Mycenaean stirrup vessel, the piriform body swelling at the shoulder and tapering to the foot, 1400–1200 B.C., 8^3/$_4$in. high.
(Bonhams) $2,340

A substantial upper portion of a wooden sarcophagus lid, a yellow painted face with traces of blue and red on her eyes, Late Period to Ptolemaic, 21in. high.
(Bonhams) $4,056

A bronze flat-backed figure of seated Maat, goddess of Truth, the ma'at feather resting on her knees, Late Dynastic Period, after 1000 B.C., 2^1/$_2$in.
(Bonhams) $625

A gesso-painted wooden mummy mask, the white face with details in black, Late Period, after 500 B.C., 10^1/$_2$in.
(Bonhams) $858

An Assyrian gypsum relief fragment representing an inhabitant of Palestine hauling a bull, circa 700 B.C., 3^3/$_4$ x 2^7/$_8$in.
(Bonhams) $4,056

A polished indurated limestone jar with disk rim and two lug handles, Old Kingdom, circa 3rd Millennium B.C., 4^3/$_4$in.
(Bonhams) $936

A West Iranian buff-colored pottery bridge-spouted vessel with rope-twist handle, 8th–7th century B.C., 5¹/₂in. high. (Bonhams) $655

A Roman amber glass bowl on a low flared foot, with a folded thickened rim, circa 3rd-4th century A.D., 7in. diameter. (Bonhams) $1,092

A small Attic Black Figure hydria decorated with added white within a panel, early 5th century B.C., 8in. (Bonhams) $893

A Ptolemaic plaster mask of a boy, the details of his flesh-colored face picked out in black and brown, 334–31 B.C., 8in. (Bonhams) $2,652

A Campanian Red Figure bell krater attributed to the Capua Painter, with added details in white, Greek, South Italy, 360–330 B.C., 7⁵/₈in. (Bonhams) $1,170

An Etruscan terracotta antefix, molded in relief with a female head within a shell-like niche, circa 6th–5th centuries B.C., 9³/₄in. high. (Bonhams) $1,170

A Corinthian amphoriskos, the buff-colored body decorated in Black Figure with incised lines, 6th century B.C., 6¹/₄in. (Bonhams) $749

A Byzantine square terracotta tile showing a leaping jackal in relief within a box, circa 5th–7th centuries A.D., 10¹/₄in. high. (Bonhams) $455

A Roman marble Priapus, his cloak raised to expose his phallus, circa 1st–2nd century A.D., 3¹/₄in. high. (Bonhams) $893

ARMOR

A heavy mid 17th century cavalry trooper's breastplate, distinct medial ridge, deep musket ball proof test, borders pierced for liner.
(Wallis & Wallis) $480

A pair of German black-and-white mitten gauntlets, circa 1540, each with short tubular cuff embossed for the ulna, 12½in.
(Sotheby's) $3,162

An Italian half-shaffron, late 16th century, comprising a main plate formed in one piece, flattened in the middle, 17¾in.
(Sotheby's) $2,070

A late Gothic breast-plate, Italian or Flemish, circa 1490–1500, of rounded form with a very low medial ridge diminishing towards the base, 14in. high.
(Sotheby's) $2,070

A German demi-shaffron of bright steel, composed of a main plate shaped to the upper part of the horse's head and shaped round the eyes and ears, circa 1550–60, probably Landshut, 14½in.
(Christie's) $10,833

A pair of 18th century Indian arm defences Bazu Band, 13in., gold damascened overall with repeated floral and foliate designs, reinforced shaped edges.
(Wallis & Wallis) $490

A cavalry officer's cuirass, German or Danish, second half 19th century, comprising breast-plate and back-plate with shoulder straps, 20½in. high.
(Sotheby's) $1,495

A mail shirt, 16th century, formed of large riveted iron rings throughout, open at the neck, 30in. high.
(Sotheby's) $2,415

French model 1855 Cuirassier trooper's breast and backplate, both marked for Chatellerault armory and dated *Mai 1858*.
(Butterfield & Butterfield) $825

ARMOR

A German breast-plate, circa 1500, of globose form, with a strongly flanged turn across the neck, 14in. high.
(Sotheby's)   **$2,300**

A pair of German gauntlets, third quarter 16th century, each with hinged pointed cuff, roped edges, articulated metacarpus of six plates, 13in.
(Sotheby's)   **$5,750**

A mid 17th century siege weight breast plate, with turned over edges, traces of line borders.
(Wallis & Wallis)   **$428**

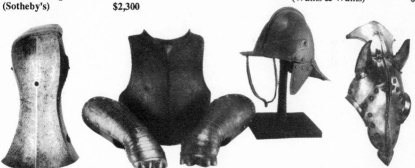

A left-hand reinforcing gauntlet for the tilt, comprising a main plate covering the back of the hand from the bases of the fingers and flaring out into a long bell-shaped cuff, early 16th century, probably Italian, 12in.
(Christie's)   **$8,124**

An English composite trooper's armor, circa 1640-50, comprising pot helmet, neck-guard, breast-plate, back-plate, pair of bridle gauntlets.
(Sotheby's)   **$2,300**

A half-shaffron, Flemish or Italian, third quarter 16th century, comprising a main plate formed in one piece, the edges cusped and tapering below the ocular flanges, 21¹/₂in.
(Sotheby's)   **$4,600**

A full shanfron, in Italian late 16th century style, 19th century, formed with a central plate rising to a low ridge over the lower half, 20³/₄in. long.
(Sotheby's)   **$1,150**

A fine and heavy 17th century Indian chain mail and lamellar shirt, the mail of alternate rows of thickly forged solid rings and riveted rings.
(Wallis & Wallis)   **$1,423**

A rare silver-mounted gorget of gilt-brass, of deep crescent shape, flanged at the throat and with turned edges, 17th century, probably French, 7in. wide.
(Christie's)   **$11,735**

ARMOR

 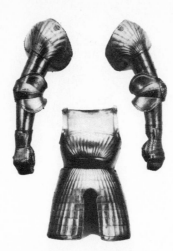 

A German composite fluted full armor, comprehensively circa 1530–40, perhaps Landshut, close helmet with one-piece skull rising to a low cabled comb.
(Sotheby's) $48,961

A German composite fluted full armor, partly first half 16th century, on a wooden stand; and together with a sword, in the 16th century style.
(Sotheby's) $10,350

A well made copy in the 16th century style of a full suit of armor, roughened black finish overall, 6ft. 3in. high overall.
(Wallis & Wallis) $3,479

A full armor, in German mid-16th century style, comprising close helmet, gorget, breast-plate, back-plate, full arm defences, gauntlets, and full leg defences.
(Sotheby's) $9,000

A full armor, in late 16th century style, including close helmet, gorget, breast-plate, back-plate, arm-defences, articulated gauntlets, full leg defences.
(Sotheby's) $4,600

A composite full armor for the field, composed of Italian close helmet, gorget, gorget of three plates, German breast-plate, skirt, and later complete legs, comprehensively 16th century.
(Christie's) $30,693

ARMOR

A half-armor, in German late
16th century style, comprising
close helmet, breast-plate and
back-plate etched in the
Augsburg style, gauntlets.
(Sotheby's) $3,450

A full armor, in the Swiss style
of the third quarter of the 16th
century, well-formed
throughout.
(Sotheby's) $9,200

Imperial German Cuirassier
armor, comprised of brass
mounted white metal helmet,
two-piece unmarked quilted
body armor.
(Butterfield & Butterfield)
                              $3,575

A full armor, for the
tournament, in late 16th century
style, including close helmet,
hinged gorget, breast-plate,
back-plate, full arm defences.
(Sotheby's) $9,000

A Japanese part suit of armor,
comprising twenty-eight plate
kabuto with lining, fukigayeshi
and shikaro; mempo with
shakaro (nose missing).
(Wallis & Wallis) $3,579

A fine full armor, of bright
steel, in mid-16th century style,
in pristine condition throughout,
on an articulated wooden stand.
(Sotheby's) $14,950

31

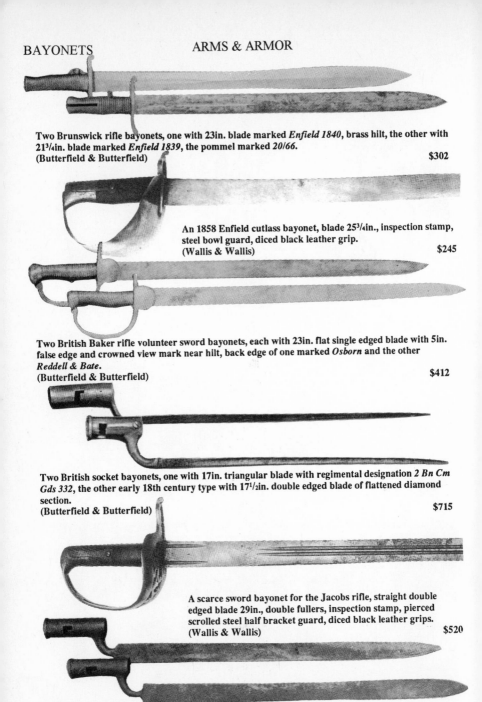

Two Brunswick rifle bayonets, one with 23in. blade marked *Enfield 1840*, brass hilt, the other with 21³/₄in. blade marked *Enfield 1839*, the pommel marked *20/66*.
(Butterfield & Butterfield) $302

An 1858 Enfield cutlass bayonet, blade 25³/₄in., inspection stamp, steel bowl guard, diced black leather grip.
(Wallis & Wallis) $245

Two British Baker rifle volunteer sword bayonets, each with 23in. flat single edged blade with 5in. false edge and crowned view mark near hilt, back edge of one marked *Osborn* and the other *Reddell & Bate*.
(Butterfield & Butterfield) $412

Two British socket bayonets, one with 17in. triangular blade with regimental designation *2 Bn Cm Gds 332*, the other early 18th century type with 17¹/₂in. double edged blade of flattened diamond section.
(Butterfield & Butterfield) $715

A scarce sword bayonet for the Jacobs rifle, straight double edged blade 29in., double fullers, inspection stamp, pierced scrolled steel half bracket guard, diced black leather grips.
(Wallis & Wallis) $520

Two Ferguson rifle type socket bayonets, one with broad 19¹/₂in. single edged blade with shallow 15in. fuller, the other with 19¹/₈in. single edged blade with 14in. fuller and marked at the base *R*.
(Butterfield & Butterfield) $330

BOWIE KNIVES

Large unmarked Bowie knife, having a 17½in. clip point blade with a long shallow fuller running the length of the blade, cylindrical grip with staghorn scales, silver inlaid quillons with recurving terminals, 23in. long overall.
(Butterfield & Butterfield) **$935**

Large Bowie knife by Marsh, having a 13in. double edged spear point blade, horn grip scales with a silver escutcheon plate, German silver quillons with ball terminals.
(Butterfield & Butterfield) **$1,320**

Ivory hilted Bowie knife, the 8½in. single edged blade with worn maker's marks and notched back edge, ivory grip with German silver cutlery style bolsters, 13¾in. long overall.
(Butterfield & Butterfield) **$770**

Exhibition Bowie knife by Rodgers, having a 13¾in. curved doubled edged blade with two fullers running the length of the blade, marked *Joseph Rodgers & Sons/6 Norfolk Street, Sheffield/ England.*
(Butterfield & Butterfield) **$3,025**

A fine English Bowie knife signed *Wm. SANSOM & Co. KING'S CUTLERS*, circa 1860–70, German silver guard and horsehead pommel each formed in two halves and cast in high relief, 16in.
(Sotheby's) **$7,909**

Unmarked Bowie knife, the 8½in. single edged blade with 3¼in. false edge, steel crossguard, marine ivory grip carved in the form of a coiled belt, 12¾in. long overall.
(Butterfield & Butterfield) **$660**

Large unmarked Bowie knife, having a 12¼in. spear point blade with a 5in. false edge, staghorn grip with iron crossguard and brass mounts and copper disk on butt, 18in. long overall.
(Butterfield & Butterfield) **$770**

CASED SETS

Cased Colt Model 1849 pocket percussion
revolver, serial No. 44690, .31 caliber, 6in. barrel
with two line New York address.
(Butterfield & Butterfield)   **$1,320**

Cased factory engraved Colt Pocket Model 1849
percussion revolver, serial No. 57493, .31 caliber,
5in. barrel engraved *Sam'l Colt*.
(Butterfield & Butterfield)   **$5,500**

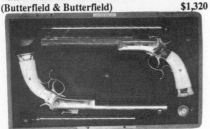

Fine cased pair of engraved Galand single
shot pistols, first pistol, a .22 caliber, having a
10in. octagonal barrel, second pistol, a .44
caliber, 10in. unusual seven sided barrel.
(Butterfield & Butterfield)   **$5,500**

A fine cased factory engraved Colt Model 1849
five-shot percussion revolver, No. 105758 for
1855, with .31 caliber blued 4in. barrel engraved
Saml. Colt, silver-plated brass trigger-guard and
grip-straps, 8³/₄in. (Sotheby's)   **$6,325**

An Adams patent 120-bore five-shot self-cocking
percussion revolver with blued octagonal sighted
barrel, the top-strap signed *F. Barnes & Co., 109
Fenchurch St., London*, London proof marks,
9³/₄in.
(Christie's)   **$1,172**

A pair of percussion duelling pistols with
browned twist octagonal sighted barrels signed
in full on the top flat, checkered butts, by Nixon,
Gun Maker, Newark, Birmingham proof marks,
circa 1850, 14¹/₂in.
(Christie's)   **$5,416**

A good cased .36 Colt Navy percussion revolver,
Serial No. 35773 (matching), 7¹/₂in. barrel
engraved with London address, engraved
cylinder and inscribed *Colt's Patent No. 35773*,
plated trigger guard and strap, walnut grips.
(Bonhams)   **$3,275**

A German cased percussion target pistol, by Jos.
Kruse in Münster, circa 1855, with signed
browned swamped octagonal sighted barrel
rifled with ten grooves and inscribed *ENGL.
STAHL LAUF*, 16³/₄in.
(Sotheby's)   **$4,887**

CASED SETS

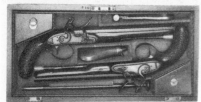

A cased pair of 16 bore flintlock duelling pistols by Mallet, 14³/₄in., swamped octagonal barrels 9¹/₂in. engraved *No 7 Charing Cross London.*
(Wallis & Wallis) $4,053

A cased John Manton & Son 20 bore grip safety double barrelled percussion fowling piece, serial No. 10554, 30in. signed browned twist barrels.
(George Kidner) $2,400

Cased Colt Model 1849 percussion pocket revolver, serial No. 287503, .31 caliber, 4in. barrel, blued and casehardened finish, varnished walnut grips.
(Butterfield & Butterfield) $2,750

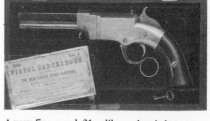

A very fine cased .31 caliber volcanic lever-action No. 1 pocket pistol, by the New Haven Arms Company, No. 1923, circa 1857–62, with sighted blued 3¹/₂in. barrel and magazine, 9¹/₄in.
(Sotheby's) $13,225

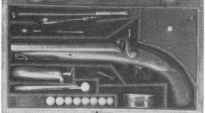

An English cased double barrelled percussion officer's pistol by J. Beattie, London, circa 1848, with signed browned twist sighted barrels, engraved case-hardened breeches, breech tang and signed back-action locks, 13¹/₂in.
(Sotheby's) $2,875

Rare cased and gold inlaid pair of deluxe Colt Brevete percussion revolvers made for the Emperor Faustin I (1847–1859) of Haiti, circa 1855, each with 6in. octagonal barrels in .36 caliber.
(Butterfield & Butterfield) $33,000

A fine English cased pair of flintlock officer's pistols by Wattell Clark, Holborn, London, circa 1810, with signed browned twist sighted barrels, gold-lined vents, 15in.
(Sotheby's) $4,887

A Webley patent 50-bore five-shot double-action percussion revolver with blued octagonal barrel, checkered walnut grips, in fitted mahogany case, Birmingham proof marks, 11¹/₂in.
(Christie's) $1,533

CASED SETS

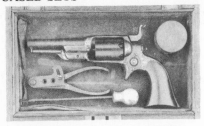

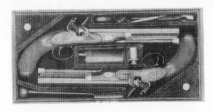

A .31 caliber Colt 'Roots Patent' (M1855 sidehammer) percussion pocket revolver, Serial No. 5687 (1862), standard 3¹/₂in. barrel model, British proof (London) in typical London Agency oak case with descriptive label. (Bonhams) $753

A pair of flintlock duelling pistols by R. Baker, Hereford, Birmingham proof marks, circa 1820, with heavy rebrowned twist octagonal barrels with silver fore-sight, patent breech with platinum lines and platinum vent, breech tangs finely engraved with scrolls and foliage, 15³/₄in. (Sotheby's) $6,035

A rare 10-bore double barrelled percussion combined shotgun and rifle with browned twist sighted barrels signed in full at the breech, blued folding leaf-sights calibrated from 100 to 300 yards, gold-plated scroll engraved tang, highly figured walnut half-stock, London proof marks, No. 3722 for 1863, 31in. barrels.
(Christie's) $6,860

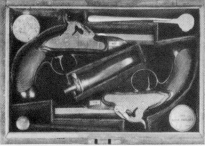

An unusual pair of German percussion traveling pistols with swamped octagonal sighted barrels signed in silver and stamped with a mark at the breech, figured walnut half-stocks, checkered butts, by F. Ulrich in Stuttgart, circa 1830, 8¹/₄in.
(Christie's) $3,069

A cased 5 shot 80 bore Tranter's patent double action percussion revolver No. 21121T, 10in. barrel 4¹/₂in. Birmingham proved, top flat engraved *Griffiths & Worsley (Late) J W Edge Manchester*.
(Wallis & Wallis) $2,026

CROSSBOWS

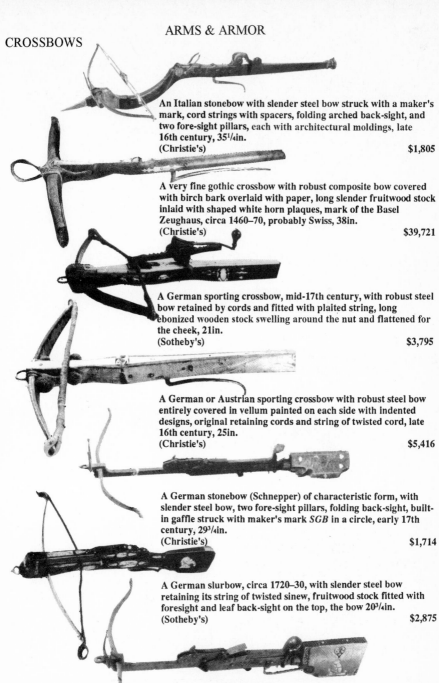

An Italian stonebow with slender steel bow struck with a maker's mark, cord strings with spacers, folding arched back-sight, and two fore-sight pillars, each with architectural moldings, late 16th century, 35¼in.
(Christie's) $1,805

A very fine gothic crossbow with robust composite bow covered with birch bark overlaid with paper, long slender fruitwood stock inlaid with shaped white horn plaques, mark of the Basel Zeughaus, circa 1460–70, probably Swiss, 38in.
(Christie's) $39,721

A German sporting crossbow, mid-17th century, with robust steel bow retained by cords and fitted with plaited string, long ebonized wooden stock swelling around the nut and flattened for the cheek, 21in.
(Sotheby's) $3,795

A German or Austrian sporting crossbow with robust steel bow entirely covered in vellum painted on each side with indented designs, original retaining cords and string of twisted cord, late 16th century, 25in.
(Christie's) $5,416

A German stonebow (Schnepper) of characteristic form, with slender steel bow, two fore-sight pillars, folding back-sight, built-in gaffle struck with maker's mark *SGB* in a circle, early 17th century, 29¾in.
(Christie's) $1,714

A German slurbow, circa 1720–30, with slender steel bow retaining its string of twisted sinew, fruitwood stock fitted with foresight and leaf back-sight on the top, the bow 20¾in.
(Sotheby's) $2,875

A German sporting stonebow, early 17th century, with steel bow, steel tiller with built-in gaffle struck with maker's mark, molded iron trigger-guard, bow 18½in.
(Sotheby's) $1,955

DAGGERS

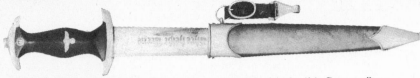

A good 1933 pattern SS dagger, by Boker, blade retaining all original polish, German silver
mounts, in its dark blued sheath.
(Wallis & Wallis)   **$1,321**

A large 17th century katar, blade 16in. with raised central rib, serrated edges and swollen forte,
steel hilt chiseled overall.
(Wallis & Wallis)   **$480**

A 19th century Indo Persian dagger pesh kabz, recurved single edged fullered blade $9^3/4$in., steel
knucklebow and quillons, grip made from sections of jade.
(Wallis & Wallis)   **$130**

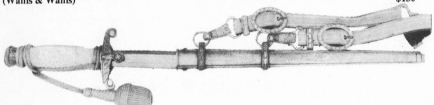

A Nazi Army officer's dagger, by Robert Klaas, plated mounts, white grip, original bullion dress
knot, in its plated sheath.
(Wallis & Wallis)   **$416**

A Nazi 1st Pattern Railway Protection Force dagger, by Eickhorn, plated mounts, black grip, in
its plated sheath.
(Wallis & Wallis)   **$603**

A late Mogul pesh-kabz, early 19th century, with cast silver lion head grip and fretwork silver
mounts, on leather covered wood scabbard.
(Bonhams)   **$309**

DAGGERS

A Nazi SA dagger, by EP & S, the blade with partly erased Rohm inscription, German silver
mounts, in metal sheath with plated mounts.
(Wallis & Wallis) $342

An old Barong, leaf blade 16in., polished wood hilt with small foliate carved beak, Eastern silver
long base mount with silver wire band at top, in its wooden sheath.
(Wallis & Wallis) $107

A Nazi Luftwaffe 1st pattern officer's dagger, by SMF, plated blade, plated mounts, wire bound
blue leather covered grip, bullion dress knot, in its blue leather covered metal sheath.
(Wallis & Wallis) $416

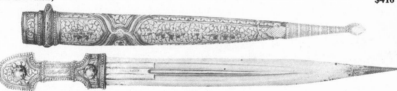

A Russian nielloed silver mounted dagger kindjal, circa 1900, 21$^{1}/_{2}$in., double edged blade with
three fullers 14in. stamped *AGAYPAINMZ*, fullers etched with scrolls, hilt and sheath deeply
foliate chiseled with scrollwork and foliage.
(Wallis & Wallis) $765

A Nazi Labor Service (RAD) enlisted man's dagger, cleaver blade 9½in. etched *Arbeit Adelt,* with
maker Carl Crebbs with RJAD mark, plated guard stamped *Ma803,* staghorn grips, in its black
painted sheath, plated mount stamps *Ma803.*
(Wallis & Wallis) $616

An Indian katar, Tanjore, 17th/18th century, with very slender blade retained by an iron
reinforce finely pierced and chiseled on both sides with a pattern of scrolls, 21¼in.
(Sotheby's) $2,875

ARMS & ARMOR

A fine Ballock dagger, Flemish or German, early 16th century, with long slender tapering blade of flattened diamond section changing to flattened hexagonal section, 17³/₄in.
(Sotheby's) $3,954

A German silver-encrusted left-hand dagger, circa 1620–30, with slender blade of flattened diamond section pierced with rows of minute circular holes and slots, 9³/₄in.
(Sotheby's) $4,331

A dagger of so-called Buckingham type, English or Dutch, second quarter 17th century, with tapering single-edged blade formed with a reinforced point of diamond section, 13³/₈in.
(Sotheby's) $1,092

A large all steel Indian recurved double dagger Haladie, 29³/₄in. overall, recurved blades 12in. with shallow fullers, spiral grip, knucklebow with 4in. blade.
(Wallis & Wallis) $275

A fine Neapolitan left-hand dagger, circa 1670–90, with slender three-stage blade pierced with small circles and squares within the narrow fuller along the notched back edge, 20⁵/₈in.
(Sotheby's) $5,175

An unusual 18th century Indian wavy bladed katar, 24in., single edged firangi blade 18in., hilt with raised chiseled edges, grip bars chiseled with fluted ornament
(Wallis & Wallis) $275

A rare left-hand dagger, circa 1560–80, probably German, in excavated condition, with tapering double-edged blade formed with a strong full-length medial ridge, 15¹/₂in.
(Sotheby's) $979

ARMS & ARMOR

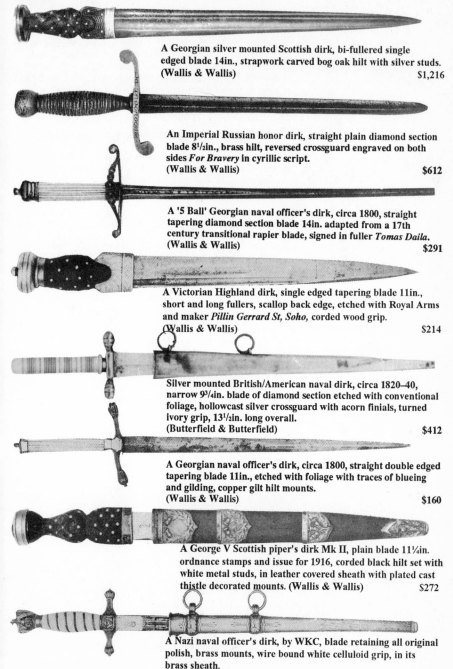

A Georgian silver mounted Scottish dirk, bi-fullered single edged blade 14in., strapwork carved bog oak hilt with silver studs. (Wallis & Wallis) $1,216

An Imperial Russian honor dirk, straight plain diamond section blade 8½in., brass hilt, reversed crossguard engraved on both sides *For Bravery* in cyrillic script. (Wallis & Wallis) $612

A '5 Ball' Georgian naval officer's dirk, circa 1800, straight tapering diamond section blade 14in. adapted from a 17th century transitional rapier blade, signed in fuller *Tomas Daila*. (Wallis & Wallis) $291

A Victorian Highland dirk, single edged tapering blade 11in., short and long fullers, scallop back edge, etched with Royal Arms and maker *Pillin Gerrard St, Soho,* corded wood grip. (Wallis & Wallis) $214

Silver mounted British/American naval dirk, circa 1820–40, narrow 9¾in. blade of diamond section etched with conventional foliage, hollowcast silver crossguard with acorn finials, turned ivory grip, 13½in. long overall. (Butterfield & Butterfield) $412

A Georgian naval officer's dirk, circa 1800, straight double edged tapering blade 11in., etched with foliage with traces of blueing and gilding, copper gilt hilt mounts. (Wallis & Wallis) $160

A George V Scottish piper's dirk Mk II, plain blade 11¼in. ordnance stamps and issue for 1916, corded black hilt set with white metal studs, in leather covered sheath with plated cast thistle decorated mounts. (Wallis & Wallis) $272

A Nazi naval officer's dirk, by WKC, blade retaining all original polish, brass mounts, wire bound white celluloid grip, in its brass sheath. (Wallis & Wallis) $326

41

FLINTLOCK GUNS

Scarce Manton Pattern 1833 flintlock cavalry carbine, the 20in.
.67 caliber barrel with swivel ramrod, casehardened bolted lock
marked *WR* with crown over *Tower* and dated *1835*.
(Butterfield & Butterfield) $2,475

Short Land Pattern flintlock musket by Barbar, circa 1760, with
42in. .78 caliber barrel, round lock with double line border,
including top jaw, trefoil spring finial and marked *Barbar*.
(Butterfield & Butterfield) $2,750

A 10 bore East India Company military flintlock musket, 54½in.
overall, barrel 39in. with London proofs, also bearing Jaipur
arsenal stamps, slightly rounded lock with ring neck cock and
raised pan.
(Wallis & Wallis) $918

Flintlock musketoon, late 17th/early 18th century, the 28½in.
three stage barrel with flared muzzle and with octagonal breech
marked with crown over *IN*, crown over *V* and a third
undecipherable mark.
(Butterfield & Butterfield) $1,760

A steel barrelled flintlock blunderbuss, 31½in., swamped barrel
15¾in., Birmingham proved, fullstocked, bolted lock engraved
Newark with roller bearing frizzen spring.
(Wallis & Wallis) $1,186

Flintlock cavalry carbine, circa 1800, the 20in. .70 caliber barrel
with Birmingham proofs, Tower marked lock with crown and
single line border, brass furniture including swivel ramrod.
(Butterfield & Butterfield) $825

An unusual Turkish miquelet flintlock rifle, 48in., deeply rifled
swamped octagonal barrel 34in. of good quality, inlaid with two
Islamic silver maker's poincons in the Spanish style, unusual
graduated folding rearsight.
(Wallis & Wallis) $612

FLINTLOCK GUNS

Scarce Baker flintlock cavalry carbine, the 20½in. barrel rifled
in .72 caliber with proofed breech, pistol grip stock with crown
and cipher and obsolete stamps, 36in. long overall.
(Butterfield & Butterfield) $3,575

American halfstocked flintlock buck and ball gun by I. Ruswell,
the 44in. two stage barrel in .56 caliber smoothbore, underside of
barrel with wood rib for attachment of ramrod thimbles.
(Butterfield & Butterfield) $1,870

A brass barrelled flintlock blunderbuss, 32¼in., half octagonal
flared barrel 16½in., bell mouthed, top flat engraved *T. Bolton &
Co. London*, fullstocked, foliate engraved lock with roller bearing
frizzen spring.
(Wallis & Wallis) $1,760

A rare flintlock blunderbuss by Durs Egg, London, circa 1780,
with iron barrel belled towards the muzzle, signed in early script
form, fitted on the right with an iron frame housing a sliding
bayonet, 34in. (Sotheby's) $3,865

A flintlock blunderbuss with sighted four-stage brass barrel
belled at the muzzle, walnut full stock with raised apron around
the barrel tang, by Robert 1 Silk, London, London proof marks,
late 17th century, 29½in.
(Christie's) $3,069

Italian flintlock fowling piece, blued two stage 35½in. .72 caliber
smoothbore barrel with swamped muzzle, roller mounted frizzen
spring with maker's name *Paolo Corsini*.
(Butterfield & Butterfield) $2,200

A rare German inlaid wheellock sporting rifle with square bore,
late 16th century, 43½in., swamped octagonal barrel 33¼in.
struck with maker's brass poincon of an owl with initials *I.E.*,
fullstocked, lock with gilt bronze wheel cover foliate engraved.
(Wallis & Wallis) $3,729

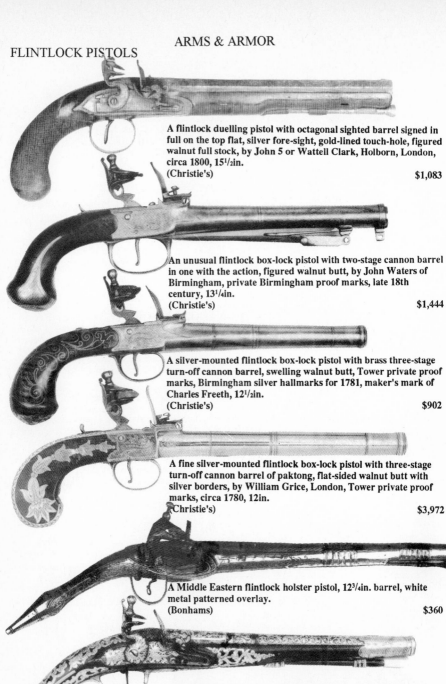

A flintlock duelling pistol with octagonal sighted barrel signed in full on the top flat, silver fore-sight, gold-lined touch-hole, figured walnut full stock, by John 5 or Wattell Clark, Holborn, London, circa 1800, 15¹/₂in.
(Christie's) $1,083

An unusual flintlock box-lock pistol with two-stage cannon barrel in one with the action, figured walnut butt, by John Waters of Birmingham, private Birmingham proof marks, late 18th century, 13¹/₄in.
(Christie's) $1,444

A silver-mounted flintlock box-lock pistol with brass three-stage turn-off cannon barrel, swelling walnut butt, Tower private proof marks, Birmingham silver hallmarks for 1781, maker's mark of Charles Freeth, 12¹/₂in.
(Christie's) $902

A fine silver-mounted flintlock box-lock pistol with three-stage turn-off cannon barrel of paktong, flat-sided walnut butt with silver borders, by William Grice, London, Tower private proof marks, circa 1780, 12in.
(Christie's) $3,972

A Middle Eastern flintlock holster pistol, 12³/₄in. barrel, white metal patterned overlay.
(Bonhams) $360

A Turkish silver-mounted flintlock holster pistol with three-stage barrel profusely encrusted with gold scrollwork, foliage and trophies of arms, spurred pommel with grotesque mask cap, dated *1224* for 1810 A.D., 18in.
(Christie's) $5,055

ARMS & ARMOR

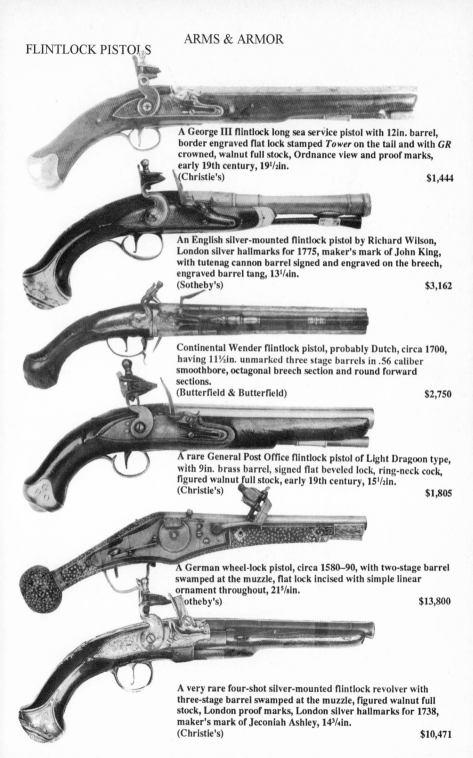

A George III flintlock long sea service pistol with 12in. barrel, border engraved flat lock stamped *Tower* on the tail and with *GR* crowned, walnut full stock, Ordnance view and proof marks, early 19th century, 19½in.
(Christie's) $1,444

An English silver-mounted flintlock pistol by Richard Wilson, London silver hallmarks for 1775, maker's mark of John King, with tutenag cannon barrel signed and engraved on the breech, engraved barrel tang, 13¼in.
(Sotheby's) $3,162

Continental Wender flintlock pistol, probably Dutch, circa 1700, having 11½in. unmarked three stage barrels in .56 caliber smoothbore, octagonal breech section and round forward sections.
(Butterfield & Butterfield) $2,750

A rare General Post Office flintlock pistol of Light Dragoon type, with 9in. brass barrel, signed flat beveled lock, ring-neck cock, figured walnut full stock, early 19th century, 15½in.
(Christie's) $1,805

A German wheel-lock pistol, circa 1580–90, with two-stage barrel swamped at the muzzle, flat lock incised with simple linear ornament throughout, 21⅝in.
(Sotheby's) $13,800

A very rare four-shot silver-mounted flintlock revolver with three-stage barrel swamped at the muzzle, figured walnut full stock, London proof marks, London silver hallmarks for 1738, maker's mark of Jeconiah Ashley, 14¾in.
(Christie's) $10,471

HELMETS

A King's Crown officer's blue cloth helmet, with 4th Battalion Border Regiment badge, leather trim to reverse.
(Bonhams) **$1,015**

A German comb morion, early 17th century, of heavy construction and formed of two halves joined by a narrow cabled comb, 10¹/₈in. high.
(Sotheby's) **$1,162**

A scarce RAF officer's parade helmet, fur trimmed black leather skull, plaited gilt lines, patent leather chinstrap.
(Wallis & Wallis) **$641**

A fine Greek bronze helmet, Corinthian, early 6th century B.C., forged in one piece, of slightly carinated domed form with out-turned flaring cheeks, 9in. high.
(Sotheby's) **$40,250**

A South German infantry burgonet, circa 1540–50, with one-piece skull formed with four segmental low ridges meeting at a chiseled acorn finial, 10¾in. high.
(Sotheby's) **$5,462**

A Victorian other rank's lance cap of The 12th (Prince of Wales's Royal) Lancers, black patent leather skull, peak and top, brass plate with battle honors to Sevastopol
(Wallis & Wallis) **$805**

An armet, designed to rotate on the rim of a gorget, with one-piece skull with high roped comb, circa 1540–50, probably French, 10¹/₂in. high.
(Christie's) **$11,735**

A Victorian trooper's lance cap of the 9th (Queen's Royal) Lancers, black patent leather skull, peak and top, eight battle honors to Lucknow.
(Wallis & Wallis) **$700**

A close helmet, in German mid-16th century style, well-formed throughout, with one-piece skull drawn up to a pronounced ridge, 13¹/₄in. high.
(Sotheby's) **$1,035**

HELMETS

A Savoyard cuirassier helmet, of blackened steel, circa 1630–50, with two-piece skull joined by a low comb, 12in. high.
(Sotheby's) $5,462

53rd Foot (Shropshire) officer's 1829–44 bell top shako, large fire gilt Universal plate mounted with diamond-cut silver star.
(Bosley's) $6,520

A Prussian General officer's Pickelhaube, gilt guard eagle helmet plate, with silver and enameled Garde star.
(Wallis & Wallis) $1,864

15th Irish Lancers officer's silver mounted czapska, early 20th century, of scarlet cloth and black patent leather with gold lacing.
(Butterfield & Butterfield) $1,760

A German burgonet with one-piece skull with roped comb, the fall and neck-plate upcurved and sharply pointed, late 16th century, perhaps Landshut, 11in. high.
(Christie's) $4,333

An extremely rare military padded quilted headdress, 18th century, perhaps Indian, formed with a domed skull built on a segmented wicker frame rising to a wooden calyx finial.
(Sotheby's) $8,050

A German black-and-white comb morion, early 17th century, with blackened broad two-piece skull joined by a high narrow comb, 13in. high.
(Sotheby's) $5,175

A German etched close helmet, for the foot tournament, in early 17th century, with two-piece skull joined by a cabled comb, 12¹/₂in. high.
(Sotheby's) $4,025

A French Second Republic shako, black beaver, patent leather peak, headband and top, crimson lace band to top, red and blue cockade.
(Wallis & Wallis) $146

HELMETS

A scarce Nazi M 1935 steel helmet of the SS Polizei Grenadier Division, original transfer badges, police shield and state emblem.
(Wallis & Wallis) $700

An officer's helmet of the Royal Horse Guards, silver plated skull, gilt mounts, leather backed brass chinchain.
(Wallis & Wallis) $1,932

French Dragoon helmet, 19th century, with unmarked brass mounted steel skull retaining its horsehair crest.
(Butterfield & Butterfield) $495

A very good late Victorian officer's gilt helmet of The 6th Dragoon Guards (Carabiniers), with gilt ear to ear wreath, top mounts, red leather backed chinscales.
(Wallis & Wallis) $1,540

An extremely rare close helmet, Innsbruck Court Workshop, in the manner of Hans Seusenhofer, circa 1515–30, with broad rounded skull drawn out in one piece to a strong rear-swept profile, 11in. high.
(Sotheby's) $43,311

17th of Foot Leicestershire Regiment, 1844–55 Albert pattern officer's shako, body of beaver skin with patent leather peak and neck peak.
(Bosley's) $5,216

A composite close helmet, Italian or Flemish, circa 1580, with two-piece skull joined by a narrow comb, fitted with plume-holder, 12$\frac{1}{2}$in. high.
(Sotheby's) $2,300

SS, a rare example of a 1936 pattern double decal steel helmet, retaining SS runes (95% present), and swastika and red shield.
(Bosley's) $1,630

Royal Fusiliers, a good post 1902 other rank's issue fur cap, to front, a brass regimental pattern flaming grenade with white hackle to right side.
(Bosley's) $293

A scarce and interesting Victorian Staff Officer's cocked hat of the Royal Guernsey Regiment of Militia, silver lace loop, with large silver plated regimental button.
(Wallis & Wallis) $489

An English trooper's pot helmet, circa 1640, with two-piece skull joined by a low comb, fitted with hinged pointed fall, 11¹/₂in. high.
(Sotheby's) $1,599

Rare U.S. Marine headgear, circa 1800, constructed of heavy black felt with brim edged in ribbon, the crown of black painted leather.
(Butterfield & Butterfield) $3,300

An Imperial German Reservist cuirassier officer's helmet, silver plated skull fluted spike and helmet badge with brass reservist cross.
(Wallis & Wallis) $2,432

A closed burgonet, German or Dutch, first quarter 17th century, with two-piece skull joined by a narrow comb and fitted with fluted plume-holder, 12in. high.
(Sotheby's) $2,259

The Yorkshire Regiment post 1902 officer's Home Service pattern blue cloth helmet, with gilt spike, rose bosses and chin chain with velvet lined backing.
(Bosley's) $1,010

A French Leib Gendarmerie trooper's helmet, brass shell, German silver foliate embossed comb with black bristle brush comb.
(Wallis & Wallis) $576

A very rare lining for a morion of brown fabric faced inside with red velvet and quilted in a lozenge pattern, late 16th/early 17th century, 16in. wide.
(Christie's) $3,972

An Imperial German cuirassier's helmet, steel skull, brass eagle badge, steel spike to brass mount, stamped inside *C E Juncker 1914*.
(Wallis & Wallis) $567

A Czarist Russian hunting knife from the Zlatoust Arsenal, straight tapered double edged blade 8³/₄in., with shallow fuller, etched with two vignettes, steel crosspiece and pommel.
(Wallis & Wallis) $138

Large single bladed dirk knife by Marx & Co., 5¹/₂in. single edged blade, grips with mother-of-pearl insets decorated with incised lines and notches, 12in. long extended.
(Butterfield & Butterfield) $1,430

English cutlery hilted dirk knife by Mason, the 6¹/₂in. single edged blade with etched panel *A Sure Defense*, German silver cutlery hilt, 11¹/₂in. long overall.
(Butterfield & Butterfield) $1,210

Unusual single bladed dirk knife by Samuel Robinson, broad 4³/₄in. spear point blade, unusual pierced German silver and tortoise shell grip scales, 10³/₄in. long extended.
(Butterfield & Butterfield) $825

A fine Augsburg silver-mounted trousse, maker's mark of Hans Selber, circa 1570–84, with two small knives and a bodkin each with silver-gilt pommel chased with strapwork on the back and cast in relief on the front, 7⁷/₈in.
(Sotheby's) $16,100

A good silver mounted Gaucho knife, 14¹/₂in., tapered single edge blade 8³/₄in. with broad fuller, silver inlaid at forte, back and octagonal stem with fruiting vine, foliate and geometric designs.
(Wallis & Wallis) $352

A late 19th century Japanese knife, approximate length 11¹/₂in., with lacquered handle and lacquered scabbard, handle decorated with applied bat motif, the scabbard with a silvered lizard, circa 1900.
(Bosley's) $358

KNIVES

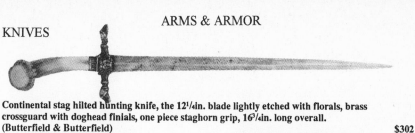

Continental stag hilted hunting knife, the 12¼in. blade lightly etched with florals, brass crossguard with doghead finials, one piece staghorn grip, 16¾in. long overall.
(Butterfield & Butterfield) $302

An early 19th century German hunting knife, swollen single edged blade 6¾in. struck with crescent moon, silver mounted deer's hoof hilt, in its silver mounted leather sheath.
(Wallis & Wallis) $199

Buck Brothers knife, the 6½in. double edged blade marked *Buck Brothers*, German silver quillons, one piece wood grip, black leather scabbard, 11¼in. long overall.
(Butterfield & Butterfield) $990

Large Mediterranean dirk knife, 19th century, acutely pointed 10¼in. single edged blade with etched florals on one side, two piece bone and horn grip scales, brass bolsters with recurved quillons at the blade, 22in. long extended.
(Butterfield & Butterfield) $990

A composite knife and fork set, comprising knife with later rounded single-edged blade struck with a mark, fork with long slender writhen steel neck made in one with two tines, ivory handle, and silver ferrule, in ivory sheath with two compartments, German or Dutch, all 17th century, 6½in., 7in. and 7in.
(Christie's) $2,708

Civil War IXL 'Liberty and Union' knife by Wostenholm, single edged 4¾in. spear point blade with 2½in. false edge, ivory grip scales, the left side with lozenge shaped German silver escutcheon, 10in. long extended.
(Butterfield & Butterfield) $3,300

A German Waidblatt, circa 1620–30, from a hunting trousse, with heavy blade double-edged over half its length towards a conventional spear point, 22¼in.
(Sotheby's) $3,450

MILITARIA

A Victorian officer's full dress embroidered scarlet pouch of the 8th (King's Royal Irish) Hussars, embroidered Royal Crest/lugs on VR.
(Wallis & Wallis) $416

A post-1902 General's blue cloth shabraque, double gilt lace border, complete with one pistol holster cover and top.
(Wallis & Wallis) $1,135

A good Nazi Party rectangular rigid car flag, laid on emblem on white silk background, the flag border edging of gold roping, 7½ x 11in.
(Wallis & Wallis) $240

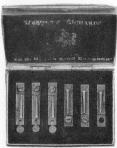 

An unusual set of extra foresights, for Westley Richards .577 double-barrelled rifle No. 17231, in brass silk- and velvet-lined and fitted presentation box.
(Christie's) $368

A Company Commander's embroidered silk pipe banner of The Highland Light Infantry, embroidered with King's Crown over HLI monogram, within wreath and thirty-one battle honors 'Hindoostan' to 'Mysore'.
(Wallis & Wallis) $1,181

2nd West Yorks Artillery Volunteers (Bradford), a good pre-1901 officer's sabretache, black melton cloth ground with silver embroidered Royal Arms oak leaf and acorn decoration.
(Bosley's) $293

5th Lancashire Volunteer Artillery (Preston), a good pre-1901 officer's sabretache, Royal Arms and oak leaf decoration in silver embroidery.
(Bosley's) $293

A pair of bronze rowel spurs, early 17th century, possibly French, decorated throughout with punched and pricked ornament, 5½in.
(Sotheby's) $1,265

A Victorian officer's full dress embroidered blue cloth sabretache of the Edinburgh Artillery (Militia), gilt lace border.
(Wallis & Wallis) $648

MILITARIA

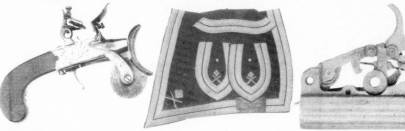

A brass flintlock powder tester, by Spencer of London, frame engraved with trophies of arms, calibrated wheel, 6in. long overall.
(Bonhams) $786

A Major General's blue cloth shabraque, double gilt lace border, complete with pistol holster covers and top.
(Wallis & Wallis) $851

Rare Volks-Sturm-Gewehr (VG1–5) trigger mechanism, of stamped steel construction throughout marked at a *4* at back of cover piece.
(Butterfield & Butterfield) $192

An American fleece lined World War II bomber jacket, type B-3, immaculately painted on front and back, bearing the artistry from the nose of the plane 'Some Pumpkins'.
(Bonhams) $1,391

A pair of iron parade stirrups, Hungarian or Transylvanian, 18th century, each with triangular sides formed in one piece with the tread, 6¹/₄in. high.
(Sotheby's) $1,495

A fine American parade saddle, mounted in German silver, unsigned, perhaps for a lady or a child, comprising saddle with the cantle and horn completely encased in German silver.
(Sotheby's) $4,600

A Georgian officer's silver colored gorget of The 62nd (The Wiltshire) Regiment, engraved with pre-1801 Royal Arms, *G* and *R*.
(Wallis & Wallis) $697

A late Georgian naval officer's sword belt, of black silk, with slings, gilt lions mask mounts and buckles to slings.
(Wallis & Wallis) $88

A Victorian officer's full dress embroidered sabretache of the 13th Hussars, buff cloth, six battle honors 'Peninsula' to 'Sevastapol'.
(Wallis & Wallis) $1,360

PERCUSSION CARBINES

Rare brass mounted U.S. Model 1855 Harpers Ferry percussion rifle, the 33in. .58 caliber barrel marked at breech *U.S./1857* with *VP* and eaglehead proofs, brass fore-end cap, barrel bands, trigger guard.
(Butterfield & Butterfield) $5,500

New York Central Schuetzen Corp. Sharps Model 1874 sporting rifle, series No. 162298, .40 caliber, 30in. octagonal barrel with open bead front and Lawrence ramp adjustable rear sights.
(Butterfield & Butterfield) $4,950

W. Wurfflein mid-range Schuetzen rifle, serial No. 5143, .32–40 caliber, 29¾in. No. 4 part round/part octagonal barrel with wind gauge/spirit level front sight, mid-range Vernier tang sight.
(Butterfield & Butterfield) $1,430

Winchester Fourth Model 1866 lever action rifle, serial No. 154701, .44 rimfire, 24½in. octagonal barrel with German silver blade fore-sight and adjustable rear.
(Butterfield & Butterfield) $4,950

Winchester Model 1873 lever action musket, serial No. 367653B, .44–40, 30in. barrel, third model configuration, walnut stock and fore-end.
(Butterfield & Butterfield) $825

Remington-Hepburn Walker underlever single shot rifle, serial No. 11, .32-40 caliber, 30in. No. 4 browned octagonal barrel marked *Geo. C. Schoyen Denver, Colo*, equipped with globe front sight and telescopic sight blocks.
(Butterfield & Butterfield) $24,200

Unique Winchester factory modified Model 1876 1 of 1000 lever action carbine, serial No. 8006, .45/60, 22in. round barrel, color casehardened frame and fore-end cap, folding adjustable rear sight marked *1876*.
(Butterfield & Butterfield) $8,800

Winchester Model 1866 lever action rifle, serial No. 16046, .44 rimfire, 24¼in. octagonal barrel marked with *HENRY'S PATENT*, folding ladder-type rear sight, varnished walnut fore-end.
(Butterfield & Butterfield) $14,300

PERCUSSION CARBINES

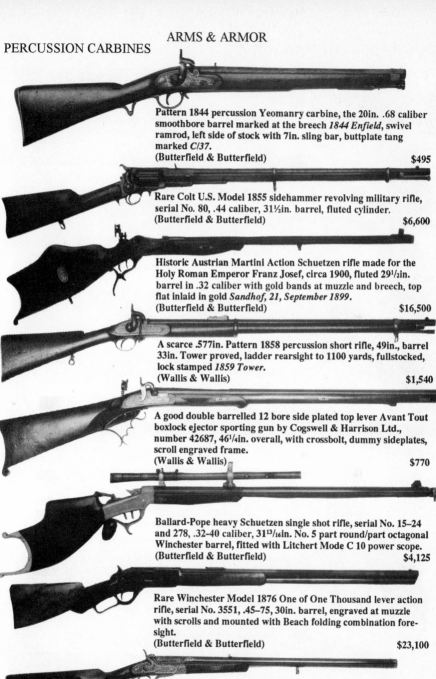

Pattern 1844 percussion Yeomanry carbine, the 20in. .68 caliber smoothbore barrel marked at the breech *1844 Enfield*, swivel ramrod, left side of stock with 7in. sling bar, buttplate tang marked *C/37*.
(Butterfield & Butterfield) **$495**

Rare Colt U.S. Model 1855 sidehammer revolving military rifle, serial No. 80, .44 caliber, 31½in. barrel, fluted cylinder.
(Butterfield & Butterfield) **$6,600**

Historic Austrian Martini Action Schuetzen rifle made for the Holy Roman Emperor Franz Josef, circa 1900, fluted 29½in. barrel in .32 caliber with gold bands at muzzle and breech, top flat inlaid in gold *Sandhof, 21, September 1899*.
(Butterfield & Butterfield) **$16,500**

A scarce .577in. Pattern 1858 percussion short rifle, 49in., barrel 33in. Tower proved, ladder rearsight to 1100 yards, fullstocked, lock stamped *1859 Tower*.
(Wallis & Wallis) **$1,540**

A good double barrelled 12 bore side plated top lever Avant Tout boxlock ejector sporting gun by Cogswell & Harrison Ltd., number 42687, 46¼in. overall, with crossbolt, dummy sideplates, scroll engraved frame.
(Wallis & Wallis) **$770**

Ballard-Pope heavy Schuetzen single shot rifle, serial No. 15–24 and 278, .32-40 caliber, 31¹³/₁₆in. No. 5 part round/part octagonal Winchester barrel, fitted with Litchert Mode C 10 power scope.
(Butterfield & Butterfield) **$4,125**

Rare Winchester Model 1876 One of One Thousand lever action rifle, serial No. 3551, .45–75, 30in. barrel, engraved at muzzle with scrolls and mounted with Beach folding combination foresight.
(Butterfield & Butterfield) **$23,100**

Fine gold inlaid sporting carbine by Novotny of Prague, circa 1880, serial No. 2300, .450 centerfire caliber, 25in. round barrel with flat top rib fitted with engraved front and single standing/single folding leaf rear sights.
(Butterfield & Butterfield) **$9,900**

PERCUSSION PISTOLS

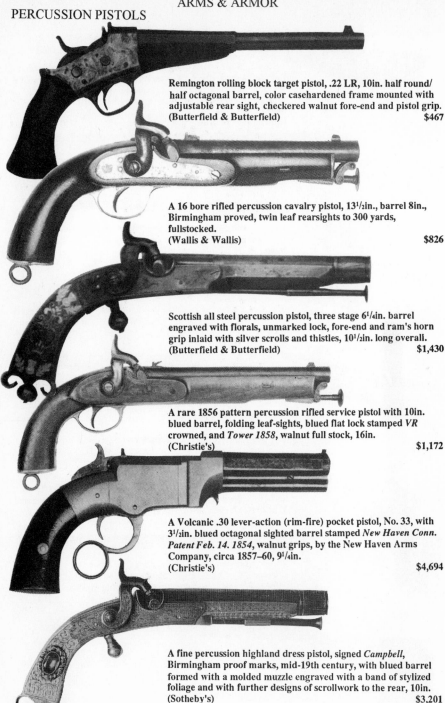

Remington rolling block target pistol, .22 LR, 10in. half round/
half octagonal barrel, color casehardened frame mounted with
adjustable rear sight, checkered walnut fore-end and pistol grip.
(Butterfield & Butterfield) $467

A 16 bore rifled percussion cavalry pistol, 13½in., barrel 8in.,
Birmingham proved, twin leaf rearsights to 300 yards,
fullstocked.
(Wallis & Wallis) $826

Scottish all steel percussion pistol, three stage 6¼in. barrel
engraved with florals, unmarked lock, fore-end and ram's horn
grip inlaid with silver scrolls and thistles, 10½in. long overall.
(Butterfield & Butterfield) $1,430

A rare 1856 pattern percussion rifled service pistol with 10in.
blued barrel, folding leaf-sights, blued flat lock stamped *VR*
crowned, and *Tower 1858*, walnut full stock, 16in.
(Christie's) $1,172

A Volcanic .30 lever-action (rim-fire) pocket pistol, No. 33, with
3½in. blued octagonal sighted barrel stamped *New Haven Conn.
Patent Feb. 14. 1854*, walnut grips, by the New Haven Arms
Company, circa 1857–60, 9¼in.
(Christie's) $4,694

A fine percussion highland dress pistol, signed *Campbell*,
Birmingham proof marks, mid-19th century, with blued barrel
formed with a molded muzzle engraved with a band of stylized
foliage and with further designs of scrollwork to the rear, 10in.
(Sotheby's) $3,201

PERCUSSION PISTOLS

A 9mm. P08 long barreled artillery Luger semi automatic pistol, 12³/₄in. overall, barrel 8in., number 5273, rearsight to 800 metres, the breech dated *1917*.
(Wallis & Wallis)   **$673**

Volcanic No. 1 lever action pocket pistol by New Haven Arms Co., serial No. 527, .30 caliber, 6in. barrel marked *New Haven Conn Patent Feb 14, 1854*, varnished walnut grips.
(Butterfield & Butterfield)   **$4,400**

A scarce .455in. Eley British Service issue Colt Government Model semi automatic pistol, 8¹/₂in. overall, barrel 5in., number W104976, the slide and frame bearing government acceptance marks.
(& Wallis)   **$765**

Approx. .38-bore percussion boxlock sidehammer belt pistol, NVN, retailed by 'Thomas Norfolk, Bury St. Edmunds', smooth bored 4in. octagonal barrel with under-rib and captive rammer.
(Bonhams)   **$294**

English swivel breech percussion pocket pistol by Hartwell, with round 1⁵/₈in. .36 caliber barrels with keyed muzzles, rounded brass frame engraved with florals.
(Butterfield & Butterfield)   **$220**

A rare French breech-loading percussion pistol for center-fire cartridges with octagonal sighted rifled barrel pivoting to the left for loading, foliate engraved case-hardened hammer, by Louis Perrin-Le Page à Paris, circa 1832, 14¹/₄in.
(Christie's)   **$1,444**

PERCUSSION REVOLVERS

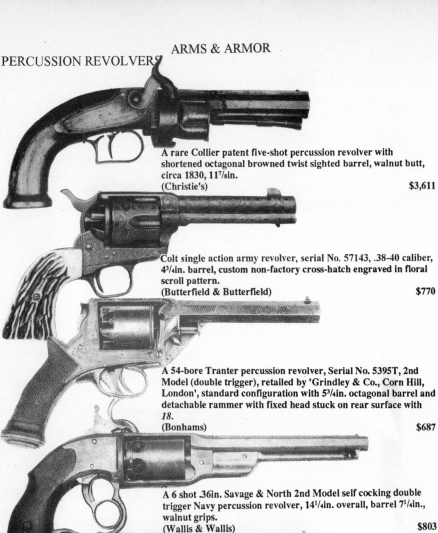

A rare Collier patent five-shot percussion revolver with
shortened octagonal browned twist sighted barrel, walnut butt,
circa 1830, 11⁷/₈in.
(Christie's) $3,611

Colt single action army revolver, serial No. 57143, .38-40 caliber,
4³/₄in. barrel, custom non-factory cross-hatch engraved in floral
scroll pattern.
(Butterfield & Butterfield) $770

A 54-bore Tranter percussion revolver, Serial No. 5395T, 2nd
Model (double trigger), retailed by 'Grindley & Co., Corn Hill,
London', standard configuration with 5³/₄in. octagonal barrel and
detachable rammer with fixed head stuck on rear surface with
18.
(Bonhams) $687

A 6 shot .36in. Savage & North 2nd Model self cocking double
trigger Navy percussion revolver, 14¹/₄in. overall, barrel 7¹/₄in.,
walnut grips.
(Wallis & Wallis) $803

A 54-bore Deane-Harding patent five-shot double-action
percussion revolver, with blued octagonal sighted take-down
barrel engraved *Deane & Son London Bridge*, London proof
marks, circa 1860–65, 12¹/₄in.
(Christie's) $992

A Belgian bar hammer cocking transitional revolver, No. 5457,
approx. 80-bore, 6in. octagonal 'smooth bore' barrel with sprung
bayonet, the action with border engraving and scrollwork,
checkered walnut grip.
(Bonhams) $736

PERCUSSION REVOLVERS

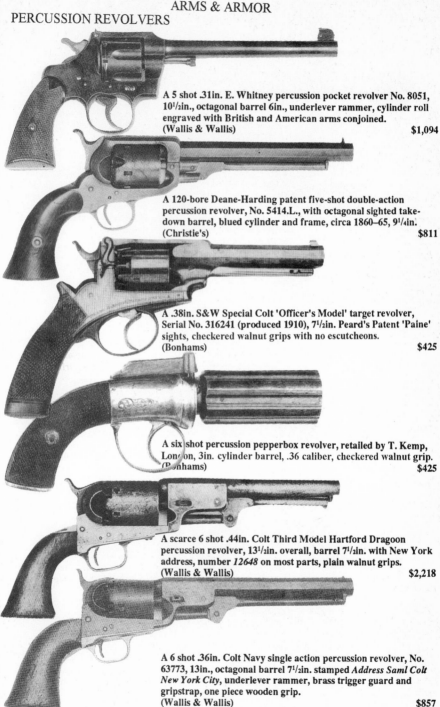

A 5 shot .31in. E. Whitney percussion pocket revolver No. 8051, 10¹/₂in., octagonal barrel 6in., underlever rammer, cylinder roll engraved with British and American arms conjoined.
(Wallis & Wallis) $1,094

A 120-bore Deane-Harding patent five-shot double-action percussion revolver, No. 5414.L., with octagonal sighted take-down barrel, blued cylinder and frame, circa 1860–65, 9¹/₄in.
(Christie's) $811

A .38in. S&W Special Colt 'Officer's Model' target revolver, Serial No. 316241 (produced 1910), 7¹/₂in. Peard's Patent 'Paine' sights, checkered walnut grips with no escutcheons.
(Bonhams) $425

A six shot percussion pepperbox revolver, retailed by T. Kemp, London, 3in. cylinder barrel, .36 caliber, checkered walnut grip.
(Bonhams) $425

A scarce 6 shot .44in. Colt Third Model Hartford Dragoon percussion revolver, 13¹/₂in. overall, barrel 7¹/₂in. with New York address, number *12648* on most parts, plain walnut grips.
(Wallis & Wallis) $2,218

A 6 shot .36in. Colt Navy single action percussion revolver, No. 63773, 13in., octagonal barrel 7¹/₂in. stamped *Address Saml Colt New York City*, underlever rammer, brass trigger guard and gripstrap, one piece wooden grip.
(Wallis & Wallis) $857

POWDER FLASKS

A German musketeer's powder-flask, early 17th century, with curved triangular wooden body bound with strips of iron, Nuremburg mark, 12³/₄in.
(Sotheby's) $846

An Italian musketeer's triangular powder-flask, early 17th century, the front almost entirely encased by an iron plate pierced and embossed with an heraldic cartouche, 11¹/₈in. high.
(Sotheby's) $903

A good copper powder flask 'Shell and Bush', brass universal pattern charger unit, retaining virtually all original lacquered finish.
(Wallis & Wallis) $160

A rare French brass-mounted lyre-shaped two-way copper pistol flask, the body embossed with sprigs of laurel and marked *Fabque De Nouchet*, circa 1830, 5¹/₄in.
(Christie's) $631

A circular priming-flask of ivory, the body of rounded form set on one face with a central iron plaque chiseled in high relief, early 17th century, probably German, 4¹/₄in. high.
(Christie's) $3,430

A fine Colonial pre-Revolutionary period engraved powder horn, mid-18th century, formed with a molded, very short nozzle, 8¹/₂in.
(Sotheby's) $3,162

A rare silver three-way pistol flask, the ball compartment with pivoting cover, the base incorporating a compartment with sliding cover, early 19th century, 4⁷/₈in.
(Christie's) $758

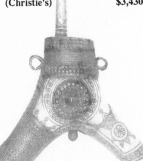

A good scarce 18th century Transylvanian staghorn powder horn, 5³/₄in., body nicely engraved with geometric designs.
(Wallis & Wallis) $474

A scarce 17th century Continental engraved bone powder flask, 7³/₄in., body engraved with a panel of an archer hunting boar with two dogs.
(Wallis & Wallis) $448

A copper powder flask 'Stars', General Service universal pattern charger unit, marked *Dixon & Sons*, with false silver hallmarks.
(Wallis & Wallis) $72

A Dixon brass-mounted copper gun flask with bag-shaped body finely embossed and chased on one side with foliage and hanging game, 19th century, 8in.
(Christie's) $686

A brass-mounted red leather-covered three-way pistol flask, the body of slightly tapering flattened oval section, early 19th century, 4⁵/₈in.
(Christie's) $505

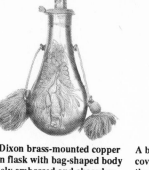

A rare Swiss circular brass priming-flask, by a member of the Oeri family of goldsmiths, Zurich, second half 17th century, the body decorated with engraved concentric lines, 4⁵/₈in. high.
(Sotheby's) $2,070

A German powder-flask in the manner of Johann Michael Maucher of Schwäbisch-Gmünd, with circular wooden body made in two parts around a central pierced hole and carved in high relief, late 17th century, 5¹/₂in. diameter.
(Christie's) $5,055

A tortoiseshell powder-flask, English or Dutch, early 18th century, with large pale body with plain gilt-metal mounts shaped over the sides and covering much of the reverse, 7⁷/₈in.
(Sotheby's) $2,070

Unmarked oak leaf powder flask, Riling 560, oak leaves and ribands decorated two compartment flask.
(Butterfield & Butterfield) $121

A German musketeer's triangular powder-flask, early 17th century, with wooden body retaining its original black velvet covering, 10in.
(Sotheby's) $941

Fine oak leaf powder flask by G. & J. W. Hawksley, Riling 562 type, varnished gilt spout marked with *DR ⁵/₈ through ³/₈.*
(Butterfield & Butterfield) $176

SHELLS

U.S. Hotchkiss bolt, missing lead sabot, 3.67-inch caliber, 7¼in. long.
(Butterfield & Butterfield)
$165

U.S. James bolt, missing sabot, 3.8-inch caliber, 7in. long.
(Butterfield & Butterfield)
$2,090

Post Civil War projectile, unidentified, 8¹⁵/₁₆in. long, 2³/₁₆in. diameter.
(Butterfield & Butterfield)
$77

U.S.N. 12-pound canister round, portion of tin side removed to expose canister shot, wooden sabot on base intact, 4.62-inch calibre.
(Butterfield & Butterfield)
$2,090

U.S. Dahlgren 'Blind Shell', brass pin in nose, lead sabot with remains of hemp rope in lubrication groove, 3.4-inch caliber, 9³/₈in. long.
(Butterfield & Butterfield)
$1,980

German Krupp canister, portion of tin side cut away to expose the canister balls for display, wooden sabot intact, circa late 19th century, 8³/₈in. long.
(Butterfield & Butterfield)
$137

U.S.N. Schenkl projectile, missing papier mâché sabot and fuse, 3.4-inch caliber, 8⁷/₈in. long.
(Butterfield & Butterfield)
$330

32-pound stand of grapeshot, complete with top and bottom plate, 8¹/₂in. long, 6.4-inch caliber.
(Butterfield & Butterfield)
$2,200

U.S. 1-pound Ketchum hand grenade, complete with paper fins marked: *Patented Aug. 20 1861*, 10⁵/₈in. long.
(Butterfield & Butterfield)
$3,300

SHELLS

Late 19th century French rifled projectile, approximate 4.5-inch caliber, large lead studs in two rows, missing fuse, 9¹/₈in. long.
(Butterfield & Butterfield)
$275

Solid shot with metal banded wood sabot, 4in. diameter.
(Butterfield & Butterfield)
$1,760

Confederate archer bolt, missing lead sabot, 3-inch caliber, 6in. long.
(Butterfield & Butterfield)
$385

U.S. Mann or Dimick projectile, patented during the Civil War but not introduced into field surface, two lead bands, 6¹/₄in. long, 3¹/₈in. diameter.
(Butterfield & Butterfield)
$495

British Whitworth rifled spherical solid shot, first appeared in 1867 Whitworth's manual, painted inscription reads: *First experimental shell for smoothbore cannon, Ft. Monroe, Va.*, 5⁷/₁₆in. diameter.
(Butterfield & Butterfield)
$1,650

U.S. 2.6-inch canister round, portion of tin side cut away to expose the canister balls for display, wooden sabot intact, 6¹/₄in. long.
(Butterfield & Butterfield)
$3,575

U.S. Sawyer pattern projectile, iron body covered by a lead jacket, missing fuse, 9⁵/₈in. long, 5in. diameter.
(Butterfield & Butterfield)
$1,870

British Armstrong projectile, three rows of brass studs three rows high, fuse missing, 8³/₈in. long, 3in. diameter.
(Butterfield & Butterfield)
$1,540

French rifled projectile, circa late 19th century, two rows of lead studs, missing fuse, 6¹/₂in. long, 3⁵/₈in. diameter.
(Butterfield & Butterfield)
$302

SWORDS

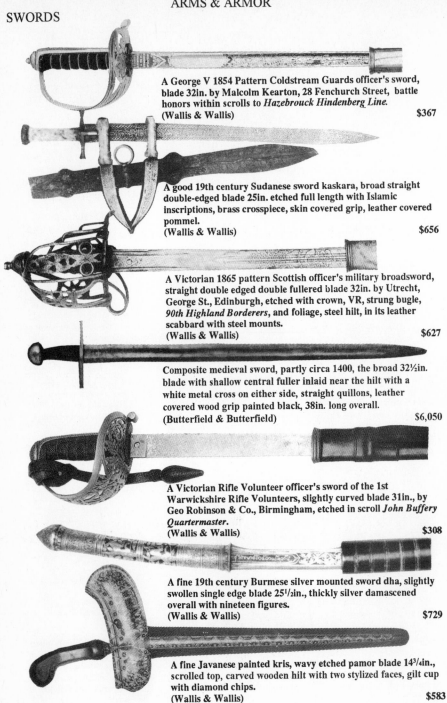

A George V 1854 Pattern Coldstream Guards officer's sword, blade 32in. by Malcolm Kearton, 28 Fenchurch Street, battle honors within scrolls to *Hazebrouck Hindenberg Line*.
(Wallis & Wallis) $367

A good 19th century Sudanese sword kaskara, broad straight double-edged blade 25in. etched full length with Islamic inscriptions, brass crosspiece, skin covered grip, leather covered pommel.
(Wallis & Wallis) $656

A Victorian 1865 pattern Scottish officer's military broadsword, straight double edged double fullered blade 32in. by Utrecht, George St., Edinburgh, etched with crown, VR, strung bugle, *90th Highland Borderers*, and foliage, steel hilt, in its leather scabbard with steel mounts.
(Wallis & Wallis) $627

Composite medieval sword, partly circa 1400, the broad 32½in. blade with shallow central fuller inlaid near the hilt with a white metal cross on either side, straight quillons, leather covered wood grip painted black, 38in. long overall.
(Butterfield & Butterfield) $6,050

A Victorian Rifle Volunteer officer's sword of the 1st Warwickshire Rifle Volunteers, slightly curved blade 31in., by Geo Robinson & Co., Birmingham, etched in scroll *John Buffery Quartermaster*.
(Wallis & Wallis) $308

A fine 19th century Burmese silver mounted sword dha, slightly swollen single edge blade 25½in., thickly silver damascened overall with nineteen figures.
(Wallis & Wallis) $729

A fine Javanese painted kris, wavy etched pamor blade 14¾in., scrolled top, carved wooden hilt with two stylized faces, gilt cup with diamond chips.
(Wallis & Wallis) $583

ARMS & ARMOR

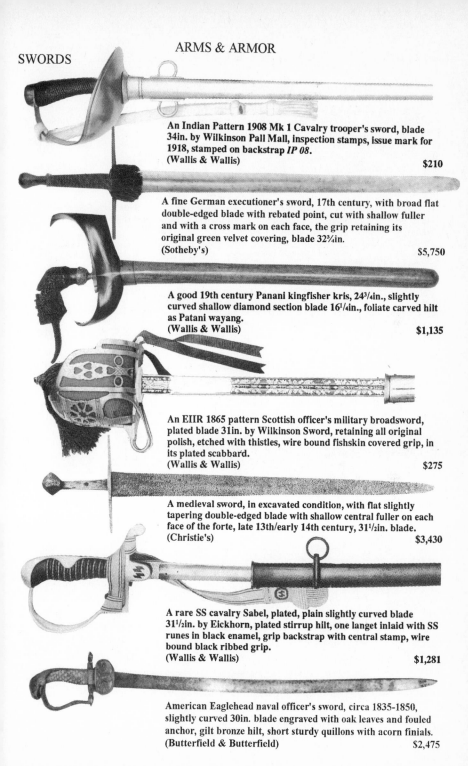

An Indian Pattern 1908 Mk 1 Cavalry trooper's sword, blade 34in. by Wilkinson Pall Mall, inspection stamps, issue mark for 1918, stamped on backstrap *IP 08*.
(Wallis & Wallis) $210

A fine German executioner's sword, 17th century, with broad flat double-edged blade with rebated point, cut with shallow fuller and with a cross mark on each face, the grip retaining its original green velvet covering, blade 32¾in.
(Sotheby's) $5,750

A good 19th century Panani kingfisher kris, 24¾in., slightly curved shallow diamond section blade 16¼in., foliate carved hilt as Patani wayang.
(Wallis & Wallis) $1,135

An EIIR 1865 pattern Scottish officer's military broadsword, plated blade 31in. by Wilkinson Sword, retaining all original polish, etched with thistles, wire bound fishskin covered grip, in its plated scabbard.
(Wallis & Wallis) $275

A medieval sword, in excavated condition, with flat slightly tapering double-edged blade with shallow central fuller on each face of the forte, late 13th/early 14th century, 31½in. blade.
(Christie's) $3,430

A rare SS cavalry Sabel, plated, plain slightly curved blade 31½in. by Eickhorn, plated stirrup hilt, one langet inlaid with SS runes in black enamel, grip backstrap with central stamp, wire bound black ribbed grip.
(Wallis & Wallis) $1,281

American Eaglehead naval officer's sword, circa 1835-1850, slightly curved 30in. blade engraved with oak leaves and fouled anchor, gilt bronze hilt, short sturdy quillons with acorn finials.
(Butterfield & Butterfield) $2,475

SWORDS

A 19th century Persian Qjar sword qama, broad single edged blade 24¹/₂in., swollen towards
pointed tip, four fullers, deeply struck with maker's cartouche, damascened Islamic inscription,
horn grips, silver gripstrap.
(Wallis & Wallis) $256

An unusual 18th century Indian khandar, recurved single edged kopis blade 26in., four shaped
fullers, geometric brass decoration, steel hilt of traditional form, pommel spike with lotus bud
finial.
(Wallis & Wallis) $612

A Japanese sword katana, blade 68cm., mumei, gunome hamon, active nie line, itame hada, iron
mokko tsuba, tape bound same tsuka, gilt menuki.
(Wallis & Wallis) $1,683

A Chinese river pirate's double sword, shallow diamond section blades 18¹/₂in. inlaid with brass
dots, brass mounts, crosspieces as makarra heads, dragons in clouds to pommels, reeded horn
grips.
(Wallis & Wallis) $275

An unusual 19th century Chinese shortsword, 20¹/₂in., slightly curved single edged blade with
narrow fuller 12¾in. with shaped brass collar at forte, finely pierced and chiseled oval brass
guard.
(Wallis & Wallis) $688

A good early 16th century Japanese wakizashi, blade with three holes to tang, one side with one
character, the reverse with six characters, swordsmith believed to be Kanesada, circa 1504, tsuba
decorated with gilt floral leaf motifs.
(Bosley's) $2,119

A fine German early 18th century ormolu hilt rococo hunting hanger, straight single edged blade
20in. extensively pierced with geometric openings in the twin fullers.
(Wallis & Wallis) $1,013

SWORDS

An unusual early 19th century Chinese sword, broad curved single edged blade 25¹/₂in., oval brass guard, leather lined, red lacquered leather bound grip with raised knobs, brass pommel and ferrule.
(Wallis & Wallis) $214

A composite Italian broadsword, circa 1600, with mid-16th century broad flat double-edged blade formed with a spear point and no ricasso, each face cut with a pair of long central fullers and struck with a serpent mark, blade 25¹/₂in.
(Sotheby's) $2,300

A good early 19th century Sumatran silver mounted sword, swollen single edged blade 19¹/₄in., large swollen octagonal ivory hilt of good color, in its wooden scabbard with eleven silver bands.
(Wallis & Wallis) $306

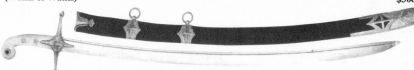

An attractive Georgian Light Cavalry officer's mameluke sword, curved single edged piped back blade 30³/₄in. nicely etched with crowned GR cypher.
(Wallis & Wallis) $2,189

A hallmarked silver mounted hunting hanger for 1739, straight single edged blade 17³/₄in. with narrow back fuller, silver hilt hallmarked for London 1739, chiseled with old man's face to gripstrap and oval shellguard.
(Wallis & Wallis) $372

A fine Japanese sword tachi, blade 70cm. suriage nakago, 2 mekugi ana, kinzoganmei, gold inlay Kinju attributed to 1st or 2nd generation, 1320–1375, hon tsukuri, midare hamon with abundant niye and kinsuji, mixed mokume itame hada.
(Wallis & Wallis) $5,350

A good 19th century Indian Muslim gauntlet hilted sword Pata, broad straight double edged blade 33¹/₂in. with narrow fullers, gauntlet hilt finely gold and silver damascened overall.
(Wallis & Wallis) $880

TSUBAS

A Hamano School Shakudo tsuba, signed *Nobuyuki*, depicting a group of warriors and priests in a grotto, 7.3cm. (Butterfield & Butterfield) $1,725

A brass 19th century tsuba forming a dragon clasping a tama, the scales and details of the dragon finely carved, 6.8cm.
(Christie's) $450

A 19th century inlaid tsuba, the oval shibuichi plate cast with a dragon in a network of clouds, 3in.
(Butterfield & Butterfield) $1,380

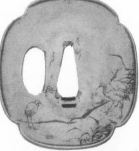

A large 16th century Yamagane tsuba of mokkogata plate, finely punched, bearing impressed flowers and hishi, 7.5cm. (Christie's) $670

A circular iron Akasaka Tadashige tsuba, signed *Gyonen Hachiju-issai, Tadashige Saku*, 18th century, the circular iron plate pierced with a design of orchid sprays, 7.9cm. (Christie's) $3,450

A mokkogata Sentoku tsuba, signed *Yoshu Tsuki Mitsuoki*, 19th century, depicting cranes among reeds in katakiri-bori, 6.2cm.
(Christie's) $1,207

An iron Kyo-Sukashi tsuba, late 16th century, the eight-lobed plate pierced with eight alternating positive and negative kiri design, 7.7cm. (Christie's) $862

A Shakudo mokkogata tsuba, signed *Matsumura Norimoto*, 19th century, depicting asagao and flowers in iroe takazogan, 6cm.
(Christie's) $1,293

A Kamiyoshi School iron tsuba, 19th century, the fine lobed iron plate pierced with a design of stylized bracken buds, 7.7cm.
(Christie's) $1,465

TSUBAS

An iron Akasaka Sukashi tsuba, 18th century, the iron plate finely pierced with sosho hiragana, 8.6cm.
(Christie's) $2,760

An Edo Period tsuba, inlaid copper plate cast with chidori in flight over crashing waves, signed *Bunko*, 6.7cm.
(Butterfield & Butterfield) $1,000

An iron Higo tsuba, 18th century, the circular plate pierced with stylized bracken buds within eight-petal piercings, 7.2cm.
(Christie's) $1,035

An inlaid silver tsuba, Meiji Period, cast in high relief with a kannon riding on the head of a dragon emerging from waves, 8cm.
(Butterfield & Butterfield) $2,587

An iron Suruga tsuba, late 16th/17th century, a large circular plate pierced and carved with five sails within an angular rim, 8.2cm.
(Christie's) $1,293

A Mito Kinko tsuba, 19th century, an oval shibuichi plate carved in relief and inlaid with Gentoku plunging his horse into the Dankai river, 7cm.
(Christie's) $1,380

An iron Kinai tsuba, signed *Echizen Jyu Kinai Saku*, 19th century, the circular plate pierced and carved with Noh masks and ropes, 7.8cm.
(Christie's) $1,725

A Higo Rakuju style tsuba, 19th century, the oval iron plate pierced with positive and negative cherry blossoms among nets, 7.5cm.
(Christie's) $1,293

An oval shibuichi tsuba with signature *Omori Teruhide* and *Kao*, 19th century, decorated with a diver in shakudo takazogan, 6.5cm.
(Christie's) $1,638

UNIFORMS

A scarce Lieutenant's service dress khaki tunic, circa 1902, of the 13th Hussars, only one bronze collar badge, medal ribbon QSA.
(Wallis & Wallis) $260

British Royal Engineers Staff Sergeant's uniform, comprising scarlet tunic, navy blue trousers, belt, sash, pillbox hat.
(Butterfield & Butterfield) $660

A World War I Captain's (Staff) service dress khaki tunic of The Royal Fusiliers, shoulder straps, scarlet gorget patches, name inside *Capt W F Cosens, 3.6.14*.
(Wallis & Wallis) $391

A George V Corporal's full dress scarlet tunic of the Grenadier Guards, blue facings, and a white serge drill jacket with George V Grenadier buttons.
(Wallis & Wallis) $160

Imperial Austrian other ranks Hussar's uniform, comprising gray green kersey wool attila, matching dolman, matching trousers.
(Butterfield & Butterfield) $715

A World War I Captain's service dress khaki doublet of The Highland Light Infantry, shoulder straps, two stripes and embroidered rank badges to gauntlet cuffs.
(Wallis & Wallis) $342

UNIFORMS

An officer's full dress drab tunic of the 23rd Sikh Pioneers, chocolate facings, drab-cord, lace and braid trim.
(Wallis & Wallis)　　　$240

1st West Suffolk Rifle Volunteers (Bury St. Edmunds), officer's scarlet 1868 pattern tunic, yellow facings to cuffs and collar.
(Bosley's)　　　$211

A post 1902 Lieut General's full dress scarlet tunic, blue facings with white piping, heavy oak leaf embroidery.
(Wallis & Wallis)　　　$400

Imperial German 15th Uhlan other ranks uniform, of the Schleswig-Holstein Regiment, comprising royal blue tunic, trousers, belt, Mutz, epaulettes.
(Butterfield & Butterfield)
　　　$825

War of 1812 U.S. officer's uniform and accessories, including U.S. infantry officer's long tailed coatee, epaulettes, belt, leather message pouch, sword, powder horn, single officer's spur.
(Butterfield & Butterfield)
　　　$3,300

Other ranks 18th U.S. Coastal Artillery uniform, circa 1902, comprising navy blue blouse, visor hat with appropriate insignia.
(Butterfield & Butterfield)
　　　$165

UNIFORMS

Other ranks Prussian Hussar's
pelisse, royal blue wool with
yellow frogging and sleeve
facings.
(Butterfield & Butterfield)
$825

A rare 1940 pattern battle-
dress blouse of the Royal
Marines Commando, Lance
Corporal chevrons to left
cuff.
(Bosley's) $498

A scarce WRNS WW2 period
officer's tunic and tricorn hat,
tailor's label for Harrods of
London.
(Bosley's) $264

A good complete RN
Commander's uniform, circa
1910, comprising cocked hat,
jacket with World War I medal
ribbons, with nameplates of
J V Wotton, RN.
(Wallis & Wallis) $580

A scarce pre-1902 Irish County
Lord Lieutenant's tunic, scarlet
melton cloth with dark blue
facings to cuffs and collar,
complete with all Queen
Victoria Crown silvered buttons.
(Bosley's) $358

A good post 1902 Royal Navy
uniform of Rear Admiral T. Y.
Greet, comprising tailcoat,
cocked hat, pair overalls, two
frock coats, three mess
waistcoats and evening shoes.
(Wallis & Wallis) $1,040

A Captain's full dress scarlet doublet of The Highland Light Infantry, and pair of tartan overalls and breeches.
(Wallis & Wallis)   **$391**

A good officer's WW2 battledress uniform of the Northamptonshire Regiment, 2nd Lt. rank insignia to epaulettes.
(Bosley's)   **$158**

A Lieutenant's full dress blue tunic of the 13th Hussars, buff collar, gilt braid and gimp trim, including six loops with olivets.
(Wallis & Wallis)   **$978**

A scarce Nazi four pocket white service dress political leader's tunic, as worn by the Nazi representative at Messina, during World War II, complete, with original Party armband.
(Wallis & Wallis)   **$885**

British Lieutenant General's dress uniform, comprising scarlet wool dress tunic, black wool trousers, belt and belt plate.
(Butterfield & Butterfield)   **$935**

A Victorian Captain's full dress scarlet tunic of The Royal Fusiliers, blue facings, gilt lace and braid trim, shoulder cords, gilt buttons.
(Wallis & Wallis)   **$277**

A painted truncheon, dated *1804*, bearing the name *Somerden*, painted with a coat of arms, 20¹/₂in. long overall.
(Bonhams) **$146**

German flanged mace, circa 1550, having seven flanges with reinforced projecting points and quadrangular knop, tubular steel shaft, the grip with spiralling fluted and herringbone panels, 25¹/₂in. long overall.
(Butterfield & Butterfield) **$4,400**

A Silesian wheel-lock axe-pistol (Fokos), second half 17th century, with two-stage barrel retaining traces of silver foliage on the breech, flat lock domed over the wheel and engraved with a stag within scrolling foliage, 32¹/₂in.
(Sotheby's) **$9,200**

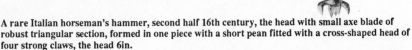

A rare Italian horseman's hammer, second half 16th century, the head with small axe blade of robust triangular section, formed in one piece with a short pean fitted with a cross-shaped head of four strong claws, the head 6in.
(Sotheby's) **$6,325**

A William IV painted truncheon, 22¹/₂in. long overall.
(Bonhams) **$163**

A large two handled Nepalese sacrificial axe, ram dao, 34¹/₂in., broad curved blade 24in., incised with plain pattern at top edge and inlaid with brass line of diamond pattern, turned wooden hilt with fluted iron domed pommel.
(Wallis & Wallis) **$551**

A German mace, the head with seven flanges with reinforced points, tubular haft (holed and slightly dented in one place), pierced for a thong, and with spirally fluted grip, mid-16th century, 24in.
(Christie's) **$4,333**

A late 19th century Hindu axe, crescent head 6½in. chiseled with lions and suns within cartouches against foliate ground, Sanskrit inscription to peen surmounted by pagoda.
(Wallis & Wallis) $320

A fine and rare silver-mounted Indian pipe-tomahawk, circa 1860, with robust blade boldly stamped on one side with the maker's initials *PF*. in a cusped stamp, 20⁵/₈in.
(Sotheby's) $16,948

An Italian halberd with long slender spike of stiff diamond section widening at the base into a shaped feature flanked by double points, flat crescentic axe-blade and beak-shaped fluke, late 16th century, 29¹/₂in. head.
(Christie's) $2,166

European goosewing axe, the head with 10in. edge and stamped with scallop and dot designs and indecipherable maker's mark, the old haft possibly original.
(Butterfield & Butterfield) $440

European war hammer, probably Eastern Europe, late 16th/early 17th century, the head having 5in. downcurving beak, hammer with square face and acorn knop, the side fitted with belt hook, 23in. long overall.
(Butterfield & Butterfield) $2,475

A Persian (Qajar) massive parade axe, 19th century, made entirely of iron, with large double-bladed head, the blades each with acutely convex leading edge, chiseled and damascened with arabesques, the head 22¹/₂in.
(Sotheby's) $1,610

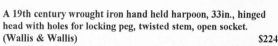

A 19th century wrought iron hand held harpoon, 33in., hinged head with holes for locking peg, twisted stem, open socket.
(Wallis & Wallis) $224

A Persian Qjar 19th century double headed all steel axe, 29¹/₂in., crescent heads 8in. etched with arabesques filled with foliage and hares, a little silver damascened ornament.
(Wallis & Wallis) $275

**Marty Feldman, signed
postcard, first name only, head
and shoulders.**
(T. Vennett-Smith) $50

**Kate Moss, signed color 8 x
10in., three quarter length
crouched, wearing black tights.**
(T. Vennett-Smith) $96

**Edvard Grieg, signed postcard,
published by C. W. Faulkner,
503D.**
(T. Vennett-Smith) $450

**The Carpenters, 8 x 10in.,
signed by both Karen and
Richard Carpenter
individually, first names only,
three quarter length standing.**
(T. Vennett-Smith) $85

**Queen Elizabeth II, signed
document, at head, two pages,
5th December 1966, being a
remission document,
countersigned by Roy Jenkins.**
(T. Vennett-Smith) $279

**Burns & Allen, signed sepia 8 x
10in., by Gracie Allen
(inscribed) and George Burns
individually, three quarter
length in evening dress.**
(T. Vennett-Smith) $163

**Ray Bolger, signed and
inscribed 8 x 10in., half-length
seated with his arms on his knee.**
(T. Vennett-Smith) $56

**Margaret Thatcher, signed
color 8 x 10in., half length
pointing getting into car.**
(T. Vennett-Smith) $163

**Valentina Tereshkova, signed
6 x 4in. to lower border, head
and shoulders.**
(T. Vennett-Smith) $62

William Gillette, signed sepia postcard as Sherlock Holmes, 1905.
(T. Vennett-Smith)　　　　$93

Muhammad Ali, signed and inscribed 8 x 10in., three quarter length in ring.
(T. Vennett-Smith)　　　$109

Enrico Caruso, signed postcard, full-length in costume, Beagles 705C, 1906.
(T. Vennett-Smith)　　　$636

Jean Cocteau, autographed signed letter, 6th November 1952, in French, thanking Dr. Badenhausen for his letter and sending a photo.
(T. Vennett-Smith)　　　$233

Marie Roze, signed and inscribed sepia cabinet photo, full-length in costume, 1900, inscribed to Mrs Kirkby Lunn.
(Vennett Smith)　　　$107

Arthur S. Sullivan, autographed signed letter, two pages, 13th February 1867, to McCaul and the proposals to change Mr. Foster's designation.
(T. Vennett-Smith)　　　$372

Bill Robinson, Bo Jangles, signed and inscribed 7¹/₂ x 8¹/₂in., 1935.
(T. Vennett-Smith)　　　$132

Lilyan Tashman, signed and inscribed sepia 10 x 7¹/₂in., first name only, photo by Pach.
(T. Vennett-Smith)　　　$59

Edith Piaf, two signed and inscribed 8 x 10in., different poses.
(T. Vennett-Smith)　　　$248

Lillie Langtry, autograph signed letter, undated, turning down an engagement.
(Vennett Smith) $220

Louis Armstrong, a good early signed and inscribed sepia, 21st July 1934, Armstrong later signed the photo a second time in 1956, obtained in person at Derby, 8 x 10in.
(Vennett Smith) $257

Margaret Thatcher, signed color, full-length seated on settee, unusual pose, 8 x 8in.
(Vennett Smith) $173

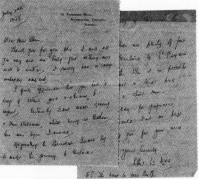

Richard F. Burton, Explorer, autograph signed letter, one page, 1st December 1886, to Mr Liseux, making an order from a catalog for an Arabic manuscript.
(Vennett Smith) $393

Ethel Le Neve, girlfriend to Dr. Crippen, two autograph signed letters, 14th June and 2nd July 1945, 3.5 pages total, to Ursula Bloom arranging a meeting and giving directions.
(Vennett Smith) $424

Charles Dickens, autograph note signed, to Messrs. Chapman & Hill, asking for *One copy of Little Dorrit and one copy of Old Curiosity Shop both cheap editions*, 8 x 2.5in.
(Vennett Smith) $487

Guglielmo Marconi, signed card, full signature, with attached magazine photo above, October 1930.
(Vennett Smith) $63

Dame Laura Knight, autograph letter signed, one page, 6th October 1965, to Mr Whitchurch, mentioning Alfred Munnings and continuing to discuss the purchase of a painting from one of her catalogs.
(Vennett Smith) $86

Bela Bartok, small signed piece, overmounted in red and black, beneath photo, 6.5 x 10in. overall.
(Vennett Smith) $251

Admiral David Beatty, a good signed, three quarter length in uniform, standing on deck, 8.5 x 6.5in.
(Vennett Smith) $94

David Lloyd George, signed postcard, full-length standing.
(Vennett Smith) $63

Francis Bacon, signed reproduction of artwork, overmounted in clay color, 9.5 x 7.5in. overall.
(Vennett Smith) $138

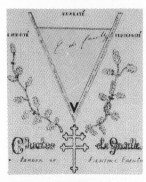

Franklin D. Roosevelt, typed signed letter, one page, 19th August 1930, to Aaron Gansey on Governor of State of New York notepaper, thanking him for some airmail covers.
(Vennett Smith) $251

Charles De Gaulle, good signature on triangular signed piece, mounted on decorative art page entitled *Leader of Fighting French*, together with an unsigned 8 x 10in.
(Vennett Smith) $157

Camille Saint-Saens, a good signed cabinet photo, *Souvenir of 3rd June 1913*, he last visited England in 1913 to conduct 'The Promised Land' at Gloucester Festival.
(Vennett Smith) $518

Arthur Conan Doyle, signed piece, overmounted in ivory, beneath reproduction photo, framed and glazed.
(Vennett Smith) $236

Guglielmo Marconi, good full signature on album page, 1936, signed to reverse slightly showing through (though well clear of Marconi), 7.5 x 5.5in.
(Vennett Smith) $122

W.S. Gilbert, signed sepia, with the additional words *born . . . 1836*, photo by Alfred Ellis, laid down to card, 4 x 4.5in.
(Vennett Smith) $361

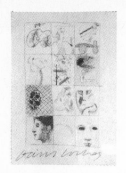

David Hockney, signed postcard
of his work The Blue Guitar
No. 1.
(Vennett Smith) $63

Sergei Rachmaninoff, signed,
head and shoulders, 4 x 4.5in.
(Vennett Smith) $102

Siegfried Sassoon, printed poem,
signed, in the form of a booklet
'In Sicily'.
(Vennett Smith) $157

American Presidents, signed
color, by Richard Nixon,
Gerald Ford, Jimmy Carter and
Ronald Reagan, full-length
standing together at Anwar
Sadat's funeral, 8 x 10in.
(Vennett Smith) $1,413

Neville Chamberlain, signed
menu to cover, Parliamentary
Press Gallery Annual Dinner,
18th March 1938, with covering
typed signed letter from
Chairman Guy Eden, 7.5 x 10in.
(Vennett Smith) $94

Queen Elizabeth II, good signed
to mount, *Elizabeth R*, being her
coronation portrait by Dorothy
Wilding, half-length in
ceremonial dress, wearing
crown, 1952, 18.5 x 25.5in.
(Vennett Smith) $628

Tod Slaughter, signed sepia, half-
length, 5 x 10in., also signed by
his wife, Jenny Lynn.
(Vennett Smith) $165

Irving Berlin, signed front cover
to Ball Program, 6th January
1944.
(Vennett Smith) $129

Beulah Bondi, signed and
inscribed, head and shoulders,
8 x 10in.
(Vennett Smith) $78

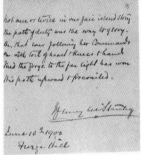

Henry Stanley, signed
handwritten poem, six lines, 10th
June 1900, Furze Hill, 4 x 4.25in.
(Vennett Smith) $330

Margaret Thatcher, signed, half-
length seated, 5 x 7in.
(Vennett Smith) $75

David Hockney, signed color,
head and shoulders, 5 x 7in.
(Vennett Smith) $102

Charles Gounod, autograph
music quotation signed, three
bars, London, 3rd July 1863,
overmounted in brown, beneath
reproduction photo, 11 x 13.5in.
overall.
(Vennett Smith) $345

Bram Stoker, signed piece, 1910,
overmounted in brown beneath
reproduction photo and original
cast list from 'Dracula'
program (18th May 1897),
framed and glazed.
(Vennett Smith) $283

S.S. Standartenfuhrer Otto
Kumm, won swords to Knights
Cross, signed to lower white
border in uniform, modern
reproduction of 1943 photo,
signed in later years, 8 x 10in.
(Vennett Smith) $82

Franz Lehar, signed sepia
postcard, full-length standing
with another gentleman.
(Vennett Smith) $181

Irving Berlin, signed copy of the
sheet music for 'Marie', to front
cover.
(Vennett Smith) $157

Tony Hancock, signed and
inscribed, half-length seated,
5.5 x 4in.
(Vennett Smith) $86

J. Miro, signed color print of one of his paintings, 7 x 9½in., taken from a magazine.
(T. Vennett-Smith) $109

George Bernard Shaw, autographed signed quotation, on board RMS Rangitare in the Pacific, 17th April 1904.
(T. Vennett-Smith) $527

Anna Pavlova, signed postcard, full-length in costume, Rotary 11719B.
(T. Vennett-Smith) $186

Cosmonauts, a rare collection of signed photos of Russian cosmonauts, being a complete set of signatures of all crew members from Vostok I (1961) to Soyuz 8 (1969).
(Vennett Smith) $2,355

Leo Tolstoy, signed postcard, 18th October 1905.
(T. Vennett-Smith) $1,116

George Bernard Shaw, signed receipt for £6.13s.2d, from Messrs. Lewis Casson & Bruce Winston for the performances of Candida, 27th May 1920.
(T. Vennett-Smith) $326

Jerome K. Jerome, signed sepia postcard, head and shoulders, Rotary 2312.
(T. Vennett-Smith) $78

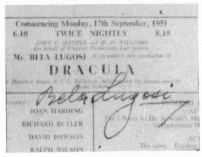

Rudyard Kipling, signed sepia
postcard, half-length wearing
boater, Beagles 346.
(T. Vennett-Smith) $465

Bela Lugosi, signed portion
from a 1951 Dracula Theatre
Program, in red ink.
(T. Vennett-Smith) $279

Tony Hancock, signed postcard,
head and shoulders in profile
wearing straw hat.
(T. Vennett-Smith) $140

David Hockney, signed
postcard, The Thirteenth V.N.
Painting.
(T. Vennett-Smith) $93

Pablo Picasso, signed 4½ x 6in.
photo, to reverse, showing him
with two other men looking at
statue, photo by Mairie de Vall,
together with a badge.
(T. Vennett-Smith) $806

The Platters, signed and
inscribed postcard, by all five
together, including Herb Reed.
(T. Vennett-Smith) $70

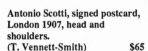

Antonio Scotti, signed postcard,
London 1907, head and
shoulders.
(T. Vennett-Smith) $65

Edward VIII, signed Christmas
Greetings Card as Prince of
Wales, overmounted alongside
5 x 6½in. photo, framed and
glazed, 18½ x 15in. overall.
(T. Vennett-Smith) $202

W. B. Yeats, autographed signed
quotation, two lines, January
1909.
(T. Vennett-Smith) $527

Will Hay, signed postcard, head and shoulders, as Schoolmaster.
(T. Vennett-Smith) $109

Emile Zola, signed piece, 3 x 2¹/₂in.
(T. Vennett-Smith) $101

H. H. Asquith, signed sepia postcard, head and shoulders.
(T. Vennett-Smith) $70

Prince Charles, typed signed letter, one page, Kensington Palace, 25th June 1986, mentioning his wife, Jimmy Saville etc., with supporting newspaper article.
(Vennett Smith) $314

Helmut Newton, signed postcard, entitled *Paloma Picasso wearing gold jewellery designed by her*, showing her half-length in black evening dress with one breast naked.
(T. Vennett-Smith) $93

Tsar Nicholas II, signed document, in Russian, one page, Tsarskay, 1st March 1914, being an instruction to the College of Russian Imperial and Royal Orders.
(T. Vennett-Smith) $790

Mike Tyson, signed 8 x 10in., three quarter length in boxing pose, wearing championship belts.
(T. Vennett-Smith) $108

Helmut Newton, signed postcard, entitled *Winnie at The Negresco*, showing naked blonde looking from balcony.
(T. Vennett-Smith) $78

Wheeler & Woolsey, signed 7 x 9in., by Bert Wheeler & Robert Woolsey, three quarter length in bar drinking beer.
(T. Vennett-Smith) $93

F. M., Earl Haig, signed postcard, half-length in uniform.
(T. Vennett-Smith) **$77**

Louis Bleriot, signed album page, 5 x 4in.
(T. Vennett-Smith) **$85**

A. Bonar Law, signed postcard, head and shoulders.
(T. Vennett-Smith) **$93**

Glen Miller, signed piece, with a typed testimonial signed stating that the signature was obtained in person at '100 Oxford Street' Jazz Club on his last performance.
(Vennett Smith) **$408**

Prince Charles, a fine signed color 6 x 8in. to mount, half-length seated in gardens, 1981, presentation frame, 10 x 13in. overall.
(T. Vennett-Smith) **$775**

Jascha Heifetz, autographed signed musical quotation, on large album page, 7 x 8½in., Edinburgh, 12th February 1921, also signed by Albert Burke 1923.
(T. Vennett-Smith) **$202**

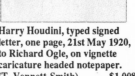

Arthur Sullivan, signed sepia cabinet photo, head and shoulders, photo by Walery of London.
(T. Vennett-Smith) **$558**

Harry Houdini, typed signed letter, one page, 21st May 1920, to Richard Ogle, on vignette caricature headed notepaper.
(T. Vennett-Smith) **$1,008**

David Hockney, signed 7 x 5in., head and shoulders in pensive pose, his hands raised to his chin.
(T. Vennett-Smith) **$77**

Percy Kilbride, signed postcard, rare, head and shoulders.
(Vennett Smith) $133

T.S. Eliot, signed Christmas card, for Faber & Faber, design by B.H. Drummond 1954.
(Vennett Smith) $126

Aldous Huxley, signed postcard, full-length standing with dog.
(Vennett Smith) $133

Joseph Lister, autograph signed letter, one page, 3rd November 1887, to Mr Newman, ...*I cannot refuse to allow my name to appear on your list of referees.*
(Vennett Smith) $243

Count Felix Von Luckner, WWI U-Boat Captain, known as 'The Sea Devil', signed and inscribed sepia, head and shoulders in cap, 3rd December 1935, 9.5 x 12in.
(Vennett Smith) $141

Robert Lincoln, son of Abraham Lincoln, US Secretary of War, signed letter, one page, War Dept., 11th December 1884, to J. Camden at Senate.
(Vennett Smith) $63

Nellie Melba, signed and inscribed to Mrs Kirkby Lunn *From her comrade and sincere friend 1902*, oval image, head and shoulders, 9 x 11.5in.
(Vennett Smith) $275

Queen Victoria, document signed at head, given at the Court of St. James's, 14th January 1852, being a military commission appointing George Henry James Mowbray Chapman a 2nd Lt. in the 5th Reg. of Foot.
(Vennett Smith) $126

Louis Armstrong, a good early signed and inscribed sepia, 21st July 1934, Derby, Armstrong later signed the photo a second time in 1956, 8 x 10in.
(Vennett Smith) $235

Nat King Cole, signed and inscribed sepia, 8 x 10in.
(Vennett Smith) $138

Siegfried Sassoon, typed poem signed, two verses from 'A Sequence', signed in ink to base.
(Vennett Smith) $149

Frederic March, signed, 1968, head and shoulders, 8 x 10in.
(Vennett Smith) $91

Sir Edward Elgar, signed and inscribed sepia cabinet photo, three quarter length seated reading at desk, inscribed to Mrs Kirkby Lunn, October 1907.
(Vennett Smith) $879

Charles Schulz, typed signed letter, one page, 17th October 1978, on Snoopy notepaper, stating that he never sells original Peanuts cartoon strips.
(Vennett Smith) $79

Louis Armstrong, a good early signed and inscribed sepia, 21st July 1934, obtained Derby, full-length with his wife Alpha, 8 x 10in.
(Vennett Smith) $267

Winston S. Churchill, signed album page, full signature, overmounted in red beneath a color reproduction of Stoneman Portrait, 7.5 x 11.5in. overall.
(Vennett Smith) $659

Queen Elizabeth the Queen Mother, signed Christmas greeting card, 1961, featuring photo of the Gardens at Royal Lodge, together with an unsigned photo.
(Vennett Smith) $91

King George VI, a good signed to mount, 1951, three quarter length seated in naval uniform, photo by Dorothy Wilding, framed and glazed, 18.5 x 25.5in.
(Vennett Smith) $274

A Blaise Bontems singing bird in cage automaton, French, circa 1890, the metal cage containing a brightly feathered bird on perch with metal foliage, 11in. high.
(Sotheby's) $1,272

A hand operated automaton, of five figures with bisque heads, two seated playing stringed instruments and three dancing, the box 42cm. wide, German.
(Christie's) $1,875

A Gustave Vichy musical automaton of a pumpkin eater, French, circa 1870, the papier-mâché head with smiling mouth, fixed glass eyes, the body with papier-mâché forearms, 20in.
(Sotheby's) $19,987

A Leopold Lambert musical automaton of a clown conjuror, French, circa 1890, the papier-mâché head with open mouth and articulated tongue, fixed blue glass eyes, 24in.
(Sotheby's) $8,177

A framed color lithographed clockwork picture of a laughing negro, with movement to head, eyes and mouth, 22in. high.
(Christie's) $603

A Gustave Vichy musical automaton of a Negro fruit seller, French, circa 1870, the keywind stop/starter musical mechanism contained within the body and playing two airs, 25¹/₂in.
(Sotheby's) $21,804

A Roullet et Decamps musical automaton of a school teacher and pupil, French, circa 1890, her head nodding and turning, her left hand holding a book, 17¹/₂in.
(Sotheby's) $4,906

A pair of Ives clockwork dancers, modeled as African Americans, in original clothes, mounted on wires on original box containing the mechanism, 10in. high.
(Christie's) $849

A Leopold Lambert musical automaton of a clown mandolin player, French circa 1910, the papier-mâché face painted with red tipped nose, a beetle on the forehead, 22in.
(Sotheby's) $8,682

AUTOMATONS

A musical automaton of a dancing girl, German circa 1900, the dancing figure in white net and red cotton dress, and red jester's hat, 14in. high.
(Sotheby's) $1,302

A Leopold Lambert musical automaton of a lady holding a fan and lorgnettes, French circa 1890, in gray and white striped silk dress, 19in.
(Sotheby's) $5,556

A Gustave Vichy musical automaton of a clown gymnast, French, circa 1870, the papier-mâché head with smiling mouth and painted teeth, 36in.
(Sotheby's) $18,170

A Gustave Vichy musical automaton of a Negro banjo player, French circa 1890, the papier-mâché head with articulated lower jaw and upper eyelids, 30in.
(Sotheby's) $12,155

A pull-along automaton toy windmill with moving sails, and bisque headed doll in original silk regional costume, 15¹/₄in. long, French circa 1900.
(Christie's) $2,415

A Roullet et Decamps musical rabbit in cabbage automaton, French circa 1890, pricking up his ears, opening his mouth and rising from inside his cabbage, 9in. high.
(Sotheby's) $3,299

A mandolin player, the Pierrot with painted composition head and bisque arms, seated, with movements to left foot, waist, head, hands, 20¹/₂in. high, possibly Roullet & Decamps.
(Christie's) $2,808

A Leopold Lambert musical automaton of a blackamoor hookah smoker, French circa 1890, the papier-mâché head with open mouth and brown glass eyes, 23in.
(Sotheby's) $10,415

A Roullet et Decamps tea-drinking mandarin in urn musical automaton, French, circa 1890, the figure with composition head, open/closed mouth, brown glass eyes, 14¹/₂in.
(Sotheby's) $3,634

Aero Shell Lubricating Oil Stocked Here, double sided sign, finished in red, yellow, blue and white and a Shell Aviation Spirit lubricant can.
(Christie's) **$927**

A silver mounted Edwardian period desk top calendar, the frame modeled with a racing car, on oak base, 5⁷/₈in. wide.
(Christie's) **$573**

Wolseley Autocars, The Leaders in Every Class, double sided, finished in white with green text, decorative scroll work surround, 18 x 30in.
(Christie's) **$713**

A glass decanter, circa 1915, in the shape of a tyre, the outside bevelled, engraved *WHEN TYRED, SCOTCH*, with hallmarked silver neck and glass stopper, 9in. high.
(Christie's) **$1,518**

Various garage accessories including a Wakefield Castrollo 'Upper Cylinder Lubricant' dispenser.
(Christie's) **$499**

A Dunhill table lighter, the silvered body engraved and enamelled with signature of *Malcolm Campbell* and inscribed *Byron House London*, 4¹/₄in. high.
(Christie's) **$590**

Grin, Grand Prix Automobile de Geneve 21st May 1936, published by Kausfelder, on linen, 102 x 64cm.
(Onslow's) **$1,163**

A detachable American wooden steering wheel by the Neville Steering Wheel and Mfg. Co., Wayne, Mich., circa 1916, 43 cm. diameter.
(Auction Team Köln) **$154**

Maurice Neumont, Guiet L'Automobile par la Carrosserie 1899, published by Chaix Paris, on linen, 198 x 125cm.
(Onslow's) **$853**

A De Dion-Bouton wooden steering wheel, circa 1900. (Auction Team Köln) $246

A. Barrere, Mors Mayol Va Arriver Avec Sa Troupe, published by Robert Paris, on linen, 115 x 167cm. (Onslow's) $465

A Michelin 'Bibendum' tyre compressor partially complete. (Christie's) $338

B.R.D.C. Silverstone Club by Marples and Beasley, Birmingham, number 390, enameled in colors with outline of circuit. (Christie's) $570

A fine pair of Lucas 'King of the Road' headlights, nickel plated and black painted bodies, bulls eye lenses, numbered *880*, 11½in. high. (Christie's) $1,883

A British Monte Carlo Rally Drivers association badge, chromed, quartered with Union Jack, Monaco flag, chain and crossed shovels, 4in. high. (Christie's) $215

Rallye Automobile Monte Carlo, a plated and enameled commemorative plaque dated *1936* (15th event), in plush lined case, 3½in. diameter. (Christie's) $1,350

Automobile Club de L'Ouest, triangular sign with date 1938, and Shell Huiles pour Moteurs, double sided, triangular, both enamel. (Christie's) $231

Automobile Club of Palestine badge, camel set within a wheel, script below, chromium plated, 4¾in. high. (Christie's) $807

Gargoyle Mobiloil, a good advertising oil crate, printed tinplate sides with original end plates, circa 1930, 20in. x 26in. x 13in.
(Christie's) $211

An original 1920s Michelin tyre compressor complete with Mr Bibendum and gauge.
(Dreweatt Neate) $735

After T. Vourihe, Hurtu – Automobiles et Cycles, a good early original poster, color lithograph, linen-backed, French circa 1904, 37in. x 53in.
(Christie's) $528

Brooklands Flying Club, a scarce late pre-war members badge depicting stylized monoplane over aerodrome buildings motif, by H. A. Shelley of London, and stamped *No. 71*, circa 1939, 4$^{1}/_{2}$in.
(Christie's) $1,584

Coupe Pilette Organisee Par l'Automobile Club de Spa 1907, published by Gouweloos Bruxelles, on linen, 80 x 119cm.
(Onslow's) $2,480

Dunlop Stock, a good and rare early sign, oval format, double sided, embossed and printed tinplate, circa 1914, 38in. x 26in.
(Christie's) $263

A 1950s Super Fina shield shaped opaque glass petrol pump globe.
(Dreweatt Neate) $330

Michelin, a pre-war advertising sign, printed and embossed tinplate, double sided, French, circa 1930s, 23in. x 23in.
(Christie's) $246

A pair of Bleriot oval headlamps, copper and brass, beveled glass lenses, (burners missing), rear mounting brackets, 13in. high.
(Christie's) $1,692

Nigel Mansell's Arai helmet, 1992, finished in red, white and blue with sponsor's decals, signed to the side *Nigel Mansell* and at the back.
(Christie's) $8,970

Mobiloil, a large enamel advertising sign, shield shaped format, 42in. x 40in.
(Christie's) $122

A 1930s Sirram picnic case with contemporary fittings for four persons and including an original kettle.
(Dreweatt Neate) $135

B.A.R.C. Brooklands, members badge, un-numbered, enameled in colors.
(Christie's) $570

Rene Vincent, Peugeot, published by Draeger, on linen, 118 x 158cm.
(Onslow's) $2,480

A Carless 'Coalene' mixture, opaque and colored glass pump globe, 15½in. high.
(Dreweatt Neate) $3,750

Grand Prix de L'A.C.F., Circuit de Dieppe 1912, advertising poster, with artwork by Dergeo, printed by Frossard, Coubet et Cie, Paris, 41¼in. x 29½in.
(Christie's) $483

A pair of Carl Zeiss headlamps, chromium plated, mounting bracket and screw, with reeded lenses, 12in. high.
(Christie's) $1,105

After Mich, Peugeot, a rare early poster for the 'Quadrilette' model, color lithograph, linen-backed, some restoration, 47in. x 31in.
(Christie's) $669

A 19th century mahogany and boxwood strung wheel barometer, signed *Pizzi, 19 Leather Lane, London,* 1.09m. high. (Phillips) $467

A 19th century carved oak stick barometer, with a mercury thermometer, 1.08m high. (Phillips) $959

A George III inlaid mahogany wheel barometer by B. A. P. Ronchetti, Manchester, 39in. high. (Dockree's) $1,672

A mahogany stick barometer, Dolland, London, circa 1840, silvered scale, 37^{1}/$_{2}$in. (Bonhams) $1,140

A French kingwood and gilt-bronze barometer, circa 1860, the paper register signed *Radiquet et Fils, opticiens,* 114cm. high. (Sotheby's) $3,565

A large mahogany wheel barometer, circa 1850, 12in. silvered dial, signed *Christanson, Cowes No. 7 Inventor,* 45in. (Bonhams) $1,064

A mahogany bowfront stick barometer, Thomas Jones, London, circa 1820, 38^{1}/$_{2}$in. (Bonhams) $4,365

A 19th century mahogany and satinwood crossbanded combination wheel barometer and wall timepiece, 1.27m. high. (Phillips) $4,354

A 19th century
mahogany and
boxwood strung wheel
barometer, signed *J.
Somalvico*, 1.1m high.
(Phillips) **$1,368**

A mahogany stick
barometer, Charles
Howorth, Halifax,
circa 1830, 39in.
(Bonhams) **$692**

A 19th century
mahogany and
boxwood strung wheel
barometer, signed
Dollond, London,
1.04m. high.
(Phillips) **$809**

A good mahogany stick
barometer, Dolland,
London, circa 1820,
silvered scale, 40in.
(Bonhams) **$2,432**

A mahogany gimballed
marine stick
barometer, circa 1860,
Bono scale, signed
*Woodruff, Dover,
Newbridge*, 37in.
(Bonhams)
$1,824

An impressive 19th
century mahogany and
crossbanded wheel
barometer, signed
C Gerletti, Glasgow,
1.28m
(Phillips)
$1,160

A Dutch walnut and
floral marquetry wall
barometer, signed
*F. Primavesi,
Amsterdam*, 1.09m
high.
(Phillips)
$2,320

An early Victorian
mahogany wheel
barometer, by Griffin
and Hyams, the clock
movement by James
McCabe, 49¹/₂in. long.
(Christie's)
$2,673

BASKETS

A coiled rye straw handled basket, Pennsylvania, 19th century, with singular bentwood carrying handle lashed to the body, 7in. high.
(Christie's) $1,265

A coiled rye straw bee skep, Pennsylvania, 19th century, with wooden collar with entry way lashed onto bottom rye straw coil, 14½in. high.
(Christie's) $863

A coiled rye straw half-basket, Pennsylvania, 19th century, with bent-wood hanging handle, 4¾in. high.
(Christie's) $288

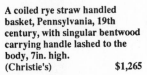

A leather key basket, probably Richmond, Virginia, early 19th century, the black oval basket decorated in silver and gold stitches, 4¾in. high.
(Sotheby's) $2,070

Two very large wool gathering splint baskets, Pennsylvania, 19th century, each with circular integrated rim with side holding handles, 15½in. and 14½in. high.
(Christie's) $2,990

A woven oak splint 'Arschbach' half-basket, Pennsylvania, 19th century, a medium size hanging half basket with pronounced cheek construction, 6½in. high.
(Christie's) $575

A coiled rye straw footed basket, Pennsylvania, 19th century, with two shaped wooden carrying handles, on a bent wood circular foot, 7¾in. high.
(Christie's) $1,093

Two woven splint baskets, Pennsylvania, 19th century, the first an oak splint garden basket, the second an ash splint basket with rectangular collar, 7¾in. and 3½in. high, the baskets.
(Christie's) $345

A coiled rye straw bee skep, Pennsylvania, 19th century, with large rye coils and a wooden top plug, landing platform and entrance slot, 20in. high.
(Christie's) $3,220

An oak splint carrying basket, Pennsylvania, 19th century, the rectangular collared basket with pronounced tapering ribs, 5¼in. high.
(Christie's) $575

A painted woven basket, New England, circa 1860, rectangular woven basket with a black-painted X-form handle, 9in. high.
(Christie's) $1,610

A large oak splint potato basket, Kutztown area, Pennsylvania, 19th century, the circular basket with large bentwood carrying handle, 6½in. high.
(Christie's) $1,265

Nantucket lightship basket, S. P. Boyer, Nantucket, Massachusetts, stamped on base *Boyer*, with paper label, 7½in. diameter.
(Skinner) $1,610

A felt and leather pannier, each side fitted with a wicker basket with hinged lid.
(Christie's) $261

A coiled rye straw dry measure, Pennsylvania, 19th century, conical, opening at either end to six inches and ten inches, 10in. high.
(Christie's) $575

A woven oak splint 'Arschbach' basket, Pennsylvania, 19th century, medium sized market basket with large defined collar and modified rib construction, 6¾in. high.
(Christie's) $1,093

An oak splint carrying basket, Pennsylvania, 19th century, the large market basket with cicular collar, bentwood center carrying handle, 7¾in. high.
(Christie's) $322

A woven oak splint 'Arschbach' basket, Pennsylvania, 19th century, with integrated collar, pronounced cheek construction and God's eye crossing splint handle, 6¾in. high.
(Christie's) $633

A Meredith & Drew Ltd 'delivery van' biscuit tin, circa 1930, advertising potato crisps to the rear door and cheese sandwiches to the front, 25cm. long.
(Sotheby's) $1,656

A large and rare tinplate passenger monoplane tin, Dutch, early 1920s, the lid formed by the domed engine section with moveable propeller, 75cm. long.
(Sotheby's) $6,992

A Carr & Co 'steam delivery truck' biscuit tin, circa 1929, with licence plate IT 1929, the lithographed tin with steam funnel to the open front, 20.5cm. long.
(Sotheby's) $3,312

A Huntley & Palmers 'globe' biscuit tin, circa 1906, the globe-shaped tin with hinged lid to the top with small handle, made up of two gores joined at the equator, on four ball feet, 57cm. diameter.
(Sotheby's) $442

A Lefèvre-Utile biscuit barrel, French, circa 1905, the brown lithographed tin finished to the sides and mice scurrying to look over the top of a wheat field, 16.5cm. high.
(Sotheby's) $883

A rare William Crawford & Sons 'barrel organ' biscuit tin, circa 1912, in the shape of a pull-along organ, lithographed to simulate mahogany with raised detailing to the front, 14cm. long including shafts.
(Sotheby's) $1,472

A Co-Operative Wholesale Society Post Office hand cart biscuit tin, circa 1920, finished in Royal Mail red and *GR* in gold to the sides upon two balloon-type wheels, 17.5cm. long.
(Sotheby's) $405

A rare Co-Operative Wholesale Society Crumpsall Cream Crackers delivery van biscuit tin, circa 1920, registration no. NC 7107, finished in mainly cream and green with well detailed advertisements to the roof, 25cm. long.
(Sotheby's) $2,944

A rare International Stores articulated delivery van tin, circa 1932, the six-wheeled lithographed delivery van finished in milk chocolate brown with brown and cream detailing, 32cm. long.
(Sotheby's) $2,576

A G. De Andreis 'racing car' biscuit tin, circa 1920, the green lithographed oval car on rectangular base, with lift off lid to the top, 16.5cm. long.
(Sotheby's) $773

A Fryer & Co. Victory-V 'church' tin, circa 1910, the well lithographed tin with tiled clerestory roof as lid, 32cm. long.
(Sotheby's) $1,067

A 'circus' biscuit tin, circa 1910, with blue and white diamond-patterned hinged lid with *Circus* against a yellow background to the sides, 12.5cm. long.
(Sotheby's) $184

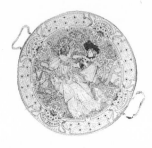

A rare Lefèvre-Utile glazed porcelain cheese or patisserie stand, French, circa 1895, transfer printed with two ladies reclining in a garden and partaking of langues de chat biscuits, 46cm. diameter.
(Sotheby's) $589

A Huntley & Palmers china 'casket' biscuit container, circa 1905, nursery rhymes to the underside of lid, the ceramic container shaped and decorated to simulate a chest of drawers, 15cm. high.
(Sotheby's) $575

An unusual Carr & Co. Ltd. 'tambourine' biscuit tin, circa 1931, the circular tin lithographed with the Pied Piper of Hamelin, the young children skipping behind, 14cm. diameter.
(Sotheby's) $920

A W. Crawford & Sons 'general' No 48 double decker biscuit tin, circa 1925, the open roofed bus from Golder's Green to Blackheath, lithographed in red with black detailing, 27.5cm. long.
(Sotheby's) $5,888

A Barringer, Wallis & Manners 'lawnmower' biscuit tin, circa 1913, with *B.W. & M. Ltd Makers Mansfield* in a shield on lid, with hinged top lid, lithographed roller, blades and freshly mown grass in the hood, 10cm. high.
(Sotheby's) $736

A William Crawford & Sons 'menagerie' biscuit tin, circa 1911, the well detailed wagon depicting caged lions, tigers, monkeys and leopards to the side, 12cm. high.
(Sotheby's) $1,288

A fine Macfarlane, Lang & Co. delivery van biscuit tin, circa 1911, with seated lithographed driver and cross-armed companion in conversation, 19.5cm. long.
(Sotheby's)　　　　$2,760

A Callard and Bowser's 'Nessie' butterscotch tin, circa 1930, in the shape of the famous Scottish monster, wearing a Glengarry, with red tinged hump and tail, 33cm. long.
(Sotheby's)　　　　$552

A Co-operative Wholesale Society 'delivery van' biscuit tin, circa 1910, with lid to the top, the red lithographed van with yellow and black detailing, 18.5cm. long.
(Sotheby's)　　　　$4,416

A Huntley & Palmers clockwork double decker biscuit tin, circa 1929, the six balloon-type wheeled vehicle, finished in red with cream roof lid to the top, 24cm. long.
(Sotheby's)　　　　$6,992

A Huntley & Palmers 'artist' palette shaped biscuit tin, circa 1900, lithographed with splashes of oil paint, raised tinplate brushes and a young man with hurdy-gurdy, 25cm. long.
(Sotheby's)　　　　$294

A rare Huntley & Palmers 'perambulator' biscuit tin, circa 1930, the lift-off sloping lid to the top lithographed with a smiling baby and teddy bear, 21.5cm. long.
(Sotheby's)　　　　$1,931

A McVitie & Price 'bluebird' novelty biscuit tin, circa 1911, the Martin Brothers type bird with detachable head which forms the lid, 24cm. long.
(Sotheby's)　　　　$736

A Lefèvre-Utile 'plates' biscuit tin, French, circa 1905, the circular tin to simulate seven stacked plates, the top as lift-off lid, 22cm. diameter.
(Sotheby's)　　　　$883

A Huntley & Palmers 'Toby Jug' biscuit tin, circa 1911, the lithographed portrait jug with raised detailing, hinged lid to the top, 16.5cm. high.
(Sotheby's)　　　　$165

A W. & R. Jacob & Co 'coronation coach' biscuit tin, circa 1936, the four wheeled coach finished in gold with red roof lid to the top with regal crown knop, 23cm. long.
(Sotheby's) $275

A Fryer & Co 'Victory-V' double decker sweetmeat biscuit tin, circa 1920, the four-wheeled oblong vehicle finished in red with cream lid to the top, 32.5cm. long.
(Sotheby's) $2,208

A G. De Andreis 'Autobus Molié' biscuit tin, French, circa 1925, *Voyage au pays des douceurs* below the windows from which the lithographed passengers look out, 29cm. long.
(Sotheby's) $2,944

A Huntley & Palmers 'Indian' biscuit tin, circa 1894, the front and back depicting regal and street scenes, the sides depicting domestic and agricultural scenes, 14.5cm. at the base.
(Sotheby's) $1,067

A Huntley & Palmers 'Gainsborough' palette-shaped biscuit tin, circa 1902, the lid lithographed with Georgiana, Duchess of Devonshire, after Thomas Gainsborough, 25cm. long.
(Sotheby's) $478

A rare W. & R. Jacob & Co. 'Alice' biscuit tin, circa 1892, with hinged lid to the top, lithographed scenes from 'Through the Looking Glass', 13cm. high.
(Sotheby's) $2,392

A Mackintosh delivery truck biscuit tin, 1920s, with lift-off lid to the top, lithographed in red with black detailing and gold lettering, 20cm. long.
(Sotheby's) $736

A W. & R. Jacobs & Co. 'caravan' biscuit tin, circa 1937, with clerestory hinged lid to the top, folding steps, finished in yellow, 13.5cm. high.
(Sotheby's) $575

A W. Crawford & Sons 'coach' biscuit tin, circa 1934, with the Royal coat-of-arms to both side doors and *GR* to the front, 20cm. long.
(Sotheby's) $1,195

South Africa: 1872 Z.A.R. £1 issued at Pretoria and printed in black on green paper.
(Phillips) $780

Guyana: 1830(c), Demerary and Essequebo 2 Joes of 22 Guilders unissued.
(Phillips) $232

China: Hukuang Rlys, 1911 £20 bond countersigned in New York by American Banks, ref.: K236.
(Phillips) $1,783

Glocester and Berkeley Canal Co. 1794 share certificate No. 720 for one share, on vellum with large yellow embossed seal.
(Phillips) $560

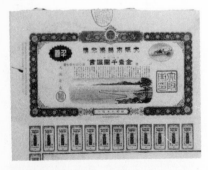

Japan: Osaka City Harbor Construction, 6% Loan, 1933, 1,000 yen bond with coupons attached, attractive vignettes of Osaka Bay and castle.
(Phillips) $387

The Company of Undertakings of the Grand Canal, Ireland 1772, £50 debenture bond with 5% interest, on vellum with a vignette depicting a canal, also an embossed paper seal.
(Phillips) $4,030

Japan: Imperial Government 5% Loan 1908, 1,000 Yen bond, with coupons dated 1942–1958.
(Phillips) **$156**

Bank of the United States of America 1837 Certificate for 20 shares, signed by Nicholas Biddle as President, a clear signature.
(Phillips) **$686**

London & Brighton Rly, 1847, 5% Bearer certificate No. 4 for £50, with vignette depicting St. Paul's and The Royal Pavilion.
(Phillips) **$651**

Stockton & Darlington Rly, 1858, £25 Class 'A' Preferential share, with a vignette depicting an early train on a viaduct.
(Phillips) **$1,209**

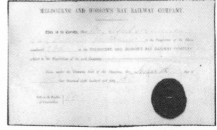

The Studebaker Corporation 1935 uncanceled 10 Common shares, vignette of a country blacksmith's workshop with a sign board headed *John Studebaker. Blacksmith.*
(Phillips) **$156**

Australia: Melbourne and Hobson's Bay Railway Co. 1853, one share on vellum, with a large embossed red wax seal depicting an early locomotive.
(Phillips) **$750**

BRONZE

Patinated bronze group of a girl and cat, cast after a model by Juan Clara, early 20th century, 10¹/₂in. high.
(Butterfield & Butterfield)
$1,610

A pair of 19th century silvered bronze and marble bookends, the silvered bronze seated classical muses set on black marble bases, 12.5cm. high.
(Phillips)
$350

J. Berré: a 19th century bronze model of a grazing faun, raised on a naturalistic base, signed, 17cm. high.
(Phillips)
$638

A cold painted bronze and ivory figure: 'Hungarian Dancer', Demetre H. Chiparus, on shaped, stepped brown onyx base, 49.5cm. high.
(Sotheby's)
$9,269

A large pair of Japanese bronze elephants, Meiji period (1868–1912), each standing four square and with a cloth covering the back, 86.4cm. x 56cm.
(Sotheby's)
$39,215

A cold painted bronze and ivory figure: 'Starlight', Demetre H. Chiparus, 1930s, the figure of a dancer wearing a pleated handkerchief skirt, 59cm. high.
(Sotheby's)
$16,934

Alexei Petrovitch Gratcheff (Russian, 1780–1850): a 19th century bronze group of a cossack and a girl on horseback, signed, 33cm. high.
(Phillips)
$1,824

A pair of late 19th century bronze figures of children, after Charles-Antoine Bridan, one playing with a dove, the other holding a bird's nest, stamped *Elkington*, 80cm. high.
(Phillips)
$3,648

'Loving Companions', an Art Deco silver metal group cast as a girl in long floral dress, standing to pet two Borzoi dogs, 45.5cm. high.
(Phillips)
$450

BRONZE

A 19th century Austrian cold painted bronze model of a Turk, seated on a rug holding a vase in his left hand, 12.5cm. high.
(Phillips) $790

A pair of 19th century bronze putti, allegorical of Autumn and Summer, raised on square Siena marble bases, 22.5cm. high.
(Phillips) $942

A 19th century Viennese cold painted group of an Arab, with horse and cart, both stamped with Bergman inverted vase stamp, 16.5cm. high.
(Phillips) $1,976

'The Flame Dancer', an Art Deco bronze and alabaster figure, modeled as an exotic dancer in crouching position, 87cm. high.
(Phillips) $4,800

A pair of French bronze figures of Eros and Psyche, circa 1890, after the models by Eugène Laurent (1832–1898), both shown kneeling, 50cm. high.
(Sotheby's) $10,695

An erotic bronze figure of a female nude, by C. Kauba, cast as a girl in long evening dress opening to reveal her naked body, 21cm. high.
(Phillips) $675

A Spanish bronze and ivory group of an Indian on horseback, circa 1910, after the model by Antoine Bofill, 41cm. high, signed.
(Sotheby's) $3,922

A pair of French bronze figures of an Arab warrior and a female water carrier, after the models by Jean Jules Salmson (1823–1902), signed, 50cm. and 43cm. high.
(Sotheby's) $10,695

A French bronze group: Hercules and The Cretan Bull, mid 19th century, the hero holding the bull by one horn, 30cm. high.
(Sotheby's) $1,693

German bronze figural tray, circa 1910, in the form of a shallow well, mounted with a man in a robe, with owls and monkeys, 8in. wide. (Skinner) $805

Gilt bronze and ivory group of a girl with her pet bulldog, on veined marble base, 6in. high, signature indistinct. (Ewbank) $936

Viennese cold painted bronze figure of a lion, early 20th century, stamped *Geschutz*, the animal shown standing on a rockwork base, 11in. long. (Skinner) $5,462

French bronze figural group of Bacchanalian putti with a goat, late 19th century, after J. M. Clodion (1738–1814), with greenish brown patina, on a red marble socle, 8¹/₂in. high. (Skinner) $805

A large Italian (?) bronze mortar, dated *1603*, the central band applied with grotesque masks interspersed with lion masks, 11in. high. (Sotheby's) $4,025

A bronze group of three athletes entitled 'Au But!', cast from a model by Alfred Boucher, the three men each shown lunging forward on one leg, French, late 19th century, 10¹/₂in. high. (Christie's) $2,193

French patinated metal figural group of a Moroccan huntsman, by A. Barye and E. C. H. Guillemin, late 19th century, in two colors, 25½in. high. (Skinner) $2,300

A gilt bronze figure of a Greek scholar, reclining on a padded stool and reading a scroll, signed *Doublemard, G.PRIX*, French, late 19th century, 11¹/₂in. high. (Christie's) $883

French Art Nouveau bronze figural group, 20th century, with indistinct signature, greenish-black patina, 19¹/₂in. high. (Skinner) $2,645

After Charles Sykes, a bronze of a passionate embrace, signed, on a rectangular green onyx plinth, 16¹/₂in. high overall.
(Hy. Duke & Son)
$5,562

Pair of Viennese cold painted bronze Arabic dancers, early 20th century, 6in. high.
(Skinner)
$1,380

19th century Japanese School, 'Fishermen Pulling in Nets', bronze group, on carved conforming wooden plinth, 31 x 16in. overall, bronze signed with seal characters.
(Schrager)
$2,250

Clodion, a bronze figure group of two classical figures and amorini with tambourine, etc., on rosewood base with brass edge, 11in.
(Russell, Baldwin & Bright)
$930

A pair of Italian or South German bird catchers, after Giambologna, perhaps 17th century, each figure stepping forward with one arm outstretched, 7³/₄in. high.
(Sotheby's)
$13,800

After Edward Onslow Ford, a bronze of a nude figure wearing a turban and holding a palmette, stamped *E. Onslow Ford, London*, 24in. high.
(Hy. Duke & Son)
$3,708

French bronze figure of a youth by Andre-Louis-Adolphe Laoust, (b. 1843), scantily clad with arms outstretched, greenish brown patina, 25¹/₂in. high.
(Skinner)
$2,530

A pair of Louis XVI style gilt bronze and amethyst glass lidded vases, the slender bowls applied with swags of fruiting vines between satyr mask head handles, each 31cm. high.
(Phillips)
$4,165

French bronze figural group of two women and a child, by A. Carrier-Belleuse, late 19th century, with light brown patina, 19in. high.
(Skinner)
$1,840

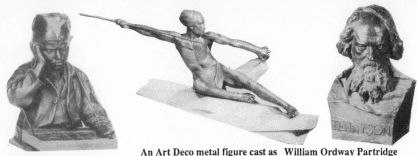

A bronze bust of a boy,
modeled as a street vendor, the
front of his tray inscribed *Que
les affaires vont mal*, 9¹/₂in. high.
(Christie's) $327

An Art Deco metal figure cast as
a male warrior, he is depicted in
hunting stance with spear in
hand, in a green patination on
shaped stone base, 73cm. long.
(Phillips) $618

William Ordway Partridge
(American, 1861–1930), portrait
bust of Alfred, Lord Tennyson,
signed, bronze with brown
patina, 20¹/₂in. high.
(Skinner) $3,450

A 19th century French brown
patinated bronze bust of a young
woman with a leaf garland in her
hair and on a square incurved
socle, 9in. high, indistinctly
signed *L. V. E. Ree*.
(Canterbury) $277

A pair of Restauration bronze
tazze, with fluted shallow bowls
and scroll handles raised on
siena marble square plinths,
each 27cm. high.
(Phillips) $1,934

A patinated bronze group of the
Farnese bull, late 19th century,
cast with a central figure of a
rearing bull, two young men
attempting to subdue it, 19¹/₂in.
high.
(Butterfield & Butterfield) $2,587

Demetre H. Chiparus,
'Bayadere', 1920s, cold painted
bronze and ivory figure of an
exotically dressed dancer
standing on tiptoes with both
arms raised, 52.75cm.
(Sotheby's) $17,080

An Art Deco bronze group,
modeled as a charioteer and
horses in racing stance, in a part
silvered patination on
rectangular marble base,
40.5cm. long, signed *Voltas*.
(Phillips) $618

Art Deco silvered bronze figure
of a dancer, cast after a model
by T. D. Guirande, circa 1925,
depicted wearing a drape over
her shoulder, 18in. high.
(Butterfield & Butterfield)
$920

Ferdinand Preiss, 'Con Brio', 1920s, cold painted bronze and ivory figure, modeled as a scantily clad dancer, 15in.
(Sotheby's) $9,994

French patinated bronze figural group, cast after a model by Ary Jean-Léon Bitter, circa 1925, depicting Pan playing the flute flanked by reclining nymphs, 42in. long.
(Butterfield & Butterfield) $3,450

Ferdinand Preiss, child with doll, 1930s, cold painted bronze and ivory figure of a young girl clasping a doll, 7in.
(Sotheby's) $2,362

Art Deco patinated bronze group of cobras, originally cast after a model by Stanislaus Szukalski, circa 1919, later cast by Roman Bronze Works, 27½in. high.
(Butterfield & Butterfield) $2,875

A pair of English parcel-gilt and patinated bronze heraldic lion-form candlesticks, 19th century, each cast in the form of a rampant lion, 10¾in. high.
(Butterfield & Butterfield) $3,450

A gilt-bronze figural group of an Arabian falconer, cast after a model by Ernest Dubois, late 19th century, depicting the rider on a rearing stallion, 27¼in. high.
(Butterfield & Butterfield) $4,600

Continental cold painted bronze bull dog wall clip, probably Vienna, painted brown, black and red with hinged backplate, 4½in. long.
(Skinner) $1,495

Art Deco style patinated bronze figure of a scarf dancer, cast after a model by R. Guerbe, on a rectangular black marble base, 23in. high overall.
(Butterfield & Butterfield) $3,162

French gilt-bronze group: Chariot of Minerva, cast after a model by Emmanuel Frémiet, F. Barbedienne, founders, early 20th century, 21¼in. high.
(Butterfield & Butterfield) $2,875

A paint-decorated leather fire bucket, first quarter 19th century, with a bail handle, 19th century, 19in. high. (Sotheby's) **$3,737**

A George III mahogany and brass-bound peat bucket, the tapering circular body mounted with two brass drop handles, 15in. diameter. (Christie's) **$1,553**

A George III brass-bound mahogany bucket, with loop handles and later base and brass liner, 43cm. diameter. (Christie's) **$5,455**

Pair of George III brass-bound mahogany peat and plate buckets, late 18th century, each with brass handle and brass binding, 14³/₄in. and 15³/₄in. (Butterfield & Butterfield) **$2,185**

A green-painted and polychrome decorated leather fire bucket, inscribed *No. 37 Benj Marshall, 1827,* American, first half 19th century, 19in. high. (Sotheby's) **$460**

A pair of George III mahogany and brass bound buckets, one designed for plates, with brass swing handles, 37cm. diameter. (Phillips) **$4,864**

A George III brass-bound mahogany peat-bucket, with part rope-twisted loop handle and later brass liner, 13³/₄in. diameter. (Christie's) **$4,399**

An oak and brass banded ship's fire bucket, bearing the name *Madeline,* 12½in. high. (George Kidner) **$151**

A brass-bound mahogany peat bucket, of George III style, with arched part-ropetwist loop handle and spirally-reeded sides, 13³/₄in. diameter. (Christie's) **$2,760**

A chip-carved poplar butter print, Pennsylvania, 1800–1820, circular, with deeply carved stylized eagle, 4½in. diameter. (Christie's) $345

A chip-carved poplar double-sided butter print, Pennsylvania, handle marked *EF*, dated *1792*, the circular print with side handle with central radial design, 3½in. diameter. (Christie's) $1,380

A chip-carved poplar butter print, Pennsylvania, 1800–1820, with applied handle, the mold decorated with a stylized flower basket and stars, 4in. diameter. (Christie's) $748

A poplar chip-carved butter print, Lititz, Lancaster County, Pennsylvania, dated 1833, ovoid, with pine cone and foliate decoration. (Christie's) $863

A chip-carved and incised butter print, Pennsylvania, 1800-1830, rectangular, with deeply carved tulips and hearts surrounded by incised squares, 4¾ in. long. (Christie's) $633

A chip-carved poplar butter print, probably Schoenck, Lancaster County, Pennsylvania, 1800–1820, with deeply carved five arm pinwheel decoration, 4in. diameter. (Christie's) $2,070

A chip-carved poplar butter print, Pennsylvania, circa 1820, circular, with deeply carved tulip atop a star flanked by leaves, 4⅝in. diameter. (Christie's) $748

A carved poplar two-piece butter mold, Pennsylvania, circa 1800, carved in two parts with a four arm pinwheel surrounded by a punctuated border, 8⅞in. wide. (Christie's) $575

A chip-carved poplar butter print, Pennsylvania, 1800–1820, circular, with stylized rooster and incised border, 4½in. diameter. (Christie's) $690

A tortoiseshell tea caddy, of rectangular outline with inlaid pewter and ivory bun feet, 19th century, 5¹/₂in. wide. (Christie's) **$640**

A Regency penwork decorated sewing box of sarcophagus form, extensively decorated with birds, urns, bell husk and acanthus motif, 19cm. high. (Phillips) **$1,186**

A late Regency tortoiseshell veneered workbox, the case of sarcophagus outline, the front with gadroon fluted frieze, 8¹/₄in. wide. (Christie's) **$2,925**

A George III brass-mounted mahogany tulipwood and floral marquetry tea-caddy, brass banded overall and inlaid with rosette trellis, 5³/₄in. wide. (Christie's) **$1,143**

A pair of George III satinwood and rosewood crossbanded knife boxes, later painted with cherubs, portrait medallions, trophies and flowers, 14in. high. (Christie's) **$8,262**

George III blond tortoiseshell ivory inlaid tea caddy, circa 1800, of octagonal form with domed conforming hinged cover with ovoid knop, 5in. high. (Butterfield & Butterfield) **$2,300**

A Regency mahogany, satinwood and checker-banded oval tea caddy, the lid with central oval paterae medallion, 5¹/₂in. wide. (Christie's) **$607**

A liqueur casket, interior fitted with four large Bohemian glass decanters, four smaller decanters, two tumblers and two small glasses, 43cm. long. (Phillips) **$988**

George III inlaid ivory ten sided tea caddy, circa 1800, of faceted oval-form beneath a domed conforming hinged cover with ovoid ivory knop, 5¹/₄in. high. (Butterfield & Butterfield) **$4,025**

A Victorian walnut and brass-bound stationery box, with hinged domed top, 9¹/₂in. wide.
(Christie's) $411

A Victorian simulated coromandel and silver mounted tantalus, fitted with three cut glass decanters of square section, frieze drawer to the base, 37cm. wide.
(Phillips) $608

Victorian burr walnut brass bound tea caddy of domed form, fitted within for two compartments, 19th century, 9in. wide.
(G. A. Key) $255

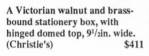

George III mottled tortoiseshell and ivory inlaid tea caddy, circa 1800, of ten-sided form, veneered with panels of strongly mottled tortoiseshell, 4¹/₄in. high.
(Butterfield & Butterfield)
$3,737

A Korean metal bound traveling storage box, the door decorated with studded and pierced mounts and handles, 15in. x 19in.
(Dreweatt Neate) $427

A hat box, New England, circa 1830, covered in a blue, white and beige-glazed wallpaper depicting Castle Garden, New York Harbor, 21³/₈in. long.
(Sotheby's) $6,900

An ebony and ormolu casket, 19th century, in the Renaissance style, the rectangular case inset with rock crystal panels, 9¹/₄in. wide.
(Christie's) $2,925

A George III parcel-gilt rolled paper tea caddy, of hexagonal outline, with brass handle to the cover, 5¹/₄in. wide.
(Christie's) $713

Victorian rosewood jewel casket, the lid of pagoda form, gadroon molded handle and inlaid throughout with brass lines and ivorine circles, 19th century, 12in. wide.
(G. A. Key) $615

A rare Federal inlaid mahogany document box, New England, circa 1815, with domed hinged lid fitted with a brass bail handle, 12in. long.
(Sotheby's) $6,325

A paint-decorated sycamore and beech covered box, probably Continental, late 18th century, painted in orange and cream with stylized floral sprays, 13in. long.
(Sotheby's) $690

A paint-decorated pine small trunk, probably Massachusetts, early 19th century, with a domed lid painted in red, yellow, white and black, 13in. long.
(Sotheby's) $68,500

A pair of brass-bound mahogany jardinières, each with the octagonal body with a molded edge with two bands and two C-scroll shaped handles, 8in. wide.
(Christie's) $3,767

A pair of early 19th century mahogany and checker inlaid urn knife boxes with elevating lids of cavetto and domed outline, 61cm. high.
(Phillips) $4,463

A Victorian red japanned post box, 'The Fawcett', with original gilt lettering and postal rates on a red ground, 32cm. high.
(Dreweatt Neate) $515

A William IV tortoiseshell veneered and pewter strung tea caddy of rectangular form with pagoda shaped lid, with later mother-of-pearl inlaid front panel, 190cm. wide.
(Phillips) $1,413

A carved and painted pine hanging wall box, New England, probably Connecticut, mid/late 18th century, the shaped rectangular backplate chip-carved with two stylized flowerheads, 15¾in. high.
(Sotheby's) $1,035

A George III mahogany satinwood, kingwood and marquetry tea-caddy, the waisted rectangular lid with boxwood and ebony simulated ribbon-edge, 9½in. wide.
(Christie's) $986

A William IV Tunbridgeware and rosewood tea caddy. (G. E. Sworder & Sons) $973

A Georgian mahogany cheese coaster, the turned ends with inset ivory roundels, molded base and leather castors, 17¼in. wide. (Andrew Hartley) $377

A paint-decorated bird's eye maple jewel box, probably New England, initialed *MN*, early 19th century, 14⅛in. long. (Sotheby's) $2,300

An ivory and whalebone-inlaid mahogany pipe box, probably New England, early 19th century, the initials *E.H.* above a drawer with a turned ivory pull, 14¾in. high. (Sotheby's) $21,850

A pair of George III mahogany and inlaid knife boxes with ogee shaped sloping lids enclosing original velvet lined interiors, each 28cm. wide. (Phillips) $1,041

A George III fruitwood pear-form tea caddy, late 18th century, with hinged lid opening to a partially lead-lined well, 19th century, 5⅞in. high. (Sotheby's) $3,162

A paint-decorated pine fall-front utility box, Continental, early 19th century, the rectangular box with a hinged lid and front, 8¼in. long. (Sotheby's) $1,150

A Napoleon III brass-inlaid ebony decanter box, the rectangular top and front inlaid with engraved brass, tortoiseshell, and mother-of-pearl cartouches, 12½in. wide. (Christie's) $2,972

An unusual painted pine tea caddy, probably New England, 19th century, the top painted with a swooping bird grasping bellflower swags, 9in. long. (Sotheby's) $3,450

A wallpaper covered oval box, Pennsylvania, circa 1841, the interior lined with newspaper 'Hannover Gazette' dated *March 11, 1841*, 9in. high.
(Christie's) **$1,380**

Miniature 16th century iron Armada chest with original polychrome paintwork, 8³/₄in. wide.
(Boardmans) **$1,246**

Early 20th century Art Nouveau oak cigar box, decorated with pewter strap work of organic form and green cabouchon stones, 5¹/₂in. high.
(Peter Wilson) **$156**

A wallpaper covered comb box with comb, Pennsylvania, 19th century, the semi-circular box covered in gray paper with geometric designs, 5¹/₄in. high.
(Christie's) **$1,380**

A pair of early Victorian japanned metal tea canisters, the black ground cylindrical bodies heightened in gilt and each painted with oval panels, 18¹/₈in. high.
(Christie's) **$1,033**

A mahogany traveling medical chest, with brass furniture, eight bottles and five drawers for pills etc.
(Auction Team Köln) **$744**

A joined chestnut butter box, Pennsylvania, possibly Oley Valley, Berks County, 1800–1840, the rectangular form with applied molded and notched surround on three sides, 16in. wide.
(Christie's) **$403**

A painted and decorated trinket trunk, Lancaster County, Pennsylvania, 1800–1840, the rectangular blue-painted box with domed lid, 5¹/₂in. high.
(Christie's) **$5,750**

A French or Spanish brass mounted leather missal box, circa 1500, the lid with three hinges connected to straps interspersed with flowerheads, 5¹/₂in. long.
(Sotheby's) **$1,725**

A yellow painted and fruit decorated slide-lid box, Pennsylvania, 19th century, the rectangular sliding lid decorated with a flowering strawberry plant and rosebud, 5¹/₂in. wide.
(Christie's) $27,600

An oak boarded box, profusely chip-carved overall, dated *1650*, inscribed to front edge *Thomas Beament Made This*, 10in. wide.
(Christie's) $2,530

George III inlaid mahogany tea caddy, 19th century, rectangular-form with dual covered compartments, shell medallion inlay, 8in. long.
(Skinner) $862

A turned painted and decorated saffron box, Joseph Long Lehn, Pennsylvania, 1849–1892, cylindrical footed, the cover with turned finial embellished with strawberries, 4⁵/₈in. high.
(Christie's) $1,495

Two wallpaper covered hat boxes, Pennsylvania, 19th century, both covered in multicolored paper with stylized foliate and geometric motifs, 8¹/₂in. and 9¹/₄in. high.
(Christie's) $748

A painted and decorated trinket trunk, Lancaster County, Pennsylvania, 1800–1840, the rectangular dark blue-painted box with dome lid, 4⁵/₈in. high.
(Christie's) $3,680

A painted and decorated bentwood 'Bucher' box, Pennsylvania, circa 1830, oval red painted box with fitted lid decorated with white freehand tulips, 4¹/₂in. high.
(Christie's) $1,610

A Regency period mahogany campaign dispatch lap desk, (Watts Patent), the baize lined fitted interior with a pen and ink tray and secret drawers to the compartment, 20in.
(Woolley & Wallis)
                    $1,824

A painted and decorated 'Bucher box', Berks and Lancaster Counties, late 18th/early 19th century, decorated with red, orange, yellow, green and white stylized flowers with yellow banded edge, 5³/₄in. high.
(Christie's) $9,200

A Nikon SP-Black camera, with Nikkor f/1.14 5 cm. lens no. 394962, with Nikon UV filter. (Auction Team Köln) $6,938

A brass bound mahogany taiboard camera by W.W. Rouch, London, 1870. (Auction Team Köln) $924

Leica M4 No. 1231127, chrome, and a Leitz Summicron f/2 50mm. lens No. 2407661 and lenshood, in maker's ever ready case. (Christie's) $2,235

Le Parvo Model K ciné camera by Debrie, Paris, for 35 mm. film, with Zeiss Jena Tessar f/1:3.5 7/5 cm. lens, in leather case, 1930. (Auction Team Köln) $577

A Nizo Heliomatic Trifo film camera for 2 x 8 mm., light gray hammered finish, with three Rodenstock lenses, 1950. (Auction Team Köln) $308

A Pathé KoK cine camera for 28 mm. film, with Special Cinema Anastigmat f/1.4, 5/45 mm. lens, in leather case, 1913. (Auction Team Köln) $846

An Eastman No. 4 Kodak Junior camera with Bausch & Lomb focusing lens, from 1890. (Auction Team Köln) $385

A French camera obscura with brass optics by Victor Chevalier, Paris, picture area circa 12 x 18 cm., circa 1840. (Auction Team Köln) $4,625

An early mahogany folding camera by W. Watson & Sons, London, with London Stereoscopic wide-angle 9 x 7" brass optics. (Auction Team Köln) $539

Leica IIIc Monté en Sarre, No. 359421 and with a Leitz/Taylor-Hobson Xenon 5cm. f/1.5 lens No. 490823.
(Christie's) $3,439

Seiki-Kogaku, Japan, a screw-fit chrome-barrel Serenar f/4 20cm. lens No. 4015, the tripod mount engraved 5, and filter ring with red filter.
(Christie's) $10,316

Leica Still Picture KE-7a, No. 1294600, the backplate with engraved contract number and with a Leitz Elcan f/2 50mm. lens No. 276–0085.
(Christie's) $8,252

F. Kochmann, Dresden, an 18 x 24mm. red-body Korelle K camera with a Carl Zeiss, Jena Tessar f/3.5 3.5cm. lens No. 2757824 in a rimset Compur shutter.
(Christie's) $550

Rolleiflex 2.8F No. 2434247, with meter, a Heidosmat f/2.8 80mm. viewing lens and a Carl Zeiss Planar f/2.8 80mm. taking lens.
(Christie's) $688

A brass and walnut Dubroni camera for oval instant pictures, complete with developing bath, 1865.
(Auction Team Köln) $2,929

Leica M3 No. 1046554, chrome, with a Leitz Summicron f/2 50mm. lens No. 1887259 and a Leica-Meter MC, in maker's ever ready case.
(Christie's) $1,891

Beaulieu, France, a 16mm. R16 Automatic ciné camera, un-numbered, with motor, instruction booklet and microscopy lens mount, in maker's box.
(Christie's) $550

Leica M3 No. 733984, doublewind, with a Leica Meter M and a Leitz Summicron 5cm. f/2 lens No. 1156287, in maker's ever ready case.
(Christie's) $1,891

Shanghai 58-II No. 5812135, with a Shanghai f/3.5 50mm. lens.
(Christie's) $175

Leica M4 No. 1286646, black-paint, with a Leitz Summicron f/2 50mm. lens No. 2408225.
(Christie's) $3,095

Leica MDa No. 12745645, chrome, with a Leitz Elmar 5cm. f/3.5 lens No. 1146223.
(Christie's) $997

Asahi Optical Co., Japan, an Asahiflex IIb camera No. 47728 with an Asahi-Kogaku Takumar f/3.5 50mm. lens No. 56262.
(Christie's) $490

Nikon S2 No. 6167324, with an internal-bayonet Nippon Kogaku Nikkor-N.C f/1.1 5cm. lens No. 119696.
(Christie's) $4,199

Misuzu Kogaku Kogyo, Japan, an Alta camera No. 700489 with a Misuzu Kogaku Altanon f/2 5cm. lens No. M170057.
(Christie's) $1,487

Leicaflex SL No. 1220157, with a Leitz Summicron-R f/2 50mm. lens No. 2303321, in maker's ever ready case and a Leitz Elmarit-R f/2.8 35mm. lens No. 1995391.
(Christie's) $910

An Iso Duplex Super stereo camera by ISO, Milan, Iriar f/1.35 35 mm. lens, in original box.
(Auction Team Köln) $462

A Contessa Nettel tropical brass bound mahogany camera with Tessar f/1.4 5/18 cm. lens, with case and original double cassette.
(Auction Team Köln) $716

Pignons S.A., Switzerland, an Alpa Standard camera No. 11172 with a P. Angénieux Type Z2 50mm. f/2.9 lens No. 32403.
(Christie's) $3,324

A Kodak K-100 Turret 16 mm. 5-speed camera with Ektar II f/1.9 25 mm. and Elitar f/1.9 5 cm. lenses.
(Auction Team Köln) $616

Leica IIIb No. 317889, with a Leitz/Taylor-Hobson Xenon 5cm. f/1.5 lens No. 288787 and SCNOO rapid winder.
(Christie's) $1,400

Leica Reporter 250FF No. 135627, (factory converted to 250GG), the backplate synchronised and with two 250 film cassettes.
(Christie's) $7,872

Reise Camera Co. Ltd., Japan, a Chiyoca 35 camera, with a Konishiroku Hexar f/3.5 50mm. lens No. 34729.
(Christie's) $1,749

Leica IIIg Three Crowns no. 987976, black, the backplate engraved with Swedish three crowns logo and with a Leitz Summaron f/2.8 35mm.
(Christie's) $12,246

Zuiho Optical Co. Ltd., Japan, a Honor camera No. 71290 with a Zuiho Optical Co. Honor f/1.9 50mm. lens No: 61633.
(Christie's) $2,099

Panon Camera Shoko Co. Ltd., Japan, a Widelux model F6 camera No. 343884 with a Lux f/2.8 26mm. lens No. 462849.
(Christie's) $490

Tanaka Optical Co. Ltd., Japan, a Tanack Type IV-S camera No. 74185 with a Tanaka Tanar HC f/2 5cm. lens No. 26999.
(Christie's) $1,574

Leica Ig No. 925870, with a SBOOI 5cm. finder and a Leitz Summitar 5cm. f/2 lens No. 679149, in maker's ever ready case.
(Christie's) $1,487

Linhof, Germany, a 120 rollfilm Technorama camera No. 7421065 with a Schneider Super-Angulon f/5.6 90mm. lens, with a viewfinder, center-filter IV.
(Christie's) $2,407

R. Gerstendörfer, Wien, a Wica camera No. 139 with slow-speeds and a Rodenstock Heligon f/2 5cm. lens No. 2039679.
(Christie's) $3,324

Leica IIIg No. 969653, with a Leitz Summaron 3.5cm. f/3.5 lens No. 1160278, in maker's box.
(Christie's) $1,574

A Leica M1 No. 950295 with Visoflex I and Pegoo-sight, double wire and Telyt f/1.5 400 mm lens, 1958.
(Auction Team Köln) $10,022

Leica M4-P Anniversary, No. 1636711 and commemorative No. A202 with instructions and passport, in maker's box.
(Christie's) $2,449

Seroa, Monaco, a Mecaflex camera No. A457 with a Kilfitt Kilar f/2.8 40mm. lens and a Kilfitt Tele-Kilar f/4 105mm. lens.
(Christie's) $2,579

Kodak Pink Petite camera with mirrored compact case, small blush case, original instruction manual.
(Skinner) $632

Nikon F2 No. 7862549, with AS photomic head, Nikon Noct-Nikkor 48mm. f/1.2 lens No. 185734, Nikon MD-2 No. 416546, Nikon MB-1.
(Christie's) $1,400

Nikon F2 H-MD No. 7850082, black, with Nikon MD-100 motordrive No. 785226 and Nikon MB-100 battery packs.
(Christie's) $7,347

Kodak 1939 New York World's Fair 'Bullet' camera, black and brass colored metal with Trylon and Perisphere medallion, original paper box.
(Skinner) $373

Simons & Co., Switzerland, a 35mm. Sico camera No. 166 with a polished teak body brass fittings and a Rüdersdorf Sico Anastigmat 6cm. f/3.5 lens.
(Christie's) $3,439

Leica CL outfit, comprising a Leica CL camera No. 1311349, Leitz Summicron-C f/2 40mm. lens No. 2568289 and Leitz Elmar-C f/4 90mm. lens No. 2579118.
(Christie's) $1,662

Zeiss Ikon, Germany, a twin-lens Contaflex camera No. A50405 with a Sucher-Objektiv f/2.8 8cm. viewing lens No. 1781432 and a Carl Zeiss Sonnar f/2 5cm. taking lens.
(Christie's) $1,203

Nikon M No. M6092538, chrome, synchronised and with a Nippon Kogaku Nikkor-S.C f/1.4 5cm. lens No. 320253, black front cap.
(Christie's) $2,624

'Coq Nain', a Post-War clear
and frosted glass car mascot,
stencil-etched *R Lalique,*
20.5cm. high.
(Christie's) $1,057

'Victoire', a clear and frosted
glass mascot, in the form of a
woman's head molded *R
Lalique,* 17cm. high
(Christie's) $2,718

A 1920s chrome plated winged
Goddess on wheel mascot,
signed *C H Soudant,* and
inscribed, 6in. high.
(Dreweatt Neate) $240

A Retriever mascot by Charles
Paillet, the dog with game in its
mouth, signed on the collar
C. Paillet, wood display base,
3¼in. high.
(Christie's) $270

'Archer', a clear and frosted
glass car mascot, the circular
disk intaglio molded with a
kneeling naked archer,
impressed *R Lalique*, 12cm.
high.
(Christie's) $1,019

'Longchamp' a frosted glass
car mascot in the form of a
horse's head, surmounted on
black glass base, molded *R
Lalique*, 12cm. high.
(Christie's) $4,228

A reclining female nude mascot,
seated on an 'O', chromium
plated, mounting screw, 5in.
high.
(Christie's) $376

'Grand Libellule' a pale
amethyst tint glass car mascot,
in the form of a dragonfly,
etched and molded *R Lalique*
21cm. high.
(Christie's) $3,737

A 'Bat Girl' mascot, mounted to
swing to horizontal position at
speed, mounted on radiator cap,
4⅞in. high.
(Christie's) $358

1936 Alvis Speed 25 open 4 seat tourer, coachwork by Cross & Ellis, chassis no. SB/13366, engine no. 14049, burgundy with original red leather interior, engine: six cylinder, overhead valves, 3,571cc, 106bhp at 3,800rpm, triple SU carburettors, gearbox: four speed manual, brakes: four wheel drums. (Christie's) $67,115

1933 Marmon V16 type 143 five passenger Victoria coupe, serial no. 16-143-907, dove gray with mulberry wheels and blue leather interior, engine: V16, 515ci, est. 250bhp at 3,400rpm, gearbox: three speed manual, brakes: four wheel mechanical, suspension: semi-elliptic leaf springs front and rear. (Christie's) $96,000

1910 Rolls-Royce Silver Ghost Shooting Brake, coachwork by Croall & Croall, chassis no. 1246, natural wood finish with black leather upholstery, engine: six cylinder, 7,428cc, side valves, 48bhp at 1,000rpm, gearbox: three speed manual, brakes: two wheel drum, suspension: semi-elliptic front and rear springs. (Christie's) $519,500

1920 Rolls-Royce Silver Ghost Torpedo Tourer, formerly owned by the Maharajah of Jodhpur, coachwork by Barker, chassis no. 50 RE, engine no. M114, polished aluminum with dark red leather upholstery, engine: six cylinder, 7,428cc, side valves, 70-75bhp at 1,250rpm, gearbox: four speed manual, brakes: two wheel drum. (Christie's) $123,500

1922 Secqueville-Hoyau sports two seater with dickey, registration no. XL 595, chassis no. 12, engine no. 14, blue with brown interior, engine: four cylinder, 1,250cc rated at 10hp, gearbox: four speed manual, brakes: rear wheel drum, suspension: semi-elliptic leaf springs, right hand drive. (Christie's) $16,043

1939 MG TA 'Tickford' two seater Drophead coupe, coachwork by Salmons of Newport Pagnell, chassis no. TA 3050, ivory with dark brown hood and beige leather upholstery, engine: four cylinder, overhead valve, 1,292cc giving 50bhp at 4,500rpm, gearbox: four speed manual. (Christie's) $33,868

**1940 H.R.G. 1500 'Square Rigger', chassis no.
W142, green with beige upholstery, engine:
four cylinder, single overhead camshaft,
1,496cc, 61bhp at 4,800rpm, gearbox: four
speed manual, brakes: drums all round,
suspension: front quarter elliptic leaf springs,
rear half elliptic springs, right hand drive.
(Christie's) $22,729**

**1914 Rolls-Royce 40/50hp Silver Ghost, open
drive landaulette coachwork by Barker,
chassis no.60 RB, gray with black coachlines
and original beige bedford cord interior,
engine: six cylinder, 7,428cc, side valves,
48bhp at 1,000rpm, gearbox: four speed
manual, brakes: two wheel rear drum.
(Christie's) $215,450**

**1912 Renault CE 20/30 tourer, coachwork by
the Regent Carriage Co., chassis no. CEC
31710, green with green hide upholstery,
engine: four cylinder, side valve cast in two
blocks of twin cylinders, 5,026cc, 24.8hp,
gearbox: four speed with reverse, brakes: rear
wheel drum, suspension: semi-elliptic leaf
springs front and rear, right hand drive.
(Christie's) $56,885**

**1898 Benz 'Comfortable' 3¹/₂ H.P. Vis-A-Vis,
chassis no. 1326K, engine no. 1527, two tone
green with black leather interior, engine:
single cylinder, rear-mounted, horizontal,
automatic inlet valve, 1,045cc, gearbox: two
speed belt and chain final drive, rear wheel
brakes, suspension, fully elliptic leaf springs
all round.
(Christie's) $49,910**

**1926 Rolls-Royce Silver Ghost Permanent Top
Landaulette, coachwork by Brewster, chassis
no. S300PL, black highlighted with canework
and gray broadcloth interior, engine: six
cylinder, 7,428cc, side valves, 65bhp at
1,250rpm, gearbox: three speed manual,
brakes: two wheel drum.
(Christie's) $74,000**

**1937 MG SA saloon, chassis no. SA 2055, two
tone blue with blue leather interior, engine: six
cylinder, 2,288cc, overhead valves, 78.5bhp at
4,200rpm, gearbox: four speed manual,
brakes: four wheel drum, hydraulically
operated, suspension: semi-elliptic leaf
springs, right hand drive.
(Christie's) $23,173**

1956 MG TD Arnolt Drophead coupe,
coachwork by Bertone, chassis no. 26718, red
with beige leather upholstery.
(Christie's) $35,650

Circa 1960 Abarth Allemano 2200 coupe,
chassis no. 112 038118, gray with red leather
interior, engine: six cylinder, overhead valve.
(Christie's) $8,912

'The Rimoldi' 1933 Alfa Romeo 8C-2300
Corto Spyder, coachwork by Carrozzeria
Touring, chassis no. 2.211.107, red with dark
red leather interior, engine: straight 8, double
overhead camshafts, supercharged, 2,600cc,
165bhp at 5,000rpm, gearbox: four speed
manual, brakes: four wheel drum.
(Christie's) $1,817,500

1914 Rolls-Royce Silver Ghost Open Touring,
coachwork believed to be by Cockshoot,
chassis no. 27LB, engine no. 80A, white with
dark red leather upholstery, engine: six
cylinder, 7,428cc, side valves, 48bhp at
1,000rpm, gearbox: four speed manual,
brakes: two wheel drum.
(Christie's) $178,500

1969 4.2 litre Jaguar E-type series II roadster,
chassis no. 1R 9218, red with black leather
interior, engine: six cylinder in-line, double
overhead camshaft, 4,235cc, 171bhp at
5,400rpm, gearbox: four speed manual;
brakes: disk all round.
(Christie's) $28,520

1956 Lincoln Continental MKII, vin. no.
C56F3037, turquoise with white interior,
engine: V8, 368ci, 285hp, gearbox: three-speed
automatic, brakes: four wheel drum,
suspension, front independent, rear, live axle,
left hand drive.
(Christie's) $21,850

1960 Bentley S2 standard saloon, chassis no.
B280AM, engine no. 302AB, black and white
with gray leather interior, engine: V8,
overhead valve, 6,230cc, 200bhp at 5,000rpm,
gearbox: four speed automatic.
(Christie's) $24,955

1988 Ferrari Testarossa, chassis no.
ZFFSG17AXJ0075283, white with biscuit
leather interior, engine: Flat 12, horizontally-
opposed cylinders, 4,942cc, est. 390bhp at
6,300rpm, gearbox: five speed manual.
(Christie's) $70,700

1968 Lotus 49 Formula 1 child's car, gasolene powered, finished in gold leaf colors with pneumatic tires and alloy wheels.
(Christie's) $13,800

1979 MGB Roadster, FKE 567V, Brooklands racing green, chassis No. GHN5 5010239, engine No. 32317, with service history.
(Holloway's) $5,320

1929 Ford Model A Phaeton, engine no. 2171192, andalucite blue with black fenders, engine: four-cylinder, in-line, 200.5ci, 40bhp at 2,200rpm, gearbox: three-speed manual with overdrive, brakes: four-wheel drums, mechanical, suspension: semi-elliptic springs front and rear, solid axle, left hand drive.
(Christie's) $19,550

1929 Lincoln 'L' Sport Phaeton, coachwork by Murray, bronson yellow with black fenders and black leather interior, engine: V8 side-valve, 384ci, gearbox: three-speed manual with overdrive, brakes: four-wheel mechanical, suspension: semi-elliptic leaf front and rear, left hand drive.
(Christie's) $51,750

1955 Jaguar XK140 MC Roadster, chassis no. S810609 DN, Pacific blue with navy blue interior and top, engine: six-cylinder in line, 3,442cc, gearbox: four-speed with overdrive, synchromesh except on first, brakes: four-wheel hydraulic drum.
(Christie's) $86,100

1962 Mercedes-Benz 220 SEB convertible, chassis no. 11102320032232, engine no. 12798420003818, ivory with red leather interior, engine: inline, overhead-cam, six cylinder, 2,195cc, 130bhp at 5,000rpm, brakes: four wheel disk; gearbox: four speed manual.
(Christie's) $19,608

1961 Mercedes-Benz 300SL Roadster, chassis no. 19804210002877, red with tan leather interior, engine: six-cylinder, in line, 2,996cc, 215bhp, gearbox: four-speed manual, brakes: hydraulic disk all round.
(Christie's) $156,500

1973 4 Litre V12 Lamborghini Espada Series III, chassis no. 9000, white with red leather interior, engine: V12 twin overhead cam, 3929cc, 365bhp at 7,500rpm, gearbox: five speed manual, brakes: front/rear disk.
(Christie's) $12,478

1925 Rolls-Royce Silver Ghost Piccadilly Roadster, coachwork by Rolls-Royce Custom Coach Works, chassis no. S54LK, cream and maroon with dark red leather upholstery, engine: six cylinder, 7,428cc, side valves, 65bhp at 1,250rpm, gearbox: four speed manual, brakes: two wheel drum.
(Christie's)   **$112,500**

1929 Ford Model A town car, coachwork by Briggs, engine no. A111313, green with black fenders, engine: four-cylinder, 200.5ci, 40hp, gearbox: standard Model A three-speed, brakes: mechanical internal expanding, suspension: semi-elliptic transverse front and rear, left hand drive.
(Christie's)   **$52,900**

1899 Daimler 6hp Wagonette, engine no. 1417, blue with ivory coachlines and black leather interior, engine: twin vertical cylinders, water cooled, sidevalve, 1551cc, gearbox: four speed forward and reverse, double chain drive, brakes: spoon, also external contracting on rear wheels.
(Christie's)   **$67,115**

1907 Ford Model K seven-passenger touring car, engine no. 516, gray with black fenders and black interior and top, engine: six-cylinder, 405.6ci, 40hp, gearbox: two-speed planetary, brakes: rear drums, suspension: front, semi-elliptic, rear, full-elliptic, right hand drive.
(Christie's)   **$72,900**

1926 Packard Series 243 Landaulet, coachwork by Lebaron, dark blue with black leather upholstery, engine: eight cylinder in line, side valve, gearbox: three speed, brakes: four wheel drum, suspension: semi-elliptic leaf spring front and rear, left hand drive.
(Christie's)   **$43,700**

1954 Bentley R type 4½ litre two door coupe, coachwork by Abbott, chassis no. B401S.P, black over silver with tan leather upholstery, engine: six cylinder in-line, overhead-valve, twin carburettors, 4,566cc, 150bhp at 4,500rpm, gearbox: four speed manual.
(Christie's)   **$30,302**

1937 MG TA open sports two seater, chassis no. TA 1025, cream over brown with beige leather upholstery, engine: four cylinder, overhead valve, 1,250cc giving 54bhp at 5,200rpm, gearbox: four speed manual, brakes: four wheel drum, suspension: semi-elliptic leaf springs, right hand drive. (Christie's) $21,390

1937 Bentley 4¼ litre sports saloon, coachwork by Barker, chassis no. B 175HM, two tone red with gray leather interior, engine: six cylinder in-line, 4,257cc, 125bhp at 4,500rpm, gearbox: four speed manual, brakes: four wheel drums assisted by mechanical servo. (Christie's) $2,3170

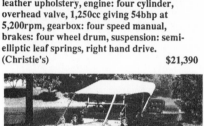

1910 Rolls-Royce Silver Ghost 'Balloon Car' Roadster, coachwork by Wilkinson & Sons, chassis no. 1322, maroon with black wings with brown hide upholstery, engine: six cylinder, 7,428cc, side valves, 48bhp at 1,000rpm, gearbox: three speed manual, brakes: two wheel drums. (Christie's) $189,500

1934 Bentley 3½ litre Sedanca Coupe, coachwork by Freestone & Webb, chassis no. B78CR, cream and black with red interior, engine: six-cylinder in-line, overhead valves, 3,669cc, twin SU carburettors, coil ignition, gearbox: four speed manual with synchromesh on 3rd and 4th. (Christie's) $63,705

1909 Rolls-Royce Silver Ghost Roi-Des-Belges Tourer, chassis no. 1179, dark green with dark green leather upholstery, engine: six cylinder, 7,428cc, side valves, 48bhp at 1,000rpm, gearbox: three speed manual, brakes: two wheel drum. (Christie's) $376,500

1903 Ford Model A two-passenger roadster, engine no. 581, red with black interior, engine: two-cylinder opposed, 8hp, gearbox: two speeds forward and reverse, brakes: two-wheel, suspension: full elliptic leaf springs, front and rear, right hand drive. (Christie's) $32,200

The Wiz Register cast iron recording till by the American Sales Book Co, circa 1919, 45 cm. wide.
(Auction Team Köln) $122

An Intercount coin counting and sorting machine, circa 1955.
(Auction Team Köln) $115

American Autographic Register cast iron till, 1888, 29 cm. long.
(Auction Team Köln)
                             $308

A National Model 92 cash register with five row keyboard for Danish currency, bronzed brass decoration, circa 1898.
(Auction Team Köln) $655

American McCaskey full keyboard cash register with printer with original wooden undercasing and till drawer, 1921.
(Auction Team Köln)

                             $423

A late 19th century pre-decimalisation till, having neo-classical boxwood stringing, in working order, 20in.
(Locke & England) $534

A miniature wooden cash register with five keys for 5, 10, 15, 20 and 25 cents, with bell, 23.5 cm. wide.
(Auction Team Köln) $115

Brandt Automatic Cashier four-row coin changer with seven coin chutes and change slide, circa 1933.
(Auction Team Köln) $92

A National Model 442X cash register with richly decorated nickel casing with crank, for German currency to 99.99 marks and receipt dispenser, circa 1908. (Auction Team Köln) $1,264

A gilt-bronze ten-light
chandelier, of inverted trumpet-
shape, the acanthine scroll arms
issuing from an engine-milled
circlet, 49¼in. high.
(Christie's) $6,769

René Lalique, plafonnier
'Charmes', after 1924, clear and
frosted glass molded with leafy
branches, 34.25cm.
(Sotheby's) $2,725

An English cut-glass chandelier,
mid-19th century, the six scroll
arms with tulip-shape sconces
radiating from a central
baluster column, 33½in. high.
(Christie's) $2,190

A cut glass and gilt bronze
ceiling light, late 19th/early 20th
century, the circlet cast with
ribband bound reeded ornament
supporting a frosted shade,
13½in. diameter.
(Christie's) $1,033

Daum and Edgar Brandt, tiered
ceiling light, 1920s, orange glass
etched with abstract scrolls,
composed of three tiers in
descending size, in a patinated
metal mount, 15in.
(Sotheby's) $6,541

A Regency style gilt bronze and
cut glass hanging dish light, 20th
century, the circular shade cut
with hobnail ornament enclosed
by a pierced and stiff-leaf cast
frieze, 22½in. diameter.
(Christie's) $3,098

An Empire style gilt bronze and
cut glass chandelier, 20th
century, of inverted trumpet-
shape, the circlet applied with a
continuous frieze of berried
laurel, 42in. high.
(Christie's) $2,237

A 19th century gilt bronze
twelve-light chandelier in the
troubadour style, the pineapple
corona above three standing
cherubs, 80cm. drop.
(Phillips) $3,040

A brass and cut-glass dish-light,
the circular stiff-leaf and
molded top suspending four
chains and a circular paneled
rim with flowerhead-filled
guilloche band, 54cm. diameter.
(Christie's) $3,671

Cobalt decorated three-gallon stoneware churn, *H. M. Whitman Havana N.Y.*, 15in. high.
(Skinner) $1,150

Newcomb College covered jar, glossy glaze, decorated with blue and green flowers and leaves on white ground, 5½in. wide.
(Skinner) $1,160

Teplitz Art pottery vase, two handles with open work, decorated in blue and gold with irises, marked *R.S.& K.,* 9¼in. high.
(Skinner) $575

Grueby Pottery vase, circular form bulbous base tapering in toward top, broad and narrow alternating leaf pattern, 4¾in. high
(Skinner) $4,025

A figural chalkware mantle garniture, Pennsylvania, 19th century, the hollow molded figure depicting a stylized group of fruit, vegetables and foliage, 13¼in. high.
(Christie's) $1,093

Weller Jap Birdimal vase, decorated by Hattie Ross, decorated with bands of birds in white, green and brown, 5¼in. high.
(Skinner) $316

Stoneware pitcher, America, 19th century, cobalt applied floral decoration, inscribed *All Life is Brief – What Now is Bud Will Soon be Leaf*, interior Albany glazed, 8in. high.
(Skinner) $1,265

Merrimac pottery jardiniere, collar rim over bulbous base, matte and glossy green glaze, unmarked, 7½in. high.
(Skinner) $201

An amusing brown-glazed stoneware face jug, Southern, signed *Robert Jackson*, late 19th century, the bulbous face with protruding ears and bail handle, 12¼in. high.
(Sotheby's) $690

A fine Union Porcelain Works white parian 'Poet's Pitcher', Greenpoint, New York, 1879–88, designed by Karl L. H. Müller, 8⁹/₁₆in. high.
(Sotheby's) $4,312

Fulper pottery three-handle vase, green crystalline glaze over blue, black vertical ink stamp, 6¾in. high.
(Skinner) $172

Amphora glazed earthenware vase, early 20th century, in gold glaze with green and violet iridescence, 13¹/₂in. high.
(Butterfield & Butterfield)
$1,265

A large figural chalkware Cheshire cat, Pennsylvania, 19th century, with a gold painted body and smoke-decorated stripes, 14³/₄in. high.
(Christie's) $10,925

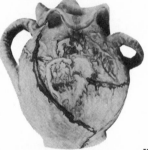

Weller silvertone vase, exquisite floral modeling on bulbous body with swirling handles and ruffled rim, 8in. high.
(Skinner) $460

Weller Sicardo glazed pottery vase, early 20th century, decorated in green, blue, fuchsia and gold iridescence, 6¹/₂in. high.
(Butterfield & Butterfield)
$690

Chelsea Keramic Art works pottery vase, flat oval form, handles at sides, blue and brown glaze, impressed mark, 13in. high.
(Skinner) $287

A rare cobalt-blue-decorated salt-glazed stoneware water cooler, American, circa 1845, of ovoid form with flared rim, 17³/₄in. high.
(Sotheby's) $1,955

A cobalt-blue-decorated salt-glaze stoneware jug, signed by Cowden & Wilcox, Harrisburg, Pennsylvania, circa 1855, 15¹/₂in. high.
(Sotheby's) $2,300

ARITA

A pair of Japanese Arita vases,
12in. high.
(Dockree's) $725

A group of three Arita models
of a cockerel, hens and stands,
late 17th/early 18th century,
decorated in iron-red, black,
aubergine and yellow enamels
and gilt.
(Christie's) $14,750

An Arita model of a cat, 19th
century, seated with head
turned over its left shoulder
and right paw raised, 24cm.
high.
(Christie's) $2,600

BELLEEK

A second period Belleek china
mask jug vase, with applied
encrusted flowers and raised on
spreading base with scroll feet,
12¹/₂in. high.
(James Adam) $515

A Belleek second period
Neptune pattern tea service,
comprising teapot, six cups, six
saucers, sugar bowl and milk
jug.
(James Adam) $589

A Belleek partially glazed
Parian bust of Clytie, after the
sculpture by C. Delpech, the
young woman with wavy hair
and off the shoulder dress,
28.5cm. high.
(Phillips) $1,188

Belleek hexagon cake plate with
grog applied twig handles, the
center having a basket weave
pattern, 9¹/₂in. diameter.
(Peter Wilson) $406

A Belleek three-strand oval
basket and cover with branch
handles and finial, 20.5cm.
wide.
(Christie's) $604

A late 19th century Belleek
circular basket, with woven
three strand base, looped rim
applied with a trail of intricately
modeled roses and thistle heads,
22cm. diameter.
(Peter Wilson) $556

134

BERLIN

A good Berlin plaque, by F. Zapf, signed, painted with a lady standing seductively in a shady grotto, 26 x 40.3cm., impressed marks.
(Phillips) $7,440

A 19th century KPM cup and saucer, the cup decorated with an armorial, the saucer with dedication and dated *16th September 1861*.
(Academy) $565

A finely painted Berlin plaque of Princess Louise, by F. Zapf, signed, the figure standing by a classical column, 25.9 x 40.5cm., impressed KPM and scepter.
(Phillips) $5,735

A Berlin (K.P.M.) porcelain cup painted with a view of figures in a landscape before a town in the distance within gilt borders, mid 19th century.
(Christie's) $440

A Berlin classical group, representing Wisdom, with Athena standing supporting her shield flanked by winged putti holding attributes, 23cm. high, late 19th century.
(Christie's) $392

A Berlin porcelain circular plaque, the central oblong panel depicting the 'Fire of Brogo', signed *A. Beer*, in gilded vitruvian scroll border, 24¹/₂in. wide.
(Andrew Hartley) $7,248

An attractive and well painted Berlin plate, painted in the center with a view of Das Rathhaus in Potsdam, 25cm., scepter and KPM in blue and orb in red, titled in black.
(Phillips) $4,030

A very fine Berlin plaque by Carl Meinelt, painted after Rubens with seven naked children supporting a garland of fruit, signed with monogram, 36.5 x 52cm., impressed marks.
(Phillips) $24,800

A finely painted Berlin plate, the center painted with a view of the Palace of the Prince of Prussia in Berlin, 24.5cm., mark of scepter, orb and KPM.
(Phillips) $8,680

A rare Bow partridge tureen and cover, the bird nesting among twisted straw and leaves around a white basket, 15cm. long.
(Phillips) $496

A pair of Bow figures of musicians, circa 1762, he in flowered breeches, his companion in a flowered skirt playing a zither, 6¾in. high.
(Christie's) $1,923

A rare Bow octagonal deep plate, printed in sepia/purple after Robert Hancock with a full version of 'L'Amour', 22cm.
(Phillips) $1,705

A pair of Bow figures of Mercury and Apollo, circa 1765, modeled with their attributes, draped, standing on flower-encrusted scroll-footed bases, 7¾in. high.
(Christie's) $961

A pair of Bow figures of 'New Dancers', circa 1770, modeled in typical pose with arms outstretched before flowering trees on scroll bases, 8¾in. high.
(Christie's) $1,923

A pair of Bow candlestick-figures, circa 1765, the supports modeled as cherubs with hounds at their sides pursuing birds among flowering foliage, 9½in. high.
(Christie's) $2,622

A pair of Derby bocage candlestick figures of Italian farmers modeled as a lady and gentleman, standing, each holding chickens, wearing 18th century dress, circa 1765.
(Christie's) $1,188

A pair of Bow models of songbirds, each perched on a woody stump applied with brightly colored leaves and flowers, 9cm.
(Phillips) $1,085

Two Bow figures of dancers, circa 1765, the lady modeled curtseying, the gentleman with one hand extended, 8¼in. high.
(Christie's) $2,622

BRITISH

Fine Mason's Ironstone ice pail of oval form, the sides applied with two scrolled handles, molded as frogs heads, 19th century, 15in.
(G. A. Key) $1,650

Ironstone large oval meat plate, the border printed in blue with panels of scenes of cattle, deer etc. within foliate scrolled cartouches, 'Parma' pattern, 19th century, 21in. wide.
(G. A. Key) $135

A Nantgarw porcelain tea cup and matching saucer, the cup interior painted in gold with a band of foliage around a central bouquet of flowers, pattern No. 822. (Bearne's) $324

A rare and fine pair of Rockingham vases of distinctive shape with flattened bodies rising from leaf molded bases, probably painted by Edwin Steele, 12cm.
(Phillips) $4,340

Antonin Boullemier: a fine Coalport cabinet plate, painted in characteristic style with a young girl seated by a fence, signed, 24.5cm., printed mark superimposed with *Chicago Exhibition 1893*.
(Phillips) $2,015

A rare pair of Davenport vases in Empire style, the ovoid bodies painted with panels of baskets overflowing with ripe fruit on marble tables, 28.5cm., circa 1820–1825.
(Phillips) $1,064

A William Brownfield plaque, handpainted with ducks and riverbank landscape, signed with initials, date to reverse *9/88*, 26cm. diameter.
(Peter Wilson) $201

Brannam Barum Ware puzzle jug, of bulbous form, the body having an incised fish and inscription against a deep green glaze, dated 1906, 13cm. high.
(Peter Wilson) $108

A large blue and white pottery meat dish, printed with the 'Hospitality' scene of a farmer's wife offering food to a lame traveler, 52.4cm. wide.
(Bearne's) $1,311

CANTON

Canton bidet, China, 19th century, 24in. long.
(Skinner) $575

Pair of unusual Canton enamel and ivory figures of foreigners, first quarter 19th century, each portrayed as a kneeling Dutchman, 20in. high overall.
(Butterfield & Butterfield) $90,500

A large Canton famille rose celadon-ground baluster vase, 19th century, with two confronted lion-cub handles, enemeled with panels of figures, 23¼in. high.
(Christie's) $961

A Canton porcelain 'Rose Medallion' hexagonal garden seat, late 19th century, painted in famille-rose enamels with three rows of panels depicting Mandarin figures, 18¾in. high.
(Sotheby's) $3,737

A pair of Canton porcelain famille rose vases mounted as lamps, late 19th century, each of tapering quadrangular shape, 25.7cm. high.
(Sotheby's) $6,325

A large Canton punchbowl, Qing Dynasty, mid-19th century, painted in 'famille-rose' enamels, the interior painted with an extensive figurative frieze, 51.5cm. diameter.
(Sotheby's) $7,486

CAUGHLEY

A very rare Caughley inkwell with separate liner, of spreading circular shape with sloping shoulder pierced with four holes for quills, 9.5cm. diameter at the base.
(Phillips) $1,705

A Caughley blue and white teapot and cover and four cups and saucers printed with the 'Pagoda' pattern, within gilt rims, circa 1785.
(Christie's) $597

A very rare Caughley pounce pot or sander of 'hour glass' shape with conical top and foot, printed with hexagonal cell borders and flower sprigs, 7.8cm. high.
(Phillips) $651

CHELSEA

A rare Chelsea bough pot, of fluted semi-circular shape bound by a central simulated ribbon, 18.5cm. wide, unmarked, red anchor period.
(Phillips) $1,163

A very rare Chelsea-Derby model of a spaniel reclining on an oval grassy base, facial features picked out in black and red, 16cm.
(Phillips) $1,085

A rare Chelsea bough pot of tapering semi-circular shape molded with flutes and encircled by a simulated length of ribbon, 18cm. wide, circa 1756.
(Phillips) $730

A pair of Chelsea figures of pilgrims, circa 1798, each with one arm outstretched and a staff in the other hand, their clothes applied with scallop-shell badges, 10¼in. high.
(Christie's) $5,244

A fine pair of Chelsea sunflower dishes, each yellow flower partially obscured by a leaf growing from a stalk handle, 23cm., red anchor mark, circa 1755.
(Phillips) $5,230

A pair of Chelsea figures of street vendors, both standing on heavily scrolled and pierced floral encrusted bases, 25cm., gold anchor marks.
(Phillips) $1,085

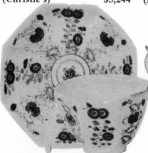

A Chelsea octagonal teabowl and saucer, in Kakiemon style, painted in red, blue and turquoise with chrysanthemums and carnations, the bowl 8.2cm. diameter.
(Phillips) $589

A finely painted Chelsea chocolate cup, both sides painted with views along the river Thames, gilt dentil border to rim, 6.5cm., gold anchor mark, circa 1765.
(Phillips) $988

A Chelsea plate of Mecklenberg Strelitz type, the border with five shell-shaped panels of flower festoons between mazarine blue panels with exotic insects, circa 1764.
(Phillips) $1,426

CHINESE

19th century Wu Ts'ai porcelain figure of the goddess Quan Yin seated in flowing robes, 9in. high.
(Eldreds) $1,000

Armorial Chinese Export porcelain soup tureen, circa 1765, decorated with the arms of Garfoote, 13in. long.
(Skinner) $4,887

A Chinese polychrome washstand bowl, the interior painted with herons and foliage around a peony, 25.5cm. wide.
(Bearne's) $224

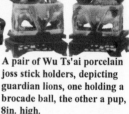

A pair of Chinese famille verte biscuit officials, Kangxi, each seated on a semi-circular chair, wearing long loose green-glazed robes splashed with aubergine, 7in. high.
(Christie's) $1,049

A pair of Chinese green, yellow and aubergine-glazed buddhistic lions, seated on tall rectangular plinths with their opposite forepaws resting on a cub and a brocaded ball, 18in. high.
(Christie's) $1,049

A pair of Wu Ts'ai porcelain joss stick holders, depicting guardian lions, one holding a brocade ball, the other a pup, 8in. high.
(Eldreds) $1,000

A Chinese Export porcelain armorial charger, circa 1740, painted in famille-rose enamels in the center with a butterfly flitting near two birds, 38.6cm. diameter.
(Sotheby's) $1,840

A Chinese Export porcelain goose tureen and cover, 1765–85, naturalistically modeled with incised plumage delineated on the back and wings in black, brown, blue and green, 32.8cm. high. (Sotheby's) $28,750

A Chinese guanyao-type crackle-glazed globular jar, 19th century, molded with two animal-mask fixed ring-handles, all under a thick widely crackled gray glaze, 12in. high.
(Christie's) $2,797

CHINESE

A pottery figure of a horse, T'ang Dynasty, in chestnut glaze, 12½in. high.
(Eldreds) $1,045

Pair of rose medallion cylindrical vases, China, 19th century, 12¾in. high.
(Skinner) $977

Nanking cider jug, China, 19th century, 11in. high.
(Skinner) $920

A pair of Chinese blue and white ginger jars and covers, late 19th century, the baluster bodies decorated with figures within fenced gardens, 10in. high.(Christie's) $835

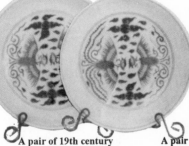

A pair of 19th century porcelain plates decorated with phoenix and clouds on exterior and interior, six character Chia Ching mark on base, 6¼in. diameter.
(Eldreds) $1,595

A pair of 19th century Chinese porcelain famille rose shouldered vases with flared gilded rim, reserves depicting interiors with figures, 24in. high.
(Andrew Hartley) $961

A Chinese porcelain jardinière, painted in bright famille rose enamels with rulers and their attendants, 35cm. high.
(Bearne's) $626

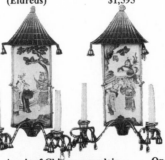

A pair of Chinese porcelain-mounted brass two-branch wall-lights, each with rectangular backplate with courtly scenes surmounted by a pagoda roof, 46cm. high.
(Christie's) $2,972

One of a pair of Chinese blue and white hexagonal garden seats with pierced sides, each painted with scrolling foliage above a lappet band, 46.5cm. high.
(Bearne's) (Two) $1,265

CLARICE CLIFF

Clarice Cliff Bizarre squat ribbed vase, shape 371, red roof design, from the Fantasque range, 11cm. high.
(Peter Wilson) $865

'Crocus', a 'Bizarre' duck egg cruet set, comprising: circular tray surmounted with a yellow duck, with six egg cups, 13cm. high.
(Christie's) $475

'Broth' , an Athens shape teapot and cover, painted in colors, printed factory marks, 15cm. high.
(Christie's) $475

A Clarice Cliff 'Orange House' pattern plate, painted with a stylized cottage and trees enclosed by orange border, 26.3cm. diameter.
(Phillips) $850

A wall pocket modeled in the form of a young girl with trellis and flowers in her hair, in shades of red, blue and brown on a mushroom glaze, 18cm. high.
(Christie's) $372

'Farmhouse', a 'Fantasque Bizarre' side plate, painted in colors, bordered by yellow, orange and black bands printed factory marks, 17.5cm. diameter.
(Christie's) $320

A Clarice Cliff twin-handled baluster vase, 'Bizarre', painted with a sunburst and geometric landscape between two broad orange borders, 11¹/₂in. high.
(George Kidner) $3,080

A pottery centerpiece modeled as a fish amongst seaweed, covered in a running delecia glaze, in shades of red, brown, green and yellow, 22.5cm. high.
(Christie's) $288

A Clarice Cliff 'Coral Firs' single handled Lotus jug, brightly painted, the rim with brown, yellow and beige banding.
(Neales) $616

CLARICE CLIFF

A 'Bizarre' charger designed by Dame Laura Knight, the well painted with a crowd of naked women, 47cm. diam.
(Christie's) $9,342

A Clarice Cliff, Fantasque conical bowl, brightly painted with the 'Lily' pattern, 19.2cm. diameter.
(Bearne's) $402

'Orange Roof Cottage', a 'Bizarre' Daffodil preserve pot and cover, 12cm. high
(Christie's) $680

'Sliced Circle', a 'Bizarre' twin-handled lotus jug, painted in colors, printed factory marks, 29cm. high.
(Christie's) $6,795

A Wilkinson's Stamford tea for two painted with orange, purple and yellow fruit, comprising: teapot and cover, milk-jug and sugar bowl, two cups, saucers and a side plate,
(Christie's) $755

'Passion Fruit', a vase, painted in colors on a turquoise ground, printed factory marks, 24.5cm. high.
(Christie's) $305

Orange 'Gardenia', a 'Fantasque Bizarre' single handled lotus jug, painted in colors, printed factory marks, 29cm. high.
(Christie's) $1,360

'Teepee', a teapot designed by M B Sylvester, the handle modeled as a totem pole, the spout as an Indian brave, 17cm. high.
(Christie's) $593

'House and Bridge', a Fantasque Bizarre' conical sugar sifter, painted in colors, printed factory marks, 14cm. high.
(Christie's) $1,360

COPELAND

A Copeland parian group, in the form of a young peasant man and woman seated on a rocky mound, 31cm. high.
(Bearne's) $801

A pair of Copeland parian porcelain busts of young women with flowers in their hair, representing 'Spring' and 'Summer', after originals by Louis Auguste Malempre, 32cm. high. (Bearne's) $1,102

One of a set of seven Copeland handpainted porcelain plates with pink, green and gilt borders enclosing a reserve decorated with floral sprays, 10.2in. diameter.
(James Adam) $347

CREAMWARE

An English creamware enameled jug, dated *1791*, the swelling body painted with two cottages with smoking chimneys, 8¹/₈in. high.
(Sotheby's) $1,380

A pair of English creamware Dutch-decorated plates, 1775–85, each painted with 'Our Lady of Kevelaar', 9³/₄in. and 9¹⁵/₁₆in. diameter.
(Sotheby's) $1,265

An English creamware enameled jug, probably Leeds, dated *1771*, the barrel-shaped body painted on the front with the inscription *John and Martha Wheeler. 1771*, 7¹/₈in. high.
(Sotheby's) $1,035

DE MORGAN

An earthenware dish, possibly William de Morgan, early 20th century, painted in ruby luster with a winged dragon and a snake, 36cm. diameter.
(Sotheby's) $980

A William De Morgan two-handled vase, Merton Abbey Period, circa 1882–1888, painted with peacocks and Iznik flowers bordered with fish on a blue scale ground, 13³/₈in. high.
(Sotheby's) $6,820

A William De Morgan ruby luster dish, painted with a scaly sea creature against a red and white ground of swirls and waves, 36cm diameter.
(Phillips) $1,736

DELFT

A fine and interesting Dutch delft polychrome plaque, of shield shape, spiritedly painted with a Chinese man standing upright on a galloping horse, in Kakiemon style, 33.5cm.
(Phillips) **$4,185**

A very rare English delft flower holder, of tapering square shape, the sides painted in blue with leafy sprays, 10.8cm. wide.
(Phillips) **$2,790**

A London delftware polychrome posset pot, 1680–1700, the cylindrical body painted in blue and manganese on the front with two chinoiserie figures, 5¹/₈in. high.
(Sotheby's) **$1,725**

A very rare and early English delft coffee cup or 'Capuchine', of bell shape with a turned central groove and a rolled loop handle, 6.2cm.
(Phillips) **$3,100**

A very unusual pair of English delft vases of baluster shape with spreading bases, painted in blue with massive stylized flowerheads.
(Phillips) **$3,255**

A Dutch delft ovoid jar, painted after a Japanese Arita original with figures in a highly stylized landscape with willow and banana trees, 31cm.
(Phillips) **$1,705**

A 19th century delft cottage pastille burner, with blue and white floral pattern, 4in. high.
(Andrew Hartley) **$76**

A Dutch delft figure of a horse, mid 18th century, cold-decorated with an iron-red muzzle, brown mane and tail, gold hooves, 8³/₄in. high.
(Sotheby's) **$1,380**

A London delftware polychrome plate, circa 1760, painted with a Chinaman seated amidst shrubbery, 9in. diameter.
(Sotheby's) **$920**

DERBY

A rare and amusing Derby (King Street) model of a boy in a boat, the child scantily clad with a blue drape, the exterior painted pale green and pink, 25cm. long, circa 1860.
(Phillips) $190

A pair of Bloor Derby figures modeled as 'Toper' and companion, typically modeled standing, 11cm. high, 19th century.
(Christie's) $755

A Derby 'Dolphin Ewer' creamboat molded as a rococo shell design with a high scroll handle and entwined dolphins below the lip, 8cm. high.
(Phillips) $403

A Royal Crown Derby baluster shaped two-handled vase, with shaped flared rim decorated in blue, green, orange and gilt with an Imari pattern, 4³/₄in. high, date code for 1909.
(Canterbury) $198

A pair of Derby models of sporting dogs, both modeled on rough grassy bases applied with flowers, and naturalistically colored, circa 1820.
(Phillips) $1,109

A Royal Crown Derby two-handled vase and cover painted by Cuthbert Gresley, of campana form, painted with trailing blooms suspending swags of flowers, date codes for 1906, 22½cm. high.
(Christie's) $1,288

A Royal Crown Derby dark blue ground plate painted by Edwin Trowell with a street scene in Bakewell, Derbyshire, 22.9cm. diam.
(Christie's) $1,460

A good pair of Derby porcelain figures of negroes, the male wearing full-length floral decorated coat and holding a sheath of arrows, William Duesbury & Co., circa 1765.
(Canterbury) $4,530

A fine Derby plate painted by George Complin, with two canaries perched in a tree beside a stream, within a gilded border, 21.5cm., crown crossed batons and D mark, circa 1790.
(Phillips) $2,432

DERBY

A fine Derby basket, the pierced sides applied with pink and yellow florets at the intersections, with green and yellow ropetwist handles, 25cm., circa 1760.
(Phillips) $1,246

A Derby group of Europa and the Bull and Leda and the Swan, painted in colors and gilt, 11¼in. high, circa 1765.
(Christie's) $2,547

A fine Derby ice pail and cover by William Billingsley painted with a series of sprays of roses, cornflowers and grasses, 24cm.
(Phillips) $3,720

A pair of Derby Crown Porcelain Co. vases and covers, the pale creamy-yellow ground decorated in gilding and silver with bamboo and other leafy branches, 40.5cm., date code for 1888.
(Phillips) $608

A finely modeled Derby white porcelain bust of a gentleman, probably modeled by William Stephan, the broad-featured face with a smiling expression, 44.5cm.
(Phillips) $930

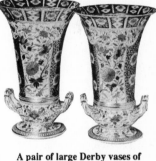

A pair of large Derby vases of rare elongated campana shape, with twin scroll molded handles painted with a bright Japan pattern, 34.5cm.
(Phillips) $2,170

A good Derby dessert plate, the center well painted with a large floral spray, within an ornate gilded border, 24cm.
(Phillips) $496

A pair of colorful Bloor Derby figures, each seated, he sitting cross legged reading a book, she sewing, 15cm. high.
(Bearne's) $864

A fine Stevenson & Hancock Derby plate, painted by W. Mosley, signed, with tulips, pink roses and other summer flowers, 8¾in. diameter.
(Neales) $631

A Royal Doulton figure: Shire horse and foal 'Pride of the Shires', on a shaped oval base, detail in green and brown, HN2523, 14¹/₂in. long.
(Russell, Baldwin & Bright)
$388

Royal Doulton ashtray, 'Dick Turpin', D5601, 4in.
(G. A. Key) $53

Doulton figure 'Two Rabbits' HN218, model number 249, introduced 1920, withdrawn 1940s.
(Peter Wilson) $196

Sung jar and cover, the cover mounted with an elephant decorated in rich flambé with mottled and veined Sung glazes, Fred Moore monogram to base, 6¹/₂in. high.
(Peter Wilson) $378

Doulton Lambeth three handled mug, the silver rim inscribed *To Joseph McWilliams*, and dated *1880*, the three handles molded with geometric designs, by Hannah Barlow, incised marks 1876, 5¹/₂in.
(G. A. Key) $675

Royal Doulton Lambeth baluster vase, the rim molded with a line of rosettes and formal foliage, decorated with a central panel, by Hannah Barlow, late 19th/early 20th century, 6¹/₂in.
(G. A. Key) $495

'Mrs Fitzherbert' HN2007, designed by M. Davies, introduced 1948, withdrawn 1953.
(Peter Wilson) $315

A Royal Doulton group entitled, 'The Wardrobe Mistress', H.N.2145, withdrawn 1967.
(Bearne's) $263

A Royal Doulton figure entitled 'Henry VIII', No. 17 of a limited edition of 200 copies.
(Bearne's) $832

DOULTON

Royal Doulton figure, 'The Potter', HN1493, painted in colors, printed marks, 7in.
(G. A. Key) $173

A pair of Doulton stoneware bottle vases with everted rims, decorated by Eliza Simmance, 25cm. high.
(Bearne's) $715

A large Royal Doulton character jug, entitled, 'Regency Beau', withdrawn 1967.
(Bearne's) $525

Doulton fluted dish, circa 1923, decorated with handpainted 'Grey Mullet', by C. Hart, signed, dated *10.23* to base, 22cm. diameter.
(Peter Wilson) $116

A near pair of Royal Doulton vases, of baluster form, with relief decoration of roses against a mottled blue ground, 14in. high.
(George Kidner) $262

Doulton, 'Blue Children' seriesware jardinière, decorated with a lady and child within garden overlooking lake, 8in. diameter.
(Peter Wilson) $575

'The Fortune Teller' D6467, designed by G. Sharpe, introduced 1959, withdrawn 1967.
(Peter Wilson) $278

A fine pair of Doulton stoneware candlesticks, each baluster stem and domed foot applied with beads and incised with leaves, 18.8cm. high.
(Bearne's) $387

Field Marshal the Rt. Hon. J. C. Smuts, no number, should be D6198, designed by H. Fenton, introduced 1946, withdrawn 1948.
(Peter Wilson) $764

DRESDEN

A very impressive Dresden model of a carriage, assembled in two large sections and with a detachable lid to the carriage, 93cm. long overall, pseudo Naples mark.
(Phillips) $2,790

A 'Dresden' porcelain two-handled pedestal vase with pierced cover, painted with alternate panels of figures in gardens and flowers, 30cm. high.
(Bearne's) $386

A Dresden oval basket with pierced sides, the whole encrusted with roses and supported by four putti, 4in. high.
(Canterbury) $228

A pair of Dresden yellow ground porcelain vases, each painted to both sides with scenes of peasants in courtyards, 21½cm. high, late 19th century.
(Christie's) $1,200

A Carl Thieme baluster flower encrusted pot pourri vase, cover and stand painted with a vignette of ladies and a child by a fountain, 98½cm. high.
(Christie's) $5,200

A pair of Carl Thieme blue ground baluster vases and covers painted with riders hunting, 46cm. high, late 19th century.
(Christie's) $1,735

A pair of Dresden blue and gilt-embellished baluster vases and covers, the bodies painted with oval scenes depicting courting couples, 14½in. high.
(Christie's) $450

A decorative Dresden dessert service with pierced trellis panels alternating with pierced flower sprays painted in colors, circa 1880.
(Phillips) $2,850

A pair of Dresden blue ground waisted beaker vases each painted with a couple walking in gardens, 16½cm. high, late 19th century.
(Christie's) $375

A Soviet porcelain dish, 'The Commissar, Uritskii Square', with underglaze mark of the Imperial Porcelain Factory, period of Alexander III and later, dated *1921*, 12in. diameter.
(Christie's) $8,446

Teplitz pottery figural group, Czechoslovakia, late 19th century, modeled as two Moroccan males riding camels, 19¹/₂in. high.
(Skinner) $575

A Soviet porcelain propaganda plate, 'The Russian and The German, Proletarians of All Nations Unite', by the Lomonosov Porcelain Factory, 9³/₄in. diameter.
(Christie's) $5,630

Continental porcelain musical group of young couple, she playing an oboe with her left hand resting on a basket of flowers, 20th century, 6in.
(G. A. Key) $87

Goebel container formed as a portly monk, wearing a brown habit; together with two matching graduated jugs, printed and incised marks, 9¹/₂in., 6in. and 4in.
(G. A. Key) $166

A 19th century Austrian porcelain vase and cover with gilt finial and loop handles, reserves depicting reclining maiden with cherubs, 18¹/₂in high.
(Andrew Hartley) $1,125

A Soviet porcelain propaganda plate, 'He who does not work does not eat', with underglaze mark of the Imperial Porcelain Factory, dated *1922*, 9⁵/₈in. diameter.
(Christie's) $3,167

Early 20th century Czechoslovakian ceramic wall mask, of a woman's head, naturalistically colored and wearing an orange cream and yellow head dress, 7¹/₂in.
(Peter Wilson) $211

A Soviet porcelain propaganda plate, by the State Porcelain Factory, blue overglaze mark, dated *1919*, painted with orange motif depicting factories, sickle and sheaf of wheat, 9⁷/₁₆in. diameter.(Christie's) $4,927

FRENCH

CHINA

A pair of Jacob Petit figural spill vases, modeled as a young man and girl, standing, wearing simple rustic dress, 21,4cm. high, circa 1840.
(Christie's) $549

A Vincennes figure of 'Le Porteur de Mouton', circa 1755, modeled as a young man kneeling and offering a beribboned sheep in a basket, 8½in. high.
(Christie's) $3,146

A pair of Vincennes figures of 'La Petite Fille a Tablier' and 'Le Jeune Supplient', circa 1753, the girl with her hair tied in a headscarf, 8in. high.
(Christie's) $9,614

A French biscuit porcelain figure of a musician modeled as a young man in 17th century dress, standing, one hand by his ear, the other on his purse, 56cm. high, circa 1870.(Christie's) $1,373

An interesting Paris part dessert service decorated for Lahoche, Palais Royal, the deep blue borders reserved with panels of birds, flowers, fruit, and trophies, circa 1870-1880. (Phillips) $2,853

Clement Massier iridescent glazed pottery vase, decorated overall with sunflowers in tones of iridescent and flat yellow ocher, 14¼in. high.
(Butterfield & Butterfield)
$977

A pair of Limoges Art Deco porcelain vases painted in colors and gilt on a yellow ground with stylized palmettes and foliage, 29.5cm. high.
(Christie's) $712

A Mennecy silver gilt mounted oval snuff box, circa 1750, the mount with Paris décharge for 1750-55, modeled as a sportswoman in blue jacket, 2¾in. (Christie's) $786

Emile Gallé, seated cat, circa 1880, yellow tin glazed earthenware body decorated with abstract blue designs, with glass eyes, 13in.
(Sotheby's) $3,634

CHINA

FRENCH

A Vincennes cup and saucer, of 'Gobelet Hébert' shape modeled with five lobes and with a double twisted handle, date letter C for 1755, painter's mark of Denis Levé. (Phillips) **$2,945**

A Continental figural centerpiece set with nymphs and a stag amongst rolling waves. (Academy) **$612**

A 'Gallé' faience model of a seated cat with green glass eyes, painted with flowers and yellow stripes, 33.5cm. high. (Bearne's) **$1,013**

A pair of Chantilly seaux à verre, circa 1745, painted in pale in colors with a gallant and companion in an arbor trapping game in a landscape, 4½in. high. (Christie's) **$8,020**

A pair of Paris porcelain twin-handled vases, each painted with a parrot, exotic and native birds by lakes in the garden of a château within chased gilt oval panels, 38.8cm. high, 19th century. (Christie's) **$4,806**

Two Paris porcelain Napoleonic portrait coffee cans and two saucers with a quarter-length profile of the Emperor, early 19th century. (Christie's) **$1,364**

A Tournai plate from the Duc de Orleans service, probably painted by Jean-Ghislain-Joseph Mayer, 24cm., titled in black on the reverse with the names of the four birds depicted, circa 1787 (Phillips) **$7,291**

A gilt metal mounted French white biscuit porcelain group modeled as a man seated at a piano, another standing by a cello, playing a guitar and two ladies, standing, 42cm. wide, late 19th/early 20th century. (Christies) **$1,373**

Round faience bowl, depicting execution via guillotine, *'Van Second de la Republique Francaise Execution de Louis Capet 21 Janvier 1793'*, decorator's initials *NV* on reverse. (Schrager) **$40**

GERMAN

Late 19th century Volkstedt figure group of cupid standing upon a plinth, a classical maiden kneeling below him, 11in. high. (Peter Wilson) **$265**

A pair of Sitzendorf porcelain lamp bases, each in the form of a flower encrusted basket weave globe, supported by three cherubs, total height 40.5cm. (Bearne's) **$680**

A large Furstenburg figure of a warrior, standing on a rocky base, wearing elaborate armor decorated in gray and gold, 33cm., *F* mark in blue. (Phillips) **$775**

German porcelain portrait plate, late 19th/early 20th century, depicting Countess of Harrington, titled on the reverse, the central enameled portrait signed *Wagner*, 9³/₈in. diameter. (Skinner) **$488**

A late 18th/early 19th century Continental white porcelain box, circa 1800, possibly German, rectangular form, depicting various putti scenes within a burgundy scroll and blue floral border, 3¹/₄in. long. (Bonhams) **$1,413**

A rare Ansbach group of three putti probably symbolic of Summer, two small boys seated with wheatsheaves and a little girl standing, 10.5cm., circa 1765–1770. (Phillips) **$1,520**

A Continental figural incense burner, fashioned as a seated clown, in yellow and black costume, 20.5cm. high, marked *Edition Kaza*. (Phillips) **$225**

A pair of German porcelain birds, 19th century, mounted as lamps, the male and female birds perched atop a tree stump over rockage, 34in. high. (Butterfield & Butterfield) **$3,162**

A large Ludwigsburg figure of a naked warrior, standing on a rocky base and leaning on a shield, well colored with armor picked out in brown and gilt, 34.5cm., blue mark. (Phillips) **$899**

GERMAN

A Limbach figure of a shepherdess, wearing a purple and white dress and hat, the sheep at her feet eating from her hand, 14cm., *LB* monogram mark.
(Phillips) $527

A Sitzendorf porcelain comport, the pierced bowl supported on a pillar surrounded by children, painted in pale enamel colors, 38.5cm. high.
(Bearne's) $525

A Mettlach pottery ewer, the cylindrical body with short neck, incised with green and brown foliage, having a metal collar and lid, 38.5cm. high.
(Phillips) $263

A pair of Sitzendorf porcelain bulbous urns and covers with cherubs-head pattern handles, the whole encrusted with floral garlands, 10¹/₄in. high.
(Canterbury) $486

A German porcelain rectangular plaque, painted with a scene from Tristram Shandy showing Uncle Toby looking in the eye of Mrs. Wadman, 33.5cm. x 23cm.
(Bearne's) $775

A pair of Potschappel porcelain jars and covers with scroll handles terminating in female heads, set on rectangular stands, 47cm. high.
(Bearne's) $1,937

A Kreussen pewter-mounted stoneware Apostle Humpen, dated *1671*, applied with figures of the twelve apostles, their names inscribed above, 6¹/₈in. high.
(Sotheby's) $2,300

A small Ludwigsburg group of a girl and boy with a goat, on oval scrolled base, decorated in pale colors, 9.5cm., blue mark.
(Phillips) $558

A large Bellarmine stoneware jar of rotund form, a bearded face on the neck, a medallion below, covered in a mottled brown glaze, 34cm. high.
(Bearne's) $507

IMARI

Japanese Imari figure of a standing maiden, late 19th century, 17³/₄in.
(Jacobs & Hunt) $1,473

A pair of Japanese Imari figures of bijin, late 19th century.
(Jacobs & Hunt) $325

A Samson Imari baluster jar and domed cover, 19th century, with shishi lion and rockwork finial, painted and heavily gilt.
(Christie's) $3,185

A foliate-rimmed Imari bowl, late 17th/early 18th century, decorated in various colored enamels and gilt with chrysanthemums and peonies 21cm. diameter.
(Christie's) $1,735

A large Japanese Imari charger, late 19th century, decorated with two roundels, one containing a bird in a flowering cherry tree, the other a dragon, 25in. diameter.
(Christie's) $3,146

A Japanese Imari porcelain charger, Meiji Period, with underglaze blue floral center surrounded by a gourd and flower landscape design, 18in. diameter.
(Eldreds) $522

A 19th century Imari porcelain charger with decoration of scroll paintings on a floral ground, 17¾in. diameter.
(Eldreds) $1,100

Pair of Japanese Imari large baluster vases with ribbed borders, decorated in the typical manner in traditional colors, 19th century, 12in.
(G. A. Key) $544

Imari charger decorated in the typical manner in colors, with central panel of jardinière and flowers etc., early 20th century, 23in. diameter.
(G. A. Key) $525

ITALIAN

An early 20th century Italian figure, modeled as a young girl, decorated in bright polychrome enamels, monogram and painted blue N & Crown marks to base, 5in. high.
(Peter Wilson) **$201**

A Savona large jar, painted in blue with a Roman soldier on horseback pursuing a stag, 23.5cm., shield mark.
(Phillips) **$2,790**

An Urbino tin-glazed earthenware inkstand, from the Patanazzi workshop, circa 1570, in the form of a large pipe organ with putti above, 17^1/2in. high.
(Sotheby's) **$28,750**

A rare Urbino maiolica accouchement shallow bowl painted with an interesting interior scene of the expectant mother seated on a stool surrounded by three attendants, 16.5cm., circa 1570.
(Phillips) **$4,560**

An early 20th century Italian figure group modeled as a child seated with a dachshund, decorated in polychrome enamels, monogram mark and blue painted N & Crown to base, 4in. high.
(Peter Wilson) **$286**

A Deruta syrup jar of baluster shape with a looped strap handle, painted with a colorful fruiting wreath and inscribed drug label *Sy:Di.Agresta.*, 16.5cm.
(Phillips) **$853**

An Italian late 17th century 7^3/4in. globular jug with crimped spout, painted panels of flowers and foliage in blue and yellow, marked *D.S.*, possibly Pesaro.
(Anderson & Garland) **$435**

An Urbino circular dish or crespina, lightly molded with a honeycomb pattern, painted with God appearing to Noah, 26cm., in a gilt stucco frame.
(Phillips) **$1,473**

A small Campanian Red Figure trefoil lipped oinochoe decorated with the profile head of a Lady of Fashion, Greek, South Italy, 4th century B.C., 4in. high.
(Bonhams) **$276**

LEEDS

A 19th century Leeds creamware loving cup, with plough and corn sheaf motifs on blue banded ground, 5in. high. (Andrew Hartley) $279

LIVERPOOL

Liverpool handpainted and transfer printed creamware jug, England, early 19th century, handpainted scene entitled *Washington in His Glory,* **10.5in. high. (Skinner)** $10,350

CHINA

A Leeds creamware three-tiered centerpiece, circa 1780, in three sections, the rockwork base rising to a lower tier of five leaf-shaped dishes on simple scroll brackets, 24½in. high. (Christie's) $6,775

A very rare Liverpool tin-glazed stoneware coffee cup, painted in blue with a curious ruined arch or folly in an otherwise Chinese style landscape, 6.2cm. (Phillips) $2,945

A documentary dated creamware snuff box, probably Leeds, of circular shape with a screw top, the lid inscribed *John Claytons Tobackah Box, Huddersfield, 1776,* **7.8cm. diameter. (Phillips)** $2,584

A Liverpool creamware transfer-printed and enameled pitcher, dated *1802,* **printed in black and enameled with initialed portraits of Samuel Adams and John Hancock. (Sotheby's)** $2,070

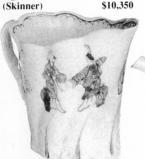

A Liverpool porcelain 'Chelsea ewer' cream-jug, probably Seth Pennington's factory, spirally fluted and molded with a band of leaves, 3in. high, circa 1780-90. (Christie's) $340

A very rare Liverpool tin-glazed stoneware teapot, painted in blue with a Chinese style house on a rocky island with pylon trees, 7.5cm. high. (Phillips) $1,163

A fine and rare Liverpool tin glazed stoneware mug, painted in blue with a highly stylized peony and lotus spray in Chinese style, 12.5cm., circa 1760. (Phillips) $5,472

LONGTON HALL

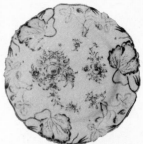

A good Longton Hall leaf dish, the border molded with six brightly colored hollyhock leaves, 21.5cm.
(Phillips) $1,860

A Longton Hall coffee cup, with rare clip handle and leaf-molded thumbrest, painted in characteristic colors with a fantastic bird on a towering rock, 6.5cm.
(Phillips) $496

A Longton Hall strawberry leaf dish, the border molded with leaves and fruit picked out in bright colors, 23.5cm.
(Phillips) $853

A rare Longton Hall mug, the angular handle with a leaf-molded thumbrest, painted with a root, chrysanthemums and bamboo by a fence, 9cm. high, circa 1755.
(Phillips) $1,347

One of a pair of Longton Hall teabowls and saucers, painted in an attractive palette of green, pink, yellow, turquoise and brown.
(Phillips)   (Two) $1,085

A rare Longton Hall coffee cup with plain loop handle, painted with Chinese buildings nestling in a wooded landscape, 5.6cm., circa 1755.
(Phillips) $1,104

LOWESTOFT

A Lowestoft globular teapot and cover painted with a Curtis type pattern of loose sprays of flowers below diaper panels suspending swags, 15cm. high, circa 1785.
(Christie's) $951

A rare Lowestoft saucer dish, the border printed in blue, the center inscribed *A Trifle from Lowestoft*, 19.5cm., circa 1790.
(Phillips) $2,736

A rare large Lowestoft tea canister of rectangular form with chamfered sides, the sides with molded medallions painted with *H, T* and *Hyson Tea*, 12cm.
(Phillips) $5,270

159

MEISSEN

A late Meissen group of two children leading a bull, the children in eighteenth century style dress, 19.5cm. wide.
(Phillips) $1,705

A pair of late Meissen figural sweetmeats, with seated figures of a lady and gentleman in eighteenth century style costumes, 31cm., crossed swords marks.
(Phillips) $1,550

A Marcolini Meissen group of two lovers, the gentleman seated and holding a basket of flowers, 20.5cm., crossed swords mark.
(Phillips) $1,705

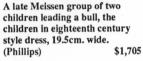

A Meissen porcelain group, after an original by Johann Carl Schoenheit, in the form of Venus sitting on a rock with doves at her side, incised *G84*.
(Bearne's) $1,298

A fine pair of large seated Meissen pugs, the bitch with her left paw raised and a puppy at her feet, 22.5cm. and 25cm., traces of crossed swords mark.
(Phillips) $9,300

A late Meissen group of two lovers, the lady standing before an ornate scrolled chair, 15.5cm., crossed swords mark, incised *0159*.
(Phillips) $1,163

A late Meissen group of a girl and boy with a rabbit, the boy holding a helmet in which the rabbit sits, 12cm., crossed swords mark, incised *H37*.
(Phillips) $1,240

A pair of late Meissen figural candlesticks emblematic of Spring and Autumn, Spring modeled as a classical lady holding a flower, 28.5cm.
(Phillips) $1,473

A late Meissen group of Cupid in disguise as a schoolteacher instructing in the art of love, 22cm. wide, crossed swords mark, incised *C2454*.
(Phillips) $2,480

MEISSEN

An early Meissen sugar box of oblong octagonal cushion form painted with chinoiseries in the manner of Heroldt, KPM and sword marks, 4¼in. high.
(Graves, Son & Pilcher) $6,869

A pair of Meissen figure candlesticks, emblematic of Summer and Winter, modeled by J. J. Kaendler, the elaborate rococo scroll supports heightened in gold, 29.5cm.
(Phillips) $2,015

A late Meissen group of three children, with a boy and a girl on a see-saw, on a circular base with gilt edge, 21.5cm.
(Phillips) $2,170

A Meissen figure of Julius Caesar representing Rome, from the set of The Four Monarchies, modeled by J.J. Kaendler, 18.5cm.
(Phillips) $961

A pair of late Meissen figural candlestick salts, modeled as a boy and girl in enameled eighteenth century dress, 23cm., crossed swords mark, incised *3024* and *3124*.
(Phillips) $1,550

A late Meissen group of a lady and gentleman, the lady seated in gilt scrolled chair, 14.5cm., crossed swords mark, incised *0151*.
(Phillips) $1,395

A late Meissen group of a lady and a putto in a chariot, the scantily clad classical lady seated and holding an apple, 18cm., crossed swords mark.
(Phillips) $2,170

Two late Meissen figures of a boy and a girl, both in eighteenth century dress and on gilt scrolled bases, 13cm. and 14cm., crossed swords and dot marks, 1924–1934.
(Phillips) $744

A 19th century Meissen porcelain Bacchanalian group, comprising two male figures, one riding an ass, a seated female, and a putto, 8½in. high.
(Andrew Hartley) $1,335

MINTON

A Minton majolica ware tavern jug, with two figures of topers on one side, green handle, 25.5cm., date code for 1864. (Phillips) **$899**

A pair of Minton majolica ware figure sweetmeat dishes, with seated figures of a girl and boy, 17.5cm., date code for 1869. (Phillips) **$1,705**

A rare Minton majolica ware triple horn flower holder, modeled as three entwined hunting horns connected by chains, 71cm. (Phillips) **$2,480**

A Minton majolica ware stemmed bowl and cover, in Renaissance style, the bowl with incised green panels below satyr masks and pendant swags, 26cm. (Phillips) **$1,240**

A Minton majolica ware 'Shell Carrier' with two Bacchic children swathed in wheat and vines and supporting a central shell, 27cm. high, date code for 1867; and another similar, 27.5cm. (Phillips) **$3,100**

A Minton majolica ware Palissy vase, with barrel shaped body, four Bacchic putti disporting themselves below the helmet shaped spout, 37cm., impressed mark and date code for 1870. (Phillips) **$1,705**

A large porcelain centerpiece, probably Minton or Copeland, circa 1860, modeled with three kneeling parian putti holding flower garlands, 33cm. high. (Sotheby's) **$4,991**

An important pair of 19th century Minton majolica jardinières on stands, the planters with green wreath rim, the bases fluted 26½in. high. (Dee, Atkinson & Harrison) **$11,400**

An Art Nouveau pottery vase of Minton majolica style, the waisted body having a flared neck and decorated in the Moorish manner, 11in. high. (Morphets) **$816**

MOORCROFT

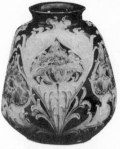

A small Moorcroft covered jar, 4in. high.
(Dee, Atkinson & Harrison)
$106

A Moorcroft large two-handled vase with design of pomegranate, grapes, etc., 14in., green signature.
(Russell, Baldwin & Bright)
$1,444

Florian Ware Moorcroft Art pottery vase, white floral form on cobalt blue ground, 8in. high.
(Skinner)
$920

A Moorcroft pair of ovoid vases, the blue/ivory ground divided by green leaves and pink buds, green signature mark, 20.8cm.
(Bristol)
$1,094

Moorcroft glazed earthenware moonlit blue landscape design vase, second quarter 20th century, painted and slipped with a scene of trees and mountains, 12½in. high.
(Butterfield & Butterfield)
$1,610

A pair of Moorcroft pottery spill vases with pomegranate pattern on deep blue ground, 12½in. high.
(Andrew Hartley)
$942

Moorcroft Florian ware squat oviform three handled vase, decorated in the 'Daisy' pattern in applied raised slipware in shades of yellow, green and blue, 5in. high.
(Peter Wilson)
$675

A Moorcroft Florian-Ware vase of squat form with tall neck, decorated in relief with blue forget-me-nots and yellow cornflowers, 13cm. high.
(Phillips)
$845

A Moorcroft brown chrysanthemum vase, the twin-handled vessel decorated with red flora against a blue green ground, 9.5cm. high, signed and dated 1913.
(Phillips)
$750

REDWARE

A figural redware whistle, attributed to Jesiah Shorb, Pennsylvania, 19th century, molded in the form of a barking Dachshund with whistle in tail, 4⁵/₈in. high.
(Christie's) $3,680

A glazed redware food mould, stamped *Willoughby Smith*, 1839–1905, Womelsdorf, Berks County, Pennsylvania, 1864–1880, in the form of a fish and glazed with manganese highlights, 12in. long.
(Christie's) $1,495

A glazed redware creamer, Pennsylvania, 19th century, daubed with manganese on a red body with a clear lead glaze, 3¹/₂in. high.
(Christie's) $1,093

A large glazed redware flower pot and saucer, stamped *John Bell*, Pennsylvania, 1860–1870, cylindrical tapering with everted brim and applied rope-twist handles, 9¹/₄in. high.
(Christie's) $5,750

A slip decorated redware plate, Smith Pottery, Norwalk, Connecticut, 1825–1880, with coggle wheel rim embellished with pretzels decorated in yellow slip, 12¹/₂in. diameter.
(Christie's) $2,070

A glazed redware one piece flowerpot and saucer, Pennsylvania, 19th century, with ruffled rim and applied base with dappled manganese glaze, 8¹/₄in. high.
(Christie's) $1,495

A yellow glazed redware food mold, stamped *John Bell*, 1800–1880, Waynesboro, Pennsylvania, 1830–1880, glazed in yellow with manganese decorated brim, 8¹/₄in. diameter.
(Christie's) $920

An unglazed redware wall pocket, stamped *George S. Freshley*, 1856–1922, Lebanon, Pennsylvania, circa 1883, with punch decorated rim and large applied medallions, 10¹/₂in. high.
(Christie's) $748

A double walled pierced glazed redware covered bowl, possibly Henry Grady, 1812–1880, Shanksville, Somerset County, Pennsylvania, 1843–1880, yellow glazed cylindrical body.
(Christie's) $12,650

REDWARE

A large slip decorated 'Moravian' redware bowl, Pennsylvania, 19th century, the everted rim with white squiggle decoration, 13in. diameter.
(Christie's) $978

A glazed redware pipe holder, possibly George A. Wagner Pottery, Weissport, Carbon County, Pennsylvania, 1875–1896, cylindrical with perforated lid and four pipe stands, 4in. high.
(Christie's) $2,760

A glazed redware mantle ornament, Pennsylvania, initialed *M M* and dated *1798*, in the form of a pelican pecking its breast, mounted on a molded plinth, 6½in. high.
(Christie's) $24,150

A glazed redware flowerpot and saucer, probably Lebanon or Berks County, Pennsylvania, 19th century, the coggle rim above applied ovoid decorations, 8½in. high.
(Christie's) $288

A glazed redware coffee pot, stamped *John Bell*, 1800–1880, Waynesboro, Franklin County, Pennsylvania, 1850–1880, the cylindrical body with fine manganese 'tortoiseshell' decoration, 9in. high.
(Christie's) $7,475

A green glazed redware flower pot, stamped *John Bell*, Pennsylvania, 1860–1870, cylindrical tapering, with everted brim and applied saucer, 7in. high.
(Christie's) $1,725

A glazed redware mug, stamped *Solomon Bell*, 1817–1882, Winchester or Strausburg, Virginia, 1843–1882, glazed yellow with green daubs, 5in. high.
(Christie's) $2,990

A glazed redware covered bowl, Adams County, Pennsylvania, 19th century, the circular lid with full-figured bird and handle, 6¼in. high.
(Christie's) $5,520

A glazed redware flowerpot and saucer, attributed to Henry Fahr, b. 1821, Pennsylvania, with ruffled rim and saucer and pressed ruffled bands, 8¼in. high.
(Christie's) $253

A glazed redware handled cheese mold, Pennsylvania, 19th century, cylindrical with applied handle, molded rim and body, 4¹/₂in. diameter.
(Christie's) **$575**

A molded redware figural group, attributed to the 'Master Hobo Potter', Pennsylvania, 19th century, depicting a dog resting on an alligator atop a turtle, 5in. high.
(Christie's) **$13,800**

A glazed redware flower pot and saucer, Pennsylvania, 19th century, cylindrical tapering, with double ruffled rim, 9in. high.
(Christie's) **$1,725**

A glazed redware fancy presentation flower pot, attributed to Enos Smedley, 1805–1892, Pennsylvania, dated *1827*, body inscribed *Earl Pell L. C. Leah Connell/5th moth, 18th dy, 1827*, 9³/₄in. high.
(Christie's) **$18,400**

A sgraffitto decorated redware plate, attributed to Conrad Mumbouer, Pennsylvania, dated *1802*, the surface decorated with an inscribed potted heart issuing stylized flowers and notched tulips, 11¹/₂in. diameter.
(Christie's) **$21,850**

A redware sgraffito decorated mug, signed *W. Roth*, possibly Berks or Mongomery County, Pennsylvania, dated *1821*, with German inscriptions and decorated with distlefink, 5in. high.
(Christie's) **$4,025**

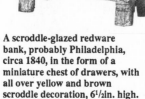

A glazed redware mug, possibly Pennsylvania, 19th century, glazed in beige decorated with vertical bands alternating in green, black and red, 6¹/₄in. high.
(Christie's) **$115**

A scroddle-glazed redware bank, probably Philadelphia, circa 1840, in the form of a miniature chest of drawers, with all over yellow and brown scroddle decoration, 6¹/₂in. high.
(Christie's) **$460**

A redware field jug, Pennsylvania, 19th century, baluster form, with applied handle, straight spout and dripped manganese glaze, 11in. high.
(Christie's) **$403**

ROOKWOOD

CHINA

Rookwood matt glaze pottery vase, decorated by Lorinda Epply, 1924, painted with clusters of periwinkle cupid's dart blossoms on green leafy stems, 12⁷/₈in. high. (Butterfield & Butterfield)
$2,875

Rookwood standard glaze three-handled presentation loving cup, painted by William P. McDonald, 1898, painted and slipped with horse chestnut pods, 7in. high. (Butterfield & Butterfield)
$1,840

Rookwood standard glaze pottery vase, painted by William P. McDonald, 1892, painted and slipped with blossoming yellow irises and green foliage, 8³/₄in. high. (Butterfield & Butterfield)
$1,725

ROYAL COPENHAGEN

Carl Hallier and Knud Andersen for the Royal Copenhagen Porcelain Manufactory Ltd., vase and cover, with base, 1937, the patinated bronze cover with spherical knop, 8¹/₂in. (Sotheby's)
$2,725

Royal Copenhagen porcelain figures of polar bears, one seated growling, another prowling. (Christie's)
$340

An impressive Royal Copenhagen 'Flora Danica' dessert dish and cover, with dentate edge, the bell-shaped cover with pierced basketwork sides, 29cm., printed marks, 20th century. (Phillips)
$3,800

ROYAL DUX

A Royal Dux pottery group in the form of a brown and white cow, feeding from a bundle of greenery, 46cm. high. (Bearne's)
$477

A Royal Dux Bohemia Art Deco figure of a naked young woman, wearing skull cap, seated on a pedestal, naturalistically painted, 27cm. high. (Christie's)
$475

A Royal Dux figure of a young woman with fish in a net, standing on a rocky outcrop with seaweed and coral, 34.5cm. high. (Bearne's)
$834

SATSUMA

A Satsuma figure, possibly of Urishima Taro, the old man seated on a rock above a stream and holding a turtle (minogame), 24cm.
(Bristol) **$502**

A richly enameled Satsuma pottery plate, Meiji Period, with gosu blue flower garden design, 8¾in. diameter.
(Eldreds) **$1,500**

A Satsuma jar and cover, with flowerbud knop, the ovoid body painted with two panels each portraying women and children by a river, 19.2cm. high, signed.
(Bearne's) **$1,565**

A Satsuma bowl, signed *Hankinzan Do,* 19th century, decorated in various colored enamels and gilt with numerous children in a pavilion and some ladies and deer on the bank, 12.1cm. high.
(Christie's) **$4,340**

A pair of trumpet-shaped Satuma vases and bases, signed *Satsuma Yasui Zo,* 19th century decorated with Bentens Daruma and other legendary figures, 23.5cm. high.
(Christie's) **$1,200**

A small Satsuma koro, signed *Satsuma,* 19th century, decorated in various enamels and gilt with various fans, the neck with aoi mon between the bands of stylized chrysanthemum, 10cm. high.
(Christie's) **$2,600**

A Satsuma jar and cover, the lobed ovoid body painted with numerous women and children, 16.5cm. high, and wood stand, signed *Satsuma Hotoda.*
(Bearne's) **$447**

A Satsuma tripod koro, 19th century, decorated in various colored enamels and gilt with lobed square panels each filled with two ho-o birds, 12.5cm. high.(Christie's) **$2,775**

Late 19th century Japanese Satsuma ovoid vase, decorated with women and children and men robed, heavily gilt, 5in. high.
(Peter Wilson) **$148**

SEVRES

A pair of very large Sèvres style earthenware vases with ovoid bodies painted with rustic lovers in Boucher style, signed *Maglin,* circa 1860.
(Phillips) $45,706

A Sèvres style white biscuit porcelain group modeled as Bacchus and attendants, flanked by maidens, before the god two putti at play above devices, 36cm. high, late 19th century.
(Christie's) $1,545

A pair of Sèvres-style vases and covers, of straight-sided form, painted with continuous scenes of cherubs and putti at play, 12¾in. high, 19th century.
(Christie's) $2,718

A Sèvres-style 'jeweled' coffee can and saucer painted in two-tone gilt with bands of flowerheads and scrolling foliage, 19th century.
(Christie's) $938

Two Sèvres style 'jeweled' pink ground plates, one painted with a classical scene, 24.5cm. diameter, 19th century.
(Christie's) $1,030

A richly decorated and jeweled Sèvres-style coffee can and saucer, painted with half-length portraits of Louis XV, Mme. de Montesson and Mme. Elizabeth in gilt-bordered panels, mid 19th century.(Phillips) $2,219

A Sèvres later-decorated blue ground plate with central roundel of exotic birds within floral swags, 23.5cm. diam., the porcelain 18th century.
(Christie's) $190

A Sèvres style gilt metal mounted circular table, the *blue celeste* table top printed to the center with a half-length portrait of Henri VI, 77cm. high, late 19th century.
(Christie's) $1,545

A fine and rare Sèvres plate from the Service de Départements, commemorating the Département des Basses Pyrenées, painted by A. Poupart, signed and dated *1823.*
(Phillips) $7,440

STAFFORDSHIRE

Historic blue Staffordshire soup tureen, England, second quarter 19th century, 14in. length.
(Skinner) $575

Staffordshire style fairing of a child lying in a cot, painted in colors, 5in.
(G. A. Key) $68

Late 18th century Staffordshire Bull Baiting group, strongly modeled with the bull, its head lowered, gazing malevolently at the small dog, 18cm. long.
(Peter Wilson) $571

Historic blue Staffordshire plate. Enoch Wood & Sons, England, 19th century, *Boston State House*, marked on base, 10.25in. diameter.
(Skinner) $201

A pair of Staffordshire pottery groups, probably representing the Prince of Wales and the Princess Royal, 22cm. high.
(Bearne's) $1,328

A Staffordshire green spatterware 'Schoolhouse' sugar bowl and cover, circa 1840, painted on either side in red with a schoolhouse and trees, 5in. high.
(Sotheby's) $1,495

19th century Staffordshire pottery watch stand, three maidens standing under a bower of roses, pale coloring, 11½in. high.
(Peter Wilson) $133

19th century Staffordshire pottery figure group of a cow with a milk maid on a milking stool, well colored, 6½in. high.
(Peter Wilson) $187

Late 18th century Staffordshire pearlware mask cup, modeled with three faces of Bacchus bordered with fruiting vines, 9cm. high.
(Peter Wilson) $142

STAFFORDSHIRE

18th century Staffordshire 'squire' toby jug, decorated in brown, turquoise and blue slip glazes, 11³/₄in. high.
(Lawrences) $1,034

A pair of Staffordshire pottery poodles with clay fragmented coats, separate front legs, 19th century, 8in. high.
(Locke & England) $298

19th century Staffordshire pottery figure of David Garrick playing Richard III, 26cm.
(Peter Wilson) $226

A glazed earthenware bank, George A. Wagner Pottery, Pennsylvania, 1875–1876, in the form of a Staffordshire spaniel, glazed in yellow with green and brown daubs, 6¹/₂in. high.
(Christie's) $1,093

A pair of Staffordshire cow and calf figure groups, enameled colors, coved base, 8in. high.
(Locke & England) $565

A glazed earthenware bank, George A. Wagner Pottery, Pennsylvania, 1875–1876, in the form of a Staffordshire poodle with coleslaw mane, 6¹/₂in. high.
(Christie's) $1,495

A very rare and large Staffordshire model of a cat, seated on oval base with markings sponged in black and beige, on oval base, 26cm.
(Phillips) $1,860

Pair of late 19th century Staffordshire dalmations sitting on cobalt blue oval bases, the collars and chains painted in gold, 5in. high.
(Peter Wilson) $390

Staffordshire group of a child standing by a zebra with panniers on its back, 19th century, 7in.
(G. A. Key) $248

A salt glazed and cobalt decorated stoneware batter jug, stamped *Cowden & Wilcox, Harrisburg, Pennsylvania*, 1869–1887, baluster form with lid and spout cover, 9¼in. high.
(Christie's) $1,610

Jean Carriès, grotesque head wall plaque, circa 1880, stoneware, with gray/green glaze, modeled as the head of a grinning bearded man, 14in.
(Sotheby's) $4,179

A salt glazed and cobalt decorated stoneware jug, stamped *Cowden & Wilcox, Harrisburg, Pennsylvania*, 1869–1887, decorated with 'Man in the Moon', 13¾in. high.
(Christie's) $3,220

A salt glazed and cobalt decorated stoneware puzzle jug, attributed to Richard Clinton Remmy, 1835–1904, Philadelphia, 1859–1870, baluster shaped, with circular rim with seven applied spouts and applied strap handle, 6½in. high.(Christie's) $8,625

A salt glazed and cobalt decorated stoneware lady's spittoon, stamped *Cowden & Wilcox, Harrisburg, Pennsylvania*, 1869–1887, circular, with tapering top opening to a receptacle, 3½in. high.
(Christie's) $2,070

A salt glazed stoneware bank, attributed to Richard Clinton Remmy, dated *December 16, 1851*, the stepped conical top with coin slot surmounted by a spherical finial (now lacking) handle, 5¾in. high.
(Christie's) $5,175

A salt glazed and cobalt decorated stoneware crock, stamped *Cowden & Wilcox, Harrisburg, Pennsylvania*, 1869–1887, decorated with face of an Amish man and a plume, 12in. high.
(Christie's) $20,700

A rare ocher-decorated salt-glazed stoneware double-handled jug, signed by Lyman & Clark, Gardiner, Maine, circa 1830, of bulbous form, 15½in. high.
(Sotheby's) $4,025

A salt glazed stoneware water cooler, attributed to Charles and William Wingender, New Jersey, late 19th century, barrel shaped, with domed lid decorated with concentric bands of blue, 14½in. high.
(Christie's) $863

A Vienna porcelain plate, the painted reserve depicting figures at an easel, on gilded and jeweled deep blue ground, 9¹/₂in. wide.
(Andrew Hartley) $623

A good Vienna figure of a street vendor, standing on an oval base before a tree stump, in maroon coat and breeches and a green waistcoat, 20cm., impressed *P* mark.
(Phillips) $543

A late 19th century Vienna porcelain lidded bowl of circular outline and gros bleu ground, painted with Hercules and Omphale beneath a tree, signed *Knoelle*, 7.25in. diameter.
(Morphets) $565

A Vienna (Du Paquier) teabowl, circa 1725, of flared form, painted en grisaille with a continuous scene of falconers on horseback before a church in a wooded landscape, 3½in. diameter.
(Christie's) $489

One of a pair of early 20th century Vienna plates, 13in. diameter.
(Dockree's) (Two) $488

A Vienna purple ground lobed sugar bowl and flattened cover with fruit finial, painted with loose sprays of flowers within quatrefoil panels, 11.5cm. high, early 19th century.
(Christie's) $346

A Vienna style large octagonal wall plate, attractively painted within a rectangular panel with a young maiden scattering flower petals, signed *Bison*, 34.5cm., circa 1890.
(Phillips) $1,064

A Vienna figure of a man wearing red cape and hat, striped doublet and hose, naturistically painted, date code for 1849, 14.5cm. high.
(Christie's) $138

A Vienna cabinet plate, date code for 1802, painted with Cupid in a chariot drawn by two serpents on clouds on a dark-brown ground, 10in. diameter.
(Christie's) $1,573

WEDGWOOD

A Wedgwood 'Fairyland Luster' large circular bowl decorated with black Fairyland pattern, of poplar trees, bridge over a river and views of a park with gilt trees and foliage, 26.5cm.
(Phillips) $3,328

A pair of Wedgwood white jasper pot-pourri vases, set on square bases, each exterior applied with an encircling band of green fruiting vines, circa 1800.
(Bearne's) $371

A Wedgwood luster Moonlight Fairyland fruit bowl, the inside with Jumping Fawn, Elf on Toadstool, the outside a variant of Woodland Elves III Feather Hat, No. Z5462, 9¼in. wide.
(Andrew Hartley) $1,520

An oval black basalt plaque of Josiah Wedgwood, modeled by William Hackwood, attributed to Wedgwood and Bentley, circa 1782, 9cm. long.
(Christie's) $450

A Wedgwood yellow-ground wash basin set printed in black with vignettes of Classical ruins, Italianate boating view and figures before lakes.
(Christie's) $1,364

A Wedgwood caneware cream jug and cover, the cover with recumbent lion finial, circa 1790, 11.5cm. high.
(Christie's) $450

A Wedgwood blue dip jasper 'Staites Patent' pipe-bowl of baluster form, fitting a terminal formed as an acorn, 8.8cm. high, circa 1849.
(Christie's) $155

Pair of Wedgwood gold embossed creamware covered vases, having four sculpted heads of Bacchus at shoulders, 11½in. high, circa 1795.
(Schrager) $1,200

A Wedgwood black and white oval portrait medallion of Richard, first Earl Howe, modeled by John de Vaere, 12cm. high., 19th century.
(Christie's) $376

WEMYSS

A Wemyss Ware globular teapot and cover painted with cabbage roses painted Wemyss mark, 8in. wide.
(Christie's) $330

A Wemyss Ware Audley bowl-on-stand, painted with cabbage roses, impressed and painted Wemyss marks, 6½in. high.
(Christie's) $695

A Wemyss Ware soap-dish, liner and cover painted with cabbage roses, painted Wemyss mark, 5¾in. diam.
(Christie's) $312

A Wemyss preserve jar and cover painted with grapes and vine leaves in green and purple, impressed *WEMYSS* to underside, 4.75in. high.
(Morphets) $628

A pair of Wemyss Ware plates painted with cabbage roses impressed Wemyss Ware R.H. & S. and printed T. Goode & Co. South Audley St., London W. marks, 7½in. diameter.
(Christie's) $312

A Wemyss Ware pear-shaped jug, painted with cabbage roses, impressed Wemyss and printed T. Goode & Co., Audley St. London W. marks, 5in. high.
(Christie's) $260

A Wemyss Ware teacup and saucer, painted with cabbage roses and a sugar bowl ensuite impressed Wemyss and printed T. Goode & Co., South Audley St., London W. marks
(Christie's) $225

Two Bovey Tracey Wemyss Ware models of pigs, mid 20th century, green printed *Plichta, London England* to both, both signed Nekola Pinxt, 18¾in. and 12in. long.
(Christie's) $1,955

A Wemyss Ware chamber candlestick, painted with cabbage roses, with scroll handle, painted Wemyss mark, 5½in. high.
(Christie's) $660

WORCESTER

A Royal Worcester figure, Nursery Rhyme series, "Little Jack Horner", 4in. high, and with date code for 1952. (Canterbury) $339

A Worcester tea canister of plain oval shape, the 'Wet Blue' ground richly gilt with caillouté, 13cm. (Phillips) $232

A Royal Worcester figure, Nursery Rhyme series, "Little Miss Muffet", 4in. high. (Canterbury) $339

A fine Worcester 'fable' plate, painted in the center with a fox reclining on a tree trunk, the scalloped rim gilt with trellis and flowers, 21.5cm., crescent mark. (Phillips) $2,325

A pair of Royal Worcester porcelain beaker vases signed *H Stinton*, the ivory ground painted with highland cattle, cypher mark for 1913. (Morphets) $1,382

Royal Worcester circular porcelain plaque, 1912, painted with highland cattle, signed *H. Stinton*, in a silver frame, Birmingham 1912, 4in. diameter. (Peter Wilson) $483

An unusual Royal Worcester vase and cover decorated in 'Prismatic Enamels', in delicate pink, turquoise and primrose, 26cm., date code for 1891. (Phillips) $744

A very rare Worcester teabowl and saucer, delicately painted in blue with the 'Heron on a Floral Spray' pattern after a Chinese original, the saucer 11.8cm. (Phillips) $2,170

A Royal Worcester figure, 'June', modeled by F.G. Doughty, a young boy sitting on a stump with a dog on his lap, 6.25in. high, date code for 1955. (Canterbury) $169

WORCESTER

A Royal Worcester porcelain tapering vase with flared rim, pierced grotesque handles, applied masks, painted clematis on ivory ground, 13¼in. high.
(Andrew Hartley) $1,099

A rare Worcester 'Blind Earl' sweetmeat dish, mounted with rosebuds and rose bush leaves, with woody stem handle, 15cm., open crescent mark, circa 1765.
(Phillips) $1,824

A fine Royal Worcester two handled covered vase, hand painted swans, signed *C. Baldwyn*, No. 1515, 8in. high.
(Dee, Atkinson & Harrison) $3,473

A Royal Worcester blush porcelain figure of a man sharpening a scythe, wearing a hat, open neck shirt and breeches, on rustic base, 8½in. high.
(Andrew Hartley) $534

Two rare Royal Worcester models of ladies' shoes, decorated with gilded dots on a matt gold ground, pink pierced laces, 15.5cm., date codes for 1879.
(Phillips) $1,473

Samuel Ranford: a Royal Worcester reticulated vase and cover of baluster shape, finely pierced with an irregular pattern of flowers and leaves, 24.5cm., date code for 1879.
(Phillips) $8,525

A Worcester milk jug of barrel shape, painted in blue with the 'Barrel Jug Scroll' pattern, 8cm. crescent mark, circa 1765.
(Phillips) $456

Richard Sebright, a good Royal Worcester oval plaque painted with a basket overflowing with apples, grapes, peaches, pears and strawberries, signed, 15cm. x 21cm. date code for 1913.
(Phillips) $5,472

James Hadley: a Royal Worcester fountain group of a girl and a boy by a waterfall, decorated in blush ivory, 17cm., date code for 1886.
(Phillips) $899

BRACKET CLOCKS

An ebony veneered pull quarter repeating bracket timepiece, 7in. dial with a silvered Roman and Arabic chapter ring, signed *Jn° Blundell, Greenwich*, 15¹/₂in.
(Bonhams) $2,333

A late Victorian bracket clock, the movement chiming on two gongs, arched brass and silvered dial, carved oak case, 67cm.
(Bearne's) $958

A walnut veneered bracket clock, Alldworth, London, circa 1690, twin fusée and wire line six vase shape pillar movement, converted excapement, 15¹/₂in.
(Bonhams) $4,665

An 18th century bell topped bracket clock, the arched engraved silvered dial with subsidiaries for date and for strike/silent signed *Thos. Hunter, Junr., London*, 50cm. high.
(Phillips) $2,177

A George III mahogany and gilt brass mounted quarter chiming bracket clock, the arched brass dial with circular enamel dial plate signed *Eardley Norton, London*, 53cm. high.
(Phillips) $6,188

A good George III mahogany and brass mounted quarter chiming bracket clock by Ellicott, London, the case with inverted bell top and carrying handle, glazed to the sides, 46cm. high.
(Phillips) $9,641

A large ebonized and gilt mounted chiming bracket clock, English, circa 1880, 8¹/₂in. dial, silvered Roman and Arabic numeral chapter ring, with a matted center, 31½in.
(Bonhams) $3,888

A William IV pollard oak cased bracket clock by Walker of Clerkenwell, the silvered dial with strike / silent dial to arch, 22.5in. high.
(Canterbury) $2,849

A George III mahogany and brass mounted bracket clock, the arched silvered dial signed *Thomas Gray, London*, the twin fusée movement with verge escapement.
(Phillips) $3,266

BRACKET CLOCKS

A German chiming bracket clock, the Junghans gong striking movement with brass arch-top dial, in a carved oak rectangular case, 48cm. (Bristol) $251

A mahogany quarter chiming bracket clock, Robert Burgess, London, circa 1770, with calendar aperture and strike/silent hand in the arch, 52cm. (Bonhams) $4,560

A 19th century mahogany and brass inlaid bracket clock, the 5in. painted dial signed *M. Wing, London,* 37cm. high. (Phillips) $2,320

An ebonized bracket clock, William Owen, London, 1775, 6³/₄in. dial with a silvered Roman and Arabic dial matted center with calendar aperture, 19³/₄in. (Bonhams) $2,799

A substantial 19th century quarter chiming ebonized and gilt brass bracket clock, the arched case centered by a mask of Father Time, backplate signed *J. C. Jennens, London,* 80cm. high. (Phillips) $2,552

A mahogany bracket timepiece, A.J. Barnsdale, circa 1880, 7in. dial with a silvered Roman chapter ring, matted center and calendar subsidiary in the arch, 21in. (Bonhams) $1,368

An ebonized bracket clock, Thomas Cartwright, circa 1720, 7¹/₂in. dial with a silvered Roman and Arabic chapter ring, 15³/₄in. (Bonhams) $2,333

A fruitwood bracket clock, George Graham, circa 1800, 6³/₄in. dial with a silvered Roman and Arabic chapter ring, matted center with a calendar aperture, 19³/₄in. (Bonhams) $2,799

A Georgian bracket clock, the twin-fusée bell-striking movement with 8in. white dial signed *Maddack, Bath,* strike/silent to arch, 45cm. (Bristol) $2,052

BRACKET CLOCKS

A Georgian mahogany and brass mounted bracket clock, the arched repainted dial inscribed *Thos Hunter London*, 53cm. high.
(Phillips) $2,475

A 19th century rosewood bracket clock, the 5.5in. circular silvered dial with subsidiary seconds and signed *G.P. Tode, 248 Regent Street*, 26cm. high.
(Phillips) $1,423

A good early 18th century red tortoiseshell and silver mounted musical bracket clock, mock pendulum aperture, signed *Peter Garon, London*, 55cm. high.
(Phillips) $43,540

An early 18th century ebonized and brass mounted quarter chiming bracket clock, the arched brass dial signed around *Stephen Asselin, London fecit*, 47cm. high.
(Phillips) $6,842

A 19th century mahogany and brass inlaid bracket timepiece, with 4½in. circular painted dial indistinctly signed, the fusée movement with anchor escapement, 28cm. high.
(Phillips) $1,431

A fine small mahogany bracket clock, Allam and Clement, London, circa 1770, the twin fusée movement with a verge escapement, engraved backplate, 11¼in.
(Bonhams) $15,550

A George III mahogany bracket clock, the arched engraved silvered dial with date aperture signed *Willm. Swaine, Woodbridge*, 56cm. high.
(Phillips) $2,877

A 19th century mahogany bracket clock, the engraved dial with strike/silent and signed *Archard, 70 South Audley St, London*, 26cm. high.
(Phillips) $1,702

A mahogany quarter chiming bracket clock, the arched brass dial with silvered chapter ring inscribed *J. Green, London*, 56cm. high.
(Phillips) $3,577

BRACKET CLOCKS

Joseph Knibb, London, an ebonized and gilt brass mounted bracket clock, the movement with five ring-turned latched pillars, 32cm. high.
(Phillips) **$4,177**

A 19th century rosewood bracket timepiece, the pointed arched case with gilt metal mounted plinth base on flat bun feet, 34cm. high.
(Phillips) **$541**

James McCabe, Royal Exchange, London, a Regency repeating bracket clock, the ebonized case with inlaid brass foliate decoration, 49cm.
(Bearne's) **$2,704**

An ebonized chiming bracket clock, **David Murray, Edinburgh,** circa 1780, the triple fusée movement with a converted half dead beat escapement, 21in.
(Bonhams) **$2,584**

A mahogany bracket clock, **Stear, London,** circa 1840, the twin fusée bell striking movement in break arch single pad top case, 18¹/₂in.
(Bonhams) **$1,089**

A 19th century mahogany bracket timepiece, the shaped painted dial signed *Taylor, Regents Park,* the fusée movement with anchor escapement, 41cm. high.
(Phillips) **$560**

A 19th century rosewood bracket clock, the shallow arched case with applied carved decoration and scrolls on bun feet, 24cm. high.
(Phillips) **$1,089**

A 19th century ebonized bracket clock, the rectangular case with beveled glass panels, scrolled base and brass feet, 23cm. high.
(Phillips) **$1,856**

A George III ebonized and brass mounted bracket clock by **Ellicott,** five pillared twin fusée movement with verge escapement, 46cm. high.
(Phillips) **$5,598**

CARRIAGE CLOCKS

A French repeating carriage clock, with escapement striking movement having white enamel dial with subsidiary alarm dial, 7¼in. high.
(Andrew Hartley) $875

Late 19th century brass carriage clock with eight day striking repeating lever movement, 6½in.
(Ewbank) $507

A miniature gilt carriage timepiece, French, circa 1900, the movement with a lever escapement in a corniche style case, 3¾in.
(Bonhams) $608

A 19th century gilt brass and porcelain paneled carriage clock by Drocourt, the dial, sides, back and top panels of bleu celeste Sèvres style porcelain, 6in. high.
(Phillips) $6,380

A solid silver limited edition carriage clock, 2¼in. silver chapter ring with Roman numerals, surrounded by a pierced gilt foliage mask, signed below *Garrard Crown Jeweller 1843–1993*, 7½in.
(Bonhams) $2,107

Silver and tortoiseshell eight day carriage clock, small rectangular movement with gilt lever platform, hallmarked *Birmingham 1912*, 73mm. high.
(Pieces of Time) $1,661

A French gilt-brass and enamel miniature carriage timepiece, unsigned, the dial enameled with green, white, pink and red flowers, 3in. high.
(Christie's) $1,645

A 19th century gilt brass carriage clock, the polychrome dials set within a pierced and engraved mask, in a pillared Anglaise style case, 8in. high.
(Phillips) $1,036

A 19th century French brass miniature oval carriage timepiece, the movement with replaced lever platform escapement, 4in. high.
(Phillips) $797

CARRIAGE CLOCKS

Brass carriage clock with eight day striking and repeating lever movement with alarm, maker's mark *AB*, 7in. high, with leather carrying case.
(Ewbank) $1,043

A late 19th century French carriage clock, the eight day movement striking and repeating on a gong, with beveled glass panels, 6½in.
(Woolley & Wallis) $1,359

A French gilt-brass and enamel miniature carriage timepiece, Drocourt, the movement with bimetallic balance to silvered lever platform, 3¼in. high.
(Christie's) $7,680

A Victorian gilt-brass giant striking carriage clock, the typical heavy molded case with reeded scroll handle to the glazed top with repeat button, 8½in. high.
(Christie's) $8,777

Late 19th century brass carriage clock, with angular handle and four turned finials, reeded column corners, on four feet, the dial enameled with flowers and foliage, eight day repeating lever movement, 7in.
(Ewbank) $1,043

A French gilt-brass and porcelain-mounted miniature carriage timepiece, Drocourt, the movement with bimetallic balance to gilt lever platform, 3¼in. high.
(Christie's) $7,314

A 19th century lacquered and silvered brass carriage clock, the movement with lever platform escapement, alarm and push repeat, dated *1881*, 19cm. high.
(Phillips) $765

A French brass cased carriage clock, the eight day movement with replaced platform lever escapement, the back plate signed *Moser à Paris*, 18cm. high overall.
(Dreweatt Neate) $1,067

A French engraved gilt-brass striking carriage clock, unsigned, the movement with bimetallic balance to silvered lever platform, 5¼in. high.
(Christie's) $3,291

CLOCK SETS

A 19th century French garniture de cheminée, the clock with an eight day striking movement striking on a bell inscribed *C.V.* (Charles Vacheron), 15in.
(Woolley & Wallis) **$1,329**

A French 19th century garniture de cheminée, the gilt bronze mounts to the brass cased clock with enamel porcelain panels, repeated on the pair of urns, eight day striking movement.
(Woolley & Wallis) **$1,225**

Third Republic parcel-gilt and patinated bronze and marble clock garniture, circa 1900, eight-day, half-hour strike, set in a siena marble plinth, the flanking gilt-bronze kylix raised on rectangular marble plinths over square bases, 26¹/₂in. high.
(Butterfield & Butterfield) **$4,887**

Three-piece Dresden porcelain garniture: mantle clock depicting mother and child in rococo base, brass works by Lenzkirch, 12in. high; and pair of three-branch candelabra, blue/white glazed with sculpted figures, Germany, mid 19th century.
(Schrager) **$550**

A gilt metal clock garniture set, French, circa 1880, 3¹/₂in. enamel dial with Roman and Arabic numerals, signed *Boursier Jne, Elve De Le Pautre A Paris,* together with a matching pair of four light candelabra, 14¹/₂in.
(Bonhams) **$1,064**

A 19th century French gilt brass and porcelain mounted clock garniture, the twin train movement bearing the Japy trademark and striking on a bell, 30cm. high, together with the similar pair of twin handled vases.
(Phillips) **$2,955**

CLOCK SETS

A French bronze, gilt-bronze and marble clock garniture, by E. Boisseau, circa 1870, with a Florentine youth in Renaissance dress playing a mandolin, clock: 77.5cm. high.
(Sotheby's) $7,711

A French gilt-bronze and marble clock garniture, Paris, circa 1890, the clock with a white enamel dial painted with swags of summer flowers, in a lyre case, clock: 47cm. high.
(Sotheby's) $7,711

A gilt bronze and marble clock garniture, French, circa 1880, 5in. dial with Arabic numerals and floral swags, signed for *Thiebaut Frea, Paris, 32 Avenue de l'Opera,* the bell striking movement, signed *Marti,* together with a pair of matching six light candelabra, 57cm. (Bonhams) $4,104

A 19th century French ormolu clock garniture, the shaped clock case surmounted by an urn, bearing the Marti trademark, 53cm. high, together with the matching pair of five branch candelabra.
(Phillips) $1,555

A white marble and ormolu clock garniture, French, circa 1890, applied Roman numeral chapter ring on a bronzed globe, bell striking movement, the bronzed case held by three gilt putti standing on a marble column, 15^{1}/$_{2}$in.
(Bonhams) $1,976

A 19th century French gilt and oxidized brass clock garniture, the clock case in the form of a temple, the 4^{1}/$_{2}$ inch chapter ring with Chinese characters, the twin train movement stamped *Marti,* 38cm. high.
(Phillips) $877

185

LONGCASE CLOCKS

A small mahogany and inlaid longcase clock, John Collier, London, 19th century, 5ft. 7in. (Bonhams)

$2,032

A mahogany longcase clock, unsigned of Hereford, circa 1820, 7ft. 3in. (Bonhams)

$1,355

A late George III mahogany longcase regulator, Douglas London, 5ft. 11in. high. (Christie's)

$5,485

A late 18th century mahogany longcase clock, Jh. Banks, Oldham, 92in. tall. (Morphets)

$3,454

A small month going walnut longcase clock, circa 17th century and later, dial bearing signature of *Chas Gretton, London*, 6ft. 1¹/₂in. (Bonhams)

$10,535

A George III mahogany longcase clock, late 18th century, dial engraved *Wm Smith, LONDON*, 6ft. 11in. high. (Butterfield & Butterfield)

$4,887

An Italian red lacquer longcase clock, unsigned, circa 1750, the case decorated overall with raised gilt chinoiserie figures, 7ft. 4¹/₂in. high. (Christie's)

$1,828

A George II red japanned longcase clock, dial inscribed *Tudor Smith, LONDON*, 8ft. 6in. high. (Butterfield & Butterfield)

$18,400

LONGCASE CLOCKS

A good walnut veneered longcase clock, Ellicott, London, circa 1740, 7ft. 9in. (Bonhams)

$11,196

A mahogany longcase clock, Wm. Taylor, Glasgow, circa 1800, 7ft. 7in. (Bonhams)

$2,408

A late 18th century mahogany longcase clock, by Wm. Leigh, Newton, 90in. (Morphets)

$3,611

An eight-day longcase clock, the 12in. white dial painted, 'Jas Harvey, Abergavenny', in an oak case, 206cm. (Bristol)

$803

A rare mahogany master regulator, Magenta, London, circa 1900, 12in. painted dial with Roman numerals, 7ft. 6in. (Bonhams)

$1,444

A black walnut and Westmorland stone year-going mean solar and sidereal longcase regulator, T. Brameld, Edinburgh 1989, 6ft. 4¹/₂in. high. (Christie's)

$14,628

An important George III mahogany month-going longcase regulator, John Grant London; the case attributed to Thomas Chippendale, 6ft. 5in. high. (Christie's)

$47,541

An 18th century simulated tortoiseshell and chinoiserie decorated longcase clock, the hood with caddy top and turned columns, 7ft. 6in. high. (Phillips)

$3,349

LONGCASE CLOCKS

An early Victorian longcase clock, signed *G. Stromier, Glasgow,* **eight day movement, 200cm. high.** (Winterton's)

$1,186

A 19th century oak and mahogany longcase clock, signed *Caleb Evans, Bristol,* **7ft. high.** (Phillips)

$2,799

An 18th century blue lacquered longcase clock by Thomas Moore of Ipswich, 96in. high. (Boardmans)

$4,560

A George III mahogany longcase clock, the 12in. arched dial signed *Jn. Austin, Bristol,* **7ft. 6¹/₂in. high.** (Phillips)

$2,644

A Manchester regulator longcase clock, by William Mayo, Manchester, in a mahogany case, 189cm. (Bristol)

$5,809

Federal mahogany inlaid tall case clock, by Levi Hutchins Concord, New Hampshire, circa 1810, 100in. high. (Skinner)

$5,750

A 17th century oyster veneered walnut and marquetry eight day longcase clock by Samuel Watson, 200cm. high. (Phillips)

$4,495

A late 17th/early 18th century walnut and floral marquetry longcase clock, signed *William Whittingham, London,* **7ft. 6in. high.** (Phillips)

$7,775

LONGCASE CLOCKS

A 19th century mahogany longcase clock, signed *Phippard, Poole*, 8ft. 2in. high. (Phillips)
$2,332

Rococo style carved oak tall case clock, 19th century, with a reticulated brass dial, 90in. high. (Skinner)
$1,955

Tiger maple tall case clock, dial inscribed *William Stillman in Hopkinton 1786*, 83in. high. (Skinner)
$7,475

J. Smerdon, Newton Abbot, early 19th century mahogany longcase clock, arched painted dial, 218cm. (Bearne's)
$2,163

A George III longcase clock having painted arched dial with moon, ship and country house rotating dial surmount, 7ft. 9in. high. (Russell, Baldwin & Bright)
$3,768

A good George III walnut longcase clock by Thomas Quested of Wye (Nr. Ashford, Kent), 12in. arched brass dial, 91in. high. (Canterbury)
$5,436

A late 17th century walnut and floral marquetry longcase clock, signed *Dan Lécount, London*, 6ft. 9in. high. (Phillips)
$20,215

A marbleised longcase clock, 20th century, of neo-classical form, the painted dial in a hood shaped as a shell, 82in. high. (Christie's)
$1,990

LONGCASE CLOCKS

A mahogany chiming longcase clock, William Withers, London, circa 1760, 8ft. 2in. (Bonhams)

$6,321

French Provincial polychrome decorated tall-case clock, 19th century, 94in. high. (Skinner)

$2,000

A Black Forest regulator, the brass dial surrounded by carved vines and surmounted by an owl. (Galerie Moderne)

$3,126

Small Federal cherry inlaid tall-case clock, probably Mass-achusetts, circa 1810, 85in. high. (Skinner)

$4,312

A Louis XVI Provincial pine longcase clock, circa 1800, 7ft. 10³/₄in. high. (Butterfield & Butterfield)

$3,162

A Directoire mahogany and ebonized month-going longcase regulator, *Janvier, au Louvre*, 80in. high. (Christie's)

$42,055

An Edwardian mahogany month-going miniature longcase regulator, Chas. Frodsham, 5ft. 10¹/₂in. high. (Christie's)

$14,628

A mahogany regulator, Scottish, circa 1840, the silvered circular 13in. dial signed *Bryson, Edinr.*, 6ft. 8¹/₄in. high. (Sotheby's)

$21,390

190

LONGCASE CLOCKS

Federal mahogany inlaid tall case clock, Southeastern US, circa 1790, 104.5in. high. (Skinner)

$9,200

A George III oak eight day longcase clock by Robert Parker of Derby, 80in. high. (Phillips)

$2,015

Rare Tiffany & Co. corner case astronomical master timepiece, circa 1880, 86in. high. (Skinner)

$56,350

An 18th century mahogany long cased clock by John Smith of Pittenweem, 83in. high. (Christopher Matthews)

$2,869

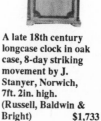

A walnut and marquetry chiming longcase clock, signed *Hobbin Fakenham* 18th/19th century, later 11in. dial, 7ft. 9in. (Bonhams)

$3,344

A Biedermeier mahogany, ebonized and satinwood-inlaid longcase regulator, *C. L. Baumgärtel in Leipzig,* 6ft. high. (Christie's)

$23,770

A late 18th century longcase clock in oak case, 8-day striking movement by J. Stanyer, Norwich, 7ft. 2in. high. (Russell, Baldwin & Bright)

$1,733

An imposing Edwardian mahogany longcase clock, 12in. arched brass dial with silvered chapter ring, 100in. high. (Canterbury)

$5,698

MANTEL CLOCKS

A Liberty Tudric pewter clock, designed by Archibald Knox, with a copper dial and blue enamel center, circa 1905, 9in. high.
(Dee, Atkinson & Harrison)
$1,444

Continental painted and parcel giltwood blackamoor and monkey mantel clock, late 19th century, 14in. high.
(Skinner) $2,300

A brass-mounted wooden mantel clock with hour and half-hour strike and musical alarm, circa 1920.
(Auction Team Köln) $423

A 19th century French ormolu and porcelain mantel clock, the arched shaped case surmounted by a twin handled urn and decorated with scrolls and swags, 51cm. high.
(Phillips) $1,866

A William IV rosewood bracket clock by Josh Wilson, Stamford, the leaf carved case on melon lobed feet with brass Gothic arch side panels, 12in.
(Hy. Duke & Son) $927

An 18th century Austrian giltwood quarter striking mantel clock, the circular restored enamel dial with concentric date and signed *Leopold Korner in Wien*, 66cm. high.
(Phillips) $2,643

Mahogany double steeple shelf clock, Birge and Fuller, Bristol, Connecticut, circa 1845, with eight-day brass wagon spring movement, 27in. high.
(Skinner) $862

A late Victorian mahogany cased clock/barometer, the instruments set side by side, the clock with ivorine chapter ring, 10in. high.
(Dee, Atkinson & Harrison)
$188

A 19th century gilt bronze mantel timepiece, the circular fusée movement with anchor escapement, signed *Payne, New Bond Street*, 29cm. high.
(Phillips) $700

MANTEL CLOCKS

A German chiming mantel clock in ebonized wooden case, with cast brass dial and Roman numerals, circa 1930.
(Auction Team Köln) $254

A French dog clock, with anchor escapement, showing the hours and minutes in the pupils of the eyes, circa 1930.
(Auction Team Köln) $269

An early 19th century boudoir mantel timepiece, the gilt brass drum shape case with an engine turned dial inscribed *Den Granges, London*, 8in.
(Woolley & Wallis) $1,413

Classical mahogany carved mantel clock, Sylvester Clark, Straitsville, Connecticut, for Hill Wells & Co., circa 1830, with brass eight-day Salem bridge-type movement, 31^1/2in. high.
(Skinner) $3,565

A Victorian novelty timepiece with an easel back, modeled as a jockey cap flanked by crossed riding crops and a bit, by William Frederick Williams, 1882, 7.5cm. high.
(Phillips) $1,064

Classical mahogany carved mantel clock, E. Terry and Sons, Plymouth, Connecticut, circa 1820–24, with eight-day weight driven wooden movement, 37in. high.
(Skinner) $575

A 19th century French mantel clock in the Louis XVI style having inset porcelain dial and panels, urn shaped pot pourri surmount, 18in. high.
(Russell, Baldwin & Bright) $1,444

An early 19th century ormolu pendule d'officier, the chased case with serpent handle and paw feet, the circular restored enamel dial signed *Meuron & Comp*, 22cm. high.
(Phillips) $4,354

Classical mahogany triple decker mirror clock, C. & L. C. Ives, Bristol, Connecticut, circa 1831, with eight-day brass wagon spring driven movement, 36^1/2in. high.
(Skinner) $3,680

MANTEL CLOCKS

A carved beech cuckoo clock, Black Forest, circa 1900, in a typical chalet style case surmounted by a bird, 22in.
(Bonhams) $677

A classic English time-clock, possibly by International Time Clocks, 50 volt battery powered.
(Auction Team Köln) $732

A bronze and gilt French 19th century mantel clock, decorated with lion masks, swags and garlands.
(Galerie Moderne) $1,125

Russian 84 standard silver clock with green onyx base, O. F. Kurlyukov, Moscow, circa 1908–1917, allegorical figure group of two classical figures with a large book, 20½in. high.
(Butterfield & Butterfield) $6,900

A German silvered and silver-mounted gilt-brass striking table clock, Schultz. Rieger; circa 1700, the hexagonal case on winged claw feet and with later winged caryatids to the glazed sides, 3¼in. high.
(Christie's) $8,777

An Austrian mantel clock, the silvered dial and Roman numerals with regulator dial above, eight day striking movement by Lenzkirch, 27in. high.
(Anderson & Garland) $960

A 19th century French gilt and enameled brass mantel clock, the spherical dial with hands in the form of a snake, surmounted by a bust, signed *Howell & Co., Paris 64*, 35cm. high.
(Phillips) $1,435

19th century Continental porcelain cased mantel clock with flowers and foliage in relief and painted panels of flowers, on scroll feet, eight day striking movement, 15in. high.
(Ewbank) $819

A 19th century French brass and champlevé enamel mantel clock, the case surmounted by an urn and flanked by quivers of arrows, movement stamped *Japy Freres*, 42cm. high.
(Phillips) $1,036

MANTEL CLOCKS

French red boulle mantel clock, crested with a gilt metal foliate scrolled urn formed finial, late 19th/early 20th century, 17in.
(G. A. Key) $1,087

A Charles X bronze and ormolu mantel clock with Atala freeing Chactas.
(Hôtel de Ventes Horta) $7,033

A Directoire bronze and ormolu mantel clock, 'Au Sauvage', the huntress seated on the dial, a lioness beside her.
(Hôtel de Ventes Horta) $19,539

A 19th century French mantel clock having white enamel dial inscribed *Deniere, Ft de Bronzes a Paris*, eight-day movement in ormolu case with frieze of cherubs, signed, 17in. high.
(Russell, Baldwin & Bright) $2,643

A Louis XIV style gilt-bronze and marble annular clock, circa 1860, the central orb mounted with fleur-de-lys and surmounted by a crown, 20¹/₂in. high.
(Butterfield & Butterfield) $5,175

A Louis XVI style gilt-bronze and Sèvres biscuit porcelain figural mantel clock, Planchon à Paris, 19th century, eight-day, half-hour strike, within an octagonal case, 17in. high.
(Butterfield & Butterfield) $5,175

An ebonised quarter chiming mantel clock, Hunt & Roskill, London, circa 1875, the substantial triple fusée movement chiming on 8 bells or 4 gongs at the quarters, 21¹/₂in.
(Bonhams) $1,244

A 30 hour pantry alarm timepiece, English, early 19th century, 6in. brass dial with Roman numerals and concentric alarm hand, with iron hanging loop, 6in.
(Bonhams) $421

A large 19th century brass and silvered sculptural mantel clock, the shaped case surmounted by the figure of Neptune, dial signed *Raingo Fres, a Paris*, 71cm. high.
(Phillips) $3,190

MANTEL CLOCKS

An ormolu mantel clock, French, circa 1840, 3¹/₄in. enamel dial with Roman numerals, signed *Raingo Freres A. Paris*, 17in.
(Bonhams) $780

A boulle mounted mantel clock, French, circa 1880, 3³/₄in. enamel dial with Roman and Arabic numerals, signed for Nathans of Birmingham, 16¹/₂in.
(Bonhams) $760

A gilt ormolu and jeweled porcelain mantel clock, French, circa 1870, 3¹/₄in. porcelain dial with Roman numeral reserves, and decorated center, 14½in.
(Bonhams) $1,824

An onyx and champlevé enamel four glass clock, French, circa 1890, the gong striking movement and mercury compensated pendulum in a case, surmounted by an urn finial, 16in.
(Bonhams) $608

An ebonized and porcelain mounted mantel clock, French, circa 1870, 6¹/₄in. porcelain dial with Arabic numeral reserves and decorated with blue and white foliage, signed for Elkington & Co., Paris, 18in.
(Bonhams) $426

A large rosewood and boxwood inlaid chiming mantel clock, English, circa 1880, 8in. silvered chapter ring with Roman numerals, matted center and subsidiaries in the arch for chime/silent, 26in.
(Bonhams) $2,280

A 19th century French ormolu mantel timepiece, now fitted with a Swiss eight day movement with enamel dial and pierced gilt hands, 26cm. high.
(Phillips) $1,011

An 8-day amboyna and brass strung mantel chronometer, the 5.5in. circular silvered dial signed *Kelvin, White & Hutton, 11 Billiter St, London 604*, 29cm. high, with a safety key.
(Phillips) $5,260

A champlevé enamel and porcelain mounted mantel clock, French, circa 1870, 3³/₄in. enamel dial with Roman numerals, signed for *Lacour A Paris*, 17in.
(Bonhams) $2,584

MANTEL CLOCKS

A 19th century French ormolu mantel clock, the enamel dial signed *Godard A Paris,* twin train movement, 54.5cm. high. (Phillips) $1,362

A 19th century French ormolu and bronze mantel timepiece, the plinth base with applied plaque inscribed *Henri Le Grand,* 38cm. high. (Phillips) $928

A 19th century French ormolu and porcelain mounted mantel clock, the circular twin train movement striking on a bell, 46cm. high. (Phillips) $2,177

An ebonized and gilt mounted chiming mantel clock, English, circa 1860, 7^1/$_2$in. silvered dial with Roman numerals, the going barrel movement chiming on seven bells, 52cm. (Bonhams) $578

An oak mantel timepiece with a silent escapement, Dent, London, No. 33680, circa 1900, 4^3/$_4$in. painted dial with Roman numerals, regulation arbor at 12 o'clock, 10^1/$_2$in. (Bonhams) $622

A gilt brass four glass mantel clock, French, circa 1880, 3^1/$_2$in. two-piece enamel dial with Roman numerals and Visable Brocourt escapement, signed for Sir John Bennett Ltd, 12^3/$_4$in. (Bonhams) $866

A 19th century French gilt brass and enamel circular four glass mantel clock, the stepped top with champlevé enamel boss and cast band above similarly decorated frieze, 33cm. high. (Phillips) $1,160

A Regency ormolu and black marble mantel timepiece, the gilt engine turned circular dial signed *Duncan, London,* the signed fusée movement with anchor escapement, 22cm. high. (Phillips) $1,083

A large beech trumpeter mantel clock, German/English, circa 1950, the triple going barrel movement sounding on a gong and playing five trumpets, in a Gothic church style case. (Bonhams) $1,368

SKELETON CLOCKS

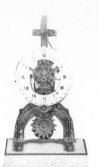

A Louis Philippe gothic striking skeleton clock, *Hry. Marc à Paris,* the frame of typical design with central arch supported on four pilasters, 17¹/₂in. high.
(Christie's) $731

A brass skeleton timepiece, English, circa 1840, the pierced Gothic style polished frame, single fusée movement standing on an oval mahogany base, 14in.
(Bonhams) $638

A Directoire ormolu and white marble skeleton timepiece, unsigned, pinwheel escapement with steel-suspended sunburst pendulum, 12in. high.
(Christie's) $2,560

A Belgian ormolu and marble astronomical striking skeleton clock, *à Paris,* circa 1795, attributed to Hobart Sarton, raised on two ormolu pillars and black marble D-ended plinth, 19³/₄in. high.
(Christie's) $27,428

A Regency ormolu and rosewood spherical striking skeleton clock, Barraud, London, the revolving silvered Roman and Arabic hour and minute rings with ormolu sunburst, 15in. high.
(Christie's) $47,541

An important Belgian ormolu and black marble complicated astronomical world-time skeleton clock, Sarton, circa 1820, the ormolu bezel cast with sunbursts and foliate beading, 23³/₄in. high.
(Christie's) $124,815

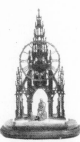

A Walter Scott memorial skeleton clock, under glass dome with white marble base, on oval mahogany stand with brass bun feet, 24in. high.
(Andrew Hartley) $2,114

An important early Louis XVI ormolu and verdi antico marble astronomical skeleton timepiece, engraved on the back of the frame *Ferdinand Berthoud inventi et fecit AParis,* 19in. high.
(Christie's) $54,855

An Empire ormolu striking skeleton clock, unsigned, the white enamel Roman and Arabic annular chapter ring within engine-turned ormolu bezels, 13³/₄in. high.
(Christie's) $2,377

SKELETON CLOCKS

A 19th century brass skeleton timepiece, the shaped pierced plates with silvered scalloped chapter ring, 33cm. high.
(Phillips) **$684**

Brass skeleton clock with single train movement, blued steel hands, 9in.
(G. A. Key) **$936**

A Victorian gilt-brass striking skeleton clock, unsigned, the circular silvered annular chapter ring with Roman chapters and blued moon hands, 17³/₄in. high.
(Christie's) **$1,553**

An Empire ormolu and marble weight-driven striking keyhole skeleton clock, unsigned, the 18cm. diameter foliate-cast bezel framing a narrow diameter white enamel Arabic annular chapter ring, 16in. high.
(Christie's) **$16,456**

A German torsion skeleton timepiece, Gustav Becker Freiburg, with silvered Arabic chapter ring and blued spade hands, the going barrel movement with anchor escapement, 11in. high.
(Christie's) **$1,370**

An important Charles X highly complicated long duration astronomical striking skeleton clock with equation of time, *J. F. Henri Motel A Paris,* the 6in. diameter silvered engraved dial with Roman mean time chapter ring, 22³/₄in. high.
(Christie's) **$116,070**

A Directoire ormolu and verdi antico marble astronomical month-going weight-driven skeleton clock, A. Paris attributed to Verneuil, 21³/₄in. high.
(Christie's) **$45,712**

A modern fusee skeleton clock with coup perdu escapement, the silvered Roman and Arabic dial of regulator layout signed *Francis Abbot* on a silvered sector, 17¹/₄in. high.
(Christie's) **$1,736**

A brass skeleton timepiece, English, circa 1880, the single fusée movement and half deadbeat escapement with a polished scroll shape frame, 11¹/₄in.
(Bonhams) **$778**

WALL CLOCKS

A 19th century Dutch stoelkok, the painted wood bracket with pierced gilt lead cresting and mermaid figures to each side, 76cm. high.
(Phillips) **$1,057**

A 30-hour weight driven wall clock, with alarm, Dutch, 19th century, the brass birdcage movement with turned columns at the corners, 15¹/₄in.
(Bonhams) **$622**

A Victorian walnut cased regulator wall clock.
(Jacobs & Hunt) **$534**

A Louis XV style gilt-bronze cartel clock, late 19th century, the circular white enamel dial painted with Roman numerals and eight-day half-hour strike, 31in. high.
(Butterfield & Butterfield) **$2,875**

A giltwood grande sonnerie picture frame clock, Austrian, early 19th century, 4³/₄in. enamel dial in a rectangular case with a molded border and oval pendulum aperture, 20in.
(Bonhams) **$684**

A beech and ebonized weight driven trumpeter wall clock, Black Forest, late 19th century, 8in. painted dial with Roman numerals, signed *A. Furtwangler, 1665 Strand, London*, 35in.
(Bonhams) **$1,355**

A beech 'Vienna' wall clock, the weight driven movement with tapered plates, deadbeat escapement and maintaining power, German, circa 1880, 45in.
(Bonhams) **$1,120**

A large painted dial sedan style timepiece, English, unsigned, early 19th century, the surround decorated with a scene of Adam and Eve in the Garden of Eden, 10¹/₂in.
(Bonhams) **$692**

A walnut 'Vienna' grande sonnerie wall clock, Gustav Becker, circa 1880, 6¹/₄in. silvered chapter ring with Roman numerals and engraved gilt center.
(Bonhams) **$1,672**

WALL CLOCKS

A gilt ormolu cartel clock, French, circa 1860, 8in. enamel dial with Roman numerals, signed *Clermont, 25 Reie de Choiseul, Paris*, 31½in.
(Bonhams) **$1,505**

A brass 30-hour weight driven lantern clock, Daniel Ray, Manningtree, 8in. dial with a silvered Roman numeral chapter ring, matted center single hand, 15in.
(Bonhams) **$812**

Mirror timepiece, James Collins, Goffstown, New Hampshire, circa 1830, with eight-day weight driven movement, painted iron dial, 30in. height.
(Skinner) **$2,185**

A 19th century wall clock, the month going movement with anchor escapement and ebonized 14in. dial inscribed *Terry Bedale*, 48½in. high.
(Andrew Hartley) **$2,356**

A wall picture timepiece, French, mid-19th century, 1¼in. enamel dial, set into a scene of a tower in a country village, 26 x 23cm.
(Bonhams) **$873**

A 19th century Austrian walnut Vienna wall timepiece, incorporating a three-tune musical box in the base, signed on the comb *A. Olbrich in Wien*, 1.05m. high.
(Phillips) **$4,641**

A black lacquer and gilt chinoiserie tavern wall timepiece, William Carter, Kingston, late 18th century, 21in. dial with gilt Roman and Arabic numerals, 5ft.
(Bonhams) **$2,558**

A 30 hour pantry alarm timepiece, unsigned, 18th/19th century, 5in. dial with a brass Roman chapter ring, single hand and concentric alarm setting dial, 8in.
(Bonhams) **$512**

Mahogany banjo timepiece, probably Boston, Massachusetts, circa 1830, with black eglomise glasses and eight-day brass weight driven movement, 50in. high.
(Skinner) **$4,600**

WALL CLOCKS

A softwood picture frame clock with pressed brass plate with flower carriers, enamel dial.
(Auction Team Köln) $169

A Mickey Mouse mechanical display clock with moving legs, right hand and eyes, 1955.
(Auction Team Köln) $655

A Waterbury Clock Co. octagonal wall clock, with small reverse painted glass panel under.
(Auction Team Köln) $169

A rosewood and shell inlaid striking drop dial wall clock, Bentley, London, circa 1840, 12in. painted dial with Roman numerals, the twin fusee bell striking movement with shaped plates, 23¹/₂in.
(Bonhams) $380

A 19th century mahogany circular wall timepiece, the 12in. circular painted convex dial signed *Dwerrihouse, Davis Street, Berkeley Square,* the fusée movement with anchor escapement, 36cm. diameter.
(Phillips) $1,011

A mahogany tavern wall timepiece, Allam and Clement, London, circa 1770, 19in. painted dial with Roman numerals, in a case with a turned surround, shaped trunk door, 46in.
(Bonhams) $5,320

A carved oak striking wall clock, W. Potts, Pudsey, circa 1850, the twin fusée gong striking movement in a carved case decorated with scroll foliage and fruit berries, 4ft.
(Bonhams) $1,672

A picture frame clock with eagle motif, the black lacquered wooden frame with glass door, stamped brass plate.
(Auction Team Köln) $214

A 19th century giltwood wall timepiece, with 10in. circular convex painted dial, the fusée movement with anchor escapement, 94cm. high.
(Phillips) $933

WALL CLOCKS

A 19th century mahogany and brass inlaid drop dial wall timepiece, the 12in. convex repainted dial with octagonal inlaid surround, 71cm. high.
(Phillips) $466

A mahogany circular wall timepiece, the 8in. painted dial signed for *B.R. (S) John Walker, London, 6385*, 26cm. diameter.
(Phillips) $902

A German wall regulator striking the hours and half-hours on a gong, also showing date, circa 1900.
(Auction Team Köln)
$1,348

An amusing Black Forest picture automaton wall clock, D. Willman, Elsenbach, mid-19th century, 3³/₄in. enamel dial with Roman numerals, set into a picture containing a lion with moving eyes, 10¹/₂ x 12³/₄in.
(Bonhams) $1,140

A mahogany and brass inlaid wall timepiece, Halfhide Hereford, circa 1840, 12in. convex painted dial with Roman numerals, the single fusée movement with shaped plates, 17³/₄in.
(Bonhams) $380

A verge bracket clock movement with a Battersea enamel dial, William Mould, London, circa 1770, the twin fusée five pillar movement with a verge escapement and bob pendulum.
(Bonhams) $1,555

A 19th century mahogany drop dial wall clock, the 12in. repainted dial signed for *J. Garland, Gray St., Newcastle,* twin fusée movement, 43cm. high.
(Phillips) $746

An 18th century Austrian carved wood quarter chiming wall clock, with circular enamel dial with concentric date, signed *Andreas Kullman, Wien,* 94cm. high.
(Phillips) $5,287

Rosewood octagon wall timepiece, probably Atkins Whiting & Co., Bristol, Connecticut, mid 19th century, with thirty-day wagon spring movement, 25¹/₂in. high.
(Skinner) $690

WATCHES

A gold tonneau shaped watch, Swiss, circa 1920, signed *Graziosa*, nickel movement in a polished case with a hinged back, 32 x 55mm.
(Bonhams) $467

An 18ct. gold keyless lever dress watch, the movement signed *Le Coultre Co 41718*, the silvered dial signed *Cartier*, 48mm. diameter.
(Phillips) $1,315

A silver 'Unique' Dunhill lighter with inset watch, the keyless lever watch movement jeweled to the third, marked for London 1926, 54 x 43mm.
(Phillips) $897

A gold open faced chronograph watch with split seconds, Leonidas, circa 1900, enamel dial with Arabic numerals, signed for a Shanghai retailer, 52mm.
(Bonhams) $760

An 18th century pocket chronometer movement by *Jn Arnold London*, with Arnold type spring detent escapement, with later enamel dial in a later case, 51mm. diameter.
(Phillips) $2,166

Rentzsch, London, a rare early 19th century 18ct. gold quarter repeating keyless watch, the signed gilt movement with cylinder escapement, 46mm. diameter.
(Phillips) $4,950

A 19th century Swiss gold and enamel cylinder watch, the gold cuvette signed *Vacheron & Constantin à Geneve No. 27500*, 46mm. diameter.
(Phillips) $1,238

A gold open faced watch, International Watch Co., circa 1920, enamel dial with Arabic numerals and subsidiary seconds, gilt movement, 52mm.
(Bonhams) $809

A 19th century Swiss keyless lever watch, the enamel dial signed *Lonville*, with subsidiary seconds, chased case, signed *HOL FRS*, 70mm. diameter.
(Phillips) $263

WATCHES

A George III gilt metal, pair cased verge clockwatch, the movement with pierced and engraved cock signed *Jno Ilbery, London 1060*, 67mm. diameter.
(Phillips) $3,713

A Swiss 18ct. gold half hunter cased keyless lever watch, 50mm. diameter, together with a gold guard chain and swivel fob.
(Phillips) $1,114

A Swiss keyless lever dress watch, the movement jeweled to the center and signed *International Watch Co Schaffhausen, 922984.*
(Phillips) $851

A German keyless lever deck watch, the movement jeweled to the center with compensated balance, signed *A Lange & Sohne, Glashutte, 201113*, 59mm. diameter.
(Phillips) $1,470

A silver and shagreen triple cased verge watch, made for the Turkish market, pierced and engraved cock signed *Geo Johnson London 7584*, marked *London 1778*, 69mm. diameter.
(Phillips) $2,065

A Swiss keyless lever watch, the gilt bar movement jeweled to the center with micrometer regulation, 47mm. diameter, together with a two color guard chain.
(Phillips) $495

A gilt metal enamel and paste set quarter repeating verge watch, circa 1800, enamel with Arabic numerals, *signed Fre' Wifs e Menu*, 48mm.
(Bonhams) $1,057

A good 19th century French silver pocket thermometer, the enamel dial calibrated with Fahrenheit and Reamur scales, 59mm. diameter.
(Phillips) $2,166

A French gold and enamel verge watch, the movement with pierced bridge cock, signed *L'Epine, Hr du Roy a Paris, 11461*, 41mm. diameter.
(Phillips) $2,333

WATCHES

An 18ct. gold and enamel fob watch, Swiss, circa 1860, gilt dial with a Roman chapter ring in a case with enamel Alpine scene with an engraved border, 35mm.
(Bonhams) $988

An early 19th century French gold and enamel ball watch, the verge movement with pierced bridge cock signed *L'Epine A Paris*, 23mm. diameter.
(Phillips) $1,380

A superb gold verge stop watch by George Graham, made for Sir James Pennyman at Ormesby Hall near Middlesborough in 1726.
(Tennants) $37,026

A late 18th century French verge in a five color gold consular case with shagreen covered protective, full plate gilt fusee movement, signed *Roux a Paris*, circa 1780, 43mm. diameter.
(Pieces of Time) $3,398

A 9ct. petrol burning lighter with inset watch, Dunhill, 1926, silvered dial with raised Arabic numerals, signed *Dunhill*, similarly signed nickel movement with three adjustment, 45 x 55mm.
(Bonhams) $2,128

A 17th century Swiss gold and enamel verge, the gold case decorated on almost all surfaces with polychrome enamel, signed *Pierre Duhamel*, circa 1650, 30mm. diameter.
(Pieces of Time)
$24,915

A late 17th century French oignon with cartouche dial in a decorative gilt metal consular case, signed *Francoise Delinotte a Orleans*, circa 1700, 57mm. diameter.
(Pieces of Time) $5,210

A rare early 19th century Swiss automaton in a gold open face case, as the pendant is depressed two cupids move towards the figure of Father Time, circa 1810, 57mm. diameter.
(Pieces of Time) $7,928

A fine Swiss lever silver deck watch by Ulysse Nardin in a mahogany deck box, keyless gilt bar movement with large going barrel, signed, circa 1940, 56mm. diameter.
(Pieces of Time) $3,688

WATCHES

An 18th century East European verge in a gold and enamel consular case, signed *Ant Bernard Prag*, circa 1770, 37mm. diameter.
(Pieces of Time) $3,699

A 19th century Continental gold and enamel form watch, the case in the form of a bow harp with eight strings and red, white, green and blue decoration.
(Phillips) $2,022

An 18ct. gold open faced watch, Patek Philippe, No. 92345, circa 1900, signed for *Tilden Thurber & Co. Providence*, 48mm.
(Bonhams) $1,824

A two day deck watch with power reserve indication by Hamilton in a brass drum case with fittings for gimbals, original aluminium storage case lined with rubber, bayonet fitting lid, signed, circa 1942, 75mm. diameter.
(Pieces of Time) $589

An early 19th century French quarter repeating automaton verge in a gold open face case, as the watch strikes the hours and quarters the arms of the figures move as though striking the bells between them, circa 1810, 56mm. diameter.
(Pieces of Time) $4,908

An early silver pair case verge watch, Joseph Howes, London, circa 1680, silvered repoussé dial with Roman and Arabic numerals, signed, the gilt movement with a pierced winged balance cock, 55mm.
(Bonhams) $1,064

A fine gold repoussé pair cased quarter and alarm verge watch, Joseph Martineau Sen', London, circa 1770, the outer case finely repoussé with a scene of the stag hunt, 50mm.
(Bonhams) $5,320

A lady's 19th century gold open-face pocket watch with black and white enameled foliate decoration, signed *Stace, Foulkstone, No. 9081*.
(Bearne's) $448

A rare early 19th century Swiss quarter repeating watch with musical work in a gold open face case, gilt movement, blue steel Breguet hands, signed *Freres Rey & Comp 11135*, circa 1810.
(Pieces of Time) $8,305

WRIST WATCHES

A stainless steel water resistant wristwatch, Rolex Oyster, ref. 3136, circa 1940, restored silvered dial with quarter Arabic numerals, subsidiary seconds, 30mm.
(Bonhams) $334

A 9ct. gold cushion shaped wristwatch, Rolex 'Oyster', ref. 678, 1929, enamel dial with Arabic numerals and subsidiary seconds, 32mm.
(Bonhams) $2,280

A stainless steel chronograph with triple calendar and moonphase, Universal 'Tri-Compax', circa 1960, silvered dial with baton numerals, outer tachograph scale 36mm.
(Bonhams) $1,166

A stainless steel center seconds military wristwatch, International Watch Co., Mk. XI, circa 1950, black dial with Arabic numerals, fine damascened nickel movement, 35mm.
(Bonhams) $1,824

A 9ct. gold tonneau shaped wristwatch, Rolex, ref. 2010, 1937, refinished silvered dial with Arabic numerals, subsidiary seconds, nickel movement signed beneath the dial, 28mm.
(Bonhams) $532

A stainless steel center seconds military wristwatch, International Watch Co., Mk. XI, circa 1950, black dial with Arabic numerals, the fine damascened nickel movement with hack setting, 35mm.
(Bonhams) $1,900

A plated chronograph wristwatch, Breitling, circa 1950, silvered dial with Arabic and dagger batons, subsidiary for running seconds and 45-minute recording, 36mm.
(Bonhams) $280

A Swiss silver and enamel folding watch, by Rolex, the signed circular movement with signed dial and arabic numerals, 49 x 31mm.
(Phillips) $510

An early 18ct. gold water resistant watch, Swiss, 1929, silvered dial with Arabic numerals and subsidiary seconds, signed for *Mappin*, 32mm.
(Bonhams) $529

WRIST WATCHES

A stainless steel chronograph wristwatch, Breitling Chronomat, circa 1960, silvered dial with raised baton numerals, 17 jewel movement.
(Bonhams) **$933**

A Swiss platinum and sapphire mounted keyless lever dress watch, the rectangular case with shuttered dial operated from the gem set sides, 47 x 38mm.
(Phillips) **$1,834**

An 18ct. gold automatic center seconds wristwatch, Omega, 1959, the pink movement in a heavy polished case with a snap-on back, 34mm.
(Bonhams) **$591**

A stainless steel automatic chronograph wristwatch, Breitling Navitimer, circa 1970, black dial with luminous batons, calendar aperture and subsidiaries for 12 hour and 30 minute recording, 50mm.
(Bonhams) **$274**

An early 20th century Swiss silver wrist watch with protective pierced cover, gilt three quarter plate keyless movement with going barrel, signed *Jupiter*, circa 1915, 35mm. diameter.
(Pieces of Time) **$445**

A 9ct. gold automatic center seconds wristwatch, Rolex Oyster, ref. 1500, date, 1965, signed movement in a polished case with a plain bezel and screw down button and back, 34mm.
(Bonhams) **$1,368**

An 18ct. gold square wristwatch on a 14ct. gold bracelet, Patek Philippe, Nos. 837592, circa 1960, silvered dial with raised gilt baton numerals and subsidiary seconds, 25mm.
(Bonhams) **$3,110**

A stainless steel automatic bracelet watch, Rolex Sea-Dweller, ref. 16660, black dial with luminous dots and calendar aperture, signed *Rolex Oyster Perpetual Date*, 40mm.
(Bonhams) **$1,368**

An 18ct. gold square cased wristwatch, Universal, circa 1965, silvered dial with dagger numerals, signed *Universal Geneve* and subsidiary seconds, 26mm.
(Bonhams) **$334**

WRIST WATCHES

An 18ct. gold automatic calendar bracelet watch, Rolex Day Date Perpetual 18038, pavé set dial with baguette quarters and day/date apertures, signed *Rolex Day Date*, 35mm. (Bonhams) **$13,545**

A fine 18ct. gold tourbillon wristwatch, signed *Breguet*, No. 4775, recent, the matt silvered textured dial with raised eccentric polished Roman chapter ring, 36mm. diameter. (Christie's) **$29,911**

An 18ct. gold bracelet watch set, circa 1980, plain black onyx dial, signed *International Watch Co., Schaffhausen*, with Middle East crest; with matching cufflinks and signet ring, 30mm. (Bonhams) **$2,333**

An 18ct. gold rectangular wristwatch in the shape of a gold ingot, signed *Corum*, No. 4702, 1980s, with mechanical movement, the gold dial in the shape of a gold ingot bearing the stamp of the Union Bank of Switzerland, 40 x 24mm. (Christie's) **$2,639**

A steel two time zone double dialled reversible wristwatch, signed *Jaeger-LeCoultre*, model Reverso, with mechanical movement, the first dial with matt chapter ring Arabic numerals, 42 x 27mm. (Christie's) **$4,399**

An 18ct. gold and diamond set wristwatch with moonphase, signed *Breguet*, No. 4425, recent, the matt silvered textured dial with polished Roman chapter ring, subsidiary seconds and aperture for the moon, 32mm. diameter. (Christie's) **$13,724**

A fine and rare platinum and diamond set waterproof automatic chronograph calendar wristwatch, signed *Breguet*, No. 594, 'model Marine', recent, 38mm. diameter. (Christie's) **$86,445**

An 18ct. gold self-winding triple calendar and moonphase water resistant wristwatch, signed *Ulysse Nardin*, model Michelangelo, recent, the gilt movement with gold alloy balance, 33 x 29mm. (Christie's) **$5,630**

An 18ct. white gold chronograph wristwatch, signed *Daniel Roth*, No. 214, recent, with nickel finished lever movement under sapphire glass with 21 jewels, monometallic balance, 35 x 38mm. (Christie's) **$12,316**

WRIST WATCHES

An 18ct. gold automatic bracelet watch, Rolex Day-Date, ref. 18038, gilt dial with baton numerals, sweep seconds, in a polished case with a bright cut bezel screw down button, 36mm.
(Bonhams) **$4,864**

An 18ct. gold self-winding skeletonized wristwatch, signed *Breguet*, No. 1731, recent, with finely engraved skeletonized lever movement, 35 jewels, 36mm. diameter.
(Christie's) **$12,316**

A silver cased rectangular wristwatch, Rolex Prince, ref. 971/02802, 1930, signed 15 jewel nickel movement marked *extra prima*, Glasgow import mark for 1930, 22 x 42mm.
(Bonhams) **$4,560**

A gentleman's 18ct. gold self-winding calendar wristwatch, signed *Rolex*, Oyster Perpetual Day-Date Chronometer, recent, with automatic movement, the brushed silvered dial with raised baton numerals, 36mm. diameter.
(Christie's) **$7,918**

A gentleman's white gold automatic wristwatch, signed *Patek Philippe*, model Ellipse, 1980s, the nickel plated movement with gold rim to the rotor, gold alloy balance, 36 x 33mm.
(Christie's) **$3,519**

An 18ct. gold perpetual calendar moonphase chronograph wristwatch, signed *Patek Philippe, Geneve*, No. 876310, recent, with jeweled lever movement, matt silvered dial with applied baton numerals, 37mm. diameter.
(Christie's) **$51,025**

An 18ct. gold demi-skeletonized automatic wristwatch, signed *Audemars Piguet, Rolls Royce*, No. c71977, recent, the nickel plated movement with skeletonized rotor, 36 jewels, 34mm. diameter.
(Christie's) **$9,677**

A fine 18ct. gold perpetual calendar and moonphase wristwatch, signed *Urban Jurgensen, Copenhagen*, No. 076, recent, the engine turned silver dial with polished Roman chapter ring, 38mm. diameter.
(Christie's) **$23,753**

An 18ct. gold automatic water-resistant wristwatch on a later 18ct. gold bracelet, Patek Philippe, ref. 2551, 1959, silvered dial with raised gilt baton numerals, subsidiary seconds, 35mm.
(Bonhams) **$4,214**

A pair of large 19th century cloisonné enamel vases, the turquoise ground decorated with blossoming peony sprigs, butterflies, birds, grasshoppers and other insects, 21.5in. high.
(Morphets) $2,433

Patinated sheet brass Hanukah lamp, possibly Dutch, with engraved floral decoration, 6³/₄in. high.
(Skinner) $546

A massive pair of Chinese cloisonné baluster vases, decorated in high relief with dragons chasing flaming pearls, all on a turquoise T-pattern ground, 72¹/₂in. high.
(Christie's) $15,925

A pair of red-painted and gilt tôle and brass two-branch wall-lights, each with square tapering pilaster-shaped back-plate decorated with various foliate motifs and cornucopiae, 62cm. high.
(Christie's) $5,594

Two nearly identical William and Mary brass candlesticks, Continental, probably Spanish, 1625–50, each having a baluster-form flared candle cup, 7¹/₄in. high.
(Sotheby's) $5,175

A brass warming pan, the cover punch decorated with an inscription *WAIT ON THE LORD 1670*, English, third quarter 17th century, 12¼in. diameter.
(Christie's) $1,518

A brass and stained glass hall lantern, the four multi-colored glass panels surmounted with brass finials, 42cm. high.
(Phillips) $456

Pair of Continental rococo brass candlesticks, 18th century, molded with 'C' scrolls, 9in. high.
(Skinner) $747

A 17th century Chinese cloisonné vase of Hu form, decorated with stylized flowerheads amongst scrolling foliage, Jingtai seal mark, 41cm.
(Bearne's) $1,143

A Far Eastern Shoeshine-kit with brass footrest, 15 jars, cloths and brush holders, circa 1920.
(Auction Team Köln) $539

A brass fireman's helmet (distressed).
(Bonhams) $154

A good skillet, the handle cast with the maker's name *IOHN FATHERS*, the bowl cast in high relief with the date *1704*, English, early 18th century, the bowl 7¾in. diameter.
(Christie's) $2,530

Silver plated lantern, America, late 19th century, with acid etched blue-to-clear glass shade, presentation plaque reads, *Evening Record Prize Lantern, number of votes 115537, 1890*, 11¼in. high.
(Skinner) $977

Two very fine and rare brass candlesticks, probably Spanish, circa 1700, on a domed circular base with lower faceted edge, 7³/₄in. high.
(Sotheby's) $4,312

A George II repoussé, patinated and gilt-copper coffee-pot, engraved overall with monkeys, parrots, butterflies and flowers, and a patinated and gilt copper stand and burner, 10in. high, excluding stand.
(Christie's) $4,168

An 18th-century brass horizontal garden sundial, indistinctly signed *T. Wright fecit*, with engraved calendar and time scales, with original gnomon, 9¼in. diameter.
(Christie's) $745

A 19th-century brass padlock, by Cotterill & Co., Birmingham, with iron claw and two keys, 5in. long.
(Christie's) $331

A brass chafing dish of typical form, the circular molded bowl with three tapered lugs, on a campana shaped foot, 17th century, 8¾in. diameter.
(Christie's) $303

A wrought copper kettle, stamped *D. Stoehr*, 1787–1863, West Hanover, York County, Pennsylvania, 1820–1830, serpentine spout and applied C-scroll handle, 15in. high.
(Christie's) $1,840

A pair of 16in. decorative brass candlesticks in the form of flamingoes standing on naturalistic rocky bases.
(Stainers') $480

English dry goods measure, large brass bowl with turned wood handles, circa 1800, 68 cm. diameter .
(Auction Team Köln) $693

A fine pair of Queen Anne brass candlesticks, Continental, probably French, circa 1720, each having a molded candle socket above a gadrooned and faceted stem, 9in. high.
(Sotheby's) $2,300

Two German brass alms dishes, circa 1500, one embossed with gadrooning in the center, the other embossed with Saint George and the dragon, 14³/₄in. and 14¹/₈in. diameter.
(Sotheby's) $6,325

A pair of wrought iron and brass miniature hogscraper candlesticks, Pennsylvania or England, 19th century, each with circular dished brass bobeche above a cylindrical iron shaft.
(Christie's) $2,990

A wrought copper large pot, Pennsylvania, 19th century, the tapering cylindrical form with flat bottom and rolled brim, 22in. diameter.
(Christie's) $403

A matched pair of copper buckets, each with hinged handle above the cylindrical body with a rivetted band to one side, 15¹/₂in. diameter.
(Christie's) $897

A good brass and copper gooseneck kettle, probably English, late 18th century, together with a Queen Anne pierced oval brass trivet, 13¹/₂in. high.
(Sotheby's) $1,035

A brass handwarmer of circular form, pierced and incised with foliate decoration, the internal reservoir on gimbal support, late 18th/early 19th century, 6in. diameter.
(Hy. Duke & Son) $494

A pair of Dutch style brass candlesticks, with spirally-turned stems, on circular domed bases cast with fruit and flowerheads, 9¹/₂in. high.
(Christie's) $411

A Nuremburg copper-mounted gilt brass engraved casket, by Michel Man, circa 1600, the sides and top engraved with three-quarter length figures of a king and queen and various angels, 2⁷/₈in. long.
(Sotheby's) $10,925

Arts & Crafts copper and wrought iron kettle on stand, late 19th century, the tapering ovoid body incised on the sides with a stylized blossoming thistle and leafage, 16¹/₂in. high overall.
(Butterfield & Butterfield) $862

Two fine pairs of brass candlesticks, French, circa 1700, with octagonal candle cup, shaped stem and faceted base, 9in. high.
(Sotheby's) $4,887

A pair of punch-decorated brass and iron combs, Pennsylvania, one dated 1834, each with scalloped and punch-beaded edge above a beaded band, 4¹/₄in. high.
(Christie's) $460

Densy, geometric vase, 1930s, nickel plated brass, of square section supported on four 'U' shaped interlocking elements, 30.25cm.
(Sotheby's) $2,362

A pair of Baroque repoussé-decorated large brass double-light wall sconces, probably Dutch, late 17th/early 18th century, 16in. high.
(Sotheby's) $13,800

Hagenauer, stylized female head, 1930s, patinated brass, modeled as a highly stylized female head, with martelé finish, 42cm.
(Sotheby's) $9,812

A Kestner mould 162 doll, with bisque head, jointed wood and composition body, dressed in original fairy outfit, 16in. high.
(Christie's) $713

An unusual Lenci character doll, modeled as a lady with molded felt head, downcast painted eyes and lashes, high-heeled shoes, 26in. high, circa 1925.
(Christie's) $713

A Bye-lo type baby doll, with bisque head, closed mouth, blue sleeping eyes, dressed in spotted muslin baby gown, 13^1/$_2$in. high.
(Christie's) $337

A rare Burgarella sexed composition doll, with painted features, small mouth, heavily shaded sleepy eyelids, unusual elbow and knee joints, 15^1/$_2$in., Italian, circa 1929.
(Christie's) $254

Two all-bisque dolls in original outfits, with painted features, blonde molded and painted hair, one with bare feet, 4^1/$_2$in. high; the other with molded and painted pink shoes, 4in. high. $340
(Christie's)

A Carl Bergmann composition Shirley Temple, with blue, lashed, sleeping eyes, wide, smiling mouth and blonde, curly, mohair wig, 18in. high, impressed *S. T. CB*.
(Christie's) $1,528

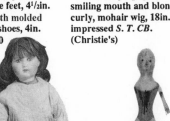

A Chad Valley doll in original state and box, with painted mask face, blonde wig, elongated limbs and blue velvet frock, 12in. high, 1950s.
(Christie's) $472

A Limoges Cherie size 9, with blue sleeping eyes, pierced ears, long, fair hair wig, jointed body and contemporary tucked frock, 24in. high, in original box.
(Christie's) $815

An early English wooden doll, carved and painted with inset enamel eyes, remains of one arm and later jointed legs, head and torso 13in. high, circa 1700s.
(Christie's) $3,398

A bisque-headed doll in original outfit, with blue eyes, blonde wig and jointed wood and composition body, 10¹/₂in. high, impressed *400/0*.
(Christie's) $815

An unusual wooden-headed doll, with chiseled brown hair, the wooden arms and feet attached to a later kid body, 13¹/₂in. high.
(Christie's) $1,273

An English wax dipped papier mâché doll, with smiling mouth, inset dark eyes, original white muslin wedding dress over pink chintz, 23in. high, circa 1866.
(Christie's) $593

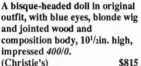

A papier mâché-headed doll with molded brown hair, blue painted eyes, kid body, wood limbs held with red paper bands, 9in. high, German circa 1840.
(Christie's) $593

A fine pair of Ichimatza Ningyos, with inset eyes, shaded brows, pierced nostrils and finely molded ears, 16½in. high.
(Christie's) $18,686

A papier mâché headed doll in original clothes, the molded black hair falling in ringlets on the shoulders and held in a bun above the nape, 9in. high, German circa 1840.
(Christie's) $476

Two cloth dolls by Norah Wellings, one modeled as a Spanish Senorita, with painted features, 25in. high; the other modeled as a red Indian Chief, 12¹/₂in. high.
(Christie's) $373

The first patented American autoperipatetikos, with original porcelain head, dress, box and key, in working order, 1862.
(Auction Team Köln)
$2,697

An all-bisque doll in original outfit, with domed head, closed mouth, blue eyes, blonde mohair wig and molded and painted black boots, 7in. high, German 1880s.
(Christie's) $2,547

An SFBJ child doll, with bisque head, brown sleeping eyes, pierced ears, fair wig, dressed in blue silk, 13¹/₂in. high. (Christie's) **$767**

A Sasha baby girl, English, 1960s–1970s, blonde, wearing a white knitted top, shorts, bootees and nappy. (Bonhams) **$133**

A Sasha doll no. 113, English, 1982, brunette, wearing her dancing dress, boxed with catalog. (Bonhams) **$218**

A Jules Steiner walking talking doll, French, circa 1885, the domed head with blonde real hair wig, stiffened body with composition lower limbs, 17³/₄in. (Sotheby's) **$1,272**

An SFBJ 251 character doll, with bisque head, blue lashed sleeping eyes, brown wig and jointed wood and composition toddler body, 15in. high. (Christie's) **$818**

A J. D. Kestner bisque character doll, German, circa 1910, impressed *185*, with open/closed mouth and simulated teeth, painted blue eyes, 11¹/₂in. (Sotheby's) **$1,817**

An Armand Marseille 'Ella' Oriental bisque head baby doll, German, circa 1920, with weighted black glass eyes, closed mouth, domed head, 8in. (Bonhams) **$749**

A Simon & Halbig 126 character doll, with bisque head, blue sleeping eyes, painted brows and blonde wig, impressed to head, 46cm. long. (Peter Wilson) **$479**

A bisque swivel head doll, French, circa 1870, fixed blue glass eyes, pierced ears, blonde plaited real hair wig over original cork pate, 18in. (Sotheby's) **$2,544**

A Jumeau bisque doll, French, circa 1895, impressed *1*, with open mouth and upper teeth, fixed blue glass paperweight eyes, 10in.
(Sotheby's) $2,907

A black Sasha 'Cara baby' No. 519, English, 1985, in crib, with catalog.
(Bonhams) $140

A Sasha baby 'Whitebird' girl, English, 1970s, brunette, wearing red tights and blue check smock.
(Bonhams) $156

A stitched face black cloth doll, American, early 20th century, with embroidered eyes, eyebrows, nose and mouth, looped hair, 37in. high.
(Sotheby's) $2,300

A Shirley Temple composition doll, with sleeping eyes, smiling mouth and curly blonde wig, 21in. high, marked *Shirley Temple Ideal*.
(Christie's) $597

A black Sasha baby girl, English, 1960s–1970s, wearing a blue printed long dress, including extra items of clothing.
(Bonhams) $172

A carved and painted wooden doll, French, circa 1825, with open mouth and painted blue eyes, with elaborate molded hair, 24in.
(Sotheby's) $1,999

A Lenci reclining baby felt doll, Italian, circa 1930, with painted features, blonde real hair wig, jointed at the neck, shoulders and hips, 20in.
(Sotheby's) $999

A Simon and Halbig bisque head girl doll, German, circa 1900, wearing a sheer cotton embroidered dress, underwear, black heeled shoes, 20in.
(Bonhams) $717

An unusual Hertel Schwab character doll, jointed wood and composition toddler body, dressed in white cotton frock, 16½in. high, impressed *149 5*.
(Christie's) $9,342

A china-headed doll circa 1850, with hair arranged in ringlets and stuffed body with kid arms and china legs, 16in. high.
(Christie's) $655

A bisque shoulder-headed lady doll with blue glass eyes, molded blonde curls and stuffed body with kid arms, 23in. high, German circa 1860.
(Christie's) $863

An Armand Marseille bisque head doll, having blonde curly mohair wig, weighted blue glass eyes, 10½in., impressed *Germany 390*.
(Phillips) $165

A rare papier-mâché shoulder-head 'kitchen' doll, German circa 1850, the yellow painted papier-mâché skirt centrally opening to reveal a tile and brickwork effect papered kitchen, 47cm. high.
(Sotheby's) $12,510

An early and rare Emile Jumeau pressed portrait bisque doll, French circa 1881, impressed *9 E.J.* with open/closed mouth showing white between lips, 61cm.
(Sotheby's) $10,766

A Bru Jeune pressed bisque doll, French circa 1880, kid-leather gusseted body with bisque forearms, checked jacket and skirt, 24in.
(Sotheby's) $15,629

A Simon & Halbig bisque head walking doll, having key wound mechanism with walking leg movement that also operates the voice box, 60cm.
(Phillips) $1,275

A François Gaultier pressed bisque swivel-head doll, French circa 1865, blonde real hair wig over cork pate and gusseted kid-leather body, 15in.
(Sotheby's) $2,084

A George III wooden doll, English circa 1765, the carved head with a thin layer of gesso, her original dress with leading strings, of cream cotton, 47cm.
(Sotheby's) $6,946

A Gebrüder Heubach bisque piano baby, German circa 1915, the seated figure with clenched hands and painted downturned mouth, 5in. high.
(Sotheby's) $521

An early 20th century Armand Marseille bisque china head doll impressed *990.4*, 43cm., together with a stained white wood rush seat chair, 41.5cm. high.
(Bearne's) $340

A good mid-19th century wax over composition shoulder head doll, with inserted blonde hair, blue glass eyes and on a soft body, 56cm.
(Bearne's) $757

A J. D. Kestner bisque character 'Hilda' doll, German circa 1914, blonde lambswool wig and five-piece composition body in a cream floral embroidered dress, 20in.
(Sotheby's) $3,473

A Simon & Halbig 1129 Oriental doll, with brown sleeping eyes, pierced ears, black mohair wig, jointed and composition body, 14in. high.
(Christie's) $2,243

A Jules Steiner Bourgoin C series pressed bisque doll, French, circa 1880, blonde real hair wig, jointed papier-mâché body, 29in.
(Sotheby's) $7,268

A papier mâché-head doll in original condition, 16in. high, German with possibly French body and clothes, circa 1850.
(Christie's) $1,868

An unusual molded bisque doll on Jumeau body, French, circa 1890, impressed *V 11 G*, with open mouth, simulated upper teeth and dimple in chin, 22in.
(Sotheby's) $3,452

A mouse trap, oak with ash block, of rectangular dead-fall type, first half 19th century, 11¼in. wide.
(Christie's) $303

A tin samovar with ivory handle, circa 1875, 34 cm. high.
(Auction Team Köln) $192

A Chr. Gaier pasta machine with three blades (5 cm. cutting width), circa 1910.
(Auction Team Köln) $107

A small American safe by the Herring Hall Marvin Safe Co., with combinations on a roller, circa 1900, 35 x 38 x 48 cm.
(Auction Team Köln)
$423

A wrought iron scold's bridle, the mouthpiece incised with the maker's initials *I.G.*, and with rotating drum, possibly 17th century, 20.6cm. high.
(Christie's) $675

A safe by Diebold Safe & Lock Co, Ohio, with four-part combination lock, owned by B N Adams, great grandson of Quincy Adams, circa 1890.
(Auction Team Köln) $498

A heart-carved walnut yarn winder, Pennsylvania, late 18th century, the scrolled support with heart-carved crest, 32½in. high.
(Christie's) $2,530

An early German coffee dispenser with original onion shape porcelain containers, circa 1900.
(Auction Team Köln) $539

A large turned pine wool spinning wheel, attributed to Daniel Danner, 1803–1891, Lancaster County, Pennsylvania, 59¾in. high.
(Christie's) $1,035

An AEG Model 44610 electric coffee machine, complete with equipment and filter.
(Auction Team Köln) $136

A pair of Charles I elm and leather bellows, the circular panels with concentric ring moldings, 11½in. diameter.
(Christie's) $1,855

A flower basket doorstop, cast in the half round, 21.5 cm. high.
(Auction Team Köln) $53

An American Electric Luminous Radiator, a General Electric heater with three matt glass bars, circa 1920.
(Auction Team Köln) $136

Mid 19th century mahogany tapestry frame, adjustable rectangular stretcher on trestle base, 36in. wide.
(Peter Wilson) $374

An American Vegetable Cutter No. 49, by the Enterprise Mfg. Co., Philadelphia, with rotary blades, circa 1900.
(Auction Team Köln) $115

An early American wire basket for milk bottles, with six original bottles from various dairies.
(Auction Team Köln) $103

A turned chestnut and oak 'castle-type' spinning wheel, attributed to Daniel Danner, 1803-1891, the molded and grooved wheel centering turned spindles, 54in. high.
(Christie's) $2,070

A mouse trap, oak, of triple dead-fall type, 18th or 19th century, 14½in. wide.
(Christie's) $1,518

Elvis Presley turquoise and black leather belt set with ornate silver medallions and large squares of natural lone mountain turquoise.
(Butterfield & Butterfield)
$5,750

Elvis Presley signed one thousand dollar bill, United States paper currency signed across the face of bill *Merry Christmas Elvis Presley* in red ink.
(Butterfield & Butterfield)
$6,900

Elvis Presley personal sunglasses, neo-style silver plastic and chrome with non-prescription brown plastic tint lenses.
(Butterfield & Butterfield)
$2,588

Elvis Presley color autograph photograph in the 'Peacock' jumpsuit, inscribed *To Romano Thank you for the beautiful wardrobe through the years. Sincerely Elvis Presley*, framed, 22¼ x 19⅛in.
(Butterfield & Butterfield)
$2,300

Elvis Presley Confederate Air Corps card, small thick paper card with black lettering, reading, *The Confederate Air Corps – This card will serve to identify Colonel Elvis Aaron Presley, C.A.C.*
(Butterfield & Butterfield)
$805

Elvis Presley handwritten outline for karate movie, this is the original concept for Elvis's dream to create the ultimate karate documentary film, with letter of authenticity from Joe Esposito.
(Butterfield & Butterfield)
$17,250

Elvis Presley signed one sheet for Elvis On Tour, Metro-Goldwyn-Mayer, 1972, signed on middle right *Elvis Presley* in black ink, 41 x 28in.
(Butterfield & Butterfield)
$1,840

Elvis Presley signed acetate for How Great Thou Art, Elvis Presley's personal copy, signed on original Transco envelope *To Dick Thanks Elvis Presley*.
(Butterfield & Butterfield)
$1,725

Black and white photograph of Elvis Presley from The Memphis Press Scimitar, wearing a black blazer standing behind a guitar shaped cake, framed, 15 x 12in.
(Butterfield & Butterfield)
$138

Elvis Presley Hamilton electric gold wristwatch from Blue Hawaii, Paramount, 1961, having a black triangular-shaped dial together with two lobby cards from the film.
(Butterfield & Butterfield)
$17,250

Elvis Presley Center Courts, the racquet presented to Elvis at the Memphis opening of the club in April 1976. A plaque on the grip reads *Ground breaking site No 1 Presley Center Courts April 21, 1976.*
(Butterfield & Butterfield)
$633

Elvis Presley signed album sleeve of Elvis Presley's 1957 RCA record release Elvis Presley/Loving You signed *To Mary Jane "With Love" Elvis Presley.*
(Butterfield & Butterfield)
$1,380

Original prototype for Elvis Presley's jacket from Elvis, NBC, December 3, 1968, shiny black polyester knit motorcycle style jacket with *Elvis Presley* handwritten in black ink on label.
(Butterfield & Butterfield)
$2,070

Elvis Presley signed wedding photograph signed *To Ed With all my thanks and my Deep Respect Elvis Presley,* also *Thanks for everything from both of us Elvis and Priscilla,* 11 x 11in.
(Butterfield & Butterfield)
$1,955

Elvis Presley, a royal blue simulated silk scarf, a color photograph of Presley wearing a similar scarf, and a note from a fan stating that this scarf was given to her by Presley during a performance in Las Vegas in December, 1976.
(Christie's)
$829

A German publicity postcard franked *Badnauheim 10 11 59,* signed in black ink on the front *Elvis Presley,* additionally signed and inscribed on the reverse, 5¹/₂ x 3¹/₂in.
(Christie's)
$1,380

1950s Elvis Presley merchandising cap, black canvas with black brim and top, multi-colored images screened around the white canvas center section.
(Butterfield & Butterfield)
$633

Elvis Presley signed one sheet for Change of Habit, Universal, 1969, signed on bottom right *Elvis Presley* in black ink, 41 x 28in.
(Butterfield & Butterfield)
$920

Large color ceramic bust of Elvis Presley wearing a white studded jumpsuit, black hair and aqua blue eyes.
(Butterfield & Butterfield)

$518

Elvis Presley Gold Sales award for King Creole, mounted in the floater style black mat with a gold 33¹/₃rpm LP and cassette.
(Butterfield & Butterfield)

$1,150

Elvis Presley off-white soft leather coat with three knotted leather button front closure and two front slit pockets.
(Butterfield & Butterfield)

$1,380

Framed black and white photograph of a young Elvis Presley leaning forward on his elbows, signed on left in blue ink *To Jo Ann From Elvis Presley*, framed 11¹/₄ x 8³/₄in.
(Butterfield & Butterfield)

$1,265

Elvis Presley personal and concert boots, white leather, mid calf high, inside zip-closure boots and squared tip, with a photograph of Elvis wearing the boots.
(Butterfield & Butterfield)

$4,600

Elvis Presley autographed photograph, signed on center left, *To Bob My Sincere Thanks for everything and the best of luck to you in the future, Elvis Presley*, framed.
(Butterfield & Butterfield)

$10,350

Elvis Presley signed air travel card issued to Elvis Presley and V E Presley, expired in October of 1979, signed on verso, *Elvis Presley* in blue ink.
(Butterfield & Butterfield)

$3,738

Elvis Presley make-up chair from the Lisa Marie, deep ocher colored folding metal chair.
(Butterfield & Butterfield)

$575

Elvis Presley concert stage belt, white leather with gold medallions studded with faux moodstones, cabochon, sapphire and gold faceted studs.
(Butterfield & Butterfield)

$25,300

Elvis Presley signed one sheet for Jailhouse Rock, Metro-Goldwyn-Mayer, 1957, 41 x 28in.
(Butterfield & Butterfield)
$2,587

Elvis Presley, 1956, pink pillow with sketch depicting a young Elvis playing the guitar and belting out a song, 10¹/₂ x 10¹/₂in.
(Butterfield & Butterfield)
$633

Elvis Presley signed one sheet for Kid Galahad, United Artists, 1962, signed in the middle in black ink, 41 x 28in.
(Butterfield & Butterfield)
$1,150

Elvis Presley signed acetate for She Used To Be Mine, Elvis Presley's personal copy, signed on left of original envelope *Thanks Elvis Presley* in blue ink, framed 15 x 12in.
(Butterfield & Butterfield)
$1,495

Elvis Presley merchandising souvenir scarf with various images of Elvis performing, the the shades of blue, beige and brown, dated *1956 Elvis Presley Enterprises All Rights Reserved*, 32in. square.
(Butterfield & Butterfield)
$184

Elvis Presley signed album cover of Elvis Presley's 1960 RCA release His Hand In Mine with depiction of Elvis playing piano on the cover, signed *To Bud from Elvis Presley*, 14⁵/₈ x 14⁵/₈in.
(Butterfield & Butterfield)
$1,725

Commemorative Elvis Presley stand-up vinyl doll, identification, wearing a white and gold jumpsuit, 21in. high.
(Butterfield & Butterfield)
$316

Graceland street sign erected by the City of Memphis opposite Graceland to direct visitors to the mansion after Elvis's death, circa 1978.
(Butterfield & Butterfield)
$1,840

Vintage RCA microphone with chrome mesh top, used by Elvis as well as many others at the RCA studios.
(Butterfield & Butterfield)
$8,625

Elvis Presley black leather shirt having a low V-neck and zipper on left side seam.
(Butterfield & Butterfield)
$2,875

Elvis Presley, signed 7in. circular complimentary souvenir menu, for his summer festival at the Las Vegas Hilton.
(T. Vennett-Smith)
$279

Elvis Presley polka dot shirt, circa 1960s, a personal polyester navy knit, button down front with long pointed collar.
(Butterfield & Butterfield)
$1,035

Elvis Presley, signed and inscribed 4 x 5in. front to advertising brochure for the 1970 summer festival, International Hotel Las Vegas.
(T. Vennett-Smith)
$279

Elvis Presley signed early American Express card, circa 1950s, small purple and white paper American Express card issued to Elvis A. Presley, signed on front bottom center *Elvis A. Presley* in blue ink.
(Butterfield & Butterfield)
$63,000

Elvis Presley early black and white photograph of Elvis Presley, screened on lower left *Sincerely Elvis Presley* in blue ink
(Butterfield & Butterfield)
$316

Elvis Presley signed one sheet for Love Me Tender, Twentieth Century-Fox, 1956, 41 x 28in.
(Butterfield & Butterfield)
$3,163

Elvis Presley, a California Indians Honor Jacket of beige twill and a typescript letter addressed to Colonel Parker concerning the shooting jacket.
(Christie's)
$4,490

Elvis Presley signed one sheet for G.I. Blues, Paramount, 1960, 41 x 28in.
(Butterfield & Butterfield)
$1,495

Elvis Presley RCA overnight case made of black plastic with gold plastic lining, given to Elvis Presley by RCA in 1956. (Butterfield & Butterfield)
$863

Elvis Presley Rolls Royce key, small key with 14ct gold top with Rolls Royce *RR* logo in center and *Elvis Presley* along border. (Butterfield & Butterfield)
$2,070

Elvis Presley sterling silver wristwatch, Timex, signed on dial and case *Timex Electronic*, purchased while filming Stay Away Joe, on location in Arizona. (Butterfield & Butterfield)
$2,185

Elvis Presley short suede jacket from Double Trouble, Metro-Goldwyn-Mayer, 1967, pale blue colored suede waist jacket having flared cuffs with single snap closure. (Butterfield & Butterfield)
$7,475

Elvis Presley helmet from Viva Las Vegas, Metro-Goldwyn-Mayer, 1964, having a red stripe down the middle, a lightning bolt on either side with white lettering reading *Lucky*. (Butterfield & Butterfield)
$11,500

Elvis Presley, handwritten inspirational note, *Philosophy for happy life: Someone to love, something to look forward to, and something to do!* Signed *E.P. 1972*, framed, 4³/₄ x 6¹/₂in. (Butterfield & Butterfield)
$4,025

Summer Festival billboard, actual size billboard for Elvis Presley that was displayed outside of the Las Vegas Hilton. (Butterfield & Butterfield)
$690

Elvis Presley shirt, circa 1970s, a fuschia polyester personal shirt with pointed collar, button front and balloon sleeves. (Butterfield & Butterfield)
$920

Elvis Presley shirt, worn on the cover of Guitar Man album, white cotton button down shirt having two front flap pockets. (Butterfield & Butterfield)
$3,163

A mid-18th century German white enamel box, circa 1760, the hinged cover depicting two young boys overlooking a gentleman fishing, 3¹/₂in. long.
(Bonhams) $1,256

A Battersea enamel oval plaque, printed in brown with a Ravenet engraving of George II and the words *Georgius II Rex*, in gilt metal mount, 9.5cm.
(Phillips) $558

A late 18th century South Staffordshire pink enamel box, decorated with a raised white painted floral motif, the hinged cover painted with a rustic scene, 9¹/₄in. long.
(Bonhams) $1,413

A fine George IV 18 carat gold circular snuff box, cover set with a late 18th century enameled portrait miniature of a gentleman, by A. J. Strachan, 1824, 8.2cm. diameter, 6oz. gross.
(Phillips) $11,520

A 19th century Viennese gem-set silver-mounted enamel cornucopia, maker's mark of Rudolf Linke, the horn decorated with a painted scene of Mercury and Herse, flanked by her two sisters, 8¹/₄in. high.
(Bonhams) $2,041

A pair of late 18th century green enamel South Staffordshire salt cellars, cauldron shape, painted with deep magenta and blue flowers against a white background, 2¹/₂in. diameter.
(Bonhams) $471

A good English enamel plaque, printed and overpainted with a scene after Boucher to a conte of La Fontaine, depicting a harbor scene, 10.5 x 8.4cm.
(Phillips) $698

An enameled beaker in 'Alhambra' style, painted by A. Bucath, signed, with fanciful birds among scrolling plants, 18.5cm., possibly Lobmeyr.
(Phillips) $653

An enamel pug's head snuff box, circa 1800, possibly German, the white dog with cream and black markings and pink tongue, 1⁵/₈in. diameter.
(Bonhams) $1,805

ELECTRIC

An elegant MTC table fan with decorative green cast iron housing, circa 1920.
(Auction Team Köln) $423

An American cast iron standard fan, with brass blades and brass diffuser, circa 1890, 145 cm. high.
(Auction Team Köln) $577

A large AEG fan with brass blades and cage, 44 cm. diameter.
(Auction Team Köln) $346

A German Ziehl-Abegg cast iron desk fan with gold decoration, brass blades and cage, circa 1925.
(Auction Team Köln) $253

The first ever hot air fan with 2 stroke hot air motor driven by a copper petroleum lamp, on a richly decorated cast metal tripod stand with 2 wooden carrying handles, 113cm. high, only known example, circa 1860.
(Auction Team Köln) $4,173

A prototype Spontan desk fan, Swedish, with fabric blades and molded wooden base, circa 1935.
(Auction Team Köln) $539

A large swiveling General Electric fan, with brass blades, cage 43 cm. diameter.
(Auction Team Köln) $115

A German Dr. Max Levy desk fan, with brass 30 cm. diameter rotor blades, without cage.
(Auction Team Köln) $192

A Siemens Model W 250T fan with tilting facility, brass blades 26 cm. diameter.
(Auction Team Köln) $214

A fan signed *Vanoni*, the leaf painted with a
fête champêtre, the mother of pearl sticks
pierced and gilt, 11in., circa 1885.
(Christie's)   **$1,919**

A Dutch fan, the leaf painted with a lady in a
carriage beside an angel and cupid and two
vignettes of a formal garden, 11in., circa 1770.
(Christie's)   **$524**

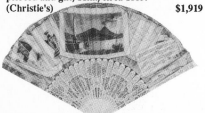

A Grand Tour fan, the leaf painted with a
trompe l'oeil with two views of Vesuvius on the
night of 14th November 1776 and the caves of
Posilipo, 10in., circa 1776, in contemporary
fan box.
(Christie's)   **$1,046**

Diana the Huntress, a painted fan, the verso
painted with brightly colored flowers against
a dark ground, the ivory sticks painted with
two double portraits recto and verso, 11in.,
circa 1690.
(Christie's)   **$5,231**

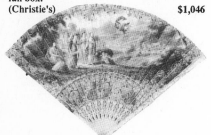

Herse espied by Mercury, a fine fan, the leaf
painted with Mercury flying over the three
sisters returning from the festival of Minerva,
10in., circa 1730.
(Christie's)   **$1,919**

One of a pair of Indian handscreens of plaited
split ivory, partly stained green and silver
thread, with ivory handles, the tips carved
with elephant's heads, 15in., late 18th century.
(Christie's)   (Two)   **$3,313**

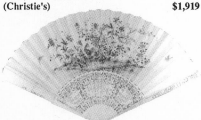

A Chinese fan, the leaf painted with a cockerel
by a flowering tree, with an inscription, the
verso with sprays of flowers, 12in., late 18th
century.
(Christie's)   **$436**

A framed fan, the leaf painted with Diana the
Huntress, the mother of pearl sticks pierced
and gilt, 11in., French, circa 1860, framed and
glazed.
(Christie's)   **$698**

A Canton tortoiseshell brise fan, carved and pierced with figures and animals, 7in., circa 1820.
(Christie's)   **$1,918**

A fine ivory brise fan, carved and pierced with a hunting scene, the guardsticks with flowers, 10in., Chinese, late 18th century.
(Christie's)   **$1,918**

A late 18th century Italian fan painted with Pompeian scenes and having intricately carved ivory guards, together with an unmounted chicken skin fan painted with the Roman Pantheon.
(McCartneys)   **$1,727**

George, Prince of Wales, a printed fan, the leaf an etching of vignettes of Queen Charlotte and the Prince, the verso with *Ich Dien*, the Prince of Wales's feathers, and prayer, with wooden sticks, 11in., circa 1760.
(Christie's)   **$1,395**

A carved ivory handscreen, Ceylon, 17th century, composed of radiating segments of ivory enclosed within gilt copper bands, the handle carved with a female deity with two attendants, 20in., 17th century.
(Christie's)   **$4,534**

The Spy Cartoon fan, a wooden brise fan painted with fifteen copies of Pelegrini's Spy and Ape cartoons of Disraeli, Palmerston, the Marquess of Hartington, the Marquess of Lorne and others, 9in., circa 1865.
(Christie's)   **$436**

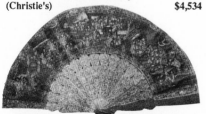

A Canton fan, painted with figures on terraces, their faces of ivory, their clothes of silk, 11in., circa 1860, in shaped red lacquer box, labeled *Volong Canton*.
(Christie's)   **$1,255**

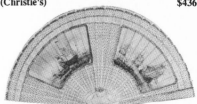

A brise fan, painted with the Luxemburg Palace and Laykente Palace, Brussels, and two naval engagements on the verso, 7in., late 19th century.
(Christie's)   **$2,615**

A circular skirt and matching bolero, of faux leopardskin, labeled *Biba, size 12*, 1970's. (Christie's) **$429**

A dress of black jersey, with oatmeal yoke forming a flower pendant, labeled *Jersey Couture by Pierre Cardin*, 1972. (Christie's) **$274**

A Teddy Boy suit of blue wool, with black velvet lapels, cuffs and pockets, labeled in nape *Rose Tailors, 19 Savile Row, London W1*, 1950s. (Christie's) **$342**

A jacket of black wool, with top stitched detail, trimmed with gilt interlocked 'C' buttons, labeled *Chanel*, 1970s. (Christie's) **$479**

A mini dress of black suede, appliqué with simulated emeralds and pastes in star bursts, labeled *Yves St Laurent, Paris*, stamped *020294*, mid 1960s. (Christie's) **$1,283**

A suit of blue and red bouclé wool, bound in blue petersham, trimmed with pierced gilt buttons, labeled in nape *Chanel*, late 1960s. (Christie's) **$650**

An evening dress of chestnut brown velvet, the sleeves embroidered with butterflies, labeled *Thea Porter,* 1970's.
(Christie's) $155

A circular cape of pale pink wool, inset with bands of felt printed with 'wiggle and check' and 'tasseled circle', 1970, Zandra Rhodes.
(Christie's) $4,446

A coat of sugar pink wool, with two asymmetrically arranged patch pockets, labeled *Courrèges Paris,* 1970s.
(Christie's) $155

A mini dress of white organza, embroidered with white daisy flowerheads with pink and green leaves, labeled *Courrèges, Paris,* 1960s.
(Christie's) $599

A pair of tartan bondage trousers, with black toweling bum flap and tartan strap between the legs, labeled *Malcolm McLaren, Vivienne Westwood, Seditionaries Personal Collection.*
(Christie's) $770

A lady's smoking suit, of black silk crepe, with white waistcoat with mandarin collar and necktie, the jacket labeled *Yves St Laurent, Rive Gauche.*
(Christie's) $223

A maxi coat of orange plush, with deep stand collar, labeled *Biba*, 1970s.
(Christie's) $291

A black satin mantle, lined with white satin, reversible, trimmed with black and white silk cord, labeled in tassel *Liberty & Co.*
(Christie's) $270

A cocktail dress of black chiffon, bound in gold lamé, embroidered with red and gilt bugle beads, mid 1920s.
(Christie's) $589

Kathryn Grayson costume from Two Sisters From Boston, Metro-Goldwyn-Mayer, 1946, a forest green wool two-piece suit.
(Butterfield & Butterfield) $460

An opera cloak of black velvet woven with gold lamé bands of geometric patterns, lined with honey colored velvet and a stenciled velvet shawl and a woven jacket.
(Christie's) $387

A mantle of mauve satin, trimmed with mauve ribbon, lined in lilac silk, the hem hobbled, circa 1910.
(Christie's) $84

A white cotton robe, woven with a sateen stripe, trimmed with slotted lilac ribbons, 1870s; and a similar white cotton jacket. (Christie's) $219

A dress of copper shot silk woven with a chine spot and trimmed with fringing and braid, early 1870s. (Christie's) $351

An evening jacket of taupe chiffon velvet woven with japonaiserie motifs and trimmed with silk fringes, 1920s. (Christie's) $438

An opera coat, of dark blue satin embroidered and appliqué with Chinese figures and flowers, adapted from a Chinese informal robe, 1920s. (Christie's) $337

An evening coat of ivory silk damask with deep cape collar trimmed with lace, lined with fleecy lambskin, 1910–20. (Christie's) $387

A gentleman's banyan, of ivory silk brocaded with stripes and posies of flowers, the silks 1760s, the gown made up in the early 19th century. (Christie's) $168

A mini dress of ivory wool crepe, the collar and cuffs embroidered with opalescent sequins, labeled *Pierre Cardin, Paris*, late 1960s.
(Christie's) $172

A blouse of emerald chiffon, with three quarter sleeves with deep chiffon frilled cuffs, labeled *BIBA*, 1970's.
(Christie's) $94

A suit of chocolate and cream checked wool, the short bell shaped jacket trimmed with three elaborate leather buttons, labeled in nape *Givenchy, 1960's*.
(Christie's) $308

A matching coat and dress ensemble, of white gabardine, trimmed with black leatherette squares on pockets, labeled *FM (Fortnum & Mason), Made in France*, 1960.
(Christie's) $172

A charcoal grey felt tunic, with large zip fastening side to side, printed with a roundel of fluorescent green 'Aztek' design, labeled *World's End*.
(Christie's) $514

A suit of scarlet ribbed wool, with sham slit vertical pockets to square collared jacket, labeled in jacket *Mary Quant, London, and Miss Fortnum, at Fortnum & Mason, London*, 1960s.
(Christie's) $172

A 'Pirate' shirt and matching culottes, of dark blue striped cotton, labeled *World's End, McLaren, Westwood, Born in England*; and a 'Pirate' sash.
(Christie's) $547

A suit of pale apricot knitted wool, trimmed with 'wet look' leatherette collar, yoke and belt, labeled *Courrèges Paris*, and a blouse piped in yellow, 1970s.
(Christie's) $155

A bolero waist coat and matching chain mail skirt, composed of silver and gilt links, with gilt shoulder bag, late 1960s.
(Christie's) $240

A dress of raspberry pink suede, flecked with gilt, with tie neck, long tapered sleeves and shaped buttons, labeled *Jean Muir, London, size 10*.
(Christie's) $304

A lady's chain mail bolero jacket, with three quarter length sleeves, the hems trimmed with deep chain fringes, Italian, circa 1967.
(Christie's) $68

A suede coat, composed of salmon pink, russet and plum colored leather, with candy pink scarf ties, labeled *Jean Muir, London, size 10*.
(Christie's) $1,198

A circa 1930 Georgian style stained pine desk belonging to Hollywood legend David Selznick and a fixture in his famous Hollywood home on Summit Drive, 106in. wide. (Christie's East)

A 1936 first edition of Gone With The Wind by Margaret Mitchell, the first copy given to Ms. Mitchell by her publishing company. (Christie's East) $11,500

Addams Family Values, 1994, a proto-type miniature electric chair for the character 'Thing', 19¹/₂in. high. (Christie's East) $1,495

$11,500

Statue from Citizen Kane, RKO, 1941, depicts an old, bearded, muscular Bacchus wearing a wrapped skirt, on a circular base, 80in. high. (Butterfield & Butterfield) $6,900

Wonder Woman, a collection of accessories worn by actress Lynda Carter in the 70s television series Wonder Woman, including her trademark lame headband and matching waist belt. (Christie's East) $4,600

Star Trek, NBC Television, 1966–1969, from the third season of the series a small, rectangular black painted prop futuristic communicator, 4¹/₂ x 3in. (Butterfield & Butterfield) $5,463

Howard Hughes autograph, inscription handwritten in black ink reads *To Carl Laemmle...I want to express the deepest admiration and respect for you, Mr Laemmle - Howard Hughes,* 5¹/₂ x 7in. (Butterfield & Butterfield) $2,300

Alfred Hitchcock, a fine signed and inscribed 8 x 10in., head and shoulders. (T. Vennett-Smith) $465

Betty Grable, a silver cigarette box engraved on the front cover *To Betty Grable"Queen of the Pin-Up-Girls" from Movie Stars Parade September 30, 1943,* 4¹/₂ x 6in. (Christie's East) $1,610

Walt Disney, signed album page, 4.5 x 4in.
(Vennett Smith) $973

Boris Karloff, a customised, 1941 Schick manufactured injector razor, the bakelite handle features the engraved *Boris S. Karloff*.
(Christie's East) $633

Mack Sennett, signed album page, with attached photo.
(T. Vennett-Smith) $109

The Howdy Doody Show, a Howdy Doody puppet constructed in the image of Buffalo Bob's best friend Howdy, dressed in the familiar red plaid shirt, faded jeans and red cowboy boots.
(Christie's East) $23,000

Bette Davis, a three page handwritten letter to Hal Wallis on Ms. Davis' personal stationery 'My Bailiwick', discussing her feelings on starring with Katharine Hepburn in Whitewater .
(Christie's East) $690

Marilyn Monroe autographed Divison of Special Services card, together with a black and white photograph of Marilyn taken while she was signing the card.
(Butterfield & Butterfield) $2,185

Steven Spielberg, signed colour 8 x 11$^{1}/_{2}$in., half-length surrounded by cartoon characters.
(T. Vennett-Smith) $101

Batman Returns, 1992, a first pair of sleek black gloves worn by Michelle Pfeiffer as Catwoman, mounted in a yellow and black lucite display case, 15in. in length, accompanied by a photograph.
(Christie's East) $4,830

A signed photograph of Walt Disney, pictured with the recipient 'Pat', a set decorator, 20.5 x 25.5cm.
(Sotheby's) $863

Jean Harlow, a pair of size four black suede and cream leather dress shoes, the interior label of the open filigree style shoes reads *Walk Over, Cabana.*
(Christie's East) **$1,955**

James Bond prop briefcase, black hard case which opens to reveal a 007 monogrammed portable pushbutton phone with antenna, a tape recorder, etc., 12½ x 16¾ x 3¼in.
(Butterfield & Butterfield) **$2,185**

Dune, 1983, a rare Flame Gun constructed of gray painted cast-resin, the oversized pistol features both front and rear handles, 24in. in length.
(Christie's East) **$748**

Cleopatra, 1962, a Roman shield from Caesar's army used in the epic film starring Elizabeth Taylor and Richard Burton, of brown painted fiberglass with attached cloth rear straps, 40½ x 22½in.
(Christie's East) **$1,495**

A horse drawn carriage used in The Wizard of Oz, 1939. The Barouche, Civil War era, circa 1865–1870 Brewster manufactured carriage is constructed of hand-forged iron work, the body of American hardwoods.
(Christie's East)
$40,250

The Andrews Sisters, a 1955 legal judgement document between the 'Andrew Sisters Eight To The Bar Ranch, Inc.', signed on the last page.
(Christie's East) **$575**

Clark Gable, a Hawkeye basket outdoor 'refrigerator' used by actor Clark Gable, circa 1950s, 15 x 19in.
(Christie's East) **$1,150**

Citizen Kane, 1941, an original pre-production script for A Mercury Production of Citizen Kane written by Orson Welles and Herman J. Mankiewicz, inscribed *To Chris, Orson Welles.*
(Christie's East) **$7,475**

Saturday Night Fever, 1977, a pair of black leather boots worn by Karen Lynn Gorney, with 3½ in. stack heels.
(Christie's East) **$4,830**

Batteries Not Included, 1987, a robot ship prop, originally wired to illuminate, constructed of vacu-form with applied detailing and two acrylic eyes.
(Christie's East) $518

An original contract for Tom Cruise to appear in Born on the Fourth of July, signed on the last page, *Tom Cruise*, together with an early color photograph of the actor, signed, 8 x 10in.
(Christie's East) $920

A model house created for The Wizard of Oz, 1939, modelled after Dorothy's farmhouse in Kansas, and constructed of painted wood and sturdy cardboard, 7½ x 16 x 20in.
(Christie's East) $11,500

A costume from the production Little Buddha, comprising a tunic in patchwork hide, wicker skirt and belt, shoulder-piece, orange turban, two gold-colored bracelets and prop dagger in scabbard.
(Sotheby's) $1,630

The Ten Commandments, 1956, a pair of Tablets from the Cecil B. deMille epic starring Charlton Heston, made of thick, richly hewn fiberglass, 24in. high.
(Christie's East)
                          $81,700

Little House on the Prairie, 1974–1983, a teaching tool from the family television series, constructed of carved wood in the shape of a paddle, 12¼in. long.
(Christie's East) $805

John Wayne, a brown felt cowboy-style hat, together with an ornate silver cigarette case engraved *John Wayne*, and a heavy gold tone shoe horn, engraved on the back *Duke*.
(Christie's East) $5,520

Elaine's portrait from The Graduate, 1967, consisting of an artist's canvas stretched over back boards with a photograph of Elaine applied to the front, 24 x 20in.
(Christie's East) $9,200

The Flintstones, 1995, an over-sized briefcase, hand painted and fashioned to look purposely distressed and primitive, three seashells serve as case locks, 15½ x 19¼in.
(Christie's East) $2,300

Mary Pickford/Douglas Fairbanks, a signed and dedicated photograph to Mrs. Cochran.
(Bonhams) $314

Adrian original prototype for Margaret Hamilton's Wicked Witch Hat from The Wizard of Oz, Metro-Goldwyn-Mayer, 1939.
(Butterfield & Butterfield)
                            $4,600

Laurel and Hardy, postcard signed by both on their last tour of the U.K.
(Bonhams) $345

John Goodman lunchbox from The Flintstones, 1994, blue and black painted styrofoam over-sized lunchbox with brown handle, printed *Flintstone* on lavender painted nameplate, 23 x 21¹/₂ x 8in.
(Butterfield & Butterfield)
                            $2,875

Marriage certificate from the state of Arizona, certifying that on June 19th, 1935, Errol Flynn and Liliane Marie Madeleine Carre were wed. Signed as the contracting parties, *Errol Flynn and Liliane Marie Madeleine Carre*, 11¹/₄ x 13¹/₂in.
(Butterfield & Butterfield)
                            $3,450

Dummy heads of Susan Sarandon and Geena Davis from Thelma & Louise, Pathe/Main, 1991, rubber casts of the actresses bearing wide-eyed and open-mouthed expressions of fear.
(Butterfield & Butterfield)
                            $4,600

Brown Derby sketch of Clark Gable, black ink caricature by Vitch, with exaggerated ears and lips, inscribed *To Bob - Best Wishes Always, Clark*, 14 x 11in.
(Butterfield & Butterfield)
                            $2,875

Creature head and hands cast from original mould from Creature From the Black Lagoon, Universal, 1954, rubber head and hands painted shades of monster green.
(Butterfield & Butterfield)
                            $2,185

Leslie Caron costume from Daddy Long Legs, Twentieth-Century Fox, 1955, an off-white jersey knit loose-fitting robe of calf length.
(Butterfield & Butterfield)
                            $230

Six-pack of J.R. Ewing Private Stock Beer, label reads, *J.R. Ewing Stock Beer 'If you have to ask how much my beer costs, you probably can't afford it.'*
(Butterfield & Butterfield)

$259

Shirley Temple autograph on cream colored parchment paper reading, *To Uncle Carl Laemmle from your little friend, Shirley Temple,* 6⁷/₈ x 8⁷/₈in.
(Butterfield & Butterfield)

$489

Alien Egg from Alien 3, 20th Century Fox/Brandywine, 1992, constructed of latex rubber and filled with polyurethane foam.
(Butterfield & Butterfield)

$1,840

Vitch Brown Derby black ink caricature sketch of a serious James Cagney, inscribed on lower right, *To The Brown Derby with condolence - if the customers stay away take it down! Jim Cagney,* 14 x 11in.
(Butterfield & Butterfield)

$1,380

Errol Flynn autographed 8 x 10in. black and white photograph, production still from The Warriors, Allied Artists, 1955, inscription reads *Hello Flower! Errol Flynn,* also British Quad poster for Roots of Heaven, 20th Century Fox, 1958.
(Butterfield & Butterfield)

$633

Magazine clipping with a photograph of Lauren Bacall from the film To Have and Have Not, clipping autographed *Lauren Bacall* and the photograph autographed *Humphrey Bogart's.*
(Butterfield & Butterfield)

$805

George Sanders coat from All About Eve, 20th Century Fox, 1950, a charcoal wool topcoat having a large black velvet shawl collar.
(Butterfield & Butterfield)

$316

Herbie 'The Luv Bug' pedal car from Disney On Ice, red and silver glittered, miniature, hollow, fiberglass Volkswagen with red, white and blue stripe, 40 x 101in.
(Butterfield & Butterfield)

$1,150

Sigourney Weaver costume piece from Alien 3, 20th Century Fox, 1992, a dull army-green short-sleeved oversized cotton sweatshirt.
(Butterfield & Butterfield)

$920

The Adventures of Don Juan, 1949, a pair of daggers used by Errol Flynn in his last big-budget motion picture, 17¹/₂in. in length.
(Christie's East) $5,750

Marilyn Monroe, a scarce signed check, 29th December 1959, to the Moss Typewriter Co., for $10.40, Marilyn Monroe Production Inc.
(T. Vennett-Smith)
    $3,178

A taped and stitched black collapsible top hat used by W.C. Fields, circa early 1900s, during his early vaudeville act as a vagabond tramp juggler.
(Christie's East) $2,300

Lana Turner, a March 29, 1956 agreement between actress Lana Turner and Metro-Goldwyn-Mayer Studios which terminates Ms. Turner's contract with them, signed on last page *Lana Turner.*
(Christie's East) $690

Batman Returns, 1992, a custom umbrella used by Danny DeVito as The Penguin, the red and white triangular umbrella panels are constructed with a brass handle, 43in. high.
(Christie's East) $2,070

Laurel and Hardy, a scarce signed and inscribed 7 x 10in. photographic caricature, by both Stan Laurel and Oliver Hardy, Spanish Edition, photo by Stax.
(T. Vennett-Smith) $930

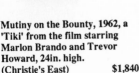

JAMES DEAN

Mutiny on the Bounty, 1962, a 'Tiki' from the film starring Marlon Brando and Trevor Howard, 24in. high.
(Christie's East) $1,840

Senior High School yearbook featuring James Dean, together with copy of the 1956 Fairmount High School Black and Gold annual with tribute to James Dean.
(Butterfield & Butterfield)
    $4,313

Gunsmoke, 1955–1975, an original poster used in the production of the popular television western, 9 x 12in.
(Christie's East) $207

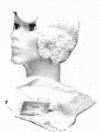

Elizabeth Taylor's MGM Studios dressing dummy, circa 1945, the padded dummy measuring 34³/₄in. bust, 22¹/₄in. waist and 36in. hip, 29¹/₂in. high. (Sotheby's) $538

Casablanca, 1943, the 1940 Buick Phaeton automobile used in the ultimate classic film, Casablanca, starring Humphrey Bogart and Ingrid Bergman. (Christie's East) $211,500

Jean Harlow, a platinum silk wig, braided and set in the flapper style, on the inside of the wig, the tag *M.G. Slattery, Boston,* handwritten *J. Harlow.* (Christie's East) $690

Tyrone Power, an early 1940s show program from The Post Theatre featuring the U.S. Marine Corps in Cherry Point, North Carolina, signed on the cover in blue ink *Tyrone Power,* 9 x 6in. (Christie's East) $575

Greta Garbo, a 1967 letter on 'Revillon at Saks Fifth Avenue' stationery, to the actress, signed at the bottom of the letter *Greta Garbo,* together with a black and white photograph, 14 x 12¹/₂in. (Christie's East) $1,610

Female skeleton from Interview with the Vampire, constructed of latex-covered plastic and having distressed remnants of a white linen top and cotton floral print skirt, 5ft 1in. high. (Butterfield & Butterfield) $1,725

Casablanca, 1943, Best Picture Academy Award presented to Hal B. Wallis, gold plated Britannia statue. (Christie's East) $145,500

Saturday Night Fever, 1977, a pair of dance shoes worn by actress Karen Lynn Gorney, black leather, 3¹/₂in. t-strap shoes specially reinforced. (Christie's East) $3,680

A cape used in the production of Superman, 1978, in red felt with yellow 'S' logo, blue ties and red nylon collar. (Sotheby's) $3,229

Jerry Lewis publicity poster, Paramount, circa 1955, French, linen backed, 47¼ x 31¾in.
(Butterfield & Butterfield)
$345

Alfred Hitchcock, signed 9 x 11½in., head and shoulders, with file holes to left-hand side and some creasing.
(T. Vennett-Smith) $202

Bright Eyes, Fox, 1936, jumbo window card, linen backed, 28 x 22in.
(Butterfield & Butterfield)
$1,840

Danny Kaye costume pieces from Merry Andrew, Metro-Goldwyn-Mayer, 1958, an extra large clown outfit, with photo still.
(Butterfield & Butterfield)
$431

Rare 1947 Mickey Mouse Ingersoll watch in-store display, the only one known to exist, together with a 1947 Ingersoll Mickey Mouse watch.
(Butterfield & Butterfield)
$23,000

Mickey Mouse store banner from The Mickey Mouse Club television program, golden burlap fabric imprinted red and black with an image of Mickey Mouse, 47 x 47in.
(Butterfield & Butterfield)
$920

Woody Woodpecker alarm clock, having Woody Woodpecker attached and pivoting with the ticking of the clock, 5 x 5in.
(Butterfield & Butterfield)
$287

Roy Rogers alarm clock, attached to the face is a small cut-out of Roy Rogers riding Trigger which pivots with the ticking of the clock, 5 x 4½in.
(Butterfield & Butterfield)
$517

Promotional ashtray from That Hamilton Woman, United Artists, 1941, inset in the center with a circular black and white photograph of Vivien Leigh, 6in. diameter.
(Butterfield & Butterfield)
$920

Psycho, Paramount, 1960, one
sheet, linen backed, 41 x 27in.
(Butterfield & Butterfield)
$575

The Wizard of Oz, Metro-
Goldwyn-Mayer, 1939, title
card, 11 x 14in.
(Butterfield & Butterfield)
$6,900

Laura, 20th Century Fox, 1944,
one sheet, framed, 41 x 27in.
(Butterfield & Butterfield)
$6,325

My Fair Lady, Warner
Brothers, 1965, Italian, style B,
linen backed, 55 x 39¹/₂in, art by
Nistri.
(Butterfield & Butterfield)
$1,150

Gone With the Wind, Metro-
Goldwyn-Mayer, 1939, half
sheet, linen backed, framed,
28 x 22in.
(Butterfield & Butterfield)
$6,325

Yvonne De Carlo portrait
poster, Universal-International,
circa 1950, Italian, one sheet,
linen backed, 39¹/₂ x 27¹/₂in.
(Butterfield & Butterfield)
$402

Lawrence of Arabia (Lawrence
d'Arabie), Columbia, 1962,
French, linen backed, 62 x 45in.
(Butterfield & Butterfield)
$1,380

How Green Was My Valley,
20th Century Fox, 1941, six
sheet, linen backed, 81 x 81in.
(Butterfield & Butterfield)
$920

The Kid, First National, 1921,
three-sheet, linen backed,
81 x 41in.
(Christie's East)
$41,400

Slave Ship, 20th Century Fox, 1937, one-sheet, linen backed, 41 x 27in.
(Christie's East) $805

A Dog's Life, First National, 1918, one-sheet, 41 x 27in.
(Christie's East)
                          $32,200

Hello Trouble, Columbia, 1932, one-sheet, linen backed, 41 x 27in.
(Christie's East) $2,990

Queen Christina, MGM, 1934, Leader Press one-sheet, linen backed, 41 x 27in.
(Christie's East) $690

The General, United Artists, 1926, half-sheet, conservation paper backed, 22 x 28in.
(Christie's East) $9,200

Riffraff, MGM, 1936, Leader Press one-sheet, linen backed, 41 x 27in.
(Christie's East) $805

The Fighting Ranger, Columbia, 1934, one-sheet, linen backed, 41 x 27in.
(Christie's East) $3,910

She Married Her Boss, Columbia, 1935, one-sheet, paper backed, 41 x 27in.
(Christie's East) $2,760

Ben Hur, MGM, 1927, original German poster, linen backed, 56 x 37in.
(Christie's East) $2,070

The Wagon Show, First National, 1927, one-sheet, linen backed, 41 x 27in.
(Christie's East) $2,300

Duck Soup, Paramount, 1933, one-sheet, linen backed, 41 x 27in.
(Christie's East) $9,200

The Kid, First National, 1921, one-sheet, 41 x 27in.
(Christie's East) $21,850

The Gilded Lily, Paramount, 1935, one-sheet, linen backed, 41 x 27in.
(Christie's East) $1,265

Breakfast at Tiffany's, Paramount, 1961, six-sheet, linen backed, 81 x 81in.
(Christie's East) $1,725

Disraeli, Warner Brothers, 1929, one-sheet, linen backed, 41 x 27in.
(Christie's East) $805

Kissing Time, Vitaphone, 1934, one-sheet, linen backed, 41 x 27in.
(Christie's East) $748

Cleopatra, Paramount, 1934, one-sheet, paper backed, 41 x 27in.
(Christie's East) $12,650

Swiss Miss, MGM, 1938, original Australian one-sheet, linen backed, 41 x 27in.
(Christie's East) $1,150

Jimmy the Gent, Warner
Brothers, 1934, one-sheet, linen
backed, 41 x 27in.
(Christie's East) $3,680

Don't Ever Marry, First
National, 1921, one-sheet, linen
backed, 41 x 27in.
(Christie's East) $518

Eight Girls in a Boat,
Paramount, 1934, one-sheet,
41 x 27in.
(Christie's East) $460

The Heart of Maryland, Metro,
1915, three-sheet, linen backed,
81 x 41in.
(Christie's East) $1,725

Napoleon Bonaparte,
Paramount, 1935, original
French poster, linen backed,
63 x 94in.
(Christie's East) $4,600

Carmen of the Border,
Goldstone, 1923, three-sheet,
linen backed, 81 x 41in.
(Christie's East) $863

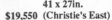

Cabaret, ABC/Allied Artists,
1972, Italian, linen backed, 55 x
39in. (Butterfield & Butterfield)
     $402

The Grim Game, Paramount,
1919, one-sheet, linen backed,
41 x 27in.
(Christie's East) $19,550

Grandma's Boy, Associated,
1922, one-sheet, linen backed,
41 x 27in.
(Christie's East) $9,200

State's Attorney, RKO, 1932, one-sheet, linen backed, 41 x 27in.
(Christie's East) $805

Blind Husbands, Universal, 1919, one-sheet, linen backed, 41 x 27in.
(Christie's East) $6,900

Love and Doughnuts, Associated, 1921, one-sheet, linen backed, 41 x 27in.
(Christie's East) $920

The Glorious Lady, Selznick, 1919, three-sheet, linen backed, 81 x 41in.
(Christie's East) $1,093

The Lawless Nineties, Republic, 1936, six-sheet, linen backed, 81 x 81in.
(Christie's East) $7,475

Creature from the Black Lagoon, Universal, 1954, three-sheet, linen backed, 81 x 41in.
(Christie's East) $6,325

Dante's Inferno, 20th Century Fox, 1935, one-sheet, linen backed, 41 x 27in.
(Christie's East) $1,725

The Maltese Falcon, Warner Brothers, 1941, window card, paper backed, 22 x 14in.
(Christie's East) $4,025

The Magnificent Ambersons, RKO, 1942, one-sheet, linen backed, 41 x 27in.
(Christie's East) $2,530

Rancho Notorious, RKO, 1952,
original Italian poster, linen
backed, 55 x 39in.
(Christie's East) $1,150

Pluto's Fledgling, RKO, 1948,
one-sheet, linen backed,
41 x 27in.
(Christie's East) $920

The Private Life of Henry VIII,
United Artists, 1933, one-sheet,
linen backed, 41 x 27in.
(Christie's East) $5,750

White Oak, Paramount, 1921,
one-sheet, linen backed,
41 x 27in.
(Christie's East) $3,220

It's a Wonderful Life, RKO,
1946, half-sheet, paper backed,
22 x 28in.
(Christie's East) $2,530

The Cold Deck, S.A. Lynch,
1917, one-sheet, paper backed,
41 x 27in.
(Christie's East) $8,625

Forbidden Planet, MGM, 1956,
original Australian one-sheet,
41 x 27in.
(Christie's East) $1,380

Dimples, 20th Century Fox,
1936, one-sheet, paper backed,
41 x 27in.
(Christie's East) $3,680

Souls for Sale, Goldwyn, 1923,
one-sheet, linen backed,
41 x 27in.
(Christie's East) $805

For A Few Dollars More, PEA, 1967, original Italian poster, linen backed, 55 x 39in.
(Christie's East) $1,150

Whoopee, United Artists, 1930, one-sheet, linen backed, 41 x 27in.
(Christie's East) $2,875

Dangerous Business, First National, 1920, one-sheet, linen backed, 41 x 27in.
(Christie's East) $1,035

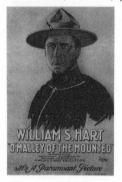

O'Malley of the Mounted, Paramount, 1921, one-sheet, linen backed, 41 x 27in.
(Christie's East) $1,380

Follow the Fleet, RKO, 1936, six-sheet, linen backed, 81 x 81in.
(Christie's East)
                          $16,100

The Invisible Man, Universal, 1933, original Danish poster, linen backed, 35 x 24in.
(Christie's East) $863

The Man from Planet X, United Artists, 1951, one-sheet, linen backed, 41 x 27in.
(Christie's East) $4,140

The Oklahoma Kid, Warner Brothers, 1939, original Italian poster, linen backed, 40 x 27in.
(Christie's East) $3,220

Outside the Law, Universal, 1921, one-sheet, linen backed, 41 x 27in.
(Christie's East) $2,760

Wine, Universal, 1924, one-
sheet, paper backed, 41 x 27in.
(Christie's East)   **$2,530**

Judge Priest, Fox, 1934, one-
sheet, paper backed, 41 x 27in.
(Christie's East)   **$690**

Sally, First National, 1930, one-
sheet, linen backed, 41 x 27in.
(Christie's East)   **$690**

Bobby Bumps Gets Pa's Goat,
Universal, 1915, one-sheet, linen
backed, folded, 41 x 27in.
(Christie's East)   **$1,495**

Good-Bye Bill, Paramount,
1918, one-sheet, linen backed,
41 x 27in.
(Christie's East)   **$575**

Exquisite Lake Louise,
Paramount, 1920, one-sheet,
linen backed, 41 x 27in.
(Christie's East)   **$690**

Showboat, Universal, 1936,
original Swedish poster, linen
backed, 48 x 36in.
(Christie's East)   **$575**

Tom Thumb, Celebrity, 1936,
one-sheet, linen backed,
41 x 27in.
(Christie's East)   **$1,495**

The Westerner, United Artists,
1940, original Argentinian
poster, linen backed, 43 x 29in.
(Christie's East)   **$2,070**

How to Eat, MGM, 1939, one-sheet, linen backed, 41 x 27in.
(Christie's East) $2,070

Cupid's Round Up, William Fox, 1918, one-sheet, 41 x 27in.
(Christie's East) $3,220

Baby, Take a Bow, Fox, 1934, one-sheet, 41 x 27in.
(Christie's East) $2,070

Camille, First National, 1927, one-sheet, linen backed, 41 x 27in.
(Christie's East) $575

The Night Before, William Fox, 1921, one-sheet, linen backed, 41 x 27in.
(Christie's East) $575

With Byrd at the South Pole, Paramount, 1930, one-sheet, linen backed, 41 x 27in.
(Christie's East) $748

The Bitter Tea of General Yen, Columbia, 1933, framed, 41 x 27in.
(Christie's East) $7,475

Dick Whittington's Cat, Celebrity, 1936, one-sheet, linen backed, 41 x 27in.
(Christie's East) $1,495

King of the Jungle, Paramount, 1933, one-sheet, linen backed, 41 x 27in.
(Christie's East) $1,725

Eddie Murphy, signed, head and shoulders from Harlem Nights, 8 x 10in.
(Vennett Smith) $63

Peter Lorre, signed and inscribed, head and shoulders, 4 x 5 in.
(Vennett Smith) $118

Peter Sellers, signed, head and shoulders as Inspector Clouseau, 8 x 10in.
(Vennett Smith) $228

Betty Grable, signed and inscribed, head and shoulders, first name only, signed in later years, 5 x 7in.
(Vennett Smith) $78

Walt Disney, an unusual large sheet, featuring three pencil sketches of Mickey Mouse, Pluto and Donald Duck, eaeh drawn and signed by three Disney artists (Franklin Thomas, Webb Smith etc.),Walt Disney himself has then signed the base of the sheet, 12 x 10in.
(Vennett Smith) $1,730

Maxie Rosenbloom, 'Slapsy', signed and inscribed, head and shoulders, smoking cigarette, 8 x 10in.
(Vennett Smith) $55

Sharon Stone, signed color half-length in dressing gown, 8 x 10in.
(Vennett Smith) $102

Pamela Anderson, signed color, three quarter length naked in bath, 8 x 10in.
(Vennett Smith) $141

Sadie Frost, signed color, full-length in costume from Dracula, 8 x 10in.
(Vennett Smith) $102

William Hartnell, signed postcard, head and shoulders in bow tie, probably 1950.
(Vennett Smith) $94

Audrey Hepburn, signed, full-length seated on floor talking on phone, 8 x 10in.
(Vennett Smith) $188

Jason Scott Lee, signed, head and shoulders, wearing large cross around his neck, 8 x 10in.
(Vennett Smith) $91

Emil Jannings, signed postcard, head and shoulders in profile, wearing hat and smoking cigarette.
(Vennett Smith) $110

Hope & Lamour, signed, by Bob Hope, Dorothy Lamour and Jimmy Van Heusen, from the Road to Zanzibar, modern reproduction signed in later years, 8 x 10in.
(Vennett Smith) $75

Walt Disney, early signature on Christmas card, cut and laid down to contemporary scrapbook page.
(Vennett Smith) $319

Robert De Niro, signed, half-length, slight smudging, 8 x 10in.
(Vennett Smith) $96

Vivien Leigh, signed postcard, as Scarlett O'Hara, from Gone With the Wind.
(Vennett Smith) $754

Klaus Kinski, signed postcard, showing a young Kinski, signed in later years, 4 x 6in.
(Vennett Smith) $44

Tom Mix, signed sepia postcard, Ross, 1654, in cowboy outfit. (T. Vennett-Smith) **$140**

Sal Mineo, signed 7¹/₂ x 9¹/₂in., head and shoulders. (T. Vennett-Smith) **$372**

Peter Finch, signed postcard, half-length seated. (T. Vennett-Smith) **$101**

Sharon Stone, signed color 8 x 10in., head and shoulders, wearing gray tee-shirt and resting her chin on her hands. (T. Vennett-Smith) **$85**

Sylvester Stallone, signed color 8 x 10in., half-length, apparently obtained in person in New York 1992. (T. Vennett-Smith) **$62**

A circa 1960's color photograph of Elizabeth Taylor in evening gown, signed *Elizabeth Taylor,* 14¹/₂ x 12in. framed. (Christie's East) **$518**

Ben Turpin, signed and inscribed 5 x 7¹/₂in., in characteristic pose. (T. Vennett-Smith) **$372**

William Boyd, signed and inscribed 8 x 10in., full-length on horseback as 'Hopalong'. (T. Vennett-Smith) **$248**

Haing S. Ngor, signed 8 x 10in., half-length from 'The Killing Fields'. (T. Vennett-Smith) **$50**

Marlene Dietrich, signed postcard, Picturegoer 598, early. (T. Vennett-Smith) $81

Montgomery Clift, signed and inscribed album page, 5 x 4in. (T. Vennett-Smith) $108

Vivien Leigh, signed postcard, Picturegoer W422. (T. Vennett-Smith) $202

Fred and Adele Astaire, early signed sepia 7 x 5in., by both Fred and Adele Astaire, full-length dancing. (T. Vennett-Smith) $186

Gary Cooper, signed made-up magazine montage of four pictures, laid down to $9^{1}/_{2}$ x $7^{1}/_{2}$in. page, signed three times. (T. Vennett-Smith) $116

Grace Kelly, a good signed sepia postcard, head and shoulders, reproduction of earlier photo, signed in later years. (T. Vennett-Smith) $372

Nigel Bruce, signed and inscribed postcard, 1941, head and shoulders, smoking pipe. (T. Vennett-Smith) $217

Bette Davis, a color window card from the 1951 film Payment on Demand, signed in black marker, 10 x 13in. (Christie's East) $437

Veronica Lake, signed 6 x $8^{1}/_{2}$in., three quarter length in low-cut dress, by statue. (T. Vennett-Smith) $481

Margaret Rutherford, signed
postcard, head and shoulders,
with hands clasped.
(T. Vennett-Smith) $163

Marissa Tomei, signed color
8 x 10in., half-length from My
Cousin Vinny.
(T. Vennett-Smith) $54

Kay Kendall, signed and
inscribed postcard, full-length
dancing.
(T. Vennett-Smith) $101

A 1944 black and white
photograph of Marlene Dietrich
from Kismet, featuring the
actress in the dance of the Lady
In The Moonlight, inscribed and
signed, 11^{1}/$_2$ x 9^{1}/$_4$in.
(Christie's East) $748

Autographed Milton Greene
photograph of a melancholy
Marilyn Monroe in a black top
hat and black scarf, signed on
upper middle, *Dear Clifton, With
admiration. Norma Jean*,
18^{1}/$_8$ x 15^{1}/$_8$in.
(Butterfield & Butterfield)
          $2,300

A black and white photograph
of actor James Dean in 1955, the
year he filmed Rebel Without a
Cause, signed and dated in black
ink *James Dean 7/6/55*, 13^{3}/$_4$ x
10^{3}/$_4$in.
(Christie's East) $3,220

Nastassja Kinski, signed color
8 x 10in., first name only, three
quarter length seated in bikini
by poolside.
(T. Vennett-Smith) $124

Orson Welles, an early black
and white photograph, circa mid
1930s, signed in blue ink *Orson
Welles*, 10 x 8in.
(Christie's East) $633

Charles Hawtrey, signed
postcard 'Charles Hawtrey
Carry On', half-length seated at
desk.
(T. Vennett-Smith) $140

Sadie Frost, signed color 8 x 10in., head and shoulders, in evening gown, from Dracula. (T. Vennett-Smith) $62

Mistinguett, signed and inscribed postcard, head and shoulders, with hands clasped. (T. Vennett-Smith) $46

Brigitte Bardot, signed color 8 x 10in., three quarter length seated in lace see-through dress. (T. Vennett-Smith) $83

An early 1950s black and white photograph of the comedy team of Dean Martin and Jerry Lewis, inscribed and signed in blue ink by both, 10 x 8in. (Christie's East) $978

Stan Laurel, typed signed letter, first name only, one page, 11th February 1960, to Jennie and Jack, advising on the foreign help situation and the real estate business. (Vennett Smith) $102

Clark Gable, a black and white photograph, together with a yellow piece of paper, signed in green ink Clark Gable, mounted together, 14 x 11in. (Christie's East) $805

Vivien Leigh, signed postcard, three quarter length as Scarlett O'Hara, from Gone With The Wind. (T. Vennett-Smith) $744

Cheers, a color photograph of the original cast of the successful television show, signatures in blue ink include Rhea Perlman, Kirsty Ally, Ted Danson, Woody Harrelson and Kelsey Grammar, 8 x 10in. (Christie's East) $805

Hedy Lamarr, signed sepia postcard, with her real name 'Hedy Kiesler', three quarter length standing, 10th May 1933. (T. Vennett-Smith) $147

Frederic March, signed
postcard, Picturegoer 702a.
(T. Vennett-Smith) $50

Mabel Normand, signed sepia
8 x 10in., full-length in costume.
(T. Vennett-Smith) $403

Peter Sellers, signed postcard,
head and shoulders.
(T. Vennett-Smith) $59

Judy Garland, signed
program to front cover
photo, London Palladium 1960,
obtained in person after the
show.
(T. Vennett-Smith) $434

Destry Rides Again, 1940, a
black and white photograph of
co-stars James Stewart and
Marlene Dietrich, signed in blue
and black ink by both, 10 x 8in.
(Christie's East) $863

Charlie Chaplin, an early 1900s
photograph card of the actor,
signed on the lower mat
Sincerely Charlie Chaplin,
7 x 5in.
(Christie's East) $1,380

Danny Kaye, signed and
inscribed 8 x 10in., head and
shoulders.
(T. Vennett-Smith) $93

Marlon Brando, signed
postcard, head and shoulders,
rare.
(T. Vennett-Smith) $403

James Cagney, signed and
inscribed 8 x 10in., head and
shoulders.
(T. Vennett-Smith) $93

Bela Lugosi, signed 8 x 10in., head and shoulders.
(T. Vennett-Smith) **$512**

Norma Shearer, signed sepia 8 x 10in., head and shoulders.
(T. Vennett-Smith) **$171**

Bing Crosby, signed and inscribed sepia 8 x 10in.
(T. Vennett-Smith) **$65**

Charles Chaplin, signed postcard, head and shoulders, early, overmounted in ivory, framed and glazed, 9¹/₂ x 11¹/₂in. overall.
(T. Vennett-Smith) **$264**

Pretty Woman, color 8 x 10in. of poster from Pretty Woman, signed by Richard Gere and Julia Roberts, inscribed by Roberts.
(T. Vennett-Smith) **$275**

Susan Hayward, a black and white photograph of the actress in evening dress, inscribed and signed, *Good Sentiments Susan Hayward*, 8 x 10in., framed.
(Christie's East) **$1,093**

Pamela Anderson, signed color 8 x 10in., full-length in white bikini.
(T. Vennett-Smith) **$74**

Clark Gable, signed postcard, head and shoulders, from Mogambo.
(T. Vennett-Smith) **$372**

Mel Gibson, signed color 8 x 10in., half-length in army uniform from 'Gallipoli'.
(T. Vennett-Smith) **$54**

Sonja Henie, signed postcard, head and shoulders, 4 x 5.5in.
(Vennett Smith) $57

Burt Lancaster, signed, 5 x 7in.
(Vennett Smith) $113

Cary Grant, signed sepia postcard.
(Vennett Smith) $149

Anna Magnani, signed postcard, trimmed, head and shoulders, 3 x 4in.
(Vennett Smith) $110

Walt Disney, signed album page, early example, also signed *Mickey Mouse*, scarce in this form, 4 x 2.5in.
(Vennett Smith) $754

Jayne Mansfield, signed and inscribed card, with small attached photo.
(Vennett Smith) $118

Lucille Ball, signed and inscribed, full signature, 8 x 10in.
(Vennett Smith) $165

Lon Chaney Jnr, signed as *The Wolfman*, with attached photo, 5 x 4in.
(Vennett Smith) $322

Phil Silvers, signed and inscribed, head and shoulders, 8 x 10in.
(Vennett Smith) $118

Judy Holliday, signed, 7.5 x 10in.
(Vennett Smith) $118

Grace Kelly, signed postcard, Picturegoer D621.
(Vennett Smith) $298

The Three Stooges, signed, first names only, 4.25 x 5in.
(Vennett Smith) $408

Robert Newton, signed postcard, head and shoulders, probably 1950.
(Vennett Smith) $63

Taylor & Hedren, signed, by both Rod Taylor and Tippi Hedren from 'The Birds', 10 x 8in.
(Vennett Smith) $50

Audrey Hepburn, signed, full-length standing, from 'Breakfast at Tiffany's, 8 x 10in.
(Vennett Smith) $298

Barbara O'Neil, signed sepia, played Scarlett's mother in Gone with the Wind, 8 x 10in.
(Vennett Smith) $251

Richard Gere, signed and inscribed, from King David, 8 x 10in.
(Vennett Smith) $55

Ruth Gordon, signed and inscribed, head and shoulders, 1963, 8 x 10in.
(Vennett Smith) $47

Hurrell black and white portrait photograph of Norma Shearer in profile, stamped on verso, 14 x 11in.
(Butterfield & Bútterfield)
$345

Hurrell black and white photograph of a smiling Jean Harlow in a white fur, stamped on verso, 10 x 8¹/₈in.
(Butterfield & Butterfield)
$173

Hurrell black and white photograph of Alice Faye resting her head upon a cushion, stamped on verso, 14¹/₈ x 11¹/₄in.
(Butterfield & Butterfield)
$633

Signed Cecil Beaton black and white photograph of a smiling Joan Crawford in a standing ³/₄ rear pose, signed on board in red crayon pencil lower left *Beaton*, 17¹/₂ x 12¹/₂in.
(Butterfield & Butterfield)
$460

Hurrell black and white photograph of Erich Von Stroheim from As You Desire Me, Metro-Goldwyn-Mayer, 1931, as the character Salter, stamped, 13 x 10in.
(Butterfield & Butterfield)
$345

Hurrell black and white photograph of Greta Garbo from Romance, Metro-Goldwyn-Mayer, 1930, in a long dark gown with a string of pearls, stamped, 13 x 10¹/₈in.
(Butterfield & Butterfield)
$403

Hurrell black and white photograph of Joan Crawford with her chin resting on her arm, stamped on verso, 10¹/₈ x 8in.
(Butterfield & Butterfield)
$403

Hurrell black and white publicity photograph of Errol Flynn in a light colored turtleneck, stamped on verso, 9¹/₂ x 7¹/₂in.
(Butterfield & Butterfield)
$230

Hurrell black and white photograph of Joan Crawford from No More Ladies, Metro-Goldwyn-Mayer, 1935, stamped on verso, 10 x 8¹/₈in.
(Butterfield & Butterfield)
$288

Hurrell black and white photograph of a dashing Leslie Howard in a suit and tie, stamped, 13 x 10in.
(Butterfield & Butterfield)

$230

Black and white photograph of Marlene Dietrich as Leda the Swan, with a handwritten note on a blue note card.
(Butterfield & Butterfield)

$1,380

Hurrell black and white photograph of Joan Crawford in a beret and fur, stamped, 13 x 10in.
(Butterfield & Butterfield)

$374

Signed Hurrell black and white photograph of Carole Lombard peering seductively with lowered eyelids, signed in black ink lower left *Hurrell*, matted, 14 x 11in.
(Butterfield & Butterfield)

$805

Hurrell black and white photograph of Rita Hayworth and Fred Astaire from You Were Never Lovelier, Columbia, 1942, stamped on verso, $10^{1}/_{4}$ x $8^{1}/_{4}$in.
(Butterfield & Butterfield)

$374

Hurrell black and white photograph of Johnny Weissmuller from Capture of Tarzan, Metro-Goldwyn-Mayer, 1935, stamped on verso, 13 x $10^{1}/_{8}$in.
(Butterfield & Butterfield)

$460

Hurrell black and white photograph of Tallulah Bankhead smoking in a mirror, stamped on verso *Please credit Hurrell Hollwood*, 10 x $8^{1}/_{8}$in.
(Butterfield & Butterfield)

$575

Hurrell black and white photograph of Kay Johnson from Madame Satan, Metro-Goldwyn-Mayer, 1930, stamped, 13 x $9^{7}/_{8}$in.
(Butterfield & Butterfield)

$316

Hurrell black and white photograph of Joan Crawford in a dramatic pose with her arm raised up across her face, stamped, 13 x 10in.
(Butterfield & Butterfield)

$460

Hurrell black and white photograph of Buster Keaton ashing his cigarette in a long vase, stamped, 13¼ x 10¼in. (Butterfield & Butterfield) $690

A black and white photograph of Vivien Leigh as Scarlett O'Hara in Gone With The Wind, 15 x 11in. (Christie's East) $805

Hurrell black and white photograph of Robert Montgomery in an overcoat and scarf, stamped, 13 x 10¼in. (Butterfield & Butterfield) $345

Hurrell black and white photograph of Jean Harlow, illegible faded signature from Jean Harlow's mother, who often signed her daughter's name, 13 x 10in. (Butterfield & Butterfield) $345

A circa 1948 black and white portrait photograph of Marilyn Monroe, inscribed on lower left *To Sylvia your realle (sic) wonderful Thanks Marilyn Monroe*, 18 x 15½in. (Butterfield & Butterfield) $2,300

Hurrell black and white photograph of a young and debonaire Douglas Fairbanks, Jnr., in a top hat, stamped on lower right *Hurrell*, matted, 14⅛ x 11in. (Butterfield & Butterfield) $403

Hurrell black and white photograph of a sultry Ann Sheridan in a satin robe holding a mirror, stamped on verso, 13⅝ x 10⅜in. (Butterfield & Butterfield) $345

Hurrell black and white photograph of Norma Shearer in a satin gown with velvet top and a white fur, stamped on verso, 13⅛ x 10in. (Butterfield & Butterfield) $345

Black and white photograph of Humphrey Bogart in a white shirt with a tie, signed on middle right, *Good Luck Carol - Humphrey Bogart*, 10⅛ x 10¼in. (Butterfield & Butterfield) $1,495

Hurrell black and white photograph of platinum blonde beauty Jean Harlow in a white dress, stamped, 13 x 10in. (Butterfield & Butterfield)

$345

Hurrell black and white photograph of Jean Harlow in a white satin dress, stamped on verso, 10 x 13in. (Butterfield & Butterfield)

$1,035

Gloria Swanson, a 11 x 14in. picture (portrait), extremely early, framed and glazed, signed to Ben Lyon. (Bonhams)

$236

Autographed black and white portrait photograph of a debonaire Rudolph Valentino, signed lower right, *To Miss Alexandra, With Best Wishes From Rudolph Valentino, Nov. 17-1924*, 10 x 7¹/₂in. (Butterfield & Butterfield)

$1,265

Hurrell black and white photograph of Joan Crawford and Robert Taylor from Gorgeous Hussy, Metro-Goldwyn-Mayer, 1936, signed on mat lower right, *Hurrell '36* in pencil, 18 x 12³/₄in. (Butterfield & Butterfield)

$575

Hurrell black and white autographed photograph of Joan Crawford leaning forward with her hands folded, signed upper right, *For Jack Henry - from Joan Crawford,* 14 x 11¹/₈in. (Butterfield & Butterfield)

$633

Hurrell black and white photograph of Buster Keaton resting his cheek against his hand, stamped *Hurrell* on lower right, 13 x 10in. (Butterfield & Butterfield)

$489

Hurrell black and white photograph of Bette Davis from Dark Victory, Warner Brothers, 1939, Davis dressed in black with a fur hat and jacket, 7¹/₂ x 9¹/₂in. (Butterfield & Butterfield)

$460

Hurrell black and white photograph of Bette Davis from All This and Heaven Too, Warner Borthers, 1940, stamped on verso, 9¹/₂ x 7¹/₂in. (Butterfield & Butterfield)

$316

A brass club fender, early 20th century, with padded ends on turned uprights and joined by a U-shaped apron, 60in. wide.
(Christie's) $3,787

A Victorian brass footman, the rectangular top with side handles and cabriole front legs centered by a trefoil leaf, 19½in. wide.
(Christie's) $548

A baroque style cast metal coal scuttle, circa 1900.
(Auction Team Köln) $137

A pair of cast iron sun-face andirons, stamped *B & H*, late 19th/early 20th century, the cicular fluted finial centering an articulated face, 16³/₄in. high.
(Christie's) $1,380

Cast bronze fireplace surround, Murdoch Foundry, Boston, in the manner of Eliho Vedder, 30½in. wide.
(Skinner) $2,530

A pair of early 18th century brass andirons, baluster turned with portrait busts of Queen Anne to iron frames, on scroll legs.
(Woolley & Wallis)

                                $4,256

A fine walnut Art Nouveau fireplace surround, inlaid with satinwood flowers and scrolls, the frieze inset with a central needlework panel of roses, 5ft. 8in. wide.
(Christopher Matthews)
                                $1,806

A Victorian gothic colored marble fireplace, with red veined shelf above white and green quatrefoil frieze, 106 x 134cm. maximum.
(Bristol) $6,437

A rare and important pair of Chippendale cast-brass and wrought-iron fireplace andirons, probably English, made for the American market, circa 1785, 31in. high.
(Sotheby's) $43,700

A pair of bronze and gilt-bronze chenets, of Transitional style, each modeled as a winged dragon resting on acanthus scrolls, 17³/₄in. and 17in. high. (Christie's) **$1,702**

A pair of cast-iron satyr andirons, American, 20th century, each cast in the half-round with the head of a satyr with pierced eyes and mouth, 11³/₈in. high. (Sotheby's) **$1,035**

A nickel alloy fire grate with railed serpentine basket over a pierced frieze centered by an eagle, 20¹/₂in. wide. (Andrew Hartley) **$868**

A pair of cast-iron Columbia-on-shell andirons, American, 20th century, each cast in the half-round with the figure of Columbia holding a flaming torch, 17¹/₂in. high. (Sotheby's) **$402**

Baroque style carved white marble fire surround, the rectangular mantle over a stepped leaf-carved arched opening, 4ft. 11in. wide. (Butterfield & Butterfield) **$5,325**

A pair of cast-iron dachshund andirons, American, 20th century, each cast in the half-round with a dachshund seated on its haunches, 13¹/₄in. high. (Sotheby's) **$2,587**

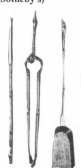

A set of three brass and steel fire-irons, each with cylindrical handle surmounted by an urn-shaped finial, 28³/₄in. long. (Christie's) **$1,883**

A pair of Louis XVI ormolu chenets, each with breakfront plinth centered by a circular paneled medallion with ribbon-twist edge and mask, 14¹/₂in. wide. (Christie's) **$13,984**

A set of three brass and steel fire-irons, each with paneled cylindrical spreading handle with lozenge leaves, 30³/₄in. long. (Christie's) **$717**

A Hardy, the 'Silex Multiplier', 2³/₄in., alloy reel, rounder ivoril thumb bar and quadrant regulator, notched brass foot.
(Christie's) $660

A Wm. H. Talbot, No. 23, German silver baitcasting reel, ivoril handle on an S-shaped counter-balanced arm, drag button.
(Christie's) $695

An E. Paton, Perth, 4¹/₂in., hardwood reel, the brass face with crown logo, brass foot bent.
(Christie's) $451

2872
A stuffed and mounted roach in river bed setting in bow fronted glazed wood case, inscribed in gilt *Roach, caught by Mr R.V.D. White at Downton 5th September 1936, weight 2 lbs. 7 ozs.,* 21 x 12.5in. overall.
(Stainers') $853

A M. Aitken and Son, Crieff, 4in., brass reel, horn handle, inscribed *gunmakers*.
(Christie's) $225

An H. Snowie, Inverness, 3¹/₂in., hardwood reel, inscribed *gunmaker*, to brass face, crack to rim.
(Christie's) $521

A Hardy, the 'Perfect', 4¹/₄in., brass faced reel, ivoril handle, strapped rim-tension adjuster with turk's head locking nut.
(Christie's) $694

A Charles Farlow pot-bellied wicker creel, with engraved name and 191 Strand address to fastening catch, 14¹/₂in. wide overall.
(Christie's) $660

A Hardy, the 'Perfect', 4in., brass faced reel, ivoril handle, strapped rim-tension adjuster with turk's head locking nut.
(Christie's) $694

A B. F. Meek, No. 3, German, silver baitcasting reel, ivoril handle on a counter-balanced arm, drag button, serial No. 2881.
(Christie's) $659

A Hardy oak and brass line-drier, marked *Hardy's W Fitting, Reg'd, 16.8.73*, 12in. wide.
(Christie's) $660

An Edward Vom Hofe, 504, reel, 4in., 4–0 size, counter-balanced central S-shaped handle, marked with *May 20, 02* patent.
(Christie's) $1,302

A Hardy, the 'Cascapedia', 3⁵/₈in., salmon reel, size 3/0, S-shaped counter balanced crossbar with ebonite handle, ebonite backplate with nickel-silver circular Hardy Bros logo.
(Christie's) $10,419

A stuffed and mounted trout in river bed setting in bow fronted glazed wood case, inscribed in gilt *Trout 2 lbs. 8 ozs., caught at Downton Bull Hotel Water by R.V.D. White 25th May 1938*, 22.5 x 10.25in. overall.
(Stainers') $930

A Hardy, the 'Bougle', 3in., alloy reel, Duplicated Mark II, ebonite handle, brass foot, three offset pillars.
(Christie's) $2,690

A Hardy, the 'Perfect', 2⁵/₈in., early alloy reel, ivoril handle, strapped rim-tension adjuster, oval, brass foot.
(Christie's) $1,000

A fly box, with five lift-out card trays containing eight-six gut-eyed salmon flies up to 3in., in length.
(Christie's) $954

A Hardy, the 'Perfect', 4¹/₂in., brass faced reel, ivoril handle, rim-tension adjuster with later brass strap, straightline and rod-in-hand logos.
(Christie's) $382

A Louis XVI carved and décapé frame, with cartouche at top center flanked by garlands of imbricated husks, 27¹/₈ x 21⁵/₈ x 5in.
(Christie's) $7,038

A Dutch 17th century ebonized and tortoiseshell frame, the outer and inner edges with various ripple and wave moldings, diameter 8 x 2⁵/₈in.
(Christie's) $1,232

An Italian 15th or 16th century carved, gilded and painted tabernacle frame, with taenia outer edge, segmented cavetto, 39³/₈ x 23⁷/₈ x 4¹/₂in.
(Christie's) $2,463

A Florentine 17th century carved and gilded reverse profile frame, the pierced foliate outer border running from anthemia at centers to acanthus leaves at corners, 26⁷/₈ x 14⁵/₈ x 5¹/₂in.
(Christie's) $2,463

An Italian 16th century carved, gilded and painted frame, the raised outer edge with dentil molding running to acanthus leaf corners, diameter 27¹/₂ x 4¹/₂in.
(Christie's) $3,167

An Italian 16th century carved and gilded tabernacle frame, the cornice with various moldings, bar-and-triple-bead courses at outer and inner edges, 31 x 24³/₈ x 5¹/₄in.
(Christie's) $28,152

An Italian 16th century carved, painted and gilded tabernacle frame, the entablature with pastiglia harpies and scrolling foliage on blue ground, 10⁷/₈ x 9³/₄in.
(Christie's) $6,158

A Dutch mid 16th century painted and gilded cassetta frame, the central plate with scrolling foliage in pastiglia, 6⁵/₈ x 4³/₈ x 1⁵/₈in.
(Christie's) $4,926

A Louis XIV carved and partly décapé frame, the pierced centers with anthemia and flowers in high relief over a raised central edge, oval 17¹/₂ x 13⁷/₈ x 2³/₄in.
(Christie's) $1,495

BEDS & CRADLES

A 19th century mahogany half-tester child's bed, with canopy and spindles to all sides, 49in. long.
(Boardmans) $730

A Flemish oak cradle, fitted with a liner, with pierced fret S-scroll toprails and shaped sides with lozenge panels, 37in. long.
(Christie's) $1,035

A George III Hepplewhite mahogany canopy bed, the framed canopy with dentil cornice.
(Boardmans)   **$4,560**

A Flemish baroque oak four poster bedstead, with overhanging molded canopy carved with swags and bunches of fruit, 66¹/₂in. wide.
(Sotheby's) $19,550

One of a pair of French thuya, bois satiné and ormolu-mounted beds, each with a bowed end, the headboard with floral swags, 48in. wide.
(Christie's)
(Two) $3,098

An English carved oak tester bedstead, in Charles II style, the molded tester with the frieze below carved with panels of interlaced foliage and flowers, 70in. wide.
(Sotheby's)   **$21,850**

A Victorian mahogany full tester bed with original iron pelmet support, 57in. wide.
(Boardmans) $1,900

A fine Edwardian mahogany and floral inlaid five foot double bed, probably Waring & Gillow.
(Academy) $1,193

An inlaid oak full tester bed, 17th century and later.
(G. E. Sworder & Sons)
    $4,864

A Napoleon III walnut and
burr-walnut lit en bateau, each
paneled and arched end fronted
with canted and paneled
uprights, 79in. wide.
(Christie's) $933

A walnut low-post bed, York
County, late 18th/early 19th
century, with peaked head and
footboards and shaped
truncated sideboards, 73in. long.
(Christie's) $1,035

A Louis Philippe mahogany lit
en bateau, with paterae-
decorated shaped uprights and
U-shaped center on split roundel
feet, 51in. wide.
(Christie's) $1,325

A green-painted maple pencil-
post bedstead, New England,
circa 1800, with four tapering
octagonal posts centering a
pitched red-stained pine
headboard, 55¹/₂in. wide.
(Sotheby's) $6,900

A Napoleon III mahogany and
brass mounted bed, the cresting,
tailboard and sides applied with
tablets with turned urn finials,
144cm. wide.
(Phillips) $760

A very rare maple folding
pencil-post bedstead, New
England, 1770–1800, the tapered
and faceted head posts centering
the original shaped pine
headboard, 4ft. 4in. wide.
(Sotheby's) $5,750

A good Federal red-stained
birchwood, maple and pine
four-poster bed, New England,
circa 1800, with four flaring
octagonal posts, 4ft. 4in. wide.
(Sotheby's) $3,162

An Empire ormolu-mounted
plum-pudding mahogany lit en
bateau, the dished paneled
front with confronting winged
maidens supporting a wreath,
83¹/₄in. wide.
(Christie's) $10,419

A Federal turned birchwood
bedstead, New England, circa
1820, with flaring octagonal
head posts centering an arched
pine headboard, 45in. wide.
(Sotheby's) $2,070

BEDS

An Italian polychrome-decorated bed, 18th century, decorated overall with floral panels, the outscrolled foliate ends with paneled center, 45in. wide.
(Christie's) $2,952

A carved and joined walnut cradle, Pennsylvania, late 18th century, the arched headboard with heart-pierced crest flanked by rectangular posts, 30¾in. wide.
(Christie's) $2,300

L. & J. G. Stickley oak daybed, model 291, 1906–1912, the square slatted end set with an angled rattan woven headrest, 6ft. 4in. long.
(Butterfield & Butterfield) $1,265

An Elizabethan oak bedstead composed of 17th and 19th century elements, the full canopy with compartmented panel, over large baluster-turned posts, 4ft. 9in. wide.
(Butterfield & Butterfield) $1,610

An early George III mahogany tester bed with a molded serpentine cornice and fluted frieze with riband and flowerhead border, 185cm. wide.
(Phillips) $23,312

A Regency engraved brass-inlaid rosewood four-post bed, inlaid overall with brass lines, the square spreading front-supports inlaid in the upper part with a stylized lyre, 81in. wide.
(Christie's) $27,784

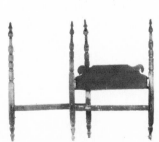  

Painted tall post bed, Northern New England, 1825–35, with original tester, headboard and side rails, original red paint with black accents, 52in. wide.
(Skinner) $3,335

An oak four-post bed, the headboard with three deep panels with rusticated and egg-and-dart edges, English, late 16th century, 74½in. wide.
(Christie's) $33,750

Spanish parcel-gilt and painted bedstead, late 18th century, the headboard painted with a central armorial coat-of-arms, 4ft. wide.
(Butterfield & Butterfield) $2,587

BOOKCASES

A good Victorian figured walnut and gilt metal mounted dwarf open-front bookcase, the whole of slightly shaped outline and with three shaped uprights, each with ornate caryatid, 90in. wide.
(Canterbury) $4,928

A mahogany bookcase-on-stand, with broken foliate-carved pediment above a molded cornice, 60in. wide.
(Christie's) $1,688

An Italian baroque style gilt-bronze-mounted burled walnut bookcase, circa 1860, coved and leaf-cast cornice over inlaid frieze drawers, 8ft. 4in. wide.
(Butterfield & Butterfield) $7,475

A late Georgian oak, walnut crossbanded breakfront bookcase, the upper part with bead molded cornice and deep frieze with reed moulding, 87in. wide.
(Peter Francis) $3,863

A pair of cedar dwarf open bookcases, each with rounded mottled gray marble top above a plain frieze and a column with two adjustable shelves, 25$^{1}/_{4}$in. wide.
(Christie's) $6,599

A Louis XVI style gilt-bronze-mounted mahogany and rosewood bibliothèque, signed *V. Raulin*, last quarter 19th century, the outset cornice with egg-and-dart edge above a paneled cornice, 4ft. 1in. wide.
(Butterfield & Butterfield) $6,900

A George III satinwood secrétaire-bookcase, the base section with molded top above a secrétaire drawer simulated as two graduated drawers, 40in. wide.
(Christie's) $11,661

A Victorian oak breakfront bookcase, the molded cornice above six astragal glazed doors, four frieze drawers and a pair of glazed doors, 112in. wide.
(Christie's) $3,159

A George II oak library bookcase, the upper section with glazed panel doors surmounted by molded cornice, 39in. wide.
(Hy. Duke & Son)
    $3,863

BOOKCASES

A Victorian mahogany breakfront bookcase, by Marsh Jones and Cribb, the ebonized molded edged top with three quarter gallery, 74in. long. (Andrew Hartley)

$2,713

An early 19th century Dutch mahogany bookcase-on-stand, with a fret-carved gallery above the dentil cornice, with tapering square legs, 34in. wide. (Bearne's)

$2,008

A mid-Victorian rosewood-veneered serpentine-fronted open bookcase, the three shelves flanked by scroll-carved canted corners, 52in. wide. (Bearne's)

$4,094

An elm bookcase, the molded cornice above a pair of glazed doors, two frieze drawers and two paneled cupboard doors, French, mid 19th century, 55in. wide. (Christie's)

$2,297

A good pair of mahogany open-front library bookcases in the William IV style, the cornices with twin molded cresting and rectangular panels, 63in. wide. (Canterbury)

$5,390

A Victorian walnut veneered bookcase on cupboard, molded cornice decorated with whitewood inlaid decoration above two glazed doors, 47in. wide. (Peter Wilson)

$3,322

A large Italian baroque walnut bookcase, the upper section with overhanging molded cornice, formed with four niches, 97¹/₂in. wide. (Sotheby's)

$20,700

A composed George IV mahogany bookcase with scroll cornice above twin lancet top, astragal glazed panel doors, 38¹/₂in. wide. (James Adam)

$1,877

A mahogany library bookcase with molded cornice, three pairs of astragal-glazed doors, on a plinth base, 118in. wide, basically George III. (Bearne's)

$4,944

BOOKCASES

A late Victorian oak bookcase, the dentil-molded cornice surmounted by a foliate and bobbin-turned cresting, 67in. wide.
(Christie's) $3,058

George III style mahogany breakfront bookcase, late 19th/20th century, 62¹/₂in. wide.
(Skinner) $4,600

A Victorian oak bookcase, the molded and dentilled cornice, above three glazed doors enclosing adjustable shelves, 72in. wide.
(Christie's) $2,344

A good Victorian figured walnut breakfront library bookcase, base with carved oval and leaf edging, two pairs of mirror paneled doors, on plinth base, 95in. wide.
(Canterbury) $13,590

A Regency rosewood revolving bookstand, the later circular green leather-lined top above an octagonal frieze and four sides with simulated shelves with bookspines, 24in. diameter.
(Christie's) $14,760

An early George III mahogany breakfront library bookcase, the upper part with a swan neck pediment terminating in foliate scrolls with dentil ornament, 282cm. wide.
(Phillips) $24,320

A fine 19th century mahogany breakfront library bookcase, the molded cornice above a pair of central glazed doors enclosing adjustable shelves, 77¹/₂in. wide.
(Diamond Mills & Co.) $5,662

A Biedermeier satinbirch and ebonized bookcase, with two cupboard doors applied with stylized foliate moldings and enclosing shelves, 62in. wide.
(Christie's) $5,574

A walnut and mahogany revolving bookcase, the feather-banded and stellar inlaid top with molded rim above two undertiers with vertical splats, 19¹/₂in. wide.
(Christie's) $544

BOOKCASES

A late Victorian mahogany bookcase, with a pair of glazed doors, two frieze drawers and a pair of paneled cupboard doors below, 50in. wide.
(Christie's) $1,699

A George II mahogany breakfront library bookcase in three parts, the dentil molded cornice with a broken swan neck pediment trellis, 250cm. wide.
(Phillips) $30,400

A Victorian mahogany bookcase, the molded cornice fitted with a pair of arched glazed doors enclosing adjustable shelves, 57in. wide.
(Christie's) $2,815

A 19th century mahogany and inlaid breakfront library bookcase, with a molded dentil cornice and blind fret carved frieze enclosed by four glazed astragal doors, 2.82m. wide.
(Phillips) $12,920

An English bookcase, circa 1870, in three parts, mahogany, the central glazed cabinet flanked by slightly smaller conforming glazed elements, 187cm. wide.
(Sotheby's) $4,543

A Louis XVI mahogany and brass mounted bibliothèque mounted by a gray marble top with rounded corners, containing a frieze drawer, 98cm. wide.
(Phillips) $3,952

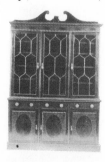

A mahogany line-inlaid bookcase, the broken swan neck pediment with paterae terminals, above three astragal glazed doors, 72in. wide.
(Christie's) $5,436

A mahogany breakfront bookcase, the reeded cornice above a blind-fret frieze, shaped foliate-carved apron, on hairy paw feet, 102in. wide.
(Christie's) $3,089

A late Victorian carved oak bookcase, with overall foliate decoration, the gadrooned cornice above three glazed doors with three drawers, 78in. wide.
(Christie's) $2,473

BUREAU BOOKCASES

A German green and gilt-japanned bureau-cabinet, decorated overall with chinoiserie scenes, mid-18th century oak carcase, 45in. wide. (Christie's) $31,464

A Venetian painted and silvered bureau-cabinet, mid-18th century, decorated overall with C-scrolls, foliate cartouches and sprays of flowers, 45in. wide. (Christie's) $10,419

An oak bureau bookcase, with molded cornice and a pair of fielded paneled cupboard doors, English, the base late 18th/early 19th century, the top late 19th century, 34¹/₂in. wide. (Christie's) $2,185

Queen Anne oyster burl walnut veneer secretary bookcase, in two sections, the upper case with broken rounded arch pediment over two paneled doors, 41½in. wide. (Butterfield & Butterfield) $14,950

A South German ivory-inlaid, walnut, marquetry and parquetry bureau-cabinet, the bow-fronted breakfront rectangular top and plain frieze above a central door, second quarter 18th century, 45¹/₂in. wide. (Christie's) $8,335

A George I walnut bureau-cabinet, feather-banded overall, the molded cornice above two later glazed doors enclosing three adjustable shelves, 41in. wide. (Christie's) $22,874

A George III mahogany secretary bookcase, the base circa 1770, the later upper case with elevated swan's neck pediment, above a plain frieze, 40¹/₂in. wide. (Butterfield & Butterfield) $7,475

A Queen Anne walnut double dome bureau cabinet in three parts, the upper part with a molded arched cornice and fitted interior, 104cm. wide. (Phillips) $39,520

A mahogany bureau bookcase, 18th century, the associated upper part with a molded cornice, the sloping fall enclosing a fitted interior, 45in. wide. (Christie's) $6,885

BUREAU BOOKCASES

An Edwardian mahogany bureau bookcase, the dentil-molded cornice above a pair of astragal glazed doors, 35¹/₂in. wide.
(Christie's) $3,227

An Italian polychrome-decorated bureau-cabinet, the pediment with baluster finials decorated with a central shaped cartouche, 50in. wide.
(Christie's) $19,101

An English oak bureau cabinet, 18th century, the associated top with a molded cornice and enclosed by a pair of paneled doors, 37in. wide.
(Christie's) $2,787

A George I burr-walnut and walnut bureau-cabinet, the rectangular cavetto cornice above a single feather-banded door inset with a later beveled plate, 32in. wide.
(Christie's) $22,575

A Dutch satinwood and purple-wood crossbanded bureau cabinet, 18th century, the upper part with an undulating molded arched cornice and mirrored frieze decorated with a scallop-shell and foliage, 49in. wide. (Christie's) $23,887

An English walnut bureau cabinet, early 18th century, the upper part with a molded cornice, the feather-strung lower part enclosing a fitted interior and well with slide.
(Christie's) $7,962

An early Georgian figured walnut bureau-cabinet, the inverted breakfront cavetto cornice above a single door with a central mirror plate with beveled plate, 31in. wide.
(Christie's) $15,629

A George III mahogany cylinder bureau, crossbanded overall and inlaid with boxwood lines, the molded rectangular cornice above a plain paneled frieze, 43¹/₂in. wide.
(Christie's) $4,575

An Edwardian satinwood crossbanded mahogany bureau bookcase, the broken swan neck cresting above a pair of astragal glazed doors, on bracket feet, 37in. wide.
(Christie's) $1,580

BUREAUX

A walnut 'Eastlake-style' bureau, having a broad corniced rectangular top over two cupboards enclosing shelves and with turned supports, 137.3cm. wide.
(Phillips) $720

A large George III mahogany bureau with a rectangular fall flap enclosing a hinged reading slope fitted to the reverse, 45in. wide.
(Anderson & Garland) $780

A good small early 18th century walnut bureau, with double herringbone inlay, fall flap enclosing a fitted interior, 2ft. 2in. wide.
(John Nicholson) $4,082

A Louis XVI period mahogany, tulipwood crossbanded and marquetry bureau à cylindre, the top with pierced brass gallery and interlaced border, 141cm. wide.
(Phillips) $9,120

A Dutch walnut and crossbanded bombé bureau of 'arc-en-arbelette' form, the rectangular top above a slope enclosing a burlwood interior, 88cm. wide.
(Phillips) $3,344

A Louis XV ormolu-mounted inlaid tulipwood bureau en pente, third quarter 18th century, the shaped surface over a shaped slant lid opening to an inset tooled leather writing surface, 46$\frac{1}{2}$in. wide.
(Butterfield & Butterfield) $3,737

A William and Mary red-painted walnut slant-front desk, New England, early 18th century, the base molding on ball feet, 36in. wide.
(Sotheby's) $10,637

Queen Anne cherry slant lid desk on frame, Norwich, Connecticut, circa 1750, 34³/₄in. wide.
(Skinner) $5,462

An early Georgian oak bureau, the fall front enclosing stepped fitted interior with drawers, pigeon holes and well, 36in. wide.
(Andrew Hartley) $2,198

BUREAUX

A George III mahogany slant-front desk, third quarter 18th century, the case with two short and three long cockbeaded drawers, 43³/₄in. wide.
(Butterfield & Butterfield) $5,750

A good Empire mahogany cylinder bureau, with rich ormolu mounts, the top fitted with three small drawers, over folding cylinder front, 4ft. wide.
(John Nicholson) $16,485

A fine and rare Chippendale carved mahogany block-front slant-front desk, Boston, Massachusetts, circa 1770, 42in. wide.
(Sotheby's) $60,250

An Italian baroque style inlaid walnut slant-front desk, the rectangular top with incurvate sides above an inlaid shaped slant-lid, 46in. wide.
(Butterfield & Butterfield) $2,300

An attractive kingwood bureau de dame in the Louis XV style, the slightly concave rectangular superstructure with pierced gilt metal foliate cast three quarter gallery, 30in. wide.
(Phillips) $6,510

An Italian baroque walnut slant-front desk, first half 18th century, with four graduated long drawers of serpentine outline over a conforming outset molded base, 45in. wide.
(Butterfield & Butterfield) $27,600

A George III oak and banded bureau, the sloping fall enclosing a fitted interior, with drawers below 36in. wide.
(George Kidner) $1,540

Federal walnut slant lid desk, probably Pennsylvania, circa 1800, 41in. wide.
(Skinner) $2,760

A Queen Anne walnut bureau, the rectangular top with a hinged fall enclosing eight pigeonholes and four drawers, 91cm. wide.
(Phillips) $3,040

BUREAUX

Chippendale maple slant lid desk, Connecticut, late 18th century, replaced brass, old refinish, 36in. wide.
(Skinner) **$2,300**

A Queen Anne cherrywood desk-on-frame, Connecticut, 1740–60, on short cabriole legs and pad feet, 34¼in. wide.
(Sotheby's) **$4,025**

Painted maple slant lid desk, New England, late 18th century, with stepped valanced multi-drawer interior, 35.75in. wide.
(Skinner) **$7,475**

A Dutch walnut and burr-veneered bombé bureau, 19th century, the sloping fall enclosing a baize-lined writing surface, a graduated fitted interior and well with slide, 40½in. wide.
(Christie's) **$5,176**

Federal birch and butternut slant lid desk, probably Massachusetts, circa 1810, the interior with ten valanced compartments flanked by three drawers, 39.75in. wide.
(Skinner) **$2,185**

An early George II walnut veneered bureau, with herringbone banding, the fall flap reveals a fitted interior, two short and two long drawers, 3ft. 1in.
(Woolley & Wallis)
$3,952

A George III mahogany rectangular slope-front bureau, the fall front opening to reveal a fitted interior with central cupboard, 42in. wide.
(James Adam) **$1,082**

Mid 18th century walnut veneered bureau, flap with book rest, crossbanding and herring bone string, bracket feet, 32in. wide.
(Peter Wilson) **$2,808**

Dutch neoclassical style mahogany and marquetry slant-lid desk, late 19th century, 37in. wide; together with a similar side chair.
(Skinner) **$2,875**

BUREAUX

Chippendale mahogany oxbow slant lid desk, probably Massachusetts, circa 1780, replaced brasses, 42in. wide. (Skinner) $5,175

George III oak bureau, flap covering fitted interior above four graduated drawers, each fitted with original oval brass plate handles, 37in. wide. (Peter Wilson) $1,389

Diminutive George III oak slant-lid desk, early 19th century, with later carved decoration, 30in. wide. (Skinner) $1,380

A George I walnut-veneered bureau, outlined with boxwood and ebony stringing, the crossbanded sloping flap enclosing a fitted interior, 36in. wide. (Bearne's) $3,553

A late 18th century North Italian inlaid walnut slope front bureau, with profusely engraved inlaid ivory figural and leaf decoration, 43$\frac{1}{2}$in. wide. (James Adam) $12,656

A George II mahogany bureau, the sloping fall enclosing a fitted interior above two short and three long graduated drawers, 45in. wide. (Christie's) $1,931

A George III mahogany bureau, the sloping fall enclosing a fitted interior, above four graduated long drawers, on bracket feet, 40in. wide. (Christie's) $2,297

A Queen Anne oak two-part bureau, the fall front above two short and one long drawers, the lower part with two further drawers, 25in. wide. (Boardmans) $6,840

A late Victorian mahogany and satinwood crossbanded bureau, the indented rectangular molded top surmounted by a turned gallery, 30$\frac{1}{2}$in. wide. (Christie's) $1,128

CABINETS

A 21in. Edwardian mahogany and satinwood inlaid music cabinet, fitted four fall front drawers with shelf below on tapering supports.
(Stainers') $341

A William and Mary lacquered brass-mounted black and gilt-japanned cabinet-on-stand, in the manner of John Stalker, decorated overall with pagodas, 34in. wide.
(Christie's) $10,405

A large Continental gothic style oak cabinet, incorporating 15th century panels, with molded cornice over two large doors, 56½in. wide.
(Sotheby's) $6,325

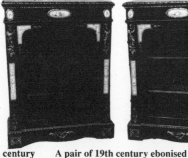

A late 17th/early 18th century black lacquer cabinet on later stand, the doors decorated and heightened in gilt with storks in a watery landscape with a jetty, 92cm. wide.
(Phillips) $2,826

A pair of 19th century ebonised and ormolu side cabinets, each having a breakfront, ovolo and foliate ormolu detailing and single glazed door, 35in. wide.
(Morphets) $6,280

A George III satinwood and marquetry bombé cabinet, crossbanded with rosewood and amaranth, the eared serpentine top above a pair of doors, 39¾in. wide.
(Christie's) $8,073

A French carved walnut two-part cabinet, in Lyon Renaissance style, the recessed upper section with molded cornice and fitted with two doors, 43in. wide.
(Sotheby's) $5,750

An American Renaissance inlaid maple and walnut console cabinet, circa 1870, the rectangular top with incurvate sides with outset canted corners and applied molded edge, 4ft. 2in. wide.(Butterfield & Butterfield)
                         $2,070

A late 19th century Korean hardwood cabinet applied with etched metal mounts, the rectangular projecting top above four short drawers, 99cm. wide.
(Phillips) $836

CABINETS

A Queen Anne walnut cabinet on chest with molded cornice, single glazed door enclosing shelving, 29in. wide.
(Andrew Hartley)
$4,340

A pair of Chinese Export brass-mounted red and gilt-lacquer cabinets-on-stands, decorated overall with chinoiserie landscapes, 22in. wide.
(Christie's)
$7,176

Victorian figured walnut music cabinet with glazed door and turned side pillars.
(Jacobs & Hunt)
$558

A George III brown and black Japanned cabinet on later stand, circa 1800, painted overall with birds, moths and trees on a brown or black ground, 39¼in. wide.
(Butterfield & Butterfield)
$5,750

A pair of Regency rosewood and parcel-gilt side cabinets, each with inset rectangular top with satinwood banding and three-quarter gothic-arched pierced brass-gallery, 42¼in. wide.
(Christie's)
$32,292

A Flemish baroque style walnut cabinet on stand, late 19th century, raised on ring-turned and spiral-carved legs, 42¼in. wide.
(Butterfield & Butterfield)
$8,050

A 22.5in. Victorian ebonized and amboyna wood cross banded bow fronted dwarf music cabinet, with glazed panel door enclosing shelves.
(Stainers')
$305

A pair of George IV inlaid mahogany sideboard cabinets, each outset square top with crossbanded and ebony-strung edge, 38½in. high.
(Butterfield & Butterfield)
$2,875

A mid-Victorian walnut-veneered and marquetry side cabinet, applied throughout with gilt-brass moldings and inlaid with floral sprays, 30in. wide.
(Bearne's)
$2,318

CABINETS

A Victorian gilt metal mounted inlaid figured walnut side cabinet, the straight front with single inlaid door enclosing a velvet lined interior with shelves, 58in. wide.
(Peter Francis) **$2,935**

Austrian Art Deco walnut bar, circa 1930, of asymmetrical form, the rectangular superstructure with a rounded end and glazed sliding doors, max. length 7ft. 2^1/$_2$in.
(Butterfield & Butterfield) **$1,495**

An attractive mahogany side cabinet by Christopher Pratt & Sons of Bradford, the raised center section with interlaced ribbon carved border, 163cm. wide.
(Phillips) **$1,064**

Koloman Moser, cabinet 'Die Verwunschenen Prinzessinnen' (The Enchanted Princesses), circa 1900, of almost triangular section, with two doors applied with six carved opaque green glass teardrops, 21in. wide.
(Sotheby's) **$167,480**

English Arts & Crafts inlaid walnut and rosewood side cabinet, in the style of Charles Bevan, circa 1870, the elevated backsplash carved with gothic motifs, 4ft. 4^1/$_2$in. wide.
(Butterfield & Butterfield) **$2,587**

Russian neoclassical style brass-mounted side cabinet, 19th century, galleried superstructure over a rectangular case fitted with mullioned cabinet doors, 39^1/$_4$in. wide.
(Skinner) **$9,200**

A French composite gothic oak cabinet, late 15th/early 16th century, fitted with four doors and drawers all carved with gothic tracery, 49^1/$_2$in. wide.
(Sotheby's) **$5,462**

A grain-painted poplar side cabinet, Pennsylvania, circa 1830, the oblong top surmounted by a scrolling three-quarter gallery, 45^1/$_2$in. wide.
(Sotheby's) **$8,050**

An English Charles II two-part oak cabinet, the dentilled paneled upper section fitted with a large drawer applied with raised panels, 44in. wide.
(Sotheby's) **$5,750**

CABINETS

A Flemish rosewood and ivory-mounted table cabinet with geometric 'ivory' line inlay, the front with a door flanked by six drawers, 11¼in. wide.
(Hy. Duke & Son) $1,082

A pair of Chinese Export black lacquer table cabinets of rectangular form, the exteriors decorated in shades of gilt with mountainous landscapes, 18th century, 21¼in. wide.
(Hy. Duke & Son)

$2,858

One of a pair of Japanese lacquer Export cabinets, 17th century, the doors with lake scenes in takamakie, supported on an elaborate Flemish gilt wood stand, total height 4ft. 10in. (Sotheby's) $16,042

A Regency style satin-veneered and tulipwood-banded side cabinet, with a pair of frieze drawers and a pair of roundel decorated grille and silk paneled doors flanked by two concave-shaped shelves, 56in. wide.
(Christie's) $1,931

An Eastern European cabinet, veneered in Hungarian ash, banded in sycamore and oak, having engraved steel mounts and lock plates, 4ft. ½in.
(Woolley & Wallis)

$3,800

A Victorian mahogany Sheraton Revival serpentine side cabinet, enclosed by a pair of doors inlaid with harewood and boxwood, the slender out-turned legs supporting an undertier, 48in. wide, circa 1900.
(Neales) $2,504

An Art Nouveau stained oak dentil cabinet, arched pediment with white wood inlay, above two glazed doors flanking twelve graduated small drawers, 36in. wide.
(Peter Wilson) $1,174

A gilt-metal-mounted floral marquetry walnut side cabinet, the eared rectangular top above a pair of paneled doors, on plinth base, some veneer missing, 55in. wide.
(Christie's) $4,239

Art Deco bird's-eye maple cabinet, circa 1930, in two parts, the upper case with lobed cornice over conforming cupboard doors, 4ft. 7in. wide.
(Butterfield & Butterfield)

$4,025

CABINETS

A Victorian walnut, amboyna, crossbanded and inlaid music cabinet, with gilt metal spindle gallery on turned columns, 61cm. wide.
(Phillips) $1,292

Renaissance Revival ebonised, rosewood and marquetry side cabinet, late 19th century, with handpainted porcelain plaques, 57in. long.
(Skinner) $1,955

A 1930s mirrored glass and ebonized cabinet, the rectangular form with two doors enclosing a partly mirrored interior, 89cm. wide.
(Phillips) $390

A late 17th century Japanese lacquer cabinet on later stand, the rectangular top above a pair of cupboard doors decorated with pavilions and flowering trees, 91cm. wide.
(Phillips) $6,694

A pair of japanned lacquer cabinets-on-stand, late 19th/ early 20th century, each cabinet decorated with figures in pagoda landscapes, on floral knopped legs terminating in scroll feet, 145cm. wide.
(Christie's) $13,770

A japanned cabinet on stand, the cabinet Queen Anne, circa 1710, decorated throughout with chinoiseries, the associated stand probably late 17th century, 115cm. wide.
(Sotheby's) $6,774

A mid 19th century rosewood parquetry side cabinet applied with gilt metal mounts in the Louis XV/Transitional style, molded rectangular brescia marble top, 125cm. wide.
(Phillips) $2,432

A George III satinwood and ebony strung duet music cabinet, the dividing sliding top concealing a compartment and with brass insets to take the mahogany lyre shaped rests, 68cm. wide.
(Phillips) $5,652

A French parquetry and gilt-bronze side cabinet, Paris, circa 1870, the shaped brêche violette top above a frieze applied with ribbons and a pair of 'S' bowed doors, 112cm. wide.
(Sotheby's) $8,912

CANTERBURYS

A Victorian walnut music canterbury, crossbanded in rosewood and strung with ebony and box, 22in. wide.
(Phillips) $578

A Victorian walnut canterbury with four carved divisions above single drawer and on turned legs.
(Academy) $1,585

A late 19th century mahogany four division canterbury, with bobbin turned side and corner columns joined to a platform, 44cm. wide.
(Phillips) $1,064

A Federal mahogany canterbury, attributed to Duncan Phyfe, New York, circa 1805, each side fitted with a striped mahogany molded panel with a roundel on each end, 23in. wide.
(Sotheby's) $7,475

A Regency mahogany canterbury with four 'X' shaped divisions above a drawer, on turned legs and castors, 47cm. wide.
(Phillips) $2,584

A George III satinwood canterbury, the dished rectangular top with three columned divisions above an amaranth-crossbanded mahogany-lined drawer, 18in. wide.
(Christie's) $7,918

A George IV mahogany four-division canterbury, with ring-turned corner uprights and two apron drawers, on ring-turned tapering legs, 18¹/₂in. wide.
(Christie's) $3,270

A late Georgian mahogany canterbury of rectangular form, the five slatted divisions with concave top rails, 18in. wide.
(Peter Francis) $1,700

A George IV rosewood canterbury, the four compartments with X-shaped ends and with foliate carrying-handle, on a rectangular base, 22¹/₂in. wide.
(Christie's) $12,236

DINING CHAIRS

Marcel Breuer, pair of chairs, designed in 1932, with padded back and seat on curved aluminium frame.
(Sotheby's) $3,634

Carlo Bugatti, side chair, circa 1900, the vellum seat bordered by beaten copper mount, strung with circular vellum back rest.
(Sotheby's) $3,452

Pair of Renaissance Revival rosewood side chairs, attributed to Pottier and Stymus, circa 1865, 35in. high.
(Skinner) $920

Two of a set of six Regency brass-inlaid rosewood-grained side chairs, circa 1815, each concave rectangular crest with brass-inlaid scrolling foliage.
(Butterfield & Butterfield)
(Six) $4,025

One of a pair of Venetian walnut chairs, with cane seats and Cupid's bow crestrails, mid 18th century.
(Finarte)
(Two) $3,533

Two of a set of six George III style carved mahogany side chairs, each rocaille carved crest above a pierced scroll and ribbon carved splat.
(Butterfield & Butterfield)
(Six) $4,025

Two of a set of eight Regency rosewood, simulated rosewood and brass marquetry dining chairs, forming two carvers and six single.
(Boardmans)
(Eight) $8,900

Stained Queen Anne maple side chair, New England, 18th century, with old rush seat and early surface.
(Skinner) $1,150

Two of a set of eight George II style mahogany dining chairs, circa 1870, each shaped crestrail with scrolled ears over a shaped pierced splat.
(Butterfield & Butterfield)
(Eight) $5,175

296

DINING CHAIRS

A pair of classical paint-decorated, parcel-gilt and brass-mounted side chairs, Baltimore, Maryland, circa 1820.
(Sotheby's) $1,265

Chippendale mahogany carved side chair, Connecticut, circa 1780.
(Skinner) $1,092

A pair of Victorian oak hall chairs, of Carolean design, the carved scrolling toprails centered by a pierced crown.
(Christie's) $1,308

Two of a set of six Regency gilt-metal-mounted caned beechwood side chairs, circa 1815, each baluster and ring-turned crest over two scrolled horizontal splats.
(Butterfield & Butterfield)
(Six) $3,565

One of a pair of late Victorian mahogany framed side chairs, with carved crest rail above padded panel and vase splat.
(James Adam)
(Two) $712

Three of a set of eight late 18th century design mahogany dining chairs, each having an open shield-shape back with pierced vertical splat carved with corn husks, circa 1920.
(Morphets)
(Eight) $5,338

  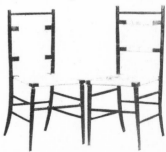

A pair of William and Mary turned maple rush-seat bannister-back side chairs, Massachusetts, 1730–50, each with a shaped swan's-neck crest above four split balusters.
(Sotheby's) $4,312

One of a set of twelve Chippendale style mahogany dining chairs with carved and pierced urn-shaped splats and claw and ball feet, circa 1900.
(Sworder)
(Twelve) $9,000

E. W. Godwin, three side chairs, designed circa 1869, ebonized turned and grooved wooden frames, with cane seats and backs.
(Sotheby's) $1,454

DINING CHAIRS

A fine pair of George II mahogany hall chairs, with shaped backs and welled bell shape seats and stretchered trestle legs.
(Woolley & Wallis) $1,064

A Queen Anne walnut sidechair, Southeastern Pennsylvania, late 18th/early 19th century, the arched crestrail above a solid vase-shaped splat, 37½in. high.
(Christie's) $863

A pair of Louis Seize walnut framed salon chairs, with oval padded panel backs, surmounted with ormolu ribbon and foliate mounts.
(James Adam) $935

Two of a good set of ten William IV mahogany balloon back dining chairs (including two armchairs) the shaped and molded backs with twin C scroll and leaf cartouche to center. (Canterbury)
(Ten) $10,780

One of a set of eight Victorian mahogany dining chairs, the scrolling reeded backs and padded panels with upholstered seats.
(Anderson & Garland)
(Eight) $2,400

Two of a set of six Victorian mahogany framed balloon back dining chairs, with upholstered seats covered in green fabric, raised on turned tapering supports.
(James Adam)
(Six) $1,438

Two of a set of twelve Victorian oak dining chairs, including two carvers with arched crest, maker's label Charles Mills and Co. Bradford.
(Andrew Hartley)
(Twelve) $3,565

A Liberty & Co. ebonized 'Moorish' chair, the design attributed to Leonard Wyburd, the back of mushrebiyeh lattice work with turned finials on the uprights.
(Phillips) $278

A pair of mahogany Hepplewhite style armchairs, with gothic arched and ribbon splats, curved arms and reeded square legs.
(Christopher Matthews)
          $1,256

DINING CHAIRS

Two of a set of six George III mahogany single chairs having arched top rails, pierced and interlocking vase splats.
(Morphets)
(Six) $2,120

One of a set of four Victorian walnut parlor chairs, with pierced toprails and back splats, on cabriole legs.
(George Kidner)
(Four) $570

Two of eight spindle back oak and elm dining chairs, 19th century, with rush seats, turned legs and hoof feet, 19in. wide.
(Hy. Duke & Son)
(Eight) $1,854

A pair of late 18th century Continental red walnut framed dining chairs finely decorated with winged angels, grotesque masks and flowers in ivory and pewter.
(Stainers') $930

A set of six early Victorian mahogany framed carved balloon back dining chairs with leaf scroll decoration and drop-in seats.
(James Adam) $2,239

Two of a set of seven Morris & Co. ebonised Sussex chairs, comprising six upright and one elbow chair, each having a spindle and turned stretcher back.
(Phillips) (Seven) $1,004

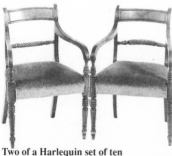

Two of a Harlequin set of ten George III mahogany dining chairs (including two armchairs) all with paneled rectangular crest rails and molded uprights.
(Canterbury)
(Ten) $2,233

One of a set of six William IV mahogany dining chairs, each with arched scrolling top-rail, lotus horizontal splat above drop-in seat.
(Christie's) (Six) $1,500

A pair of George III mahogany single chairs, each having an arched top rail, pierced and interlocking splat with leaf terminals.
(Morphets) $722

299

DINING CHAIRS

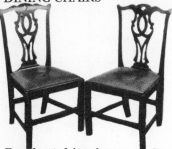

Two of a set of six mahogany dining chairs, each with a serpentine toprail, pierced vase splat, five chairs George III, one chair of later date.
(Bearne's) (Six)   **$3,399**

Cherry turned and carved side chair, Connecticut, circa 1780, with pierced splat and Spanish feet.
(Skinner)   **$805**

Two of a set of six Regency mahogany dining chairs, with reeded curved cresting rails and stiles, on turned and tapering front supports.
(Phillips)   (Six)   **$1,860**

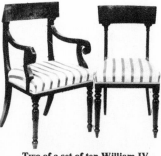

Two of a set of eight 19th century mahogany dining chairs in the Chippendale style having shaped cresting rails, gothic pierced splats, on chamfered square supports.
(Russell, Baldwin & Bright)
(Eight)   **$5,495**

One of a set of six mahogany dining chairs in George I style, the molded hoop backs with solid vase shaped splats, early 20th century.
(Neales)   (Six)   **$1,722**

Two of a set of ten William IV mahogany dining chairs, the molded backs with scroll capitols and deep bowed crestings.
(Woolley & Wallis)
(Ten)   **$7,904**

Two of a set of six George III mahogany side chairs, the molded frame open backs with reeded vertical rails and a paneled crest, circa 1790.
(Woolley & Wallis)
(Six)   **$3,040**

Maple crooked back side chair, Boston area, 1740–50, with original leather upholstered seat.
(Skinner)   **$25,300**

Two of a set of ten William IV mahogany dining chairs, each with curved and leaf carved bar back with similarly carved middle rail on turned tapering legs.
(Phillips) (Ten)   **$4,560**

DINING CHAIRS

Two of a set of eight William IV mahogany dining chairs, mid 19th century, 35in. high. (Skinner)

(Eight) $6,900

One of a set of eight Victorian rosewood balloon back dining chairs. (Sworder)

(Eight) $4,470

Two of a set of four Biedermeier fruitwood dining chairs, early 19th century, comprising two armchairs and two side chairs. (Skinner)

(Four) $2,645

Two of a set of seven 19th century fruitwood and elm dining chairs having vertical reeded rail backs, rush-upholstered drop-in seats on square tapering legs. (Russell, Baldwin & Bright)

(Seven) $1,915

One of a set of four late 18th century Dutch elm and marquetry dining chairs, the tapering arched rectangular backs inlaid with trailing flowers and foliage. (Bearne's)

(Four) $1,854

Two of a set of eight George IV rosewood dining chairs with curved cresting rails, scroll carved horizontal splats, on turned and fluted tapering front supports. (Russell, Baldwin & Bright)

(Eight) $6,437

Two of a set of six Queen Anne design walnut dining chairs, having fiddle splats and shell carved cabriole legs with pad feet, wine tapestry seats. (Christopher Matthews)

(Six) $911

One of a pair of late George III mahogany hall chairs, each with molded oval back on waisted fluted supports. (Bearne's) (Two) $1,452

Two of a set of eight Georgian mahogany dining chairs with reeded bar backs, reeded uprights and reeded splats. (Boardmans)

(Eight) $5,390

EASY CHAIRS

A George III giltwood open armchair in the French Hepplewhite manner, the cartouche shaped buttoned back with a floral carved cresting. (Phillips) $1,785

Two of a set of four Louis XV Provincial walnut chaises en cabriolet, late 18th century, raised on shaped scroll-carved legs. (Butterfield & Butterfield) (Four) $3,162

A mahogany open armchair in the Hepplewhite manner, cartouche shaped padded back, outswept arms and serpentine seat. (Phillips) $1,636

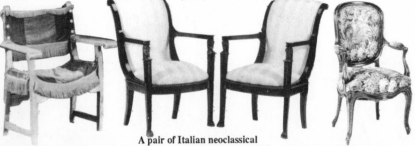

One of three Spanish walnut armchairs, part 18th century, each with a padded back and seat and scroll arms on square supports. (Christie's) (Three) $774

A pair of Italian neoclassical ebonized armchairs, circa 1810, each rectangular roll-over backrest applied with rosettes, joined by angular armrests over a bow-fronted upholstered drop-in seat. (Butterfield & Butterfield) $4,025

One of a pair of walnut fauteuils, of Louis XV style, the cartouche padded back and padded downswept arms above serpentine padded seat, late 19th century. (Christie's) $2,472

A William IV mahogany armchair, the rectangular padded button-down back and padded seat flanked by carved padded arms with caned sides. (Christie's) $1,236

A pair of Italian rococo style giltwood armchairs, 19th century, each rectangular backrest of molded undulating outline centered by a rocaille and scroll-carved cartouche. (Butterfield & Butterfield) $5,175

A late Regency mahogany bergère, the curved cane panel back with a stylized gadrooned bar top-rail, with scroll arms and caned seat. (Christie's) $1,463

EASY CHAIRS

A George III beechwood armchair, the oval panel back later upholstered in floral gros point needlework, with padded scroll arms and serpentine seat. (Christie's) **$1,721**

A pair of Louis XVI grey painted beechwood fauteuils, with oval upholstered backs and splayed scroll arm supports. (Phillips) **$1,672**

A cream and gray painted chair, early 19th century, the pierced, curved, arched back with ogee arched and quatrefoil decoration. (Christie's) **$1,118**

One of a pair of Régence giltwood fauteuils à la reine, the arched back, uprights and seat carved with repeating floral sprays on a hatched ground. (Christie's) (Two) **$119,320**

A pair of George III mahogany open armchairs, having outswept scroll arm supports with eagles' heads, on cabriole legs, probably Irish. (Phillips) **$15,400**

The Joseph Wharton Chippendale carved mahogany upholstered open armchair, Philadelphia, Pennsylvania, circa 1770, raised on frontal square molded legs. (Sotheby's) **$585,500**

A walnut wing armchair, early 18th century, with a padded arched back, scroll arms and seat with cushion, on cabriole legs. (Christie's) **$1,548**

A matched pair of Louis XV beechwood fauteuils, each with channelled cartouche-shaped padded back, arms, serpentine seat and squab-cushion. (Christie's) **$9,090**

A George IV library armchair, upholstered in green and red floral Kinsai linen, the padded back and downswept arms, on ring-turned legs. (Christie's) **$688**

EASY CHAIRS

Ron Arad for One Off, 'Rover chair', 1984, black patinated and chromium-plated metal frame with black leather seats.
(Sotheby's) $1,817

A pair of Louis XV style carved giltwood bergères, each slightly elevated molded crest carved with rocaille, flowerheads and trailing foliage.
(Butterfield & Butterfield)
$2,587

A fine and rare Chippendale carved mahogany wing armchair, New York, circa 1770, the serpentine crest flanked by ogival-shaped wings.
(Sotheby's) $29,900

One of a pair of 'Polaris' easy chairs, of rounded winged shape, upholstered in black mock leather, with loose cushion, on sprung swivel column base.
(Phillips)   (Two) $402

A pair of William IV style rosewood-grained mahogany tub chairs, each elevated rounded crestrail continuing to downward sloping armrests.
(Butterfield & Butterfield)
$3,737

A George III mahogany wing armchair, circa 1770, the arched crest and backrest with projecting curved wings.
(Butterfield & Butterfield)
$2,300

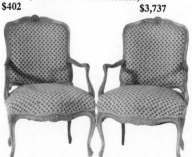

An early Victorian rosewood nursing chair, in the manner of James Mein of Kelso, with bobbin-turned and sparred back, on bobbin-turned tapering supports.
(Christie's) $653

A pair of Louis XV style painted and upholstered fauteuils en cabriolet, 19th century, each with cartouche-shaped upholstered back with molded frame.(Butterfield & Butterfield)
$1,955

A Venetian baroque style giltwood armchair, 19th century, the elevated crest carved with a central shell fronted by a male mask.
(Butterfield & Butterfield)
$2,875

EASY CHAIRS

An unusual pine corner chair, 19th century, with a shaped back, padded serpentine seat, on ring-turned tapering legs, possibly Swedish.
(Christie's) $438

A pair of Louis XVI style parcel-gilt and green-painted child's fauteuils, raised on tapering turned stop-fluted legs ending in button feet.
(Butterfield & Butterfield)
                              $1,725

A George II mahogany library open armchair, the acanthus-carved arms with cabochon terminals.
(Christie's) $6,458

Art Deco bird's-eye maple club chair, circa 1930, the rectangular upholstered back with rounded corners and sides.
(Butterfield & Butterfield)
                    $1,150

A pair of Louis XV Provincial caned beechwood fauteuils, mid 18th century, each backrest of undulating outline joining curved armrests and shaped arm supports.
(Butterfield & Butterfield)
                    $3,737

An Italian rococo tapestry upholstered walnut armchair, circa 1740, the upholsteries 19th century, the rectangular backrest with undulating outline carved with a central rocaille cartouche.
(Butterfield & Butterfield)
                              $12,650

A William IV rosewood slipper chair, circa 1835, raised on tapering leaf-carved ring-turned faceted legs.
(Butterfield & Butterfield)
                    $1,840

Two of a set of four Italian rococo carved elm armchairs, circa 1750, raised on shaped molded scroll-carved legs ending in button feet.
(Butterfield & Butterfield)
(Four) $8,050

A Chippendale carved mahogany lolling chair, Portsmouth area, New Hampshire, circa 1785, the upholstered back with serpentine-shaped crest.
(Sotheby's) $35,650

EASY CHAIRS

A George III giltwood open armchair, the oval padded back with lappeted frame, arms and serpentine seat.
(Christie's) $3,229

A pair of Edwardian mahogany framed armchairs, with pierced splats, raised on cabriole legs.
(James Adam) $353

Chippendale mahogany easy chair, New England, 18th century, with molded legs and stretchers.
(Skinner) $5,175

A fine and rare Federal inlaid mahogany lolling chair, Northeastern Massachusetts, circa 1815, on ring-turned bulbous tapered reeded legs and turned tapering feet.
(Sotheby's) $25,875

Pair of Art Deco black lacquer club chairs, circa 1930, each rectangular angled upholstered back flanked by sloped rounded armrests.
(Butterfield & Butterfield) $517

A William and Mary birchwood upholstered open armchair, American or Canadian, circa 1700, on vase-and-block-turned legs joined by an arched and scrolled frontal stretcher.
(Sotheby's) $4,025

A Chippendale mahogany wing armchair, New England or New York, circa 1785, the arched crest flanked by ogival wings and outscrolled arms.
(Sotheby's) $6,037

A pair of George IV brass-inlaid rosewood bergères, attributed to Gillows of Lancaster, on spirally-turned reeded and gadrooned turned legs.
(Christie's) $32,292

A Chippendale carved mahogany wing armchair, Boston, Massachusetts, circa 1755, the arched crest flanked by ogival wings.
(Sotheby's) $17,250

EASY CHAIRS

Aesthetic Movement ebony inlaid maple slipper chair, circa 1870–80, attributed to Herter Brothers, New York, with India Rubber Co., casters.
(Skinner) **$690**

Pair of late 19th century American rocking chairs, stained hardwood frames with turned decoration.
(Peter Wilson) **$577**

A Charles X mahogany fauteuil, second quarter 19th century, the horizontal molded ormolu-mounted crest flanked by molded stiles.
(Sotheby's) **$2,990**

A Queen Anne walnut wing armchair, Boston, Massachusetts, 1735–50, on cabriole legs ending in pad feet joined by block- and vase-turned stretchers.
(Sotheby's) **$85,000**

A pair of Victorian walnut framed tub shaped salon chairs with pierced decoration, padded seats and backs on turned front supports.
(Stainers') **$372**

A pair of Edwardian white-painted wing armchairs, with ivory floral cotton loose covering, on fluted square tapering supports ending in brass castors.
(Christie's) **$1,495**

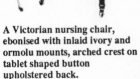

A Queen Anne walnut and maple wing armchair, Boston, Massachusetts, 1740–60, the upholstered back with arched crest.
(Sotheby's) **$34,500**

A pair of Regency painted "bamboo" pattern bergère armchairs with slender square backs, sides and seats cane paneled.
(Canterbury) **$6,006**

A Victorian nursing chair, ebonised with inlaid ivory and ormolu mounts, arched crest on tablet shaped button upholstered back.
(Andrew Hartley) **$356**

ELBOW CHAIRS

A Queen Anne carved walnut open armchair, Pennsylvania, circa 1750, the serpentine shell-carved crest above a vase-form splat.
(Sotheby's) $10,350

A late 18th century yew wood gothic Windsor elbow chair.
(Tennants) $3,534

A turned and carved Windsor comb-back armchair, Pennsylvania, circa 1760–80, the shaped crest with volute-carved ears.
(Sotheby's) $5,462

A slat-back high chair, Delaware Valley, late 18th/early 19th century, centering four shaped and graduated slats flanked by cylindrical stiles, 37¼in. high.
(Christie's) $3,910

A pair of black-painted, parcel-gilt and turned maple continuous-arm Windsor chairs, Rhode Island, circa 1760.
(Sotheby's) $37,950

Charles Rennie Mackintosh, green Windsor chair for the Dutch Kitchen, Argyle Street Tea Rooms, Glasgow, 1906, shaped rounded back with fifteen slightly swollen spindle uprights.
(Sotheby's) $3,271

A mahogany cockpen style open armchair, the rectangular lattice-work back above a gros point and petit point needlework drop-in seat.
(Christie's) $1,121

A mahogany corner armchair, of mid-Georgian style, the shaped armrests surmounted by a yoked chair-back.
(Christie's) $2,990

A good carved and turned Windsor comb-back armchair, Philadelphia, Pennsylvania, circa 1760–80, the serpentine arched crest terminating in volute-carved terminals.
(Sotheby's) $7,475

ELBOW CHAIRS

A paint-decorated maple rush-seat 'Spanish foot' armchair, New England, 1750–80, the arched volute-carved crest above a vase-form splat.
(Sotheby's) $4,887

A Chippendale carved walnut open armchair, Philadelphia, Pennsylvania, circa 1750, the shaped crest with incised edge.
(Sotheby's) $129,000

A fine black, green and red-painted carved comb-back Windsor armchair, Pennsylvania, circa 1785, on vase- and ring-turned legs.
(Sotheby's) $13,225

A very fine and rare green- and yellow-painted and turned Windsor sack-back child's highchair, New York, circa 1760–80, the arched crest above seven spindles.
(Sotheby's) $51,750

A pair of George III green-painted open armchairs, each with green lines on a lime ground, the pierced entrelac table toprail above a caned back.
(Christie's) $3,229

A William and Mary black and painted and carved maple bannister-back armchair, New England, probably Connecticut, 1730–50, the arched crest with scrolled ends.
(Sotheby's) $8,912

A William and Mary carved and turned maple bannister-back rush-seat armchair, Boston, Massachusetts, 1730–50, the pierced crest comprising C-scrolls and stylized leaves.
(Sotheby's) $21,850

A fine and rare Chippendale carved mahogany corner armchair, New York, New York, circa 1770, the convex molded crest with scrolled hand holds.
(Sotheby's) $20,700

One of a set of eight George III-style mahogany dining chairs, including two armchairs, with foliate-carved serpentine toprails, pierced gothic splats.
(Bearne's)
(Eight) $4,017

ELBOW CHAIRS

An Edwardian satinwood armchair, the top-rail with a stylized pagoda cresting and pierced scroll lyre splat, on square tapering legs.
(Christie's) $2,066

A pair of Regency bamboo armchairs, the openwork design of the back with geometric Chinese paling.
(Christie's) $4,195

An oak open armchair, early 18th century, the shaped toprail with three domes with geometric blind tracery.
(Christie's) $986

Josef Hoffmann, manufactured by Jacob & Josef Kohn, 'Sitzmachine', model No. 670, circa 1905, bent and stained beechwood, laminated wood, with pierced backrest and arm supports.
(Sotheby's) $13,082

A pair of mahogany armchairs, each with an undulating top-rail with a stylized pagoda cresting and foliate scrolled ears, on scallop-shell headed cabriole legs.
(Christie's) $4,820

One of a set of eight mahogany dining chairs, early 19th century, including one elbow chair, of a later date, each with a reeded curved bar top-rail and stylized lotus-carved horizontal scroll splat.
(Christie's)
          (Eight) $6,022

One of a set of eight mahogany dining chairs, including two open armchairs, each with bobbin-turned back, 19th century.
(Christie's)
          (Eight) $1,325

A pair of Italian neoclassical fruitwood armchairs, circa 1790, each backrest with trellis splat joining sloped armrests and arm supports.
(Butterfield & Butterfield)
          $3,162

A 19th century Dutch mahogany and floral marquetry armchair, in the Queen Anne taste, the cartouche shaped back with shaped splats with bird and floral inlay.
(Phillips) $818

ELBOW CHAIRS

A mahogany corner elbow chair, the curved back with padded scroll arms on reeded and turned splats.
(Christie's) $1,170

A George III white-painted and parcel-gilt open armchair, the pierced trellis splat flanked by a composite column.
(Christie's) $3,146

One of a set of eight carved mahogany dining chairs, 20th century, in George III style, including a pair of armchairs.
(Sotheby's)
     (Eight) $6,774

A walnut, ash and elm Windsor armchair, the comb back with central solid vase splat and wavy top-rail with scroll ends, Thames Valley, late 18th century.
(Christie's) $2,858

Two Chinese scarlet and gold lacquer folding chairs, possibly 17th century, each with U-shaped everted toprail, one with Greek-key trellis pierced and panelled splat.
(Christie's) $8,390

One of a set of six Regency mahogany dining chairs, including two open armchairs, each with bar top-rail and padded seat.
(Christie's)
     (Six) $2,119

An Edwardian satinwood and decorated elbow chair, the shield-shaped back with foliate and drapery swag splats, the padded seat on square tapered gaitered legs.
(Christie's) $1,548

An Italian walnut and ivory inlaid chair, of Savonarola type, decorated with floral and foliate tendrils with mythical beasts and stylized lilies.
(Christie's) $601

One of a pair of Regency ebonized and decorated elbow chairs, each with reeded ornament and fan-decorated curved bar top-rail.
(Christie's)
     (Two) $3,270

CHESTS OF DRAWERS

A George III oak chest of drawers.
(Dockree's) $598

Chippendale mahogany chest of drawers, Norwich, Connecticut area, 18th century, 38in. wide.
(Skinner) $8,050

A George III serpentine mahogany chest of two drawers.
(Dockree's) $1,338

A Queen Anne walnut bachelor's chest, the quarter veneered folding rectangular top with herringbone border, 31in. wide.
(Hy. Duke & Son)
                    $13,133

Charles II style bone inlaid oak chest of drawers, 19th century, in two parts, rectangular molded top over a case fitted with three paneled drawers, 39³/₄in. wide.
(Skinner) $2,415

An early George III mahogany small chest of drawers, the rectangular top with molded border above brushing slide and four long graduated drawers, 31in. wide.
(Hy. Duke & Son)
                    $2,472

A compact late George II oak chest, fitted two short and two long graduated and cockbeaded drawers beneath a brushing slide, 35in. wide, circa 1760.
(Neales) $1,440

A George III mahogany serpentine chest, with a molded edge and rounded fluted corners and angles, possibly German, 101cm. wide.
(Phillips) $5,168

A Charles II oak cabinet, with overhanging top above two short drawers and six false drawers, 38in. wide.
(Sotheby's) $2,070

CHESTS OF DRAWERS

Smoke grained child's chest over drawer, New England, 1830s, with recessed panel sides, original surface and wooden pulls, 31in. wide. (Skinner) **$1,380**

George III mahogany dwarf chest, the molded top over two short and three long graduated drawers with brass handles and bracket feet. (Lawrences) **$2,280**

Victorian mahogany bachelor's chest with molded edge, four long drawers below, on bracket feet, mid 19th century, 31in. (G. A. Key) **$1,057**

A George III mahogany chest of two short and three long drawers with molded edged top, brushing slide, pierced brass handles, 35in. wide. (Andrew Hartley) **$2,590**

A 19th century oak Norfolk chest of drawers with molded edged top, wave pattern frieze, arched central star inlaid cupboard. (Andrew Hartley) **$2,433**

A William and Mary elm and burr elm chest, the molded quarter-veneered rectangular top with a central crossbanded oval above four graduated feather banded drawers, 30½in. wide. (Christie's) **$26,047**

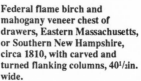

An antique oak chest, of eight short drawers, four set side by side, with shaped pierced brass escutcheons, 49in. wide. (Dee, Atkinson & Harrison) **$760**

Federal flame birch and mahogany veneer chest of drawers, Eastern Massachusetts, or Southern New Hampshire, circa 1810, with carved and turned flanking columns, 40½in. wide. (Skinner) **$1,610**

A George III bow front commode chest, mahogany veneered, the molded edge top above a slide and four long graduated drawers, 3ft. 7in. (Woolley & Wallis) **$6,080**

CHESTS OF DRAWERS

A late 17th century oak two sectional molded front chest of four long drawers with applied beaded borders, on a later stand, 3ft. 5in. wide.
(Holloway's) **$1,748**

A fine Chippendale figured mahogany serpentine-front chest of drawers, Boston-area, Massachusetts, circa 1780, 39in. wide.
(Sotheby's) **$25,300**

A William and Mary walnut chest, inlaid overall with boxwood lines, the molded rectangular top inlaid with concentric circles, 37^1/$_2$in. wide.
(Christie's) **$6,817**

A George III inlaid mahogany bow-fronted chest of drawers, early 19th century, the shaped rectangular top with reeded edge and banded reserve, 42in. wide.
(Butterfield & Butterfield) **$3,450**

An extremely rare William and Mary blue- and red-paint-decorated pine two-drawer blanket chest, Eastern Massachusetts, 1700–50, with a hinged rectangular top opening to a well, 39^1/$_2$in. wide.
(Sotheby's) **$129,000**

A George III mahogany bachelor's chest of drawers, last quarter 18th century, the rectangular top with molded edge over a brushing slide, 37in. wide.
(Butterfield & Butterfield) **$5,175**

Grain painted chest over drawers, Massachusetts, 1825-35, with burnt sienna and mustard putty paint and green sponging, 40in. wide.
(Skinner) **$31,050**

A French kingwood bombé small chest, circa 1860, the parquetry agate top of serpentine outline above two quarter veneered drawers, 75cm. wide.
(Sotheby's) **$7,487**

A Dutch parquetry mahogany chest, the eared rectangular top with fan marquetry corners and ribbon-tied and foliate medallion, late 18th/early 19th century, 37in. wide.
(Christie's) **$2,457**

CHESTS OF DRAWERS

An Edwardian mahogany and chequer lined miniature chest, the frieze fitted with two short above three long graduated drawers, 18in. wide.
(Christie's) $1,027

A mahogany chest, of George III style, the molded rectangular top above three long drawers, on bracket feet, 22¹/₂in. wide.
(Christie's) $1,308

A Queen Anne carved mahogany block-front chest of drawers, Boston, circa 1750, the oblong, thumb-molded top with blocked front, 36in. wide.
(Sotheby's) $321,500

A late Federal paint-decorated birchwood chest of drawers, Parish Hill, Maine, 1825–45, the rectangular top surmounted by a shaped scrolling splashboard, 41¹/₂in. wide.
(Sotheby's) $4,600

A grain-painted seed chest, possibly John Boyer, Pennsylvania, 19th century, the rectangular hinged slant-lid opening to a fitted interior with three compartments, 18³/₄in. wide.
(Christie's) $23,000

An important Chippendale block- and shell-carved cherrywood chest of drawers, Colchester-Norwich area, Connecticut, circa 1770, 40in. wide.
(Sotheby's) $398,500

A rare Pilgrim century oak, pine and birchwood chest of drawers, Massachusetts, 1660–1700, case fitted with three long drawers, each drawer front with geometric moldings, 37in. wide.
(Sotheby's) $13,225

A Federal inlaid mahogany and birchwood bow-front chest of drawers, Portsmouth, New Hampshire, circa 1810, 41in. wide.
(Sotheby's) $189,500

A William and Mary red-painted poplar one-drawer blanket chest, Connecticut, 1700-1750, the hinged molded top above two false drawers and one long drawer 40in. wide.
(Sotheby's) $3,162

CHESTS ON CHESTS

Chippendale cherry chest on chest, New England, circa 1800, early red stained surface, original brass, 38¼in. wide. (Skinner) **$4,600**

Chippendale walnut carved chest on chest, Massachusetts or New Hampshire, late 18th century, some original brass, 41in. wide. (Skinner) **$13,800**

George III mahogany tallboy of small proportions, the upper part with molded and dentil molded cornice, on bracket feet, 37in. wide. (Canterbury) **$4,082**

Late George III inlaid mahogany chest on chest, circa 1810, in two parts, the upper case with an outset molded and dentilated cornice over an inlaid frieze, 44in. wide. (Butterfield & Butterfield) **$7,475**

A Queen Anne walnut tallboy chest in two parts, with a molded cornice containing three short and three long drawers above and two short and three long drawers below, 95cm. wide. (Phillips) **$2,677**

A George III mahogany chest on chest, the upper section with key pattern carved cornice over two short and three long graduated drawers, 113cm. wide. (Phillips) **$1,520**

An early George III mahogany secrétaire tallboy chest, the upper part with a dentil cornice and blind fret carved canted angles, 116cm. wide. (Phillips) **$4,462**

A George III mahogany chest-on-chest, the dentil-molded cornice above two short and three long drawers flanked by fluted angles, 43½in. wide. (Christie's) **$2,120**

A late George III mahogany tallboy, with boxwood stringing, simulated dentil cornice, 43¾in. wide. (Bearne's) **$2,008**

CHESTS ON STANDS

An early 18th century
Continental oak chest with iron
mounts and carrying handles, a
pair of fielded panel doors
enclosing a fitted interior, 32in.
wide. (Anderson & Garland)
$1,800

Queen Anne style stained oak
chest of two short and three long
graduated drawers raised on
stand, fitted three short
drawers, 42in. wide.
(Peter Wilson) $1,310

A Queen Anne carved
mahogany bonnet-top highboy,
Goddard-Townsend School,
Newport, Rhode Island, circa
1765, 38$\frac{1}{2}$in. wide.
(Sotheby's) $398,500

A William and Mary burl-
veneered walnut and maple
highboy, Boston-Ipswich area,
Massachusetts, 1700–1720, on
trumpet- and vase-turned legs,
39in. wide.
(Sotheby's) $167,500

A William & Mary style walnut
marquetry chest on stand, 19th
century, the upper section with
rectangular floral inlaid surface
over a molded cornice, 38½in.
wide.
(Butterfield & Butterfield)
$5,750

A Queen Anne burl maple-
veneered diminutive flat-top
highboy, Boston, Massachusetts,
1720–50, in two parts, the
shaped beaded skirt hung with
turned pendants, 37in. wide.
(Sotheby's) $65,750

A fine burr walnut veneered
walnut chest on stand, feather
banded, the top with quartering,
two short and two long drawers,
3ft. 6in.
(Woolley & Wallis)
$3,952

A William and Mary lignum
vitae oyster veneered acacia and
marquetry chest on stand,
crossbanded in elm, the upper
part with geometrically inlaid
top, 94cm. wide.
(Phillips) $7,437

An 18th century and later oak
chest on stand, the upper part
with molded cornice over a
drawer in a cushion frieze,
41$\frac{1}{2}$in. wide.
(Andrew Hartley)
$1,748

CHIFFONIERS

A late Regency mahogany chiffonier of small size and serpentine outline, with foliate cresting and shelved superstructure, 55cm. wide.
(Phillips) $4,104

A Regency brass-mounted rosewood chiffonier, the breakfront top surmounted by a superstructure with two tiers, 78¼in. wide.
(Christie's) $6,686

A Regency rosewood chiffonier, the raised paneled back with galleried shelf on ring turned column supports, 31½in. wide.
(Andrew Hartley) $1,531

A William IV chiffonier, faded rosewood veneered, the mirror backed superstructure with a shelf and a pierced brass gallery, circa 1830, 3ft.
(Woolley & Wallis)
                             $2,584

A Regency rosewood carved chiffonier, the shelved superstructure with pierced brass three-quarter gallery and supported upon brass scrolls, 136cm. wide.
(Phillips) $7,600

A brass-mounted rosewood chiffonier, the two-tiered superstructure with gadrooned border and trellis-filled spreading sides terminating in blocks, basically early 19th century, 50in. wide.
(Christie's) $5,279

Grain painted bucket bench with drawer, probably New England, early 19th century, painted dark brown to resemble mahogany over an earlier green, 25.75in. wide.
(Skinner) $1,610

Grain painted dresser, Canada or northern New England, circa 1840, open grooved shelves above two raised panel doors which open to a single-shelf interior, 54.5in. wide.
(Skinner) $5,462

A George III satinwood and marquetry chiffonier, crossbanded overall in kingwood and inlaid with boxwood and amaranth lines, 36in. wide.
(Christie's) $7,176

CHIFFONIERS

A Victorian walnut chiffonier with raised shelf back, pierced gallery on turned supports, the base fitted pair of glazed doors. (Russell, Baldwin & Bright) **$1,854**

An unusual George IV rosewood chiffonier, the upper part with shelf with arcaded front apron and turned and carved pendant drops, 42in. wide. (Canterbury) **$1,510**

A Regency rosewood-veneered chiffonier, the raised back applied with scrolls and foliage, on turned feet, 33¾in. wide. (Bearne's) **$2,781**

A rare mid-Victorian slate and decorated chiffonier, with gilt and polychrome decoration of floral sprays, the pointed arched ledge back with a shelf, 48in. wide.
(Christie's) **$1,377**

A Victorian rosewood chiffonier, the arched mirror-back carved and pierced with leaf scrolls, rosettes and lotus, on a deep molded plinth, 58in. wide, circa 1850.
(Neales) **$2,426**

A late Regency rosewood chiffonier with a mirror back and shelf over, single frieze drawer and a pair of pleated silk paneled doors under, 3ft. 6in. wide.
(Holloway's) **$1,976**

A William IV brass-mounted rosewood chiffonier, rectangular crossbanded top with beaded edge and single shelf mirrored superstructure, 48¼in. wide.
(Christie's) **$4,020**

A parcel-gilt and simulated rosewood-painted chiffonier, the raised shelved back on scroll supports above simulated marble top with two paneled doors, 36in. wide.
(Christie's) **$1,060**

A George IV rosewood chiffonier, the ledge back with a foliate three-quarter pierced gallery and shelf, on ring-turned uprights, 49½in. wide.
(Christie's) **$2,295**

COMMODE CHESTS

An 18th century kingwood and marquetry bombé commode in the manner of Pierre Langlois, surmounted by a serpentine molded rance marble top with canted corners, 140cm. wide.
(Phillips) $12,160

A fine late 18th century Italian seaweed marquetry commode, the top, front and sides profusely inlaid with walnut, mahogany and ivory panels, with two frieze drawers, 61^{1}/$_{2}$in. wide.
(Academy) $28,388

An 18th century South German walnut and crossbanded petite commode of undulating outline, with a molded overhanging top, containing two drawers, 67cm. wide.
(Phillips) $2,888

A Régence ormolu-mounted and boulle brass-inlaid amaranth and ebony commode, the bow-fronted rectangular top with interlaced ebony and brass geometric inlays and stylized foliate border, basically 18th century, 124cm. wide.
(Christie's) $65,816

A late 18th century North Italian walnut, satinwood checker inlaid, crossbanded and marquetry rectangular commode, containing three long drawers with stylized floral garlands, 122cm. wide.
(Phillips) $13,680

A Louis XV style gilt-bronze-mounted kingwood and marquetry commode in the style of Cressent, mid 19th century, the serpentine molded black and peach-veined white marble top over a bombé case, 38^{1}/$_{4}$in.
(Butterfield & Butterfield) $6,900

An Italian neoclassical walnut commode, with bowed front over two short drawers, two conforming long drawers and inlaid sides, 37in. wide.
(Butterfield & Butterfield) $2,070

A good Continental figured walnut petit commode of shaped outline, the top inlaid with bandings and wide crossbanding, 25in. wide.
(Canterbury) $1,727

Baltic neoclassical karelian birch and part-ebonized commode, early 19th century, with ivory escutcheons, 41in. wide.
(Skinner) $3,737

COMMODE CHESTS

A late 18th century Italian walnut and marquetry commode, in the manner of Maggiolini, the rectangular top and sides with central oval paterae above a frieze drawer, 118cm. wide.
(Phillips) $8,627

A late 18th century Italian walnut marquetry commode, fitted two shallow drawers flanking a deep drawer, on fluted and turned tapering feet, 4ft. 2in. wide.
(Russell, Baldwin & Bright)
                            $17,670

A South German walnut and marquetry bombé commode, inlaid throughout in bone and various woods with hunting scenes, the serpentine top with foliate-carved edge, $30^1/_2$in. wide.
(Bearne's) $2,317

A Louis XV ormolu-mounted kingwood and marquetry commode, by Pierre Roussel, the molded sepentine brêche d'alep marble top above two long drawers, 82cm. wide.
(Christie's) $57,456

A Louis XV bois satiné and parquetry bombé commode, by Jean-François Leleu, the eared molded brêche d'alep marble top above two drawers veneered sans traverse, $26^1/_2$in. wide.
(Christie's) $19,228

A French kingwood, marquetry and gilt-metal mounted bombé commode, early 20th century, with a marble top, fitted with three drawers, $37^1/_2$in. wide.
(Christie's) $2,151

A Victorian yellow-painted simulated-bamboo commode, decorated overall with stylized anthemion-sprays and black ebonized lines, $28^3/_4$in. wide.
(Christie's) $3,049

A pair of Italian walnut petit bombé commodes, the serpentine molded tops above a cavetto frieze and two long drawers, each 97cm. wide.
(Phillips) $5,950

A George III mahogany serpentine commode, the top crossbanded and with boxwood lines, above a green baize-lined brushing-slide, $39^1/_2$in. wide.
(Christie's) $16,146

321

COMMODES & POT CUPBOARDS

Victorian cylinder shaped pot cupboard, white marble top, single door with turned handle, blind base, 30in. high.
(Peter Wilson) $604

A pair of George IV mahogany bedside commodes, attributed to Gillows of Lancaster, each with sarcophagus-shaped top with gadrooned edges and finial, 16¾in. wide.
(Christie's) $6,279

Queen Anne walnut commode roundabout chair, Philadelphia, Pennsylvania, 1740–60.
(Skinner) $920

An 18th century Italian maggiolini night table with a shallow frieze drawer with marquetry decoration of griffons in foliate surround, 22in. wide.
(Boardmans) $7,390

A George III mahogany tray top bedside commode, with tambour shutter and frieze drawer, on chamfered square legs, drawer front adapted, 20in. wide.
(Christie's) $965

A good 19th century Continental rosewood and marquetry bedside commode of bombé outline, the shaped tray inset with yellow and red veined marble slab, 20in. wide.
(Canterbury) $1,884

A German fruitwood bedside cabinet, 19th century, with a marble top and frieze drawer, enclosed by a panel door, on square legs, 15¼in. wide.
(Christie's) $612

A pair of Italian rococo inlaid walnut bedside cupboards, each rectangular top with molded edge and serpentine front, 20½in. wide.
(Butterfield & Butterfield) $8,625

A French maple bedside cupboard, 19th century, with a marble top and frieze drawer, enclosed by a panel door flanked by column stiles, 15in. wide.
(Christie's) $946

CORNER CUPBOARDS

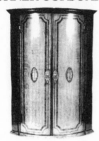

A George III oak bow fronted corner cupboard, with mahogany crossbanding and shell marquetry inlay, 28¼ x 37in.
(Andrew Hartley) $1,124

Walnut glazed corner cupboard, probably Pennsylvania, circa 1820, 48in. wide.
(Skinner) $1,840

A pine corner cupboard, possibly Scandinavian, 18th century, the center opening to reveal a two shelved interior, on a molded base, 16in. deep.
(Christie's) $920

An early 19th century Welsh oak double corner cupboard, of small proportions, the upper part with single glazed door with arched glazing bars, 36in. wide.
(Peter Francis) $1,444

A pair of late 18th/early 19th century Continental kingwood and tulipwood parquetry serpentine encoignures, the shaped green and red molded marble tops above a pair of cupboard doors, 67cm. wide.
(Phillips) $5,950

An inlaid mahogany corner cupboard of Sheraton design, the upper section with glazed door and interior shelves flanked by canted corners, 32in. wide.
(Hy. Duke & Son) $1,360

George III oak double floor standing corner cupboard, molded cornice mahogany crossbanded frieze decorated with inlaid ovals depicting urns of flowers, 82in. high.
(Peter Wilson) $2,964

A George III oak bow front corner cupboard, molded cornice above mahogany veneered frieze decorated with whitewood shell inlay, 102cm. high.
(Peter Wilson) $1,174

A late 18th century bow front corner cupboard, mahogany veneered with satinwood banding, the molded cornice above a frieze with marquetry shell inlay, 31in.
(Woolley & Wallis) $1,216

CORNER CUPBOARDS

A German giltwood and cream-painted corner cabinet, late 18th century, the arched molded cornice with foliate cresting flanked by foliate urn finials, 42in. wide.
(Christie's) $7,564

A George III mahogany corner display cabinet, with a domed concave interior decorated with foliate stems and with shaped shelves, 53in. wide.
(Christie's) $5,508

A fine late Victorian satinwood bow-front corner cupboard in the Neo-Classical Revival style, the whole crossbanded in rosewood and inlaid with stringings, 25.5in. wide.
(Canterbury) $7,238

A George III oak and mahogany crossbanded corner cabinet, the later scrolled pediment above a molded frieze fitted with a pair of paneled cupboard doors, 42in. wide.
(Christie's) $2,815

A pair of Italian walnut and crossbanded corner cabinets, each with a shaped shelved superstructure and enclosed by a pair of paneled doors, 20½in. wide.
(Christie's) $3,280

A Chippendale carved poplar scroll-top corner cupboard, Pennsylvania, late 18th century, the overhanging cove molding with canted corners surmounted by a swan's-neck pediment, 4ft. wide.
(Sotheby's) $7,475

A Dutch mahogany and marquetry upright corner cabinet, decorated with meandering floral and foliate stems with urns issuing floral sprays, 55in. wide.
(Christie's) $13,536

A French red japanned bowfront encoignure, mid 18th century, by Wolff, with a marble top and enclosed by a panel door with figures amongst pagodas with rocks, 28½in. wide.
(Christie's) $4,643

A Federal grain-painted corner cupboard, New England, early 19th century, the upper section with a molded cornice above a case fitted with two six-lighted doors, 54½in. wide.
(Christie's) $3,450

COURT CUPBOARDS

An oak court cupboard, carved with panels of foliage, hunting scenes and caryatid uprights, on plinth base, 47in. wide.
(Christie's) $2,193

An oak court cupboard, 17th century, with two pairs of geometrically paneled and coffered doors divided by split bobbins, 64½ in. wide.
(Christie's) $1,552

Mid 20th century Titmarsh and Goodwin, Jacobean style oak press cupboard, top section with central door flanked by carved cup and cover pillars, 107cm.
(Peter Wilson) $1,020

A late Georgian Cardiganshire oak cwpwrdd deuddarn, the canopied upper part with molded cornice and spirally turned angle pendants, 56in. wide.
(Peter Francis) $3,952

A fine early 17th century 'Elizabethan' oak court cupboard from the Leeds area of Yorkshire, the chevron-banded frieze in bog oak and holly, 55in. wide.
(Boardmans) $12,090

A French press cupboard, part 17th century, the upper section with foliate and guilloche frieze above a central figure flanked by paneled doors, carved *1663* and *F: TANGVY*, 58in. wide.
(Christie's) $3,982

An English oak court cupboard, dated *1722*, of country manufacture, the frieze carved with the date and the monograms *IS* and *MS*, 65in. wide.
(Sotheby's) $1,380

A small English Jacobean style oak court cupboard, in 17th century style, the upper section formed with overhanging top and frieze carved with flower-heads, 45in. wide.
(Sotheby's) $1,955

An oak standing cupboard, the upper section with gouge-carved decoration and ribbed frieze enclosed by a pair of paneled doors, Lake District, late 17th century, 41½in. wide.
(Christie's) $10,968

CREDENZAS

Victorian figured walnut veneered credenza, central single panel door with whitewood inlay in the form of urns and flowers, 58in. wide.
(Peter Wilson) $2,340

Italian Renaissance walnut credenza, 68in. long.
(Skinner) $2,645

A mid 19th century serpentine credenza, inlaid with tortoiseshell and brass and applied with gilt bronze mounts, 208cm. wide.
(Phillips) $2,584

A George III satinwood, tulipwood crossbanded and decorated dwarf cabinet of 'D' shaped outline, in the manner of Seddon, the top with riband tied garlands of flowers, 128cm. wide.
(Phillips) $19,337

A Victorian walnut crossbanded and gilt-metal mounted dwarf side cabinet, by Gillow, of D-shaped outline, with sycamore, tulipwood and purpleheart moldings, 41½in. wide.
(Christie's) $4,302

A Victorian walnut, ebonized and inlaid credenza with gilt metal, incised and 'Wedgwood' style applied plaques, the shelved superstructure with mirrored spindle back, 153cm. wide.
(Phillips) $2,888

An Italian rococo walnut credenza, the rectangular top of stepped serpentine outline over a frieze drawer and conforming cupboard doors, 5ft. 5in. wide.
(Butterfield & Butterfield) $6,900

A 19th century Louis XVI style ebonized and gilt bronze mounted side cabinet with slate top.
(Jacobs & Hunt) $4,082

A Victorian walnut, ebonized, floral marquetry and ormolu mounted credenza, the panel door with ebonized panels of flowers heightened in harewood, 176cm. wide.
(Phillips) $5,776

CREDENZAS

A mid Victorian burr walnut side cabinet, the center door inlaid in satinwood with floral urns, flanked by bow glazed compartments, 59in. wide.
(Morphets) $3,611

A large Victorian ebonised and ormolu mounted credenza, the upper frieze decorated with boulle panel and the center door with oval Sèvres type panel.
(Academy) $3,850

A Victorian walnut credenza, marquetry inlaid and gilt metal mounted, with central panel door flanked by glazed bowed doors, 172cm. wide.
(Bristol) $3,245

A Victorian walnut and marquetry inlaid breakfront credenza, with gilt metal mounts, central cupboard door flanked on either side by a glazed door, 69in. wide.
(Andrew Hartley)
$3,648

A mid-Victorian ebonized and gilt-metal mounted credenza, marquetry inlaid, the bowed breakfront with beaded rim above a foliate-inlaid paneled door, 59in. wide.
(Christie's) $1,359

A Victorian burr walnut credenza, with serpentine shaped front, rich ormolu mounts, the front with marquetry frieze, central panel door with marquetry panel, 5ft. 5in. wide.
(John Nicholson) $8,007

A Victorian walnut, marquetry and amboyna banded side cabinet, inlaid with satinwood lines and applied with gilt metal mounts, on a plinth base, 165cm. wide.
(Phillips) $3,496

A fine Victorian walnut breakfront credenza, the central paneled door inlaid and set between glazed doors enclosing three shelves, 71in. wide.
(Dee, Atkinson & Harrison)
$2,584

A Victorian ebonized and brass inlaid credenza, with serpentine front with central cupboard door having oval brass inlaid panel, 72in. wide.
(Andrew Hartley)
$2,759

A 19th century Korean hardwood cupboard in three parts, the rectangular top above a pair of paneled doors, on a plinth base, 118cm. wide.
(Phillips) $1,672

A pair of George III mahogany dining room pedestals, the divided and hinged molded tops above candleslides to the sides, 48cm. wide.
(Phillips) $8,816

A rosewood and ebony cupboard, the molded cornice above a foliate-carved cartouche and four foliate-carved panel doors, 72in. wide.
(Christie's) $9,954

An oak cupboard, with a molded cornice and enclosed by a pair of linen fold panel doors, possibly German, 65in. wide.
(Christie's) $2,448

Louis XV oak bas de buffet, stamped Roussel, second quarter 18th century, the rectangular brown and white marble top with molded edge over a frieze, 44in. wide.
(Butterfield & Butterfield) $7,475

A German carved oak cupboard, early 19th century, decorated with birds amongst fruiting foliage, cornucopiae figures and grotesque masks to a molded cornice, 60in. wide.
(Christie's) $3,384

An early 19th century Dutch mahogany and floral marquetry side cupboard, with a molded cornice enclosed by a pair of panel doors, on a plinth base with lunette feet, 1m. wide.
(Phillips) $3,040

Pair of American marquetry small cupboards, designed and executed by T. F. Adelhelm, 1938, with glazed doors enclosing shelves over a frieze drawer, 21in. wide.
(Butterfield & Butterfield) $3,737

A Dutch walnut and crossbanded cupboard, with ebonized moldings, the upper part with a shaped molded arched cornice and enclosed by a pair of paneled doors, 72in. wide.
(Christie's) $6,769

CUPBOARDS

A Dutch burr-walnut feather-
banded cupboard, 18th century,
the molded cornice above two
doors enclosing a fitted interior,
69in. wide.
(Christie's) $8,759

An oak cupboard, late 17th
century, with a part molded
cornice, enclosed by three
fielded paneled doors above and
below, 99in. wide.
(Christie's) $8,759

A Dutch polychrome-painted
cupboard, early 19th century, of
bombé form, the arched
molded cornice centered by a
stylized foliate clasp, 55in. wide.
(Christie's) $9,157

A late 19th century French
mahogany and brass molded
bedside cupboard, the inset
marble top above a drawer and
a door, 38cm. square.
(Phillips) $912

Two similar Italian dwarf
cupboards, one walnut and ash,
the other in walnut with a plain
molded top, 55cm. and 61cm.
wide.
(Phillips) $4,760

An Edwardian satinwood
painted and parcel gilt
serpentine bedside cupboard,
the frieze with a drawer above a
drawer, on fluted tapering legs,
52cm. wide.
(Phillips) $1,064

A Louis Philippe ebonized and
gilt-brass mounted meuble
d'appui, with projecting canted
angles and a marble top with an
egg-and-dart foliate decorated
frieze, 44in. wide.
(Christie's) $6,024

A Dutch mahogany and
marquetry cupboard, 19th
century, inlaid with lines and
decorated with foliate scrolls
and meandering floral and
foliate tendrils, 68in. wide.
(Christie's) $11,187

A good punch-decorated
tinware and painted poplar pie
safe, Pennsylvania, early 19th
century, two cupboard doors
each depicting a star- and heart-
decorated pot, 43¹/₂in. wide.
(Sotheby's) $7,475

329

DAVENPORTS

Victorian pollard oak davenport desk, late 19th century, 25³/₄in. wide.
(Skinner) **$1,840**

A Victorian walnut and inlaid davenport, the hinged back with a brass gallery, the fall revealing two drawers, 21¹/₂in. wide.
(George Kidner) **$1,267**

Early Victorian mahogany desk top davenport, six drawers to the interior, sliding top, pen drawer, 20in. wide.
(Peter Wilson) **$2,130**

A late Victorian walnut davenport, with three-quarter pierced gilt-metal gallery, leather-lined sloping fall enclosing fitted interior, 21in. wide.
(Christie's) **$1,528**

A Victorian rosewood and marquetry davenport, with rich floral inlay, the top with pierced gallery, sloping writing surface with green baize cover, 1ft. 10in. wide.
(John Nicholson) **$3,847**

A Victorian burr walnut davenport with hinged lid enclosing the stationery compartment with leather lined writing slope, 31in. wide.
(Anderson & Garland) **$1,770**

A Victorian walnut davenport, the rectangular top with pierced brass gallery and hinged leather-lined writing slope, 22in. wide.
(Christie's) **$1,493**

An early Victorian rosewood davenport, the sliding top with three-quarter gallery, the leather lined slope enclosing a fitted interior, 24in. wide.
(Christie's) **$1,944**

A Victorian walnut davenport desk, the slope lift top opening to reveal a fitted interior raised above four slide drawers, 22in. wide.
(James Adam) **$1,413**

DAVENPORTS

A Victorian rosewood davenport, on turned, spiral fluted and carved bracket front supports, 21½in. wide.
(Canterbury) $1,287

A Victorian walnut davenport, the rising back panel with three center small drawers and niches, 'piano' top, 21½in. wide.
(Dreweatt Neate) $4,077

Victorian walnut davenport, stationery compartment with hinged lid, writing slope with red leather inset, 21in.
(Peter Wilson) $803

Victorian walnut veneered harlequin davenport, rising pop-up stationery compartment with gallery, fitted interior with leather inset writing slope, fitted four true and four false drawers, 22in. wide.
(Peter Wilson) $3,588

An early Victorian Holland and Sons rosewood davenport, the sliding top with pierced three-quarter gallery above a leather lined writing slope, 23½in. wide.
(Anderson & Garland) $3,300

A William IV rosewood davenport, attributed to Gillows, the three-quarter galleried top with beaded molding and sloped fall-front with gilt leather-lined writing-surface, 22in. wide.
(Christie's) $6,946

A Victorian burr walnut piano top davenport, with hinged stationery compartment above the enclosed sliding writing slope, 85cm.
(Bristol) $2,280

An early Victorian rosewood davenport in the manner of Gillows of Lancaster, on barley-twist supports ending in a concave base with bun feet, 27in. wide.
(Christie's) $2,080

A Victorian rosewood davenport, with raised stationery compartment, tooled leather insert to the sloping flap, 22¼in. wide.
(Bearne's) $1,159

DISPLAY CABINETS

Pine architectural glazed cupboard, Connecticut, 1750, traces of old color, 65in. wide.
(Skinner) **$5,750**

A Dutch floral marquetry walnut display cabinet, early 19th century, the arched foliate-carved cornice above two doors, three drawers, 82in. wide.
(Christie's) **$17,518**

An Edwardian Revival Sheraton style mahogany display cabinet.
(Dockree's) **$2,048**

An Edwardian inlaid mahogany rectangular display cabinet with raised panel back, the open center mirror back compartment above twin panel door cupboard, 55in. wide.
(James Adam) **$2,022**

A Victorian walnut display cabinet, the top with molded edge over an inlaid frieze, the plain glazed door set between inlaid supports, 29¹/²in. wide.
(Dee, Atkinson & Harrison) **$755**

A Victorian walnut, crossbanded and marquetry inlaid display cabinet, the raised back and molded edged top supported by turned and fluted columns, 45¹/²in. wide.
(Andrew Hartley) **$1,727**

An attractive French kingwood and giltwood vitrine in the Louis XVI style, the upper section with bowed side panels and plate glass door, 160cm. wide.
(Phillips) **$2,280**

Edwardian mahogany display cabinet, mirror back drop center, two display cupboards with carved and shaped glazing bars, flanking central cupboard, 54in. wide.
(Peter Wilson) **$718**

A late Georgian mahogany display cabinet, the dentil cornice above astragal glazed doors enclosing adjustable shelves, 120cm. wide.
(Bristol) **$4,104**

DISPLAY CABINETS

An early 20th century inlaid and painted satinwood display cabinet in the George III manner, and of semi-serpentine outline, 60¹/₄in. wide.
(Bearne's) $4,017

Louis XVI style 19th century vitrine, 220cm. wide.
(Jacobs & Hunt) $7,850

A Louis XV style kingwood and ormolu-mounted side cabinet, the lugged molded rectangular crossbanded and quarter-veneered top above a pair of glazed doors, 55¹/₂in. wide.
(Christie's) $5,232

A mahogany breakfront display cabinet on stand by Christopher Pratt Bradford, the raised center section with pierced fretwork gallery and urn surmounts, 77in. long.
(Andrew Hartley) $4,864

Art Nouveau carved mahogany vitrine, early 20th century, the rectangular top with molded edge and outset canted corners, 35in. wide.
(Butterfield & Butterfield) $2,530

An Edwardian painted satinwood display cabinet, with string inlay, straight crest over a frieze painted with musical trophies and scrolling foliate banding, 39³/₄in. wide.
(Andrew Hartley) $4,832

An Edwardian mahogany breakfront display cabinet with broken arch cornice centered by an urn, 48in. wide.
(Anderson & Garland) $1,950

A Louis XV style kingwood and ormolu-mounted side cabinet, the molded serpentine brech d'alep marble top above a pair of glazed doors enclosing two shelves, 48in. wide.
(Christie's) $4,485

A late Victorian mahogany, satinwood, boxwood and checker lined serpentine display cabinet, on satinwood and ebony lined square tapering supports, 54in. wide.
(Christie's) $6,949

DRESSERS

A George II oak and crossbanded mahogany dresser, the rectangular molded top above an arrangement of six drawers and two cupboards, 59in. wide.
(Hy. Duke & Son)
$2,936

Early 18th century style walnut 'low dresser', circa 1920.
(Dockree's) $760

An oak dresser base, the inverted breakfront top above a central drawer and cupboard between reeded half columns, English, early 18th century, 72in. wide.
(Christie's) $6,727

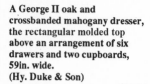

A pine dresser, the inverted breakfront partitioned plate-rack with an arrangement of shelves and molded cornice, English, late 19th century.
(Christie's) $1,176

An 18th century oak Welsh dresser, the shelves having pierced shaped frieze fitted five small spice drawers, 5ft. wide.
(Russell, Baldwin & Bright)
$6,594

An oak dresser, the plate rack with molded cornice and reeded frieze above two open shelves, South Wales, late 18th/early 19th century, 66in. wide.
(Christie's) $2,691

A George II oak dresser having upper delft rack with projecting molded cornice, shaped frieze, side shelves projecting, three plate racks, 74in.
(Locke & England)
$3,400

A carved pine hutch, Mid-Atlantic States, probably New Jersey, 1750–1800, the upper section with a reverse break-fronted cornice with dentil molding, 4ft. 4in. wide.
(Sotheby's) $4,600

An antique elm dresser fitted three frieze drawers with shaped apron, on squared tapering legs, 6ft. 4in. wide.
(Russell, Baldwin & Bright)
$3,549

DRESSERS

A George II oak dresser base, the shallow back with a row of three drawers and four blind drawers, 74in. wide, circa 1760. (Neales) $2,426

An oak dresser, the molded cornice over three shelves with beaded edges, the base fitted with three paneled drawers. (George Kidner) $1,386

17th century oak dresser base, four drawers with raised panel fronts, double arch frieze separating three turned front legs, 72in. (Peter Wilson) $9,360

A late George III oak Welsh dresser, outlined with mahogany banding and boxwood stringing, the upper section with a pierced frieze and three open shelves, 73in. wide. (Bearne's) $5,098

A George III Provincial oak Welsh dresser, in two parts, the upper with outset coved cornice above graduated open shelves, 5ft. 9^1/$_2$in. wide. (Butterfield & Butterfield) $3,737

An 18th century oak open dresser, the delft rack with molded cornice and three shelves, the base with three frieze drawers, 73^1/$_2$in. wide. (Andrew Hartley) $8,240

An antique oak dresser, the later top with molded pediment over a shaped frieze and with two shelves, 78in. wide. (Dee, Atkinson & Harrison) $2,416

A 19th century oak open dresser, the delft rack with molded cornice, shaped sides and two molded edged shelves, 60in. wide. (Andrew Hartley) $3,297

18th century oak dresser, replacement three-shelf rack with shaped frieze, two cupboards and five small spice drawers, 76in. (Peter Wilson) $5,889

KNEEHOLE DESKS

An Edwardian mahogany and boxwood lined bowfront dressing table, the molded top surmounted by a brass three-quarter gallery, on bracket feet, 54in. wide.
(Christie's) $4,485

A mahogany kneehole desk, with canted angles and frieze drawer fitted with a slide and side opening drawers, 37¹/₂in. wide.
(Christie's) $2,410

A Victorian 'Boulle' kneehole desk, circa 1860, with a leather inset top above an arrangement of nine small drawers, 124cm. wide.
(Sotheby's) $6,774

A German walnut kneehole desk, late 19th century, the serpentine molded top above seven bowed paneled doors and a recessed cupboard door between square uprights, 35in. wide.
(Christie's) $2,190

A Chippendale carved mahogany block-front bureau-table, Newport, Rhode Island, 1750–1770, the rectangular thumbmolded top above a blocked case fitted with one long drawer, 39in. wide.
(Christie's) $156,500

An early Georgian walnut kneehole desk, shaped kneehole enclosing a door, flanked by two tiers of four graduated short drawers, 30¹/₄in. wide.
(Christie's) $5,382

A Victorian mahogany partners' pedestal desk, the top inset with a panel of tooled leather and with a stylized gadrooned edge, fitted with three frieze drawers to either side, 48in. wide.
(Christie's) $6,541

A Queen Anne mahogany block-front bureau-table, Boston, 1740–1760, the rectangular top with rounded blockfront above a conforming case, on straight bracket feet, 22in. wide.
(Christie's) $32,200

A George III mahogany secrétaire pedestal estates desk, the frieze with a drawer with a dummy drawer fall front, three drawers to each pedestal, 50in. wide.
(Christie's) $4,302

LINEN PRESSES

A Regency mahogany linen press, with dentil cornice above panel doors with anthemia to the incurved corners, 127cm. wide.
(Bristol) $2,086

A George III mahogany linen press, the molded cornice above a pair of panel doors, with two short and two long drawers below, 50in. wide.
(Christie's) $1,783

Mid 19th century figured mahogany press cupboard, top section with two single panel doors decorated with white wood stringing, 47in. wide.
(Peter Wilson) $1,585

A Regency mahogany clothes-press, attributed to Gillows of Lancaster, the upper section with two paneled doors with applied rectangular banding, 52in. wide.
(Christie's) $9,867

A line-inlaid mahogany linen press, the molded cornice above a pair of paneled cupboard doors enclosing slides above two short and two long drawers, late 19th century, 50in. wide.
(Christie's) $1,931

A George III mahogany and string inlaid linen press, with paneled doors enclosing slides, over two short and two long drawers, 49in. wide.
(Andrew Hartley) $1,705

A Regency mahogany and ebony clothes-press, the molded rectangular cornice with inlaid dentils above a paneled frieze, 53¼in. wide.
(Christie's) $6,686

A Regency mahogany clothes-press, attributed to Gillows of Lancaster, the upper section with two paneled doors with applied rectangular banding, 52in. wide.
(Christie's) $8,611

An early 19th century mahogany linen press, with reeded cornice, two paneled doors enclosing trays, 48½in. wide.
(Bearne's) $1,931

LOWBOYS

A Queen Anne cherrywood lowboy, Connecticut, circa 1760, the shaped skirt continuing to cabriole legs, 34in. wide. (Sotheby's) $7,475

A Queen Anne walnut and featherstrung lowboy, the top quarter veneered with a molded edged and re-entrant corners, 84cm. wide. (Phillips) $3,570

A George II walnut lowboy, the molded rounded rectangular cross and feather-banded top above a long drawer and two short drawers, 31¹/₂in. wide. (Christie's) $11,965

George III style laburnum wood oyster veneered lowboy, composed partially of antique elements, the rectangular crossbanded top oyster veneered, 36¹/₄in. wide. (Butterfield & Butterfield) $3,000

An American cherrywood lowboy, 19th century, with molded rectangular top above three long drawers, the lowest centered by a sunburst motif, 42in. wide. (Christie's) $4,579

An antique oak and elm lowboy fitted with three shallow drawers over shaped apron on cabriole legs and pad feet, 2ft. 5in. wide. (Russell, Baldwin & Bright) $1,725

A fine Queen Anne carved cherrywood lowboy, Connecticut, circa 1760, the triple arched skirt below with a turned pendant finial, top 36in. wide. (Sotheby's) $25,300

A William and Mary carved and turned walnut lowboy, Boston, Massachusetts, 1720–50, the molded and crossbanded-top above three herringbone-inlaid drawers, 34in. wide. (Sotheby's) $6,325

A Chippendale carved and figured walnut lowboy, the carving attributed to Bernard and Jugiez, Philadelphia, Pennsylvania, circa 1765, 34¹/₂in. wide. (Sotheby's) $29,900

SCREENS

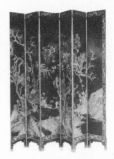

A Louis XV-style three-fold screen, the giltwood frame carved with foliate scrolls and plumes, glazed upper panels, 75¹/₂in. high.
(Bearne's) $1,421

A Chinese coromandel eight-leaf lacquer screen, 19th century, the central field with courtly figures within an architectural setting, each panel 78 x 16in.
(Christie's) $5,740

A twelve-fold Oriental screen in two parts, red-painted and decorated with birds amid foliage, on later bracket feet, 97in. high.
(Christie's) $2,193

H. Thomas, five panel lacquer screen, circa 1919, in sealing wax red and black lacquer, with stylized foliage and exotic birds on perches, each panel 185.5 x 50cm.
(Sotheby's) $12,719

A French painted canvas three-fold screen, late 19th/early 20th century, painted with a scene of a classical garden and buildings from within a gazebo, width of central panel 5ft. 7in.
(Butterfield & Butterfield) $6,037

Chinese Export wallpaper four-fold screen, late 18th century, each panel painted with birds amid flowering and fruiting branches, 6ft. 10in. long.
(Butterfield & Butterfield) $4,025

A French painted canvas four-fold screen, mid 19th century, the screen painted with an interior with a woman at a piano and a young man leaning against it, 6ft. wide.
(Butterfield & Butterfield) $6,325

A Chinese Export bantamwork eight-leaf low screen, 18th century, decorated on both sides with an extensive scene, one side with a mountainous landscape, each leaf 49¹/₂in. x 9³/₄in.
(Christie's) $5,210

A Chinese painted glass and ebonized eight-leaf miniature screen, the central panels showing a garden landscape with dignitaries and pagodas, each panel 26¹/₂ x 6in.
(Christie's) $1,256

SECRETAIRE BOOKCASES

A good Federal bird's-eye maple and flame-birch inlaid mahogany desk and bookcase, Northeastern Shore, New England, circa 1815, 41in. wide. (Sotheby's) $10,350

A George III mahogany and satinwood inlaid secrétaire bookcase, the curved ogee molded cornice inlaid with a central conch, 110cm. wide. (Phillips) $5,206

A Federal maple desk-and-bookcase, in two parts. the upper section with arched shaped pediment surmounted by urn-turned finials, 32in. wide. (Christie's) $3,450

A George IV mahogany secrétaire bookcase, the upper part with arched pediment inlaid in ebony with star motif, fitted three adjustable shelves, 42in. wide. (Canterbury) $5,436

A Regency brown oak and rosewood secrétaire-cabinet, attributed to George Bullock, the upper section with a pair of arched paneled doors below an arched pediment, 61¹/₂in. wide. (Christie's) $16,146

A line-inlaid mahogany secrétaire bookcase, the molded cornice above a pair of astragal glazed doors and fall front, early 19th century, parts associated, 50in. wide. (Christie's) $2,106

A William IV mahogany secrétaire bookcase, the upper part with a molded cornice with later foliate scroll angles, fitted with adjustable shelves, 32in. wide. (Christie's) $6,541

A George III mahogany secrétaire bookcase, the deep dummy drawer front fall enclosing a baize lined writing surface and fitted interior, 48in. wide. (Christie's) $3,443

A fine and rare Federal satinwood-inlaid églomisé and ivory-mounted mahogany secretary-bookcase, Boston or North Shore, Massachusetts, circa 1810, 36in. wide. (Sotheby's) $16,100

SECRETAIRE BOOKCASES

Large late George III mahogany
and inlay secrétaire bookcase,
early 19th century, 49in. wide.
(Skinner) $2,300

A George III mahogany
secrétaire bookcase, with a
dentil cornice, two fifteen-pane
astragal-glazed doors, on later
bracket feet, 48³/₄in. wide.
(Bearne's) $5,253

Federal mahogany veneer glazed
desk and bookcase,
Massachusetts, circa 1790-1810,
40.5in. wide.
(Skinner) $2,760

An early Victorian mahogany
secrétaire bookcase with a flared
cornice above astragal panel
doors enclosing adjustable
shelves, 41¹/₂in. wide.
(Anderson & Garland)
                             $1,950

Austrian Art Deco walnut
secretary bookcase, circa 1930,
the rectangular top with
rounded edges above glazed
sliding doors, max. width
4ft. 7in.
(Butterfield & Butterfield)
                             $1,092

A fine George III satinwood,
tulipwood crossbanded and
inlaid kneehole bookcase, the
upper part with a molded
cornice and pear drop pendant
frieze, square tapered gaitered
legs, 87cm. wide.
(Phillips) $31,237

A Regency mahogany secrétaire
bookcase, inlaid with ebony
lines, the upper part with a
molded arched cornice and
lozenge decorated frieze, 41in.
wide.
(Christie's) $3,098

A George III satinwood
secrétaire-bookcase,
crossbanded overall in
tulipwood, amaranth and
mahogany, and inlaid with
boxwood lines, 68¹/₂in. wide.
(Christie's) $8,970

A George III mahogany
secretary bookcase, circa 1800,
the upper case with a
rectangular outset cornice over
an arched frieze, 47¹/₄in. wide.
(Butterfield & Butterfield)
                             $4,600

341

SECRETAIRES & ESCRITOIRES

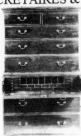

A George III mahogany tallboy, the dentil molded cornice above two short and three long drawers, with a secrétaire drawer below, 47in. wide.
(Christie's) **$3,510**

A William and Mary style oak and walnut escritoire, the upper section with arched panel front and fitted interior with stepped convex drawers, 38in. wide.
(Hy. Duke & Son) **$649**

A George I walnut secrétaire chest on chest with inlaid sunburst and pierced bracket feet, secrétaire drawer perhaps added later, 41in. wide.
(Sworder) **$13,112**

An unsual Louis XVI kingwood, tulipwood parquetry and marquetry secrétaire à abattant by J. B. Hedouin, with a molded cornice and central fall enclosing a fitted interior, 119.5cm. wide.
(Phillips) **$4,462**

A 19th century burr walnut secrétaire military chest by Hill and Millward, 7 Dun Cannon Street, London, patented 1873, in two parts with brass corners, 39in. wide.
(Boardmans) **$4,300**

Art Nouveau bird's-eye maple and oak secrétaire à abattant, early 20th century, the rectangular brown-veined white marble top above a frieze drawer, 31in. wide.
(Butterfield & Butterfield) **$1,610**

A French secrétaire à abattant, rosewood veneered with marquetry inlay, the rouge marble top above a flared frieze, late 19th century, 26in.
(Woolley & Wallis) **$2,120**

A Spanish baroque parcel-gilt polychrome bone and iron-mounted walnut vargueño, the 17th century upper section on a later chest, 50¹/₂in. wide.
(Sotheby's) **$26,450**

An Empire period Karelian birch secrétaire à abattant, surmounted by a rance marble top fitted with an ogee cushion frieze drawer, possibly Russian, 1m. wide.
(Phillips) **$4,165**

A small oak escritoire on chest, the molded cornice above a paneled fall front with molded decoration, reveals a nest of drawers, 3ft. 2in.
(Woolley & Wallis)   **$1,444**

George III mahogany military secrétaire chest, fitted with three long drawers, on bracket feet.
(Hobbs & Chambers)
                               $2,508

A 19th century lady's kingwood and tulipwood small secrétaire on stand, with inset porcelain plaques and gilt metal mounts, 21in. wide.
(Andrew Hartley)
                               $4,560

An Empire gilt-bronze-mounted mahogany secrétaire à abattant, circa 1815, rectangular gray-flecked black marble top above an outset frieze drawer, 37³/₄in. wide.
(Butterfield & Butterfield)
                               $2,875

A 19th century mahogany Biedermeier secrétaire chest of drawers, the molded edged top with protruding corners, on plinth base with wave pattern frieze, 42in. wide.
(Andrew Hartley)   **$1,473**

A Sheraton period secrétaire cabinet, banded in satinwood, the dwarf top with an adjustable shelf enclosed by a pair of oval panel doors, on splay French feet, 34in.
(Woolley & Wallis)
                               $4,710

A Biedermeier mahogany secrétaire à abattant, the fall front opening to interior fitted with leather lined writing surface, 37in. wide.
(Hy. Duke & Son)
                               $2,627

An early 19th century brass bound teak secrétaire military chest, the top section with secrétaire drawer fitted with pigeon holes and five small drawers, 30in. wide.
(Canterbury)   **$2,039**

An early 19th century floral marquetry inlaid walnut secrétaire à abattant, the concave frieze above a fall front enclosing a fitted interior, above three long drawers, 44in. wide.
(Peter Francis)   **$3,862**

SETTEES & COUCHES

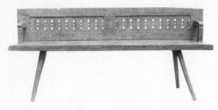

A 19th century veranda settle in the American style with pierced back, jointed arms and stick legs, 73in. wide.
(Boardmans) $760

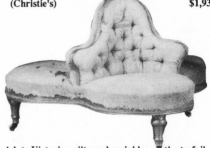

An early Victorian rosewood chaise longue, the overscrolled end and undulating back above a padded seat, with a reeded frieze, 79in. wide.
(Christie's) $1,931

A George III mahogany triple chair back settee in the Sheraton taste, with curved bar top rails and reeded vertical splats, 130cm. wide.
(Phillips) $1,824

A late Victorian giltwood sociable, the trefoil-shaped stuffed seat with conforming buttoned-back covered in pale calico, 50in. diameter.
(Christie's) $2,797

A Victorian walnut three-piece salon suite, comprising low chair, armchair and sofa, the button upholstered backs with carving, sprung seats and on carved turned supports, width of sofa 182cm.
(Bristol) $2,240

An early 19th century Swedish painted and gilded settee, the straight crest rail with applied florets and acanthus leaves, upholstered back and overstuffed seat, downswept padded arms, on four square tapering supports with castors, 11 1/2in wide. (Andrew Hartley) $831

A William and Mary turned and carved beechwood daybed, 1720–50, the arched molded crest continuing to molded stiles centering an adjustable caned back, 5ft. 2in. long.
(Sotheby's) $4,600

A Regency mahogany window seat, the Egyptian style show-wood frame carved lotus details, fluting and scroll finials, on down-turned supports.
(Russell, Baldwin & Bright) $10,850

344

SETTEES & COUCHES

Regency style mahogany finish settee, scroll back
and arms with carved frame, two cushion seat,
five molded cabriole legs.
(Peter Wilson) **$513**

Classical carved mahogany veneer settee,
probably Philadelphia, 1810, with scrolled arms
and turned legs on castors, 74in. wide.
(Skinner) **$1,955**

A William IV brass-inlaid rosewood sofa,
attributed to Gillows of Lancaster, the arms
carved with scrolling acanthus and terminating
in an acanthus-spray, 79in. wide.
(Christie's) **$6,099**

A late Victorian walnut sofa, paneled carpet
upholstery with tasseled fringe, on ring-turned
legs, 62in. wide.
(Christie's) **$2,025**

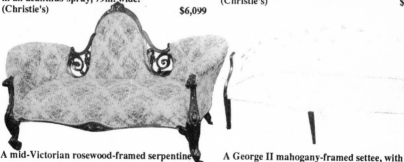

A mid-Victorian rosewood-framed serpentine
settee, the arched button back pierced and
carved with scrolls and foliage, scroll-carved
arm supports continuing into cabriole legs with
knurl feet.
(Bearne's) **$2,163**

A George II mahogany-framed settee, with
arched rounded button-upholstered back,
serpentine feet and molded S-shaped arm
supports continuing into tapering square legs,
72in. wide.
(Bearne's) **$2,858**

A Regency scroll-end sofa with simulated
rosewood frame carved leafage, upholstered in
cut figured velvet, on saber legs and brass
casters.
(Russell, Baldwin & Bright) **$1,900**

A Victorian walnut settee, with twin upholstered
high back ends, pierced and scrolled central
splat, downswept arms with scrolled ends on
barley twist supports, 64in. wide.
(Andrew Hartley) **$1,473**

SETTEES & COUCHES

Arts & Crafts oak settle, early 20th century, the rectangular crestrail above fifteen vertical slats over broad arms, 6ft. 6in. long.
(Butterfield & Butterfield) $2,875

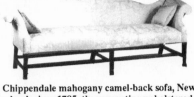

A Chippendale mahogany camel-back sofa, New England, circa 1785, the serpentine upholstered back flanked by downsloping outscrolled arms, on square tapering legs joined by stretchers, 7ft. 6in. long.   (Sotheby's) $9,200

A classical carved mahogany sofa, Baltimore, Maryland, circa 1820, the pierced and reeded crest rail carved with pinwheels and flanked by scrolled arms, 7ft.8in. long.
(Sotheby's) $3,737

A classical carved mahogany sofa, Boston, Massachusetts, circa 1825, the shaped crest with projecting center section with scrolling leaf-carved terminals, 7ft. long.
(Sotheby's) $4,600

Classical carved mahogany veneer small settee, Boston area, third quarter 19th century, with rolled and carved crest, scrolled leaf-carved arms and veneered seat rail, 53½in. wide.
(Skinner) $2,070

A mid-Victorian walnut conversation settee, with a foliate and floral cresting above three buttoned backs, with foliate scrolling arm divisions, 48in. wide.
(Christie's) $1,404

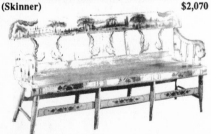

A cream-painted and polychrome-decorated plank-seat settee and four matching side chairs, Pennsylvania, circa 1825, the settee with horizontal crest with shaped ears, 6ft. long.
(Sotheby's) $4,025

A Louis XVI gray-painted canapé, stamped *I.B. Lelarge,* last quarter 18th century, the cove-molded backrest of D-shaped outline joining over-scrolled armrests, 5ft. 4in.
(Butterfield & Butterfield) $3,737

SETTEES & COUCHES

Regency faux bois settee, England, early 19th century, old brown grain painted wood surfaces, 63.25in. wide.
(Skinner) $2,070

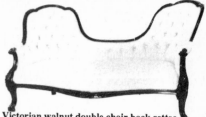

Victorian walnut double chair back settee, carved show wood frame with molded decoration, button back serpentine front, 71in. wide. (Peter Wilson) $1,560

Philadelphia camel back sofa, eight legs, circa 1800, with extensive restoration, scroll arms, tight upholstered seat, serpentine front, 76in. long.
(Du Mouchelles) $3,250

A turned and painted Windsor knuckle-arm settee, signed by John Wire, Philadelphia, Pennsylvania, 1791–1813, the shaped back above thirty-three tapered spindles, 6ft. 7in. long.
(Sotheby's) $8,050

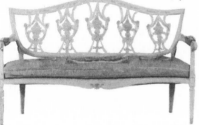

One of a pair of Italian neoclassical style needlepoint settees, each arched channel-molded foliate-carved crestrail, above graduated pierce-carved urn-form splats, 6ft. long.
(Butterfield & Butterfield) $3,450

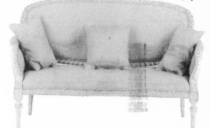

An Italian neoclassical parcel-gilt and cream-painted settee, last quarter 18th century, the slightly arched and rounded backrest carved with guilloche centered by a ribboned cartouche, 4ft. 11½in. long.
(Butterfield & Butterfield) $1,955

A fine and rare classical ormolu-mounted carved mahogany sofa, Philadelphia, Pennsylvania, circa 1825, the horizontal reverse-scrolled crest mounted with ormolu masks, 7ft. long.
(Sotheby's) $5,175

A George IV mahogany sofa, attributed to Gillows of Lancaster, the rectangular caned back flanked by scrolled arms centered by a turned flowerhead, on gadrooned and reeded turned feet, 79in. wide. (Christie's) $5,023

A George III giltwood wall-bracket, the shaped top with a band of concave stylized leaves above laurel swags on three scrolled supports, 14¼in. high.
(Christie's) $2,084

A pair of oak wall brackets, the rectangular platforms with canted corners, supported by foliate carved tapering back-plates, 18in. high.
(Christie's) $577

A scrolled five-tier hanging corner shelf, Pennsylvania, 19th century, centering five graduated quarter-fan shelves flanked on each side by scrolling serpentine support, 51in. high.
(Christie's) $2,185

A pair of Federal carved giltwood brackets, American, 19th century, each shaped shelf above a carved spread winged eagle support, on a tassel carved pendant, 13in. high.
(Christie's) $6,900

A pair of mahogany open bookcases, of George III style, each fitted with four molded rectangular shelves supported by pierced scrolled sides, 21in. wide.
(Christie's) $1,362

A pair of George II white-painted plaster wall brackets, attributed to John Cheere, each with waved molded top above an asymmetrically-cast rockwork C-scroll and foliate backplate, 16in. wide.
(Christie's) $13,024

A scroll-carved chestnut hanging shelf, possibly Northern Chester County, Pennsylvania, 19th century, centering three rectangular shelves with repeating serpentine fronts, 23in. wide.
(Christie's) $2,990

A pair of early George III giltwood wall brackets, the serpentine galleried platforms supported upon ho ho birds with outswept wings, 35cm. wide.
(Phillips) $11,856

A set of George II grained hanging shelves, the broken pediment with egg-and-dart cornice and foliate carved spandrels centered by a double scallop-shell finial, 43in. wide.
(Christie's) $6,334

348

A mahogany pedestal sideboard, early 19th century, with a crossbanded shaped top and fitted with two frieze drawers, 97in. wide.
(Christie's) $2,754

An Art Deco Mercier Frères walnut and rosewood sideboard, having a stepped top and two central cupboard doors enclosing an adjustable shelf, 169cm. wide.
(Phillips) $825

A William IV painted breakfront pedestal sideboard, the raised back with foliate scroll carving above a gadrooned edge, 90in. wide.
(Christie's) $1,688

A magnificent Victorian mahogany marquis cabinet of monumental form, the tall raised arched mirror back surmounted with two putti, 102in. wide.
(James Adam)
                      $16,539

17th century oak three shelf buffet, top with 7 inch frieze decorated with thumb mold and concealing single drawer, 45in. wide.
(Peter Wilson) $2,496

A French walnut buffet, circa 1860, in Henry II style, the upper part with a recess flanked by figures of Hercules and Minerva enclosing further panels, 147cm. wide.
(Sotheby's) $5,704

A George III mahogany sideboard, banded overall with fruitwood, the semi-elliptical crossbanded top above a frieze drawer and a recess with tambour shutter, 66in. wide.
(Christie's) $4,399

Victorian Arts and Crafts oak canted breakfront sideboard, low panel back pierced with heart motifs, 54in. wide.
(Peter Wilson) $630

A carved oak buffet in the Gothic taste, the geometric molded top above a leaf carved and pierced arch frieze, 2nd/3rd quarter 19th century, 163cm. wide.
(Phillips) $1,976

SIDEBOARDS

Late 18th century Sheraton design serpentine front mahogany sideboard, on six square tapering legs, 42in. wide.
(Locke & England) $3,140

Federal cherry inlaid half sideboard, Northern Windsor County, Vermont, 1810–15, the top hinged drawer opens to a desk-like interior, 43³/₄in. wide.
(Skinner) $3,220

A late George III mahogany serpentine sideboard, the frieze with a long drawer above 'C' scroll and paterae carved brackets, 188cm. wide.
(Phillips) $4,462

An Elizabethan oak, sycamore and walnut buffet with carved frieze above a central carved arcaded door, 48in. wide.
(Boardmans) $16,720

A classical carved mahogany parcel-gilt and ormolu-mounted sideboard, New York, New York, circa 1830, the rectangular top surmounted by a reverse breakfronted black backsplash, 42in. wide.
(Sotheby's) $2,185

A Victorian walnut mirror back sideboard, top section with arched central glass flanked by two oval mirrors, 60in. wide.
(Peter Wilson) $803

A George III mahogany sideboard, the crossbanded serpentine top above a central crossbanded drawer and a kneehole with fan-shaped angle brackets, 54¹/₄in. wide.
(Christie's) $7,535

Art Deco style burled walnut buffet, the shaped splashboard and central-oval top over bow-fronted long drawers, 5ft. 7in. wide.
(Butterfield & Butterfield) $3,450

A fine Sheraton period faded mahogany bow front sideboard, crossbanded and inlaid stringing, on square tapering legs with collar feet, 5ft. 4in.
(Woolley & Wallis) $7,600

SIDEBOARDS

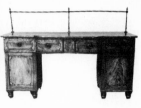

A Regency mahogany twin pedestal sideboard, the bowfront center with brass rail back and two frieze drawers, 185.5cm. wide.
(Bristol) **$1,483**

A George III-style inlaid mahogany bow-front sideboard, crossbanded throughout and outlined with ebony lines, 66¼in. wide.
(Bearne's) **$3,090**

A Regency mahogany semi bow front sideboard having a brass curtain rail, center drawer, flanked by two smaller drawers with brass ring handles, 74in. wide.
(Morphets) **$2,120**

Arts and Crafts enameled copper mounted pollard oak and carved walnut breakfront sideboard, amber glass door panels, center mirror, English, 85in. wide.
(Skinner) **$7,475**

A classical mahogany and mahogany veneer sideboard, Massachusetts, circa 1800, old refinish, old brasses, 47½in. wide.
(Skinner) **$4,370**

A 49in. Victorian mahogany sideboard with mirror back in floral carved decorative frame, two frieze drawers and cupboard below, enclosed by paneled doors.
(Stainers') **$1,193**

A good George III mahogany bow-fronted sideboard, the central drawer above an arched fronted napery drawer, approx. 60in. wide.
(Diamond Mills & Co.) **$4,470**

A line-inlaid mahogany breakfront sideboard, the crossbanded top above a frieze drawer and arched apron drawer with reeded molding, 19th century, 64in. wide.
(Christie's) **$3,886**

A Federal inlaid and crossbanded figured mahogany serpentine-front sideboard with slide, New England, circa 1810, on line-inlaid square tapering legs, 1.66m. long.
(Sotheby's) **$34,500**

STANDS

A mahogany pot cupboard, the circular belge granit marble top above a cupboard door, 17in. wide.
(Christie's) $1,990

A Chinese Export porcelain charger on an English polychrome-painted mahogany stand, the porcelain Daoguang (1821–1850), the stand 19th century, 63cm. wide. (Christie's) $5,210

Bird's eye maple stand, New England, circa 1820, with opalescent glass pulls, 19in. wide.
(Skinner) $747

A Queen Anne figured mahogany dish-top candlestand, Philadelphia, Pennsylvania, circa 1750, tilting above a turned flaring compressed ball standard, 23¹/₂in. diameter.
(Sotheby's) $12,650

Pair of Louis XV style mahogany and burl walnut coiffeuses, each heart form hinged surface opening to a reserve with beveled mirror plate over a small front, 19¹/₂in. wide.
(Butterfield & Butterfield) $4,025

A Regency mahogany architect's table, the double-hinged molded-rectangular rising top with two later reading-supports and on square tapering end-supports, 40in. wide.
(Christie's) $5,210

A carved solid mahogany model of a four-headed horse, mid-18th century, of X-shaped design centered by a foliate scallop-shell, on splayed legs, 17in. wide.
(Christie's) $16,497

Tiger maple and cherry stand, Connecticut River Valley, early 19th century, with beaded drawer and skirt, 24in. wide.
(Skinner) $2,760

Gallé marquetry waste paper basket, circa 1900, of flaring rectangular outline, the front inlaid with stylized flowerheads and foliage, 21¹/₄in. high.
(Butterfield & Butterfield) $1,035

STANDS

A mahogany jardinière, the slatted concave body with carrying handle and brass liner, on turned column and quadripartite platform, Dutch, early 19th century, 20¹/₂in. high.
(Christie's) $668

Federal cherry candlestand with drawer, Connecticut, circa 1790, old cherry color top with moulded edge, 16.75in. wide.
(Skinner) $19,550

Painted and grained stand, New England, circa 1825, the top and drawer facade have brown and yellow vinegar painting outlined in black, 18in. wide.
(Skinner) $4,600

A Chippendale carved mahogany dish-top candlestand, Philadelphia, Pennsylvania, circa 1765, the circular top tilting and revolving above a bird-cage support, 24¹/₂in. diameter.
(Sotheby's) $129,000

Pair of Louis Philippe mahogany and parcel-ebonized chevets, circa 1840, each with white marble top over a frieze drawer projecting above a cupboard, 16in. wide.
(Butterfield & Butterfield) $3,162

Charles Rennie Mackintosh, easel for the Glasgow School of Art, 1910, ebonized pine, rectangular section canvas support on splayed pegged stand on H-frame base, on castors, 197cm. high.
(Sotheby's) $7,268

A Chippendale carved and figured mahogany serpentine-top candlestand, Salem, Massachusetts, circa 1780, on C-scroll-carved cabriole legs, 27¹/₂in. high.
(Sotheby's) $35,650

Federal cherry and bird's-eye maple stand, Connecticut River Valley, circa 1815-25, cherry top above two drawers with bird's-eye maple facades, dark stained legs, 19in. wide.
(Skinner) $2,300

Chippendale cherry and tiger maple candlestand, Connecticut River Valley, 1770-90, with cherry tray top, tiger maple pedestal and tripod base, 25.5in. high.
(Skinner) $16,100

STEPS

A set of mahogany library steps, comprising three steps with a turned handrest, on molded outswept legs joined by a stretcher, 17in. wide.
(Christie's) $373

A set of Victorian mahogany bedsteps with three green leather-lined tiers, the top and central ones hinged.
(Christie's) $1,035

A Victorian oak metamorphic library stepchair, the arched and pierced gothic back centered by a shield, panel seat.
(Andrew Hartley) $780

A Regency mahogany metamorphic library step armchair in the manner of Morgan and Sanders, with scroll arm supports and cane seat.
(Phillips) $4,800

A set of Regency mahogany four-tread metamorphic library steps, by Gillows, the beige material-lined rectangular top above paneled sides, opening to reveal four beige material-lined treads, 35³/₄in. wide.
(Christie's) $15,628

A Regency satinbirch metamorphic open armchair and steps, the paneled tablet toprail on scrolled arms on turned supports.
(Christie's) $7,245

A set of mahogany library steps, early 19th century, the green leather-lined top step above two further steps, molded supports and curved feet, 13¹/₄in. wide.
(Christie's) $2,952

A set of William IV metamorphic library steps with leather-lined top, fitted with drawer and hinged to reveal four treads.
(Christie's) $1,200

A set of elm simulated-bamboo library steps, 19th century, each spreading side with turned treads and shafts and the top with iron hinges, 77¹/₄in. high, open.
(Christie's) $2,257

STOOLS

An early Victorian mahogany X-frame stool, with floral needlework seat, 21in. wide. (Christie's) $702

A William and Mary turned and paint-decorated birchwood joint stool, New England, 1710–40, on vase-turned legs joined by stretchers, 22in. long. (Sotheby's) $6,325

A Regency mahogany hallbench, the rectangular top with canted corners and molded rim and two cylinder handles, 35in. wide. (Christie's) $878

A pair of Victorian walnut X-framed stools, each with rectangular padded seat covered in gros point patterned needlework, 50cm. and 47cm. (Christie's) $4,664

A George IV brass-mounted mahogany piano stool, attributed to Gillows of Lancaster, on four reeded turned baluster legs joined by an X-shaped stretcher, 16½in. diameter. (Christie's) $1,435

A pair of Charles II ebonized stools, the rectangular top upholstered in black horsehair above block and volute feet, 20½in. wide. (Christie's) $6,817

A Louis XV style giltwood tabouret, the shaped square seat upholstered in floral needlepoint, the seatrails carved with scrolls and scallop shells, raised on cabriole legs. (Butterfield & Butterfield) $3,737

Edwardian mahogany stool, with four triple pillar cluster column legs, 'X' stretcher upholstered rectangular seat, 19in. diameter. (Peter Wilson) $468

A Regency mahogany X-frame stool, attributed to Gillows of Lancaster, the rectangular bowed caned seat with scroll ends above the chaneled S-shaped X-frame, 21¼in. wide. (Christie's) $9,328

STOOLS

A Continental baroque walnut choir stall, with molded shaped top over the conforming paneled back and sides, 29¼in. wide.
(Sotheby's) **$2,875**

A tapestry covered walnut stool in the Jacobean style, the rectangular padded seat on block and reel turned legs joined by stretchers, 108cm. long.
(Phillips) **$547**

A Victorian walnut piano stool, on turned baluster legs with upturned fluting centered by a conforming baluster.
(Christie's) **$986**

A classical carved mahogany footstool, Boston, Massachusetts, circa 1830, the rectangular seat with a molded and scrolling X-form base, 21in. wide.
(Sotheby's) **$1,150**

An Italian parcel-gilt and gray-painted stool, 19th century, the rectangular padded seat and anthemion decorated frieze on acanthus headed cabriole legs, 16½in. wide.
(Christie's) **$2,237**

A Victorian mahogany rectangular piano stool, the padded seat with height adjustment mechanism, raised on turned and fluted tapering supports.
(James Adam) **$177**

A George II mahogany dressing stool, with drop in needlework top above plain frieze, 20in. wide.
(Hy. Duke & Son)
$2,086

A walnut dressing stool, of early Georgian design, the shaped rectangular top with a gros point needlework upholstered drop-in seat, 22¼in. wide.
(Christie's) **$840**

A Victorian rosewood cross frame dressing stool, on fluted formal foliate sheathed cross supports tied by a baluster turned stretcher.
(Phillips) **$243**

STOOLS

A Regency simulated rosewood window seat, each end as a chair back with scrolled toprail and mid-rails with central bullseyes, 36in. wide. $770
(George Kidner)

Continental neoclassical mahogany and parcel-gilt bench, early 19th century.
(Skinner) $1,725

A carved poplar and walnut footstool, American, possibly Hudson River Valley, 1780–1820, the oblong top with concave ends, 12in. wide.
(Sotheby's) $460

A North Italian walnut prie dieu, in baroque style, with molded rectangular top, the slanted front fitted with four molded drawers, 24in. wide.
(Sotheby's) $1,265

Pair of Victorian polychrome decorated benches, late 19th century, distressed silk upholstery, 22½in. long.
(Skinner) $2,185

One of a pair of 17th century joined stools, the thumbnail molded top above a lunette carved frieze, 18in. wide.
(Boardmans) $3,565

Modern gothic walnut tabouret, third quarter 19th century, the side inset with tiles, upholstered top, 24in. long.
(Skinner) $402

An Edwardian mahogany lyre shaped dressing stool, the raised ends with bar slats centrally inlaid with shells and scrolls.
(Dee, Atkinson & Harrison) $302

A North Italian walnut seat, the open scroll arms with leaf carved terminals supported by putti.
(Woolley & Wallis) $1,287

SUITES

A good set of twelve Federal grain-painted and stencil-decorated cane-seat side chairs and matching bench, New York, circa 1820, each with an arched crest with projecting center section.
(Sotheby's) $5,462

A good Victorian walnut framed nine-piece drawing room suite, the molded frames with carved leaf cresting, comprising three-seat settee, gentleman's open-arm easy chair, lady's chair and six drawing room chairs.
(Canterbury) $2,567

Art Deco tubular steel salon suite, second quarter 20th century, comprising a settee and two club chairs, each rectangular backrest joined by continuous scrolled armrests continuing to supports, settee 4ft. long.
(Butterfield & Butterfield) $4,312

SUITES

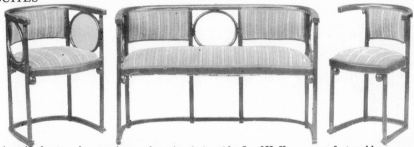

Austrian bentwood seven-piece parlor suite, designed by Josef Hoffman, manufactured by Pancotta, circa 1915, comprising a settee, two armchairs and four side chairs, the settee with a curved roll-over U-shaped crestrail, settee 4ft. 1¹/₂in. long.
(Butterfield & Butterfield) $2,875

English Art Deco bird's-eye maple dining seven-piece suite, circa 1930, the table with rectangular divided top and rounded corners over trestle ends, each side chair with a lobed incurvate laminated backrest, length of table closed 5ft. 5³/₄in.
(Butterfield & Butterfield) $4,600

An inlaid Edwardian mahogany part salon suite, the two seater settee with shaped crest rail centered a floral inlaid cartouche over a part upholstered back.
(Dee, Atkinson & Harrison) $1,057

BREAKFAST TABLES

A William IV rosewood breakfast table, the rounded rectangular top on lotus-lappeted turned column and quadripartite platform on lappeted bun feet, 52in. wide. (Christie's) **$1,229**

Dutch neoclassical walnut and marquetry breakfast table, 19th century, 42¹/₂in. long extended. (Skinner) **$3,220**

A Regency plum pudding mahogany, satinwood and rosewood crossbanded breakfast table, on a ring turned shaft and quadripartite base with outswept legs, 152cm. wide. (Phillips) **$6,247**

Federal mahogany inlaid breakfast table, New York City, circa 1790, with a working and a simulated drawer, 31¹/₄in. wide. (Skinner) **$11,500**

A fine George III mahogany tilt-top breakfast table, the 'D' ended rectangular top, raised on a turned cannon barrel stem with four downswept reeded legs, 60in. x 47in. (Diamond Mills & Co.) **$2,682**

Chippendale mahogany breakfast table, New London County, Connecticut, 18th century, with chamfered legs, shaped stretchers and early brass, 20.75in. wide. (Skinner) **$3,105**

A Regency pollard oak and ebony strung breakfast table in the manner of George Bullock, with circular quarter veneered snap top inlaid with ebony lines, 105cm. diameter. (Phillips) **$5,206**

A William IV rosewood breakfast table, the circular tilting top with plain frieze on turned tapering shaft, 54in. diameter. (Hy. Duke & Son) **$2,472**

A William IV rosewood breakfast table, with bead decoration and circular hinged top on turned column, 48in. diameter. (Christie's) **$5,508**

CARD & TEA TABLES

An early Victorian rosewood card table, the hinged leather-lined top with shaped frieze, on turned column, 36in. wide.
(Christie's) $1,589

A pair of George III mahogany tea tables inlaid with satinwood lines, the 'D' shaped tops above inlaid friezes, on square tapering legs, 92cm. wide.
(Phillips) $9,880

A fine and rare Queen Anne walnut and parcel gilt half round card table, the baize lined top crossbanded and featherstrung, 81cm. wide.
(Phillips) $32,725

A George III satinwood and rosewood crossbanded card table, the 'D' shaped baize lined hinged top with crossbanded frieze, on square tapered gaitered legs, 92cm. wide.
(Phillips) $6,384

A pair of Regency brass-inlaid rosewood swivel-action card-table, on a dished central support with spreading plinth and concave-fronted rectangular platform, 35in. wide.
(Christie's) $19,734

One of a pair of Federal inlaid mahogany card tables, Baltimore, 1790–1810, each with radiating veneered demi-lune top with banded edge, 36in. wide.
(Christie's)
(Two) $222,500

An early George II mahogany half round tea table, the hinged top enclosing a frieze compartment, on hipped tapered legs, 71cm. wide.
(Phillips) $1,672

A pair of early George III mahogany card tables in the Chippendale style, the rectangular baize lined hinged tops with riband and paterae edges, 92cm. wide.
(Phillips) $22,800

A William IV burr-elm tea table, with a crossbanded hinged top, on a square baluster column, 36in. wide.
(Christie's) $2,323

CARD & TEA TABLES

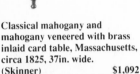

Classical mahogany and mahogany veneered with brass inlaid card table, Massachusetts, circa 1825, 37in. wide. (Skinner)   **$1,092**

Classical mahogany veneer carved card table, New York, 1820–30, 36¼in. wide. (Skinner)   **$632**

A Dutch walnut and floral marquetry card table, with hinged demi-lune top, on square tapering supports, 32¼in. wide. (Christie's)   **$1,213**

A Chippendale carved mahogany card table, Boston-Salem, Massachusetts, circa 1760, the hinged oblong top with squared outset corners, 32in. wide extended. (Sotheby's)   **$134,500**

An important classical gilt-metal mounted mahogany and rosewood swivel-top card table, labelled *Charles Honoré Lannuier, New York*, circa 1810, 35¾in. wide. (Sotheby's)   **$310,500**

A yew-wood card table of George II style, the eared crossbanded hinged top enclosing a needlework lining, on scallop-shell headed cabriole legs, 32½in. wide. (Christie's)   **$1,766**

A Victorian burr walnut card table with a serpentine shaped swivel top, raised on a carved and turned column, 36in. wide. (Anderson & Garland)   **$1,320**

A George III mahogany D-shaped card table, the plain baize lined top with wide satinwood crossbanding, 36in. wide. (Canterbury)   **$1,309**

A fine classical carved mahogany and rosewood brass-inlaid swivel-top card table, Philadelphia, Pennsylvania, circa 1825, 38in. wide. (Sotheby's)   **$4,025**

CARD & TEA TABLES

An early Victorian rosewood rectangular card table, the plain baize lined top with bead mounts, plain apron, 36in. wide. (Canterbury) $1,694

Federal mahogany veneer card table, Massachusetts, early 19th century, 37.4in. wide. (Skinner) $1,495

An early Victorian rosewood serpentine card table, with hinged top and bulbous cabochon column, with downswept legs and scrolling foliate-carved feet, 36in. wide. (Christie's) $1,237

A Regency brass-mounted satinwood-inlaid rosewood card table, circa 1815, the rectangular divided top with inlaid reserve and canted corners, 36in. wide. (Butterfield & Butterfield) $1,725

A Chippendale figured mahogany diminutive serpentine-front stop-fluted card table, Goddard-Townsend School, Newport, Rhode Island, circa 1780, 32in. wide. (Sotheby's) $41,400

A George II walnut triple-top games table, circa 1760, the serpentine triple fold-over top with outset rounded corners, 32¼in. wide. (Butterfield & Butterfield) $4,025

A William IV rosewood card table, the hinged rectangular top with gadrooned edge enclosing a baize interior, above carved frieze, 36in. wide. (Christie's) $1,942

An Edwardian floral-marquetry rosewood envelope card table, the quarter hinged top enclosing a lined playing surface, above a frieze drawer, 22in. wide. (Christie's) $1,931

A classical ebony and rosewood-inlaid mahogany swivel-top card table, Boston, Massachusetts, circa 1820, 35½in. wide open. (Sotheby's) $2,185

CARD & TEA TABLES

A classical mahogany carved and inlaid gaming table, New England, circa 1820, with tiger maple crossbanded borders and brass inlaid stringing, 35½in. wide.
(Skinner) $1,955

A Colonial carved hardwood envelope card table, the hinged top enclosing green baize above four frieze drawers, late 19th century, 24in. wide.
(Christie's) $680

A late 19th century carved pine half round card table in the George II style, the hinged molded top with a velvet inset surface and overlapping laurel frieze, 82cm. wide.
(Phillips) $684

A mid-Victorian burr-walnut card table, the hinged top of serpentine outline enclosing a baize, interior, swiveling to reveal a compartment below, 36in. wide.
(Christie's) $1,019

A pair of mahogany card tables, George IV, possibly Scottish, circa 1820, the crossbanded chamfered rectangular tops above quadruple turned and dolphin carved supports, 94cm. wide.
(Sotheby's) $58,590

Regency gilt-bronze mounted and brass-inlaid rosewood games table, early 19th century, the rectangular brass inlaid hinged surface opening to a tooled leather playing surface, 35¾in. wide.
(Butterfield & Butterfield)
                            $9,200

A George III mahogany D-shaped tea table inlaid with ebony stringings, with plain folding top, on molded saber legs, 36in. wide.
(Canterbury) $1,117

A mid-Victorian rosewood tea table, the rectangular hinged top above a foliate-carved shaped apron, on a fluted baluster-turned shaft, 37in. wide.
(Christie's) $1,188

A George III satinwood, mahogany banded card table, of D-shaped outline with a baize lined hinged top and panel front, 36in. wide.
(Christie's) $3,442

CENTER TABLES

Painted chair table, New England, early 18th century, old red painted surface, 44.5in. diameter.
(Skinner) $8,625

A mahogany circular extending table, with five extra leaves and a leaf cabinet, the circular top on four turned columns, 82in. fully extended.
(Christie's) $2,193

A bamboo, simulated bamboo and cane table, the canted rectangular top lined with woven trellis and with a slide to each end, 45^1/$_2$in. wide.
(Christie's) $4,862

A mid-Georgian Provincial mahogany Manx tripod table, the ring-turned spreading columnar shaft on three shaped legs carved with buttoned and buckled britches and buckled shoes, 38^1/$_2$in. diameter.
(Christie's) $4,862

A mahogany and hardwood center table, 19th century, the circular rosewood crossbanded top with foliate border above four true and four false frieze drawers, 29in. wide.
(Christie's) $2,987

An English ebonized, brown tortoiseshell and brass-inlaid center table, 19th century, decorated with interlaced and undulating foliate scrolls, 53^1/$_2$in. diameter.
(Christie's) $15,925

A mid-Victorian mahogany dining table, the top of serpentine outline with molded rim above a plain frieze, 58in. wide.
(Christie's) $1,510

A marble top center table, 19th century, with circular top and brass-mounted concave sided triform base, 36in. diameter.
(Christie's) $1,513

A walnut circular table, the molded and radially-veneered tip-up top with bulbous column and splayed legs, 19th century, 49^1/$_2$in. diameter.
(Christie's) $1,528

CENTER TABLES

A French ebonized gilt-metal mounted and marquetry center table, late 19th century, of undulating outline, veneered in scarlet tortoiseshell, on cabriole legs, 59in. wide.
(Christie's) $2,581

A gilt-metal circular center table, with a marble top and rope-twist border, on S-scroll supports with gadrooned feet, 33in. diameter.
(Christie's) $7,229

A Victorian carved oak center table, the radial octagonal tip-up top with leaf carved edge, deep frieze with trailing vine divided by protruding panels, 48in. wide.
(Andrew Hartley)
$2,038

An oak center table, the hinged rectangular top opening to reveal a green-leather surface, above deep frieze carved with portrait medallions, 33¹/₂in. wide.
(Christie's) $527

A superb George IV circular center table, the top with quarter walnut veneer within a floral marquetry and ribbon band and molded rosewood rim, 51in. diameter.
(James Adam) $7,942

A Regency mahogany center table, the rounded rectangular top above end supports joined by a turned and reeded stretcher, 91cm. wide.
(Phillips) $1,934

A Louis Philippe mahogany center table, with a circular marble top and later frieze, on a turned and reeded vase column, 37in. diameter.
(Christie's) $3,787

A Dutch ebonized, floral marquetry and bone banded center table, the rectangular top inlaid with a vase issuing acanthus scrolls and foliage, 36in. wide, open.
(Christie's) $3,363

A Regency brass-inlaid rosewood library table, attributed to Gillows of Lancaster, the circular top with arabesque band along the border, 48in. diameter.
(Christie's) $17,940

CENTER TABLES

A George III mahogany center table, the rectangular double-hinged top with two fold-out leaves, with two frieze drawers, 121cm. wide, open.
(Christie's) **$5,023**

A fine William IV inlaid mahogany circular center table, the top crossbanded in rosewood and having reeded rim, 45in. diameter.
(James Adam) **$2,166**

An early 20th century French kingwood and marquetry center table, in the style of Louis XV, top with serpentine outline, frieze drawer, 100cm. wide.
(Peter Wilson) **$1,545**

Jules Leleu, mirror top table, circa 1940, the circular mirrored top set in a gilt metal frame on columnar support, 35½in. diameter.
(Sotheby's) **$3,997**

Good quality Victorian mahogany center table, circular top with sixteen segment matched flame veneers, guilloche carving to rim, 60in. diameter.
(Peter Wilson) **$4,524**

An Italian walnut drum-top center table, 19th century, with a star inlaid top and four frieze drawers, possibly Maltese, 26½in. diameter.
(Christie's) **$4,131**

A mahogany center table, the circular top on turned column, quadripartite platform and bun feet, Central European, 19th century, 31¾in. wide.
(Christie's) **$741**

A German walnut circular center table, 19th century with a marble top on three scroll acanthus-headed cabriole legs, 39in. diameter.
(Christie's) **$3,614**

Baltic neoclassical tilt-top karelian birch center table, early 19th century, possibly Russian, circular top on a hexagonal support, raised on three paw feet, 36in. diameter.
(Skinner) **$4,025**

CENTER TABLES

A Regency classical inlaid rosewood center table on twin fluted supports with carved terminals on downturned bases, 27½in. wide.
(Graves, Son & Pilcher) $10,644

An Italian walnut center table, circa 1890, in Renaissance style, with a rectangular top on supports carved with female masks and harpies, 99cm. wide.
(Sotheby's) $14,260

A walnut center table, Pennsylvania, late 18th/early 19th century, on tapering block and ring-turned legs with flattened ball feet, 71in. wide.
(Christie's) $10,350

An early 19th century parquetry library table inlaid with specimen woods, the octagonal baluster shaft with a chamfered and turned socle, 111cm. diameter.
(Phillips) $8,181

A Louis XV style gilt-bronze-mounted marquetry mahogany and tulip table de milieu, late 19th century, the circular top inlaid with a radiating reserve and inlaid crossbanded edge, 37in. diameter.
(Butterfield & Butterfield) $3,450

A George IV rosewood and specimen marble center table, the circular inset top with central panel of fossil banded with sections of specimen marbles, 33½in. diameter.
(Christie's) $7,038

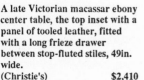

A late Victorian macassar ebony center table, the top inset with a panel of tooled leather, fitted with a long frieze drawer between stop-fluted stiles, 49in. wide.
(Christie's) $2,410

Chinese root wood center table, 19th century, rosewood top, 38½in. diameter.
(Skinner) $2,760

A silvered and ebonized center table, 19th century, in the early 18th century style, with a marble top and S-scroll frieze, 40in. wide.
(Christie's) $3,098

CONSOLE TABLES

A late 19th century giltwood and composition console table, the bowed breakfront white marble top above a fluted frieze, on fluted legs, 114cm. wide.
(Phillips) $3,800

A pair of giltwood consoles, each with a variegated marble top and Greek key carved frieze, on a support in the form of an eagle, 39in. wide.
(Christie's) $10,328

A William IV rosewood console table, lacking marble, the molded rectangular top above a foliate-scroll frieze with lotus corners, 31in. wide.
(Christie's) $3,473

A Louis XVI style gilt-bronze and porcelain-mounted mahogany console-vitrine, early 20th century, the lower case with ovolo-shaped marquetry inlaid surface, 4ft. 3¼in.
(Butterfield & Butterfield)
                              $4,600

A pair of Louis XVI giltwood pier tables, design attributed to Antoine-Mathieu Le Carpentier, each with later rounded rectangular breakfront portor marble top, 76cm. wide.
(Christie's) $319,960

A Regency console table with simulated rosewood graining, the shallow rectangular top of rosewood veneer, with brass anthemion mount to the frieze, 4ft. 3in.
(Russell, Baldwin & Bright)
                              $3,410

An Empire gilt-bronze-mounted mahogany console, early 19th century, rectangular white marble top above a plain frieze, 42in. wide.
(Butterfield & Butterfield)
                              $4,312

A pair of late 18th century kingwood and purplewood console dessertes, in the Louis XVI style, the 'D' shaped marble tops with pierced three-quarter gallery, possibly Dutch, 56cm. wide.
(Phillips) $6,247

A Louis XVI tulipwood console desserte, stamped G. Schlichtig, banded in amaranth and inlaid with boxwood and checker lines, 96cm. wide.
(Phillips) $4,864

DINING TABLES

A George II mahogany drop leaf dining table, with an oval hinged top and arched apron, on cabriole legs, 126cm. x 150cm. extended.
(Phillips) $1,339

A Victorian mahogany extending dining table with half-round ends and molded edge, on floral-carved cabriole legs and casters, 12ft. 3in.
(Russell, Baldwin & Bright)
                              $4,455

A Victorian mahogany oblong dining table, winding out with one leaf, on turned tapering fluted supports with castors, 182cm. wide.
(Bristol) $1,130

An early 19th century loo table, the figured mahogany veneered octagonal top inlaid stringing quartering, centered a satinwood panel, 3ft. 5in. diameter.
(Woolley & Wallis)
                              $2,660

A mahogany extending dining table comprising two drop-leaf end sections and central drop-leaf section, the rectangular top with reeded edge, 162in. fully extended.
(Christie's) $3,886

A fine quality Victorian oval burr walnut loo table, the burr walnut segmented top with parcel carving to the edge, 60 x 47in.
(Boardmans) $3,875

A good early Victorian mahogany extending dining table with three extra leaves, the top with plain molded edges and rounded corners, 118 x 54in. extended.
(Canterbury) $6,930

An early George III mahogany drop-leaf dining table, the oval top on turned club legs with pad feet, 49¹⁄₂in. wide.
(Christie's) $1,053

A Federal inlaid mahogany three-part dining table, New England, circa 1800, in three parts; with a drop-leaf center section flanked by D-shaped ends, 8ft. 11¹⁄₂in. long.
(Sotheby's) $74,000

DINING TABLES

A mid-Victorian mahogany dining table, the oval top with four extra leaves, on cabriole legs terminating in pad feet, 62in. closed.
(Christie's) $2,297

Good quality mahogany dining snooker table, fitted three leaves, slate bed base with four cabriole legs, 76 x 40in.
(Peter Wilson) $1,092

A mahogany circular table, extending radially with four extra leaves, above ring-turned column uprights joined by a stretcher, 78in. fully extended.
(Christie's) $2,826

A Regency rosewood, satinwood crossbanded and brass dot inlaid breakfast table, the rectangular snap top with rounded corners on a beechwood turned column quatrefoil platform, 138cm. wide.
(Phillips) $3,867

A mid-Victorian burr-walnut loo table, the shaped oval top on turned column, on foliate-capped carved cabriole legs, 56in. wide.
(Christie's) $1,589

An Austrian Biedermeier mahogany extension dining table, circa 1830, the circular divided top extending over an octagonal baluster-form standard, extended 9ft. 1/2in. diameter.
(Butterfield & Butterfield) $3,450

A Victorian mahogany extending dining table, including four extra leaves, the rectangular top on faceted turned tapering legs, 147in. fully extended.
(Christie's) $4,592

A George IV mahogany breakfast table, the rectangular tilt top crossbanded in rosewood to a molded edge, on crenellated hip splay legs, 4ft. 6 1/2in. wide.
(Woolley & Wallis) $2,826

Federal mahogany veneer three part dining table, Boston, Massachusetts, circa 1800, 161 1/4in. long extended.
(Skinner) $4,600

DRESSING TABLES

An Empire mahogany dressing table, the lyre-shaped mirror with eagles' head terminals, the base with single frieze drawer, 36in.
(Hy. Duke & Son) **$1,082**

Tiger maple and maple dressing table, Massachusetts or New Hampshire, circa 1740, old refinish, 32¼in. wide.
(Skinner) **$6,000**

An Art Deco style coromandel vanity table, after a design by Ruhlman, having a circular glass mirror on a u-shaped support, 64cm. across.
(Phillips) **$600**

A George III mahogany kneehole dressing table or sideboard, containing five drawers about an arched apron on splayed square legs, 106cm. wide.
(Phillips) **$1,976**

Mahogany carved dressing table, probably Massachusetts, circa 1750, overhanging top with chamfered edge, above a central concave carved drawer.
(Skinner) **$17,250**

A George III satinwood and crossbanded enclosed dressing table, with a yew-wood veneered oval panel hinged top enclosing a fitted interior, 27in. wide.
(Christie's) **$2,323**

Art Deco bird's-eye maple vanity and stool, second quarter 20th century, the elevated partially framed mirror plate swiveling within a U-shaped bracket, 38½in. wide.
(Butterfield & Butterfield) **$862**

A Regency mahogany dressing-table, attributed to Gillows of Lancaster, the rectangular molded top with a concave center surmounted by a three-quarter reeded gallery, 46in. wide.
(Christie's) **$7,535**

A Louis XV kingwood parquetry and amaranth banded poudreuse inlaid with boxwood lines and applied with gilt metal mounts, on cabriole legs with sabots, 75cm. wide.
(Phillips) **$2,280**

DRESSING TABLES

A George III mahogany dressing table, the rectangular twin-flap hinged top enclosing a fitted interior with a toilet mirror, 28in. wide.
(Christie's) $1,588

A Regency mahogany kneehole dressing table, outlined with boxwood stringing, the central fitted drawer flanked by four small drawers, 46¾in. wide.
(Bearne's) $1,112

A George III mahogany dressing-table, the central drawer with a red baize-lined slide, flanked to each side by narrow drawers, 44in. wide.
(Christie's)   **$7,176**

A Louis XV style brass, tortoiseshell and polychrome inlaid coffre de toilette, by Befort Père, second quarter 19th century, decorated with birds of paradise with stylized foliage, 33½in. wide.
(Christie's) $29,859

A Louis XV Provincial inlaid walnut poudreuse, the rectangular divided hinged top enclosing a central mirrored well flanked by hinged covered wells, 32¼in. wide.
(Butterfield & Butterfield)
                    $3,162

A Directoire ormolu-mounted mahogany table de toilette, the rectangular hinged top to the reverse with an inset mirror, 91cm. wide.
(Christie's) $5,594

An Edwardian satinwood kneehole dressing table, fitted with a central checker strung oval panel frieze drawer in the arched apron flanked by two short drawers.
(Christie's) $3,098

A George II ormolu-mounted walnut and oak dressing-table commode, the molded rectangular twin-flap top above a paneled walnut and mahogany brushing-slide, 68½in. wide.
(Christie's) $10,419

A Federal painted dressing glass, Massachusetts or New Hampshire, circa 1810, painted cream with outline of red and gray pinstriping, top with painted foliate devices, 17¾in. wide.
(Skinner) $1,092

DROP-LEAF TABLES

Chippendale mahogany drop leaf table, Massachusetts, circa 1800, 48³/₄in. long extended. (Skinner) **$1,495**

Chippendale cherry drop leaf table, attributed to Samuel Sewall, York, Maine, 18th century, with molded legs and shaped skirts, 38¹/₂in. deep extended. (Skinner) **$1,955**

Queen Anne mahogany drop leaf table, New England, 18th century, 45in. long extended. (Skinner) **$2,875**

A rosewood Sutherland table, the twin-flap oval top on lotus carved dual end standards, 36¹/₂in. wide. (Christie's) **$1,434**

A fine Chippendale carved mahogany drop-leaf table, Boston or Salem, Massachusetts, circa 1760, the oblong top flanked by rectangular leaves, 44¹/₄in. wide open. (Sotheby's) **$8,050**

An Export Chinese padouk dropleaf table, second half 18th century, the circular molded top above a deep frieze and four cabriole legs, 37in. diameter. (Christie's) **$3,588**

Federal cherry drop leaf table, Eastern Massachusetts or Rhode Island, circa 1820, with one drawer and old finish, 34¹/₂in. wide extended. (Skinner) **$1,150**

Classical mahogany veneer table, Northern New England, circa 1820, with a single hinged drop leaf in the rear, 28in. wide. (Skinner) **$1,725**

A late Victorian burr-walnut Sutherland table, with molded top and fluted legs with gadrooned collars, 42in. extended. (Christie's) **$1,273**

DROP-LEAF TABLES

Tiger maple drop leaf table, New England, early 19th century, 42in. wide.
(Skinner) $3,335

Dutch inlaid oak drop-leaf dining table, late 18th/19th century, shaped molded hinged top over a frieze drawer, 71in. long extended.
(Skinner) $7,475

Pine table, Massachusetts, early 19th century, scrubbed top with single drop leaf over red painted base with paint loss, 47in. wide.
(Skinner) $977

A classical carved mahogany drop-leaf library table, New York, circa 1820, the rectangular top flanked by oblong leaves with notched corners, 48in. wide open.
(Sotheby's) $1,265

A Victorian walnut Sutherland table, with molded edged serpentine oval top, on six barley twist supports, 44 x 31½in.
(Andrew Hartley) $1,155

A Queen Anne walnut drop-leaf table, Salem, Massachusetts, 1740-70, the shaped molded skirt below on cabriole legs ending in pad feet, 41½in. wide open.
(Sotheby's) $4,025

A Victorian walnut Sutherland table, with a twin-flap top of serpentine outline, on baluster-turned supports joined by a turned stretcher, 40in. extended.
(Christie's) $612

A fine and rare Queen Anne mahogany single-drawer drop-leaf dining table, New York, 1735–60, on six cabriole legs ending in pointed slipper feet, 42in. wide open.
(Sotheby's) $14,950

A George III mahogany 'spider leg' table, the rectangular single flap top on turned legs and pad feet, 84cm. wide.
(Phillips) $912

FURNITURE

DROP LEAF TABLES

Queen Anne red painted cherry and birch dining table, probably Connecticut River Valley, 18th century, 40½in. wide.
(Skinner) $20,700

An English oak gate-leg table, 18th century, with a single drop-leaf rectangular hinged top and frieze drawer, 40in. wide extended.
(Christie's) $797

A William and Mary maple butterfly table, New England, 18th century, refinished, 28in. wide.
(Skinner) $1,150

A late Victorian mahogany Sutherland table, the rounded rectangular twin flap tops on dual baluster turned and ribbed end columns, 102cm. wide.
(Phillips) $912

A pair of Federal cherry drop leaf tables, Nantucket, Massachusetts, circa 1820, 23in. wide.
(Skinner) $978

A diminutive Queen Anne drop-leaf table, New England, 1740–1760, the oval top with drop leaves above a conforming rectangular apron, 32in. wide (open).
(Christie's) $18,400

An early Georgian walnut drop-leaf table, the oval twin flap top with molded edge, on slightly cabriole legs and hoof feet, 66¼in. wide.
(Christie's) $5,279

A 1930s limed oak drop-leaf occasional table/bookcase, the narrow rectangular top raised on plank supports with shelves at either end, 63.5 x 80cm. open.
(Phillips) $195

A classical carved mahogany and mahogany veneer breakfast table, New York, circa 1815–1820, with one working and one faux drawer, 37½in. wide.
(Skinner) $4,312

DRUM TABLES

A George IV mahogany drum-top library table, with inset gilt tooled green leather panel, the cockbeaded frieze fitted three drawers, 50³/₄in. diameter, circa 1825.
(Neales)   **$6,000**

A Regency mahogany drum table, the circular black leather-lined top above a frieze with four drawers and four simulated drawers on a turned baluster column, 42in. wide.
(Christie's)   **$5,210**

A mahogany drum table with leather-lined and crossbanded top above four frieze drawers, on ring-turned column, probably French, 51in. diameter.
(Christie's)   **$1,060**

A George III mahogany and satinwood drum table, the circular crossbanded revolving top above four crossbanded drawers, 42cm. diameter.
(Christie's)   **$2,622**

An early 19th century mahogany drum top library table, with a red tooled leather inset top containing four drawers and dummy drawers, 91cm. diameter.
(Phillips)   **$3,570**

A mahogany drum table, the later oval top above the ebony-lined frieze with two drawers, 22¹/₂in. wide.
(Christie's)   **$1,836**

A Regency mahogany drum top table, the circular green tooled leather inset top containing four drawers and four simulated drawers, 112cm. diameter.
(Phillips)   **$5,472**

George III mahogany drum table, circular leather inset top over alternating frieze and sham drawers, splayed legs, 48in. diameter.
(Skinner)   **$3,737**

A Regency mahogany drum table, the circular revolving top with a tan leather insert above four drawers and four simulated drawers, 96cm. diameter.
(Phillips)   **$6,688**

DUMB WAITERS

A George III mahogany three tier dumb waiter raised on a turned column with carved tripod supports, 44½in. high. (Anderson & Garland)
$480

Mahogany circular two tier dumb waiter, baluster turned central column, tripod base with scrolled feet, 19th century, 22½in. diameter. (G. A. Key)
$1,125

George III style mahogany dumbwaiter, 19th century, three circular tiers, raised on cabriole legs ending in pad feet, 44¼in. high. (Skinner)
$920

A George II mahogany three-tier dumb-waiter, the dished circular top tier above two further tiers supported by spirally-fluted baluster shafts, 19½in. diameter. (Christie's)
$14,956

A George IV mahogany two-tier dumb waiter, on a reeded column and channeled splayed legs with lappeted foliate scroll feet, 24in. wide. (Christie's)
$3,098

A Regency mahogany two tier dumb waiter, the wreathed and turned knop above two circular molded tiers joined by a baluster turned shaft, 105cm. high. (Phillips)
$2,280

Victorian mahogany metamorphic circular dumb waiter, central reeded spreading column, with dished under tier, mid 19th century, 24in. diameter. (G. A. Key)
$1,200

A late Georgian mahogany dumb waiter of three graduated revolving tiers on baluster-turned stem and cabriole tripod, 23½in. diameter. (Russell, Baldwin & Bright)
$1,601

A Georgian mahogany three tier dumb waiter, the graduated circular tray top tiers raised on a ring turned center column, 46in. high. (Diamond Mills & Co.)
$1,714

GATELEG TABLES

An oak gate-leg table, with circular top and long frieze drawer, on turned legs with faceted cappings, English, late 17th century, 50½in. diameter.
(Christie's) $4,725

An English oak gate-leg drop-leaf circular table, in 17th century style, incorporating early elements, the top formed with two drop-leafs, 70in. long.
(Sotheby's) $18,400

An English oak gate-leg table, part early 18th century, with an oval hinged top on turned and baluster supports terminating in bun feet, 54in. wide, extended.
(Christie's) $1,620

A rare William and Mary turned maple and birchwood diminutive gateleg dining table, New England, 1720–50, on ring-and-vase-turned legs joined by similarly turned stretchers, 4ft. wide open.
(Sotheby's) $13,800

A pine and blue painted drop-leaf gate-leg table, 19th century, the oval top above a frieze drawer, on bobbin-turned legs, 35½in. wide.
(Christie's) $464

Late 17th century jointed gate leg table, oval top with two drop leaves, plain gates, two turned pillars, trestle base, 33 x 26in.
(Peter Wilson) $2,106

An antique elm gate leg table, with D shaped drop leaves, on baluster supports united bobbin stretchers on turned feet, 45½in. open.
(Dee, Atkinson & Harrison) $706

A very fine and rare William and Mary maple gate-leg dining table, New England, 1730–60, the oblong top with two hinged D-shaped leaves, 50½in. wide extended.
(Sotheby's) $63,000

A George II Irish red walnut gateleg table, the rounded rectangular top on leaf and scroll carved cabriole legs with claw and ball feet, 164cm. extended.
(Phillips) $7,600

LARGE TABLES

A George III mahogany dining table, late 18th century, comprising two demilune sections, each with a shaped frieze, 7ft. 2in. long. (Butterfield & Butterfield) $1,840

A mahogany twin pedestal 'D' end dining table with 'D' shaped snap tops, on ebonized ring turned columns and tripod legs, 2.24m. x 1.22m. (Phillips) $4,560

A Regency mahogany extending dining-table, attributed to Gillows of Lancaster, the rounded rectangular top with reeded edge with seven extra leaves above a shallow frieze with beaded edge, 201in. long, fully extended. (Christie's) $30,498

A Regency mahogany extending dining-table, with four extra leaves, the molded and rounded rectangular top collapsible to a side table, 138in. long, fully extended. (Christie's) $11,661

A pine refectory table, of large size with twin-plank top, plain molded friezes and square chamfered legs joined by flattened stretchers, English, 19th century, 160in. wide. (Christie's) $2,018

A Victorian mahogany extending dining table, the top with a double molded edge, on foliate-headed tapering legs terminating in brass caps and castors, including five extra leaves, 171in. long. (Christie's) $18,934

A late Victorian mahogany extending dining table, on cabriole legs headed with acanthus scrolls and terminating in claw and ball feet, including three extra leaves, 120in. long. (Christie's) $4,475

An unusual walnut baroque refectory table, probably Spanish, with two frieze drawers in front carved in relief with scrolls and animals, 82¼in. long. (Sotheby's) $11,500

LARGE TABLES

A classical mahogany drop leaf dining table, New England, circa 1830, old refinish, 71¼in. wide extended.
(Skinner) $690

Regency mahogany hunt table, first quarter 19th century, the semicircular surface with two hinged leaves, 6ft. 8in. wide.
(Butterfield & Butterfield) $6,325

A Victorian carved oak center table, the lugged rectangular top inlaid with rosewood lines, in a trellis-work pattern, on spirally-turned supports and ball feet joined by waved and foliate-carved shaped stretchers, 66in. wide.
(Christie's) $1,868

A Federal mahogany inlaid dining table, Mid-Atlantic, 1790–1810, in three sections, the whole forming a rectangular top with demi-lune ends and line-inlaid edge, 117in. deep (open).
(Christie's) $9,200

A mahogany dining table, early 19th century, the top with rounded corners and a molded edge on turned tapering legs, 112in. long extended.
(Christie's) $5,508

A Regency mahogany extending dining-table, in the manner of Gillows of Lancaster, comprising two semi-circular end-supports, a central single flap gateleg-section and three extra leaves, the top with reeded edge, 152in. long, with all but one leaf. (Christie's) $6,458

A Federal inlaid mahogany three-part dining table, New England, circa 1800, in three parts, the center section with rectangular drop leaves above a crossbanded frieze, 7ft. 6in. long open.
(Sotheby's) $5,750

A mahogany drop-leaf extending dining table, early 19th century, the top with a reeded edge extending on a concertina action, on standard and dual splayed supports, 119in. wide extended.
(Christie's) $6,885

OCCASIONAL TABLES

A walnut stretcher-base table, Pennsylvania, 18th century, the rectangular top above a conforming case fitted with two offset thumb-molded drawers, 47³/₄in. wide.
(Christie's) $2,300

An early 18th century red walnut china table with tray top and three frieze drawers, 29in. wide.
(Locke & England) $667

A French Henry II style walnut extension table, incorporating Renaissance elements, with quartered solid top and similar sliding extensions, 96¹/₂in. extended.
(Sotheby's) $16,100

A George II walnut architect's table, second quarter 18th century, the hinged rectangular top with molded edge and notched corners, 32³/₄in. wide.
(Butterfield & Butterfield) $8,625

A pair of French bird's-eye maple and simulated-bamboo two-tier tables, late 19th/early 20th century, each with shaped rectangular galleried tiers with polychrome and parcel-gilt decoration, 22in. wide.
(Christie's) $7,342

A very fine and rare William and Mary turned and carved maple and pine 'Spanish-foot' tea table, Massachusetts, possibly Ipswich, 1720–50, 35in. wide.
(Sotheby's) $29,900

A Queen Anne figured maple single-drawer tavern table, New England, circa 1740–80, the oblong molded top above a frieze drawer, 22in. wide.
(Sotheby's) $8,050

Art Deco two-tier table, circa 1925, marble and onyx, the square top with cut corners, the legs and frieze of open work bronze, 80cm. high.
(Sotheby's) $3,271

A fine Queen Anne mahogany tray-top tea table, Goddard-Townsend School, Newport, Rhode Island, circa 1750–80, on cabriole legs, 20³/₄in. long.
(Sotheby's) $28,750

OCCASIONAL TABLES

A Victorian walnut tripod-bookstand, with circular top on a turned and fluted stem, rotating galleried undertier, 17¼in. diameter.
(Bearne's) $989

A set of four scarlet-lacquer, parcel-gilt and carved nesting tables. Chinese, second half 19th century, 19¾in. wide.
(Sotheby's) $6,325

A Regency mahogany three-tier étagère, each rounded rectangular tier with brass gallery and on solid end-supports, 24in. wide.
(Christie's) $7,390

A Federal carved and figured mahogany adjustable drawing table, the carving attributed to Samuel McIntire, Salem, Massachusetts, circa 1800, 30½in. long.
(Sotheby's) $189,500

A French Second Empire circular parquetry table with single frieze drawer, arched tapered legs with stretchers, and center basket undertier, 3in. diameter.
(Holloway's) $3,344

A japonaiserie lacquer, specimen-wood and bamboo étagère, late 19th/early 20th century, the rectangular two-handled top with molded border inset with a lacquer panel, 35½in. wide.
(Christie's) $3,146

A Chippendale carved mahogany piecrust tilt-top tea table, Philadelphia, Pennsylvania, circa 1770, 33in. diameter.
(Sotheby's) $530,500

A pietra dura rectangular table top, centered by an agate moth within an oval reserve, now on an early Victorian oak base, 38¾in. wide.
(Bearne's) $4,790

A nest of seven Japanese lacquer stacking-shelves, 19th century, each with rounded square tray top decorated with red and gilt foliage, 56in. high overall.
(Christie's) $2,447

OCCASIONAL TABLES

Modern gothic walnut, part-ebonized and parcel-gilt occasional table, third quarter 19th century, 24¹/₄in. long. (Skinner) $690

A George III plumbago mahogany architect's table, the molded edge hinged easel top with a sprung folio rest above a drawer, 35in. (Woolley & Wallis) $2,280

Maple and pine turned tea table, New England, 18th century, partial red paint, some refinishing, 27.75in. diameter. (Skinner) $2,300

A 19th century German oak humidor, of stepped rectangular form, the superstructure surmounted by a carved figure group depicting a hound chasing a deer, 22in. wide. (Phillips) $760

A contemporary circular revolving drum coffee table, designed by Willy Rizzo, the wooden frame covered with black laminated plastic and bands of polished metal. (Phillips) $278

A rare William and Mary turned birchwood and pine tavern table, New England, 1730–50, the oval top above a molded rectangular frieze, 32¹/₂in. wide. (Sotheby's) $4,025

William and Mary maple tavern table, New England, 18th century, old natural surface on the top, dark red painted base, 23.4in. wide. (Skinner) $6,325

A mahogany occasional table, in Chippendale style, the circular piecrust molded edge tilt top on a revolving bird-cage, 25in. (Woolley & Wallis) $4,864

A George II red walnut D-shaped supper table, the folding top opening to vacant interior above plain frieze, basically early 18th century, 28in. wide. (Hy. Duke & Son) $711

OCCASIONAL TABLES

A yellow painted guéridon, of Louis XV style, the oval gray marble inset top above a trelliswork carved frieze, 18in. wide. (Christie's) $261

A red painted stretcher-base table, Lancaster County, Pennsylvania, late 18th/early 19th century, on tapering blocked legs joined by flat stretchers, 47¹/₄in. wide. (Christie's) $5,750

Victorian black painted iron and parcel-gilt tilt-top tripod table, mid 19th century, the top with foil decoration, 19in. diameter. (Skinner) $632

A late 19th century French bijouterie table, veneered in faded rosewood with ormolu mounts, the serpentine edge beveled glazed lid with a brass moulding, 25in. (Woolley & Wallis) $1,570

Painted poplar and pine table, Pennsylvania, 1780–1810, with removable top having carved pins doweled through the supporting battens, two thumb-molded drawers, 30½in. wide. (Skinner) $6,440

A Continental Art Nouveau bois satiné two-tier table, attributed to Serrurier-Bovy, having a square top with raised fluted edges, raised on four curved supports, 84cm. long. (Phillips) $695

An Edwardian inlaid mahogany oval tray table with brass handles, undertray with splay square tapering supports, 2ft. (Russell, Baldwin & Bright) $408

An early 19th century occasional table, veneered in gold burr elm with stringing, the concave side top banded in burr walnut, 24in. (Woolley & Wallis) $2,280

A William and Mary turned birchwood and pine tavern table, New England, the rectangular molded top above a frieze drawer, 23in. wide. (Sotheby's) $4,600

PEMBROKE TABLES

Classical mahogany veneer Pembroke table, New York, 1820s, with reeded edges on the falling leaves and cockbeaded end-drawers, one simulated, 39in. wide.
(Skinner) $1,840

Classical carved mahogany veneer Pembroke table, New York, circa 1835, with shaped corners, 56¼in. wide extended.
(Skinner) $1,495

A George III ebony-inlaid mahogany Pembroke table, the canted rectangular twin-flap top banded with satinwood, above two frieze drawers, 40¾in. wide.
(Christie's) $4,844

A small late 19th century satinwood butterfly flap Pembroke table, with a center oval mahogany inlaid paterae, cross-banded and line inlaid border, 2ft. 4in. x 2ft. 10in., open.
(Holloway's) $3,268

A George III mahogany Pembroke table, the molded serpentine rectangular twin flap top crossbanded in satinwood above a mahogany-lined frieze drawer, 35in. wide.
(Christie's) $3,579

A George III mahogany and satinwood banded oval Pembroke table with ebony stringing, the molded hinged top containing a bowed drawer, 1m. x 86cm. overall extended.
(Phillips) $4,760

A late George III mahogany and satinwood banded Pembroke table inlaid with ebony and boxwood lines, the shaped rectangular top with a frieze drawer, 106cm. wide.
(Phillips) $1,976

Regency mahogany Pembroke breakfast table, rounded rectangular top tulip wood crossbanding with black string, turned pedestal support, 42 x 36in.
(Peter Wilson) $1,087

A Federal inlaid mahogany Pembroke table, New York, circa 1795, the oblong line-inlaid top with bowed ends flanked by D-shaped leaves, 40½in. wide extended.
(Sotheby's) $17,250

PEMBROKE TABLES

A George III fiddleback mahogany Pembroke table, crossbanded in tulipwood and inlaid with ebonized and boxwood lines, 38¹/₂in. wide.
(Christie's) $3,049

Chippendale walnut Pembroke table, probably Maryland, 18th century, with single drawer, 34in. wide extended.
(Skinner) $1,150

A Chippendale figured mahogany Pembroke table, New England, circa 1780, the rectangular top with two hinged rectangular leaves, 37¹/₂in. wide.
(Sotheby's) $2,875

A Federal inlaid mahogany Pembroke table, Mid-Atlantic States, probably Baltimore, Maryland, circa 1795, the oblong top with bowed ends flanked by hinged D-shaped leaves, 40in. wide open.
(Sotheby's) $3,450

Regency rosewood crossbanded satinwood Pembroke table, early 19th century, the rectangular crossbanded hinged surface with rounded corners, 45in. wide, open.
(Butterfield & Butterfield) $5,500

A Chippendale figured mahogany Pembroke table, Philadelphia, Pennsylvania, circa 1785, the oblong molded top with bowed ends flanked by serpentine leaves, 41in. long extended.
(Sotheby's) $145,500

A George III mahogany Pembroke table, the oval hinged top containing a bowed drawer inlaid with boxwood lines and dot inlay, 76cm. x 92cm. overall.
(Phillips) $1,487

A Victorian decorated Pembroke table, crossbanded overall and inlaid, later decorated overall with mythological figures, 40¹/₄in. wide, extended.
(Christie's) $4,223

A Sheraton period mahogany Pembroke table, the veneered rectangular top crossbanded in satinwood and tulipwood with stringing, 30in.
(Woolley & Wallis) $1,824

SIDE TABLES

A Queen Anne giltwood and gesso side table, surmounted by a rectangular verde antico marble top, the cavetto frieze with strapwork panels, 108.5cm. wide.
(Phillips) $4,560

A mid 17th century Dutch oak side table, the rectangular molded edge top above a frieze drawer with walnut panels, 3ft. 1in.
(Woolley & Wallis) $1,292

A rosewood, brass-inlaid and parcel-gilt side table, with a marble top and frieze decorated with anthemion and scrolls, part early 19th century, 45½in. wide.
(Christie's) $3,787

A kingwood and ormolu-mounted side table, of Louis XV design, the shaped rectangular brass-bordered top, inlaid with a panel of ribbon-tied marquetry, 27¾in. wide.
(Christie's) $4,485

An early Victorian yellow-painted simulated bamboo bow-fronted side table, overall with chinoiserie figures and rustic landscapes, 39in. wide.
(Christie's) $4,126

A Dutch marquetry side table, the rectangular checker-banded top centered by an urn with trailing foliage and flowers, 33in. wide.
(Christie's) $2,383

A mahogany side table, of mid-Georgian design, the rectangular hinged top with rounded angles above a deep frieze, partly 18th century, 33in. wide.
(Christie's) $1,308

A late 18th/early 19th century Dutch mahogany and floral marquetry hall table, with oval checker strung top with vase of flowers and a bird inlay, 76cm. wide.
(Phillips) $2,082

A 19th century demi-lune side table in the Louis XVI style having pierced brass gallery and quarter-veneered top with chevron stringing, 3ft. 2in. wide.
(Russell, Baldwin & Bright)
                       $1,413

SIDE TABLES

A Regency mahogany side table, gray fossil marble top above a plain molded frieze on quadripartite pillars, 72¼in. wide.
(Christie's) $60,684

A late Victorian walnut side table, with a variegated green marble top and cavetto frieze with palmettes and foliate scroll decoration, 50½in. wide.
(Christie's) $4,302

A George II walnut side table, the molded rectangular brêche violette marble top with inset serpentine angles, above a waisted frieze, 50in. wide.
(Christie's) $20,102

A William and Mary turned birchwood and pine single-drawer stretcher-base side table, New England, 1710–40, the rectangular molded top above a single-drawer frieze, 31½in. wide.
(Sotheby's) $6,325

Pair of Frank Lloyd Wright oak side tables, executed for the Aline Barnsdall Hollyhock House, Los Angeles, circa 1917, 30in. wide.
(Butterfield & Butterfield)
                    $10,925

A silvered carved side table, the verde antico marble top above pierced foliate frieze centered with ovolo cartouche, on scrolling acanthus legs, 29in. wide.
(Christie's) $1,148

A Federal inlaid mahogany marble-top mixing table, New England or New York, circa 1800, rectangular white and gray veined marble top, 41in. wide.
(Sotheby's) $35,650

18th century oak jointed side table, two plank top, single drawer with applied molding decorative apron, four turned legs, 35in. wide.
(Peter Wilson) $842

An Irish George II gilt-mahogany side table, the later simulated gray-veined rectangular white marble top above a tapering plain frieze, 49¾in. wide.
(Christie's) $10,764

SOFA TABLES

A Regency rosewood, crossbanded and brass mounted sofa table attributable to John McLean, inlaid with ebonized lines, 158cm. wide.
(Phillips) $19,760

A fine Regency rosewood and brass marquetry sofa table, the dropleaf top with a wide line border of brass marquetry, 36in. wide.
(Boardmans) $6,665

A Regency mahogany sofa-table, the rectangular twin flap top crossbanded in satinwood above two cedar lined frieze drawers, 59½in. wide.
(Christie's) $4,399

A Regency mahogany and satinwood inlaid sofa table, the satinwood crossbanded top with rounded corners and tulipwood crossbanding, top 168cm. x 61cm. extended.
(Phillips) $3,867

A Regency rosewood draw leaf sofa or dining table, the pull-out rectangular top with rounded corners and frieze applied with a brass foliate spray, 150cm. x 76cm. extended.
(Phillips) $5,950

Classical mahogany veneer sofa table, probably New York, 1820–40, with two veneered cockbeaded drawers, 23³/₈in. wide.
(Skinner) $4,025

A Regency rosewood and brass inlaid sofa table, the hinged top with scroll stylized fleur-de-lys inlay to the corners, the top 147cm. x 61cm. extended.
(Phillips) $5,355

A Regency brass-inlaid rosewood sofa table, circa 1815, raised on four outswept legs ending in scroll and foliate-cast feet, extended 4ft. 11in. long
(Butterfield & Butterfield) $4,025

A Regency giltmetal-mounted rosewood sofa table, inlaid overall with boxwood lines, crossbanded in yewwood, 58³/₄in. wide.
(Christie's) $6,099

SOFA TABLES

A satinwood crossbanded line-inlaid rosewood sofa table, the twin-flap rounded rectangular top above two frieze drawers and a U-shaped support, early 19th century, 60in. wide
(Christie's) $3,712

A Regency brass-inlaid and ebonized sofa-table, the rounded rectangular twin-flap top crossbanded in rosewood, above a pair of cedar and mahogany-lined drawers, 66¼in. wide.
(Christie's) $7,038

A Regency bronze-mounted plum-pudding mahogany sofa table, trestle end-supports joined by a flat associated stretcher with central cartouche of a Greek key, 65¾in. wide.
(Christie's) $20,631

A Sheraton period sofa table, veneered in figured satinwood, the drop leaf top crossbanded in rosewood, two frieze drawers in front, 35in.
(Woolley & Wallis) $4,256

A child's rosewood and simulated rosewood sofa table, the divided rectangular twin flat top above a pair of paneled drawers, first half 19th century, 85cm. wide.
(Phillips) $912

A Regency brass-inlaid rosewood sofa table, the rounded rectangular twin-flap top above a pair of mahogany-lined frieze drawers and two simulated drawers, 44in. wide.
(Christie's) $8,797

A rosewood sofa table, George IV, circa 1820, the satinwood banded rectangular top above a sycamore banded frieze, 156cm. long extended.
(Sotheby's) $5,347

A mahogany sofa table, the twin-flap rounded rectangular top above two frieze drawers, early 19th century, 58½in. wide.
(Christie's) $2,193

A Regency mahogany sofa table, banded overall, the reeded rounded rectangular top above two drawers, on downswept reeded legs, 59in. wide.
(Christie's) $13,110

TEAPOYS

Early Victorian teapoy, veneered in plum pudding mahogany sarcophagus box, containing four lead lined wooden tea canisters, 31in. high. (Peter Wilson) **$1,020**

A George IV mahogany sarcophagus-shaped teapoy, the hinged rectangular paneled top enclosing a divided interior, 21in. wide. (Christie's) **$1,380**

A Victorian black papier mâché rectangular teapoy, painted with birds and floral sprays within gilt borders, on turned central column, 31in. high. (Canterbury) **$510**

A George IV mahogany teapoy, attributed to Gillows of Lancaster, the hinged canted rectangular molded top enclosing a green baize-lined interior, 18¹/₄in. wide. (Christie's) **$1,530**

A fine Regency rosewood teapoy with brass string inlay, the top with deep molded edge and enclosing a fitted interior, 32¹/₂in. high. (Dee, Atkinson & Harrison) **$1,976**

Regency penwork and découpage decorated teapoy, circa 1820, the sarcophagus form hinged tea caddy with penwork decoration, 13¹/₄in. wide. (Butterfield & Butterfield) **$4,000**

A William IV mahogany teapoy, the rectangular hinged lid with a molded handle and molded rim, enclosing a fitted interior, 15¹/₂in. wide. (Christie's) **$617**

A Regency amboyna and ebonized teapoy, the hinged rectangular top with gadrooned handle enclosing three mahogany-lined lidded wells, 17in. wide. (Christie's) **$1,737**

A Regency rosewood and brass-inlaid teapoy, the stepped hinged top enclosing a fitted interior with four tin lined canisters, 16in. wide. (Christie's) **$2,039**

A Victorian rosewood work-table, the hinged octagonal top with foliate-carved and molded border, 17¼in. wide.
(Christie's) **$1,935**

A gilt-metal-mounted parquetry inlaid work table of Transitional style, the crossbanded oval hinged top above a frieze drawer, 22in. wide.
(Christie's) **$1,148**

A 19th century walnut sewing table, carved and with colored marquetry inlay, 64 cm. wide.
(Arnold) **$3,913**

A Regency rosewood and inlaid drop flap work table, the top inlaid for chess with scroll inlay, with fitted pen drawer and sliding well to each side, 83 x 46cm. extended.
(Phillips) **$2,100**

A Regency ormolu-mounted rosewood games-table, the bow-ended rectangular green leather-lined twin-flap top with central sliding-section veneered to the reverse with a checkerboard, 53½in. wide.
(Christie's) **$22,575**

A rosewood and engraved mother-of-pearl inlaid work-table, 19th century, the shaped rectangular hinged top, enclosing a mirrored and fitted interior, possibly Colonial, 52cm. wide.
(Christie's) **$1,345**

A Victorian rosewood oblong work table, with frieze drawer above basket, and pierced standard supports joined by stretcher.
(Bristol) **$1,080**

A George III mahogany and satinwood inlaid sofa games table, the hinged crossbanded top in rosewood, inlaid with a sliding panel, 109 x 52cm., extended.
(Phillips) **$7,800**

Federal mahogany veneer work stand, Portsmouth, New Hampshire, 1708–1815, with bird's-eye maple and flame birch veneer, mahogany crossbanding, 17in. wide.
(Skinner) **$2,760**

WORKBOXES & GAMES TABLES

A classical cherry and mahogany veneer two-drawer work stand, New England, circa 1820, with opalescent glass pulls, refinished, 18in. wide.
(Skinner) $1,035

A Regency rosewood games-table, banded overall, the rounded rectangular top with sliding panel with chessboard to the reverse, 36¼in. wide.
(Christie's) $6,118

An Edwardian mahogany, satinwood inlaid and rosewood crossbanded work table, the oval top inlaid with an oval paterae, above a frieze drawer, 22in. wide.
(Christie's) $598

A Victorian kingwood and gilt-metal mounted work table, of Louis XV design, the hinged rectangular top inset with a panel of parquetry and fitted with a mirror to the reverse, 23½in. wide.
(Christie's) $2,242

A Regency rosewood brass inlaid and gilt mounted games table, the tulipwood crossbanded top inlaid for chess; and another similar with walnut and purplewood top, the top 49cm.
(Phillips) $4,462

A George IV rosewood work-table, banded overall in fruitwood and ebony, the rectangular removable reading-slide concealing a leather-lined backgammon playing surface, 34¼in. wide.
(Christie's) $2,639

A fine and rare Federal maple-inlaid mahogany sewing table, Boston, Massachusetts, circa 1795, the hinged octagonal top with inlaid edge above a conforming frieze, 19¾in. wide.
(Sotheby's) $11,500

A Regency mahogany and ebony inlaid drop flap work table, the hinged top with scroll inlay containing two cedar lined drawers, on turned column, 67cm. wide extended.
(Phillips) $5,168

Federal mahogany veneer serpentine work stand, Boston, 1790, possibly the Seymour Workshop, with side opening bag drawer, original turned pulls, 19.25in. wide.
(Skinner) $6,325

WORKBOXES & GAMES TABLES

A Louis XV-style kingwood and marquetry work table, applied with gilt-brass edge moldings 24¼in. wide.
(Bearne's) $1,545

An early Victorian rosewood games table, the square top enclosing reverse-painted glass chessboard above a sliding well, 23in. wide.
(Christie's) $529

Federal mahogany and mahogany veneer work table, probably Massachusetts, 18.5in. wide.
(Skinner) $862

A late Victorian ebony-inlaid satinwood secrétaire games-table, crossbanded in kingwood, the rectangular top with sliding central section inlaid with a checkerboard to the reverse 29½in. wide.
(Christie's) $5,630

A George IV mahogany work table, with two drop leaves, a drawer and a false drawer, with fitted interior, 45cm. x 72cm. open.
(Dreweatt Neate) $1,178

A Federal mahogany worktable, Massachusetts, 1800–1810, the rectangular top with outset rounded corners above three cockbeaded drawers flanked by ring-turned engaged colonettes, 20¾in. wide.
(Christie's) $1,150

A Federal satinwood and burlwood inlaid sewing table, attributed to John and/or Thomas Seymour, Boston, Massachusetts, circa 1800, 21in. wide.
(Sotheby's) $189,500

A late Regency rectangular burr walnut work table with a drawer, pleated pouch on 'U' shaped support, 20in. wide.
(Dreweatt Neate) $1,001

An Edwardian mahogany work table, banded with fruitwood, the shaped eared top with removeable shaped superstructure, 16½in. wide.
(Christie's) $2,098

WRITING TABLES & DESKS

A Louis XV style gilt-bronze-mounted mahogany bureau plat and an associated fauteuil, raised on shaped legs headed by female mask, 5ft. 3in. wide. (Butterfield & Butterfield)
$3,737

A mahogany pedestal chest, the molded rectangular top above a frieze fitted with a brushing slide, 19th century, 25in. wide. (Christie's) $2,415

A French kingwood, marquetry and gilt-bronze bureau plat, circa 1880, by Frederic Schmit, Paris, the leather inset top of arc en arbalette form above three frieze drawers, 151cm. wide. (Sotheby's) $18,716

A late Regency rosewood and brass inlaid writing table, the rectangular top with gadrooned edge above a beaded secrétaire drawer, 70cm. wide. (Phillips) $3,952

Arts and Crafts drop front desk, Paine Furniture retail tag, brass stamp hinges and pulls with copper patina, 36in. wide. (Skinner) $747

A Regency mahogany writing-table, attributed to Gillows of Lancaster, the rounded rectangular top with molded edge above a shallow frieze with beaded rim, 32in. wide. (Christie's) $4,927

Painted pine stand-up desk, western Massachusetts, early 19th century, original red wash with grained pull-out writing surface, 31.25in. wide. (Skinner) $1,380

A Federal mahogany inlaid tambour fall desk, probably Massachusetts, circa 1810, refinished, replaced brasses, 37³/₄in. wide. (Skinner) $3,680

An Edwardian Sheraton mahogany bonheur du jour with delicate box line stringing, 31in. wide. (Locke & England) $1,295

A Victorian walnut crossbanded and ormolu-mounted bureau plat, of undulating serpentine outline, the top inset with a panel of tooled green leather, 62¹/₂in. wide.
(Christie's) **$23,236**

A Napoleon III ebonised, ormolu mounted and brass marquetry bureau plat in the Louis XVI style, the fluted tapered legs joined by an 'X' stretcher, 131cm. wide.
(Phillips) **$532**

A William IV rosewood and parcel-gilt writing-table, on gadrooned and foliate-wrapped spreading trestle end-supports joined by a ring-turned and reeded baluster stretcher, 58¹/₄in. wide.
(Christie's) **$6,158**

A French mahogany clerk's desk, 19th century, the tooled leather-lined hinged sloping fall with a stay and a pen compartment to one side, 44¹/₂in. wide.
(Christie's) **$2,389**

A Victorian walnut writing table, circa 1860, with a crossbanded and marquetry top above a frieze drawer on cabriole legs, 123cm. wide.
(Sotheby's) **$4,100**

A 19th century rosewood bonheur du jour with swan neck pediment to tray top, five shallow drawers enclosed by a pair of solid doors, 23in. wide.
(Dreweatt Neate) **$1,988**

A Louis XV ormolu-mounted kingwood bureau plat, altered in England in the early 19th century by E. H. Baldock, 57¹/₂in. wide.
(Christie's) **$19,312**

An Art Nouveau walnut writing table, having a flat rectangular top that hinges open to reveal a compartmentalised interior, 66.8cm. wide across.
(Phillips) **$958**

A mid-Victorian walnut writing table, the sloping center section with shaped and fretted gallery enclosing four small drawers, 42in. wide.
(Canterbury) **$2,869**

WRITING TABLES & DESKS

Desk, 1930s, shaped, rectangular top, veneered in burrwood and zebrawood, one side with open shelf, 184.5cm. wide.
(Sotheby's) $6,541

A mahogany writing desk with rounded front corners converted from a William IV square pianoforte with satinwood banding, checkered and ebony stringing and six gilt mounts.
(Russell, Baldwin & Bright) $1,240

Art Deco black lacquer and mahogany desk, circa 1930, the top rounded at one end above a frieze drawer and sold cross-support, 4ft. 2in. wide.
(Butterfield & Butterfield) $1,150

Gallé marquetry table à écrire, circa 1900, the hinged and divided rectangular top with galleried edge inlaid with stylized foliage, 21in. wide closed.
(Butterfield & Butterfield) $2,300

Painted sewing desk, attributed to Ezra Haskell, Sweden, Maine, 1860-70, old brown paint with orange drawer facades, 36.13in. wide.
(Skinner) $3,737

A mahogany and gilt-metal-mounted bonheur du jour, of Louis XVI style, the brass-lined tambour top enclosing three short drawers above a hinged writing slide, 26^{1}/$_{4}$in. wide.
(Christie's) $2,055

Carlo Bugatti, lady's writing desk, circa 1900, rectangular vellum covered writing surface bordered by beaten copper, with galleried upper section, 24^{3}/$_{4}$in. wide.
(Sotheby's) $7,631

Fine Majorelle marquetry table à ecrire, circa 1900, the top of irregular rectangular outline inlaid with flowerheads, foliage and butterflies, 37^{1}/$_{2}$in. wide.
(Butterfield & Butterfield) $6,325

A red painted oval writing table, Ephrata Cloister, Lancaster County, 19th century, the elongated oval top above a straight-sided applied apron, 30in. wide.
(Christie's) $6,900

WRITING TABLES & DESKS

A gilt-metal-mounted crossbanded walnut serpentine bureau plat of Louis XV style, the leather-lined top above a frieze drawer, on cabriole legs, mid 19th century, 49in. wide.
(Christie's) **$2,297**

A William IV mahogany writing table, in the manner of Gillows, with three-quarter gallery and five drawers about a kneehole, 122cm. wide.
(Bristol) **$2,508**

Austrian ebonized oak writing desk, manufactured by Kohn & Kohn, circa 1900, the rectangular three-quarter galleried top with green felt reserve, 5ft. 3in. long.
(Butterfield & Butterfield) **$1,380**

An Edwardian satinwood and floral-painted cylinder desk, the rectangular top with three-quarter pierced brass gallery, the frieze fitted with two drawers, 90cm. wide.
(Christie's) **$3,737**

A William and Mary red-stained figured maple and birchwood diminutive slant-front desk-on-frame, New England, circa 1730, in two parts, 27$\frac{1}{2}$in. wide.
(Sotheby's) **$27,600**

A late 19th century rosewood and brass marquetry and line inlaid bonheur du jour, the shaped arched back with shelf on turned brass columns, 29$\frac{1}{4}$in. wide.
(Andrew Hartley) **$2,826**

Grain painted stand-up desk, probably Canada, second quarter 19th century, original grained surface with recessed panel sides and shaped skirts, original brass, 29$\frac{1}{4}$in. wide.
(Skinner) **$6,900**

A late Victorian pine clerk's desk, the shaped raised back with hinged frieze enclosing letter racks above a pair of bowed paneled doors, opening to reveal pigeon holes, drawers and hinged writing surface, 37in. wide.
(Christie's) **$3,002**

A mid-Victorian burr walnut-veneered bureau de dame, applied with gilt-brass foliate mounts and inlaid throughout with foliate arabesques, 34$\frac{1}{2}$in. wide.
(Bearne's) **$3,245**

TRUNKS & COFFERS

A 16th century Gothic plank chest, front carved with blind Gothic tracery, 52in. wide. (Boardmans) **$3,192**

19th century Chinese black and gold lacquered coffer on stand. (Jacobs & Hunt) **$3,140**

Small James I oak coffer, the lunette/foliate frieze above two arcaded panels, 45in. wide. (Boardmans) **$2,888**

An 18th century oak coffer with scroll carved frieze, two carved panels to front, molded frame, paneled ends, 3ft. 10in. wide. (Russell, Baldwin & Bright) **$638**

A paint-decorated pine blanket chest, signed John Selzer, Dauphin County, now Lebanon County, Pennsylvania, dated *1793*, 52in. wide. (Sotheby's) **$12,650**

An 18th century oak mule chest with lift-up top, six dummy drawers and three drawers to the base, on ogee bracket feet, 62in. wide. (Morphets) **$2,120**

A painted and decorated blanket chest, York County, Pennsylvania, late 18th/early 19th century, the rectangular top with molded edges centering two red and green painted pinwheel motifs, 47in. wide. (Christie's) **$29,900**

A brass-studded leather coffer, 18th century, with rectangular hinged top and carrying handles to the sides, on later walnut stand, 41in. wide. . (Christie's) **$2,389**

An Alpine pine blanket chest, probably Tirolean, 18th/19th century, raised on the stiles decorated with birds within vine foliage, 43in. wide. (Sotheby's) **$2,587**

A sulpher inlaid sycamore blanket chest-over-drawers, Lancaster County, Pennsylvania, dated *1781*, the rectangular top with applied molding, 55¾in. wide. (Christie's) **$46,000**

A late 17th/early 18th century coromandel lacquer coffer, all over decorated on a black ground with Chinese landscapes and figures, 127cm. wide. (Phillips) **$1,540**

An 18th century oak Carmarthen coffer having four 'cupid's bow' panels over five rectangular fielded panels on bracket feet, 4ft. 9in. wide. (Russell, Baldwin & Bright) **$836**

400

TRUNKS & COFFERS

A 17th century American pine chest attributed to Essex County MA, the rising plank top enclosing a lidded till, 50in. wide.
(Boardmans) **$7,904**

An Italian giltwood cassone, early 19th century, with front inset with a painted panel on board representing a scene of courtiers, 71in. wide.
(Christie's) **$5,164**

Grain painted poplar six board chest, Pennsylvania, 1830–40, with molded top and lidded till, early graining simulates tiger maple, 42in. wide.
(Skinner) **$805**

A 19th century Dutch oak and mahogany veneered marquetry nonesuch chest, heavy three plank lid with molded edge, 51in. wide.
(Peter Wilson) **$834**

A late 17th/early 18th century Continental walnut and ivory inlaid coffer of Moorish influence, the hinged top with a central 'chess' panel, possibly Italian or Spanish, 125cm. wide.
(Phillips) **$4,560**

Grain painted pine dower chest, Pennsylvania, early 19th century, with lidded till, two drawers, original red and yellow graining, 47.25in. wide.
(Skinner) **$690**

An Arts and Crafts oak and copper log box, the rectangular form with hinged cover having an oak frame set with beaten copper panels, 45cm. high.
(Phillips) **$433**

An inlaid walnut blanket chest, Lancaster County, Pennsylvania, dated *1772*, the exterior centering two raised lozenge panels with molded surrounds, 48³/₄in. wide.
(Christie's) **$5,520**

A George III mahogany blanket chest-on-stand, with hinged lid and carrying handles, the stand with two frieze drawers and squat cabriole legs, 48in. wide.
(Christie's) **$1,237**

Late 16th century oak jointed chest, two plank cleated top, with wire hinges, front with two panels, linen fold decoration, 36in. wide.
(Peter Wilson) **$7,020**

A red painted child's blanket chest-over-drawers, Schaefferstown, Pennsylvania, circa 1838, the rectangular hinged top with applied molding, 31¼in. wide.
(Christie's) **$5,520**

A sulphur inlaid walnut blanket chest, attributed to Peter Holl (d. 1775) or Peter Holl II (d. 1784), Pennsylvania, dated *1765*, 51½in. wide.
(Christie's) **$19,550**

WARDROBES & ARMOIRES

An 18th century Dutch padouk and purplewood armoire, the upper part with a molded cornice with foliate fruit and riband cresting, 2m. wide.
(Phillips) $5,168

Edwardian satinwood wardrobe with dentil cornice above a frieze inlaid with scrolling foliage and a central female mask, plinth base, 91in.
(Ewbank) $3,791

A Victorian mahogany and crossbanded wardrobe, with molded gothic cornice, two pointed arched doors, 54$^1/_2$in. wide.
(Andrew Hartley) $1,094

A Second Empire plum pudding mahogany and gilt bronze mounted bibliothèque, the rectangular breakfront cornice above an arched central frieze, 2.06cm. wide.
(Phillips) $3,040

A William and Mary paneled sycamore kas, Hudson River Valley, New York, circa 1730–60, the rectangular molded overhanging cornice above two raised paneled cupboard doors, 5ft. 11in. wide.
(Sotheby's) $6,900

A good Victorian mahogany two piece bedroom suite by Sopwith & Co., Newcastle upon Tyne, comprising a pedestal dressing table and breakfront wardrobe to match, 6ft. 9in. wide.
(Anderson & Garland) $1,950

An antique Normandy garde-robe in oak, extensively carved floral bouquets, leafage ribbons and birds, on scrolled feet, 5ft. wide.
(Russell, Baldwin & Bright) $1,510

A George III Sheraton breakfront wardrobe, the dentil decorated cornice above a central part of two long doors enclosing a shelved interior, 100in. wide.
(Boardmans) $5,890

A Victorian yellow-painted simulated-bamboo wardrobe, the doors simulated as four short and two long drawers and enclosing a plain interior, 39in. wide.
(Christie's) $3,229

WARDROBES & ARMOIRES

A 68in. fine quality Victorian figured walnut wardrobe, the two paneled doors enclosing hanging space, five linen shelves and three deep drawers, 7in. tall. (Stainers') $899

An Austrian floral and green-painted armoire, 19th century, the molded cornice above a pair of doors depicting lakeside landscapes, 82in. wide. (Christie's) $3,982

A late 18th/early 19th century French Provincial oak and elm armoire, with two paneled doors with scrolled brass lock plates and hinges, 41¹/₂in. wide. (Andrew Hartley) $1,473

A German baroque walnut 'Wellenschrank', early 18th century, veneered with well-figured walnut throughout, with overhanging stepped and molded cornice, 77in. wide. (Sotheby's) $8,625

A mid-Victorian burr-walnut triple section breakfront wardrobe, with molded cornice and a central arched mirrored door flanked by arched paneled doors, 92in. wide. (Christie's) $2,378

A Colonial hardwood armoire, the gadrooned cornice and fleurs de lys carved frieze above a pair of paneled cupboard doors, mid 19th century, 52in. wide. (Christie's) $2,473

A Louis XV Provincial oak armoire, the molded paneled doors with high relief floral and grape bouquets above panels with pairs of doves, 60in. wide. (Peter Francis) $4,326

A Flemish oak armoire, the molded cornice above a foliate and acanthus-carved frieze and fitted with a pair of paneled cupboard doors, 58in. wide. (Christie's) $1,868

Early 19th century mahogany hanging wardrobe, dentil cornice two paneled doors with three simulated short drawers to each, 51in. wide. (Peter Wilson) $1,482

WASHSTANDS

A fine Federal inlaid mahogany corner washstand, Northeastern Shore, New England, circa 1805, the convex surface pierced with three circular holes, 22in. wide.
(Sotheby's) $3,000

An early Victorian oak washstand, the rectangular top surmounted by a three-quarter gallery, on ring-turned tapering supports, 47¼in. wide.
(Christie's) $660

A Federal mahogany and mahogany veneer inlaid one-drawer wash stand, probably Massachusetts, circa 1800, with tambour door, 18½in. wide.
(Skinner) $1,495

A George III mahogany and ebony string inlaid quadrant washstand with folding top, undershelf with drawer below having brass knob handle, 28in. wide.
(Andrew Hartley) $597

A pair of George III mahogany washstands, each with rectangular double-hinged top with molded edge enclosing a fitted interior, 21½in. wide.
(Christie's) $9,867

A rare classical mahogany washstand, Boston, Massachusetts, circa 1815, the hinged square molded top opening to three circular recesses, 18½in. wide.
(Sotheby's) $1,955

George III mahogany washstand, twin flap rectangular top enclosing circular divisions and mirror compartment, 21in. wide.
(Peter Wilson) $600

A Victorian mahogany washstand, the rectangular molded top surmounted by a three-quarter gallery, on ring-turned baluster supports, 48in. wide.
(Christie's) $834

A mahogany and line inlaid corner washstand, the bowed top above a tambour shutter and a single long drawer, 22½in. wide.
(Christie's) $486

WHATNOTS

Victorian walnut two-tier
whatnot.
(Jacobs & Hunt) $816

A Victorian three-tier rosewood
whatnot, with fluted uprights
and frieze drawer, on turned
feet, 28¹/₂in. wide.
(Christie's) $1,766

A Victorian rosewood three-tier
whatnot, each serpentine tier on
ring-turned uprights, 15in. wide.
(Christie's) $1,140

A late 19th century rosewood
and simulated rosewood
canterbury whatnot, with four
serpentine molded tiers
supported upon turned columns,
45cm. wide.
(Phillips) $1,216

A Victorian rosewood and
simulated rosewood canterbury/
what-not, the rectangular
molded top surmounted by a
three-quarter gallery, on turned
baluster supports, 23in. wide.
(Christie's) $1,736

A Regency yewwood etagère,
circa 1815, of rectangular
outline, each shelf held by ring-
turned baluster-form supports
over a lower drawer, 24in. wide.
(Butterfield & Butterfield)
                    $4,887

A Victorian walnut three tier
canterbury/whatnot with
pierced scrolling foliate galleried
top, baluster turned supports
with turned finials, 24in. wide.
(Andrew Hartley) $1,178

A Victorian papier-mâché four
tier whatnot, inlaid with
colored mother-of-pearl floral
swags and heightened in gilt,
37cm. wide.
(Phillips) $1,824

An Edwardian burr walnut
marquetry ebonized three tier
whatnot with pierced brass
gallery on splayed feet, 38cm.
wide.
(Dreweatt Neate) $589

WINE COOLERS

A Regency brass-bound wine-cooler, the open round rectangular top above plain sides with pilaster angles, 87cm. wide.
(Christie's) $4,223

Mahogany Adam style cellaret of canted rectangular form, the raised lid molded with a central oval rosette, late 19th/early 20th century, 35in.
(G. A. Key) $3,000

George III oval brass bound mahogany bottle carrier, early 19th century, with hinged sides, 10in. high.
(Skinner) $2,185

A George III mahogany and satinwood crossbanded oval cellaret, the hinged lid with a divided later zinc liner, on square tapered legs with spade feet, 53cm. wide.
(Phillips) $2,736

A George III mahogany rectangular cellaret, the compartmented bottle holder top opening to reveal a fitted interior, 22in. wide.
(James Adam) $3,466

A George III brass-bound mahogany cellaret, the oval hinged top enclosing a later lead-lined interior, the sides with carrying-handles, 21in. wide.
(Christie's) $5,279

A George III mahogany cellaret, of octagonal form, the hinged octagonal top with eight radiating veneers, strung with box, 46cm. wide.
(Phillips) $1,900

A Chinese Export 18th century Paktong wine-cooler, on a Regency bronze and ebonized stand, the bulbous body with grotesque Chinese mask ring-handles, 27in. wide.
(Christie's) $15,835

George III satinwood wine cooler, circa 1800, with pomegranate finial, faceted top and sides with lion mask handles, 21in. high.
(Skinner) $2,530

WINE COOLERS

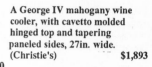

A Victorian mahogany cellaret of sarcophagus shape with fitted interior and bun feet, 2ft. 2in. (Russell, Baldwin & Bright) **$851**

A fine Victorian mahogany rectangular sarcophagus wine cooler, the domed lid with applied carved fruit and leaves, 33 x 24in. (James Adam) **$4,890**

A George IV mahogany wine cooler, with cavetto molded hinged top and tapering paneled sides, 27in. wide. (Christie's) **$1,893**

A George III mahogany wine cooler of octagonal form, the rising crossbanded top above three brass bindings and raised upon a period stand, 16in. wide. (Boardmans) **$2,170**

A Regency mahogany cellaret, the canted rectangular top with central raised crossbanded panel and with molded edge enclosing a plain interior, 31½in. wide. (Christie's) **$2,111**

A mahogany wine cooler, with recessed rounded angles and hinged top with simulated panel sides, on square chamfered legs, 17½in. wide. (Christie's) **$1,893**

A Georgian mahogany octagonal lead lined wine cooler, brass bound with lion mask ring handles, 24in. high. (Dee, Atkinson & Harrison) **$3,040**

A George III brass-bound mahogany wine-cooler-on-stand, the later reeded stand on splayed reeded square tapering legs, 24in. wide. (Christie's) **$2,870**

Mid 19th century Georgian style mahogany wine cooler, oval brass coppered body with two lion mask handles, on cabriole legs, metal liner, 24in. diameter. (Peter Wilson) **$725**

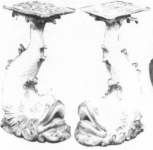

A bronze figure of an elephant, 34½in. high.
(Sotheby's) **$1,840**

A pair of figural side tables, each formed as dolphins with a rectangular top, 26in. high.
(Sotheby's) **$5,750**

A bronze frog, 24in. high.
(Sotheby's) **$1,380**

A set of four wrought-iron armchairs, circa 1950, each with a domed head.
(Sotheby's)
(Four) **$3,162**

A pair of marble lions, 45in. long.
(Sotheby's) **$20,700**

Benjamin Edward Spence (1822–1866), a marble figure of a boy holding a flute, signed *B.E. Spence, T.T. Rome*, 37in. high.
(Sotheby's) **$5,175**

A bronze bust of a Buddha, the head hollowed, 24in. high.
(Sotheby's) **$4,600**

Two of a set of four stone sphinxes, 31in. high.
(Sotheby's)
(Four) **$2,300**

A wrought-iron fishing basket, diameter 36in.
(Sotheby's) **$690**

One of a pair of stone lions, 41in. high.
(Sotheby's)
(Two) $4,600

A pair of cast-iron falcons, each majestically perched, 33in. high.
(Sotheby's) $4,600

A stone fountain mask, depicting a lion, 16in high.
(Sotheby's) $1,380

G. de Kerveguen (French, late 19th century), a bronze figural group, circa 1900, depicting three nude female figures hanging from chains, 29in. high.
(Sotheby's) $12,650

A pair of terracotta garden seats, early 20th century, the arms formed as griffins with intertwining wings as backrests, circular stamp, 29in high.
(Sotheby's) $34,500

A bronze figural fountain, the central font flanked by two smiling youths, possibly by Evelyn Beatrice Longman, 39¾in. high.
(Sotheby's) $36,800

A stone figural console, the standard formed as a cherub, 35½in. high.
(Sotheby's) $2,875

A pair of marble urns, each of compana form, the base with a gadrooned band, 28in. high.
(Sotheby's) $10,350

A marble group of Urania-Muse of Astronomy, late 19th century, 5ft. 1in. high.
(Sotheby's) $10,350

GARDEN ORNAMENTS

A pair of fine 19th century terracotta garden urns, of campana shape, the circular foot fluted and on square base, 43in. high.
(Dee, Atkinson & Harrison)
$1,216

A Continental carved marble wellhead, 17th/18th century, the square top with circular well, carved with a shield on two sides within arches, 24½in. high.
(Butterfield & Butterfield)
$3,162

A pair of 19th century cast iron garden urns, the campana shaped bodies decorated with scrolling arabesques, 4ft. overall.
(Woolley & Wallis)
$1,649

A pair of recumbent lions, 27in. high.
(Sotheby's)
$2,185

A set of stone figures of The Four Seasons, depicting females, 42in. high.
(Sotheby's)
$5,175

A pair of stone sphinxes, 44½in. long.
(Sotheby's)
$4,600

A Portland stone and bronze sundial, 19th century and later, on a square shelf over a ringed baluster standard on a stepped square base, 3ft. 10½in. high.
(Butterfield & Butterfield)
$3,162

A pair of Neoclassical style cast stone urns, each tapering cylindrical two-handled body with domed cover, cast in relief, 27in. high.
(Butterfield & Butterfield)
$1,725

A Neoclassical style large marble urn, mid 19th century, the low bowl with everted rim, the sides with scroll handles over a gadrooned lower section, 39in. diameter.
(Butterfield & Butterfield)
$4,312

Victorian mustard-painted cast iron garden settee, late 19th century, 46in. long.
(Skinner) $460

A pair of 19th century Coade stone type garden urns, with tongue carved edges and partly ribbed bodies, on turned stems to square bases, 24^1/$_2$in.
(Woolley & Wallis) $691

A good 19th century cast iron, white painted garden bench, with slatted wood seat, 48in. wide.
(Canterbury) $1,444

A Victorian cast iron bench with 'dragon' ends.
(G. E. Sworder & Sons) $2,888

A set of four stone musicians, 34in. high.
(Sotheby's) $8,625

A Victorian iron bench with 'branch ends'.
(G. E. Sworder & Sons) $3,648

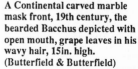

An Italian carved marble jardinière of rectangular outline, the frieze carved with putti at various pursuits amid grapevines, 30in. high.
(Butterfield & Butterfield) $2,875

A pair of Neoclassical style marble urns, 19th century, of campana form, with gadrooned everted lip over fluted and beaded upper section, 41in. high.
(Butterfield & Butterfield) $11,500

A Continental carved marble mask front, 19th century, the bearded Bacchus depicted with open mouth, grape leaves in his wavy hair, 15in. high.
(Butterfield & Butterfield) $2,300

411

A bronze figure of a male archer, 45in. long. (Sotheby's) $5,750

One of a pair of lead urns, the tapering body applied with dancing cherubs, beneath a Greek key border, 39cm. high. (Phillips) (Two) $1,596

A cast-iron figure of a hound, 4ft. 1in. high. (Sotheby's) $4,025

A marble sarcophagus, late 19th/early 20th century, centered on opposing sides with a shield, the corners with carved mermaids, 36in. long. (Sotheby's) $4,887

One of a pair of classical style marble urns, late 19th/early 20th century, each with a continuous allegorical band, the loop handles ending in masks, 41in. high. (Sotheby's)

(Two) $1,495

One of two American painted cast-iron urns, late 19th century by J.W. Fiske, New York, stamped *J.W. Fiske*, 18in. high. (Sotheby's)

(Two) $1,035

A stone fountain, early 20th century, the baluster shaped standard carved with masks, swags and figural terms, 5ft. high. (Sotheby's) $10,925

An Indian marble low table, the circular top carved with a central flower, raised on leaf-tip form base, diameter 35^1/2in. (Sotheby's) $2,070

A marble wall font, the undulating font raised on a scrolled rectangular standard carved with cattails. (Sotheby's) $1,150

An alabaster figural group, depicting the three Graces, 35½in. high.
(Sotheby's) $7,475

One of a pair of marble walking lions, late 19th/early 20th century, 4ft. 9in. long.
(Sotheby's)
(Two) $11,500

One of a pair of stone finials, of sphere form, 23in. high.
(Sotheby's)
(Two) $1,265

One of a pair of marble urns, late 19th century, each carved with four masks of angels joined by fruited swags, 23½in. high.
(Sotheby's)
(Two) $14,950

One of a pair of stone cornucopiae, 19th century, each naturalistically carved ending in a bearded mask, raised on a rectangular double plinth, 4ft. 3in. high.
(Sotheby's)
(Two) $17,250

A Coalbrookdale painted-iron and glass miniature greenhouse, circa 1840, the domed paneled removable top above a conforming base, 24in. high.
(Sotheby's) $1,092

One of a pair of lead eagles, 28in. high.
(Sotheby's)
(Two) $3,737

One of a pair of cast-iron 'Woodbury' urns, 21in. high.
(Sotheby's)
(Two) $2,300

One of a pair of clay tub chairs, after the antique.
(Sotheby's)
(Two) $11,500

BEAKERS

A Transparentmalerei Bohemian beaker of hexagonal trumpet shape, painted in pale colors with a lady and a man in a clown type hat, 12cm.
(Phillips) $1,011

A Transparentmalerei beaker of trumpet shape, painted with a kneeling figure of Cupid writing *Ich liebe...*, 10.5cm.
(Phillips) $1,088

A Bohemian blue overlay beaker of waisted form, in clear glass with six panels painted in colors with sprays of flowers, 12.8cm.
(Phillips) $902

A Vienna Transparentmalerei Ranftbecker, by Anton Kothgasser, painted with an orange blossom spray, the gilt inscription *Meine Liebstes* below, 10.7cm.
(Phillips) $5,909

A Bohemian Transparentmalerei beaker in clear glass with hexagonal bucket bowl, enameled in colors in the workshop of Friedrich Egermann, Haida, 13.5cm.
(Phillips) $1,244

A Transparentmalerei Bohemian beaker, each panel with an amber stained circle between pendant sprays of grapes in colors, 10.8cm.
(Phillips) $1,011

An attractive Vienna Ranftbecher with a view of St. Stephen's, by Kothgasser, with a carriage, riders and pedestrians, 11cm.
(Phillips) $7,464

A finely engraved German armorial beaker in clear glass, engraved with a coat of arms crested by a crowned eagle, 11.2cm.
(Phillips) $809

A Silesian ruby cased beaker of trumpet shape, engraved on one side with views of Kynast, Warmbrunn and Erdmansdorf, 13.2cm.
(Phillips) $653

BEAKERS

A Bohemian white overlay and painted beaker with two panels, one painted with a view of Warmbrunn, 12.5cm.
(Phillips) $560

A 'Glasperlen' beaker with a wide white band decorated with scrolling sprays of flowers in colors beneath an engraved border, 10.8cm.
(Phillips) $809

A North Bohemian 'Glasperlen' beaker with a broad band of colored glass beads forming a panoramic scene, 11cm.
(Phillips) $295

A rare dated 'Glasperlen' beaker with wide white band decorated with vases of flowers, the Sacred Monogram, initials *ZA* and *KT* and the date 1833, 9.5cm.
(Phillips) $622

A Bohemian Transparentmalerei topographical beaker of trumpet shape, painted with a view of 'Die Metropolitankirche z. St. Veit i. Prag', en grisaille, 12.5cm., 19th century.
(Phillips) $882

A Dresden Transparentmalerei beaker by Samuel or August Mohn, of cylindrical shape with everted rim, painted with the initials *LEY* in amber, red and blue, 10cm., early 19th century.
(Phillips) $1,976

A Bohemian 'granitic' beaker of faceted flared shape, on octagonal bulbous foot, with blue and white marvered inlays, 12.2cm.
(Phillips) $466

A Bohemian white and blue overlay beaker in clear glass with five panels in two rows, with cameo cut leaf motifs, 12cm.
(Phillips) $653

A Bohemian white overlay painted beaker with trumpet bowl, painted in an oval panel with a view of Fürstenstein, 13cm.
(Phillips) $560

BOWLS

Bohemian pale green overlay glass cut and etched punch bowl, late 19th century, depicting a forest scene with deer, on a shaped foot, 7¹/₂in. high.
(Skinner) $402

20th century pressed green glass bowl and cover, in the shape of a turkey, 22cm. high.
(Peter Wilson) $75

Rare Carder Steuben dark blue jade grotesque bowl, involuted rim on oval form with extraordinary blue shading, 7in. high.
(Skinner) $4,255

Orrefors Swedish Ariel bowl, Edvin Ohrstrom design with air trap bubbles and aubergine stripes, 8in. diameter.
(Skinner) $690

A pair of George III silver-mounted cut-glass confitures and covers, each clear glass bowl and spreading circular base cut with diaper decoration, 15.8cm. high, London 1815, in a fitted oak case.
(Bearne's) $1,714

Murano Studio iridescent leaf bowl, attributed to Barovier & Toso, heavy deeply ribbed colorless glass with occasional gold leaf intrusions, 6½in. high.
(Skinner) $345

Daum cameo glass grapevine bowl, heavy walled mottled purple and yellow bowl with tooled trefoil inturned rim, 6¼in. high.
(Skinner) $3,450

An Irish 19th century cut glass circular covered bowl, the domed lid with flat print finial, with reed rim and diamond cut and facet body, 7in. diameter.
(James Adam) $149

Carder Steuben etched acanthus bowl, design 6415, molded of heavy walled colorless glass deeply acid etched with leaf decoration, 6¼in. high.
(Skinner) $1,035

CANDLESTICKS

A miniature baluster candle or taperstick with cylindrical nozzle with slightly everted rim, on a ball knop, 11.8cm., circa 1730.
(Phillips) $760

Steuben glass tear drop candlesticks, pair, 8¾in. high, baluster form, No. 7792, signed.
(Du Mouchelles) $700

A rare miniature taperstick with cylindrical nozzle with turned-over rim, above a ball knop and a drop knop containing a tear, 12.3cm., circa 1730–1740.
(Phillips) $2,128

A façon de Venise diamond point engraved candlestick, 17th century, the cylindrical sconce with everted rim and gadrooned collar, 8½in.
(Sotheby's) $9,804

In the style of Jacques Adnet, Modernist four light candelabra, 1930s, clear glass, the four square section arms on a spherical base, 13.75cm.
(Sotheby's) $1,272

One of a very fine pair of Regency cut-glass and ormolu table candelabra, the cylindrical columns cut with diamonds, surmounted by ormolu leaves and pine cones, 33.8cm.
(Phillips)   (Two) $3,110

Tiffany gold iridescent candlestick, flared cupped integrated bobèche on ten-rib twisted stick with lustrous iridised surface, 7in. high.
(Skinner) $600

A pair of Edwardian cut glass candlesticks, the trumpet-shaped stems and bases cut with hob-nail ornament, 15in. high.
(Christie's) $1,463

A composite-stemmed candlestick, circa 1750, the cylindrical nozzle with vertically molded ribs, the stem with a center octagonal tapering pedestal section, 26cm. high.
(Christie's) $886

DECANTERS

An early 19th century Dutch decanter set, comprising six oblong clear glass decanters engraved with flowers and a pair of glasses, 16in. wide.
(Andrew Hartley) **$744**

A late Victorian tantalus, with three cut glass spirit decanters, the frame with a swing handle, 13in.
(Woolley & Wallis) **$450**

A Victorian liqueur set, comprising four gilt banded clear glass decanters and fifteen glasses, in burr walnut case with hinged lid, 13in. wide.
(Andrew Hartley) **$682**

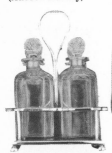

A George III Scottish decanter stand, Edinburgh 1817, maker's mark of George Fenwick, also marked *G. F. Tobago*, fitted with four glass decanters, 11in. high, approx. weight 36oz.
(Bonhams) **$1,178**

A set of four Victorian cut glass decanters together with a matching serving salver in the early 19th century style, contained in a silver-mounted wooden box, decanters 21cm. high, salver 15.5cm. diameter.
(Phillips) **$1,174**

A pair of 'Bristol' blue glass decanters, with matching lozenge stoppers, each decorated in gold, one inscribed *Hollands* the other *Rum*, 24cm. high.
(Bearne's) **$536**

Silver overlaid glass decanter, colorless angular molded vessel with conforming silver decoration depicting Alpine dancers, 8½in. high.
(Skinner) **$431**

Edwardian oak mirror back tantalus, fitted with three square section decanters and compartments with hinged lid above a secret drawer, 12½in. high.
(Peter Wilson) **$287**

German sterling and cut glass decanter, circa 1930–40, neck marked *hand made sterling Erik Magnussen*, elephant finial, flattened faceted bell shaped bottle, 12¾in. high.
(Skinner) **$1,495**

DISHES

René Lalique, coupe 'Muguet', after 1931, green tinted glass molded with lilies of the valley, 9¹/₈in. diameter.
(Sotheby's) $3,271

Emile Gallé, sea shell coupe, circa 1900, green glass, slightly opalised around the rim, realistically enameled with trailing flowering sprays, 4³/₄in.
(Sotheby's) $3,997

René Lalique, coupe 'Perruches', after 1931, opalescent glass heightened with blue staining and molded with a frieze of budgerigars, 23.75cm.
(Sotheby's) $3,452

A façon de Venise tazza, circa 1650, the shallow rib-molded circular tray set on a hollow inverted baluster knop, 3½in. high.
(Sotheby's) $2,139

René Lalique, coupe 'Cyprins', after 1921, opalescent glass molded on the inside with swimming fish, 14in. diameter.
(Sotheby's) $3,089

Libbey-Nash Art Glass compôte, optic ribbed crystal with dotted green internal decoration in colorless crystal, 6⅜in. high.
(Skinner) $632

A Baccarat crystal table centerpiece, the shallow bowl with etched flower decoration, supported by a dolphin on lobed circular base, 32cm. high.
(Phillips) $836

Gabriel Argy-Rousseau coupe 'Lierre', 1919, pâte-de-verre, clear glass decorated with yellow and molded around the rim, 9cm.
(Sotheby's) $3,997

Empire style gilt bronzed cut glass centerpiece, late 19th century, 12in. high.
(Skinner) $977

A rare sweetmeat glass, the double ogee bowl with pincered crenellated rim, on an opaque twist stem, 14.5cm., circa 1765–1770
(Phillips) $1,368

A mead glass, the cup-shaped bowl molded around the base with gadroons, on a triple-knopped stem containing a tear, 13.2cm., circa 1730.
(Phillips) $1,444

A sweetmeat glass with ogee bowl molded with vertical ribs above two collars, on a domed and folded foot, 12.7cm., circa 1740.
(Phillips) $289

A rare diamond-point engraved royal armorial roemer, dated 1653, signed *JM,* of emerald green tint, the ovoid bowl engraved with a bust portrait of King Philip III of Spain, 26.2cm. high.
(Sotheby's) $56,885

A 'Façon de Venise' drinking vessel, late 16th/early 17th century, the oval globular bowl with everted rim supported on a short hollow stem, 10.5cm. high.
(Christie's) $1,771

A bluish-green tinted Berkemeyer, Germany or Netherlands, circa 1600, the flared bowl merging into a cylindrical section applied with three rows of watery pointed prunts, 5½in.
(Sotheby's) $73,935

EPERGNES

A fine Victorian flower épergne fitted four part ruby tinted flower trumpets with clear crimped mounts.
(Anderson & Garland)
                    $840

A cranberry and clear glass épergne, comprising: three vases hung from barley twist branches, three trumpet vases between, 40.5cm. high.
(Bearne's) $649

A cranberry épergne of four trumpet vases and dish base, with crinkled rims and pinched trailed decoration, 21in.
(Russell, Baldwin & Bright)
                    $730

420

FLASKS

A Webb style 'Chinese chimera' glass moon flask, decorated with mythological dragon-like creatures amongst swirling waves, 31.7cm. high.
(Bearne's) **$1,545**

A glass flask complete with stopper, painted on one side with a man holding a wine glass, 18.4cm. high.
(Bearne's) **$448**

A façon de Venise flask, early 17th century, the ovoid lobed form with slender flared neck and pointed octafoil rim, 9¼in.
(Sotheby's) **$2,582**

A façon de Venise diamond point engraved silver mounted flask and stopper, circa 1680, in the manner of Willem Mooleyser (circa 1640-1700), 27cm. high.
(Sotheby's) **$9,269**

A diamond point engraved silver mounted flask, circa 1685, in the manner of Willem Mooleyser, engraved with two hawks perched among foliage, 17cm. high.
(Sotheby's) **$7,130**

A Netherlandish turquoise blue tinted silver mounted bottle and stopper, late 17th century, the cork stopper with lobed mount and cast final figure, 7½in. high.
(Sotheby's) **$3,923**

A diamond point engraved flask, circa 1685, in the manner of Willem Mooleyser, the flattened ovoid form molded with vertical ribs, 11¼in.
(Sotheby's) **$8,021**

A Central European pewter mounted glass flask, the front panel painted with a woman in country costume, 17.5cm. high, mid-18th century.
(Bearne's) **$386**

A façon de Venise diamond point engraved silver mounted flask, circa 1685, attributed to Willem Mooleyser, engraved with exotic birds, 20cm. high.
(Sotheby's) **$16,934**

GOBLETS

A baluster goblet, circa 1715, of drawn form with a flared funnel bowl merging into a slender true baluster stem, 15.5cm. high.
(Christie's) $1,062

A Bohemian green cased opaque white goblet with hexagonal faceted funnel bowl cut with leaf motifs, 14cm.
(Phillips) $715

A baluster goblet, circa 1710, the stem with a wide angular knop and basal knop and enclosing an elongated tear, 18.7cm. high.
(Christie's) $1,771

A façon de Venise 'jeweled' and gilt goblet, possibly Antwerp, second half 16th century, the thistle shaped bowl applied with three gilt lion masks, 6¼in. high.
(Sotheby's) $7,130

A fine and unusual diamond point engraved façon de Venise winged goblet, early 17th century, turquoise blue cup-shaped bowl, 13.8cm. high.
(Sotheby's) $10,695

A façon de Venise diamond point engraved calligraphic goblet, circa 1685, the cup-shaped bowl with the inscription *Kent eer gy Mint*, 21.1cm. high
(Sotheby's) $17,825

A façon de Venise diamond point engraved calligraphic goblet, dated *1686*, by Willem Jacobz. van Heemskerk, 20.5cm. high.
(Sotheby's) $49,910

A fine façon de Venise 'ice glass' goblet, perhaps South Netherlands or Antwerp, late 16th/early 17th century, the elongated funnel bowl set on a ribbed ovoid knop, 21.2cm.
(Sotheby's) $13,904

A Baccarat faceted goblet, mid 19th century, enameled with the crowned Badge of the Legion d'Honneur, the centre with a portrait of Napoleon, 16.2cm. high.
(Christie's) $885

JUGS

Roman glass ewer, 1st/2nd century A.D., crimped spout, ribbed handle and baluster body, 6¾in. high.
(Skinner) $488

An English enameled 'ice glass' sugar bowl and milk jug painted in colored enamels with fish, 14cm. and 12cm., and a silver gilt sifter spoon, marks for London 1883. (Phillips) $933

A silver-mounted glass pitcher, Tiffany & Co., New York, circa 1880, the brilliant-cut glass with stylized flowerheads, 9¾in. high.
(Christie's) $2,760

An electroplated mounted clear glass claret jug, the tapering glass body decorated with wading birds within a surround of rushes and palm trees, 27cm. high.
(Bearne's) $402

Dr. Christopher Dresser for James Couper & Sons, 'Clutha' glass pitcher, circa 1890, green glass internally decorated with streaks of milky white and gold aventurine, 21.5cm.
(Sotheby's) $3,997

An electroplated mounted clear glass claret jug, the ovoid body cut with circular motifs, the electroplated neck and hinged cover embossed with flowers and scrolls, 28.7cm. high.
(Bearne's) $432

A cranberry ewer painted blue enamel forget-me-nots, with crimped clear handle and stopper.
(Russell, Baldwin & Bright)
                              $91

Late 19th century ewer and goblet, probably Murano, decorated with vertical blue bands interspersed with aventurine and opaque twists, ewer 17cm. high.
(Peter Wilson) $209

Gallé enamel decorated carafe, transparent ribbed topaz colored cruet-form with applied twist handle, 6¼in. high.
(Skinner) $862

MISCELLANEOUS

René Lalique, pendulette 'Inseparables', after 1926, opalescent glass, the square frame molded with a pair of budgerigars, 11cm.
(Sotheby's) **$2,180**

Almaric Walter, fish, 1920s, pâte-de-verre, in shades of green and blue, marked *A. Walter Nancy* and monogrammed *R.D.*, 14.5cm.
(Sotheby's) **$4,179**

Hawkes Gravic inkstand, solid colorless glass with deep cut and polished scroll pattern, 4¼in. high.
(Skinner) **$1,725**

A Bohemian amethyst-flash and cut three-tiered stand, circa 1860, the central clear hexagonal column flashed in amethyst at the angles above a plinth, 58cm. high.
(Christie's) **$1,681**

An interesting verre églomisé commemorative picture by Aug. Forberger, signed, of the Ameshoff family with a profile portrait of a lady, and an obelisk with her name, 52 x 39cm., gilt frame.
(Phillips) **$2,333**

Austrian iridescent glass humidor with American silver plate mounts, circa 1900, the ovoid body with dimpled sides decorated with iridescent amber and violet 'oil spot' striations, 8in. high.
(Butterfield & Butterfield)
$920

Sabino opalescent glass figure of a nude, circa 1930, with arms outstretched holding a curtain of billowing drapery, 9in. high.
(Butterfield & Butterfield)
$1,725

Daum box and cover parlant, 'Plus Fait Douceur que Violence', 1890s, amethyst glass, with asymmetrical etched decoration including stylized pansies, 6⅞in.
(Sotheby's) **$4,543**

Steuben crystal champagne cooler vase, of classic urn form with applied reeded handles, 12in. high.
(Skinner) **$373**

MISCELLANEOUS

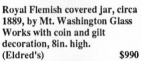

Royal Flemish covered jar, circa 1889, by Mt. Washington Glass Works with coin and gilt decoration, 8in. high.
(Eldred's) $990

A pair of early 19th century cut crystal and ormolu cornucopiae, the finials in the form of ram's heads, on marble base with cast bronze face, 9in. high.
(Locke & England) $440

A German green-tinted Daumenglas and cover, 18th century, of barrel shape with six thumb-holes between applied triple milled bands, 33cm. high.
(Christie's) $2,479

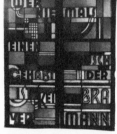

Thomas Webb & Sons George Woodall plaque, six-inch oval of deep amethyst colored glass layered in opal white, carved with a barefoot woman, 6¼in. high.
(Skinner) $12,650

A pair of German Art Deco stained glass panels, possibly by Hoffman, the mauve, red and blue patterned panels with verse *'Wer Niemals Einen Rausch Gehabt Der Ist Keiner Braver Mann'*, each 46½ x 19½in.
(Canterbury) $1,812

Two René Lalique Quatre Saisons statuettes, Automne and Printemps, originally mounted as lamps, glass 7¾in. high.
(Skinner) $862

A rare diamond point engraved blue tinted bottle, probably Leiden, dated *1687*, attributed to François Crama, the squat body engraved in a fine calligraphic script, 9in. high.
(Sotheby's) $24,955

Pair of late 19th century ruby glass two tier lusters, each decorated with polychrome floral enameling embellished with gilt, turned ebonized bases, glass domes, 14½in. high.
(Peter Wilson) $604

One of a pair of Bohemian amber jars and covers with faceted bodies cut with a doe and a stag in woodland, 26cm., circa 1880.
(Phillips) (Two) $578

A St. Louis crown weight, mid
19th century, the twisted lime-
green and iron-red ribbon
alternating with entwined
latticinio thread, 8cm. diameter.
(Christie's) $2,125

Almaric Walter, butterfly
paperweight, 1920s, pâte-de-
verre, in shades of yellow, blue
and brown, marked *AWN*,
11.5cm.
(Sotheby's) $3,089

A Clichy white flower weight,
mid 19th century, the flower
with six white petals about a
pink and white center, 7cm.
diameter.
(Christie's) $2,302

A St. Louis carpet-ground
patterned millefiori weight, mid
19th century, the central pale-
blue, white and red setup within
a circle of red-lined hollow pale-
blue tubular canes, 7.3cm.
diameter.
(Christie's) $6,021

A Bacchus white and blue
carpet-ground weight, third
quarter of the 19th century, the
central square setup surrounded
by four concentric
arrangements of canes, 8.3cm.
diameter.
(Christie's) $2,656

A St. Louis dated amber carpet-
ground concentric millefiori
weight, 1848, the central dark-
blue, pale-green and pink setup
surrounded by five large
silhouette canes, 6.7cm.
diameter.
(Christie's) $7,969

A Baccarat dated scattered
millefiori weight, 1847, the large
brightly colored canes
including silhouettes of animals
and with a cane inscribed
B 1847, 8cm. diameter.
(Christie's) $2,479

Antique Baccarat
paperweight, blue, red, green
and white millefiore garland
with central medallion on
claret ground, 2¾in. diameter.
(Skinner) $1,495

A Baccarat mushroom weight,
mid 19th century, the brightly
colored tuft within a torsade of
white gauze cable entwined by
cobalt-blue latticinio thread,
8cm. diameter.
(Christie's) $1,416

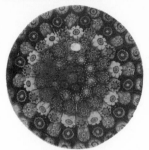

A Clichy concentric millefiori pedestal weight, mid 19th century, the central pink rose surrounded by six circles of canes, 6.5cm. diameter.
(Christie's) $4,250

Henri Bergé for Almaric Walter, chameleon, 1920s, pâte-de-verre, in shades of green and black with red spotting, 8.5cm.
(Sotheby's) $5,088

A St. Louis faceted mushroom weight, mid 19th century, the tuft with three circles of canes about a central pink tube, 8cm. diameter.
(Christie's) $2,125

A Clichy blue-ground patterned millefiori weight, mid 19th century, the three circles of canes in shades of pink, turquoise and white surrounded by five large white and pale-blue canes, 7.8cm. diameter.
(Christie's) $973

Debbie Tarsitano faceted butterfly paperweight, millefiori winged butterfly over fanciful blossom and buds, 2¾in. diameter.
(Skinner) $690

A Clicht red-ground patterned millefiori weight, mid 19th century, the large central white star cane enclosed within a cinquefoil garland of alternate blue and green-centered white canes, 7.2cm. diameter.
(Christie's) $1,682

A St. Louis red and blue crown weight, mid 18th century, the red, white and blue twisted ribbon alternating with entwined latticinio thread, 8cm. diameter.
(Christie's) $2,302

Tiffany bronze and favrile paperweight, swirling wave designed dark bronze frame on green iridescent damascene glass insert, 3¾in. long.
(Skinner) $2,070

A Clichy turquoise-ground daisy weight, mid 19th century, the flower with five white petals tipped in crimson about a green and pale-pink stamen center, 6.5cm. diameter.
(Christie's) $4,782

SCENT BOTTLES

A Victorian novelty scent flask, modeled as a rose, by E.H. Stockwell, 1880, 11.5cm. long, 3oz.
(Phillips) $782

A Pellatt & Co. patentees scent bottle and stopper intaglio molded with a profile head of Queen Adelaide, 10.5cm.
(Phillips)   £1,244

An 18th century Continental scent bottle of teardrop form, with projecting points at either side, probably mid-18th century, 7cm. high.
(Phillips) $501

A George III scent étui of tapering octagonal form, velvet-lined and complete with glass scent bottle inside, by Samuel Pemberton, Birmingham, 1795.
(Phillips) $250

Pair of Daum Nancy silver-mounted gilt cameo glass scent bottles, circa 1900, each cylindrical bottle overlaid with emerald green, 6¹/₄in. high.
(Butterfield & Butterfield)
                           $3,450

An amethyst cut and enameled scent-bottle and gold screw cover, circa 1760, one side enameled in colors with billing doves perched on a tree-trunk, 7cm. high.
(Christie's) $3,010

'Relief', a clear glass scent bottle and stopper, of circular design, molded in relief with beaded spirals, moulded *R Lalique*, 17cm. high
(Christie's) $407

A pair of late Victorian silver-mounted cut glass cologne bottles, the domed hinged covers and the mounts die-stamped with flowers, foliage and C-scrolls, Drew & Sons, London 1892, 6in.
(Christie's) $1,944

'Vers le Jour' a Lalique scent bottle and stopper, yellow glass shaded with amber, molded in relief with panels of chevrons, 16cm. high.
(Christie's) $1,510

SCENT BOTTLES

A rare Lithyalin scent bottle and stopper in brown-red tones with agate-type markings, with ten-faceted bulbous body, 15.5cm.
(Phillips) $622

A cased pair of Stourbridge cameo scent bottles of flattened tear shape, one in ruby the other yellow, overlaid in white, silver hallmarked London 1866.
(Phillips) $1,477

A good 19th century hexagonal cut and green overlay glass table scent bottle, decorated with scroll and figural panels, and fruiting blackberries, 7in. high.
(Academy) $308

A Bohemian double overlay tall cologne bottle and stopper with pear shaped body and tall neck, in clear glass overlaid in white and dark blue, 27.5cm.
(Phillips) $435

'Coque D'Or', five graduated blue glass scent bottles and stopper, made for Guerlain, each in the shape of a bow.
(Christie's) $1,020

A St. Louis cranberry and green overlay glass perfume bottle, decorated with flowers in relief and enriched in gilt, oval etched mark, 7^{1}/2in. high.
(Christopher Matthews)
$565

One of an attractive pair of Webb & Sons cameo scent bottles of globular shape in dark olive-green with a blue-tinted overlay, silver hallmarked Birmingham 1892, 9cm.
(Phillips) (Two) $1,244

'Kustos', an unusual silvered metal scent bottle modeled as a fire extinguisher, engraved *Odenius Göteborg*, 16cm. high.
(Christie's) $755

An Edwardian VII silver-mounted clear glass scent bottle, the plain rounded square glass bottle with pierced silver shoulders, 12cm. high, William Comyns, London 1901.
(Bearne's) $170

SHADES

René Lalique, plafonnier 'Provence', after 1927, clear and frosted glass, almost spherical form, molded with leaves in high relief, 34cm. diameter.
(Sotheby's)   **$2,362**

A Loetz yellow opalescent shade with blue splashes and purple radial stripes, aperture 11cm.
(Christie's) $375

René Lalique, plafonnier 'Saint-Vincent', after 1926, yellow glass, molded with bands of scrolling vine branches with fruits, molded mark, 34.5cm. diameter.
(Sotheby's)   **$2,725**

STAINED GLASS

A French (Normandy?) stained glass panel of the head of a young man, circa 1325, of octagonal shape, the man looking to the right, 8¹/₄in. diameter.
(Sotheby's)   **$8,050**

A French stained glass panel of a group of Apostles, probably from the Miracles of Christ window, Cathedral of Saint-Pierre, Troyes, circa 1170–1180, 12¹/₄ x 10in.
(Sotheby's)   **$16,100**

An Austrian (Vienna) stained glass panel depicting Salome receiving the head of Saint John the Baptist, circa 1400, 17¹/₄ x 24¹/₂in.
(Sotheby's)   **$5,750**

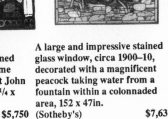

A large and impressive stained glass window, circa 1900–10, decorated with a magnificent peacock taking water from a fountain within a colonnaded area, 152 x 47in.
(Sotheby's) $7,631

An Austrian (Danube School) stained glass panel of the Annunciation, 16th century, centered by the Virgin with both hands raised and looking up, 14¹/₂ x 17¹/₂in.
(Sotheby's)   **$1,610**

TANKARDS

A Bohemian ruby-flashed tankard with octagonal faceted body engraved with a view of Munchen flanked by views of the Glyptothek and Kuhmmelhalle, 17cm.
(Phillips) $715

A German giltmetal-mounted engraved cylindrical tankard, circa 1800, engraved with a begging dog beneath the initials *IZ* enclosed within a circle, 19cm. high.
(Christie's) $1,771

An attractive Bohemian tankard in ruby glass overlaid in white, painted with a border of flowers above seven arcaded panels, 15.5cm.
(Phillips) $1,710

A Bohemian large and finely engraved amber tankard and cover of tapered cylindrical shape, finely cut with three stags, 27.5cm.
(Phillips) $1,477

A baluster coin tankard with a George II sixpence of 1757 trapped in the short stem to a spreading foot, 14cm.
(Phillips) $700

A Bohemian finely carved amber tankard and cover with decagonal faceted body deeply cut through to the clear ground with a stag, 18.3cm.
(Phillips) $809

TAZZA

A Venetian latticinio tazza, late 16th century, in vetro a retorti with an allover decoration of radiating gauze cable, a spreading conical foot with folded rim, 17.5cm. diameter.
(Christie's) $7,969

An attractive Lithyalin tazza, the shallow top cut with ten petal-shaped panels, on a faceted baluster stem, 12cm.
(Phillips) $809

Karl Massanetz for Lobmeyer, tazza, circa 1915, clear glass, the shallow bowl enameled in black with a dense stylized floral design, 12cm. high.
(Sotheby's) $2,725

TUMBLERS

A Transparentmalerei small tumbler in Kothgasser style, painted with a classical lady kneeling and making a libation, 10.9cm.
(Phillips) $933

A Baccarat molded cylindrical tumbler, mid 19th century, enameled in colors on gilt foil with Napoleon Bonaparte in military uniform, 9cm. high.
(Christie's) $885

An unusual gilt decorated Lithyalin tumbler with faceted sides, in brown and cream simulated agate tones, 12.2cm.
(Phillips) $591

An engraved German or Austrian tumbler and a cover of cylindrical shape, engraved on one side with a man in a governess cart and the date 1819 below the word 'souvenir', 13cm.
(Phillips) $684

A St. Louis faceted cylindrical tumbler, mid 19th century, enameled in colors and gilt, with the Badge of the Legion d'honneur, the center with a portrait of Henri IV, 10.5cm. high.
(Christie's) $531

A Bohemian transparent-enameled flared tumbler, circa 1845, enameled in transparent colors with a view of the Hradschin, inscribed in gilt *Das Königl Schloss in Prag*, 11cm. high.
(Christie's) $1,416

A Bohemian pink-flash 'alabaster' tumbler, circa 1845, the upper part with six cut roundels above exotic birds painted in bright colors 12.5cm. high.
(Christie's) $1,239

A Bohemian engraved and stained flared tumbler, circa 1850, engraved with two Oriental gentlemen, one jumping into a hoop held by his companion, 11.5cm. high.
(Christie's) $1,027

A Saxon engraved portrait tumbler of cylindrical shape, engraved with a profile bust portrait of *Fride. August Konig von Sachsen der Gerechte*, 11.5cm.
(Phillips) $622

432

VASES

Loetz iridescent glass vase, circa 1900, decorated around the shoulder and down the sides with iridescent blue wavy pulls, 3⅞in. high.
(Butterfield & Butterfield)
$2,185

Pair of Sandwich green pressed glass tulip vases, Boston and Sandwich Glass Co., mid 19th century, flaring scalloped rim on octagonal base, 9.9in. high.
(Skinner)
$4,485

Arsall cameo glass landscape vase, circa 1900, overlaid with green and cut with a continuous oasis scene, 8⅛in. high.
(Butterfield & Butterfield)
$1,092

Unsigned Loetz iridescent glass vase, circa 1900, decorated with light amber iridescent spotting on a cobalt blue ground, 9¾in. high.
(Butterfield & Butterfield)
$2,070

'Druides', a Lalique opalescent glass vase, the globular vessel molded with clusters of mistletoe, 17.8cm. high, moulded *R. Lalique.*
(Phillips)
$896

A Val St Lambert cameo glass vase, of tapering form, acid-etched with a bold geometric design in blue glass against a frosted ground, 14cm. high, etched *Val St Lambert.*
(Phillips)
$263

Steuben jade glass vase, circa 1930, the ovoid vase with outward flaring neck and inverted rim in jade, 12¼in. high.
(Butterfield & Butterfield)
$1,955

A pair of magnificent Bohemian ruby overlay vases deeply engraved through to the clear glass with two running horses on one and stags on the other, 43.5cm.
(Phillips)
$9,641

A Daum single overlay glass vase, decorated with purple flowers on a gray opaque ground, molded Daum Nancy mark, 7in. high.
(Christie's)
$1,121

VASES

A green Loetz vase with triple wavy everted rim, decorated with swirls of lilac iridescence, 10½in. high.
(Hobbs & Chambers) **$258**

René Lalique, vase 'Gui', after 1920, electric blue glass molded with mistletoe, 17cm.
(Sotheby's) **$4,542**

Daum, olives vase, circa 1913, gray glass internally decorated with yellow, overlaid with green, with a band of aubergine, 12in.
(Sotheby's) **$6,541**

Emile Gallé, cyclamen vase, circa 1900, dichroic opalescent/ yellow glass, overlaid with burgundy red and carved with flowering stems and leaves, 5⅝in.
(Sotheby's) **$7,631**

Emile Gallé, retailed by Escalier de Cristal, vase in the form of a Chinese bronze 'gu' vessel, circa 1900, clear glass, with a band of enameled stylized floral decoration in shades of pale blue, navy, red, white and pink, 25.25cm.
(Sotheby's) **$9,085**

Emile Gallé, rose hip 'blow-out' vase, circa 1900, gray glass shading from mustard to amber, molded in high relief with rose-hips and leaves, 24cm.
(Sotheby's) **$4,724**

Loetz vase, circa 1925, bubble-gum pink glass, the lower section overlaid with deep purple washed with peacock blue iridescent spots, 19.5cm.
(Sotheby's) **$2,180**

Muller Frères butterflies vase, circa 1910, clear glass, internally decorated with leaf green, overlaid with red and etched with butterflies and leafy stems, cameo mark, 15.5cm.
(Sotheby's) **$2,362**

René Lalique, vase 'Gobelet Six Figurines', after 1912, molded with six vertical rectangular panels each with a veiled female figure in flowing robes, 7³/₈in.
(Sotheby's) **$1,544**

VASES

Daum stylized fronds vase, circa 1920, smoked glasss, etched with fronds against a textured ground, 11³/₈in.
(Sotheby's) $1,272

A Lalique blue stained glass vase, the ovoid body molded with grasshoppers on reeds, 27cm. high, inscribed *LALIQUE*.
(Bearne's) $2,395

Loetz vase, 1902, peach glass washed with lustrous ripples of deep purple and green/gold spotting, 17.5cm.
(Sotheby's) $12,355

Emile Gallé, wild roses vase, circa 1900, gray glass internally decorated with yellow, overlaid with red and etched with flowering sprays of wild roses, 6in.
(Sotheby's) $3,634

Emile Gallé, orchid vase, circa 1900, clear green glass, internally mottled with pink and orange, etched and enameled, with flowering stems and large leaves, 5³/₄in.
(Sotheby's) $2,362

Daum, pendant flower vase, circa 1900, creamy pale blue glass cased in clear glass, overlaid with emerald green and etched with flowering sprays, 11³/₄in.
(Sotheby's) $7,268

Emile Gallé tulip vase, circa 1900, gray glass, internally decorated with apricot, overlaid with amber and etched with flowering sprays, 23cm.
(Sotheby's) $2,544

Daum, poppies vase, circa 1900, stripes of white, ocher, yellow with aventurine and green towards the base, 4⁷/₈in.
(Sotheby's) $5,814

Daum, abstract vase, 1920s, turquoise glass, etched with an abstract design of circles against a textured ground, 14¹/₂in.
(Sotheby's) $2,725

René Lalique, vase 'Bacchantes', after 1927, opalescent glass molded with a frieze of female nudes, 24.5cm.
(Sotheby's) $14,536

Daum, thistle vase, circa 1910, clear glass internally mottled with aubergine, etched with thistles and a butterfly, 7⁵/₈in.
(Sotheby's) $7,268

Loetz cased vase, circa 1900, orange glass, cased in clear glass washed with light blue and lime green iridescence, 15.25cm.
(Sotheby's) $2,180

François-Emile Décorchemont, vase, 1924–27, pâte-de-cristal, clear glass internally streaked with pink and aubergine, 11.75cm.
(Sotheby's) $4,724

Daum, wild rose vase, circa 1900, frosted glass overlaid with dichroic pink/green and etched with wild roses and rose-hips, 6³/₄in.
(Sotheby's) $5,088

Daum, sycamore vase, circa 1910, gray glass internally mottled with yellow and pink, etched with leaves and pendant sycamore seeds, 9in.
(Sotheby's) $3,997

Emile Gallé, vase parlant 'L'Inconnue est l'Ocean', circa 1900, clear glass internally streaked with milky white, turquoise and purple, 9cm.
(Sotheby's) $7,268

Emile Gallé, Libellule vase, circa 1890, clear glass enameled with a dragonfly among delicate flowering stems, heightened with gilding, 5in.
(Sotheby's) $2,362

Emile Gallé, good aquatic vase with shells, circa 1900, clear glass internally decorated with swirls of lime green, yellow and blue, 7⁵/₈in.
(Sotheby's) $39,974

René Lalique, vase 'Formose',
after 1924, emerald green glass
molded with swimming fish,
17cm.
(Sotheby's) $3,997

Daum, antelope vase, circa 1925,
clear glass, overlaid with leaf
green and etched with a stylized
stag and hind, 12in.
(Sotheby's) $5,814

René Lalique, vase 'Formose',
after 1924, mustard glass
molded with swimming fish,
17cm.
(Sotheby's) $3,089

René Lalique, vase 'Druide',
after 1924, emerald green glass
molded with mistletoe
branches with berries in high
relief, 17.5cm.
(Sotheby's) $6,178

Gabriel Argy-Rousseau vase
'Rayons de Soleil', 1926,
molded around the rim and
foot with flowerheads in shades
of red, 6in.
(Sotheby's) $8,722

François-Emile Décorchemont,
Blossoms vase, 1924–27, pâte-
de-cristal, decorated with three
panels of highly stylized flowers,
12cm.
(Sotheby's) $6,905

Emile Gallé, chrysanthemum
vase, circa 1900, dichroic yellow/
blue glass, overlaid with blue
and etched with flowerheads,
buds and leaves, 13in.
(Sotheby's) $7,268

René Lalique, vase 'Archers',
after 1921, clear and frosted
glass, molded with archers
beneath a flock of large birds,
26.5cm.
(Sotheby's) $2,725

Daum, poppy vase, circa 1895,
clear glass, overlaid with deep
red, with silvered metal mounts
at neck and foot decorated with
conforming poppy heads, 7⁵/₈in.
(Sotheby's) $6,541

WINE GLASSES

A rare engraved Jacobite wine glass, the bell bowl engraved with a six-petalled rose and two buds with a star and 'Fiat'. 16.3cm.
(Phillips) $1,555

An engraved wine glass with small ogee bowl engraved with a daffodil on one side and a small spray of flowers on the reverse, 14.8cm.
(Phillips) $202

An engraved and composite stem wine glass with drawn trumpet bowl engraved with a border of fruiting vine and two insects, 17.4cm., circa 1750.
(Phillips) $608

A finely engraved armorial light baluster wine glass with rounded funnel bowl, Dutch-engraved with the coat-of-arms of Anne, daughter of George II, 18cm., circa 1750.
(Phillips) $1,824

A white enameled wine glass with rounded funnel bowl, enameled around the rim with fruiting vine and leaves, on a plain stem and folded foot, 15.3cm.
(Phillips) $933

An enameled and mixed twist stem wine glass with small ogee bowl decorated possibly by Beilby, with star-like flowers and leaf scrolls, 14.2cm., circa 1760.
(Phillips) $1,216

An attractive Beilby enameled wine glass with bell bowl, painted around the rim in white enamel with fruiting vine and tendrils, 17cm., circa 1765.
(Phillips) $1,824

A pedestal stem wine glass, the funnel bowl with solid base containing a tear, on a six-pointed pedestal stem and domed foot, 16.5cm.
(Phillips) $467

An attractive wine glass with double ogee bowl engraved around the rim with scrolling flowers and leaves, 15.2cm., circa 1750.
(Phillips) $486

WINE GLASSES

A rare diamond-point engraved wine glass with rounded funnel bowl engraved with a youth and a seated girl in 18th century costume, 17cm., circa 1770.
(Phillips) **$1,368**

An engraved ratafia glass with slender ogee bowl molded with vertical fluting and engraved with a border of flowers and leaves, 17.8cm., circa 1770.
(Phillips) **$638**

An attractive wine glass with honeycomb-molded ogee bowl, on a double knopped multi-ply air twist stem and conical foot, 16cm., circa 1750.
(Phillips) **$274**

A commemorative facet-stemmed wine glass, circa 1780, engraved with a bird perched on the top of an opened birdcage and inscribed above *LIBERTY AND WILKES*, 13.8cm. high.
(Christie's) **$1,416**

A fine Dutch-engraved light baluster wine glass with rounded funnel bowl with a meeting of a Queen and a turbanned man, on a light baluster stem and a domed foot, 17.2cm., circa 1740.
(Phillips) **$1,976**

A color twist tall 'flute' or wine glass, on a color twist stem composed of an opaque white corkscrew edged in blue and with a blue central stripe, 20.5cm., circa 1765.
(Phillips) **$1,520**

A color twist wine glass with rounded funnel bowl molded with vertical flutes on the lower part of the bowl, 15.2cm., circa 1765.
(Phillips) **$304**

An engraved ale glass with tall ogee bowl engraved with hops and barley on an opaque twist stem of a lace corkscrew, 18.8cm., circa 1770.
(Phillips) **$289**

A color twist wine glass also with rounded funnel bowl molded with vertical fluting around the lower part, 14.5cm., circa 1765.
(Phillips) **$1,672**

WINE GLASSES

A color twist wine glass with rounded funnel bowl molded with vertical flutes on the lower part, 14.1cm., circa 1765.
(Phillips)   **$1,368**

A baluster wine glass, circa 1720, the bell bowl supported on a knop above a cushion knop and true baluster stem, on a domed foot, 16.5cm. high.
(Christie's)   **$886**

A baluster cordial glass, circa 1720, the waisted bucket bowl supported on an angular collar, on a conical foot, 15.5cm. high.
(Christie's)   **$1,027**

A color-twist wine glass, circa 1765, the stem with an opaque corkscrew spiral closely entwined by a single red thread and with a single blue spiral thread, 14cm. high.
(Christie's)   **$3,896**

An engraved facet-stemmed wine glass, circa 1780, the ogee bowl engraved with a continuous horse-racing scene with two gentleman pointing towards four horses, 15cm. high.
(Christie's)   **$1,204**

A color-twist wine glass, circa 1765, the ogee bowl supported on a stem with a laminated corkscrew core enclosed by spiral opaque, translucent green and brick-red threads, 15cm. high. (Christie's)   **$3,542**

A color-twist wine glass, circa 1765, the stem with an opaque laminated corkscrew core edged with translucent red threads, 13.5cm. high.
(Christie's)   **$1,948**

A balustroid wine glass with drawn trumpet bowl containing a small tear, terminating in an inverted baluster section also with a tear, 16.7cm.
(Phillips)   **$342**

A Jacobite air twist wine glass, circa 1750, the funnel bowl engraved with a flower-spray including Scotch thistle and honeysuckle, 16cm. high.
(Christie's)   **$673**

WINE GLASSES

A fine color twist wine glass with rounded funnel bowl on a color-twist stem, 14.4cm., circa 1765.
(Phillips) $2,736

A tall ale glass with rounded funnel bowl, on a double knopped multi-ply airtwist stem and conical foot, 20cm.
(Phillips) $342

An opaque twist wine glass with vertically ribbed rounded funnel bowl, the stem with a gauze corkscrew, 15cm.
(Phillips) $202

Toastmaster's glass with a waisted bucket bowl on a collar, above a swelling knopped stem with basal knop, on a conical foot, 15.7cm.
(Phillips) $435

A color-twist wine glass, circa 1765, the stem with a yellow laminated corkscrew core edged in white enclosed within two opaque gauze spirals, 15cm. high.
(Christie's) $4,250

An opaque twist cordial glass, circa 1760, the funnel bowl with hammered flutes to the lower part, on an angular domed foot, 17.5cm. high.
(Christie's) $886

A five-knopped air twist wine glass, circa 1750, with a bell bowl, the stem with five knops and filled with airtwist spirals, on a conical foot, 17.5cm. high.
(Christie's) $7,084

An engraved color-twist ale flute, circa 1765, the slender funnel bowl engraved with two ears of barley and a hop-spray, 17cm. high.
(Christie's) $2,656

A color-twist wine glass, circa 1765, of drawn-trumpet form, the stem with a solid blue core entwined by two opaque flat ribbons, 15.5cm. high.
(Christie's) $3,896

D. Marshall: a rare feather ball marked *D. Marshall*, with ink written weight *27*, and stamped *R.H.B.*
(Phillips) $25,500

A Copeland blue pottery teapot, the sides decorated in royal blue glaze and with white pottery golfing figures in relief, 21cm.
(Phillips) $780

The Edinburgh Burgess Golfing Society: a silver medal of oval lobed form, 1831.
(Phillips) $8,736

A studio photograph of old Tom Morris, dated *1902*, autographed by himself and photographed by A. Donnie of St. Andrews, 5¼ x 4in.
(Sotheby's) $3,435

J.H. Taylor: a 9ct. gold medal commemorating the first International Professional match at Gleneagles, America versus Britain.
(Phillips) $3,900

A framed photograph of Tom Morris, the Royal and Ancient Clubhouse in the background, in gilt frame, 14½ x 11½in.
(Christie's) $742

A golfing Hole in One coin in slot machine, circa 1955, requiring great skill to obtain your chewing gum, 18.25 x 30cm.
(Sotheby's) $891

A studio portrait of members of the Montrose Golf Club, circa 1900, 18.5 x 23cm.
(Phillips) $240

After Bernard Villemont (1911–1989), Côte Basque, lithographed poster, backed with linen, 99 x 61cm.
(Sotheby's) $578

A fine Amphora figure of a caddy boy, manufactured in Austria, early 20th century with five original clubs, 10¹/₂in. high.
(Bonhams) $720

A fine Royal Doulton Crombie series ware bowl, circa 1925, 24cm. diameter.
(Sotheby's) $1,650

A composition Dunlop advertising figure, decorated in colors upon a mound base, uninscribed, 15¹/₂in. high.
(Bonhams) $540

Golfing book: Golf at Gleneagles, by R.J. Mclennan, illustrated boards, with map.
(Phillips) $530

A Doulton Lambeth advertising jug, 1904, numbered *9073*, initialed *EB* and entitled *Colonel Bogey whiskey*, 7¹/₂in. high.
(Bonhams) $570

A signed portrait photograph of old Tom Morris in front of the Swilcan Burn, dated to the reverse *20.1.08*, with George Bruce's signature, in reasonable condition.
(Sotheby's) $1,380

After Henschoz, Villars, Chesières lithographic poster, framed and glazed, 39 x 24¹/₂in.
(Sotheby's) $891

A boxed wrapped dozen Ocobo gutta-percha golf balls, circa 1895, registered no. 210248, by J. B. Halley, 76 Finsbury Pavement, London EC.
(Sotheby's) $10,029

After Peikert, Lenzerheide, Valbella lithographic poster, framed and glazed, 39 x 24¹/₂in.
(Sotheby's) $835

A Russian portable gramophone with integral moveable horn. (Auction Team Köln) $154

An early Peter Pan gramophone, in wooden case with integral folding speaker, American, circa 1902.
(Auction Team Köln) $423

An HMV cased gramophone with original speaker.
(Auction Team Köln) $154

An His Master Voice Model 202, re-entrant tone chamber gramophone, with No. 5A soundbox, oxidised fittings and oak case, 49¹/₂in. high, 1928. (Christie's) $22,815

A Brunswick Luxury Model 105 mahogany gramophone, original speaker with interchangeable two-needle system and automatic switch-off, circa 1917.
(Auction Team Köln) $500

An HMV Model 163 standard gramophone with original speaker and two front doors for sound regulation, circa 1920.
(Auction Team Köln)
$1,232

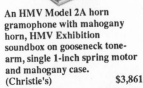

A Victor Gramophone by the Gramophone & Typewriter Ltd., with brass-belled black horn, small gooseneck tone-arm, Gramophone Company Exhibition soundbox, circa 1905. (Christie's) $965

A green-painted Nirona gramophone, with the children's disk 'Gnom', German, circa 1915.
(Auction Team Köln) $539

An HMV Model 2A horn gramophone with mahogany horn, HMV Exhibition soundbox on gooseneck tone-arm, single 1-inch spring motor and mahogany case.
(Christie's) $3,861

A French Pathé Diffusor table gramophone with unusual, round, flat, paper-membrane horn, circa 1922.
(Auction Team Köln) $500

An Emil Berliner spring-driven gramophone, American, circa 1895, in working order.
(Auction Team Köln) $3,853

A French Melophone table gramophone with integral horn, and eight shellac disks, circa 1915.
(Auction Team Köln) $616

A horn Zonophone, Model HVO, with Exhibition-pattern soundbox, oak case and gilt-lined black Morning Glory horn, 23in. diameter, dated on base *1920*.
(Christie's) $1,404

A Pathé Elf gramophone with original speaker and integral horn, circa 1915.
(Auction Team Köln) $655

A horn Pathéphone with single-spring motor, Ebonite reproducer, scrolling back bracket and walnut case, 19$^{1}/_{2}$in. diameter, and a lateral-cut soundbox with adapter.
(Christie's) $527

A Victrola Model VV1-77 with original diaphragm box and handle.
(Auction Team Köln) $293

An American Columbia Graphophone gramophone, with nickel-plated horn, circa 1906.
(Auction Team Köln) $1,155

A Bing Pigmyphone toy gramophone, with key and needle tin.
(Auction Team Köln) $254

René Lalique, sycamore seeds haircomb, circa 1902–03, horn, the seeds and twigs formed from gold modeled in high relief, 6.75cm. wide.
(Sotheby's) $26,460

René Lalique, bees haircomb, circa 1900, carved and patinated horn, as two stalks of corn, each applied with a carved and patinated bee, 16.8cm. wide.
(Sotheby's) $58,009

René Lalique, cherries (prunus cerasus) haircomb, circa 1902–03, horn, the stems picked out in rose and brilliant-cut diamonds, 9.5cm. wide.
(Sotheby's) $30,531

Charles Boutet de Monvel, Symbolist comb, 1901–02, tortoiseshell with applied upper panel in openwork silver, centered by a female head with turquoise enamel flowers, 9.5cm. wide.
(Sotheby's) $3,460

Georges Fouquet, ornamental haircomb, circa 1895–98, tortoiseshell, the shaped symmetrical panel mounted with gold scroll set with rose and brilliant-cut diamonds, 8.75cm. wide.
(Sotheby's) $7,123

René Lalique, anemones haircomb, circa 1899–1901, horn, the concave openwork upper panel with stylized wood anemones in matt gold enameled in shades of pale peach and pink, 9cm. wide.
(Sotheby's) $26,460

Maison Vever, seaweed comb, circa 1900–02, horn, gold framed openwork upper section enclosing plique à jour enamel seaweed fronds, set with amethysts, 8.4cm. wide.
(Sotheby's) $28,496

Falize Frères, dolphin haircomb, circa 1900, tortoiseshell, the shaped rectangular panel applied with openwork gold design centered by an opal vase, 8.25cm. wide.
(Sotheby's) $7,123

René Lalique, bramble haircomb with detachable hair clip, circa 1905, horn, applied with three carved glass fruits enclosed in gold fronds, comb 8.1cm., hairclip 5.5cm. wide.
(Sotheby's) $40,708

Boucheron, sycamore haircomb, circa 1900, horn, the seed pods represented by two stained green chalcedony cabochons, 7.5cm. wide.
(Sotheby's) $18,319

Lucien Gaillard, honesty haircomb, circa 1902–05, horn, containing six graduated oval pods formed from thin slivers of mother-of-pearl, 14cm. wide.
(Sotheby's) $4,274

René Lalique, beetles and fern haircomb, circa 1902–03, horn, carved in high relief as two fern sprays with applied beetles among the leaves, 10cm. wide.
(Sotheby's) $26,460

Georges Fouquet, probably from a design by Charles Desrosiers, mother-of-pearl haircomb, circa 1905, tortoiseshell applied with a fan-shaped section of mother-of-pearl, 10.5cm. wide.
(Sotheby's) $14,248

René Lalique, pair of ombellifère hair pins, circa 1902–03, horn, carved as two individual stems of ombellifère, the carved diamond-set canopies of flowers on delicate gold stems, 21cm. high.
(Sotheby's) $67,168

René Lalique, floral diadem, circa 1900, horn, carved as a hinged arched openwork design of interlaced floral stems, flowerheads centers set with brilliant-cut diamonds, 12cm. wide.
(Sotheby's) $7,633

Lucien Gaillard, wild caraway haircomb, circa 1900–02, horn, the fan-shaped plants with circular clusters of small baroque pearl fruits, 12.5cm. wide.
(Sotheby's) $48,850

Boutet de Monvel, serpent and oyster haircomb, circa 1900, the tortoiseshell comb applied with a silver serpent writhing across two large pieces of mother-of-pearl, 9.5cm. wide.
(Sotheby's) $20,354

Lucien Gaillard, blackberry blossom haircomb, circa 1900, horn, applied with three carved mother-of-pearl flowers enhanced with rose diamond stamens, 9.3cm. wide.
(Sotheby's) $50,885

Northern Greek painted icon depicting a host of Saints, mid 19th century, each with name inscriptions, crowned with halos, 8³/₄in. x 7in.
(Skinner) $402

A triptych celebrating the deliverance of Constantinople, Greek, 18th century, the central panel with an elaborate composition depicting the City of Constantinople.
(Christie's) $15,835

Russian micro mosaic icon, 20th century, with gilt glass halo, with inscriptions, 9⁷/₈ x 8in.
(Skinner) $805

The Archangel Michael, Provincial Byzantine, 13th century, the Archangel shown half-length from a Deisis composition, in a red vestment over a blue shift, an ocher garment underneath, 18¹/₈in. x 14³/₈in.
(Christie's) $150,399

Saint George slaying the dragon, School of Emmanuel Tzanes, Cretan, late 17th century, Saint George, mounted on a vigorously rearing gray charger, transfixes the dragon with his lance whilst the princess makes her escape, 10in. x 8in.
(Christie's) $24,633

The Akra Tapeinosis (Christ 'Man of Sorrows'), Cretan, beginning of the 16th century, the naked, half-length figure of Christ is depicted standing within a marble sarcophagus against the outline of the Cross, 9in. x 7¹/₄in.
(Christie's) $43,987

A small Byzantine icon of three warrior saints, circa 1400, Saints George, Dimitri and Theodore depicted in armor holding swords and lances, 10³/₄ x 7⁷/₈in.
(Christie's) $24,633

A small icon of Saint Anthony the Great, Provincial Greece, 17th century, the founder of monasticism shown in a monk's habit unfurling a scroll with both hands, 8¹/₄in. x 5³/₄in.
(Christie's) $2,463

The Mother of God of Smolensk, 18th century, finely painted on a gilt ground, the Virgin's maphorion heightened with a gold wash, 13⁵/₈in. x 11³/₄in.
(Christie's) $2,991

The Doubting of Thomas, Russian, 17th century, 16¹/₂in. x 14³/₈in.
(Christie's) $7,389

An unusual Greek triptych, early 18th century, painted on a gold ground, the central panel with the Resurrection of Christ and His Ascension, 4¹/₂ x 6³/₄in.
(Christie's) $2,815

The Birth of the Virgin, Provincial Russian, 17th century, 15³/₄in. x 14¹/₄in.
(Christie's) $3,870

A monumental icon of Christ King of Kings and Great Hierarch, Cretan, late 17th century, the Saviour seated upon an elaborate gilt throne, majestically vested as Great Hierarch, with Imperial miter.
(Christie's) $52,785

An important late Byzantine icon of the Nativity of Christ, Crete, beginning of the 15th century, against an elaborate mountain setting, the Virgin reclines upon a red pallet at the mouth of a cave, 25³/₄ x 24³/₄in.
(Christie's) $406,215

Saints Theodore of Tiron and Theodore Stratilates, probably Syria/Lebanon, possibly 13th century, the two warrior saints depicted as bearded young men, on an olive-green ground, 32¹/₄in. x 17³/₄in.
(Christie's) $145,350

The Archangel Michael, Balkan, late 17th century, brightly painted on a gold ground, the Archangel depicted half-length 'Captain of the Hosts', 27³/₄in. x 20¹/₂in.
(Christie's) $5,630

The Hodigitria Mother of God, Cretan, early 15th century, Christ Emmanuel, is seated erect on the Virgin's left arm, clothed in a gold himation, 17¹/₈in. x 12¹/₄in.
(Christie's) $52,785

The Deisis, Northern Greece, early 17th century, painted on a silver ground, the Saviour on a throne, flanked by the Virgin and John the Baptist, 13³/₈in. x 11in.
(Christie's) $2,815

Five-case inro, 19th century, decorated with a continuous scene of an inland waterway, 4½in. high.
(Butterfield & Butterfield)
$2,587

Four-case mixed metal inro, 18th century, a version of the Koseikiko legend, 3in. high.
(Butterfield & Butterfield)
$2,587

Five-case lacquer inro, 19th century, decorated in gold hiramaki-e with moored fishing boats, 9.6cm high.
(Butterfield & Butterfield)
$3,162

Fine coral inlaid inro, 19th century, of lozenge form, delicately rendered with fruiting leaves in gold hiramaki-e, 3½in. high.
(Butterfield & Butterfield)
$2,587

Fine five-case inro, 19th century, expertly rendered in gold hiramaki-e with two scenes of cranes under a blossoming cherry, 3½in. high.
(Butterfield & Butterfield)
$6,325

Good five-case inro, 19th century, subtly rendered with a crescent moon shimmering through scattered clouds, 10.3cm.
(Butterfield & Butterfield)
$1,725

Five-case inro, 19th century, decorated in gold hiramaki-e, kirikane and aogai, with a bridge spanning a narrow river, 9.3cm high.
(Butterfield & Butterfield)
$1,380

Good two-case inro, 19th century, decorated with a continuous scene of a fish by waterweeds, 6.1cm. high.
(Butterfield & Butterfield)
$2,875

Good soft metal inro, 19th century, the shibuichi cases decorated in gold, silver and shakudo takazogan, signed *Katenori*, 3in. high,
(Butterfield & Butterfield)
$2,587

A Detector Lock, ornately engraved on the backplate *Made by H. Gadsby Cutler & Silversmith late of 38 Sincil Street Lincoln*, with barrel key, in polished steel case, 10in. long.
(Christie's) $497

A lapping and grinding device, for hand-rest socket mounting, with pulley drive, adjustable protractor motion and two slides.
(Christie's) $331

A barograph, by Casella, London, the lacquered-brass mechanism mounted on a crackle-finish iron base, with drum inscribed *Gluck Co. Ltd.*, 15¼in. wide.
(Christie's) $580

An early mining theodolite, signed on the silvered compass dial *Troughton and Simms, London*, the instrument arranged for use as either a theodolite or mining dial, 10¼in. wide.
(Christie's) $1,408

A pair of Regency mahogany terrestrial and celestial globes, by John and William Cary, 1816, the terrestrial globe corrected to 1828, exhibiting the tracks and discoveries made by Captain Cook, the globe 18in. diameter.
(Christie's) $45,149

A U.S. Navy binnacle, the gimballed compass in a turned hood, on a mahogany pedestal, with label *Kelvin & Wilfred O. White Co., Boston and New York*, 51in. high.
(George Kidner) $1,118

A black-enameled and chromium-plated compound binocular laboratory microscope, by Beck, London 'London Model' No. 26490, in mahogany case, 17in. high.
(Christie's) $580

A 19th-century brass 'Culpeper'-type microscope, unsigned, with rack and pinion focusing, sprung stage, four objectives, fish-plate and other items, 13in. high.
(Christie's) $961

A specific balance by F. Leunig & Co., the stand of plated iron with brass scale crescent, on tripod base with justification screw, circa 1910.
(Auction Team Köln) $146

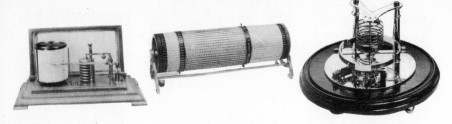

A lacquered brass barograph by Callaghan & Co. London, with eight tier vacuum in a glazed oak case, 38cm. wide, with some recording sheets.
(Phillips) **$560**

Large logarithmic calculating cylinder by Albert Nestler, with 12.5m. scale, circa 1920, 59 cm. wide.
(Auction Team Köln) **$539**

A large brass and mahogany demonstration model of the Earnshaw spring detent escapement, with a $4^3/4$in. bi-metallic balance wheel, 10in.
(Bonhams) **$753**

A fine mid-19th century '30 inch' terrestrial globe by W. & A. K. Johnston Limited, Edinburgh and London, in brass-mounted mahogany frame, 95cm.
(Bearne's) **$23,948**

An early 19th century lacquered brass universal equinoctial dial, signed on the chapter *Gilbert & Sons, London*, the sprung gnomon with scroll support, 9cm. wide.
(Phillips) **$1,036**

A lacquered brass and black enameled compound monocular microscope by Watson & Sons, London, 60816, the signed body tube inscribed *Patna*, 34cm. high.
(Phillips) **$404**

A George III brass circumferentor dial by F. Morgan, London, the signed frame of 15cm. diameter with rotating arm centred by an engraved silvered compass.
(Phillips) **$1,435**

A large 19th century compound monocular microscope by Dancer, Manchester with rack and pinion focusing, together with two fitted drawers of extensive accessories.
(Phillips) **$1,993**

A lacquered brass Culpepper type microscope, with draw tube focusing above circular stage on a circular mahogany base, 10in. high.
(Phillips) **$797**

A painted carved wood fraternal hour glass, America, 19th century, painted blue with gilt highlights, 11¹/₂in. high.
(Skinner) $431

A 19th century 3in. pocket globe by Bithray Royal Exchange, London, in a fishskin case.
(Phillips) $3,558

A late 19th century rack corkscrew with closed barrel, coat of arms, side and wind handle and bone grip, 18cm.
(Peter Wilson) $479

An 18th century mahogany and brass octant by John Williamson, the frame with double 'pin hole' sight and cover, 1769, 40cm. wide.
(Phillips) $5,263

A 19th century lacquered and oxidized brass compound binocular microscope, with rack and pinion focusing and fine eyepiece adjustment.
(Phillips) $765

A silver and leather covered traveling barometer and thermometer, retailed by Asprey, the hinge marked *London 1931*, 3in. diameter.
(Phillips) $433

A mid 19th century brass sundial by Adie & Son, the 32.5cm. circular plate engraved with regulation of time and compass points, signed *Adie & Son, Edinburgh 1842*.
(Phillips) $606

A 19th century lacquered brass compound monocular microscope, the base signed *C. Baker, 244 High Holborn, London,* with rack and pinion focusing.
(Phillips) $712

A mid 19th century bronze sundial by Watkins & Hill, the quatrefoil plate engraved with compass points, equation of time and chapter from IIII-XII-VIII, London 1847, 37cm. diameter.
(Phillips) $765

Early French Haar hygrometer, 14 cm. wide.
(Auction Team Köln) $92

A 19th century mahogany cased weather station by Negretti & Zambra, comprising timepiece, aneroid barometer, recording barograph and thermometer, 16in. high.
(Canterbury) $2,512

A W. R. Murray compass set, brass, in mahogany case/
(Auction Team Köln) $130

A rare mahogany barometer and thermometer with a perpetual regulation of time, John Alment, Dublin Fecit, circa 1770, exposed barometer tube with a silvered scale graduated from 27–34in, 39in.
(Bonhams) $19,760

A mid 18th century 2.5in. lacquered brass reflecting telescope by James Short London numbered *1741 114/306=9.5*, the 14in. long body tube with speculum mirrors, 44cm. wide.
(Phillips) $1,392

A 19th century lacquered brass compound monocular microscope by Negretti & Zambra, Hatton Garden, London with coarse and fine focusing, 40cm. high.
(Phillips) $464

A World War II German Enigma encoding machine, in original metal case, lacking batteries, 1940.
(Auction Team Köln) $10,041

A 19th century 15in. celestial table globe by J & W Cary, 181 Strand, London 1818, with engraved brass meridian, 55cm. high.
(Phillips) $2,630

A 19th century brass dial barograph, with 4.5in. silvered chapter and eight tier vacuum, 36cm. wide.
(Phillips) $897

An English brass theodolite by Troughton & Simmons, London, with silver scale, spirit level and tripod base.
(Auction Team Köln) $577

A Polish magnetic compass signed *Phos. Varsovie*, 23.5 cm. diameter, on tripod stand.
(Auction Team Köln) $323

Compass set with copper housing with petroleum burner and gimballed compass, 25 cm. high.
(Auction Team Köln) $231

A 19th century gilt brass pocket barometer and compass, the 1.75in. silvered dial marked *compensated*, by Negretti & Zambra, 10344.
(Phillips) $495

A pair of 12in. table globes by Cary, the 'New Terrestrial' inscribed *Exhibiting the different Tracks of Captain Cook and the new discoveries made by him... J.& W. Cary, September 2 1816*, 48cm. high.
(Phillips) $5,909

A small mahogany 2-day marine chronometer, Ulysse Nardin, No. 5872, circa 1900, silvered dial with Roman numerals, with power reserves indicator and subsidiary seconds, bezel diam. 90mm.
(Bonhams) $3,648

Engraved brass binocular theodolite by Richer, Paris, with silver scale, on tripod base, circa 1875.
(Auction Team Köln) $1,617

An 18th century brass universal equinoctial dial with folding rod gnomon, the octagonal base signed *Le Maire a Paris*, 8cm. long.
(Phillips) $928

An oak and engraved brass octant with pinhole sight and two shades and mirrors, on three turned brass feet, 29cm. wide.
(Phillips) $715

7329 – 1850, coffee-roaster, W. H. Trissler and Elias Brecht, Fairview, PA, lacquered brass, 7¼in. long.
(Christie's) $633

288654 – 1883, folding basket, H. J. Morse, Boston, MA, metal, cane and fabric, 11½in. wide.
(Christie's) $184

374091 – 1887, truss, Thomas Simmons, Hartford, CT, leather, canvas, wood and nickel-plated brass, 9in. diameter.
(Christie's) $920

254494 – 1882, paper-hanging machine, R. H. Miner, Elk City, PA, wood, white-metal, paper and brush, with plaque signed *R. H. Miner Inventor Elk City Pa.*, 11in. wide.
(Christie's) $173

36469 – 1862, improved sugar-evaporator, John K. Leedy, Bloomington, IL, wood, brass, painted tin and glass, lettered *John K Leedy Bloomington McLean County Ills.*, and with framed photo of the inventor, 12in. x 11in.
(Christie's) $6,670

169160 – 1875, improvement in game-counters, David Fey and Hermann Pein, Peoria, IL, mahogany and brass with spring steel, 6in. diameter.
(Christie's) $1,610

403362 – 1889, dust-collector, Orville M. Morse, Jackson, MI, mahogany and plated brass, with engraved plate, 19¼in. high.
(Christie's) $3,680

134578 – 1873, improvement in apparatus for physical culture, George B. Windship, Boston, MA, wood and brass, 8½in. x 9in., early exercise machine.
(Christie's) $2,530

50685 – 1865, combined coal-shuttle and ash-screen, A. F. Carling and L. Rockwell, Ellenville, NY, painted tin, 10¼in. high.
(Christie's) $633

238741 – 1881, life-saving chair, Alphonso Wilson, New York, NY, painted wood, galvanized tin and brass, 11¼in. high. (Christie's) $4,600

194097 – 1877, improvement in portable ice houses, John E. Lippitt, Wilmington, NC, wood, painted, 9in. x 10⅝in. (Christie's) $1,265

4166 – 1845, swing for exercising, Joel H. Ross, New York, NY, mahogany, wire and tin, 4¾in. high. (Christie's) $690

90284 – 1869, improved manufacture of deodorized heavy hydrocarbon-oils, Joshua Merrill, Boston, MA, wood, brass and copper, with finely engraved maker's plate, 8½in. x 8¼in. (Christie's) $1,093

144929 – 1873, improvement in ink stands, Thomas S. Shenston, Brantford, Ontario, painted, tin, one model in two sections, each with paper label inscribed *The Champion Air-Tight Ink Stand etc*, 5in. diameter. (Christie's) $460

208241 – 1878, improvement in smut machines, W. S. Hills, Boone, IA, wood and brass, 10¾in. high, smut is an impurity in grain, contary to popular belief. (Christie's) $1,265

19343 – 1858, rotating blast-producing chair, Leopold Richard Breisach, New York, NY, mahogany, brass and leather, 16¼in. high. (Christie's) $8,625

40088 – 1863, suspension-rack for coupon-tickets & c, Edward P. Bacon, Milwaukee, WI, oak with brass fittings, paper cards, 11½in. high. (Christie's) $633

70473 – 1867, improved hitching-strap, A. J. Ross, Rochester, NY, carved wood, painted, with leather and brass fittings, 9¾in. high. (Christie's) $1,725

A Victorian painted cast-iron horse restraint modeled as a jockey, 43in. high.
(Christie's) $1,325

A pair of wrought iron hinges, Pennsylvania, 19th century, each sheet metal, of wish-bone form with claw termini, 18in. long.
(Christie's) $253

A Victorian painted cast-iron horse restraint modeled as a negro jockey, 23in. high.
(Christie's) $529

18th century steel footman, D shaped top with fretwork decorated frieze, three slender legs with pad feet, 12½in. high.
(Peter Wilson) $624

A Persian Qajar damascened steel harpy figure, late 19th century, the acid-etched body decorated with feathers and figures within cartouches terminating in a human face, 28in. high.
(Christie's) $2,447

A cast-iron '10 Ft. No. 2' rooster millweight, American, late 19th century, the swell-bodied figure of a rooster with moulded comb, eye and wattle detail, 17in. long.
(Sotheby's) $1,840

Two brass-inlaid wrought iron utensils, Pennsylvania, early 19th century, the first a flesh fork with hooked terminus, the second a ladle with tapering rectangular handle, 19½in. long.
(Christie's) $2,990

A South German or Spanish wrought-iron strong box, 17th century, composed of overlapping iron straps, 26¼in. long.
(Sotheby's) $4,025

A pair of large wrought iron door brackets, Pennsylvania, 19th century, the mushroom-shaped top above a pointed baluster terminus, 16¾in. high.
(Christie's) $5,175

Cast iron fountain, attributed to J.W. Fiske, New York, late 19th century, 40in. high.
(Skinner) $1,092

A wrought iron trivet, stamped *J.W.*, Pennsylvania, early 19th century, the rounded open triangular form with star-punch decoration.
(Christie's) $173

An ancient Chinese iron kettle with traces of cyphers and a later bronze cover, 5¼in. high.
(Holloway's) $157

A fine and very rare cast iron fireback, Pleasant Furnace, Monongehela County, Virginia, 1799–1811, emblazoned with the Great Seal of The United States, 29¾in. high.
(Sotheby's) $31,050

A Victorian painted cast-iron console, James Yates, Rotheram, circa 1842, the rouge and gray striated rectangular marble top of serpentine outline, above a conforming frieze, 4ft. 11in. wide.
(Butterfield & Butterfield) $6,900

A French or Spanish iron missal box, circa 1500, the wood core mounted with pierced wrought-iron panels, 4³/₈ x 4³/₄ x 6in.
(Sotheby's) $5,462

A pair of wrought and cast iron tongs, attributed to E. Meninger, Clay Township, Berks County, Pennsylvania, 19th century, the scissor-action form with scalloped decoration.
(Christie's) $1,955

A pair of wrought iron hinges, Pennsylvania, late 18th/early 19th century, each ram's horn shaped, with scrolling tendrils and eagle's head ends.
(Christie's) $920

A Victorian cast iron novelty stick stand, of a Jack Russell, holding his master's whip, standing on a leaf molded plinth.
(Woolley & Wallis) $1,492

A Biedermeier brass iron, with iron handle columns, hinged closure.
(Auction Team Köln) $107

A German Keln electric travel iron set, for 110 and 220v, in purple velvet case, circa 1925.
(Auction Team Köln) $130

Iron heating set for stove top, the plate with decorated handle, with three irons.
(Auction Team Köln) $184

A cast iron long iron oven with some very early irons, by C M Hess, Veile, circa 1880.
(Auction Team Köln)

$1,540

An American Crown pleating iron by the American Machine Co, Philadelphia, circa 1880, with table clamp and cylinders.
(Auction Team Köln) $207

A Voss hexagonal flatiron oven, with six corresponding irons, circa 1890. (Auction Team Köln)
$616

A Dutch or Friesian flatiron, with wooden handle, circa 1800.
(Auction Team Köln) $370

A Crown pleating iron by the American Machine Co., Philadelphia, with table clamp and brass cylinders, circa 1880.
(Auction Team Köln) $214

An early flatiron, the sole plate either Dutch or Friesian, turned wooden handle, circa 1750.
(Auction Team Köln) $847

Dual gas fired iron heater, with
two irons, brass taps.
(Auction Team Köln) $136

A 'Dragon's Head' chimney iron,
sole plate 17 cm. long.
(Auction Team Köln) $292

A large tailor's gas iron,
American, 27 cm. long.
(Auction Team Köln) $122

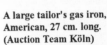

A charcoal iron with unusual
splint closure, wooden handle
and two eyes on the sides,
American, 1916.
(Auction Team Köln)

$231 A Scandinavian Anker Heegard
iron oven of cast iron, with
associated irons, circa 1890.
(Auction Team Köln)

$2,543

French Biedermeier charcoal
iron, made of sheet iron, with
unheated tip, folding handle with
spring closure, circa 1860, 14 cm.
wide.
(Auction Team Köln) $184

A Swedish Husqvarna chimney
iron, circa 1880, 24 cm. long.
(Auction Team Köln) $539

A General Electric Paperweight
iron issued for the 1960
anniversary marking the sale of
60 million GE produced irons,
in original box.
(Auction Team Köln) $97

Ox tongue iron, cast brass with
pusher and nailed on handle,
circa 1860.
(Auction Team Köln) $150

Ferdinand Preiss, Bather, 1930s, cold painted bronze and ivory figure of a kneeling male bather, his arms clasped, 6¹/₂in. (Sotheby's) **$4,543**

Ferdinand Preiss, two young children, 1930s, carved ivory figure of two young naked boys seated on the ground, with painted detail, 5.5cm. and 6cm. (Sotheby's) **$3,089**

A 19th century Northern French carved ivory figure, boy musician, 12.5cm. high. (Langlois) **$370**

An ivory okimono of a dragon and a terrified man, signed *Isshosai Shizumasa*, 19th century, 8.5cm. high. (Christie's) **$2,600**

A pair of French or English ivory writing tablet covers and three blank leaves, second half 14th century, with a French cuir boulli case, second quarter 14th century. (Sotheby's) **$409,500**

A French ivory triptych, 14th century, the Virgin and Child in the central panel, the side leaves carved with the Annunciation and the Adoration, 4⁷/₈ x 3³/₄in. open. (Sotheby's) **$25,300**

A parcel-gilt lidded tankard, the tapering oval ivory body carved in relief with a frieze of putti harvesting vines, 7in. (Christie's) **$3,105**

An ivory okimono of two carpenters signed *Muneyasu*, 19th century, one sawing a large plank of wood, the other sitting on the end chatting, 12.5cm. wide. (Christie's) **$3,473**

Ferdinand Preiss, 'Ecstasy', 1930s, carved ivory figure of a female nude standing with both arms upraised, on an octagonal green onyx base, 8in. (Sotheby's) **$3,089**

IVORY

An ivory figure of a queen, Dieppe, late 19th century, the queen with a folding triptych body revealing historical scenes, 18cm. high.
(Sotheby's) $1,336

A large ivory okimono of Takarabune, 19th century, a prow shaped as a phoenix carrying five Indian deities, some mother-of-pearl and horn inlays, 38.5cm. wide.
(Christie's) $2,430

Bubble blower, 1930s, carved ivory figure of a kneeling young girl blowing a pearlized bubble through a straw, 3in.
(Sotheby's) $1,635

A Continental carved ivory and bone tankard, late 19th century, the cylindrical body carved with a scene of a bacchanalia, on an arch-carved foot, 14in. high.
(Butterfield & Butterfield) $8,625

An ivory okimono of Benkei carrying the Bell of Miidera, signed Muneyuki, 19th century, the lantern hung on the other side of the pole, 17.5cm. wide.
(Christie's) $4,160

A 19th century ivory cane handle in the form of a phrenological head, the cranium divided into thirty seven areas listed around the neck, 72mm. high.
(Phillips) $925

An ivory okimono of a bespectacled man with a fan, 19th century, seated with a cloth cap admiring a painting on an open fan, 10cm. wide.
(Christie's) $2,604

An Italian ivory-hilted steel knife and fork, second half 17th century, each finely carved in relief with a kneeling putto, 8¼in. and 8in. long overall.
(Sotheby's) $1,840

An ivory okimono of Tsuitate of Shichifukujin, signed *Shomin,* 19th century, 11.5cm. wide.
(Christie's) $3,125

A mid 19th century gold and garnet oval brooch with central oval garnet within a surround of quartz and beaded leafy frame. (Bearne's) $462

A modern ruby, diamond and turquoise mounted flower brooch. (Bearne's) $209

A late 19th century gold and seed-pearl six-point star brooch pendant. (Bearne's) $525

A late 19th century gold and oval shell cameo brooch, the oval cameo carved depicting the Madonna within a plain gold frame in fitted case. (Bearne's) $685

A pair of early 19th century gold and carved shell cameo earrings, the cameos depicting maidens and classical portrait busts. (Bearne's) $1,118

A late 19th century gold and agate cameo portrait brooch, the oval layered cameo with the portrait of a young woman. (Bearne's) $1,788

An Indian Jaipur enameled gold, ruby and emerald oval pendant of floral design with emerald drop. (Bearne's) $510

A turquoise, chalcedony and gold-mounted brooch, the oval chalcedony panel with flowers and posy holder motif within an engraved frame. (Bearne's) $447

A late 19th century frosted gold, diamond, seed-pearl and ruby oval locket with central foliate and ribbon spray. (Bearne's) $1,192

Georg Jensen white metal brooch, of a wren sitting on a branch, stamped marks to back, 2in. diameter.
(Peter Wilson) **$227**

A late 19th century gold, seed-pearl, turquoise and diamond twelve-pointed star brooch.
(Bearne's) **$715**

A 19th century Italian gold and micro mosaic-shaped circular brooch, with central circular mosaic panel of a butterfly.
(Bearne's) **$386**

A late 19th century silver, amethyst and citrine large circular brooch, the reverse inscribed *Catherine D. Kerr*, 10.5cm. diameter.
(Bearne's) **$1,051**

A pair of diamond mounted cluster earrings, each with a crescent of graduated brilliant and eight-cut stones within a textured ribbon frame.
(Bearne's) **$507**

A 19th century gold and diamond ribbon brooch with four ribbon loops of graduated 'old-mine' brilliant and rose-cut stones.
(Bearne's) **$8,344**

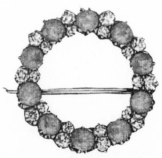

A 19th century paste-mounted heart-shaped brooch/pendant in the 17th century-style, the central portrait of a lady within a paste-mounted floral border.
(Bearne's) **$283**

A gold, opal and diamond circle brooch, with cultured opals separated by pairs of 'old-mine' brilliant-cut diamonds.
(Bearne's) **$1,112**

A sapphire and diamond mounted floral spray brooch, with two flowerheads each claw-set with a single circular diamond.
(Bearne's) **$3,278**

A 19th century silver, seed-pearl and turquoise-mounted brooch, in the form of a hand.
(Bearne's) $355

A late 19th century gold, baroque pearl and amethyst-mounted brooch, of pierced scroll design.
(Bearne's) $649

A gold and jade oval brooch, the jade panel carved and pierced with peonies, 4cm.
(Bearne's) $803

Gem-set bird brooch, set with rubies and rose-cut diamonds with removable body, in a silver mount.
(Skinner) $1,725

Burmese South Seas cultured pearl necklace, composed of thirty-one pearls, completed by a pavé-set diamond bead clasp.
(Skinner) $162,000

Antique butterfly brooch, rose-cut diamond and cultured pearl wings and body, edged in sapphires and rubies.
(Skinner) $1,322

A late Victorian shell cameo brooch, carved to depict Night personified with her attribute the owl, carrying sleeping children in her arms.
(Bonhams & Langlois)
                    $1,380

Sterling silver moonstone brooch, suspending two foliate drops, signed *Georg Jensen no. 25.*
(Skinner) $3,220

Tourmaline and diamond hat brooch, a watermelon tourmaline hat, with a baguette diamond trim and briolette yellow beryl ties, signed *Julius Cohen.*
(Skinner) $4,255

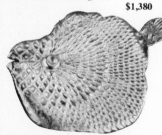

Max Ernst (1891–1976), 23ct. gold poisson, made by Francois Hugo, signed and numbered *4/6* in a fitted original wooden box.
(Skinner) $23,000

Victorian Scottish agate circle brooch, set with jasper, agate and bloodstone within a silver frame.
(Skinner) $920

Victorian Revival 18ct. gold snake necklace, alternating coiled wire and polished gold links, 16½in. long.
(Skinner) $3,105

A diamond set spray brooch, the central marquise-cut diamond to single-cut diamond leaves and buds. (Bonhams & Langlois)
$540

Strand of South Seas pearls, completed by a 14ct. yellow gold and diamond clasp, 20in. long. (Skinner) $18,400

18ct. gold and enamel flower brooch, blue enamel petals with yellow gold pistils. (Skinner) $402

Strand of cultured black pearls, comprised of thirty-seven slightly graduated pearls, completed by a pavé-set diamond barrel clasp. (Skinner) $7,475

Victorian butterfly brooch, centered by an old mine-cut diamond body, accented by red stone eyes, within a 14ct. yellow gold mount. (Skinner) $2,070

Double strand of cultured pearls, completed by a diamond flower clasp, approx. total weight 3.5ct., in a platinum mount. (Skinner) $10,925

18ct. yellow gold enamel frog brooch, designed as a green translucent enamel frog accented by gold tracery and red stone eyes, signed Webb, 34.4 dwt. (Skinner) $2,415

Antique diamond cross pendant/ brooch, designed as a Maltese cross set with old mine-cut diamonds, approx. total weight 4.25ct. (Skinner) $5,520

Art Nouveau dragonfly brooch, the body set with nine graduating emeralds and diamonds, the wings of plique-à-jour. (Skinner) $18,400

Victorian 14ct. yellow gold earpendants, each suspending three beaded drops within a tapered oval mount. (Skinner) $1,150

Etruscan Revival yellow gold pendant necklace, circa 1880, composed of beads with applied wire-twist suspending a locket/ pendant. (Skinner) $4,370

18ct. yellow gold belt buckle, designed as a head of a mythological creature in repoussé, signed Webb, 39.9 dwt. (Skinner) $1,840

A Victorian table oil lamp, the base bell-shaped and decorated in opaque white and red drawn glass, the panel-cut shade with crimped rim, 15in. high. (Canterbury) **$426**

Bronze patinated metal table lamp, with colored leaded glass shade, 23in. high, American, early 20th century. (Schrager) **$1,450**

A green-painted turned lamp stand, Pennsylvania, 19th century, the circular top with molded sides above a ring-turned shaft. (Christie's) **$1,840**

Handel interior-painted glass and patinated metal boudoir lamp, early 20th century, the shade painted with a continuous scene of sailing ships on calm waters, 14¹/₈in. high. (Butterfield & Butterfield) **$2,300**

A rare large pair of ormolu and colorless glass double-light argand lamps, circa 1830, the colorless glass lower section raised on an ormolu wreath, 24in. high. (Sotheby's) **$5,462**

Léo Laporte Blairsy, Art Nouveau figural lamp, circa 1900, painted bronze, modeled as a young woman in flowing costume, the billowing fabric concealing a light fitting, 41cm. (Sotheby's) **$6,905**

Tiffany favrile glass and patinated bronze dogwood lamp, 1898–1928, the domical shade with an overall pattern of dogwood blossoms, 21¹/₂in. high. (Butterfield & Butterfield) **$16,100**

Emile Gallé, prunus lamp, circa 1900, gray glass internally decorated with yellow, overlaid with red and etched with flowering branches, 43cm. (Sotheby's) **$32,706**

Tiffany-type bronze table lamp, on tree trunk styled base, with engraved signature of artist: *Dominowski*, approx. 27in. high, made in Poland, 1980/early 1990s. (Schrager) **$2,025**

Daum and Edgar Brandt, 'Vigne Noire Orange' lamp, circa 1920, gray glass internally mottled with orange and aubergine, overlaid with brown, 40cm.
(Sotheby's) $5,451

Art Deco lamp, bronze base in the form of an Ionic column supporting four lights, molded opalescent orange shade, 25in. high.
(Peter Wilson) $3,432

Daum, riverscape lamp, circa 1900, gray glass, internally decorated with orange, overlaid with red and etched with a river landscape, 17in.
(Sotheby's) $8,176

Argy-Rousseau pâte de verre lumière: Deux Tigres Dans L'Herbe, circa 1928, molded with two black-striped orange tigers, 7⁷/₈in. high.
(Butterfield & Butterfield)
                               $9,775

Dirk van Erp hammered copper and mica lamp, designed by August Tiesselinck, circa 1915, low-domed wide circular shade with a pierced border, 16¹/₂in. high.
(Butterfield & Butterfield)
                               $7,475

R. W. Lange, Parachute Lady lamp, 1930s, table lamp modeled as a cold painted bronze and ivory figure of a female parachutist falling to earth, her parachute forming the shade, lamp 85cm. high.
(Sotheby's) $10,539

A Fauré enamel and leaded glass table lamp, the tapering body decorated with stylized flora and leaves in turquoise, blue and orange, 30.5cm. high, signed *Fauré Marty Limoges*.
(Phillips) $386

Gabriel Argy-Rousseau veilleuse 'Masques', 1923, pâte-de-verre shade in clear glass streaked with orange and purple, divided into six segments, 14cm.
(Sotheby's) $7,268

Emile Gallé, chrysanthemum lamp, circa 1900, gray glass internally decorated with yellow, overlaid with mauve and blue and etched with flowering stems, 12in.
(Sotheby's) $12,355

Pittsburgh enamel decorated water lily lamp, frosted textured glass domed shade obverse painted as stylized blossoms, 20½in. high.
(Skinner) $805

Handel desk lamp, adjustable reading light with roll cylinder of green Teroma glass cased to white, mounted on arched shaft, 16in. high.
(Skinner) $1,265

Tiffany favrile glass twelve-light lily lamp, 1899–1928, fitted with gold glass lily-form shades, 20¾in. high.
(Butterfield & Butterfield)
     $23,000

Handel border decorated lamp, domed Teroma shade reverse painted in primary colours with Arts and Crafts stylized foliate band, 24in. high.
(Skinner) $3,335

Old Mission Kopperkraft hammered copper and mica lamp, circa 1910, the conical shade with molded domical cap fitted with four mica panels, 16in. high.
(Butterfield & Butterfield)
     $5,175

Handel cameo etched parrot lamp, shade composed of four curved frosted glass panels, acid etched with two orange enameled exotic birds, 24in. high.
(Skinner) $8,050

Rare Fulper Pottery leaded glass mushroom lamp, shade with matte gunmetal crystal trailings and brown highlighting, 16in. high.
(Skinner) $11,500

Handel bronze and glass three-light lily lamp, rare form with each blossom composed of six bent panels of opal white glass 'petals', 21in. high.
(Skinner) $4,600

Bronze and leaded glass lamp, attributed to Duffner and Kimberly, conical leaded glass shade with curved tuck-under border, 26in. high.
(Skinner) $4,485

Pairpoint puffy Papillon lamp, closed top blown-out butterflies and red roses shade with vivid coloration, 21½in. high.
(Skinner) $8,050

Pairpoint reverse painted table lamp, flared glass shade decorated in green, brick-red and yellow amber floral tapestry motif, 26in. high.
(Skinner) $2,300

American cut glass lamp, honeycomb shaft above hobstar and fan cut base with conforming mushroom cap shade, 20½in. high.
(Skinner) $1,840

Tiffany favrile glass and bronze twelve-light lily lamp, 1898–1902, composed of twelve slender cylindrical stems turning outward at the top, 19¹/₂in. high.
(Butterfield & Butterfield)
                           $12,650

Dirk van Erp hammered copper and mica lamp, circa 1911, the conical shade with three mica panels held by three tapering battens, 21¹/₂in. high.
(Butterfield & Butterfield)
                           $8,050

Pairpoint puffy Torino table lamp, closed top blown out glass shade reverse painted with colorful roses, daisies and chrysanthemums, 20in. high.
(Skinner) $7,475

Tiffany bronze and favrile glass acorn lamp, progressive green dome shade with conical taper and pink heart-shape acorn border, 18½in. high.
(Skinner) $10,350

Tiffany nautilus lamp on dragonfly enameled base, natural shell shade with silvered rim raised on Tiffany bronze base, 15in. high.
(Skinner) $4,830

Duffner and Kimberly Colonial lamp, leaded shade of quatriform design with four raised and four recessed panels, 23½in. high.
(Skinner) $8,050

MARBLE

An Italian white marble bust, of a young man, late 19th century, his hat tilted back on his head, on a socle, 51cm. high.
(Sotheby's) $2,139

A 19th century carved white marble bust of a Roman, with curly hair, 23in. high.
(Canterbury) $4,650

An 18in. Classical plaster bust of a Roman Emperor after the Antique on flecked green marble pedestal, 24in. overall.
(Stainers') $256

Continental carved white marble bust of an aristocrat of the court of Louis XIV, 19th century, wearing a Roman style breast plate, 31in. high.
(Butterfield & Butterfield) $5,462

A white marble sculpture, of an angel supporting a semi nude female figure, on mottled brown demi-lune base, 13in. high.
(Dee, Atkinson & Harrison) $283

French marble group: Salammbô (Charmeuse de Serpent), carved after a model by François Sicard, early 20th century, depicting the actress Sarah Bernhardt, 21in. high.
(Butterfield & Butterfield) $3,737

Italian carrara marble figure of the bound Cupid, circa 1880, the figure seated on a rock and looking downward.
(Skinner) $2,875

A North Italian (Campionese) marble relief of the Madonna and Child, by the Maestro della Loggia degli Osii, first half 14th century, 28¼ x 23¾in.
(Sotheby's) $35,650

A white marble bust of a lady wearing a bonnet, head inclined to dexter, on integral tapering socle, late 19th century, 23in. high.
(Christie's) $1,053

A sculpted white marble figure of the crouching Venus, Italian, 19th century, 33¹/₂in. high.
(Christie's) $4,777

An Italian white marble figure of a naked child lying on a mattress, circa 1880, cuddling a dove, 53cm. long.
(Sotheby's) $4,099

A white marble bust of a bearded Roman gentleman, 34cm.
(Bristol) $330

An Italian white marble bust of Benjamin Franklin, after Jean Jacques Caffieri, 19th century, his head inclined forward, 21in. high.
(Sotheby's) $5,175

A late 19th century Italian carved marble group of two cherubs, playing with a billy goat, and an accompanying group of two cherubs stroking a spaniel, 93cm. high.
(Phillips) $10,640

An Italian marble bust of a maiden, 19th century, shown with pulled back wavy hair, her head turned slightly to her left, 33¹/₂in. high.
(Butterfield & Butterfield) $2,875

Emile Wolff (1802-1879), carved white marble bust of a Roman senator, on turned socle, 27.5in. high, inscribed "E. Wolff Fc. Romae".
(Canterbury) $4,312

An Italian Siena marble ewer, circa 1880, carved with an eagle handle and ram spout on a fluted trumpet stem, 46cm. high.
(Sotheby's) $3,743

A white marble bust of a young girl, 18th century, probably Italian, her hair gathered in a bun in the back, 18³/₄in. high.
(Sotheby's) $2,587

A good musical seal with barillet movement, engraved bow and plain base.
(Christie's) $2,457

A rare Hohner Trumpet Call harmonica with array of trumpet horns.
(Auction Team Köln) $199

A Q.R.S. Playasax, self-playing saxophone with three rolls.
(Auction Team Köln) $338

A very decorative barrel organ by Bacigalupo Söhne, Berlin, in marquetry case with 35 cm. barrel, 15 pipes, playing eight tunes, 49 x 34 x 64 cm.
(Auction Team Köln) $4,240

An Autophone organette with twenty-two note, ratchet-advance mechanism and twin bellows in walnut case on twin pillars on plinth, 9³/₄in. wide, with approximately twenty-eight strips.
(Christie's) $966

A photograph album with musical clock, plush binding with Art Nouveau decoration, playing three melodies, circa 1900.
(Auction Team Köln) $423

A musical clock picture, of a chateau and village on a river with boats and figures, with two-train movement striking on gong, 39¹/₂ x 33in.
(Christie's) $913

A Tanzbär roll-operated accordion with sixteen-note movement, maroon leather-cloth covering and six rolls in wood-grained cardboard box with photocopy instructions.
(Christie's) $2,633

A singing bird box by Griesbaum, with filigree decoration to top, plinth with drawer, the bird with colored plumage, moving tail, wings and metal beak, 4¹/₈in.
(Christie's) $1,404

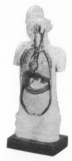

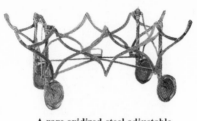

Anatomical demonstration model, with removable model organs, circa 1930, 87 cm. high. (Auction Team Köln) $477

A rare oxidized-steel adjustable stretcher-carrying frame, with embossed label inscribed *Champion Chemical Co. Springfield Ohio*, the telescopic sides and ends with handles, 47in. long extended. (Christie's) $497

A pneumatic lung volume testing device, in portable wooden case, circa 1925. (Auction Team Köln) $77

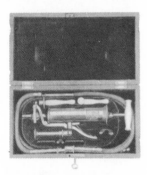

A lacquered-brass enema syringe, the body-tube with embossed label for *Savigny & Co., 67 St. James's ST*, with ivory handpieces and handle, in mahogany case, 11¹/₂in. wide. (Christie's) $580

A Pictorial Atlas of Skin Diseases Edited and Annotated by J. J. Pringle, M.B., F.R.C.P., in twelve parts, many color plates with descriptions. (Christie's) $66

A 19th-century surgeon's pocket set of instruments, signed *Birhenry á Paris*, with various scalpels with tortoiseshell guards, silver probes, needles and other items. (Christie's) $861

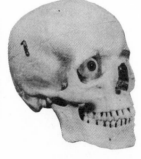

A 19th-century surgeon's part operating set, by Charrière à Paris, with saw, snips, four Liston knives, finger-saw, scalpels and other items, in mahogany case, 16³/₈in. wide. (Christie's) $1,623

An anatomical life-size model skull by Somso, West German, circa 1955. (Auction Team Köln) $154

A fine lacquered-brass auroscope, unsigned, with accessories, in fitted plush-lined leather case, 7¹/₈in. wide. (Christie's) $696

475

A George II miniature mahogany bureau, the rectangular top above a hinged fall enclosing three pigeonholes, 22cm. wide.
(Phillips) $1,140

A miniature mahogany half-tester bed, late 19th century, the shaped end with baluster turned posts on turned bun feet, 12¹/₂in. long.
(Sotheby's) $453

A mahogany miniature linen press, English, late 19th century, the top with carved cornice, the sides inlaid with burr-walnut panels, 11in.
(Sotheby's) $635

A 19th century rosewood Tunbridgeware miniature chest of drawers, with three long drawers inset with bands of mosaic decoration, 23cm. wide.
(Phillips) $578

A George III mahogany miniature commode, outlined with boxwood, the rectangular top above four graduated drawers, 16¹/₂in. wide.
(Christie's) $4,305

A William and Mary painted pine child's chest of drawers, the rectangular top above three small drawers on ball feet, 13¹/₄in. high.
(Sotheby's) $3,680

A miniature grain-painted blanket chest, inscribed John A. Forney, Pennsylvania, 1800–1820, the rectangular hinged lid opening to an interior fitted with a till, 19¹/₂in. wide.
(Christie's) $5,175

A grain-painted and comb decorated toy milk cupboard, Lancaster, Pennsylvania, circa 1875, the rectangular top surmounted by a scalloped gallery with carved turkey, 9in. wide.
(Christie's) $5,750

A painted and decorated miniature blanket chest, Centre County, Pennsylvania, late 18th/early 19th century, the rectangular red-painted hinged lid with molded edge above a conforming case, 17¹/₄in. wide.
(Christie's) $4,370

A fine mid 19th century Belgian mirror, the painted wooden frame in relief and depicting roses and foliage around the oval plate, 32cm. wide.
(Phillips) **$1,540**

A French giltwood and gesso oval girandole, 19th century, the plate with a mirrored surround with ribbon-tied interlaced foliate stems and cresting, 49in. wide.
(Christie's) **$3,098**

A George III mahogany and marquetry toilet mirror, edged overall with a boxwood line, the oval plate in scroll supports on a serpentine base, 23in. wide.
(Christie's) **$1,935**

Louis XVI painted and parcel-gilt trumeau mirror, last quarter 18th century, the rectangular mirror plate with beaded carved molded slip, 38¹/₂in. wide.
(Butterfield & Butterfield) **$2,185**

A George III mahogany toilet-mirror, attributed to Gillow, banded overall with fruitwood lines, the oval plate painted to the reverse with trailing foliage and flowers, 22in. high.
(Christie's) **$2,431**

One of a pair of walnut wall mirrors, probably Irish, late 17th/early 18th century, each with an oval plate with a bold acanthus scroll surround and cresting of a lion, 50in. high.
(Christie's)
(Two) **$24,684**

An Italian rococo giltwood mirror, mid 18th century, of asymmetrical outline, the waisted frame carved with scrolls, flowerheads, foliage and rocaille, 4ft. 1¹/₄in. high.
(Butterfield & Butterfield) **$2,875**

A 19th century Dresden porcelain oval dressing table mirror, the cresting molded in relief with two cupids holding a rose garland, 10¹/₂ x 8in. overall.
(Canterbury) **$441**

An Empire parcel-gilt mahogany mirror, early 19th century, the rectangular mirror plate flanked by cylindrical pilasters headed by petal-cast capitals, 6ft. 2in. high.
(Butterfield & Butterfield) **$1,380**

Chippendale walnut and gilt gesso looking glass, England, 18th century, 36in. high.
(Skinner) $1,265

Victorian burr walnut dressing table mirror, raised on columns, on a rectangular base with three shaped drawers, 35in. high.
(Peter Wilson) $624

Mahogany inlaid and gilt gesso looking glass, probably New England, circa 1790, old surface, 37.5in. high.
(Skinner) $1,150

An extremely large and elaborate Continental mirror frame of oval shape, surmounted by an oval plaque painted with a half-length portrait of Marie Antoinette, 76cm., crossed swords mark, circa 1870–1880.
(Phillips) $1,398

A red-painted mirror, Pennsylvania, early 19th century, rectangular, with split-baluster and cornerblocks enclosing a conforming looking glass, 11⅝ x 9½in.
(Christie's) $978

New Hampshire mirror timepiece, Abiel Chandler, Concord, New Hampshire, circa 1830, ebonized and gold painted split baluster case with eight-day weight driven brass movement.
(Skinner) $11,500

Queen Anne walnut looking glass with candle sconces, England or America, early 18th century, original finish, 31in. high.
(Skinner) $16,100

George II giltwood wall mirror, the shaped surmount decorated in floral relief and incorporating Prince of Wales feathers, 36¼ x 24¼in.
(Lawrences) $1,596

A Federal eglomisé looking glass, Pennsylvania, 19th century, the rectangular frame enclosing a rectangular eglomisé panel depicting a landscape.
(Christie's) $690

Large Renaissance Revival giltwood overmantel mirror, third quarter 19th century, 64in. wide.
(Skinner) $1,725

A Chippendale gilt framed wall mirror (poor condition).
(G. E. Sworder & Sons)
                             $3,648

Louis XVI Provincial style giltwood mirror, 40in. high.
(Skinner) $575

A George II giltwood mirror, the later rectangular plate within a foliate molded slip and auricular egg-and-dart frame carved with Vitruvian-scroll and chandelles, 66 x 50¼in.
(Christie's) $10,764

Federal mahogany carved and mahogany veneer dressing stand, Boston or Salem, Massachusetts, 1800–15, with flanking C-scrolled brackets with brass mounts and reeding, 21in. wide.
(Skinner) $2,415

An early Victorian giltwood overmantel mirror, by William Thrale Wright, the later central rectangular plate flanked by two later shaped plates, divided by trailing foliage, 78½ x 66in.
(Christie's) $3,588

A 19th century Italian looking glass of cartouche shape, the foliate apron with a removable mask revealing a sconce attachment, 40¼in. high.
(Bearne's) $417

Courting mirror in box, Northern Europe, late 18th century, box painted light blue, 17.5 x 12.5in.
(Skinner) $805

A George I gilt-gesso mirror, the associated shaped rectangular plate within a foliate-trailed slip with pounced ground, 40¼ x 20¾in.
(Christie's) $2,511

William IV mahogany framed
dressing table mirror, supported
on carved and molded lyre
shape bracket platform shelf
with four scroll feet, 33in. high.
(Peter Wilson) $332

Hagenauer, mirror, circa 1930,
brass, the rectangular mirror
plate surmounted by an
asymmetrical stylized female
head, 62cm.
(Sotheby's) $3,089

One of a pair of 18th century
Venetian wall mirrors, the
tapering giltwood frames each
surmounted by a shell, C-scrolls
and flowerheads, 23³/₄in. high.
(Bearne's) (Two) $494

A George II walnut and parcel
gilt mirror, the shaped
rectangular plate within a gilt
slip and trailing leaf and
flowerhead surround, 65cm.
wide.
(Phillips) $3,040

A pair of 19th century Italian
giltwood cartouche mirrors,
surmounted by baskets of
flowers and inset with beveled
plates with grotesque masks,
each 78cm. x 48cm.
(Phillips) $2,677

A Venetian neoclassical
engraved mirror, late 18th
century, surmounted by a shaped
engraved crest enclosing a
shaped mirror plate, 4ft. 4¹/₂in.
(Butterfield & Butterfield)
$1,840

An imported pine and églomisé
courting mirror, Continental,
18th/early 19th century, the
shaped projecting crest
depicting fruit and flowers in
polychrome, 18in. high.
(Sotheby's) $4,600

Tubular chrome and blond
wood dressing mirror, 1950s, the
elongated arched mirror plate
within a tubular chrome frame
above a rectangular shelf,
41¹/₄in. wide.
(Butterfield & Butterfield)
$575

A French giltwood and gesso
wall mirror, the shaped arched
plate with a beveled mirrored
surround and borders with
interlaced ribbon-bound foliate
stems, 59in. high.
(Christie's) $2,410

A Chippendale parcel-gilt mahogany wall mirror, circa 1780, the shaped scrolled crest centering a wing-spread phoenix 22³/₄in. wide.
(Sotheby's) $12,650

A Queen Anne walnut wall mirror, circa 1720–50, the arched and scrolled crest centering a pierced reserve, 23in. high.
(Sotheby's) $13,800

A French easel dressing table mirror, in the Louis XV style, richly embossed with scrolling foliage, late 19th century, maker's mark *MG*, 20¹/₂in. high.
(Christie's) $1,681

A Venetian rococo white-painted and parcel gilt mirror, the rectangular mirrorplate with an arched shaped crest, raising carved scrolling foliage, 4ft. 3in. high.
(Butterfield & Butterfield) $2,875

A pair of giltwood oval wall mirrors, mid 19th century, each with a stiff-leaf molded slip and bead and foliate scroll decorated molded surround, 49³/₄in. wide.
(Christie's) $13,770

Chinese Export black lacquered toilet mirror, early 19th century, the oval swivel mirror joined to supports fitted in a rectangular elevated serpentine top, 17in. wide.
(Butterfield & Butterfield) $2,070

An Italian white-painted and parcel-gilt overmantel mirror, 19th century, the rectangular plate within a molded frame flanked by two paneled pilasters, 95 x 46¹/₄in.
(Christie's) $3,846

A Chippendale parcel-gilt mahogany wall mirror, circa 1780, the scrolled crest centering a pierced giltwood acanthus leaf-carved reserve, 39in. high.
(Sotheby's) $5,750

An Empire gilt-bronze-mounted mahogany mirror, the rectangular outset cornice with leaf-cast edge over a coved frieze, 6ft 3in. high.
(Butterfield & Butterfield) $6,900

A professionally built model of a standard English hot air blower produced in 1871, with round spirit burner, 50 cm. high.
(Auction Team Köln) $693

A mid 19th century Instrument Makers models of a French single cylinder horsedrawn portable engine, with brass plate engraved *E Gaussinet a Paris 1868*, 16in. x 12in.
(Christie's) $9,280

A Doll stationary steam engine with lacquered oven and stamped stonework effect on chimney, circa 1930, 30 cm high.
(Auction Team Köln) $732

A model twin cylinder launch engine, with bronze cylinders approx. ⅝in. bore x ⅝in. stroke, entablature with hand rails, slipper type crosshead guides, 7¾in. x 6in.
(Christie's) $430

A live steam spirit fired water pumping set, comprising a cased brass smithies boiler, cylinder rotative beam engine, twin cylinder water pump and two gantry mounted water tanks, 13¼in. x 11¾in.
(Christie's) $502

A model 'V' twin reversing marine engine, by Wanitschek with bronze cylinders 1in. bore x ¾in. stroke, piston valves, pipework and reversing valve, 6½in. x 8¼in.
(Christie's) $448

A model single cylinder rotative beam engine, with cylinder 1½in. bore x 2¾in. stroke, studded stuffing box, cylinder head lubricator, 15in. x 18in.
(Christie's) $752

A 2in. scale Fowler single cylinder two speed four shaft agricultural traction engine Regn. No. BAJ389 'Victoria', built by H. Perry, finished in red, black and polished brightwork, 23in. x 33in.
(Christie's) $6,412

A brass, wrought and cast iron single cylinder six pillar beam engine, built by Chadburn Bros., Sheffield, circa 1840, with cylinder 1¼in. bore x 3½in. stroke, 20in. x 18¾in.
(Christie's) $6,478

A rare Bowmans Aeroboat II rubber band powered speedboat, wooden hull with brass gear box and fittings, circa 1935, 30in. long.
(Andrew Hartley) **$188**

A Bowmans model 'Snipe' spirit fired steam boat, single cylinder engine finished in blue and cream, in original box, circa 1935, 23in. long.
(Andrew Hartley) **$298**

A bone ship model of the 'Royal William', 19th century, the three masted vessel with three tiers of guns, deck details and rigging, the model 9in. long.
(Sotheby's) **$3,387**

A large prisoner-of-war bone ship model, early 19th century, with two masts, rigging, lifeboats, a single row of deck cannon and other details, 61cm. long.
(Sotheby's) **$11,408**

Cased whaling ship model, 19th century, D. H. Bennet maker, fully rigged, sails, hull, 34in. long.
(Skinner) **$3,220**

A large old model galleon, 57$^1/_2$in. high x 54in. long.
(Dee, Atkinson & Harrison) **$456**

A Hornby clockwork 4–4–0 tender locomotive, finished in red with gold lining, LMS to tender, 1185 to cab.
(Andrew Hartley) $314

A Hornby clockwork 4–4–0 tender locomotive 'Yorkshire', finished in green with black and white lining, LNER to tender.
(Andrew Hartley) $471

A finely engineered 5in. gauge model of the British Railways (ex. LMS) rebuilt Scot Class 4-6-0 locomotive and tender No. 46109, 'Royal Engineer', 34.5 x 178cm., with showtrack.
(Peter Wilson) $8,806

L.M.S.R. No. 6100 'Royal Scot', 3^1/$_2$in. gauge, well engineered with brazed superheated copper boiler with fittings, finished in LMS red livery and lining, 10^1/$_4$in. x 47^3/$_4$in.
(Christie's) $3,229

B.R. Class 7P No. 700060 'Britannia', 3^1/$_2$in. gauge, well engineered by N. C. King, circa 1960, with brazed superheated copper boiler with fittings, finished in BR green livery and lining, 10^1/$_4$in. x 51^1/$_2$in.
(Christie's) $3,588

(L.M.S.) 2–6–0 locomotive and tender 'Princess Marina', 3^1/$_2$in. gauge, built by D. A. J. F. Hodson to L.B.S.C. designs with brass clad brazed superheated copper boiler, finished in polished brass, copper and steel, 10^1/$_2$in. x 46in.
(Christie's) $2,331

LMS 4–6–0 locomotive and tender No. 6100 'Royal Scot', 7^1/$_4$in. gauge, built to designs by H. Greenly and completed by W. Rodie with silver soldered superheated copper boiler No. 006 with fittings, finished in finely lined LMS livery and lining, 20in. x 96in.
(Christie's) $10,968

A 7^1/$_4$in. gauge coal fired live steam 0000–4–2 tank locomotive, open cab design with two outside cylinders, finished in green and black, 33^1/$_2$in. long.
(Andrew Hartley) $1,884

L.N.E.R. Class VI 2–6–2 Side Tank locomotive No. 473, 5in. gauge finely engineered by R. Becket, finished in LNER livery and lining, 14in. x 45in.
(Christie's) $5,742

A Hornby 4–4–2 three rail electric tank locomotive, finished in maroon with gold lining, LMS to tank sides.
(Andrew Hartley) $204

A Bassett Lowke Enterprise 4–4–0 spirit fired
steam locomotive and tender, finished in BR
green with 62759 to cab.
(Andrew Hartley)   **$408**

A Bowman models 4–4–0 spirit fired steam
locomotive and tender finished in LMS red with
LMS 13000 to tender.
(Andrew Hartley)   **$267**

An 0–6–0 locomotive and tender, gauge 1, with
spirit fired center flue boiler with firebox
crosstubes and normal fittings, finished in black
with red lining, 5³/₄in. x 20¹/₂in.
(Christie's)   **$465**

L.M.S. 4–6–0 locomotive and tender No. 4815,
gauge 1, with spirit fired brazed water tube
boiler with normal fittings, finished in LMS red
livery, 5¹/₄in. x 24in.
(Christie's)   **$807**

Union Pacific Rail Road Baldwin Class F.E.F.3
4–8–4 locomotive and tender No. 843, 5in. gauge
well engineered from works drawings by D. A. F.
Hodson, finished in gray, 'silver' and black,
16¹/₂in. x 113in.
(Christie's)   **$10,766**

L.M.S.R. Class 7P No. 6200, gauge '1', well
engineered with copper center flue boiler with
syphon tubes and superheater and normal
fittings, finished in LMS red livery and lining,
5¹/₄in. x 27in.
(Christie's)   **$1,794**

G.W.R. 57XX Class Pannier Tank No. 5783, 5in.
gauge, built to exhibition standard by R. M.
Tyler with brazed superheated copper boiler by
R. R. Chambers.
(Christie's)   **$5,742**

BR Class 7P locomotive and tender No. 70021
'Morning Star', 7¹/₄in. gauge, built to exhibition
standard by W. Rodie with silver soldered
superheated copper boiler built by Swindon
Boilers, finished in finely lined BR green livery
and lining with cast plates, 19¹/₂in. x 103in.
(Christie's)   **$32,063**

A 2¹/₂in. gauge GWR 47 series locomotive and
tender 2-8-0, BR crest to tender, outside
cylinders inside motion, 85 x 19cm.
(Peter Wilson)   **$1,236**

District Railway 4–4–0 Beyer & Peacock
Condensing Side Tank locomotive, No. 27, 5in.
gauge, well engineered by D. H. Sutcliffe with
silver soldered superheated copper boiler.
(Christie's)   **$7,536**

An early 20th century negro money box, named Dinah, painted in yellow and naturalistic colors, impressed name to back, 16.5cm.
(Peter Wilson) **$185**

An Artillery Bank mechanical money bank, coin fired from the cannon to land in the tower.
(Auction Team Köln) **$235**

An unusual Harold Lloyd tinplate mechanical bank, German, early 1930s, possibly made by Sehulmer and Strauss, 5¼in. high.
(Sotheby's) **$3,271**

A fine and scarce Mickey Mouse tinplate mechanical bank, German, early 1930s, possibly made by Sehulmer and Strauss, brightly lithographed with a background of green and yellow, 6in. high.
(Sotheby's) **$22,713**

A Shepard Hardware Co. 'Punch and Judy bank', painted cast-iron, red, yellow and blue booth with squabbling couple, 6¼in. base length.
(Christie's) **$1,553**

A Shepard Hardware Co. 'Uncle Sam bank' cast iron money bank, America, circa 1885, the coin is placed in his right hand and as lever is pressed, he releases into his open suitcase, 11½in. high.
(Sotheby's) **$521**

A J. & E. Stevens 'Bull dog bank' cast iron money bank, American, circa 1880, the bull dog seated on blue fringed blanket, 5½in. long.
(Sotheby's) **$1,007**

A Saalheimer and Strauss Minstrel money bank, type I, lithographed tinplate with negro face, when lever is pressed eyes roll and tongue sticks out, 1920s, 7in. high.
(Christie's) **$293**

A J. & E. Stevens 'Teddy and the Bear' money bank, painted cast-iron, President Roosevelt with rounded hat, standing firing, 10⅛in. long.
(Christie's) **$750**

A 1940 Levis Model SV, 350cc, side valve single port single (downswept), frame No. 26914, engine No. 33018, V.5 green log book.
(Holloway's) $1,596

A 1934 Levis Model B.34, 250cc, OHV twin port single, frame No. 23678, engine No. 26283, V.5 green log book.
(Holloway's) $2,280

A 1939/40 Levis Model SV, 350cc, side valve single (single port downswept), upswept system included, no documents.
(Holloway's) $1,292

A 1935 Levis Model A.35, 350cc, OHV twin port single, frame No. 24270, engine No. 29952, V.5 buff log book.
(Holloway's) $2,204

A 1934 Levis Model A.34, 350cc, OHV twin port single, frame No. 24030, engine No. 29883, fitted twin tool boxes and pillion, V.5 buff log book.
(Holloway's) $1,672

A 1937 Levis Model L, 350cc, OHV single port single, frame No. 25461, engine No. 28442, V.5 buff log book.
(Holloway's) $1,368

1940 Triumph speed twin, French registered, frame No. 474963475, engine No. 86049635, black.
(Christie's) $3,743

A 1936 Levis Model, Model D Special fitted 350cc, OHV twin port engine single, frame No. 24877, V.5 buff log book.
(Holloway's) $2,052

A tabatière, playing three airs with tune card and N.L. Van Gruisen and Son, Liverpool retailer's label, in wood case of basket-weave form, 6in. wide.
(Christie's) $421

A musical box by Henriot, No. 12148, playing six airs, in grained case with endflap and inlaid lid, 17³/₄in. wide, the cylinder 10¹/₂in.
(Christie's) $966

A late 19th century Swiss musical box, with 33cm. cylinder and zither attachment playing twelve tunes as listed on the tune sheet, 68cm.
(Bearne's) $1,174

A Swiss bells-in-sight musical box, late 19th century, the 6¹/₄in. brass barrel playing ten airs, with three chromed and enamel bells with butterfly strikers, 18¹/₂in. wide.
(Christie's) $1,275

An interchangeable cylinder, musical box by Nicole Freres, with three cylinders playing eight airs each, figured walnut case with bird's-eye maple lid lining, 38in. wide.
(Christie's) $4,563

A six-bell musical box by Georges Bendon & Co., playing eight airs accompanied by six optional engine-turned bells with bird, butterfly and flower strikers, 21in. wide.
(Christie's) $1,931

A Harpe Harmonique Picolo, musical box by Ami Rivenc, No. 28806, playing six airs (Gamme 126), with zither on main comb and tune sheet, 22in. wide, the cylinder 13in.
(Christie's) $2,808

19th century Swiss music box, with marquetry inlaid walnut case, interior with three painted metal Chinamen playing six bells, eight tunes, 22in. long.
(Eldred's) $2,200

A mandolin musical box by PVF, No. 692, playing eight airs, with teeth in groups up to six, full-length zither attachment and tune sheet, 26in. wide, the cylinder 16in.
(Christie's) $2,633

VIOLINS

A good Danish violin labeled *Emil Hjorth i Kjöbenhavn/Anno 1893*, the length of back 35.7cm. (Christie's)

$6,440

A very fine English viola labeled *Forster London 1775/Amatus Copy*, the length of back 39.4cm. (Christie's)

$18,400

An interesting violin labeled *Carlo Tononi*, the length of back 35.1cm. (Christie's)

$23,920

An interesting violin, probably Milanese, indistinctly labeled, the length of back 35.2cm. (Christie's)

$12,880

A French viola by Jean-Baptiste Vuillaume labeled *St Cécile des Thernes Paris 1849 Nr 337*, the length of back, 39.7cm. (Christie's)

$20,240

An Italian violin labeled *Antoniazzi Romeo Cremonese/fece a Cremona l'anno 1916*, the length of back 35.2cm. (Christie's)

$6,992

An interesting violin circa 1770, bearing the label *Vincenzo Trusiano Panormo fecit anno 1770 Palermo*, l.o.b. 14¹/₈in. (Phillips)

$15,708

A violin labeled *Mathijs A. Heyligers/Cremona/No 35 1981*, the length of back 35.9cm. (Christie's)

$7,728

An ivory netsuke of two hares, eyes inlaid in dark and red horn, 18th century, 3.6cm. high.
(Christie's) $1,150

An ivory netsuke of a rat, seated and holding its tail, 19th century, 4.7cm.
(Christie's) $1,681

An ivory netsuke of a dragon writhing around a large sacred jewel, unsigned, late 18th century, 5.5cm. wide.
(Christie's) $3,364

A fine boxwood netsuke of a rat, its compact body curled tightly in a ball, signed *Masanao*, 19th century, 1½in. high.
(Butterfield & Butterfield) $4,312

An ivory netsuke of Okame, the mirthful goddess kneeling over to trim her toenails, signed *Shinsan*, Meiji Period, 1½in. high.
(Butterfield & Butterfield) $862

An ivory seal netsuke of a ram, the recumbent bearded animal with three legs turned under, late 18th/early 19th century, 3.7cm. high.
(Butterfield & Butterfield) $690

An ivory netsuke of Sennin and Karako, Sennin seated turning its head laughing, unsigned, 18th century, 4.5cm. high.
(Christie's) $796

A ivory netsuke of two skeletons, one standing on an uchiwa pouring sake from a flask, signed *Kazumasa*, 19th century, 5cm. high.
(Christie's) $1,681

A wood netsuke of a seated man cutting a gourd held between his feet, signed *Shuraku* and *Kao*, 19th century, 4cm. wide.
(Christie's) $1,327

A wood netsuke of a cockerel, perched on a half open fan, signed *Masanao*, 19th century, 4cm. high.
(Christie's) $3,896

An 18th century ivory netsuke of a dragon writhing among flames, 4cm. wide.
(Christie's) $3,719

A Shibayama netsuke of a horse in saddle and harness, signed *Shibayama*, 19th century, 4.5cm. high.
(Christie's) $6,375

A boxwood netsuke of a monkey with a young monkey clambering on its back, signed *Masanao*, 19th century, 2.8cm high.
(Butterfield & Butterfield) $3,162

A rare ivory netsuke of a boar resting by a rocky outcropping, signed *Kaigyoku[sai] [Masatsugu]* (1813-1892), 3.2cm high.
(Butterfield & Butterfield) $18,400

An ivory netsuke of a wolf with bared teeth, hunched over the severed head of a beauty, inscribed *Tomochika*, 19th century, 3.2cm. high.
(Butterfield & Butterfield) $862

Ivory netsuke of a tiger crouched protectively over her young, signed *Hakuryu (II)*, 3.2cm. high.
(Butterfield & Butterfield) $920

A wood netsuke of Gama Sennin carrying a toad on his shoulder, signed *Toyomasa*, late 18th/early 19th century, 5.2cm.
(Christie's) $6,729

An ivory netsuke of a tiger and cub, both with inlaid eyes, signed *Hakuryu (II)*, 19th century, 1in. high.
(Butterfield & Butterfield) $1,035

Lantern, wood-body with brass fittings, brass bound lens support, rack and pinion focusing lens and chimney. (Christie's) **$219**

E. Reynauld, Paris, a hand-cranked Praxinoscope and a quantity of picture strips. (Christie's) **$1,096**

A Mechanical Puzzle amusement machine, circa 1930. (Auction Team Köln) **$385**

Biunial lantern, a mahogany-body biunial lantern with lacquered-brass fittings, a pair of rack and pinion focusing lenses, brass shutter and chimney. (Christie's) **$2,868**

William Greenwood, England, a mahogany-body and lacquered-brass Greenwood-Wallwork projecting microscope with two sets of three rotating objective holders. (Christie's) **$1,350**

J. H. Steward, London, a fine wood and lacquered-brass fitted triunial lantern, dividing into two section, the upper single lantern with side door, decoratively gilded japanned metal chimney and lens mount. (Christie's) **$50,625**

A Dissolving Magic Lantern by J.H. Steward, London, brass mounted mahogany case, with duplex burners with reflectors and condensors, 74 cm. high. (Auction Team Köln) **$1,309**

Kinora viewer, with hand-crank, metal label *The Kinora. Registered Trade Mark. Letchworth and London* and retailer's label *Hamley's*, six Kinora reels. (Christie's) **$1,032**

Carpenter & Westley, London, a metal-body Improved Phantasmagoria lantern with chimney, lens, spirit burner and plate, slides each with three or four circular pictures. (Christie's) **$1,012**

A table stereo viewer with progressive holder for fifty 9 x 18 cm. slides, 44 cm. high. (Auction Team Köln) $500

Zoetrope, 11-inch diameter drum, hand-crank, turned-mahogany base and quantity of picture strips and disks. (Christie's) $927

Lapierre, France, a metal-body Carrée lantern with pierced-metal design, lens and chimney. (Christie's) $235

Duboscq lantern, a metal-body Duboscq-pattern lantern with a brass bound John Browning, London lens, Stock's patent illuminant and chimney. (Christie's) $338

Projection mechanism, a 35mm. metal-body hand-cranked Bioscope projection mechanism with beater movement, intermittent, rack and pinion focusing lens. (Christie's) $370

C. G. Bush, U.S.A., kaleidoscope, metal-fittings and liquid-filled vials, the wood stand stamped *C. G. Bush. Patented Nov 17 1873.* (Christie's) $708

A. H. Baird, Edinburgh, a mahogany and lacquered-brass fitted biunial magic lantern with a pair of brass bound lenses, chimney, and two slide carriers. (Christie's) $6,017

Zoetrope, the drum and base with colored paint and gilt decoration and a quantity of picture strips. (Christie's) $759

A Laterna Magica by Jean Schoenner, Nürnberg, for 3.5 cm. glass slides and three glass plates, circa 1890, 27 cm. high. (Auction Team Köln) $192

Treasury Note: J. Bradbury: £1 August 1914, HH prefix.
(Phillips) $315

South Africa: 1917 National Bank of South Africa £1 issued at Bloemfontein.
(Phillips) $600

Bulgaria: 1929 National Bank 5,000 leva Specimen.
(Phillips) $270

Sudan: 1955c. Sudan Government Specimen set of 25 and 50 piastres, £1, £5 and £10, printed by Waterlows, all notes with 000000 serial numbers.
(Phillips) $405

Ireland, Provincial Bank: £5 proof on card, 5 November 1884, vignette of Queen Victoria upper left.
(Phillips) $345

Hong Kong: 1921 Hongkong & Shanghai Banking Corporation $10 Specimen, overstamped Specimen across middle.
(Phillips) $1,380

Bank of England Note: K.O. Peppiatt: £100 17 January 1938, London issue.
(Phillips) $720

Albania: 1926 Banca Nazionale D'Albania 100 franka ari, President Zogu at right.
(Phillips) $1,575

Ulster Bank: £50 1 June 1929, No. 365 (P.310)
(Phillips) $498

Bank of Scotland: £100 2 April 1959.
(Phillips) $589

Zambia: 1963 Bank of Zambia £1 color essay in
blue and lilac, Elizabeth II at right, by Harrison
& Sons Ltd., London, lion head sketched in
watermark oval.
(Phillips) $2,480

New Zealand: 1916–23 Bank of New Zealand £10
uniface color trial in dark blue on multicolor
background and lilac-green border, perforated
Specimen at bottom.
(Phillips) $620

Bank of England: J. B. Page, £1, 1978 A01
000135 together with D. H. Somerset £1 AN01
000135 and £50 A01 000135.
(Phillips) $623

Falkirk Union Bank: £5 1814 (Douglas 3).
(Phillips) $155

Ulster Bank: £100 uniface proof in black on
white.
(Phillips) $343

U.S.A.: 1775 (June issue) South Carolina £10,
part of a total issue of 40,000 notes.
(Phillips) $311

A Mabie Todd & Co. gold lever-fill pen, with original No. 2 gold nib, circa 1928.
(Auction Team Köln) $346

An Art Deco silver fountain pen, engraved *Sterling*, American or English, circa 1925.
(Auction Team Köln) $323

A Parker 18ct. gold 51 'Barley' pen, with very broad nib, English, 1954.
(Bonhams) $585

A turquoise Waterman Patrician pen with Patrician nib, Canadian, circa 1930.
(Bonhams) $1,080

A Parker 18(?) Jacknife turban cap, with Lucky Curve pen 5 nib with keyhole vent, American, circa 1912.
(Bonhams) $825

A white metal Scheaffer filigree overlaid pen, with self-filling No. 2 nib, American, circa 1917.
(Bonhams) $870

Mabie, Todd & Co. early American eyedropper pen, with original 14 ct. gold nib, circa 1915.
(Auction Team Köln) $254

Waterman's Safety Pen No. 12½, with retractable 14 ct. gold nib, and wavy guilloche decoration, circa 1925.
(Auction Team Köln) $92

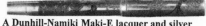

A Dunhill-Namiki Maki-E lacquer and silver pen, decorated with a geisha beneath a cherry tree, with Namiki No. 2 nib, Japanese, circa 1926-30).
(Bonhams) $4,950

An 18ct. white gold Parker model 180, with delicate hand engraved wave pattern decoration, and panel set with diamonds and lapis lazuli, French, 1980s.
(Bonhams) $630

Laurie London's Parker 9ct. gold 51 pen and clutch pencil set, in presentation case with engraved plaque on lid.
(Bonhams) $1,500

An oversized Parker Vacumatic fountain pen in streaked silver gray, with original two-color gold nib, circa 1944.
(Auction Team Köln) $231

Montblanc No. 234½ G black cartridge pen with original 14 ct. gold nib, circa 1949.
(Auction Team Köln) $137

A Waterman 0556 filigree pen with No. 6 nib, American, 1920s.
(Bonhams) $900

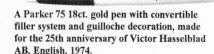

A Parker 75 18ct. gold pen with convertible filler system and guilloche decoration, made for the 25th anniversary of Victor Hasselblad AB, English, 1974.
(Auction Team Köln) $423

Montblanc Masterpiece No. 20 safety fountain pen, hard black rubber with retractable original nib No. 20 in 18 ct. gold, circa 1932.
(Auction Team Köln) $308

Montblanc No. 254 black plastic cartridge
pen with 14 ct. gold wing nib, circa 1954.
(Auction Team Köln) $107

A Mabie Todd L445-88 Green Lizard leverless,
with No. 4 nib, English, circa 1938, boxed.
(Bonhams) $570

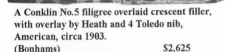

A Conklin No.5 filigree overlaid crescent filler,
with overlay by Heath and 4 Toledo nib,
American, circa 1903.
(Bonhams) $2,625

Montblanc Masterpiece No. 144, black, gold-
decorated cartridge pen with original 14 ct.
gold nib, circa 1950.
(Auction Team Köln) $231

A Mordan yellow and pink metal pencil set
with three bands of rubies and bloodstone
finial, with floral engraved decoration,
English, circa 1850.
(Bonhams) $1,500

A Conklin Endura lady's pen and propeling
pencil set, black and pastel plastic, in original
case, circa 1935.
(Auction Team Köln) $184

A Mont Blanc 128 PL pen and pencil set, with
two-color nib, German, circa 1935
(Bonhams) $900

A Pelican 500 writing set in striped brown
with gilt cap, in matching brown case, circa
1955.
(Auction Team Köln) $268

Soennecken Präsident with original 18 ct.
gold nib, in snakeskin case, circa 1940.
(Auction Team Köln) $184

A Mont Blanc Lapis 30 Masterpiece pen with
4810 nib, German, late 1920s.
(Bonhams) $1,425

A Dunhill Namiki lacquer and enamel pen
with band of floral decoration, Dunhill Namiki
No. 3 nib, Japanese, 1930s.
(Bonhams) $1,500

Montblanc 12½ safety fountain pen,
octagonal, in black hardened rubber, circa
1932.
(Auction Team Köln) $385

A Mordan bone pen/pencil/
thermometer/compass combination with
engraved yellow metal mounts, English, 1860-
1880s.
(Bonhams) $690

A Parker Duofold 'Streamlined' model,
writing set, in original burgundy red and
black marled colorway, circa 1932
(Auction Team Köln) $242

A Waterman 114 mottled pump-filler, with
No. 4 nib, American, circa 1905.
(Bonhams) $1,050

An extremely rare Waterman 20S Prohibition
pen, its one piece barrel and dummy turning
knob creating a pen-shaped liquor flask,
American, 1920s.
(Bonhams) $2,400

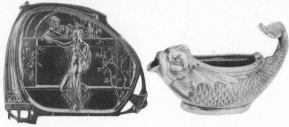

Kayserzinn centerpiece, circa
1907. pewter, modeled with two
kneeling female figures on either
end of the organic oval dish,
62cm. maximum width.
(Sotheby's) $5,088

A W.M.F. wall plaque,
stamped in relief with a
classical scene of two lovers by
a wall, 29cm. wide.
(Christie's) $440

A pewter pap boat, modeled in
the form of a mythical sea
creature, on oval base, 5¼in.
long.
(Christie's) $273

A good WMF Art Nouveau
shaped rectangular dressing
table mirror, cast with flowers
and diaphanously clad girl
looking into the glass, 14in. high.
(Neales) $1,150

A pair of German Jugendstil
candle holders, each formed as a
classical maiden supporting two
vase-shaped sconces,
Goldschmidt, circa 1900, 23cm.
high.
(Christie's) $7,101

A white metal table lighter in
the shape of a monkey, marked
Faberge, realistically modelled,
the upright monkey turning to
look at its tail, 4¼in. high,
13.5oz.
(Christie's) $21,994

WMF glass and pewter duck
pitcher, hinged mouth, scroll
work wings and base, impressed
marks, 14in. high.
(Skinner) $575

Three piece WMF pewter set,
pair of candlesticks with harp
players, centerpiece with cut
glass insert, impressed mark,
12in. wide.
(Skinner) $747

A rare pewter covered flagon,
Thomas and Samuel Boardman,
Hartford, Connecticut, circa
1825, with hinged molded lid
with urn finial, 14⅛in. high.
(Sotheby's) $3,450

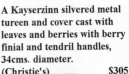

Gustav Stickley plate, ruffled edge, impressed mark, light patina, 6¾in. diameter.
(Skinner) $345

A pewter creamer, John Will (circa 1707–circa 1774), New York, 1752–1766, on three cabriole legs with incised and leaf-shaped knees, 4¼in. high.
(Christie's) $18,400

A Kayserzinn silvered metal tureen and cover cast with leaves and berries with berry finial and tendril handles, 34cms. diameter.
(Christie's) $305

A Liberty & Co. pewter and enamel box and cover, designed by Archibald Knox, of square shape, cast in relief with horizontal bands of square shape leaves, 14cm. high, stamped *Tudric 0194*.
(Phillips) $1,081

Georg Jensen, pair of two light candelabra, 1933–1944 manufacture, silver colored metal, each with two candleholders with light martelé finish, 6in.
(Sotheby's) $3,997

Austrian Art Glass metal mounted vase, bulbous baluster form yellow striped red glass vessel fitted within bronzed metal foliate frame, 11¼in. high.
(Skinner) $517

Josef Hoffmann for the Wiener Werkstätte, a pair of 'Ivy pattern' egg cups, circa 1907, circular section with pierced and repoussé design of stylized ivy leaves, 2in.
(Sotheby's) $2,362

Large Liberty Tudric pewter Stein, embossed floral pattern, impressed *Tudric 054*, 9½in high.
(Skinner) $862

A pair of Dutch japanned pewter chestnut urns, early 19th century, of ovoid-shape, the sepia ground painted with figures in rural landscapes, 12¾in. high.
(Christie's) $4,302

An American Edison Standard Phonograph dictating machine, electric, circa 1920.
(Auction Team Köln) $462

A small Swiss Mikiphone pocket phonograph in bakelite box form, 11.5 cm diameter.
(Auction Team Köln) $616

An undocumented phonograph, with Pathé soundbox and decorative horn arm, circa 1910.
(Auction Team Köln) $269

A French Le Merveilleux Phonograph Système Lioret with two disks.
(Auction Team Köln)
                                  $2,004

A Pathé Le Menestrel phonograph with gold decorated cast case, with original aluminium horn, circa 1905.
(Auction Team Köln)
                                  $2,543

A large cabinet phonograph incorporating a Model A Edison Triumph mechanism 45035 with two-speed pulley and Diamond B reproducer, 49in. high.
(Christie's S. Ken)
                                  $3,887

A coin operated phonograph, The Graphophone Model BS, by the Columbia/American Phonograph Company, circa 1898.
(Auction Team Köln)
                                  $2,929

A Thornwood phonograph, No. 47448, with Type N Graphophone upper chassis with bullet-shaped mandrel and endgate, Type A bedplate and motor with single spring, circa 1898.
(Christie's) $1,755

A French Pathé Chante Clair phongraph for large Inter cylinders, with wooden lid and three cylinders, circa 1902.
(Auction Team Köln) $693

George Rodger (1908–1995), Wrestlers of the Korongo Nube tribe of Kordofan, Sudan, 1949, printed 1991, gelatin silver print, 16⅝ x 13in.
(Christie's) $4,312

Franz Fiedler (1885–1956); Yousef Karsh and others, tonal separation portrait of a woman wearing a head scarf, late 1920s–early 1930s.
(Christie's) $2,760

Auguste (1862–1954) and Louis (1864–1948) Lumière, Self portrait with Louis seated crocheting with pink wool, early 1900s, autochrome, 7 x 5in.
(Christie's) $5,175

Diane Arbus/Neil Selkirk, Man and a Boy on a Bench in Central Park, N.Y.C., 1962/later, gelatin silver print, signed by Doon Arbus, titled, dated and editioned 35/75 in ink, 14½ x 13¾in.
(Butterfield & Butterfield) $1,725

Lewis Carroll (Charles Lutwidge Dodgson) (1832–1898), 'Queen Eleanor – Fair Rosamund', June 1863, albumen print, 8⅛ x 6in., arched top, mounted on card, titled, dated and inscribed.
(Christie's) $5,520

Diane Arbus/Neil Selkirk, Russian Midget Friends in a Living Room on 100th Street, N.Y.C., 1963/later, gelatin silver print, signed by Doon Arbus, titled, editioned 23/75, 14¾ x 14¾in.
(Butterfield & Butterfield) $1,725

Max Yavno, 'Two Chinese', 1947/later, gelatin silver print, signed in pencil on the mount, 13⅜ x 10⅜in.
(Butterfield & Butterfield) $1,035

Dorothy Wilding (1893–1976), 'Silver Turban', 'Etude', and 'Venez Jouer Avec Moi', 1920s, three gelatin silver prints, each approximately 11¼ x 8⅞in.
(Christie's) $1,380

Julia Margaret Cameron, Maude, 1870s, albumen print, signed and titled in ink on the mount, framed, 4⅞ x 4in.
(Butterfield & Butterfield) $2,875

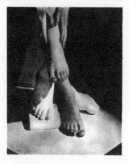

Horst P. Horst (b. 1906), 'Barefoot Beauty' advertisement, New York, 1939, printed 1987, platinum-palladium print from an edition of 10, 23⅝ x 19¼in.
(Christie's) $7,762

Aaron Siskind, 'Max Rothschild House, Chicago', 1952, gelatin silver print, mounted flush to board, signed in pencil, 7½ x 9⅜in.
(Butterfield & Butterfield) $1,265

Robert Doisneau, 'La Dent', 1956/later, gelatin silver print, signed in ink in the margin, titled and dated in ink on verso, 16½ x 11in.
(Butterfield & Butterfield) $805

Arnold Newman, Portrait of Yasuo Kuniyoshi, New York City, 1941, printed 1950s, gelatin silver print, 7¾ x 9¾in.
(Christie's) $2,415

W. Eugene Smith, 'Guardia Civil', 1951, gelatin silver print, signed and titled in pencil on the mount, 9⅞ x 12⅝in.
(Butterfield & Butterfield) $3,450

William Heike, 'Hats', 1952, gelatin silver print, signed and dated in pencil on the modern mount, 8 x 10in.
(Butterfield & Butterfield) $1,092

Diane Arbus/Neil Selkirk, Mother Holding Her Child, N.J., 1967/later, gelatin silver printed, signed by Doon Arbus, titled, dated, editioned 4/75, 14¼ x 14¼in.
(Butterfield & Butterfield) $1,380

Possibly Toussaint Barthélémy (1850–1906) and Paul Oudin (1851–1923), Experimental X-ray photographs of malformed hands, a shoe, a rat and a purse, 1896–97, album of fifteen gelatin silver prints.
(Christie's) $3,105

Diane Arbus/Neil Selkirk, Masked Man at a Ball, N.Y.C., 1967/later, gelatin silver print, signed by Doon Arbus, titled, dated, editioned 8/75, 14⅝ x 14½in.
(Butterfield & Butterfield) $1,955

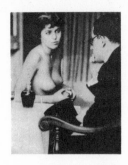

Josef Breitenbach, Dr. Riegler and J. Greno, Münich, 1933/1989, photogravure, printed on a larger sheet with embossed border, 11³/₄ x 9¹/₂in.
(Butterfield & Butterfield)
$373

Weegee, Woman Holding Chimp, 1950s/later, gelatin silver print, the photographer's circular credit stamp in ink on verso, 8³/₄ x 7⁵/₈in.
(Butterfield & Butterfield)
$1,035

Robert Doisneau, 'Baiser Blotto', 1950/later, gelatin silver print, signed in ink in the margin, titled and dated in ink on verso, 16¹/₂ x 13³/₈in.
(Butterfield & Butterfield)
$1,092

André Kertész, 'Broken Bench in Borban', 1962/later, gelatin silver print, signed and dated in pencil on the mount, 6¹/₂ x 9⁵/₈in.
(Butterfield & Butterfield)
$1,725

Robert Doisneau, 'Le Petit Balcon', 1953/1980, gelatin silver print, signed in ink in the margin, 9¹/₈ x 13³/₈in.
(Butterfield & Butterfield)
$632

Marion Post Wolcott, Main Street After a Blizzard, 1940s/later, gelatin silver print, signed in pencil on verso, 6³/₈ x 8⁷/₈in.
(Butterfield & Butterfield)
$1,150

Diane Arbus/Neil Selkirk, Seated Man in a Bra and Stockings, N.Y.C., 1967/later, gelatin silver print, signed by Doon Arbus, titled, dated and editioned *10/75*, 14³/₈ x 14³/₄in.
(Butterfield & Butterfield)
$862

Diane Arbus/Neil Selkirk, Identical Twins, Roselle, N.J., 1967/circa 1970, gelatin silver print, signed by Doon Arbus, titled, dated and annotated, 4⁵/₈ x 15in.
(Butterfield & Butterfield)
$13,800

Bill Brandt, 'Evening Light in Burslem, St. Paul's Church', 1940, gelatin silver print, titled and the photographer's copyright stamp in ink on verso, 9 x 7³/₄in.
(Butterfield & Butterfield)
$1,380

Peter Lavery, Tribal portraits, circa 1990, two gelatin silver prints, image sizes 14$\frac{1}{2}$ x 12in. and 15$\frac{3}{4}$ x 12in.
(Christie's) $1,120

Roger Fenton, Melrose Abbey, 1856, albumen print, 12$\frac{1}{2}$ x 17$\frac{1}{4}$in.
(Butterfield & Butterfield) $862

Anonymous, Portait of a lady wearing a turban, circa 1870s, albumen print, 17$\frac{1}{2}$ x 11$\frac{1}{2}$in., oak frame.
(Christie's) $775

Margaret Bourke-White, 'Machinery Abstraction', 1929, sepia-toned gelatin silver print with black borders, mounted on cardstock, 12$\frac{7}{8}$ x 8$\frac{7}{8}$in.
(Butterfield & Butterfield) $18,400

George Zimbel, Irish Dancehall, The Bronx, 1954/1995, gelatin silver print, signed and dated in ink in the margin, 8 x 11$\frac{1}{2}$in.
(Butterfield & Butterfield) $517

Roman Vishniac, Jewish Peasant, Carpatho-Ukraine, 1937/1977, gelatin silver print, signed in ink on the mount, 19$\frac{5}{8}$ x 13$\frac{1}{4}$in.
(Butterfield & Butterfield) $1,265

David Octavius Hill (1802–70) and Robert Adamson (1821–48), Miss Binney, mid 1840s, calotype, approximately 8$\frac{5}{8}$ x 6$\frac{5}{8}$in.
(Christie's) $3,277

Edward S. Curtis, Aphrodite, 1920s, blue-toned gelatin silver print, signed in the negative, 7$\frac{1}{4}$ x 9$\frac{1}{8}$in.
(Butterfield & Butterfield) $2,300

William Mortensen, 'The Indian Girl', 1927, gelatin silver print, signed and titled in ink in the margin, 14$\frac{1}{4}$ x 10$\frac{1}{4}$in.
(Butterfield & Butterfield) $1,035

Helmut Newton (b. 1920), 'Arielle after haircut, Paris', 1982, gelatin silver print, image size 22¹/₂ x 15in., signed, titled.
(Christie's) $2,242

Alfred Erhardt, 'Wotten Meer, Nordsee', 1934, gelatin silver print, 11¾ x 19in.
(Christie's) $3,795

Carl Moon (1879–1948), 'Navaho Boy', circa 1905–07; 'Apache Prince', circa 1910, two carbon prints.
(Christie's) $3,795

Herb Ritts, 'Stephano Seated, Milano, 1985, platinum print, the photographer's copyright blindstamp in the margin, 19¹/₄ x 14¹/₄in.
(Butterfield & Butterfield)
                                $3,162

Alexander Rodchenko, 'Rhythmic Gymnastics', 1936/1989, gelatin silver print from the May Parade series, titled in Russian, 9 x 12in.
(Butterfield & Butterfield)
                    $1,610

Edward Weston, 'Guadalupe Marin de Rivera', 1924, gelatin silver print, initialed and dated in pencil on the mount, 8¹/₄ x 7in.
(Butterfield & Butterfield)
                                $4,312

Oscar G. Rejlander, Portrait of Lewis Carroll, 28 March 1863, albumen print mounted as a carte-de-visite, inscribed *C. L. Dodgson* in pencil.
(Christie's) $3,450

T. R. Williams, Victoria, Princess Royal, circa 1856, stereoscopic daguerreotype, hand-tinted and with gilt highlights.
(Christie's) $81,450

Elliot Erwitt, Marilyn Monroe and Clark Gable on the set of 'The Misfits', Reno, Nevada, 1960, printed 1996, gelatin silver print, image size 17³/₄ x 12in.
(Christie's) $775

PHOTOGRAPHS

John K. Hillers (1843–1925), 'Moki spinning', 1870s, albumen print, 9¹/₁₆ x 7¹/₄in., signed and titled in the negative. (Christie's) **$1,466**

Philippe Halsman, 'Dame Edith Sitwell', 1959, gelatin silver print, 19¹/₂ x 15¹/₂in. (Christie's) **$1,120**

Jean-Francois Jonvelle (b. 1943), Sandrine Bonnaire, 1987, gelatin silver print, 19¹/₂ x 13¹/₄in., signed and dated. (Christie's) **$948**

Edouard Boubat, 'Cyntia', 1975/later, gelatin silver print, signed in ink in the margin, 12¹/₂ x 8¹/₂in. (Butterfield & Butterfield) **$345**

Brassaï, 'Le Bar: à gauche: Lulu de Montparnasse', 1932/later, gelatin silver print, signed in ink in the margin, titled, and dated, 10⁷/₈ x 9in. (Butterfield & Butterfield) **$2,300**

Henri Cartier-Bresson (b. 1908), 'At the Derby of Longchamps, France', 1950s, gelatin silver print, 15³/₈ x 10⁵/₈in., mounted on hardboard. (Christie's) **$725**

Robert Frank, Los Angeles, 1955, gelatin silver print, signed, titled and dated in ink in the margin, 13¹/₂ x 9in. (Butterfield & Butterfield) **$5,750**

Félix Nadar (1820–1910), François Guizot, circa 1857, albumen print, 9¹/₄ x 7³/₈in., corners trimmed, signed in ink on recto. (Christie's) **$2,070**

David Seymour (Chim) (1911–1956), 'Richard Avedon and Fred Astaire' in 'Funny Face', 1956, printed 1996, gelatin silver print, image size 18³/₄ x 13¹/₈in. (Christie's) **$2,415**

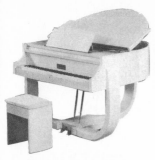

Strohmenger, baby grand piano, 1930s, white lacquer, 136cm. wide.
(Sotheby's) $5,088

A classical mahogany and mahogany veneer piano, John Osborn, Boston, circa 1820, with paper label and brand, 66½in. wide.
(Skinner) $1,840

A rosewood cased grand pianoforte, by Steinway & Sons, New York, number 154257.
(Holloway's) $6,123

J. S. Henry for Bechstein, upright piano, circa 1905–10, oak, with two panels with stylized marquetry leaves, 151.5cm. wide.
(Sotheby's) $2,180

A Strohmenger baby grand piano, 1930's, in a mahogany case numbered *20363*, 55in. wide.
(Sotheby's) $4,223

A rare Victorian papier mâché and mother-of-pearl inlaid upright cottage piano by John Bettridge, 69¾in. wide.
(Christie's) $11,285

An Empire style gilt-bronze-mounted mahogany Weber grand piano and a bench, serial no. 63318, circa 1913, the case mounted with escutcheons, 7ft. 2in. long.
(Butterfield & Butterfield) $20,700

A George IV square pianoforte, in Sheraton mahogany case with satinwood banding, 5ft. 6½in., by George Moore, London and Liverpool.
(Russell, Baldwin & Bright) $1,341

A Bechstein rosewood grand piano, No. 42684, circa 1900, the sides decorated with ribbon-tied bows and husk swags with oval paterae, 80in. long.
(Christie's) $13,770

A Symphonion No. 10 German record player with 41-tone comb, for 19.5cm. disks, circa 1905.
(Auction Team Köln) $770

A table-top barrel organ, with four 30.5cm. diameter tin disks, circa 1900.
(Auction Team Köln) $338

An 11-inch Polyphon, disk musical box, with single-comb movement in walnut case with Douglas & Co., London retailer's label, with thirty disks.
(Christie's) $1,580

An upright 19⅝-inch Polyphon, with coin mechanism, two combs and typical walnut case with spandrels and flat-fronted coin drawer, 41in. high, with ten disks.
(Christie's) $5,265

A 19⅛-inch Symphonion, upright disk musical box with coin mechanism and replacement drawer, 48in. high, with one Symphonion and four modern disks.
(Christie's) $3,335

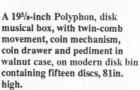

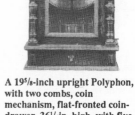

A Symphonion No. 10 record player, with four bells, 41-tone comb and handle, with 13 disks.
(Auction Team Köln) $1,078

A 19⅝-inch Polyphon, disk musical box, with twin-comb movement, coin mechanism, coin drawer and pediment in walnut case, on modern disk bin containing fifteen discs, 81in. high.
(Christie's) $7,020

A 19⅝-inch upright Polyphon, with two combs, coin mechanism, flat-fronted coin-drawer, 36¼in. high, with five disks.
(Christie's) $3,159

A 16½-inch Adler, table disk musical box, with twin comb movement, glazed motor cover and carved walnut case, 26¾in. wide, with twenty-four disks.
(Christie's) $5,265

A Calliope musical Christmas tree stand, with Art Nouveau decoration, for 23.3.cm. tin disks, lacking comb, tree stand and handle, with two disks.
(Auction Team Köln) $847

A 15⅝-inch Polyphon, table disk musical box with two combs, paneled case with inlaid Polyphon name in lid and twenty-one disks.
(Christie's) $2,633

A Calliope player for 23.4 cm. disks with 49-tone comb.
(Auction Team Köln) $385

A Symphonion record player for 20.5cm. disks, with 40-tone comb, with 13 disks.
(Auction Team Köln) $693

A 15½-inch Polyphon Excelsior, table disk musical box, with single comb movement in walnut case with drawer in plinth and tune list in lid, 24in. wide, with sixteen disks.
(Christie's) $3,861

A 25¼-inch Symphonion, upright disk musical box with side-by-side combs, coin mechanism and drawer, in typical walnut-veneered case, 82½in. high, with nine disks.
(Christie's) $8,775

A Polyphon vertical record-player for 28cm. tin disks, with 54-tone comb, coin slot, with 18 disks.
(Auction Team Köln)

$2,697

Philippe A. Peticolas, circa 1805, miniature of a child, almost full length seated in a landscape, with blonde hair, oval, 2³/₄in. high.
(Sotheby's) $1,610

George Engleheart (1750–1829), a young gentleman, facing right in blue coat, white waistcoat, oval, 2³/₁₆in. high.
(Christie's) $1,910

A George II Irish two-handled cup, with a campana shaped bowl, by William Townsend, Dublin, circa 1745, 19.5cm. high, 32oz.
(Phillips) $1,575

Attributed to Anton Rafael Mengs (1728–1779), King Augustus III of Poland, facing right in gilt-studded armor, watercolor on vellum, oval, 1⁷/₁₆in. high.
(Christie's) $1,302

Louis Marie Dulieu de Chenevoux (born 1752), the miniaturist Rouvier, facing right in lilac coat with five alphabetized buttons, signed and dated *Dulieu 1790,* enamel on copper, oval, 2⁷/₈in. high.
(Christie's) $2,084

John Bogle (1746–1803), General Prescott, facing right in scarlet uniform with gold embroidered blue facings, signed *JB/1789,* oval, 1³/₈in. high.
(Christie's) $4,168

Louis-François Aubry (1767–1851), a young gentleman, in dark-blue coat, white waistcoat, elaborately knotted silk cravat, signed, oval, 2in. high.
(Christie's) $1,042

Joseph Deranton (1756–1814), a young lady, facing right, wearing a long sleeved low-cut aubergine-colored silk dress, signed, 2⁵/₁₆in. diameter.
(Christie's) $2,084

Richard Cosway, R.A. (1742–1821), Lord John Augustus Hervey, facing right in blue coat with gold buttons, oval, 2¹/₄in. high.
(Christie's) $8,335

Isaac Oliver (died 1617), a portrait miniature of a young gentleman, facing left in embroidered black silk doublet, watercolor on vellum laid down on card, oval, 2¹/₁₆in. high. (Christie's) $68,705

Georg Nicolas Ritter (1748–1809), a young lady, facing right in frill-edged white muslin dress with fichu and scarlet bodice, signed *G. Ritter. fecit/1790*, 3³/₈in. diameter. (Christie's) $2,257

Christian Friedrich Zincke (1683/84–1767), a young gentleman, facing left in silver-embroidered light-blue coat, frilled white lace cravat, enamel on copper, oval, 1¹³/₁₆in. high. (Christie's) $3,299

Jean Petitot (1607–1691), an enamel miniature of George Villiers, Duke of Buckingham, facing left in grey and white striped slashed doublet, signed and dated, enamel on gold, oval, 2in. high. (Christie's) $417,515

French School, circa 1790, a double-portrait of two children in an interior; a young girl with long brown hair, holding a silver rattle, the younger child seated in its blue-covered cradle, 2¹/₂in. diameter. (Christie's) $1,737

William Naish (circa 1760–1800), Lieutenant John Henry Bates of the 2nd Regiment of Life Guards, facing left in scarlet uniform, oval, 2³/₄in. high. (Christie's) $3,299

French School, circa 1840, a young lady hiding her face with a black mask, in low-cut white silk dress with lace-embroidered décolleté, oval, 1⁵/₈in. high. (Christie's) $1,128

Bouvier (fl. circa 1820–1840), a young boy, facing left in brown coat, striped yellow waistcoat and open white shirt, signed, 2⁹/₁₆in. diameter. (Christie's) $1,389

Luc Sicardi (1746–1825), King Louis XVI of France, facing left in coronation robes, powdered curled wig, signed *Sicardi/1787*, oval, 2¹/₈in. high. (Christie's) $15,629

Philip Jean (1755–1802), a young lady, facing left in white dress and overcoat, pale-blue bow at corsage, oval, 2⁵/₈in. high. (Christie's) $4,341

French School, circa 1800, three young children, the two elder girls in white frill-edged pink silk dress and blue dress, rectangular, 2in. x 1⁵/₈in. (Christie's) $1,563

N. Freese (fl. 1794–1814), a young lady, facing left in white dress with blue waist sash, large straw bonnet, oval, 3in. high. (Christie's) $2,084

Richard Crosse (1742–1810), a young gentleman, facing right in brown coat, white waistcoat and frilled cravat, oval, 1⁷/₈in. high. (Christie's) $1,302

A pair of rare and finely painted portrait miniatures by Thomas Frye, signed and dated *1761*, of a lady nearly full face, and a man with hair en queue, 3.5cm. (Phillips) $9,300

John Smart (1742/43–1811), a young lady, facing left in pearl-bordered white dress and fur-edged blue overcoat, signed *J.S./ 1773*, 1¹/₈in. high. (Christie's) $4,341

Attributed to Horace Hone, a gentleman, head and shoulders, with powdered hair and wearing a blue jacket over a white waistcoat, oval, 7.5cm. (Bearne's) $462

Attributed to Richard Cosway, R.A., a lady, head and shoulders, her powdered hair tied with a blue ribbon and wearing a white dress, oval, 5cm., in a later frame. (Bearne's) $1,267

French School, circa 1795/1800, a young lady, her arms crossed, wearing a blue-bordered white silk dress, 2⁷/₈in. diameter. (Christie's) $2,257

AERONAUTICAL

Jean Colin, Air France Caravelle, double royal, 102 x 64cm., 1959.
(Onslow's) $155

Rowland Hilder, Fly To The Far East BOAC (Short S25 Sandringham Flying Boat resting amongst craft in Hong Kong's Victoria Harbor), double royal, 102 x 64cm., 1948.
(Onslow's) $1,085

Perceval, Air France Dans Tous Les Ciels, on linen, double royal, 102 x 64cm., 1948.
(Onslow's) $775

Renluc, Madagascar and Mauritius via East Africa Air France (DC4), on linen, 50 x 31cm., 1950.
(Onslow's) $264

BEA (Vickers Viking Airliner cutaway), double royal, 102 x 64cm., 1948.
(Onslow's) $465

Holz, Flying Holidays At All In Rates We Arrange Flying Holidays As Air France Authorised Agents.
(Onslow's) $248

Paul Lenglly, Potez Aero Service En Liaison Avec Air France, 1935, on linen, double royal, 102 x 64cm.
(Onslow's) $713

Frank Wootton, Fly To India by BOAC, double royal, 102 x 64cm., 1950.
(Onslow's) $450

KLM Amsterdam-Batavia Twice Weekly Speed Comfort Reliability (Fokker-Douglas DC2), 1935.
(Onslow's) $1,008

Kenneth D. Shoesmith, South America by Royal Mail, double royal, 102 x 64cm. (Onslow's) **$1,178**

Fastest To The Orient The White Empresses of the Pacific, published by Canadian Pacific, double royal, 102 x 64cm. (Onslow's) **$527**

Melbourne Brindle, Australia America and South Seas Matson Line, double royal, 102 x 64cm. (Onslow's) **$419**

A Baltic Bridge Daily Services to Sweden via Harwich Ferries Konung Gustaf V and Deutschland, published by Swedish State Railways, double royal, 102 x 64cm., 1933. (Onslow's) **$310**

Frank H. Mason, SS Arnhem New Luxury Ship Harwich Hook of Holland Service (LNER SS Arnhem approaching the Hook of Holland), published by LNER, double royal, 102 x 64cm. (Onslow's) **$465**

Feldtmann, Nord Deutscher Lloyd Bremen 4¹/₂ Days Ocean Crossing Shortest Passage To New York, double royal, 102 x 64cm., 1932. (Onslow's) **$388**

K. Herkomer, Normandie The World's Most Perfect Ship French Line, double royal, 102 x 64cm., 1939. (Onslow's) **$2,325**

Odin Rosenvinge, Royal Line from Bristol Fastest To Canada (Royal Edward), double royal, 102 x 64cm. (Onslow's) **$465**

Union Castle Mail Steamship Coy Ltd. South African Royal Mail Service, on linen, double royal, 102 x 64cm. (Onslow's) **$775**

OCEAN LINER

Leonard Padden, Union Castle Holiday Tours, double royal, 102 x 64cm.
(Onslow's) $589

Kenneth D. Shoesmith, Canadian Pacific To Canada & USA (Empress of Britain), double royal, 102 x 64cm.
(Onslow's) $1,860

Ottomar Anton, Hamburg-Sud Brazil-Africa MS Monte Rosa, 84 x 60cm., 1935.
(Onslow's) $403

K. Herkomer, Paris, Paris All The Way To New York When You Board Any French Line Ship You Step Right Into Paris Itself!, published by French Line CGT, double royal, 102 x 64cm., 1934.
(Onslow's) $837

Kenneth D. Shoesmith, Cruises To The Northern Capitals of Europe by Ellerman's Wilson Line Turbine Steamship City of Paris Sailings From Immingham, quad royal, 102 x 127cm.
(Onslow's) $837

Kenneth D. Shoesmith, Canadian Pacific To Canada & USA Great Southern Railways, blue background (Empress of Britain), printed by The Baynard Press, double royal, 102 x 64cm.
(Onslow's) $1,240

Arnold, Nord Deutscher Lloyd Bremen 4½ Days Ocean Crossing To USA, double royal, 102 x 64cm.
(Onslow's) $434

Feldtmann, Nord Deutscher Lloyd Bremen Fastest Service To New York, double royal, 102 x 64cm.
(Onslow's) $930

Odin Rosenvinge, Royal Line from Bristol Fastest To Canada (Royal Edward), double royal, 102 x 64cm.
(Onslow's) $496

PSYCHEDELIC UNDERGROUND

Silkscreened, white on black for
The Incredible Crazy World of
Arthur Brown performing in
Aylesbury.
(Bonhams) $283

Silkscreened poster, white on
black background, promoting
Cyril Davies All Stars featuring
Long John Baldry playing in
Guildford, 20 x 30in.
(Bonhams) $283

Silkscreen, black on yellow
poster advertising John Mayall
playing at the Ricky Tick Club,
Guildford on 17th March 1966.
(Bonhams) $236

Silkscreened red on yellow
poster promoting Georgie Fame
and The Blue Flames, together
with Long John Baldry and The
Hootchie Cootchie Men playing
at the Ricky Tick Club,
Windsor, 30 x 20in.
(Bonhams) $393

A rare silkscreened poster for
The Plaza, Newbury where the
Jimi Hendrix Experience were
playing on 10th February 1967,
yellow and brown on black and
yellow, 30 x 20in.
(Bonhams) $2,983

Hapshash and The Coloured
Coat poster for the Jimi
Hendrix Experience at The
Saville Theatre, Shaftesbury
Avenue, 27th August 1967,
framed and glazed,
30½ x 20½in.
(Bonhams) $1,130

A rare psychedelic poster for
Andy Warhol's Velvet
Underground 'The Wildflower',
the Trauma, Philadelphia 1967,
by Karen Fritz.
(Bonhams) $628

A rare silkscreened poster for
the Rolling Stones at the Ricky
Tick Club, Windsor, bold black
lettering on blue, circa 1963,
20 x 30in.
(Bonhams) $1,539

A rare silkscreened poster for
Jimi Hendrix at the Ricky Tick
Club, Hounslow on 3rd
February 1967, yellow on blue,
30½ x 20½in.
(Bonhams) $2,826

PSYCHEDELIC UNDERGROUND

Silkscreened pink on black background, concert poster presenting the Cream playing at The Assembly Hall, Aylesbury.
(Bonhams) $502

A black, silver and blue metallic 'Sunshine Superman', Donovan poster, by Martin Sharp.
(Bonhams) $267

Silkscreen promotional poster, blue on black background, for the Cream playing at the Ricky Tick, Windsor on 7th January 1967, 30 x 20in.
(Bonhams) $502

A Rick Griffin poster 'Flying Eyeball', featuring Jimi Hendrix Experience, John Mayall and the Bluesbreakers at the Fillmore Auditorium, 1968, framed and glazed, 15 x 23in.
(Bonhams) $973

A Track Record promotional poster of Hendrix in black and white, together with a double-sided handbill for The Newport Festival at Devonshire Downs, 20th June 1969.
(Bonhams) $864

A poster for 'It's Anarchy in the U.K. Tour' starring The Sex Pistols, The Damned, Johnny Thunder's Heartbreakers, The Clash at the King's Hall, Derby, 4th December 1976.
(Bonhams) $346

Silkscreened poster, black on yellow background promoting Martha and The Vandellas and the Night People, at the Galaxy Club, Basingstoke, 30 x 20in.
(Bonhams) $251

Silkscreened poster, black on pink background, promoting The Who and supporting group playing at the Birdcage Club, Portsmouth, 30 x 20in.
(Bonhams) $785

Silkscreened poster, white on black background, announcing the appearance of Graham Bond at the Ricky Tick, Windsor, 30 x 20in.
(Bonhams) $267

TRAVEL

Moy Thomas, Egypt The Premier Winter Rendezvous, double royal, 102 x 64cm. (Onslow's) $233

Gordon M. Forsyth, Harrogate, published by LNER, double royal, 102 x 64cm. (Onslow's) $853

H. L. Plessen, Germany Wants To See You, double royal, 102 x 64cm. (Onslow's) $171

Grif Teller, Washington The City Beautiful Pennsylvania Railroad, double royal, 102 x 64cm. (Onslow's) $806

Doris Zinkeisen, The Coronation Streamline Train 1937, published by LNER, double royal, 102 x 64cm. (Onslow's) $1,318

Nordman, Egypt Calls You Egyptian State Railways, printed by Amirayan & Co. Cairo, double royal, 102 x 64cm. (Onslow's) $667

Schoellenen Goeschenen-Andermatt, printed by Wolfensburger Zurich, double royal, 102 x 64cm. (Onslow's) $155

Terence Cuneo, Royal Border Bridge Berwick On Tweed, published by RE(NER), double royal, 102 x 64cm. (Onslow's) $760

Frank H. Mason, Fano Holidays In Denmark via Harwich-Esbjerg, published by LNER, double royal, 102 x 64cm. (Onslow's) $78

TRAVEL

C. S. Bergstrom, Colorado
Rockies Black Hills and Utah,
104 x 69cm., 1934.
(Onslow's) $419

Austin Cooper, Scarborough,
published by LNER, double
royal, 102 x 64cm., 1932.
(Onslow's) $1,318

P. Irwin Brown, Japan,
published by Japanese
Government Railways.
(Onslow's) $465

E. V. Kealey, West Indies and
Spanish Main by French Line
CGT SS Colombie & Cuba,
double royal, 102 x 64cm.
(Onslow's) $341

Gyrth Russell, Glorious Devon
(Hope & Anchor Inn and view
of harbor with yacht),
published by RE(WR), double
royal, 102 x 64cm.
(Onslow's) $1,008

E. Paul Champseix, Biarritz,
published by Chemins de Fer
Paris Orleans Midi, double
royal, 102 x 64cm., 1935.
(Onslow's) $295

Sellheim, Great Barrier Reef
Queensland; and Koala No. 31,
photographic, double royal,
102 x 64cm.
(Onslow's) $620

Doris Zinkeisen, Coronation
LNER Ancestry Coronation
1831, published by LNER,
double royal, 102 x 64cm.
(Onslow's) $651

Ledgard Lemaire, Belgium The
Coast, published by De Greve &
Co. Brussels, double royal, 102 x
64cm., 1933.
(Onslow's) $589

TRAVEL

Beautiful Japan, published by
Japanese Government Railways,
double royal, 102 x 64cm.
(Onslow's) $279

A. Cossard, Nice-Coni Nouvelle
Ligne, published by PLM,
double royal, 102 x 64cm., 1929.
(Onslow's) $295

Albert Fuss, Mediterranean
Cruises Hamburg-Amerika
Linie, double royal, 102 x 64cm.
(Onslow's) $279

Denmark The Little Belt Bridge
Between Jutland and Funen
Danish State Railways, printed
by Andreasen & Lachmann,
double royal, 102 x 64cm., 1935.
(Onslow's) $341

Augusto Giacometti, The
Grisons The Land of Sunshine,
printed by Wolfensburger
Zurich, double royal, 102 x
64cm.
(Onslow's) $1,008

Ludwig Hohlwein, Madeira
Beautiful Isle of Flowers and
Sunshine Royal Netherlands
Steamship Company, double
royal, 102 x 64cm.
(Onslow's) $403

Leonard Squirrel, Richmond
Yorkshire, published by
BR(NER), double royal, 102 x
64cm.
(Onslow's) $325

Leon Benigni, En Savoie Brides
Les Bains, published by PLM,
on linen, double royal, 102 x
64cm.
(Onslow's) $2,093

Kenneth Steel, Royal Deeside
Balmoral Castle, published by
BR (Scottish Region), double
royal, 102 x 64cm.
(Onslow's) $147

TRAVEL

Lucien Peri, Corsica The Isle of Beauty, published by PLM, double royal, 102 x 64cm.
(Onslow's) $341

Ottomar Anton, Hamburg-Sud MS Monte Rosa, 84 x 60cm., 1936.
(Onslow's) $78

Boccasile, Lugano, published by Trub Arrau, double royal, 102 x 64cm.
(Onslow's) $275

Stanley Roy Badmin, Come and Explore (villages), published by British Travel & Holiday Association, double crown on linen, 76 x 51cm., 1953.
(Onslow's) $248

S. Bailie, Middelkerke Belgium Free Baths 15 Minutes from Ostende, printed by Rycker Brussels, double royal, 102 x 64cm., 1923.
(Onslow's) $930

Melai, Ireland Invites You (fisherman mending), published by National Tourist Organisation, double royal, 102 x 64cm.
(Onslow's) $15

Roger Broders, Summer On The French Riviera Eternal Sunshine, published by PLM, double royal, 102 x 64cm., 1930.
(Onslow's) $589

F. C. Herrick, Hearing The Riches of London by London's Underground, double royal, 102 x 64cm., 1927.
(Onslow's) $604

Vogue, This Weeks Ramble Penshurst of the Sydneys, 1933, on card, double royal, 102 x 64cm.
(Onslow's) $78

WINTER SPORTS

Paul Ordner, Mont Revard
Altitude 1550m, published by
PLM, on linen.
(Onslow's) $750

Herbert Matter, Grindelwald,
photographic, printed by
Ringier, 100 x 70cm.
(Onslow's) $620

Alo, Chamonix-Mont Blanc,
published by PLM, on linen,
108 x 79cm.
(Onslow's) $1,085

Herbert Matter, Engelberg
Trubsee Switzerland,
photographic, printed by A.
Trub Aarau, double royal, 102 x
64cm.
(Onslow's) $1,008

H. R., SFR Winter Sports Ste
Croix et Les Rasses, printed by
E. Studer Yverdon, double
royal, 102 x 64cm.
(Onslow's) $3,100

Roger Broders, Winter Sports
In The Vosges The Munster
Valley and The Hohneck Alsace
& Lorraine Railways, double
royal, 102 x 64cm.
(Onslow's) $853

Winter Sports In The French
Alps, printed by Blampied
London, double royal, 102 x
64cm.
(Onslow's) $248

Louis Tauzin, Les Vosges,
published by Chemins de Fer de
L'Est, on linen, 108 x 79cm.
(Onslow's) $1,705

Herbert Matter, Pontresina
Engadin, photographic, printed
by Conzett & Huber Zurich,
double royal, 102 x 64cm., 1936.
(Onslow's) $2,945

WINTER SPORTS

Erling Nielsen, Winter Sports Week Oslo Norway 1935, double royal, 102 x 64cm. (Onslow's) $325

Huszar, Winter Season In Oslo Norway. (Onslow's) $450

Roger Soubie, Chamonix-Mont Blanc, published by PLM, on linen, 108 x 79cm. (Onslow's) $930

Lothar Rubelt, Come For Winter Sport to Austria, photographic, printed by Elbemuhl Wien, double royal, 102 x 64cm. (Onslow's) $310

M. Rozanski & R. Wylcan, Winter In Poland, published by Kosianskich, Warsaw, 100cm x 69cm. (Onslow's) $1,085

Freda Lingstrom, Norway For Real Winter Sport, published by Norwegian State Railways, double royal, 102 x 64cm. (Onslow's) $310

Julian Lacaze, Route Des Alps et Du Jura, published by PLM, double royal, 102 x 64cm. (Onslow's) $248

Ludwig Hohlwein, IVth Olympic Winter Games 6–16th February 1936, double royal, 102 x 64cm. (Onslow's) $1,395

Joseph Binder, Austria, printed by Reissers Sohne Wien, 95 x 63cm. (Onslow's) $496

Nathaniel Currier, Publisher, The Road, –
Winter, by O. Knirsch, lithograph with hand-
coloring and gum arabic, 1853, 17½in. x 26⅜in.
(Christie's) $17,250

John James Audubon (After), Pied Duck (Plate
CCCXXXII), hand colored etching, engraving
and aquatint, by R. Havell, 1836, plate 530 x
770mm.
(Sotheby's) $5,462

Thomas Johnston (Engraver and Printer),
Quebec, The Capital of New-France, a
Bishoprick, and Seat of the Soverain Court,
hand colored engraving, 1759, on laid paper,
framed, sheet 204 x 254mm.
(Sotheby's) $11,500

Edward Savage (Engraver), The Washington
Family, stipple engraving, 1798, after the
painting by Savage, published by Edward
Savage and Robert Wilkinson, London, image
18¼ x 24½in.
(Sotheby's) $920

Currier and Ives (Publishers), Brook Trout
Fishing, 'An Anxious Moment', hand colored
lithograph, with touches of gum arabic, 1862,
after the painting by Arthur F. Tait, framed,
469 x 686mm.
(Sotheby's) $6,325

John James Audubon (After), Trumpeter Swan
(Plate CCCCVI), hand colored etching,
engraving and aquatint, by R. Havell, 1838, on
paper with the watermark *J. Whatman 1837*,
sheet 662 x 988mm.
(Sotheby's) $37,375

N. Currier (Publisher), The Life of a Fireman, 'Take Up', 'Man Your Rope', hand colored lithograph, with touches of gum arabic, 1854, L. Maurer del., 435 x 660mm.
(Sotheby's) $1,150

Currier and Ives (Publishers), Autumn in New England, Cider Making, hand colored lithograph, with touches of gum arabic, a fresh impression, 1866, after the painting by George H. Durie, framed, 375 x 638mm.
(Sotheby's) $16,100

N. Currier (Publisher), Arguing the Point, hand colored lithograph, with touches of gum arabic, 1855, after the painting by Arthur F. Tait, framed, 467 x 606mm.
(Sotheby's) $4,600

Currier and Ives, Publishers, The Gunboat Candidate at the Battle of the Malvern Hill; Storming the Castle; and 'Taking the Stump', three lithographs, one in color, circa 1860.
(Christie's) $1,610

Bufford and Sons Lithographers (American, 19th century), 'The International Contest between Heenan Seyers at Farnborough, 17th of April, 1860.', lithograph printed in colors, with margins, image size 26in. x 39in.
(Skinner) $1,495

John Carwitham, A View of Fort George with the City of New York from the SW, hand colored engraving, published by Carington Bowles, London, circa 1794, on laid paper, framed, image and sheet 277 x 456mm.
(Sotheby's) $5,750

B. P., Austria, printed by Rosenbaum, double royal, 102 x 64cm.
(Onslow's) $124

Louis Icart, Spring Time Promenade (Promenade au Bois), 1948, etching with drypoint and aquatint printed in colors, signed in pencil, $14^7/_{16}$ x $19^3/_{16}$in.
(Butterfield & Butterfield) $1,955

Shep, Austria Calling, printed by The Baynard Press, double royal, 102 x 64cm.
(Onslow's) $116

Louis Icart, Lou Lou, 1921, etching with drypoint printed in colors with touches of pochoir on MBM paper, signed in pencil and numbered 184, $17^5/_{16}$ x $12^1/_8$in.
(Butterfield & Butterfield) $1,955

Louis Icart, Perfect Harmony (Accord Parfait), 1932, etching with drypoint and aquatint printed in color with touches of pochoir on wove paper, signed in pencil, $13^5/_{16}$ x 17in.
(Butterfield & Butterfield) $3,450

Theophile Steinlin, Racahout des Arabes, 1905, lithograph printed in colors on wove paper, English version, printed by Eugène Verneau, Paris, 22 x $15^1/_4$in.
(Butterfield & Butterfield) $690

Alphonse Mucha, Precious Stones: La Topaze, 1900, lithograph printed in colors on wove paper, printed by F. Champenois, Paris, $23^3/_4$ x $9^1/_2$in.
(Butterfield & Butterfield) $5,175

Louis Icart, Coursing III, 1930, etching with drypoint printed in colors with touches of pochoir on wove paper, signed in pencil, $15^{15}/_{16}$ x $25^{11}/_{16}$in.
(Butterfield & Butterfield) $4,312

Louis Icart, Youth (Jeunesse), 1930, etching with drypoint printed in colors with touches of pochoir on wove paper, signed in pencil, $24^1/_2$ x $15^{15}/_{16}$in.
(Butterfield & Butterfield) $4,312

Manuel Robbe, Plasson Cycles, 1897, lithograph printed in colors on wove paper, 47 x 33¹/₂in. (Butterfield & Butterfield) **$977**

Louis Icart, Guest (L'Invitée), 1941, etching with drypoint printed in colors with touches of pochoir, signed in pencil, 17³/₈ x 11⁵/₈in. (Butterfield & Butterfield) **$3,450**

Attributed to Philip Dawe (1750-1785), The Bostonians Paying the Excise Man, or Tarring and Feathering, mezzotint with hand coloring, 1774. (Christie's) **$5,520**

Alphonse Mucha, Monaco Monte-Carlo, 1897, lithograph printed in colors on wove paper, printed by F. Champenois, Paris, 41¹/₄ x 27³/₄in. (Butterfield & Butterfield) **$9,200**

Alphonse Mucha, JOB cigarette papers 1896, a colored lithograph poster in purple, red, green and brown, image area 51 x 38cm. (Phillips) **$2,008**

Louis Icart, Lilies (Les Lis), 1934, etching with drypoint and aquatint printed in colors with touches of pochoir on wove paper, signed in pencil, 28⁷/₁₆ x 19¹/₄in. (Butterfield & Butterfield) **$4,025**

Charles Gesmar, Mistinguett, 1925, lithograph printed in colors on wove paper, printed by H. Chachoin, Paris, sheet 63 x 46in. (Butterfield & Butterfield) **$1,725**

Louis Icart, Symphony in Blue (Symphonie en Bleu), 1936, etching with drypoint printed in colors, signed in pencil, 23¹/₂ x 19¹/₂in. (Butterfield & Butterfield) **$2,875**

Louis Icart, Spanish Dancer (Danse Espagnole), 1929, etching with drypoint printed in colors with touches of pochoir on wove paper, 21¹/₄ x 14¹/₁₆in. (Butterfield & Butterfield) **$1,092**

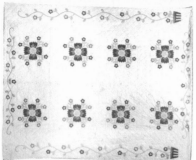

'Ohio Rose' quilt, the cream ground with Turkey reds, plain yellow and printed red and yellow small print cottons with eight 'roses', 76 x 92in., American, late 19th century.
(Christie's) $506

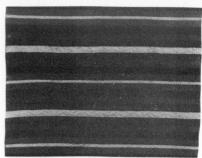

A pieced cotton 'Rainbow' quilt, probably Pennsylvania, circa 1859, composed of brightly colored green, blue, orange and brown cotton patches, approximately 84 x 70in.
(Sotheby's) $747

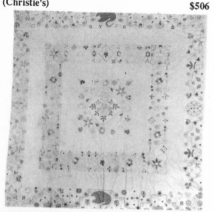

A fine appliqué coverlet, 1817, the central panel and two frames of white cotton applied with detailed and varied motifs of printed cotton, 101in. square.
(Christie's) $843

A pieced and appliquéd calico blazing star quilt, Ohio, late 19th century/early 20th century, the borders with trailing vines, the whole heightened with shell quilting, approximately 96 x 90in.
(Sotheby's) $1,610

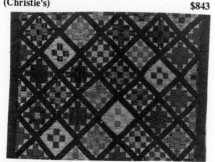

A pieced cotton and calico 'Album Blocks' quilt, American, circa 1878, composed of red, brown, blue and yellow pieced calico patches, approximately 74 x 66in.
(Sotheby's) $920

A pieced cotton 'Pine Tree' quilt, American, circa 1900, composed of coral and white cotton patches, the field heightened with outline and leaf quilting, approximately 72 x 72in.
(Sotheby's) $862

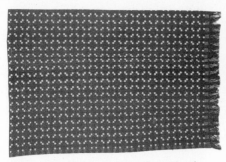

A woven wool coverlet, probably Pennsylvania, late 18th/early 19th century, woven in two double-sided panels, featuring a red, white and blue checker pattern on the obverse, 69½ x 87in.
(Christie's) $863

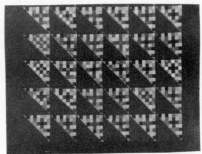

A pieced calico bird-in-flight quilt, American, circa 1900, within a wide green calico border heightened with rope quilting, approximately 76in x 76in.
(Sotheby's) $1,035

An Amish pieced wool sunshine and shadows quilt, probably Pennsylvania, 20th century, composed of pink, beige, red, black, blue, green, yellow and lavender patches, 80 x 73in.
(Sotheby's) $1,035

A pieced and appliquéd cotton floral quilt, American, 19th century, composed of green, yellow and red patches in a Tulip and Vine pattern, approximately 88 x 84in.
(Sotheby's) $575

A Tulip quilt, the large flowers of deep and pale pinks and ocher cotton, each stem with two side buds, quilted with waves, 78 x 80in., mid 19th century.
(Christie's) $438

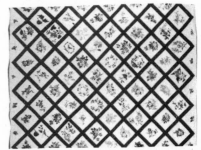

Applique friendship quilt, squares signed and dated 1844-47, panels with cut chintz flowers and birds appliqued onto white ground within printed green cotton borders, 104 x 106in.
(Skinner) $2,300

A Friendship quilt of printed cottons, of many colors plain and with small patterns, arranged in squares, 74 x 92in., second half 19th century. (Christie's) $546

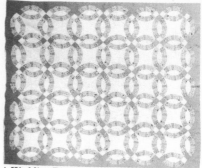

A Wedding Ring quilt, of brightly colored printed cottons against a white ground and within a rich pink border, 76 x 90in., 1930s. (Christie's) $640

A jacquard woven wool coverlet, American, 1830–1850, woven in two reversible panels, the central field decorated with crossed tulips, 103¹/₂ x 86in. (Christie's) $2,300

An appliqué quilt, of pale sea green and Turkey red cotton on a white ground, the center with a flower urn and leafy stems within a frame, 80 x 86in., American, late 19th/early 20th century. (Christie's) $286

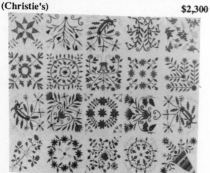

A pieced and appliquéd cotton floral album quilt top, American, circa 1850, composed of twenty-five squares each with green, red, yellow, blue and pink solid and calico patches, approximately 85 x 85in. (Sotheby's) $690

A pieced cotton 'Irish Chain' quilt, American, circa 1890, composed of slate blue, red and white cotton patches, the field heightened with cube and diagonal line quilting, approximately 84 x 72in. (Sotheby's) $575

Pieced and appliqued quilt, 19th century, red and yellow pin wheel design within blue and yellow borders, 86 x 88in.
(Skinner) $402

A wool jacquard woven coverlet, Emanuel Grube, 1813–1890, Warwick Township, Lancaster County, Pennsylvania, dated *1843*, 104 x 87¹/₂in. (Christie's) $1,725

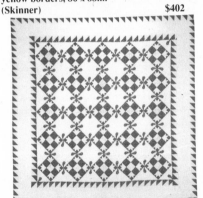

A pieced and appliqued cotton quilted coverlet, Lancaster County, Pennsylvania, dated *1847–50*, worked in twenty-five offset squares of green printed cotton calico, 92 x 89¹/₂in.
(Christie's) $1,725

A fine patchwork coverlet, of fresh printed cottons with predominantly pinkish and light colors, bordered by wide oblongs of flower prints, 92 x 96in., 19th century.
(Christie's) $438

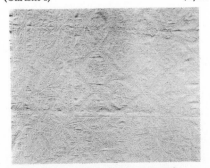

A cord quilted coverlet of white cotton, the field with flower stems arranged within a lattice design, the inner border with urns at each corner and spilling trailing flowers, 66 x 93in., possibly Portuguese, early 19th century.
(Christie's) $2,106

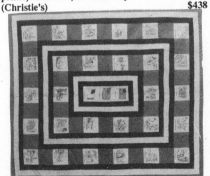

A pieced and embroidered cotton historical quilt, signed *Alice Mahoney*, Salmon, Idaho, dated *1931*, composed of red, white and blue fabric, at center the Colonies, United States and Confederate flags, 90 x 76in.
(Sotheby's) $3,450

A SABA 31W twin band receiver, circa 1931.
(Auction Team Köln) $231

5408 A Tefifon Holiday portable radio with tape recorder and one tape.
(Auction Team Köln) $500

A Crosley Model 56TD American bakelite radio.
(Auction Team Köln) $115

Pye 'Cambridge International' model P.E.80 radio, circa 1953.
(Chapman, Moore & Mugford) $21

A Siemens 'Giant dial' Type 41 W-134 two band mains receiver, circa 1929.
(Auction Team Köln) $577

A Siemens 22W mains single band receiver with 3 tubes and 'giant' dial, circa 1930.
(Auction Team Köln) $254

An AEG Deutschlandmeister 215WL single band straight receiver, circa 1935.
(Auction Team Köln) $154

A Telefunken 230W radio.
(Auction Team Köln) $423

An ARJ short wave transmitter.
(Auction Team Köln) $192

A SABA 311 WL two-band straight receiver, circa 1933.
(Auction Team Köln) $231

A Nora bakelite loudspeaker, circa 1930.
(Auction Team Köln) $254

An Ever Ready case radio, circa 1954.
(Auction Team Köln) $68

Bush VHF model 90A radio.
(Chapman, Moore & Mugford)
$15

A Johnson & Phillips induction
tuner in mahogany case.
(Auction Team Köln) $293

Westminster model Z.A.818
radio in a brown bakelite case,
LMS, circa 1948.
(Chapman, Moore & Mugford)
$48

Wartime civilian receiver,
battery model, MW only, circa
1944.
(Chapman, Moore & Mugford)
$30

An Ekco Mod. A22 Radio,
English, 1945.
(Auction Team Köln) $616

Bush BAC model 90A radio in a
bakelite case, circa 1950.
(Chapman, Moore & Mugford)
$38

RAP Translantic LMS radio in
a stepped walnut case, circa
1936.
(Chapman, Moore & Mugford)
$98

Fada maroon and yellow Catalin
Streamline 'Bullet' radio, model
1000, circa 1945, in maroon
plastic with yellow ocher handle,
$6^{3}/_{4}$in. high.
(Butterfield & Butterfield)
$1,150

A Siemens RFE 22 4-valve
neutrodyne receiver, circa 1928.
(Auction Team Köln)

$3,468

A 1-Telefunken-Super radio,
circa 1932.
(Auction Team Köln) $693

Ekco type AD 76 radio with
cracked top and non-original
dial separator.
(Chapman, Moore & Mugford)
$294

Mullard model MB 4 radio,
battery powered, circa 1935.
(Chapman, Moore & Mugford)
$24

The Beatles, a song sheet for 'Can't Buy Me Love', signed by all four on the picture cover.
(Bonhams) $2,512

Billy Fury, a brown knitted jumper featured on several record sleeves and a favorite of Billy's.
(Bonhams) $659

The Beatles, a plastic Beatle 45 single carry case to hold twelve singles.
(Bonhams) $329

Courtney Love, the well known Fender Jazzmaster acquired at the Empire Shepherds Bush on 10th May 1995 when Courtney smashed this instrument on stage and then threw it into the audience.
(Bonhams) $4,082

Jimi Hendrix, signed album page, with additional words *Be Groovy*, 3.75 x 2.5 in., together with a handbill advertising the Hendrix concert with The Move at the Theatre Royal Nottingham, Sunday 3rd Decmber 1967, 7 x 10in.
(Vennett Smith) $942

Clipped signature on white paper inscribed *Jim Morrison* in blue ink, together with black and white photocopied photograph, framed 17 x 13in.
(Butterfield & Butterfield) $748

The Who, signed album page by Pete Townshend, John Entwistle and Keith Moon individually, not signed by Daltrey.
(Vennett Smith) $235

Elton John shoes, a pair of oxford platform shoes of beige canvas with metallic lime green covering the quarter.
(Butterfield & Butterfield) $1,380

A black and white print of Madonna in an erotic pose smoking a cigarette, 8 x 10in., mounted, framed and glazed.
(Bonhams) $597

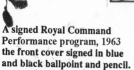

A signed Royal Command
Performance program, 1963
the front cover signed in blue
and black ballpoint and pencil.
(Sotheby's)   **$5,203**

Yoko Ono, signed color
postcard, of John and Yoko, by
Annie Leibovitz.
(Vennett Smith)   **$63**

Madonna, a tambourine, signed
boldly *Love Madonna* in large
red felt tip.
(Bonhams)   **$722**

Black and white studio
photograph of Bruce
Springsteen wearing jeans and
leather, signed *Bruce
Springsteen* in gold felt-tip
marker, framed 21^1/$_2$ x 17^1/$_2$in.
(Butterfield & Butterfield)
     $460

Album cover of the Blues
Brothers 1978 Atlantic Records
release Briefcase Full of Blues,
signed on middle, *Dan Aykroyd*
in blue marker and *John
Belushi* on upper right in blue
marker, 12^3/$_8$ x 12^3/$_8$in.
(Butterfield & Butterfield)
     $3,163

The Yardbirds, a full set of
signatures of the original line up
mounted with an 8 x 10in.
photograph of the group and a
ticket for a Blackpool gig 11th
September 1965.
(Bonhams)   **$408**

A black and white photograph
of Buddy Holly playing guitar,
signed by him in black biro,
mounted, framed and glazed,
6^1/$_2$ x 8^1/$_2$in.
(Bonhams)   **$440**

Bob Dylan custom 1990 burnt
siena Softail Harley Davidson,
includes State of California
Certificate of Title signed *Bob
Dylan* twice in black ink and
issued on 10/30/93.
(Butterfield & Butterfield)
     $28,750

A music song sheet for the song
that put The Who on the Mod
map 'My Generation', signed by
all group members on the front
page, mounted, framed and
glazed.
(Bonhams)   **$502**

Buddy Holly, and The Crickets, signed small album page, also by Joe Mauldin and Jerry Allison, dated in another hand *17th March 1958.*
(Vennett Smith) $816

A large banner of black cotton edged in red felt decorated at the center with a printed emblem of two crossed hammers, 7 x 136in., a prop from the film Pink Floyd The Wall, MGM, 1982.
(Christie's) $1,382

The Rolling Stones, a souvenir tour program 1965, signed on the cover in blue ink by all five members of the group.
(Christie's) $640

An album slick Born in the U.S.A., 1981, signed in black felt pen by Bruce Springsteen, Clarence Clemons, Max Weinberg, Danny Federici, Garry Tallent, Roy Bittan and Nils Lofgren.
(Christie's) $1,122

A rare poster Southern Sounds '63, *Brian Poole & The Tremeloes and for the first time on Merseyside The Rolling Stones...*, New Brighton Tower, Friday, August 30th, 1963, 20 x 20in.
(Christie's) $1,553

A piece of paper signed in blue biro by *Jimi Hendrix* and *Noel Redding* and additionally signed and inscribed *Love Mitch xxx*, with a reproduction photograph of Hendrix and the Experience, $18^1/_4$ x $16^1/_2$in.
(Christie's) $1,553

Jimi Hendrix, a portrait photograph by Dezo Hoffmann of Hendrix dressed as Father Christmas, November, 1967, 12 x 10in.
(Christie's) $484

Genesis, a tambourine, signed and inscribed in black felt tip pen *luv Phil Collins, Mike Rutherford and Tony Banks*, $9^3/_4$in. diameter.
(Christie's) $448

The Beatles, an album, With The Beatles, 1963, Parlophone Records, signed on the front cover in black biro by all four members of The Beatles.
(Christie's) $2,244

Michael Jackson, signed and inscribed 8 x 10in., half-length in leather jacket.
(T. Vennett-Smith) $108

A rare ¼ inch reel-to-reel tape recording of Mick Jagger and Keith Richards performing at home with their first band in 1961, the mono recording made by one of Jagger's Dartford Grammar School classmates.
(Christie's) $77,134

Abba, signed edition of the Abba Magazine to front cover photo, by all four individually.
(T. Vennett-Smith) $85

A Swedish concert poster Led Zeppelin, February 26th, 1970, the lettering printed over details for a canceled concert scheduled for October 7th, 1969, 39 x 27½in.
(Christie's) $1,122

A piece of paper signed and inscribed in blue biro *Love To You forever Jimi Hendrix,* in common mount with a black and white reproduction of Hendrix, 16¾ x 16in.
(Christie's) $1,467

Buddy Holly And The Crickets, a Coral Records publicity postcard, 1958, signed on the front in black or blue biro by *Buddy Holly, Jerry Allison* and *Joe Mauldin,* 5⅛ x 3½in.
(Christie's) $829

The Beatles, a color photograph of The Beatles performing on The Ed Sullivan Show, February 9th, 1964, (printed later), 29 x 20in.
(Christie's) $310

The Beatles, a single record Love Me Do, 1962, Parlophone, signed on the label in blue ink by all four members of the group.
(Christie's) $3,626

A military police notebook signed and inscribed inside in pencil *Be Groovy Keep Kool, the Best of Success to you Jimi Hendrix,* May or August, 1967.
(Christie's) $1,033

THE BEATLES

An Elton John stage bodice, 1970s, black suede with multi-colored leather Egyptian design with matching belt.
(Sotheby's) $1,615

An autographed fan club card, 1963/1964, signed in blue ballpoint, 14 x 11cm.
(Sotheby's) $2,870

A life mask of David Bowie from the film The Man Who Fell To Earth, 1976, in white plaster, 24cm.
(Sotheby's) $933

John Lennon, a Ministry of Education printed application form for Admission To The Examinations in Art, 1959, Liverpool College of Art and completed in the candidate's hand.
(Christie's) $3,786

A scrap of paper signed and inscribed in black ink, circa 1955, *Best Wishes to you and A.S.T. luck & love yea Elvis Presley*, 2³/₄ x 5¹/₄in., and a membership card for the Elvis Presley Fan Club, 1955–60.
(Christie's) $550

A piece of paper signed in pencil Buddy Holly, circa 1957, in common mount with a photograph of the group signed recently *Jerry Allison* and *The Crickets, Joe Mauldin*, 20 x 12¹/₄in.
(Christie's) $653

Paul McCartney's handwritten lyrics for 'Getting Better', 1967, in black ink on headed paper for the Million Volt Light and Sound Rave, 21 x 30cm.
(Sotheby's) $251,160

A pair of Keith Moon's cowboy boots, 1970s, in tan leather and skin, size 9A, labeled *Sheplers Inc. The World's Largest Western Stores*.
(Sotheby's) $753

A signed cover of 'Radio Times', December 1963, signed by The Beatles in black ballpoint, additionally signed and insribed by *Roger Moffat*, 23 x 27cm.
(Sotheby's) $3,588

A Them concert poster, British, 1960s, in pink, yellow, black and white, 44.5 x 57cm.
(Sotheby's) $718

John Lennon, a head and shoulders portrait by Robert Freeman, 1965, 9 x 9in.
(Christie's) $482

A portrait poster, 1990, signed in blue felt pen *Madonna*, 35 x 25in.
(Christie's) $361

Printed sheet music for I Should Have Known Better, signed and inscribed in red felt pen on the cover *John Lennon '74* and annotated with a small self-portrait caricature, 10³/₄ x 8¹/₄in., framed.
(Christie's) $1,807

A 'Valentine' awards coupon completed by John Lennon, 1969, the cutting from Disc and Music Echo completed in black ink by John, nominating himself as 'Mr Valentine 1969' and Yoko as 'Miss Valentine 1969'.
(Sotheby's) $12,917

John Lennon, two portrait photographs by Robert Freeman, one of the subject in a suit of armor, the other of Lennon disguised in a long beard and hat for a scene in the film Help!, both 1965.
(Christie's) $774

A pair of black suede gloves with shaped cuff decorated with gilt metal studs, labelled *Givenchy Paris*, the left glove signed in gold felt pen *Madonna*.
(Christie's) $688

A page taken from an autograph album, signed in black felt pen *Jimi Hendrix*, in common mount with a black and white publicity photograph of Hendrix.
(Christie's) $688

An original Rolling Stones' bass drumskin, 1960s, handpainted in black with the group's name and printed with the Gretsch trade mark.
(Sotheby's) $9,867

A concert poster for Canned Heat and Thin Lizzie (sic), Flamingo, Redruth, August 17th, circa mid 1970s, 30 x 20in. (Christie's) $414

The Beatles, small signed album page by all four individually, 3¹/₂ x 2¹/₂in., collected in person at a concert. (T. Vennett-Smith) $1,503

A poster for a Bob Dylan film Don't Look Back, Marquay Club, Town Hall, Torquay, July 18th, 1970, 30 x 20in. (Christie's) $345

John Lennon, a printed reproduction of a Bob Freeman portrait photograph inscribed *all the best John Lennon '79* and annotated with a self-portrait caricature, 11³/₄ x 11³/₄in. (Christie's) $1,467

A hand colored c-type portrait photograph by Elliot Landy of Bob Dylan, 1969 (colored later), inscribed in the margin in blue ink *Bob Dylan, Woodstock, For Eddie & Elizabeth from Elliot*, 16 x 11⁷/₈in. (Christie's) $1,036

John Lennon, a tan suede jacket with breast pockets and light brown cotton top-stitching, worn by Lennon in the photo session for the cover of the 1965 album Rubber Soul. (Christie's) $31,084

Bob Dylan, a two page typescript letter, signed, (n.d. but New York 1962), to a friend in Chicago and written in the form of a poem. (Christie's) $5,180

The Beatles, a piece of paper signed in black biro by all four members of the Beatles, circa 1964, with a reproduction of an early black and white publicity photograph. (Christie's) $1,381

The Bee Gees, an American presentation 'gold' single disk, How Deep Is Your Love, R.I.A.A. certified, Presented to Alan Kendall, 17 x 13in. (Christie's) $310

Paul McCartney, signed and inscribed 8 x 10in., half-length seated playing organ.
(T. Vennett-Smith) $233

The Beatles, a Beatles football of cream vinyl printed in black with portraits of the four Beatles, 23in.
(Christie's) $379

Michael Jackson, signed color 8 x 10in., three quarter length from one of his videos.
(T. Vennett-Smith) $74

The Beatles, a rare concert poster *The Beatles also The Fabulous Fortunes,* Town Hall Ballroom, Abergavenny, Saturday, June 22nd, 1963, 20 x 15in.
(Christie's) $2,590

Madonna, an album sleeve I'm Breathless, inspired by the film Dick Tracy, 1990, Sire Records, signed on the front in blue felt pen *Love Madonna and Warren Beatty.*
(Christie's) $438

John Lennon, a piece of paper signed in blue biro *John Lennon and Yoko Ono,* in common mount with a reproduction of a black and white photograph of John and Yoko, 16^1/$_4$ x 12^1/$_4$in.
(Christie's) $655

John Lennon, a portrait photograph by Bob Whitaker, taken in the garden at Kenwood, Lennon's Weybridge home, 1965, 20 x 16in.
(Christie's) $1,381

Marc Bolan, a canceled British Passport issued on March 31st, 1967 with black and white photograph and signature of bearer Marc Feld and a certificate of vaccination against smallpox, signed *Mark (sic) Feld.*
(Christie's) $1,899

The Beatles, a souvenir concert program for The Beatles/Roy Orbinson Tour, May–June 1963, signed inside in black biro by all four Beatles and Roy Orbison.
(Christie's) $6,908

Brian Epstein/Bill J. Kramer, an autograph picture postcard, signed, frankmarked Malaga, May 6th, 1963, to Billy J. Kramer & The Dakotas *Sincere congratulations on the initial success of "Secret"!*
(Christie's) $655

A marine band Hohner harmonica signed by Bob Dylan in black felt tip, the case marked with a strip of white tape marked *C* for easy identification whilst in concert.
(Bonhams) $2,041

The Beatles, a Parlophone Records publicity postcard, 1963, signed on the front in blue biro by all four members of the group and inscribed in Lennon's hand *Best Wishes, John Lennon*, $3^1/2$ x $5^1/4$in.
(Christie's) $1,899

A black and white studio portrait photograph of Lulu standing beside a seated David Bowie, circa early 1970s, signed and inscribed in black felt pen *Love Lulu and Bowie '93 "the odd couple"*, $19^3/4$ x 13in.
(Christie's) $691

Elton John, a two piece suit of yellow cotton and a jacket of emerald green velvet trimmed in navy at the shoulders, both outfits circa 1970s.
(Christie's) $2,244

Nirvana, signed 8 x 10in., by Kurt Cobain, David Grohl and Krist Novessic, each with first names with typed provenance from their production and tour managers April 1994.
(T. Vennett-Smith) $341

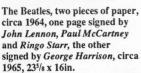

The Beatles, two pieces of paper, circa 1964, one page signed by *John Lennon, Paul McCartney* and *Ringo Starr*, the other signed by *George Harrison*, circa 1965, $23^5/8$ x 16in.
(Christie's) $880

An album cover Sgt. Pepper's Lonely Heart Club Band, 1967, Parlophone Records, signed in blue biro on the gatefold sleeve by all four members of the group.
(Christie's) $4,302

The Beatles, a page from a notepad signed in blue biro by each member of the group, circa 1963 and inscribed in McCartney's hand *Beatles*, 5 x $2^1/2$in.
(Christie's) $1,899

An Australian presentation 'platinum' sales award, The Best of The Doors, A.R.I.A. certified, Presented to Elektra International, 16¼ x 24in.
(Christie's) $1,294

The Beatles, an Apple Corps, pottery cheese dish shaped as a guitar, the cover decorated with photographic portraits of The Beatles and their printed names, 12½in.
(Christie's) $777

The Beatles, an early publicity postcard, April 5th 1962, signed and inscribed on the reverse, 4 x 6in., and a membership card for The Cavern Club, 1961.
(Christie's) $517

A rare poster *Eric Clapton presents his new group Derek and The Dominoes....* Marquay Club, Torquay Town Hall, Friday, August 21st, 1970, 30 x 20in.
(Christie's) $725

The Beatles, signed sheet of Royal Turks Head Hotel notepaper, Newcastle, 7 x 9in., collected by the receptionist Kathy, upon their visit to Newcastle in the early 1960s.
(T. Vennett-Smith) $946

The Jimi Hendrix Experience, a Track Records promotional postcard, August 1967, signed in blue biro by *Jimi Hendrix, Mitch Mitchell* and *Noel Redding*, 6 x 3¾in.
(Christie's) $1,208

Freddie Mercury, signed color 6 x 4in. composite postcard, featuring three images of Mercury.
(T. Vennett-Smith) $171

U2, an album cover War, 1983, Island Records, signed on the front in black felt pen in 1988 by all four members of the group.
(Christie's) $863

Keith Richards, an autograph letter, signed (n.d. but circa 1965), to a fan called Sal, telling her *I am glad you enjoyed the show at Rochester.*
(Christie's) $603

A Melody Maker' poster, 1964, red, black and white, 51 x 76cm. (Sotheby's)   **$897**

The Rolling Stones, signed, magazine photo (trimmed), by Jagger, Richards, Wyman, Watts and Jones, 13 x 8.5in. (Vennett Smith)   **$377**

Paul McCartney, signed postcard, half-length with guitar. (Vennett Smith)   **$82**

A rare Cavern handbill, 1963, for the period 27th March–12th April listing The Beatles and others, black on buff paper, 23 x 29cm. (Sotheby's)   **$3,588**

A questionnaire completed by John Lennon, 1963, as compiled by a fan, the questions/ categories regarding his likes and dislikes in food, drink, women etc., postmarked *Mossley Hill 2 Jly 1963 Liverpool.* (Sotheby's)   **$1,794**

Donovan, a presentation 'gold' single disk, Mellow Yellow, R.I.A.A. certified, white matte format, *Presented to Ashley Kozak*, 17¼ x 13¼in., framed. (Christie's)   **$2,066**

The Beatles, signed sheet of Imperial Hotel Torquay notepaper, by all four, together with a letter of provenance. (Vennett Smith)   **$1,068**

Jimi Hendrix, a shirt of pink satin hand-embroidered on the front with a pattern of flamingos and trees in multi-colored silks, accompanied by a letter of authenticity from Ralph Berenson. (Christie's)   **$3,098**

A concert poster, *James Brown and Revue*, Fri. Oct. 4, Rhode Island Auditorium, circa early 1960s, 28¼ x 21½in. (Christie's)   **$653**

Paul McCartney, signed postcard, 6 x 4in. (Vennett Smith) $97

Take That, signed color, by all five, 12 x 9.5in. (Vennett Smith) $235

Simon & Garfunkel, signed color, by both, 8 x 10in. (Vennett Smith) $95

A silkscreened Global Promotions tour poster presenting the American recording star Ben E. King. (Bonhams) $345

Bob Dylan's harmonica, the Hohner 'Marine Band' instrument signed in black marker, with a copy of a statement of authenticity from César Diaz, Dylan's equipment technician. (Sotheby's) $3,409

Roy Orbison, signed postcard, head and shoulders, also with stamped signature. (Vennett Smith) $97

A concert poster *Canned Heat and Lindisfarne*, Marquay, Torquay Town Hall, August 18th, circa mid 1970s, 30 x 20in. (Christie's) $550

A black wool beret, signed and inscribed in gold felt pen *Love Madonna*, and a black and white machine-print photograph of Madonna wearing a similar beret, 14 1/4 x 11 1/2in. (Christie's) $1,033

Queen, signed magazine photo, from a German magazine, signed by Freddie Mercury and the other three, 8 x 11.5in. (Vennett Smith) $353

The Rolling Stones, a publicity postcard, circa 1965, signed on the front in blue ink by all five members of the group, 3$^1/_2$ x 5$^1/_2$in.
(Christie's) $516

A pair of John Lennon's glasses, thin, gold-colored frames with oval, yellow-tinted prescription lenses.
(Sotheby's) $6,638

An album The Beatles & Frank Ifield On Stage, 1964, rare black rainbow Vee-Jay label with bracketed logo and 'portrait' sleeve, mono.
(Christie's) $1,893

John Lennon/Kenwood, a leather-clad metal-lined bulbous barrel and cover, 9$^1/_2$in. high with a letter from Cynthia Lennon stating that John used this barrel for *...stashing his marijuana and cigarette papers at Weybridge....*
(Christie's) $8,262

A concert ticket for The Beatles, at the Grosvenor, Prince of Wales Road, Norwich, Friday, May 17th, 1963, and signed in blue ink by all four members of the group, 2$^3/_8$ x 3$^5/_8$in.
(Christie's) $2,237

A white Remo Weather King drumhead, signed and inscribed in black felt pen *The Beach Boys, Bruce Johnston, Brian Wilson, Carl Wilson, Al Jardine and Love, Mike Love,* 14in. diameter.
(Christie's) $516

A silkscreen print of a photograph of Jimi Hendrix by Gered Mankowitz, signed and numbered in pencil 119/500 by photographer, 40 x 30in., framed.
(Christie's) $223

Led Zeppelin, a color print of the cover image of Houses Of The Holy, signed in blue or silver felt pen by Robert Plant, Jimmy Page and John Paul Jones, 10$^1/_4$ x 11$^1/_4$in.
(Christie's) $344

A souvenir concert program for The Beatles/Roy Orbison Tour, May-June 1963, signed inside in blue biro by all four Beatles, Roy Orbison, Gerry and the Pacemakers and others.
(Christie's) $2,754

A signed copy of the star special 'Meet the Beatles' magazine, 1963, the central double-page black and white photograph signed in blue ballpoint.
(Sotheby's) $3,947

A pair of John Lennon's glasses, circa 1961, circular prescription lenses, metal frames with reinforcing cotton to bridge and one ear-piece.
(Sotheby's) $3,409

Stuart Sutcliffe, a rare five and a half page autograph letter, signed, (n.d. but Oct/Nov 1960) to an old girlfriend and fellow art student Susan Williams.
(Christie's) $2,237

Queen, a miniature pocket diary for 1974 signed and inscribed on the back cover *Love to Hev, Freddie Mercury,* additionally signed and inscribed inside, 3 x 2^1/$_8$in.
(Christie's) $515

A postcard made from a snapshot of Elvis Presley standing between two women, signed on the reverse in blue ink *Elvis Presley,* circa late 1950s, 5^1/$_2$ x 3^1/$_2$in.
(Christie's) $551

John Lennon, a publicity photograph, 1963, signed by subject in blue biro, 10 x 8in., with a concert ticket for the Roy Orbison/The Beatles Show, June 5th, 1963.
(Christie's) $1,118

A copy of the program for the Garden Fête, St. Peter's Church Field, Woolton, Liverpool, Saturday, 6th July 1957. It was on this day that John Lennon first met Paul McCartney.
(Sotheby's) $7,176

A wide-brimmed hat of black felt, the brim signed and inscribed in silver felt pen *Love Stevie Nicks,* accompanied by a concert program for Fleetwood Mac, 1987.
(Christie's) $413

An EP sleeve, King Creole, 1958, RCA Records, signed on the reverse in black ink by Elvis Presley, with a reproduction of the EP front cover and a printed songsheet for King Creole, 9^1/$_4$ x 15in.
(Christie's) $601

A concert poster for Bruce Springsteen and The E Street Band and The Clash, Spanish, 1981, in green, 70 x 98cm.
(Sotheby's) $502

A good signed poster of The Rolling Stones, 1963/4, black and white with signatures in blue ballpoint, 58.5 x 49cm.
(Sotheby's) $1,345

A French presentation 'gold' sales award, The Doors, *Presented to Elektra Records*, $18^{1}/_{2}$ x $14^{1}/_{2}$in., framed.
(Christie's) $447

Jimi Hendrix's peacock feather waistcoat, 1967/8, sold with a color poster and two photographs of Jimi wearing the garment and a letter of provenance.
(Sotheby's) $37,674

An EP The Rolling Stones, 1964, Decca, the sleeve signed on reverse in blue biro or ink by Brian Jones, Keith Richards, Mick Jagger, Bill Wyman and Charlie Watts.
(Christie's) $344

The Beatles, a publicity postcard, 1963, signed on the reverse in blue ink or biro by all four members of the group and inscribed *love...* in McCartney's hand, 5 x $3^{1}/_{2}$in.
(Christie's) $2,066

A Who concert poster, 1971, for the Top Rank Suite, Sunderland, black and white, 51 x 76cm., mounted, framed and glazed.
(Sotheby's) $448

A signed photograph of Jimi Hendrix, 1967, the color picture from Record Mirror, mounted on paper backing, 20.5 x 16cm.
(Sotheby's) $1,794

A Buddy Holly and the Crickets concert poster, British, 1958, for their appearance at the Liverpool Philharmonic Hall, 20th March, 43.5 x 63cm.
(Sotheby's) $1,794

A concert poster for The Move and The Nice, British, circa 1967, red and black on fluorescent yellow, 51 x 76cm.
(Sotheby's) $753

An early signed publicity photograph, 1963, the black and white group portrait signed in blue ballpoint, 20 x 21.5cm.
(Sotheby's) $3,946

Four photographs of John and Yoko Ono Lennon at their wedding in Gibraltar, 20th March 1969.
(Sotheby's) $2,511

An album Two Virgins, 1968, Apple records, signed and inscribed on the front cover in black biro *JohnLennon '79* and annotated with a small self-portrait caricature.
(Christie's) $1,634

John Lennon, a portable reed organ with three and a half octave keyboard, seven stops and lyre shaped supports containing airways, with a letter from Cynthia Lennon.
(Christie's) $6,885

A black and white fold-out poster of Lennon recording at his white Steinway piano issued with the Imagine album 1971, signed and inscribed *love John Lennon*, 22 x 22in.
(Christie's) $1,548

John Lennon, a scrap of paper signed and insribed in blue biro *love to Noreen from The Beatles, John Lennon xxx, 1963*, 4¼ x 3¼in.
(Christie's) $774

U2, an album cover The Joshua Tree, 1987, Island Records, signed on the front in silver felt pen by all four members of the group.
(Christie's) $413

John Lennon, printed sheet music for She Loves You, signed and inscribed in red felt pen of the cover *John Lennon, 74 (really 63)*.
(Christie's) $1,463

A fine Kashmir rug, North India, of Mughal design, the soft red field decorated with a leaf latticework, within a red border, 2.88m. x 1.57m.
(Phillips) **$6,247**

A Sultanabad carpet, Central Persia, the indigo field with all over interlocking mina khani decoration, 3.64m. x 2.67m.
(Phillips) **$2,082**

Pictorial hooked rug, America, 20th century, central reserve of eagle in flight on gray and green field with double border of stars and oak leaves, 72in. x 47½in.
(Skinner) **$2,415**

A fine Heriz carpet, the ivory field with overall design of various polychrome stylized hooked palmettes, surrounded by shaded indigo border, 342cm. x 271cm.
(Christie's) **$4,475**

Navajo Two Grey Hills rug, centering on elongated terraced diamond medallion, within hooked and plumed outlines, 7ft. 1in. x 4ft.
(Butterfield & Butterfield) **$1,092**

A fine antique Heriz carpet, the deep indigo field with angular vines connecting various polychrome serrated palmettes and leaves around large rust medallion, 354cm. x 268cm.
(Christie's) **$4,302**

Senneh rug, Northwest Persia, late 19th century, large stepped red hexagonal medallion on the Herati decorated midnight blue field, 6ft. 4in. x 4ft. 7in.
(Skinner) **$690**

Karabagh prayer rug, South Caucasus, dated 1899, rows of flowering plants in red, gold, violet, red-brown, green, and dark blue-green on the camel field, 5ft. 8in. by 3ft. 5in.
(Skinner) **$1,610**

An antique silk Tabiz rug, North West Persia, the plain copper-red field containing a large floral medallion within ivory floral spandrels, 1.76m. x 1.3m.
(Phillips) **$5,950**

A fine Lesghi rug, North East Caucasus, the indigo field with scattered rosettes and pairs of hooked motifs, 1.92m. x 1.28m. (Phillips) **$3,040**

A Kerman pictorial rug, South East Persia, the indigo field with figures, angels and birds, within complementary indigo border, 7ft. 3in. x 4ft. 11in. (Sotheby's) **$5,348**

A Kashan prayer rug, Central Persia, the indigo mihrab with a central decoration of vases of flowers, 2.02m. x 1.33m. (Phillips) **$1,216**

Navajo pictorial rug, centering an eight-pointed Vallero star, large rooster figures above and below, in red, brown, gray-brown and white, 4ft. 9in. x 3ft. (Butterfield & Butterfield) **$1,610**

An antique Fereghan kelleh, West Persia, circa 1850/60, the shaded indigo field with overall stylized open lattice containing polychrome angular palmettes and floral sprays, 13ft. 5in. x 6ft. 10in. (Christie's) **$2,797**

Navajo Germantown rug, the borderless weaving in a serrated diamond lattice pattern, the finely toothed lozenges in contrasting colors, 5ft. 3in. x 3ft. 4in. (Butterfield & Butterfield) **$1,725**

A Bijar rug, brick field with pale blue jewel pendant center medallion, all over mina-khani design, 7ft. 6in. x 4ft. 10in. (Woolley & Wallis) **$1,805**

Bidjov rug, Northeast Caucasus, last quarter 19th century, columns of palmette and leaf motifs on the midnight blue field, ivory border, 5ft. 4in. by 4ft. 4in. (Skinner) **$1,495**

A Fachralo Kazak rug, South West Caucasus, the medium blue field with stylized animals and rosettes around three medallions, 2.02m. x 1.40m. (Phillips) **$4,560**

RUGS

An antique silk Kashan carpet, Central Persia, the ivory field decorated with a profusion of flowering trees with various animals, 3.62m. x 2.52m.
(Phillips) $1,413

A Karagashli rug, indigo field with center row of three brick palmettes, flanked by snowflake motifs and brick split palmettes, 4ft. 4in. x 3ft. 6in.
(Woolley & Wallis) $1,216

A Yuruk rug, East Anatolia, comprising: two geometric medallions on an indigo and copper-red field, 1.73m. x 1.11m.
(Phillips) $669

An antique Kuba rug, North East Caucasus, the copper-red field with an all over symmetrical design of geometric lozenges, within a rosette border, 94cm. x 73cm.
(Phillips) $1,116

A fine Heriz carpet, the shaded rust field with angular vines connecting multicolored hooked and serrated palmettes and large leaves, 12ft. 5in. x 8ft. 6in.
(Christie's) $1,237

A fine Fachralo Kazak prayer rug, South West Caucasus, the bottle-green mihrab filled with rosette shrubs centered by an ivory and copper-red medallion, 1.9m. x 1.16m.
(Phillips) $1,184

Kurd rug, Northwest Persia, early 20th century, stepped hexagonal medallion with "anchor" pendants in midnight and royal blue, 6ft. 4in. by 3ft. 8in.
(Skinner) $1,150

A Kazak prayer rug, pale blue mihrab, indented at the base, two winged diamond shape brick center motifs, 4ft. 5in. x 3ft. 7in.
(Woolley & Wallis) $2,052

Kazak rug, Southwest Caucasus, late 19th century, very large gabled square medallion on the rust field, sky blue floral meander border, 6ft. 6in. by 4ft. 6in.
(Skinner) $1,092

An antique Heriz rug, North West Persia, the orange-red field with pale blue stylized vines around a light beige and ivory medallion, 1.97m. x 1.57m.
(Phillips) $3,570

Karadja rug, Northwest Persia, early 20th century, two large medallions on the navy blue field, red star border, 4ft. 4in. by 3ft. 6in.
(Skinner) $977

An antique Shirvan rug, East Caucasus, the indigo field with scattered rosettes and hooked motifs around the two lozenge medallions, 1.5m. x 1.13m.
(Phillips) $2,082

An antique Cheleberd rug, South Caucasus, with characteristic singular sunburst medallion within an ivory rosette and vine border, 1.73m. x 1.45m.
(Phillips) $1,636

A large Tekke carpet, Turkmenistan, late 19th century, the blood-red field with vertical rows of linked Tekke guls divided by cruciform motifs, 16ft. 2in. x 11ft. 9in.
(Christie's) $3,670

Hamadan rug, Northwest Persia, second quarter 20th century, rosette medallion and floral sprays on the red field, midnight blue border, 5ft. x 3ft. 6in.
(Skinner) $373

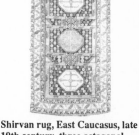

Karabagh rug, South Caucasus, late 19th century, two large hexagonal medallions inset with cloud bands on the rust field, royal blue border, 6ft. 10in. x 4ft. 4in.
(Skinner) $1,035

Edouard Bénédictus for Aubusson, Art Deco carpet, circa 1925, wool, profusely decorated with polychrome cascades of stylized flowers, 400 x 290cm.
(Sotheby's) $19,079

Shirvan rug, East Caucasus, late 19th century, three octagonal medallions and numerous small rosettes on the midnight blue field, ivory border, 6ft. 2in. x 3ft. 9in.
(Skinner) $1,035

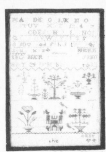

A sampler by Mary Herring, 1793, worked in colored silks in cross stitch with alphabets and numerals, 9½ x 13½in., framed and glazed.
(Christie's) $342

A sampler by Elizabeth Palfrey, 1811, finely worked on colored in cross and satin stitch with three verses 'Parent of good...', 11½ x 15in., framed and glazed.
(Christie's) $2,808

A needlework sampler, signed *Phebe Giles*, English, dated *June 23, 1826*, worked on a linen ground with alphabets above a pious verse, 18 x 12¾in.
(Sotheby's) $2,587

A wool-on-linen needlework sampler, signed *Susana Schultz*, Southeastern Pennsylvania, circa 1800–1820, the square plain woven linen ground worked in three enclosed horizontal registers, 10⅝ x 10⅝in.
(Christie's) $3,450

A cotton-on-linen needlework sampler, signed *Elmanda Donges*, Stouchsburg, Berks County, and dated *1845*, with two taupe and blue alphabetical bands above wrought verse, 17 x 12in.
(Christie's) $4,600

A sampler by Elizabeth Clarkson, 1826, worked in colored wools in cross stitch with mainly alphabets and numerals and a verse 'We stand expos'd...' 11½ x 16½in., framed and glazed.
(Christie's) $381

A sampler by Sarah Wilkinson, MDCCCII, worked in fine cross stitch in mainly shades of green, brown and cream with 'The Lords Prayer', 11½ x 16in., framed and glazed, 1802.
(Christie's) $702

A needlework sampler, Hannah Ford, Norwich, Connecticut, dated *October 12, 1764*, bands of alphabets centering a blossoming vine above a pious verse, 9½ x 7¼in.
(Sotheby's) $10,350

A sampler by Mary Ann Merscy, 1821, of brightly colored silks in fine cross stitch, with various alphabets and numerals and a verse 'On Benevolence', 13 x 17in.
(Christie's) $1,539

A charming sampler by Sarah White, 1831, worked in mainly shades of green, brown and cream silks in cross stitch, 12¹/₂ x 16in., framed and glazed.
(Christie's) $1,454

Needlework sampler, wrought by *Ruth Leach 1732*, silk threads on linen ground, 11.75 by 8.5in. (sight), framed.
(Skinner) $977

A sampler by Mary Kendell, 1786, worked in pink, brown, green silks in cross stitch with 'A Part of the 16th Psalm 7 Verse', 13 x 16¹/₃in.
(Christie's) $193

A sampler by Elizabeth Ann Warden, 1839, worked in cross stitch in shades of green, blue, cream and brown silks with a verse 'Lord What is Life?...', 13 x 15in.
(Christie's) $527

A sampler by Alice Watson, 1797, worked in cross stitch in mainly shades of green, brown, blue and black silks with a verse 'Honour bestow...', 12 x 20in., framed and glazed.
(Christie's) $1,140

Needlework sampler, *L.H. 1842* birds, flowers and patterns worked in silk, metallic, wool and chenille threads decorated with beads and sequins, 21.5 x 20.75in., framed.
(Skinner) $1,725

A sampler by Emma Parker, 1828, worked in colored silks with three verses, spot motifs including angels, windmills and stags, Adam and Eve, 12 x 15in., framed and glazed.
(Christie's) $193

A sampler by Elizabeth Morris, 1808, worked in brightly colored silks in cross stitch on a coarse linen ground, with alphabets and numerals, 9¹/₂ x 17in.
(Christie's) $479

A sampler by S. Hodginson, worked in mainly shades of green, brown and cream silks with a verse 'Religion' in black silk, 12¹/₂ x 12in., framed and glazed, circa 1830.
(Christie's) $438

A sampler by Hestera Harmer, 1843, worked in mainly shades of green, brown and ivory silks with a verse 'All you my Friends...', 12 x 17in.
(Christie's) $589

An Adam and Eve sampler by Mary Clark, 1798, Adam and Eve standing on a hillocked ground flanked by birds and animals, 18½ x 16½in.
(Christie's) $640

A sampler by Mary Clark, 1826, worked in colored silks with a verse 'Remember thy creator...', with Adam and Eve above, 13 x 17in., framed and glazed.
(Christie's) $810

A sampler by Mary Ann Cater, 1839, worked in green silks with alphabets and numerals and a verse 'Advice' flanked by colored flower posies, 11in. square., framed and glazed.
(Christie's) $472

A fine needlework sampler, signed *Sarah W. West*, Bennington School, probably New Jersey, dated *1824*, with an imposing manor house flanked by blossoming vines and trees, 20 x 24½in.
(Sotheby's) $4,600

A sampler by Mary Ann Thomas, 1846, worked in shades of green, cream and brown silks with a verse 'Jesus permit...', 19½ x 21½in., framed and glazed.
(Christie's) $927

A fine needlework sampler, signed *M. Campbell, Philadelphia*, dated *1797*, executed in a variety of green, blue, ocher, brown and cream silk stitches, 17 x 14⅝in.
(Sotheby's) $14,950

A needlework sampler, signed *Eunice Ladd*, Canterbury region, New Hampshire, early 19th century, olive-green wool ground with bands of alphabets and numerals, 15¾ x 18in.
(Sotheby's) $4,025

A needlework sampler, signed *Sarah Jenckes*, Bristol, Rhode Island, circa 1786, central panel divided into horizontal registers with elegantly dressed figures, 15⅝ x 11⅛in.
(Sotheby's) $20,700

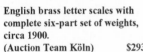

English brass letter scales with complete six-part set of weights, circa 1900.
(Auction Team Köln) $293

Portable beam-balance, brass on mahogany base with drawer.
(Auction Team Köln) $137

Fairbanks cast iron and brass scales, with three weights.
(Auction Team Köln) $115

The Twentieth Century Scale, large American grocery scales of brass mounted cast iron, 1909, 85 cm. high.
(Auction Team Köln) $207

French precision balance by Mulatière, Lyon, brass stand with bronze pans, on turned wood foot, with twelve weights, circa 1900.
(Auction Team Köln) $693

A decorative English Lion Quick Action counter scales, with ten brass weights.
(Auction Team Köln) $184

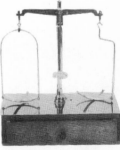

A grocery inspection balance by De Grave, London, marked *London County Council,* aluminium in mahogany case.
(Auction Team Köln) $169

Large brass grain scales, with wooden base with drawer and with brass weights, Austrian, circa 1930.
(Auction Team Köln) $423

Chemist's scales by Sanger, London, to weigh 2 oz., on wooden base with drawer and 5 brass and 16 fine weights, circa 1900.
(Auction Team Köln) $115

A Singer electric table sewing machine with wooden case and spares in wooden box, with shuttle, circa 1920.
(Auction Team Köln) $65

A German Guhl & Harbeck Original Express chainstitch machine, circa 1890.
(Auction Team Köln) $95

An early American New England chain stitch sewing machine with fiddle-shaped sewing plate, circa 1865.
(Auction Team Köln) $293

A Davis sewing machine, with bow shuttle head, with shuttle and on carved wood housing, circa 1878.
(Auction Team Köln) $423

A Monarch sewing machine, with C-frame, brass end-plate embossed *The Monarch – Smith & Co. 30 Edgware Rd. and Charles St. Soho London.*
(Christie's) $663

A Raymond English chainstitch machine with cast iron plate for *Louis Beckh, Mannheim,* circa 1873.
(Auction Team Köln) $423

A rare German 'Mary' chain stitch machine by Müller, circa 1890.
(Auction Team Köln)
$2,929

An early American Gold Medal bow shuttle machine with gold line and floral decoration, lacks shuttle, circa 1875.
(Auction Team Köln) $293

A Shaw & Clark American chain stitch machine with closed tower, US patents 1863 and 1865 (copies attached), circa 1866.
(Auction Team Köln) $924

A Bartlett type American chain stitch machine with Swedish retailer's plate, *Joh. Hedlund,* circa 1870.
(Auction Team Köln) $323

An H J Hancock American cast iron chain stitch machine, circa 1867.
(Auction Team Köln) $2,004

A Howe-type bow shuttle machine , on plinth, with shuttle, circa 1880.
(Auction Team Köln) $196

The Tabitha Sewing Machine, a small chain stitch tinplate toy machine by Daniel Judson & Son, London & New York, circa 1885.
(Auction Team Köln) $423

Victorian walnut veneered sewing machine cabinet, in the form of a davenport, top with stationery compartment, writing slope with leatherette inset fitted interior, 24in.
(Peter Wilson) $1,087

French Avrial Legat bow shuttle machine with 'pump' drive, on cast iron plinth and with gold decoration and mother of pearl inlay, circa 1880.
(Auction Team Köln) $1,522

A Meitiz Model 2 Russian child's chain stitch sewing machine, after the Casige No. 16, circa 1925.
(Auction Team Köln) $85

A rare example of the American Fairy/Mme Demorest Gold Medal running stitch machine, circa 1865.
(Auction Team Köln) $1,155

Rare German Original Express chain stitch machine, by Casige, circa 1935.
(Auction Team Köln) $462

Rocking chair, Mount Lebanon, New York, maple, three slat back, rockers pinned through legs, #4 on back of slat. (Skinner) **$402**

Stove, cast iron, wooden knob, canted sides, rare three-leg form with penny foot, hinged door with latch, 17$\frac{1}{2}$in. high. (Skinner) **$805**

Tall two-door cupboard, circa 1800, pine, door over door, applied bracket base with arched cut-outs, 49$\frac{1}{4}$in. wide. (Skinner) **$17,250**

Cupboard (top section of secretary), circa 1860, chestnut, pine, porcelain knobs, brass hinges, two paneled doors, interior containing numerous pigeonholes, 42$\frac{1}{2}$in. wide. (Skinner) **$747**

Double cupboard over case of drawers, probably Groveland, New York, circa 1840, pine, built in two sections with removable cupboard top, 36$\frac{1}{2}$in. wide. (Skinner) **$27,600**

One-door cupboard, believed to have come from Sabbathday Lake, Maine, circa 1790, pine, case pegged together, single board overhanging top, 36$\frac{1}{2}$in. wide (at base) (Skinner) **$17,250**

Wood box, purchased at Canterbury, New Hampshire, pine, iron hinges and hooks, chest with hinged lid and one drawer, 23$\frac{3}{4}$in. wide. (Skinner) **$3,220**

Swing-handle basket, wooden bottom, ash, iron nails, sawn-handle attached through ear handles which are double notched, 11in. diameter. (Skinner) **$316**

Tool cupboard, Harvard, Massachusetts, circa 1875, pine, walnut drawer fronts, gray paint, later iron hardware, 38$\frac{3}{4}$in. wide. (Skinner) **$1,955**

Four-door cupboard, circa 1860, butternut and pine, wooden pulls, iron hinges, shellac or varnish finish, 49in. wide. (Skinner) $2,760

Round grain measure, oak and pine, natural color, circa 1880-1896, 7¹/₂in. diameter. (Skinner) $230

Rocking chair, Canterbury, New Hampshire, maple, woven multi-colored tape seat, three-slat back. (Skinner) $920

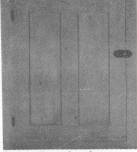

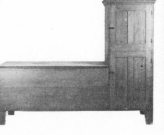

Cupboard, purchased at Canterbury, New Hampshire, circa 1870, pine, original bright yellow stain, replacement iron latch, 25¹/₂in. wide. (Skinner) $1,955

Lift-top chest and cupboard, circa 1840, a unique furniture piece acquired at Canterbury, New Hampshire, pine, cupboard has two paneled doors, each with sliding spring latch and original lock, 63⁵/₈in. high, 81in. long overall. (Skinner) $4,600

Sewing desk, Canterbury, New Hampshire or Sabbathday Lake, Maine, circa 1840, pine, fruitwood pulls, salmon paint, plank-sided case with ogee-shaped base, 26in. wide. (Skinner) $8,625

Hanging cupboard, from The Tailor's Shop building in Shaker Village, Harvard, Massachusetts, pine, old red paint, brass knob, 19in. wide. (Skinner) $977

One-drawer table, Enfield, New Hampshire, circa 1840, curly birch and pine, well-shaped deep ogee apron, finely turned legs, 36in. wide. (Skinner) $8,050

Pail, Canterbury or Enfield, New Hampshire, pine staves and bottom, original ocher-orange paint, diamond shaped bail plates, 10in. diameter. (Skinner) $1,380

Dust pan, acquired at Canterbury, New Hampshire, birch handle, inscribed on bottom *Harriet Johns 1880*, 13in. long.
(Skinner) **$3,680**

Oval carrier, Canterbury, New Hampshire, pine, maple or birch and ash handle, brown stain, shellac finish, 9in. diameter.
(Skinner) **$805**

School desk, possibly Harvard, Massachusetts, pine, grain-painted red-orange, slant-top school desk, fitted with leather straps on each side, 66in. long.
(Skinner) **$1,150**

Apple corer and slicer, acquired at Canterbury, New Hampshire, round base, riveted construction, four quarter-round cutting blades, 4⁵/₈in. diameter.
(Skinner) **$86**

Stipple-line engraving, *SHAKERS near LEBANON state of N YORK,/their mode of Worship./Drawn from Life.*, artist unknown, hand-colored circa 1830, 8³/₄ x 12³/₄in.
(Skinner) **$1,955**

Basket, square bottom, round top, bonnet-shaped handle single notched, single wrap over shaped rims, 10¹/₂in. diameter.
(Skinner) **$172**

Side chair, Mount Lebanon, New York, maple, rush seat, tilters, three arched slats, boldly turned acorn finials.
(Skinner) **$1,035**

Rare three-drawer blanket box, Enfield or Canterbury, New Hampshire, circa 1848, with through mortised paneled lid, pine, original red-orange paint, iron hinges and lock, 49⁵/₈in. long.
(Skinner) **$140,000**

Collapsible swift, pine, maple, yellow wash, dated on blade *1852*, in ink on base *Laundry No. 12*, 25¹/₂in. high overall.
(Skinner) **$1,840**

Lap-desk, butternut, cherry and poplar, old varnish finish, finely doveetailed, slant top writing surface, with breadboard end, 21in. wide.
(Skinner) $3,737

Drop leaf table, pine, ash, and birch, retains traces of red paint, boldly turned legs, 71½in. long.
(Skinner) $2,070

One-drawer table, Canterbury, New Hampshire, circa 1850, pine, red paint, two board top, mortised case, finely turned tapered legs, 60¾in. long.
(Skinner) $2,300

Pail, Canterbury or Enfield, New Hampshire, pine staves and bottom, original chrome yellow paint, interior painted white, 5⅜in. high.
(Skinner) $1,035

Lithograph, Shaker Village, Alfred, Maine, circa 1880, after a drawing by Phares F. Goist, titled below image, sheet 10½ x 14½in.
(Skinner) $115

Side chair, Canterbury, New Hampshire, maple, three graduated arched slats, front legs are tapered.
(Skinner) $805

Small strainer with handle, formed flared bowl with integral punched-screen bottom, turned handle painted black, bowl 4¼in. diameter.
(Skinner) $46

Oval carrier, probably Canterbury, New Hampshire, circa 1840–70, pine, maple and ash (?) handle, original yellow paint, three fingers, 9⅜in. diameter.
(Skinner) $28,750

Foot stool, pine, brown stain, nailed five board construction, sides have semi-circular cut-outs at feet, 14¾in. wide.
(Skinner) $747

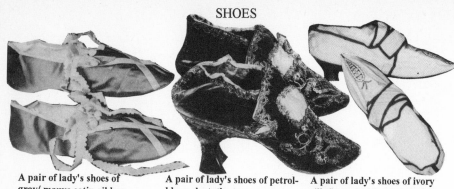

A pair of lady's shoes of gray/mauve satin ribbon, inscribed *Shoes worn at a fancy ball in 1828.*
(Christie's) $1,648

A pair of lady's shoes of petrol-blue velvet, the toes embroidered with gilt metal threads and spangles.
(Bonhams) $425

A pair of lady's shoes of ivory silk figured with a tiny check design, the latchets, pointed tongue and edges bound with crimson silk, 1780's.
(Christie's) $7,135

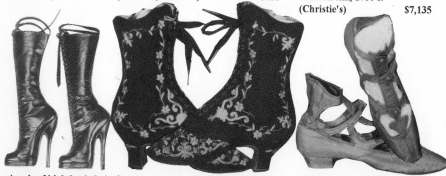

A pair of high-heeled platform boots, of chocolate brown leather with twenty-six hole lacing, 7in. shaped heel and 1/2in. sole, with strap at top of leg, 1940s.
(Christie's) $1,012

A pair of laced lady's boots of fine grosgrain crimson silk, embroidered in yellow silks with trailing flowers and strapwork, *F. Pinet, Paris,* the sole also stamped, *1867.*
(Christie's) $2,375

A pair of lady's shoes of sea green silk, with rounded toe and cut-out button straps securing over a central bar, late 19th/early 20th century.
(Christie's) $1,100

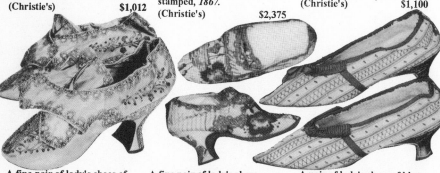

A fine pair of lady's shoes of pale blue and ivory satin, the toes and sides embroidered with stylized fruit and floral sprays, mid 18th century.
(Bonhams) $875

A fine pair of lady's shoes covered in ivory silk with a self-colored design and brocaded in shades of bright crimson, mid 18th century.
(Christie's) $7,645

A pair of lady's shoes of blue and white ticking embroidered in pale blue and maroon silk with a fleck design and herringbone pattern, late 18th century.(Christie's) $6,950

American School, 19th century, a painted full-length silhouette portrait of a young woman, watercolor and gouache on paper, 9 x 7¹/₈in. (Sotheby's) $1,380

Auguste Edouart (1789–1861), the Josiah Quincy family: a silhouette conversation group, free-hand cut black paper mounted on a wash paper ground, 16¹/₂ x 28¹/₂in. (Sotheby's) $17,250

American School 19th century, a hollow-cut silhouette bust portrait of Lydia Watson, cut white paper mounted over brown fabric, 15 x 11¹/₄in. (Sotheby's) $920

Silhouette portrait of a lady, full-length with hollow-cut head, watercolor and ink body, 7.4 x 3.5in. (Skinner) $4,312

American School, dated 1841, a pair of reverse painted silhouette conversation groups depicting notable American statesman, reverse painting on glass, 9³/₈ x 11³/₈in. (Sotheby's) $2,587

A fine full-length silhouette-on-glass portrait of Nicolo Paganini on stage, inscribed *Paganini*, attributed to J. Woodhouse circa 1830, 22.5 x 30cm. (Phillips) $1,848

American School, a full-length free-cut silhouette portrait of a gentleman, free-cut black paper mounted on a lithograph ground, circa 1830. (Sotheby's) $1,035

An oval framed silhouette picture of Nicolo Paganini performing, 8cm. high, ebonized frame with brass acorn decoration. (Phillips) $616

American or English School, 19th century, a full-length portrait of a young gentleman, watercolor on paper, 8½ x 6¹/₂in. (Sotheby's) $1,288

BASKETS

An Edwardian swing-handled cake basket, chased with fruit, flowers, foliage and shells, Elkington & Co., Birmingham 1906, 12in., 22.75oz.
(Christie's) $775

A Victorian plated egg basket, formed as a hen, with detachable cover.
(Christie's) $1,105

A George III silver cake basket, maker's mark indistinct, 1812, the rim applied with insects, flowerheads and foliage, 15$\frac{1}{2}$in. wide, 78oz.
(Christie's) $4,658

A Victorian circular fruit basket, pierced and stamped with foliage, shells and scrolls, by John Brashier, 1881, 10in. diameter, 19oz.
(Christie's) $625

A George V Art Nouveau swing-handled circular sugar basket, the sides pierced with stylized flowers and foliage, 11.5cm. diameter, Adie Bros. Ltd., Birmingham 1926, with blue glass liner.
(Bearne's) $283

A George II silver bread basket, Paul de Lamerie, London, 1738, the fluted sides pierced with panels of latticework, scrolls and foliage, 12$\frac{1}{2}$in. long, 45oz.
(Christie's) $51,750

An 18th century Dutch oval sweetmeat basket, with drop scroll side handles, shaped rim with shell and scroll border, by Cornelis Hilberts, Amsterdam, 1743, 13.2cm. long, 4.25oz.
(Phillips) $3,840

A plated swing-handled shaped circular cake basket, embossed with flowers within acanthus edging on a spreading circular base, 25.5cm. diameter.
(Bearne's) $82

An Old Sheffield plate swing-handled cake basket, of rounded oblong form, on ball feet and with applied gadroon and shell friezes, unmarked, probably circa 1810, 13in.
(Christie's) $270

BEAKERS

A French early 18th century beaker, of inverted bell shape and on a part-fluted domed circular foot, 3¹/₂in., 3.75oz.
(Christie's) $1,552

A French silver beaker and cover, Louis Tassin, Paris, circa 1815, slightly tapering cylindrical and with detachable turned part-wood side handle, 5in. high, 7oz. gross.
(Christie's) $261

Russian enameled silver beaker, singular enameled scene of peasants in a horse drawn wagon, 3⁵/₈in. high.
(Skinner) $632

A George III Channel Islands beaker with flared lip inscribed with script monogram on side, Pierre Amiraux, Jersey, overstruck by Jacques Quesnel, Jersey, circa 1800, 8.1cm. high, 3.75oz.
(Phillips) $657

A George IV silver gilt beaker, London 1827, maker's mark of Rebecca Emes & Edward Barnard, initialed, tapering cylindrical body, with an upper and lower band of stylized motifs, cased, 4¹/₈in. high, approx. weight 4.5oz.
(Bonhams) $471

German silver-gilt beaker, maker's mark: # 755, Rosenberg, Augsburg, circa 1685–1700, with broad repeat band of heart shaped lobes at the base, 4³/₄in. high, 7oz.
(Butterfield & Butterfield) $1,840

An 18th century Russian beaker of tapering shape embossed with birds and foliate scrolls, maker's mark *AE* in heart-shaped punch, Moscow, 1741, 9cm. high, 3oz.
(Phillips) $501

Guillaume Henry of Guernsey, a flared beaker with molded foot, engraved *à N.D.G. Don de Son Pere & de Sa Mere 1758*.
(Woolley & Wallis) $780

An 18th century Irish beaker, Cork, circa 1760, maker's mark of John Hillery or John Humphreys, plain tapering cylindrical form, 3³/₄in. high, approx. weight 5.5oz.
(Bonhams) $1,577

BOWLS

A French silver bowl and cover, Aucoc Ainé, Paris, second half 19th century, circular and on rim foot, with two knotted foliage handles, 8³/₄in. wide, 13oz.
(Christie's) $350

Chinese silver bowl, possible Sing Fat and Chao-Ch'ang, early 20th century, chased and applied chrysanthemum motif on open basket weave, 8⁷/₈in. diameter, approx. 24 troy oz.
(Skinner) $920

A bowl and cover, maker's mark of E. Silver and Co., London, 1951, 18ct., cast and chased with stylized wave ornament and water lilies, 13¹/₄in. long, 88oz gross.
(Christie's) $27,427

A fruit bowl of shaped circular form, on a rising circular foot and with an applied trailing vine border, Asprey & Co. Ltd., London, 12in., 30.75oz.
(Christie's) $794

An Edwardian rose bowl, the body decorated with spiral-fluting, fruit and foliage and with a vacant rococo C-scroll cartouche, Charles Stuart Harris, London 1904, 8in., 14.25oz.
(Christie's) $414

Gorham sterling footed bowl, late 19th century, retailed by Matson & Hoes, Classical Revival, interior bowl with chased scrolling design, 11¹/₂in. high, approximately 39 troy oz.
(Skinner) $1,610

An important silver and copper stone-set 'Aztec' bowl, designed by Paulding Farnham, Tiffany & Co., New York, 1905, in the form of an Indian basket, 9¹/₂in. high.
(Christie's) $112,500

George V silver two-handled presentation bowl, Crichton Brothers, London, 1922, engraved dedication and signatures, 9in. diameter, 44 troy oz.
(Skinner) $632

A silver fruit bowl, William Gale & Son, New York, 1852, circular, on spreading circular and domed base applied and chased with grapevine, 7¹/₈in. high, 32oz.
(Christie's) $1,265

An 18th century Dutch mounted mother-of-pearl cartouche-shaped box, with incurved sides and reeded rim, by Hendrik Koop, Amsterdam, 1768, 11.3cm. long.
(Phillips) $1,312

An Edward VII shaped rectangular box with serpentine fronted sliding drawer, the top embossed with a scene of a couple and a child, 26cm. wide, William Comyns, London 1904.
(Bearne's) $1,073

An 18th century German silver-gilt spice box, interior with fixed divider, raised on four scroll feet, by Peter Christian Roser, Augsburg, 1767/69, 6.1cm. long, 2oz.
(Phillips) $1,248

An unusual cigar box, on stepped rectangular base applied with lions to each corner, 1914, 10in. high overall, 48oz.
(Christie's) $1,042

A German silver-gilt sugar box and cover, Johann Martin Satzger, Augsburg, 1763–1765, the body and domed cover chased with spiral flutes, birds, fruit and foliage, dated 1765, 5¼in. wide, 11oz.
(Christie's) $10,605

A good Victorian folding biscuit box, of characteristic double shell form, with pierced liner, cast rustic branch stand and handle, 9½in. high, late 19th century.
(Neales) $462

A George III Irish silver freedom box, Carden Terry and Jane Williams, Cork, circa 1805, the centre with a coat-of-arms within a motto, the base with presentation inscription, 9.3cm. long, 3oz.
(Christie's) $8,228

A pair of George III silver-gilt spice-boxes, covers and stands, John Wakelin and Robert Garrard, London, 1800, shaped-oval, the boxes on four curved feet, the stand 8³/₄in. long, 4¼in. high overall, 37oz.
(Christie's) $53,026

A late 18th/early 19th century American pill box, engraved with a neo-Classical shield cartouche, stamped inside Revere, circa 1800, 3.4cm. long.
(Phillips) $970

CADDY SPOONS

A George III bright cut caddy spoon, the circular bowl with a border of arrowheads, by George Brazier, 1799.
(Phillips) $241

A George III caddy spoon, the oval bow with bright-engraved zig-zag borders, by Samuel Pemberton, Birmingham, 1801.
(Phillips) $344

A George III caddy spoon with a green stained turned ivory handle, by Cocks & Bettridge, Birmingham, 1801.
(Phillips) $76

An Edwardian stamped vine leaf caddy spoon with a coiled tendril and grapes handle, Birmingham, 1903.
(Phillips) $150

A George III caddy spoon with a bifurcated coffee end stem and a heart shaped bowl, by Josiah Snalt, 1802.
(Phillips) $120

Cast Scottish caddy spoon with a heart shaped bowl depicting Balmoral in relief, by Robb of Ballater, 1924.
(Phillips) $90

A George III caddy spoon with a bright cut feathered stem, engraved in the bowl with flowers, by Joseph Wilmore, Birmingham, 1804.
(Phillips) $310

A George III silver gilt shovel caddy spoon with a mother of pearl handle and embossed bowl, by Samuel Pemberton, Birmingham, 1814.
(Phillips) $135

A George III engraved caddy spoon with a hollow fiddle handle and a part-covered bowl, by Cocks & Bettridge, Birmingham, 1815.
(Phillips) $207

A George III leaf pattern caddy spoon with a tendril stem, by Lawrence & Co., Birmingham, 1793.
(Phillips) $127

A commemorative caddy spoon with a pierced thistle stem, inscribed *Empire Exhib - Scotland, 1938*, Birmingham, 1937. (Phillips) $105

A George III filigree caddy spoon with a fluted bowl and a row of graduated roundels up the stem, unmarked, circa 1800.
(Phillips) $105

CANDELABRA

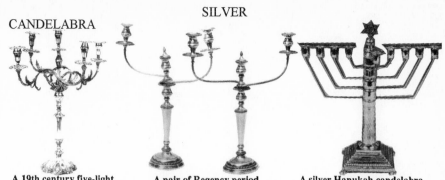

A 19th century five-light candelabrum, on a fluted rising shaped circular base and with a baluster stem, 24in.
(Christie's)   **$923**

A pair of Regency period Sheffield Plate candelabra, with turned stems to circular bases and campana shape candleholders, 21¹/₂in.
(Woolley & Wallis)   **$1,350**

A silver Hanukah candelabra, makers E. H. P. Co., Ltd., Sheffield, modern, on beaded stepped square base and bun feet, 10in. high.
(Christie's)   **$340**

Georg Jensen, pair of two light candelabra, 1920, silver colored metal, on saucer-shaped bases, the branches molded with berries and leaves, 27cm.
(Sotheby's)   **$5,814**

A William IV plated table candelabrum of classical form, with three rococo style scrolled foliate detachable branches, 22in. high, by Waterhouse Hatfield & Co.
(Dreweatt Neate)   **$3,092**

Victorian electroplated pair of seven light candelabra, Elkington & Co., Ltd., Birmingham, dated *1867*, each on a stepped shaped circular base, 28in. high.
(Butterfield & Butterfield)   **$5,175**

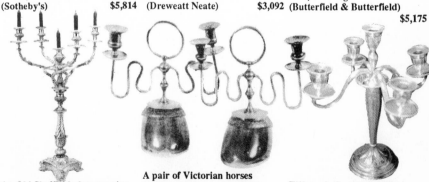

An Old Sheffield plate massive five-light candelabrum, on a foliate-decorated trefoil base with lion's mask and paw feet, 29in.
(Christie's)   **$2,650**

A pair of Victorian horses hooves, mounted with silver plated two light candelabra and inscribed *'Dapper' 27 Feb. 1886* and another mounted as a pin cushion.
(James Adam)   **$149**

Tiffany & Co., sterling silver candelabra, dated 1905, five light, reeded baluster form shaft with beaded edging, made by Charles T. Cook, 14¹/₂in. high.
(Du Mouchelles)   **$1,100**

CANDLESTICKS

John Cafe, a pair of George II cast tapersticks, the baluster stems with fluted shoulders, 4¹/₂in., London 1749.
(Woolley & Wallis) $2,432

Georg Jensen sterling candlesticks, 20th century, grapevine design, 5³/₄in. high.
(Skinner) $4,600

A pair of Queen Anne Scottish candlesticks, Robert Bruce, Edinburgh, 1708, plain and on spreading faceted slightly sunken base, 7¹/₂in. high, 26oz.
(Christie's) $13,714

Sterling pair of candlesticks, reproduction, original made in London, 1784, by John Schofield, Tiffany & Co., New York, New York, circa 1907–1947, 15in. high, 64oz. 14dwt.
(Butterfield & Butterfield) $3,737

A pair of plain silver candlesticks, in the mid-Georgian manner, each on a shaped square base, by Hawksworth Eyre Ltd., Sheffield, 1929, 8in. high.
(Christie's) $695

An Old Sheffield plated pair of candlesticks, circa 1765, maker's mark of John Hoyland & Co., Corinthian column form, fluted columns, on stepped square bases, ovolo borders, 11³/₄in. high.   (Bonhams) $628

A pair of Edwardian Corinthian column candlesticks, decorated with swags and beaded edging, by Harrison Bros. & Howson, Sheffield 1905, 8¹/₂in. high.
(Christopher Matthews) $816

A pair of late Victorian dwarf candlesticks, on part spiral-fluted stepped square bases, Hawksworth, Eyre & Co. Ltd., Sheffield 1885, 4³/₄in.
(Christie's) $635

A pair of George III neo-Classical candlesticks, with sunken round bases, urn shaped capitals, by John Wakelin & William Taylor, 1786, crested, 28cm. high, 36.5oz.
(Phillips) $6,000

CANDLESTICKS

A pair of 18th century style candlesticks of octagonal section, each on a rising base and with a tapering stem, Mappin & Webb, Sheffield 1957 and 1958, 8¼in.
(Christie's) $848

Victorian silver candlestick, London 1849–50, baluster-form, chased floral design, gold wash, monogram, 2¾in. high, approx. 5 troy oz.
(Skinner) $373

A pair of George II/George III Channel Islands cast candlesticks, fluted baluster columns, by Guillaume Henry, Guernsey, circa 1760, 20.2cm. high, 28.75oz.
(Phillips) $5,634

A pair of Edwardian candlesticks, in the mid 18th century taste, each on a rising shaped square base and with a knopped baluster stem, Goldsmiths & Silversmiths Co. Limited, London 1907, 10in.
(Christie's) $972

A pair of silver-gilt Rococo Revival openwork Irish candlesticks, on C and S-scroll trefoil bases and with scrolling supports, import marks, 6½in., 38.5oz.
(Christie's) $884

A fine pair of Regency candlesticks, in rococo taste, embossed leafy scrolls with panelled silesian stems, 11in. (loaded), Hadfield, Watson & Co., Sheffield 1814.
(Woolley & Wallis) $2,100

A pair of Louis XVI silver candlesticks, Edmé-François Balzac, Paris, 1771, on shaped-circular base and with shaped-triangular baluster stem, 10½in. high, 40oz.
(Christie's) $5,851

A pair of 18th century Portuguese cast candlesticks, with spirally fluted baluster stems, French style maker's mark *BP*, Lisbon, circa 1770, 25.8cm. high, 28.75oz.
(Phillips) $6,720

George II silver pair of candlesticks, Henry Morris, London, 1748, shaped square base with shells at the corners, 8⅝in. high, 36oz. 16dwt.
(Butterfield & Butterfield) $2,070

CARD CASES

An early Victorian 'Castletop' card case, one side chased in relief with Abbotsford, by Nathaniel Mills, Birmingham, 1837.
(Phillips) $900

A George III gold-mounted sharkskin card case, with a hinged flap and a hexagonal clasp set with three diamonds, 11cm. x 6cm., unmarked, circa 1800.
(Phillips) $600

A Victorian engraved card case, of shaped oblong form depicting a view of London Bridge, by Nathaniel Mills, Birmingham, 1848, 10cm. x 7cm., 2oz.
(Phillips) $1,080

A Victorian embossed 'Castletop' card case, of shaped oblong form depicting a view of Exeter Cathedral, by Nathaniel Mills, Birmingham, 1848, 10cm. x 7cm., 2.25oz.
(Phillips) $2,175

A Victorian engraved 'Castletop' card case, of shaped oblong form engraved with a view of The Houses of Parliament, by Foxall & Co., Birmingham, 1850, 10cm. x 7.5cm., 2.5oz.
(Phillips) $1,275

A Victorian embossed 'Castletop' card case, of shaped oblong form with a view of Gloucester Abbey, by Taylor & Perry, Birmingham, 1844, 10cm. x 7.5cm., 2.5oz.
(Phillips) $2,700

An Edwardian oblong card case, stamped in low relief, both sides with a view depicting a cathedral, by J. Gloster, Birmingham, 1905, 7cm. x 9.5cm., 1.75oz.
(Phillips) $540

A Victorian 'Castletop' card case, set on one side with an oblong panel depicting a view of Windsor Castle, by Nathaniel Mills, Birmingham, 1840, 9.75cm. x 7cm., 2oz.
(Phillips) $870

An early Victorian 'Castletop' card case, of plain oblong form depicting on one side a view of Warwick Castle, by Nathaniel Mills, Birmingham, 1838, 10cm. x 7.25cm., 2.5oz.
(Phillips) $720

CASTERS

A Victorian novelty owl sugar caster, the pull-off head with red and black glass eyes, by George Richards, 1850, 12cm. high, 4.25oz.
(Phillips) $2,400

An Edwardian sugar caster and matching cream jug, decorated with fruiting, flowers and foliage and with vacant C-scroll cartouches, William Morton & Sons, Sheffield 1903, 9¼in., 24oz. (Christie's) $810

A George III caster of inverted pear shape, with gadrooned bands and an acorn finial, Hester Bateman, London 1788, 5½in.
(Christie's) $675

A George I caster, London 1724, maker's mark of Thomas Bamford, the pull-off cover pierced with scrolls and roundels, 6½in. high, approx. weight 5oz.
(Bonhams) $785

A Victorian parcel gilt, novelty three-piece 'owl' condiment set, modeled as a pair and one larger owl, by Charles Thomas & George Fox, 1849/51/53, the largest 9.5cm. high, 12oz. weighable.
(Phillips) $9,300

An 18th century Dutch sugar caster, of baluster form on a rounded square pedestal, cast in relief with foliate tendrils, by Cornelis de Haan, The Hague, 1783, 24cm. high, 12oz.
(Phillips) $4,000

A set of three Scottish silver casters, Robert Clark, Edinburgh, 1771, each of inverted pear form and on spreading circular foot, with molded borders, the largest 7¼in., 17oz.
(Christie's) $2,415

A pair of American silver Japanese style casters, Tiffany & Co., New York, circa 1875, tapered quadrangular form, engraved with flowerheads, 8oz., 5¼in. high.
(Sotheby's) $2,070

Three George II silver casters, Ann Craig and John Neville, London, 1740, one smaller caster by Samuel Wood, London 1756, each inverted pear-shaped and on spreading circular foot, 9¼in., two 8¼in. high, 42oz.
(Christie's) $10,350

CENTERPIECES

George IV silver and cut glass épergne, circa 1805, P C maker not traced, inscription on base panel, fan and diamond cut bowl, 17⅞in. high, approximately 258 troy oz. (Skinner) **$14,375**

A parcel-gilt silver centerpiece bowl, Gorham Mfg. Co., Providence, 1870, surmounted by a gilt figural group of an Eskimo driving a sled drawn by a reindeer, 10¼in. high, 16½in. long, 63oz. 10dwt. (Christie's) **$16,100**

A George III Irish chinoiserie 'pagoda' épergne, on four large scroll supports terminating in pierced pad feet, by Charles Townsend, Dublin, circa 1775, 43.75cm. high, 123.5oz. (Phillips) **$9,000**

A centerpiece, the circular base with pierced decoration raised on scrolled feet, the circular basket with pierced decoration, Jackson & Fullerton, London 1910, 6½in. high, 17.5oz. (George Kidner) **$693**

A silver figural centerpiece, Tiffany & Co., New York, circa 1885, on tripod hoof feet, the circular dish with guilloche rim, 8½in. high, 29oz. 10dwt. (Christie's) **$1,725**

An early 19th century plated on copper épergne, the frame with circular gadrooned top, raised on four husk sheathed square supports, 13in. high overall. (Phillips) **$434**

A foliate-pierced centerpiece, on a rising circular base, the plain tapering central vase applied with scrolling foliate branches, London 1913, 12¾in., 38oz. (Christie's) **$1,638**

A silver centerpiece bowl, Black, Starr & Frost, New York, circa 1900, shaped oval, the rim applied with undulating scrolls, 14½in. long, 34oz. 10dwt. (Christie's) **$2,875**

A large table centerpiece, on a hexafoil base rising to a conforming fruit bowl, Walker & Hall, Sheffield 1911, 14¼in., 69oz. (Christie's) **$2,784**

CHAMBERSTICKS

A George III circular chamber candlestick, crested, the circular tray and nozzle with thread edging, Richard Crooke, London 1800, 8.2oz.
(Bearne's) $536

Attractive William IV silver taper stick, having veined leaf formed base, scrolled stemmed floral holder, complete with snuffer, 3¹/₂in. wide, Birmingham 1830, maker J W. (G. A. Key) $495

Late 19th century Sheffield plated chamber stick and extinguisher with rope twist decoration, pineapple mark to base, 4¹/₂in. high.
(Peter Wilson) $68

Pair of George III silver chambersticks, with beaded border and double monogrammed crest, hallmarks for London, 1784, maker's mark of Johnathan Alleine, 4in. high, 21.4 troy oz.
(Eldred's) $2,200

An American parcel-gilt silver Japanese style chamber candlestick, Tiffany & Co., New York, circa 1880, the pan of stylized maple leaf form, 10ozs. 15dwts., 6in. wide.
(Sotheby's) $28,750

A pair of Victorian circular chamber candlesticks with conical extinguishers, crested, 15.2cm. diameter, Robert Garrard, London 1849, the nozzles and one extinguisher 1850, 31.7oz.
(Bearne's) $2,682

A pair of William IV chambersticks, the bases shaped like the flower of a Tudor rose, probably by William Eaton, 1831, 15cm. diameter, 20oz.
(Phillips) $2,191

Two Tiffany & Co. diminutive sterling chambersticks, 1875–91, spotted design and thistle design, approx. 4 troy oz.
(Skinner) $402

A pair of Old Sheffield plated chambersticks of shaped circular form, urn-shaped capitals, crested, with conical snuffers.
(Bonhams) $180

CIGARETTE CASES

An early 20th century English silver cigarette case of rounded rectangular form, with enamel female figure on lid, 7.5 x 8.5 cm., 130 gr.
(Finarte) $2,155

A pre-war turned cigarette case presented to the Berlin opera singer Manowarda by Hermann Goering, inscribed *In grateful remembrance of the 21.1.1936., Hermann Goering.*
(Dockree's) $410

A white metal and enamel cigarette-case, maker's mark *SB*, Moscow, circa 1908–1917, the cover decorated with an en plein enamel plaque depicting a rocky bay scene, 4³/₈in. long.
(Christie's) $1,143

A 900 silver cigarette case, the lid decorated with an enamel picture of a nude girl reclining on drapery, French import marks for 1893, 10 x 8.5cm., 170gr.
(Finarte) $1,725

A jeweled, yellow metal-mounted silver-gilt cigarette-case, marked *Fabergé*, Workmaster Anders Nevalainen, St. Petersburg, 1908, the cover applied with gold cypher *HH*, 3¹/₂in. long, 4.2oz. gross.
(Christie's) $2,023

An early 20th century sterling silver cigarette case, of rounded rectangular form, the lid decorated in enamels with a reclining nude female figure, 9 x 7.5cm., 160 gr.
(Finarte) $1,563

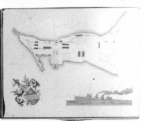

A German 935 silver cigarette case, the top enameled with a scene of girls bathing in a stream, early 20th century, 8 x 9 cm., circa 150 gr.
(Finarte) $1,563

A yellow metal enameled cartographic cigarette-case, by Fabergé, Workmaster Henrik Wigström, St. Petersburg, 1908–1917, the cover enameled with a ship, 3³/₄in. long, 8.7oz. gross.
(Christie's) $12,317

An early 20th century 900 silver cigarette case of rectangular form, a picture of a naked girl in polychrome enamels on the lid, 8 x 9 cm., circa 150 gr.
(Finarte) $2,155

CLARET JUGS

A Victorian novelty claret jug, formed as a monkey with dimpled glass body and plated mounts, 11in. high.
(Christie's) $1,076

A pair of French silver-mounted glass claret jugs, Tetard Frères, Paris, second half 19th century, each on shaped-square base, cast and chased with flutes and shells, foliage and diaper-work, 12¹/₂in. high.
(Christie's) $6,900

A late 19th/early 20th century clear glass claret jug, the fluted compressed molded circular body with plain mount and spout, Roberts & Belk, Sheffield, 8in.
(Christie's) $279

A Victorian parcel-gilt claret jug, of vase-shape, on a rising circular base decorated with broad flutes, masks, strapwork and berried foliage, Stephen Smith, London 1875, 11¹/₂in., 34oz.
(Christie's) $1,590

A pair of electroplated mounted glass claret jugs, the tapering glass bodies cut with stars, the electroplated mounts with foliate decoration and twig handles, 28cm. high.
(Bearne's) $492

A good Victorian plain glass claret jug, on inverted pear shape with a palm leaf calyx at the base, circa 1870, Sheffield, James Dixon and Sons, 10¹/₂in. high.
(Dee, Atkinson & Harrison) $486

A Victorian silver-mounted clear glass claret jug, the bottle shaped body with diamond band decoration and a faceted neck, 22.5cm. high, Hilliard & Thomason, Birmingham 1894.
(Bearne's) $479

A pair of silver-mounted cut-glass claret jugs, Tiffany & Co., New York, circa 1885, baluster, the glass rock-crystal engraved with scrolls and foliage, 9³/₄in. high.
(Christie's) $5,175

A Victorian silver-mounted glas claret jug, in the style of Dr Christopher Dresser, on a star-cut spreading base and with a plain mount, Edward Hutton, London 1890, 8¹/₂in.
(Christie's) $837

COASTERS

A pair of Regency Sheffield Plate decanter stands, the open frames to turned wood bases, with old baize.
(Woolley & Wallis) $577

A set of four Victorian Sheffield circular decanter coasters, with leaf decoration and timber bases.
(James Adam) $546

A pair of Old Sheffield plate shallow wine coasters, each with a wirework superstructure and turned wood base, 6in.
(Christie's) $384

A pair of late Victorian cylindrical decanter coasters, the bodies decorated with repoussé and chased trellis and foliate scrolls with pierced fretwork and wavy rims, Sheffield 1900.
(James Adam) $791

A pair of 'Bacchanalian' wine coasters, with gadrooned borders and vertical sides, embossed and pierced in low relief, by John Roberts, Samuel Mosley & John Settle, Sheffield, 1809, 14.5cm. diameter.
(Phillips) $2,113

A highly important pair of American silver wine coasters made for Samuel Cornell by Myer Myers, New York, 1760–1770, with scrolling openwork fret-sawn sides, 5in. diameter.
(Christie's) $299,500

A pair of Victorian wine coasters, of circular form, each on a spreading foot and with a turned wood base, Elkington & Co., Birmingham, 7in.
(Christie's) $319

A set of four William IV silver wine coasters, T. J. and N. Creswick, Sheffield, 1836, with fluted sides and everted shell and scroll rim, 7¹/₂in. diameter.
(Christie's) $4,388

A pair of George III wine coasters of circular form and with tall wirework sides, Charles Aldridge & Henry Greenaway, London 1774, 4³/₄in.
(Christie's) $2,129

COFFEE POTS

A George III pedestal coffee pot, of part-fluted tapering oval form, Richard Cooke, London 1799, the handle with Victorian hallmarks, 12¼in., 38.25oz.
(Christie's) $2,500

An Austro-Hungarian 19th century pedestal coffee pot and matching hot milk jug, each on a foliate-chased rising circular base, 10¼in. and 8½in., 35oz. gross.
(Christie's) $1,552

An 18th century style coffee pot, of tapering circular form, on a skirted foot, one side engraved with an armorial, crest and motto, 9½in., 23oz. gross.
(Christie's) $506

A George IV coffee pot, of fluted pear shape and on a rising shaped circular foot, with a molded rim, Robert Garrard, London 1829, 11in. overall, 45oz. gross.
(Christie's) $1,940

Georgian style silver coffee pot of oval baluster design, with scrolled treen handle, slightly domed lid, Birmingham 1910, 21oz. all in.
(G. A. Key) $345

A late 18th century Portuguese coffee pot, of baluster form with domed cover and leafy knop finial, maker's mark *MG*, for Manuel Alves Fendas, Oporto, last quarter 18th century, 30cm. high, 35oz.
(Phillips) $3,520

A Continental coffee pot, of part-fluted baluster form, on a spreading circular foot and with a molded short spout, possibly German, late 18th century, 7½in., 15.25oz. gross.
(Christie's) $1,293

Two silver café-au-lait pots, James Dixon & Sons, Birmingham, 1941, the baluster bodies with gadroon borders and carved composition handles, 42oz. (all in), 24cm. high.
(Sotheby's) $1,248

An 18th century Channel Islands coffee pot, of tapering shape, the cover with bell-shaped finial, by Guillaume Henry, Guernsey, circa 1735, 25cm. high, 35oz.
(Phillips) $7,500

CREAM JUGS

A George II cream jug of plain baluster form, on a spreading foot and with a molded rim, maker's initials probably G.I., London 1731, 3in.
(Christie's) $927

Continental silver creamer, 19th century, gadrooned edges, engraved 'S' with crown, 3^1/$_8$in. high, approximately 6 troy oz.
(Skinner) $115

Good Victorian silver cream jug, melon patterned on four scrolled feet and having leaf capped scrolled handle, London 1839 by the Barnards, 9.5oz.
(G. A. Key) $248

George III silver creamer, with chased foliate decoration and pedestal foot, hallmarks for London, 1778, maker's mark of Charles Henter, 5in. high, 2.6 troy oz.
(Eldred's) $192

A silver covered sugar bowl and cream jug, Harvey Lewis, Philadelphia, circa 1820, on four lion's-paw feet with a band of anthemion above, covered sugar 7in. high, 40oz.
(Christie's) $3,450

A silver cream jug, maker's mark IP, probably for Isaac Parker, Boston, circa 1775, baluster, on circular domed base, 6^1/$_8$in. high, 4oz. 10dwt.
(Christie's) $1,035

Russian silver cream jug, Moscow, A.P., 1892, made for Tiffany & Co., chased scrolling and floral design, gold wash interior, 5in. high, approximately 9 troy oz.
(Skinner) $690

An Austro-Hungarian silver jug, Vienna, 1840, maker's mark CJ, of baluster form and with scroll handle with shell terminal, 5^1/$_2$in. high, 12oz.
(Christie's) $1,035

A Dutch late 18th century cream jug, on a beaded pedestal foot and with a beaded and bright-cut tapering oval body, maker's initials T.H., Amsterdam 1788, 7^1/$_2$in., 8.50oz.
(Christie's) $483

CRUETS

A George III silver cruet stand, Robert and David Hennell, London, 1800, two bottle mounts 1801, one caster mount 1826, 8¼in. long, the stand 18oz. (Christie's) $1,207

A George III silver cruet stand and six cut-glass bottles, John Touliet, London, 1791, boat-shaped and on four bracket feet, with two reeded loop handles, 9¾in. long, 10oz. (Christie's) $828

A late Victorian six bottle plated table cruet, open-work frame with ball feet and central T-bar handle, by J. Dixon & Sons, Sheffield, circa 1890. (Christie's) $298

A small George III oil and vinegar frame, with a boat-shaped stand, stud feet, beaded borders and loop handles, the frame by John Schofield, 1782, the labels by Margaret Binley, circa 1775, 5oz. weighable. (Phillips) $1,440

A twin-bottle cruet by Martin & Dejean, Paris 1838-1846, the bottle holders with rocaille, foliate and shell decoration, 32 cm., 560 gr. (Finarte) $938

An early George III London cruet frame of handled five petalled flower form, solid based on claw and ball feet, below foliate openwork, the frame with two marks for Thomas Nash I. (Dee, Atkinson & Harrison) $825

An 18th century Genoese cruet, the bottle holders with foliate rocaille ornament, the baluster shaft ending in a beaded ring handle, 26cm., 400gr. (Finarte) $2,340

An eight-bottle cruet by Daniel Pontifex, London 1810/11, of shaped rectangular form with gadrooned edge with shell ornament, 25.5cm. high, 1,030gr. (Finarte) $2,812

A good Victorian circular cruet frame, the bowed sides pierced with fretwork, beaded border, posted loop handle, five cut-glass bottles, 9½in. high, Sheffield 1874. (Neales) $1,463

An 18th century two-handled cup, of inverted bell shape, on a rising circular foot and with a molded body band, probably Ireland circa 1730, 5³/₄in., 21oz. (Christie's) $3,282

A George II tumbler cup, gilt interior, engraved with initials *R*C*, probably 1746, 7.1cm. diameter, 4oz. (Phillips) $626

A Victorian silver-gilt-mounted agate cup, on foliate and hoof feet joined by half paterae, possibly William Nichols, London 1846, 5³/₄in. (Christie's) $1,237

A good George II Irish two-handled cup of baluster shape with cast caryatid handles, applied on either side with a rococo cartouche, by Edward Raper, Dublin, circa 1750, 16.5cm. high, 27.75oz. (Phillips) $4,069

A pair of George III silver stirrup cups, Tudor and Leader, Sheffield, 1786, each formed as a fox's mask, realistically chased, 4³/₄in. long, 8oz. (Christie's) $6,900

A small chalice-shaped cup chased with two bands of overlapping stylized feathers or flutes, inscribed around rim K.A.L.D. 26 November 1933, by Omar Ramsden, London 1927, 8.8cm. high, 3oz. (Phillips) $501

A George IV gilt-lined cup and cover, of part-fluted campana shape, engraved with the arms of the town of Stratford-upon-Avon, 12in. overall, 48oz. (Christie's) $2,025

1907 Fernando Nelson trophy in sterling silver for Fernando A. Nelson to present to the winner of the San Francisco to Los Angeles race, approx. 15in. high. (Christie's) $23,000

Samuel Hennell, a fine Regency cup and cover, applied cast openwork bands of grape vines, 13in., London 1818, 57oz. (Woolley & Wallis) $2,175

CUPS

A mid 18th century Irish cup, the inverted bell-shaped body engraved with an armorial, probably William Townsend, Dublin circa 1740, 7in., 31.5oz. (Christie's) $2,839

A George III tumbler cup, Edinburgh 1760, initialed on base, conventional form, with slightly flared rim, 2¹/₄in. high, weight 4oz. (Bonhams) $754

A Victorian cup, on a molded spreading foot, 8¹/₄in., by Aldwinkle and Slater, London 1882, 35oz. (Woolley & Wallis) $720

A George II cup, on a rising circular foot and with a molded body band and rim and two scroll handles, maker's mark indistinct, London 1743, 5¹/₂in., 15oz. (Christie's) $698

A fine William IV silver gilt cup and stand, London 1830, maker's mark of John Bridge, stand London 1836, maker's mark of William Bateman for Rundell Bridge & Co., 15¹/₂in. high overall, approx. weight 106oz. (Bonhams) $5,652

An American silver large two-handled cup signed by the designer, Gorham Mfg. Co., Providence, RI, 1904, martelé, signed W. C. Codman 1903, 124oz. 10dwt., 12¹/₂in. high. (Sotheby's) $18,400

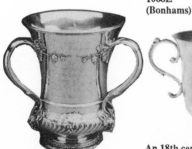

Tiffany & Co. sterling presentation loving cup, 20th century, applied grapevine design, engraved dedication, 9in. high, approximately 56 troy oz. (Skinner) $2,645

An 18th century Channel Islands christening cup, of porringer form with beaded rat-tails to 'S'-scroll side handles, attributed to John Hardie, Guernsey, circa 1750, 6.6cm. high, 7.8cm. diameter, 3oz. (Phillips) $900

An important Queen Anne race cup and cover, Louis Mettayer, London, 1713, the cover engraved with the cypher of Queen Anne within the Garter motto, 7in. high, 23oz. (Christie's) $325,950

DISHES

George Fox III, an Edwardian oval dessert dish, the pierced sides with a crested medallion and paterae linked by swags, 9¹/₂in., London 1902, 13.5oz. (Woolley & Wallis) $720

A pair of parcel-gilt silver olive dishes, Gorham Mfg. Co., Providence, each realistically formed as a cured olive on a stem, 5³/₄in. long, 10oz. 10dwt. (Christie's) $1,725

EPNS oval breakfast dish, with two loose trays (one pierced), hinged, domed lid with ivory button, reeded handles and four reeded feet, 37cm. (Peter Wilson) $255

A silver shell-form covered dish, Ball, Black & Co., New York, 1851–1876, oyster shaped, on openwork cattail and grass base, 3⁵/₈in. long, 4oz. (Christie's) $1,150

A pair of George III silver vegetable dishes, covers and liners, Richard Cooke, London, 1804 and 1805, cylindrical and with two hinged drop-ring side handles, 7¹/₄in. high, 145oz. (Christie's) $31,050

An Art Nouveau comport, the plain circular bowl and base with hammered finish and three curved supports, 20cm. high, Pearce & Sons, London 1910, 30.1oz. (Bearne's) $596

  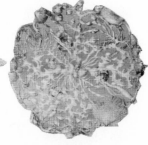

A Martelé silver tazza, Gorham Mfg. Co., Providence, 1899, the everted brim chased with a wide border of stylized foliage, 9¹/₂in. diameter, 22oz. (Christie's) $2,300

Charles Stuart Harris, a pair of late Victorian oval sweetmeat dishes, fitted blue glass liners, on oval feet, 7¹/₂in., London 1892, 14oz. (Woolley & Wallis) $930

An unusual American 19th century shallow bon-bon dish, of shaped circular form and on three shell feet, Gorham & Co., 6¹/₄in., 6oz. (Christie's) $759

DISHES

A silver butter dish, Gorham Mfg. Co., Providence, 1871, with two strapwork handles with stiff leaf and matted scroll joins, 7³/₄in. long over handles, 23oz. 10dwt.
(Christie's) $1,265

A fine pair of silver vegetable dishes and cover, Tiffany & Co., New York, circa 1880, in the Persian style, each oval, on molded oval base with crenellated band, 12³/₄in. long over handles, 95oz.
(Christie's) $17,250

Georg Jensen, dish, manufactured post 1945, silver colored metal, the shallow dish on a pierced low stem with a frieze of leaf and pine cone motifs, 17.5cm.
(Sotheby's) $1,362

A silver butter dish, Jones, Ball & Poor, also marked *W&G*, Boston, circa 1849, circular, on four pad feet, 5³/₄in. diameter, 13oz. 10dwt.
(Christie's) $920

A pair of silver vegetable dishes and covers, Gorham and Howard & Co., New York, 1886, the removable finial with a calyx of swirling flutes, 7⁵/₈in. long, 69oz.
(Christie's) $4,025

German 800 standard silver compôte, 20th century, bowl base with embossed scene of a lady alighting from a sedan chair, 8in. high, 37oz. 18dwt.
(Butterfield & Butterfield) $2,070

A pedestal sweetmeat dish, of lobed design, with wavy rim, knopped column, spreading base, 5¹/₂in. high, by Heming & Co. Ltd., 1906, 8oz.
(Neales) $169

An unusual pair of silver vegetable dishes on silver and copper warming stands, Robert Wilson, Philadelphia, circa 1840, on four ivory ball feet, 13¹/₂in. long over handles, weighable silver 73oz.
(Christie's) $4,025

A Victorian pedestal cake dish, decorated with graduated beading, spiral fluting and foliage, Charles Stuart Harris, London 1887, 7³/₄in., 11oz.
(Christie's) $391

FLATWARE

A George II mote spoon with cast scalloped bowl, by Francis Harache, circa 1750.
(Phillips) $344

A George III Irish miniature marrow spoon, by William Ward, Dublin, circa 1800, 9.25cm. long.
(Phillips) $407

A rare set of five George III picture back teaspoons depicting a three-masted sailing ship, fully rigged, on a choppy sea, initialed *P* possibly by William Withers, circa 1765, 2oz.
(Phillips) $563

A Charles II silver trefid end fork, London, 1680, maker's mark *MC*, three pronged, the handle pricked with the initials *EB*, 7¼in. long, 1oz.
(Christie's) $4,023

A good George II Hanoverian pattern basting spoon, the bowl with double drop, the back of stem with engraved crest above initials *H.T*, by James Wilks, 1751, 35.7cm. long, 6oz.
(Phillips) $814

A George III fish slice, the blade engraved with stylized foliate and floral border, the blade by Hester Bateman, 1784, the bead-edged handle probably by John Chapman (II).
(Phillips) $900

A pair of rare Charles II silver trefid end forks, maker's mark of Lawrence Coles, London, 1673, three pronged, the handles each engraved with a crest, 7in. long, 2oz.
(Christie's) $12,434

A pair of Victorian cast sugar nips, of leaf and floral design with butterfly, one either side at junction of arms, by Yapp & Woodward, Birmingham, 1847, 2.75oz.
(Phillips) $420

An early 18th century Dutch parcel-gilt spoon with 'Charity' terminal, bowl engraved with a whale about to envelop a man in a boat, inscribed *188 Duckatons*, Amsterdam, 1709 or 1733.
(Phillips) $689

A Victorian silver-gilt christening knife, fork and spoon, in a fitted case, the handles cast in relief with the figure of a young dancing maiden, by George Adams, 1863 (knife handle loaded), 4oz. weighable.
(Phillips) $720

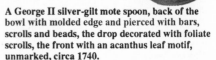

An early Victorian Scottish marrow scoop, die stamped with the crest and motto of the Scottish Marrowbone Club, Edinburgh, inscribed *Robert Ainslie* and dated *1835*, by W. Cunningham, Edinburgh, 1840, 23.25cm. long, 3.5oz.
(Phillips) $720

A George II silver-gilt mote spoon, back of the bowl with molded edge and pierced with bars, scrolls and beads, the drop decorated with foliate scrolls, the front with an acanthus leaf motif, unmarked, circa 1740.
(Phillips) $407

FLATWARE

A George III Irish fiddle pattern straining spoon, the bowl with fixed divider pierced with slats, crested, by Samuel Neville, Dublin, 1808, 5.5oz.
(Phillips) **$563**

A George I rat-tail mote spoon, bowl pierced with foliate scrolls and engraved with initials *MC*, struck with maker's mark and lion's head erased, by Andrew Archer, circa 1715.
(Phillips) **$313**

A George III Irish fish serving fork, with a pointed terminal and nine tines, by Isaac D'Olier, Dublin, 1793, initialed and crested 33cm. long, 4oz.
(Phillips) **$930**

Two very similar rare Charles I stump-top spoons of good gauge with tapering octagonal stems and deeply curved fig-shaped bowls, by David Cary, 1635, 18.2cm. long, 3.5oz.
(Phillips) **$14,868**

A pair of George III silver asparagus tongs and a pair of French silver asparagus tongs, the former Eley, Fearn and Chawner, London, 1809, the latter Paris, second half 19th century, 9¹/₄in. and 9¹/₂in. long, 11oz.
(Christie's) **$559**

An early Victorian Scottish marrow scoop, die stamped with the crest and motto of the Scottish Marrowbone Club, Edinburgh, inscribed *Cosmo Innes* and dated *1835*, by W. Cunningham, Edinburgh, 1840, 23.25cm. long, 3.5oz.
(Phillips) **$750**

A George III marrow spoon, with a teaspoon size bowl and a long narrow scoop, initialed, by Messrs Eley, Fearn & Chawner, 1813.
(Phillips) **$240**

A William III engraved trefid teaspoon with a notched terminal, a foliate rat-tail bowl and an oval cartouche on the reverse, initialed *WO*, by Jean Harache, circa 1695, 4.75cm. long.
(Phillips) **$330**

A George III fish slice, London 1820, maker's mark of Paul Storr, King's Husk pattern, the blade with pierced decoration, reeded border, crested, 11³/₄in. long, approx. weight 5.5oz.
(Bonhams) **$597**

A set of six James II silver trefid end spoons, London, 1686, maker's mark indistinct, each with rat-tail bowl, the handles each engraved with a coat-of-arms, 7³/₄in. long, 12oz.
(Christie's) **$7,680**

A mid-17th century West Country double seal top spoon (later gilded), stamped once in the bowl and three times on the reverse of the stem, possibly Salisbury, tapering hexagonal stem, fig-shaped bowl, 7¹/₄in. long, approx. weight 2oz.
(Bonhams) **$408**

A George II Channel Islands basting spoon of Hanoverian pattern, inscribed with initials *C.D.F.* above a script monogram, by Guillaume Henry, Guernsey, circa 1750, 37.5cm. long, 6.75oz.
(Phillips) **$1,534**

GOBLETS

A good George III wine goblet on bead-edged trumpet foot, by James Young, 1789, 17.2cm. high, 8oz.
(Phillips) $1,017

A good pair of George III goblets with gilt interiors, engraved with a band of flowers, leaves and berries, by Wallis & Hayne, 1816, 15cm. high, 16.5oz.
(Phillips) $2,817

An early Victorian goblet, on a rising circular foot chased with rural vignettes, Benjamin Smith, London 1839, 6¹/₂in., 9.25oz.
(Christie's) $619

A mid-Victorian goblet, Birmingham 1878, maker's mark of Frederick Elkington, crested, the tulip-shaped bowl applied with a frieze of various game dogs, 4³/₄in. high, approx. weight 5oz.
(Bonhams) $550

A pair of George III gilt-lined goblets, on reeded rising square bases, the plain tapering circular bowls engraved with crests, Peter & Ann Bateman, London 1779, 6¹/₂in., 15oz.
(Christie's) $1,944

A small early 18th century German parcel-gilt goblet, front engraved with baroque cartouche, by Johann Michael Winckelmann or Johann Michael Wecker, Dresden, circa 1715, 9.9cm. high, 3.25oz.
(Phillips) $2,660

A George III goblet on square pedestal foot, engraved with a band of stylized fruiting vines, gilt interior, by Thomas Hayter, 1808, 15.7cm. high, 9oz.
(Phillips) $501

A pair of late 18th/early 19th century silver-mounted coconut goblets, on rising circular bases, the bowls with strap work mounts, 6³/₄in.
(Christie's) $2,415

A Charles I goblet, London 1637, maker's mark I. M., a bear below, plain tapering bowl with knopped stem, 6¹/₂in. high, approx. weight 10oz.
(Bonhams) $2,198

A George IV inkstand, the oval base chased around the rim with flowers and ivy, by John Bridge, 1823, 21cm. long, 12.5oz. (Phillips)　$1,565

A Victorian inkstand, the central taperstick of foliate pattern with bluebell extinguisher, by Messrs. Barnard, 1846, 36cm. long, 42oz. (Phillips)　$2,035

An Edwardian rectangular inkstand, with two cut glass inkwells having silver hinged shell covers, 9¹/₄in. (Woolley & Wallis)　$750

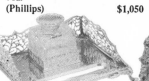

An unusual George III inkstand of small size, trefoil-shaped with pen tray in front, by Hester Bateman, 1788, 13.85cm. long, 7oz. (Phillips)　$1,050

A Victorian inkstand of shaped circular form, pierced with stylized scrolling foliage, Charles & George Fox, London 1865, 4¹/₂in. (Christie's)　$604

A William IV silver-gilt inkstand, the shaped oblong base with floral and leafy scroll border, by Messrs. Barnard, 1835, 31cm. long, 47oz. (Phillips)　$3,287

Victorian silver ink stand with single cut glass bottle, George Fox, London, 1890, nearly square form platform in a three-quarters galleried frame, 7³/₈in. long, 16oz. 4dwt. (Butterfield & Butterfield)　$1,380

A 19th century Sheffield plate shaped rectangular standish, glass wells with conforming hinged covers, rectangular chamber stick, detachable sconce, on bold lion paw feet, 13¹/₂in. long. (Neales)　$688

A Victorian silver inkstand, Barnard Brothers, London, 1895, on four lion's paw, scroll and foliate feet with pierced sides and gadrooned border, 36cm., 70oz. stand only. (Christie's)　$2,272

A George IV silver inkstand, Paul Storr, London, 1822, with two acanthus leaf scroll bracket handles and with shell and acanthus foliage border, 15¹/₂in. long, 52oz. (Christie's)　$11,885

Charles T. and George Fox, a Victorian partner's inkstand, with a pierced fretwork crested gallery, 11in., London 1851, 29oz. (Woolley & Wallis)　$1,672

A Victorian oval inkstand with two cut glass bottles and a taperstick, Martin Hall & Co., Sheffield 1895, weighable silver 11oz. (Christopher Matthews)　$408

SILVER

A Victorian water jug, embossed with stylized ribbon-tied swags above a reeded lower body, 16.8cm. high, Walker & Hall, Sheffield 1888, 12.1oz.
(Bearne's) $328

A George III silver hot water jug, Henry Chawner, London, 1795, oblong section vase-form, fluted at the angles, 28oz. (all in), 13.5cm. high.
(Sotheby's) $1,961

A late 18th century Italian hot water jug of plain baluster form, with wrythen knop finial and raffia-bound handle, Venice, circa 1780, 18cm. high, 17.5oz.
(Phillips) $783

Fine George III hunting jug, the handle in the form of a running fox, the body engraved with two huntsmen, by Peter and William Bateman, London 1811, 10in. high, 50oz.
(Ewbank) $2,265

Silver covered hot milk jug, Ball, Black and Co., New York, circa 1851–76, with repoussé floral and rococo decoration, 6in. high, 12 troy oz.
(Skinner) $258

An Old Sheffield plate cylindrical hot water jug, crested, with threaded girdles and a wood scroll handle, the detachable cover with a ball finial, 20cm. high.
(Bearne's) $164

A George II Provincial silver beer jug, Richard Richardson, Chester, 1751, with wicker covered handle, 7¼in. high, 29oz. gross.
(Christie's) $8,970

An 18th century style hot water jug, on a stand with scroll and baluster supports and with a burner, William Comyns, London 1911, height of coffee pot on warming stand 11¼in.
(Christie's) $1,419

A George II silver beer jug, Richard Bayley, London, 1750, with leaf-capped scroll handle and with short curved spout, 7¼in. high, 29oz.
(Christie's) $5,865

MISCELLANEOUS

An ivory and silvered casket, German, probably Augsburg, 17th century, surmounted by a sleeping putto with three 17th century and one later oval ivory panels, 32cm. high.
(Sotheby's) $32,976

A Continental silver-gilt and garnet-set table timepiece with alarm, unsigned, probably Viennese circa 1870, the rectangular case on elaborate foliate feet, 3¹/₂in. high.
(Christie's) $3,657

A rare late 18th century French officer's paste set gilt étui with a verge watch in the lid, full plate gilt fusee movement, signed *Le Roy Paris 336*, circa 1780, 130mm. high.
(Pieces of Time) $12,665

An Old Sheffield plate campana shape warming vessel and cover, crested and applied with two cast acanthus handles on a spreading circular base, 17cm. high.
(Bearne's) $447

Georg Jensen, bottle holder, circa 1920, silver colored metal, the molded surround with four concave panels with fruit-laden vines in high relief, 12cm.
(Sotheby's) $7,268

A George III argyle, of vase shape, on a beaded rising circular foot and with a rising curved spout, incompletely marked, Wakelin & Taylor, London circa 1780, 7³/₄in., 16.25oz. gross.
(Christie's) $2,109

Roger, Smith & Co. silver plated server, late 19th century, in the form of a four-wheeled carriage, bowl with a squirrel form finial, 11¹/₂in. high.
(Skinner) $690

A George IV silver toast rack, Paul Storr, London, 1829, oblong and on four scroll feet, with central shell and foliate scroll ring handle, 6¹/₂in. wide, 13oz.
(Christie's) $3,795

A silver-plated duck press, unmarked, late 19th century, on four leaf-capped scroll feet, the shaped body with hinged curved door, 16¹/₄in.
(Christie's) $2,070

A silver model of an elephant, import marked London, 1924, realistically modeled as a charging tusker, 28oz., 23cm. high.
(Sotheby's) $2,317

Three bottle pickle tantalus, scrolled surround on baluster feet by Mappin and Webb.
(G. A. Key) $277

Mappin & Webb, an electroplated spoon warmer in the form of a nautilus shell, engraved with shell and seaweed motifs, 14cm. high.
(Bearne's) $209

A set of fifteen George III silver dinner plates, John Wakelin and William Taylor, London, 1781, with beaded borders, engraved with crests, 9¹/₂in. diameter, 214oz.
(Christie's) $11,885

Jean E. Puiforcat, tazza, 1920s, silver colored metal, the shallow bowl on eight wooden segment supports, their outside edges faced with silver colored metal, 19.5cm. high.
(Sotheby's) $7,450

Continental silver trefoil oinochoe, second half 19th century, with mask terminal at the back supporting a standing figure of a satyr, 14¹/₂in. high, 81oz. 14dwt.
(Butterfield & Butterfield) $4,887

Contemporary sterling silver sculpture, titled A Mother's Song by Ramon Parmenter, ed. #17 in a limited edition of 100, 17in. high, 760 troy oz.
(Skinner) $4,140

A Louis XV Provincial silver chocolate pot, Jacques Lelarge, Reims, circa 1750, pear-shaped and on three scroll feet and with detachable turned wood side handle, 7¹/₄in. high, 15oz.
(Christie's) $3,657

A Victorian silver-gilt oval barrel-shaped vinaigrette, cover set with a citrine, sides set with panels of different colored agates and bloodstone, circa 1850, 5cm. high.
(Phillips) $2,269

MISCELLANEOUS

A George III silver gilt vinaigrette, London, 1815, maker's mark of Thomas Brough, the chased hinged cover depicting a classical figural scene, 1¼in. long.
(Bonhams) $600

A Continental parcel-gilt model of a stag, in the early 17th century taste, on a fluted oval base engraved with deer, 6in., 10oz.
(Christie's) $11,212

A Victorian castle top purse form vinaigrette, chased with scrolling foliage, the hinged cover with a view of Windsor Castle, 4.2cm. long, Cronin & Wheeler, Birmingham 1852.
(Bearne's) $433

A German parcel-gilt chalice, on a spreading hexafoil foot and with a baluster stem and plain tapering bowl, Philipp Heinrich Schonling, Frankfurt 1700, 8½in., 14oz.
(Christie's) $2,242

German 800 standard silver table garniture as a pair of strutting peacocks, hollow bodies with detachable heads, 15½in. high, 92oz. 6dwt.
(Butterfield & Butterfield) $2,300

An early 18th century German 'Turkenkopf' chocolate pot, the hemispherical lower part rising to tapering sides with a bulbous cover, by Conradt Blom, Hamburg, 1728/32, 23.5cm. high, 29.5oz.
(Phillips) $19,563

A Victorian silver-mounted mirror, the beveled oval mirror within a silver surround embossed with a figure, birds, vases and a mask, 28cm. high, Fredrick James Wiltshire, London 1879.
(Bearne's) $328

A George III Irish silver dish ring, Dublin, circa 1750, maker's mark EB, circular, the sides pierced with shaped-oval cartouche engraved with a crest, 7¼in. diameter, 10oz.
(Christie's) $4,140

An American silver and other metals Japanese style hexafoil tazza, Tiffany & Co., New York, circa 1880, the top with scalloped rim and spot-hammered, 12oz., 7⅛in. diameter.
(Sotheby's) $21,850

MUGS

A mug of tapering circular form and with a molded rim and scroll handle, maker's initials J.W. & Co., London 1937, 4³/₄in., 11.50oz.
(Christie's) $303

A silver gilt strip handled mug, with everted lip stamped to the plain surface with alternate vertical plain and multi-leaved stems, Chester 1913, 3in. high, 5oz.
(Dee, Atkinson & Harrison) $172

A Victorian gilt-lined christening mug, the body flat-chased with flowers and foliage and engraved with a monogram, Thomas Watson, Newcastle 1858, 4¹/₂in., 5.25oz.
(Christie's) $293

A late Victorian baluster mug richly repoussé, with an oval panel inscribed *A Slight Remembrance of Ecclesall*, Sheffield 1895, 262 grams approximately.
(Phillips) $310

A George III baluster mug, the baluster body later engraved with scrolling flowers and foliage, on pedestal foot, London 1779, 399 grams approximately.
(Phillips) $372

A China Trades 19th century mug, of tapering circular form, extensively decorated with numerous figures, some mounted on horseback, dated *1888*, Wang Hing, 6in., 13.25oz.
(Christie's) $1,070

A George III baluster mug, the curving and recurving handle decorated with formal foliage, London 1767, 334 grams approximately.
(Phillips) $527

A George III mug of baluster form, on a rising circular foot and with a molded rim and leaf-capped double scroll handle, Langlands & Robertson, Newcastle 1778, 5in., 12oz.
(Christie's) $568

A Regency gilt-lined mug, of tapering circular form and with a leaf-capped bracket handle, maker's initials probably C.F. for Charles Fox, London 1811, 4¹/₂in., 9.75oz.
(Christie's) $380

MUSTARDS

George V oval silver mustard in Adam style, pierced with conjoining scrolls and flower heads, engraved with trailing fern leaves, Chester 1912.
(G. A. Key) $270

A George III mustard pot, London 1796, maker's mark of Robert Jones I, engraved with two reeded bands, plain hinged cover, 2¹/₂in. high, approximately 6oz.
(Bonhams) $450

A William IV drum mustard pot, inscribed with presentation initials within thread and gadroon edging, 7.5cm. high, Thomas James, London 1831.
(Bearne's) $268

A late Victorian electroplated novelty condiment set, circa 1880, modeled as a chinaman holding a simulated bamboo carrying yoke, terminating in baskets holding a salt and pepper pot, 6¹/₄in. high.
(Bonhams) $300

A George III mustard pot, London 1782, maker's mark of Robert Hennell, pierced with vertical slats and oval cartouches, plus a late Victorian spoon, London 1895, 2¹/₄in. high, approx. weight 2.5oz.
(Bonhams) $707

A late Victorian electroplated novelty condiment set, by Elkington & Co., 1877, the pepper pot and mustard pot modeled as riding boots, the salt cellar modeled as a jockey's cap.
(Bonhams) $450

An Edwardian silver mustard pot of drum form, the body with pierced scroll decoration, London 1908, with a spoon and blue glass liner, approximately 3oz.
(Bonhams) $150

A William IV silver mustard pot, Charles Fox, London, 1831, melon-fluted and on spreading shaped-circular foot, with leaf-capped scroll handle, 3¹/₂in. high, 5oz.
(Christie's) $138

A late Victorian Aesthetic Movement mustard pot, London, 1879, maker's mark of Henry Holland, engraved with swallows and herons in flight over a river scene, 2¹/₄in. high, approximately 2oz.
(Bonhams) $450

PITCHERS & EWERS

Ball, Black and Company silver ewer, 1860s, chased floral and scroll decoration, engraved monogram, approx. 40 troy oz.
(Skinner) **$1,380**

An American 19th century ewer, the ovoid body decorated with friezes of shells, foliage and scrolls, Gorham, 9¹/₂in., 31.25oz.
(Christie's) **$897**

A Victorian parcel-gilt Cellini pattern wine ewer, 31cm. high, Daniel Houle & Charles Houle, London 1870, 25.8oz.
(Bearne's) **$1,013**

Frank W. Smith Silver Co., Inc. sterling pitcher, 19th century, rococo style, baluster form, chased leaf and diamond quilting design, 9¹/₂in. high, approximately 35 troy oz.
(Skinner) **$1,150**

Silver barrel-form pitcher and two beakers, Fletcher and Gardiner, Philadelphia, circa 1811, marked *Fletcher & Gardiner, Philada*, various engravings, 32 troy oz.
(Skinner) **$2,300**

Gorham sterling water pitcher, 1893, retailed by Theodore B. Starr, raised and chased German Renaissance design, monogrammed *CML EMC*, approximately 73 troy oz.
(Skinner) **$8,625**

S. Kirk & Son Co. sterling pitcher, 1896–1925, repoussé village scene on a stippled ground, surrounded by foliage, 12in. high, approx. 41 troy oz.
(Skinner) **$2,185**

Tiffany sterling presentation ewer, late 19th century, vintage pattern, engraved dedication, 14¹/₂in. high, approximately 80 troy oz.
(Skinner) **$11,500**

A Victorian gilt-lined ewer, on a rim foot and with an egg and dart rim and scroll handle, Messrs. Barnard, London 1880, 6¹/₂in., 16.25oz.
(Christie's) **$621**

PITCHERS & EWERS

Stebbins & Co., coin silver ewer, New York, 1836–1856, chased vintage pattern, approx. 31 troy oz.
(Skinner) $1,380

European silver ewer, 19th century, baluster-form, overall chased and applied floral shell and scroll design, 10in. high, approx. 29 troy oz.
(Skinner) $805

Gorham mixed metal wine ewer, 1888, hammered copper with applied silver birds in a landscape, 13in. high.
(Skinner) $2,760

An American silver large iced water pitcher, Tiffany & Co., New York, circa 1920, St. Dunstan pattern, with ice guard and faceted body, 48oz., 11in. high.
(Sotheby's) $3,737

An American silver water pitcher, Tiffany & Co., New York, circa 1885, of baluster form, embossed and chased all over with chrysanthemums and other flowers, 26oz., 7^1/$_4$in. high.
(Sotheby's) $4,887

An American silver Japanese style water pitcher, Whiting Mfg. Co., Providence, RI, circa 1880–90, with spot-hammered surface, the front ribbed below the spout, 40oz. 10dwt., 9in. high.
(Sotheby's) $14,375

An American silver water pitcher, Saunders Pittman, Providence, Rhode Island, circa 1800, of Liverpool pottery type, plain barrel-shaped body, 22oz., 9^1/$_6$in. high.
(Sotheby's) $6,900

An American silver Japanese style water pitcher, Dominick & Haff, New York, 1879, of baluster form, engraved with a pond scene, 20oz. 10dwt., 8in. high.
(Sotheby's) $3,162

American silver presentation ewer, Gale & Will, New York, circa 1860, inscribed *In Gratitude To Our Distinguished Rabbi and Leader 1860*, 8^3/$_4$in. high.
(Skinner) $2,300

599

PORRINGERS

A good Charles II porringer embossed with acanthus leaves and having caryatid handles, by Sir Thomas Fowles, 1678, 10.1cm. high, 12oz.
(Phillips) **$7,199**

An American silver porringer, Paul Revere, Sr., Boston, circa 1740–50, keyhole handle engraved with contemporary initials *P* above *IM*, 7oz. 8dwt., 4³/₄in. diameter.
(Sotheby's) **$4,887**

A George III porringer, the body decorated with spiral fluting and a rope-twist band, London 1767, 4¹/₂in., 8oz.
(Christie's) **$888**

An American silver porringer, Paul Revere Jr., Boston, Massachusetts, circa 1790, of wide circular form, keyhole handle engraved with script initial *L*, 8oz., 5⁵/₈in. diameter.
(Sotheby's) **$13,800**

A George III Channel Islands porringer or christening cup of Guernsey type, the 'S'-scroll handles with beaded rat-tails, attributed to John Hardie, Guernsey, circa 1769, 7cm. high, 4oz.
(Phillips) **$1,377**

An American silver porringer, Samuel Vernon, Newport, Rhode Island, circa 1730, double-arched keyhole handle engraved with early initials *A* over *IA*, 9oz.
(Sotheby's) **$4,312**

A George III porringer, of inverted bell shape, on a spreading foot and with a molded rim, maker's initials possibly W.S. or S.M., London 1766, 4¹/₂in., 8.50oz.
(Christie's) **$590**

An American partially gilded Japanese style covered porringer, Tiffany & Co., New York, circa 1880–90, the sides decorated with beaded scrolls, 13oz. gross, 5¹/₂in. diameter.
(Sotheby's) **$3,737**

A William and Mary silver porringer, John Hodson, London, 1691, the cylindrical body with two scroll handles and slightly everted lip, 4¹/₄in. high, 11oz.
(Christie's) **$2,933**

SALTS & PEPPERS

A Victorian novelty pepperette, modeled as a knight's helmet, the hinged visor engraved with a crest, George Unite, Birmingham 1879, 2½in.
(Christie's) $267

Robert Hennell, a set of four George III oval salts, crested, with fret sides, beaded borders, fitted blue glass liners, London 1773.
(Woolley & Wallis) $870

A pair of Edwardian novelty salt cellars, modeled as ducks, each with white and black glass boot button eyes and a blue glass liner, Crisford & Norris, Birmingham 1906, salt cellars 3¾in. long.
(Christie's) $1,000

A 17th century German parcel gilt capstan salt cellar, Nuremberg, circa 1660, embossed with trailing foliate scrolls, plain waisted neck, crimped borders, 3in. high, approx. weight 1.75oz.
(Bonhams) $785

A set of four George III gilt-lined salt cellars, of octagonal form, each with a reeded rim and engraved crest, Robert & David Hennell, London 1795, 3in., 10.25oz.
(Christie's) $888

A Victorian novelty pepper, in the form of a four identical sided turreted and inhabited Tudor gateway, Birmingham 1888, 3⅛in. high, 2.75oz.
(Dee, Atkinson & Harrison) $720

A good set of four George IV salts of squat circular form, with flared wavy rims decorated with ribbing, by Robert Garrard, 1826, 11cm. diameter, crested, 60oz.
(Phillips) $7,825

A pair of Victorian cast silver-gilt figural salts modeled as 18th century child street vendors, each one with a pannier over one arm, by Hunt & Roskell, 1870, 18.5cm. high.
(Phillips) $11,268

A pair of George III Irish boat-shaped salts on reeded supports, engraved and pierced, by Christopher Haines (Jnr), Dublin, 1792, 10cm. wide, 3.25oz. weighable.
(Phillips) $626

SAUCEBOATS

A pair of George III oval sauce boats, the scalloped bowls with everted rims and gadroon edging, 18cm. long, stamped with unregistered marks of David Whyte and William Holmes, London 1764, 20.2oz.
(Bearne's) $2,086

A George III pair of sauceboats, London 1807, maker's mark of John Emes, crested, plain oval form, approx. weight 24.5oz.
(Bonhams) $2,826

A matched pair of George IV oval sauce boats, the scalloped bowls with reed and scroll edging, 21cm. long, Richard Sibley I, London 1824 and 1826, 37.8oz.
(Bearne's) $4,023

A pair of early Victorian sauce boats, each engraved with two crests with a coronet above, Robert Hennell, London 1845, 8¼in., 30oz.
(Christie's) $2,363

Pair of Victorian silver sauce boats, marked *H.S.*, London, 1899–1900, shell form bowl, applied shell and scroll border, engraved crest, approximately 35 troy oz.
(Skinner) $1,495

A pair of George III sauceboats, on shaped oval spreading bases, gadroon borders and leaf-capped, by David Whyte & William Holmes, 1764, 33.25oz.
(Phillips) $3,450

A George III Irish Provincial sauceboat, with a flying scroll handle, a beaded border and a near vertical spout, by Carden Terry, Cork, circa 1785, 19.5cm. wide, 11oz.
(Phillips) $1,575

A pair of modern Irish sauce boats, each with a scalloped rim and leaf-capped flying scroll handle, 17.6cm. wide, Dublin 1969, 13.2oz.
(Bearne's) $358

One of a pair of silver sauce boats, Sheffield 1934, made by Mappin and Webb, each with shaped rim and scroll handle, 6.54 troy oz., 6in. long.
(Peter Wilson)
(Two) $250

602

SAUCEBOATS

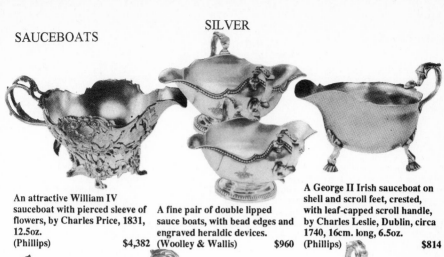

An attractive William IV sauceboat with pierced sleeve of flowers, by Charles Price, 1831, 12.5oz.
(Phillips) $4,382

A fine pair of double lipped sauce boats, with bead edges and engraved heraldic devices.
(Woolley & Wallis) $960

A George II Irish sauceboat on shell and scroll feet, crested, with leaf-capped scroll handle, by Charles Leslie, Dublin, circa 1740, 16cm. long, 6.5oz.
(Phillips) $814

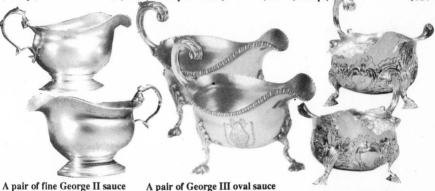

A pair of fine George II sauce boats, Paul de Lamerie, London, 1730, Britannia Standard, engraved with bands of latticework, strapwork, shells and matting, 7³/₄in. long, 30oz.
(Christie's) $72,345

A pair of George III oval sauce boats, on shell applique cast scroll legs with shell feet, possibly William Lancaster, London 1774, 14.5oz.
(Woolley & Wallis) $2,025

A pair of George II silver sauce boats, Elizabeth Hartley, London, 1748, with leaf-capped flying scroll handle and shaped rim, 12¹/₄in. long, 25oz.
(Christie's) $4,388

The Mackay Service, an American silver sauce boat and stand, Tiffany & Co., New York, circa 1877, the oval boat embossed and chased, 47oz. 10dwt., 9⁷/₈in. long.
(Sotheby's) $19,550

A fine pair of George III oval sauce boats, with gadroon edges, Benjamin Stephenson, London 1774, 24oz.
(Woolley & Wallis) $3,750

A mid-18th century Scottish sauceboat, Glasgow, circa 1750, maker's mark of Milne & Campbell, plain oval bellied form, wavy border, approx. weight 8oz.
(Bonhams) $597

SNUFF BOXES

A George III Scottish oval snuff box, cover engraved with crest and monogram in bead-edged navette cartouche, Edinburgh, 1784, 9.2cm. long.
(Phillips) $1,440

An early 19th century Russian novelty snuff box, formed as the figure of a guard dog crouched and ready to pounce, Moscow, circa 1805, 7.25cm. long, 2oz.
(Phillips) $1,283

A George III silver-gilt snuff-box of oblong engine-turned form, with acorn and oak leaf borders, by Linnit & Atkinson, 1814, 7.6cm. long, 3.75oz.
(Phillips) $1,221

A late 17th/early 18th century Norwegian oval snuff box, cover chased with scrolling foliage on matted ground, by Adrian Setsen Bogarth, Trondheim, circa 1700, 6.2cm. high.
(Phillips) $960

An early 19th century French gold and enamel snuff box, the rock crystal cover carved with rococo shells and scrolls, by Augustin-André Héguin, Paris, 1819/38, 5.5cm. long.
(Phillips) $1,956

An early 18th century oval snuff box, the tortoiseshell cover inlaid with silver and mother-of-pearl leaf designs, circa 1700, 6.7cm. long.
(Phillips) $657

An attractive 18th century Continental mounted mother-of-pearl double-lidded snuff box of rectangular form, etched with flowers, probably French, circa 1750, 7cm. long.
(Phillips) $689

A Victorian 18ct. gold oval snuff box, cover decorated with a large armorial, the arms of Chichester quartering Itchingham, by John Linnit, 1849, 8.1cm. long, 5.5oz.
(Phillips) $13,772

A George IV oblong engine-turned snuff box, with floral thumbpiece cover set with oval agate panel carved with crest and motto, by Charles Rawlings, 1822, 7.1cm. long.
(Phillips) $672

A French gold snuff-box, maker's mark LT, circa 1840, chased and engraved with two ladies in classical costume, 3^1/$_8$in. long.
(Christie's) $5,851

A gold and lapis lazuli snuff-box, probably German, circa 1810, the hinged cover and base of polished and beveled lapis lazuli, 3^1/$_4$in. long.
(Christie's) $2,743

A Swiss gold and enamel snuff-box, circa 1810, the hinged cover painted with a couple and two dogs in a river landscape, 3^1/$_2$in. long.
(Christie's) $7,680

SNUFF BOXES

A George III double compartment snuff box with a double hinged cover, of rounded curved oblong form, by Samuel Pemberton, Birmingham, 1809, 7.5 x 4cm., 2oz.
(Phillips) $910

An unusual Victorian silver-gilt novelty double-lined snuff box modeled as a kennel with hinged roof, by John Keith, 1852, 8cm. long, 3.5oz.
(Phillips) $313

An early Victorian Scottish mounted cow horn snuff mull, with a vacant cartouche, a decorative chain suspension handle and five belcher chains, circa 1850, 26cm. long.
(Phillips) $1,252

A George III silver-gilt oblong snuff box with crested cartouches, the plain surfaces with wide engine-turned band at either end, by Henry Tippen, 1815, 9.8cm. long, 4oz.
(Phillips) $438

A Charles II snuff box, of oblong form with rounded, 'squeeze' sides, maker's mark only struck twice TR monogram?, unascribed, circa 1670, 4.5cm. wide.
(Phillips) $720

An early Victorian table snuff box, cover with later inscription encircled by raised flowers and scrolls, by Nathaniel Mills, Birmingham, 1840, 8.7cm. long, 5.5oz.
(Phillips) $626

A good early 18th century Dutch gold and tortoiseshell snuff box, cover inlaid with a cartouche of birds and animals, probably by Johan Doede or Johannes van Deventer, The Hague, 1736, 8cm. (Phillips) $11,520

An attractive porcelain snuff box in the form of a carnation flowerhead, the closely modeled petals edged in bright pink, 5.8cm., diameter, possibly Meissen, early 19th century.
(Phillips) $988

A good 18th century French Provincial snuff box of oblong form, cover chased with a drummer dancing, gilt interior, by I. D. Tiron, Lille, 1741, 7.6cm. high, 3.5oz.
(Phillips) $2,560

An 18th century German cartouche-shaped snuff box, by Johann Jakob Biller (II), Augsburg, 1755/57, 7.5cm. wide. (Phillips) $1,920

A late 18th century Schleswig-Holstein silver-gilt snuff box, mark SNB for Sven Nordberg, Heide, circa 1780, 8.1cm. x 6.4cm., 5.5oz.
(Phillips) $1,600

A George I tortoiseshell oval snuff box, with gold piqué work decoration of a large Baroque style shell, circa 1720, 6.5cm. long. (Phillips) $1,248

TANKARDS

A George II silver tankard, by
Fuller White, 1746, of plain
waisted baluster form on
spreading circular foot, 8¹/₂in.
high, 24oz.
(Christie's) $1,786

A George III lidded tankard, of
tapering cylindrical form, on a
flaring foot and with a molded
body band and rim, Jacob
Marsh, London 1766, 7in., 21oz.
(Christie's) $2,297

An early Queen Anne Irish
tankard, of tapering shape with
twisted scroll thumbpiece, by
David King, Dublin, 1702,
17.5cm. high, 23.75oz.
(Phillips) $5,400

A late 17th century lidded
tankard, of plain tapering
circular form, on a rim foot,
maker's initials E.G., London,
the date letters indistinct,
probably 1681 or 1691, 5³/₄in.,
17.75oz.
(Christie's) $3,968

A William IV silver-gilt
tankard, William Eaton,
London, 1832, the slightly
tapered cylindrical body applied
with an oval plaque depicting a
horse race, 122oz., 31.5cm. high.
(Sotheby's) $9,804

A George I style quart tankard
with flat cover, scroll thumb
piece and S-scroll handle, the
plain body with stepped foot,
Reid & Son, London 1937,
7¹/₂in., 41oz.
(Christie's) $1,096

A George I silver tankard,
Humphrey Payne, London,
1726, plain tapering cylindrical
and on a molded rim foot, 7¾in.
high, 34oz.
(Christie's) $4,830

A George III tankard of
baluster form, subsequently
chased and with added spout,
20.5cm. high, maker's mark I.K.,
London 1791, 29.9oz.
(Bearne's) $1,192

A George III lidded tankard, of
tapering circular form, on a
flaring foot, Thomas & Richard
Payne, London 1778, 7¹/₄in.,
24.25oz.
(Christie's) $2,025

SILVER

A George II tapering pint
tankard, Exeter 1736.
(Tennants) $2,693

An American silver tankard,
John Edwards, Boston, circa
1720–30, plain tapered
cylindrical form, 26oz., 8¼in.
high.
(Sotheby's) $6,900

A Georgian tankard by Peter
and William Bateman, London,
1807, approximately 25oz.
(Academy) $1,256

A George II tankard of baluster
circular form, subsequently
chased and with later added
spout, the domed hinged cover
with openwork thumbpiece,
20cm. high, William Shaw II
and William Priest, London
1758. (Bearne's) $1,341

A very fine American silver
tankard, Simeon Soumaine, New
York, 1725–1740, the S-scroll
handle applied with punch-
beaded rattail, 7in. high, 32oz.
(Christie's) $57,500

A Norwegian silver peg tankard,
Jens Christensen Seestell,
Trondheim, circa 1685, the body
later engraved with two names,
the date 1775 and a quotation
from the Book of Proverbs,
7¼in. high, 26oz.
(Christie's) $20,700

Silver tankard, John Burt,
Boston, Massachusetts, circa
1745, the handle with initials
W/WE on an applied plaque,
8in. high, 25oz.
(Butterfield & Butterfield)
                     $3,737

An early 18th century lidded
tankard, of tapering circular
form, on a domed foot and with
a scroll handle, probably
London circa 1720, 7½in.,
30.25oz.
(Christie's) $1,518

An American silver tankard,
John David, Philadelphia, circa
1760–70, of baluster form,
engraved with contemporary
foliate monogram ECS, 31oz.,
8½in. high.
(Sotheby's) $24,150

TEA CADDIES

A fine Victorian tea caddy, in 18th century high rococo style, the shaped body with repoussé chinoiserie panels, 6in., Thomas Smily, London 1863, 18.5oz. (Woolley & Wallis)

$2,508

A Dutch 19th century tea caddy, the sides chased with grotesque masks, swags and foliage and with vacant oval cartouches, 3½in. (Christie's)

$384

Fine Victorian silver tea caddy of bombé-sided square design, heavily embossed shell and bead decoration, 4in. tall, London 1869 by S. W. Smith & Co. of Birmingham, 11oz. (G. A. Key)

$540

A German mid 18th century tea caddy, of fluted tapering shaped oblong form and on a conforming spreading foot, probably by Arnold Krullre, Bremen, circa 1740, 4¾in., 6.75oz. (Christie's)

$1,587

A pair of George I silver tea caddies, Anthony Nelme, London, circa 1720, Britannia Standard, each engraved with a coat-of-arms within a shell, scroll and foliage cartouche, 4in. high, 13oz. (Christie's)

$18,112

A George III tea caddy, London 1794, maker's mark of Henry Chawner, crested, with an upper and lower border of wrigglework and bright-cut decoration, 6in. high, approx. weight 13.5oz. (Bonhams)

$2,355

An American silver and other metals Japanese style tea caddy, Tiffany & Co., New York, circa 1880, of baluster form, applied with a mokume butterfly, 9oz., 4½in. high. (Sotheby's)

$3,737

An Edwardian tea caddy, of oval form, with swing scroll handle, Elkington & Co., Sheffield 1907, 4¾in.; and an Old English pattern caddy spoon, London 1911, 11.25oz. (Christie's)

$837

A Regency tea caddy, of oblong bombé shape, on scrolling foliate feet and with chased and applied floral and foliate decoration, Joseph Angell, London 1819, 5½in., 17.25oz. (Christie's)

$2,473

TEA KETTLES

Spirit kettle and stand, by
Walker & Hall, Sheffield, the
oval ribbed kettle with ebonized
handle and finial, 13½in.
(Peter Wilson) $180

Georgian sterling kettle on a
stand, John Schofield, London,
1791–92, chased floral design,
14in. high., approximately 73
troy oz.
(Skinner) $1,092

A German Jugendstil plated tea
kettle, circa 1900, in the WMF
style, the circular kettle with
fixed handle, 11½in. high
overall.
(Christie's) $380

A reproduction of a George I
kettle, compressed circular with
waisted neck and faceted spout,
the stand on three scroll
supports, 1934, 33cm. high,
57oz.
(Phillips) $1,330

A tea kettle of tapering circular
form, with a rising curved spout,
on a warming stand with
burner, Boardman, Glossop &
Co. Ltd., Sheffield 1915, 9½in.,
39oz. gross.
(Christie's) $959

Chinese Export kettle and stand,
late 19th century, Woshing 'An
Ch'ang, diamond shape, applied
and chased birds among
blossoming prunus, 12in. high,
approximately 38 troy oz.
(Skinner) $1,380

An Edwardian tea kettle, of
part-fluted molded oblong
form, maker's initials R. & S.,
London 1910, the burner a
different maker, London 1911,
12in. overall, 52.75oz. gross.
(Christie's) $948

A George IV tea kettle, stand
and burner, the former of
compressed pear shape and with
a rising curved spout, Robert
Hennell, London 1824, 12in.
overall, 64.25oz. gross.
(Christie's) $1,148

A George II silver tea kettle,
stand, lamp and stand, Gabriel
Sleath, London, 1727, part
wicker covered swing handle
and plain hinged cover, 15in.
high overall, 116oz. gross.
(Christie's) $36,570

TEA & COFFEE SETS

An Edwardian three-piece tea service, of compressed molded circular form and on rim bases, each with an applied gadroon, shell and scroll rim, William Comyns, London 1907, height of teapot 5in., 46oz. gross.
(Christie's) $972

A China Trades 19th century three-piece tea service, of compressed molded circular form, each extensively decorated with vignettes, Wang Hing, each also struck with character marks, height of teapot 4³/₄in., 34oz.
(Christie's) $884

Tea service, 1930s, comprising: teapot, milk jug and sugar basin, electroplated metal, each piece in the form of a stylized car with the mascot forming the spout, teapot 11cm. high.
(Sotheby's) $2,725

A late Victorian three-piece tea service, each piece of shaped oval form, embossed with flowers and scrolling foliage, W. Hutton & Sons Ltd., London 1900, 36.5oz.
(Bearne's) $726

Georg Jensen three-piece sterling demitasse set, coffee pot, creamer, covered sugar, blossom pattern, creamer, circa 1919, coffee pot and sugar 1925–32, with ivory handles, with tray, approximately 33 troy oz.
(Skinner) $4,887

A French silver-gilt six-piece breakfast coffee service, Paris, second half 19th century, of Empire style, comprising tray, coffee pot, cream jug, sugar vase and cover, a coffee cup and circular saucer, coffee pot 6¹/₂in. high, 56oz. gross.   (Christie's) $6,992

Italian sterling three piece coffee set with matching tray, M. Buccellati, Milan, comprising: coffee pot, cream pitcher and sugar bowl with cover, footed pyriform vessels with spiral fluting, cartouche form tray, gross weight 101oz. 4dwt.
(Butterfield & Butterfield) $2,300

A good Victorian tea and coffee service, the hexagonal paneled and flared bodies with bold C scroll and cartouche pattern mounts, coffee pot 11.25in. high, by E.J. & W. Barnard, London 1843 (gross weight 75oz.)
(Canterbury) $2,387

TEA & COFFEE SETS

An Edward VII three-piece circular tea service, each piece with a reeded lower body, gadroon edging and leaf-capped scroll handles on a spreading circular foot rim, Nathan & Hayes, Chester 1906, 41oz.
(Bearne's) $626

An Art Deco four-piece tea and coffee service, each piece of oblong form with reeded corners and a scalloped rim, Mappin & Webb, Sheffield 1946–47, 62.1oz., together with a pair of electroplated sugar tongs.
(Bearne's) $1,565

Four-piece English silver tea and coffee service, teapot, London, 1800–01, Richard Cooke; coffee pot, creamer and sugar, London, 1884–85, J.B. monogram, approx. 64 troy oz.
(Skinner) $1,265

N. J. Bogert sterling three-piece tea set, New York, circa 1830, fluted sides with repeating stylized floral border, floral finials, approximately 76 troy oz.
(Skinner) $1,840

Federal silver four piece tea service, Joel Sayre, New York, New York, circa 1800–1810, comprising: pointed oval teapot, sugar bowl with cover, cream pitcher and waste bowl, teapot 7³/₄in. high, gross weight 48oz.
(Butterfield & Butterfield) $2,587

A George V three-piece tea service, each piece of plain tapering form with an undulating rim and scroll handles, the teapot with leaf-capped scroll handle and ivory finial, Coles & Fryer, Birmingham 1910, 24.7oz.
(Bearne's) $834

Three-piece Irish silver tea service, lobed-form with chased and applied scroll and floral design, teapot and sugar, George IV, 1827, possibly by Edward Parer; creamer, William IV, 1830–01, possibly by Chas. Marsh, approx. 47 troy oz.
(Skinner) $1,092

A fine George IV tea and coffee service comprising: teapot and cover with flower knop, similar pedestal coffee pot, two handled sugar basin and milk jug, London 1826, makers Rebecca Emes and Edward Barnard, 2560 grams gross. (Phillips) $3,410

TEAPOTS

Large Georgian styled silver teapot, circular shaped with body bands, composition handle, London 1899, 26oz.
(G. A. Key) **$317**

A William IV teapot of circular form with pineapple finial on domed lid, 11½in. wide, 24oz. 2dwts, London 1837, makers mark *I W*.
(Andrew Hartley) **$713**

John Emes, a George III oval teapot, on a foliage engraved rim foot, London 1803, 17oz. all in.
(Woolley & Wallis) **$860**

A George IV teapot of lobed compressed circular form, embossed with acanthus decoration, 14cm. high, John Bridge, London 1824, 26.2oz.
(Bearne's) **$433**

An unusual George III teapot, of shaped oval form, the sides molded with simulated bamboo, London 1770, 4in., 11.25oz. gross.
(Christie's) **$405**

A George IV pedestal teapot, on a rising rounded oblong base with ball feet, Adey Bellamy Savory, London 1828, 7¾in., 25oz.
(Christie's) **$888**

Dutch 833 standard silver teapot, A. de Groot-Boersma, Sneek, circa 1875–1909, pyriform vessel with pull-off lid and figural spout, 6½in. high, 14oz. 4dwt.
(Butterfield & Butterfield) **$1,092**

Tiffany enameled sterling demitasse pot, 1875–1891, mid-Eastern influence, acid-etched Arabesque design with champ shaded opaque enamel accents, 2½ gills.
(Skinner) **$3,105**

A large Regency teapot, scroll handle with Chinaman thumb piece, gadroon and foliate everted rim, Thomas Wallis & Jonathan Hayne, London 1819, 8¾in., 34oz.
(Christie's) **$873**

A 19th century Indian Colonial teapot, of melon-fluted form, on foliate and bun feet and with a molded everted rim, Hamilton & Co., Calcutta circa 1830, 5¾in., 36oz.
(Christie's) **$672**

Continental 12 standard silver teapot, maker's initials: *IWGB*, circa 1805, straight sided oval vessel with coved collar with gallery, 6in. high, gross weight 19oz. 2dwt.
(Butterfield & Butterfield) **$1,380**

A Georgian teapot of dished oblong form with flower finial on domed lid, gadrooned edging flattened loop handle, 10½in. wide, 1784 maker's mark *N H*, 23oz. 6dwt.
(Andrew Hartley) **$589**

A George II Provincial miniature or saffron teapot of bullet shape, Samuel Willmott, Plymouth, circa 1730, 4oz.
(Phillips) $2,817

A good early 18th century Dutch (Friesland) teapot, of squat circular form embossed with panels of flowers, by Gerard van Velsen, Bolsward, 1729, 13oz.
(Phillips) $4,160

A Victorian teapot of lobed baluster form, 18cm. high, Edward Barnard & John Barnard, London 1852, 23.4oz.
(Bearne's) $402

Russian silver teapot, Khlebnikov, 19th century, ovoid-form with inlaid enamel floral bouquets, 4$\frac{1}{2}$in. high, approximately 13 troy oz.
(Skinner) $920

A China Trades teapot, of compressed molded circular form, decorated with sinuous dragons amidst clouds, Wang Hing, also struck with a character mark, 5$\frac{1}{4}$in., 24.25oz.
(Christie's) $698

A George II Channel Islands bullet teapot engraved with Baroque cartouche (with later monogram) on one side, Jersey, circa 1745, 14.5oz.
(Phillips) $5,947

A Victorian silver-gilt squat baluster teapot in the style of Edward Farrell, of squat baluster shape, decorated in high relief, by F. B. Thomas, 1875, 15.75oz.
(Phillips) $720

A mid-18th century Dutch teapot, Rotterdam 1753, crested, maker's mark unknown, squat baluster form, each section engraved with rococo scroll cartouches and fish-scales, 6in. high, approx. weight 11oz.
(Bonhams) $3,611

George Angell, a Victorian teapot, in Graeco-Egyptian Revival style, the globular body engraved with anthemions with a flared lip, London 1863, 19oz. all in.
(Woolley & Wallis) $570

A William IV teapot, of part-fluted compressed molded circular form, on a rim foot, Richard Pearce & George Burrows, London 1836, 4$\frac{3}{4}$in., 14.25oz. gross.
(Christie's) $454

A mid-18th century miniature/ toy teapot, stamped twice with maker's mark only *T. P* in a rectangular shield, circa 1740, plain bullet-shape, with a pull-off cover, 2$\frac{1}{2}$in. high, weight 2.5oz.
(Bonhams) $3,297

A William IV teapot, the compressed everted melon paneled body embossed foliage, William Theobalds and Lockington Bunn, London 1835, 27oz. all in.
(Woolley & Wallis) $729

A William III silver tazza, Alice Sheen, London, 1699, Britannia Standard, on spreading foot, with gadrooned borders, 8½in., 9oz.
(Christie's) $1,280

Renaissance Revival silver plated oval tray, late 19th century, mounted with seated cherubs, border in low relief with flowerhead design, 30in. long.
(Skinner) $1,610

A Victorian shaped circular salver, engraved with stylized scrolls, scale and diaperwork, 36.5cm. diameter, Martin Hall & Co., London 1861, 42.2oz.
(Bearne's) $556

A silver and mixed-metal fruit plate, Gorham Mfg. Co., Providence, 1880, the spot-hammered shallow bowl applied with silver dragonfly and silver and copper fruit branches, 12in. diameter, gross weight 33oz. 10dwt.
(Christie's) $20,700

A George I silver-gilt salver, Abraham Buteau, London, 1723, on four bracket feet and with molded reeded rim, 12¼in. square, 45oz.
(Christie's) $19,199

A George III Irish wine funnel stand or counter tray, with beaded border and bright-engraved star cartouche centered by an armored arm crest, by William Bond, Dublin, circa 1785, 8.5cm. diameter, 1.25oz.
(Phillips) $376

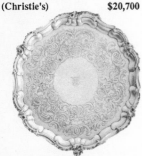

A large Victorian circular salver, the center engraved a crest within a band of scrolling foliage, 14½in., Charles Rawlings and George Summers, London 1846, 41oz.
(Woolley & Wallis) $973

A fine George I silver salver, Benjamin Pyne, London, 1718, Britannia Standard, the center later engraved with a coat-of-arms within a rococo cartouche, 15½in. diameter, 56oz.
(Christie's) $45,713

S. Kirk & Son Co. sterling salver, 1896–1925, raised on three ball and claw feet, chased and applied scroll and foliate border, 12in. diameter, 28 troy oz.
(Skinner) $805

TRAYS & SALVERS

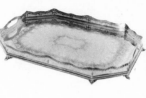

A George II waiter, London 1749, maker's mark of Henry Brind, circular form, shell and scroll border, 8¼in. diameter, approx. weight 13oz.
(Bonhams) $628

A fine late Victorian rectangular tray, with angled corners, 25in., Gibson and Langman (for the Goldsmiths and Silversmiths Co., London), Sheffield 1898, 125oz.
(Woolley & Wallis) $5,550

A George IV Sheffield Plate salver, the center engraved a contemporary armorial within a chased scrolling foliage surround, 12in.
(Woolley & Wallis) $165

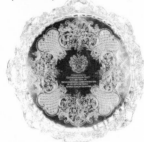

A large Victorian salver, of shaped circular form, on openwork rococo shell feet, with presentation inscription, armorial, crest and motto, John Mortimer & John Samuel Hunt, London 1842, 20in., 100.25oz.
(Christie's) $2,650

A 19th century American mixed metals tray in the Japanese style, the copper tray with bark finish, applied with a silver figure of a Japanese boy, by Gorham & Co., circa 1880, 23.5cm. long.
(Phillips) $800

A George III circular salver, the center engraved with a crest and motto *Per Ardua Ad Alta*, London 1763, probable makers Thomas Hannam and Richard Mills, 760 grams approximately.
(Phillips) $744

A George III circular salver, with gadrooned border, engraved with scrollwork, London 1770, 1350 grams approximately, maker Richard Rugg, 35cm. diameter.
(Phillips) $608

A late Victorian salver, of shaped circular form, with presentation inscription of naval interest, Henry Archer, Sheffield 1898, 11in., 23oz.
(Christie's) $873

A George III salver, of plain circular form, on shell-fluted bracket feet and with a beaded rim, Daniel Smith & Robert Sharp, London 1782, 10in., 19.75oz.
(Christie's) $1,237

TUREENS

A large Old Sheffield plate two-handled oval tureen and cover, crested above armorials with gadroon, shell and acanthus edging, 40.8cm. wide.
(Bearne's)   **$1,266**

Jean Desprès, soup tureen and cover, 1930's, silver colored metal with a martelé finish, the bowl with two handles, 27.5cm. maximum diameter.
(Sotheby's)   **$3,816**

A Georgian crested Adam style oval tureen by Henry Greenway, with urn finial on domed lid, reeded loop handles, 9in. wide, London 1779, 18oz. 7dwts.
(Andrew Hartley)   **$882**

A pair of George III silver soup tureens, covers and liners, Paul Storr, London, 1812, each on four cast acanthus leaf scroll and pad feet, 15in. wide, 372oz.
(Christie's)   **$81,090**

A pair of Old Sheffield plate soup tureens and covers, of tapering rounded oblong form, each applied with gadrooned friezes and on ball feet, 11³/₄in.
(Christie's)   **$843**

A pair of George III oval sauce tureens, engraved a contemporary armorial with a baron's coronet, Henry Chawner, London 1788, 25oz.
(Woolley & Wallis)
                             $2,775

Danish sterling soup tureen with cover and stand, Georg Jensen, Copenhagen, circa 1933–1944, circular bowl with flat base and bombé sides, 8in. high, 62oz. 12dwt.
(Butterfield & Butterfield)
                             $9,775

A pair of George III sauce tureens and covers, with beaded oval bodies, oval beaded pedestals, by John Kidder, 1780, crest and initialed, 22.25cm. wide overall, 41oz.
(Phillips)   **$3,600**

George III silver soup tureen with cover and plated liner, Robert Garrard, London, 1808, the stepped domed lid with a finial as a spray of roses, 9³/₄in. high, 100oz. 18dwt.
(Butterfield & Butterfield)
                             $11,500

URNS

19th century EPNS tea urn, half reeded body and lid, scroll and acanthus leaf handles, the brass tap with shield shaped horn handle, 15½in. high.
(Peter Wilson) **$128**

Antique oval Sheffield silver plated hot water urn, on stand with burner, sphinx-form finial, 16in. high.
(Eldred's) **$550**

Russian samovar, the ribbed urn shaped body with geometric handles and spout, ebonized finials, 20in.
(Peter Wilson) **$165**

A silver presentation punch urn, Paul Revere, Boston, 1796, one side engraved with the elevation of the Boston Theater, the other with inscription, 11⅝in. high, 31oz.
(Christie's) **$68,500**

An Old Sheffield plate coffee urn of reeded barrel shape, on a square base with ball feet, 10¾in.
(Christie's) **$675**

Rare sterling silver tea urn, cover with urn-form finial, beaded acanthus leaf handles, hallmarks for London, 1785, Hester Bateman, 46.2 troy oz.
(Eldred's) **$5,060**

A silver tea urn, Gorham Mfg. Co., Providence, 1868, the body with a spigot with a tap in the form of a putto raising a glass, 18¼in. high, 102oz. 10dwt.
(Christie's) **$14,950**

George III silver covered tea urn, in vasiform with engraved shield, two handles and square base, hallmarks for London, 1793, maker's mark of Paul Storr, 18in. high, 96.6 troy oz.
(Eldred's) **$9,350**

Copper samovar, baluster form with brass tap, foliate borders, ceramic handles and on four scrolled feet, 19th century, 24in. high.
(G. A. Key) **$188**

VASES

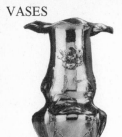

A Martelé silver vase, Gorham Mfg. Co., Providence, circa 1908, shaped baluster form, on four feet, with everted undulating rim, 10¼in. high, 36oz. (Christie's) $6,900

A pair of tulip shaped vases, with alternating panels of stylized foliage, spreading circular bases, 6in. high, 1924, 10oz.
(Neales) $215

An early 19th century Maltese sugar vase of inverted pear shape, on pedestal foot, by Gaetano Cauchi, circa 1805, 15.5cm. high, 10oz.
(Phillips) $1,956

A George III silver sugar vase, makers mark, George Cowdery or George Cowles, London, 1766, the pear-shaped body raised on mermaid caryatid supports, 13oz., 13cm. high.
(Sotheby's) $2,139

Pair of Gorham sterling covered vases, circa 1900, trumpet form, pierced chased and applied Classical Revival style, articulated handles, cobalt liner, 17⅝in. high, approx. 86 troy oz.
(Skinner) $6,037

A fine silver and enamel presentation vase, Tiffany & Co., New York, 1889–1892, in the Persian taste, lobed baluster, 9¼in. high, gross weight 73oz. 10dwt.
(Christie's) $21,850

One of a pair of Cymric rocket vases, pierced with stylized flowerheads beneath a wavy border, on three buttress supports, green glass liners, 6½in. high.
(Neales)   (Two) $285

Pair of French vermeil vases, Bointaburet, Paris, 19th century, high shouldered-form, raised leaf band with floral medallions, 7⅜in. high.
(Skinner) $862

A Chinese Export vase of bellied form with flared lip, the lips applied with prunus, by Wang Hing & Co., Hong Kong, circa 1900, 27.5cm. high, 75oz.
(Phillips) $3,443

VESTA CASES

An Edwardian vesta case, enameled on front with a mallard in flight, cover with ring attachment, by J. M. Banks, Chester, 1904.
(Phillips) $416

An American yellow-colored metal vesta case, nielloed with two heraldic lions, by Tiffany & Co., early 20th century.
(Phillips) $576

A late Victorian vesta case, enameled on front with a coach and four, Birmingham, 1896.
(Phillips) $1,088

A Victorian enameled silver rectangular vesta case, decorated on one side with a woman in a black dress walking down steps, 5.2cm. long, C. H. Cheshire, Birmingham 1891.
(Bearne's) $626

A late Victorian rectangular vesta case enameled with a mounted field officer of the Royal Artillery, with sabretache at his side, by Sampson Mordan & Co., 1890, 5.6cm. high.
(Phillips) $2,560

A rare late Victorian vesta case, enameled in large white letters *MAJUBA*, the word crossed out by three red enamel bars, the central one with the words *WIPED OUT*, by John Millward Banks, Chester, 1900.
(Phillips) $908

A Victorian vesta case, front enameled with a circular panel showing a man in red and white striped shirt rowing, maker's mark *C^E &F^D*, Birmingham, 1893, 3.9cm. long.
(Phillips) $626

A brass vesta case made in the form of a half hunter pocket watch, pendant can be hinged back to open case which stores matches, circa 1900, 49mm. diameter.
(Pieces of Time) $272

An Edwardian vesta case, chased with an interlaced 'D' like motif with turquoise blue enamel, Liberty & Co., Birmingham, 1901.
(Phillips) $288

A pair of Old Sheffield plate wine coolers, of tapering circular form and on rising circular bases, 10in.
(Christie's) $1,265

Hungarian silver wine cooler, circa 1924, ovoid-form on four raised feet, peaked lid with figural finial, decorated with repoussé mythical sea creatures, approx. 54 troy oz.
(Skinner) $2,300

A pair of magnificent silver presentation wine coolers, plaques attributed to Eugene J. Soligny, maker's mark of Tiffany & Co., New York, 1873, 13⅝in. high, 246oz.
(Christie's) $68,500

A pair of George IV Old Sheffield plate wine coolers, unmarked, circa 1825, campana-shaped, the lower part of the bodies applied with acanthus foliage and with two foliate scroll bracket handles, 9¹/₂in. high.
(Christie's) $2,070

A George IV Irish two-handled wine cooler, Dublin 1826, maker's mark of Edward Power and also Edward Twycross, raised on a circular foot with a stylized leaf border, 11½in. high, approx. weight 104oz.
(Bonhams) $5,966

A pair of Old Sheffield plated two-handled wine coolers, circa 1840, crested, maker's mark of Waterhouse, Hartfield and Co., campana form, leaf-capped scroll handles, 10¹/₄in. high.
(Bonhams) $2,512

A pair of Regency Sheffield Plate wine coolers, the campana shape bodies partly ribbed, engraved contemporary armorials, 8in.
(Woolley & Wallis) $2,356

Georgian silver champagne bucket, with liner, Wm. Fountain, London, 1805–06, vase-form, on circular foot, base chased with flutes, 9⅝in. high, approximately 92 troy oz.
(Skinner) $6,325

Two silver-gilt wine coolers and liners, William Eley II, London, 1828 and 1830, each on spreading circular waved sea foam base and with similar everted rim, 11³/₄in. high, 325oz.
(Christie's) $27,428

WINE FUNNELS

A Georgian Scottish presentation wine funnel, on stand, Edinburgh maker's mark 1 D, 4¼in. high.
(Andrew Hartley) $423

A George III silver wine funnel, Dublin, 1803, maker's mark indistinct, with a detachable strainer and reeded borders, 6in. long, 6oz.
(Christie's) $405

George III two part silver wine funnel of usual form with gadrooned edge and plain clip, London 1771.
(G. A. Key) $180

Modern silver wine funnel in traditional style of two parts with beaded and reeded detail, London Assay.
(G. A. Key) $155

A George III wine funnel with thread edging, the detachable liner with a shaped clip, 15cm. high, Alice & George Burrows II, London 1806, 5.5oz.
(Bearne's) $476

A George IV silver wine funnel, Charles Fox, London, 1827, campana-shaped and with fluted detachable bowl, 5¼in., 4oz.
(Christie's) $690

A George III silver wine funnel and a Scottish silver wine funnel stand, the funnel Naphthali Hart, London, 1805, the stand Edinburgh, 1814, maker's mark WP, 6½in. long, 7oz.
(Christie's) $518

A George III silver wine funnel, London, 1796, maker's mark indistinct, with reeded spout and detachable strainer with plain clip, engraved with a crest, 7in. long, 6oz.
(Christie's) $405

Victorian wine funnel applied with three tapering bands to the neck, having curved spout, the liner with foliate tab, London 1840, maker Robert Garrard II, 7.75oz.
(Hobbs & Chambers) $425

WINE LABELS

A Victorian vine leaf wine label with applied title *MADEIRA*, by Reily & Storer, 1849.
(Phillips) $225

A 19th century Scottish Provincial wine label, incised *BRANDY*, by R. & R. Keay, Perth, circa 1825.
(Phillips) $150

A George II plain escutcheon wine label, incised *CHAMPAGNE*, by Sandilands Drinkwater, circa 1740.
(Phillips) $195

Silver metal snuff bottle, circa 1900, in pilgrim flask form with inlaid semi-precious stones, conforming stopper, 3in. high. (Eldred's) $220

Amber snuff bottle, circa 1800, in pebble form with relief carving of a horse and a monkey, 2in. high, coral stopper. (Eldred's) $1,265

Yellow glass snuff bottle, circa 1900, in ovoid form with relief bird and flower design, conforming stopper, 3^{1}/$_4$in. high. (Eldred's) $55

Engraved overlay glass snuff bottle, 19th century, with red mask and mock ring handles, engraved on one face with bird and flowers, 2in. high, coral stopper. (Eldred's) $1,045

Carved porcelain snuff bottle, 19th century, with high relief scene of figures in a boat, clouds and cherry trees, four-character Ch'ien Lung mark, 2^{1}/$_4$in. high, glass stopper. (Eldred's) $1,925

Five-color overlay glass snuff bottle, late 19th century, with pink, green, red, yellow and black birds and flowers in relief on a milk white ground, 2^{3}/$_4$in. high. (Eldred's) $1,980

Cameo agate snuff bottle, early 19th century, in ovoid form with a white crane, deer and jui design on a gray ground, 2^{2}/$_s$in. high, agate stopper. (Eldred's) $990

Interior painted crystal snuff bottle, in rectangular form painted with a portrait of an Empress, signature and seal of Jie Ru, 3in. high, coral stopper. (Eldred's) $302

Soochow School agate snuff bottle, early 19th century, with a design of a lohan with a basket on his back, 2in. high, lapis lazuli stopper. (Eldred's) $1,870

Opal snuff bottle, early 20th
century, in temple jar form with
relief carved phoenix and chih
lung dragons, 3¼in. high.
(Eldred's) $688

Opal snuff bottle, circa 1900, in
the form of a Buddha's hand
fruit with relief carved leaves,
conforming stopper, 2¼in. long.
(Eldred's) $495

Ivory snuff bottle, 19th century,
in temple jar form with relief
figural landscape design,
conforming stopper, 4½in. high.
(Eldred's) $495

Painted enamel snuff bottle,
18th century, in pear shape with
western style scene of cherubs,
four-character Ch'ien Lung
mark, 2in. high, gilt bronze
stopper.
(Eldred's) $2,750

Enamelled milk glass snuff
bottle, circa 1935, attributed to
Yeh P'eng-ch'i, painted with
mocking birds in a flowering
tree, four-character Ch'ien
Lung mark, 2½in. high.
(Eldred's) $5,060

Celadon jade snuff bottle, 18th
century, in flattened ovoid form
with carved brown skin area
depicting a sage in a boat
approaching a rustic pavilion,
2⅝in. high, jadeite stopper.
(Eldred's) $5,720

Rich green jadeite snuff bottle,
19th century, in ovoid form with
relief carved carp above waves
design, 2¼in. high, coral
stopper.
(Eldred's) $3,520

Porcelain double snuff bottle,
mid 19th century, in spade
shape with relief figural design,
2½in. high, amber glass
stoppers.
(Eldred's) $715

Jade inlaid Mongolian style
snuff bottle, in pilgrim flask
form set with turquoise and
coral, conforming stopper,
3¾in. high.
(Eldred's) $357

A Brussels mythological tapestry, 17th century, a young man in soldier's garb kneeling before a bejeweled lady with elaborate plumed headdress, 8ft. 10in. x 11ft. 6in.
(Sotheby's) $16,100

A Flemish verdure tapestry, early 18th century, woven with formal gardens before a palace incorporating various fountains and plant life, 9ft. 11in. x 12ft. 1in.
(Sotheby's) $32,200

A Beauvais mythological tapestry of Boreas and Orithyia, from the series 'Les Amours des Dieux', after François Boucher, circa 1760, depicting Orithyia being carried away by Boreas, 9ft. 11in. x 10ft. 1in.
(Sotheby's) $17,250

A Beauvais mythological tapestry of The Rape of Europa, from the series 'Les Amours des Dieux', after cartoons by François Boucher, circa 1760, 9ft. 4$^{1}/_{2}$in. x 9ft. 7$^{1}/_{2}$in.
(Sotheby's) $9,775

An Aubusson pastoral tapestry, last quarter 18th century, after a design by Jean-Baptiste Huët the Elder, woven in wools and silks, depicting three shepherdesses and children with a cow and sheep in the foreground, 92$^{1}/_{2}$in. x 137in.
(Christie's) $17,365

Psyche's Banquet: a French mythological tapestry from The Story of Psyche, Paris, circa 1650, atelier of Raphael de la Planche, faubourg Saint-Germain, or workshops of the Louvre (?) after Michel Coxie, 12ft. x 9ft.
(Sotheby's) $56,885

A 17th century verdure tapestry wall hanging of a hunting scene before a castle, with a wide floral border, 130 x 107in.
(Boardmans) $11,780

A Flemish verdure tapestry, 17th century, the center with lightly wooded landscape, the sides with associated border, 12ft. 7in. x 8ft. 6½in.
(Sotheby's) $14,950

A Franco-Flemish verdure tapestry, early 18th century, the foreground with two cranes, trees and a flowering bush, the middle ground with formal gardens and a castle, 9ft. 6½in. x 10ft.
(Sotheby's) $17,250

A French (Marche) feuilles de choux tapestry, second half 16th century, an elephant, tiger and a stag amidst a heavily wooded area, 9ft. 2in. x 8ft. 10in.
(Sotheby's) $71,250

An Aubusson historical tapestry, 17th century, woven in wools and silks, depicting a lady (possibly Rebecca), surrounded by various maidens and before a large urn, 95½in. x 147½in.
(Christie's) $13,024

An Oudenaarde hunting tapestry depicting 'Les Picadors', circa 1620, gentleman in contemporary costume on horseback roping steer, within lightly wooded landscape, 10ft. x 14ft. 8in.
(Sotheby's) $46,000

A Bing teddy bear with golden mohair, black boot button eyes, pronounced clipped snout, 15in. tall, circa 1910.
(Christie's) $1,023

A 'growling' teddy bear in old gold plush, with orange glass eyes and felt nose, 15in. overall.
(Canterbury) $42

A Steiff cinnamon plush teddy bear, German, circa 1908, with button in ear, black stitched snout, black boot button eyes, with growler, 28in.
(Sotheby's) $4,361

A good Steiff white plush teddy bear, German, circa 1908, with button and remains of white label, excelsior stuffed and with press growler, 11in.
(Sotheby's) $2,726

The Three Bears, German miniature teddy bears, with short brown mohair, amber and black bead eyes, 5in., 4¹/₄in. and 3¹/₂in. tall, in original box.
(Christie's) $450

A Steiff gold plush teddy bear, German, circa 1925, together with a black and white photograph of the bear and owner in 1929, 19in.
(Sotheby's) $1,272

A Steiff centre seam gold plush teddy bear, German, circa 1910, with button in ear, with black stitched snout, black boot button eyes, 28in.
(Sotheby's) $7,631

A pale golden plush covered teddy bear, with large clear and black glass eyes, pronounced clipped snout, black stitched nose, 23in. tall, circa 1910, possibly American.
(Christie's) $692

A Steiff white plush 'teddy baby', German, circa 1930, with button in ear, with beige stitched snout, clipped plush muzzle and open felt mouth, 11in.
(Sotheby's) $2,180

A cinnamon Steiff teddy bear, elongated jointed shaped limbs, hump and button in ear, 16in. tall, circa 1910. (Christie's) $2,216

A pale green 'soldier' teddy bear with amber and black glass bead eyes, clipped snout and jointed padless limbs, 3½in. high, circa 1914. (Christie's) $528

A Steiff teddy bear, with golden mohair, cream felt pads, hump, growler and button in ear, 17in. tall, circa 1920. (Christie's) $6,477

A brown, short plush, Schuco two-faced teddy bear, German, circa 1913, one face with stitched snout and metal-pin eyes, the other with metal snout and eyes on white disks, 3½in. high. (Anderson & Garland) $390

A Chiltern teddy bear, with rich golden curly mohair, clear and black glass eyes painted on black, large cardboard lined feet and hump, 26in. tall, 1930s. (Christie's) $933

An Eduard Cramer teddy bear, with white curly mohair, clear and black glass eyes painted on reverse, clipped plush cut muzzle, 12in. tall, 1920s. (Christie's) $1,534

A Steiff centre seam teddy bear, with golden curly mohair, black boot button eyes, large spoon shaped feet and hump, 22in. tall, circa 1910. (Christie's) $6,795

A Farnell teddy bear, with golden mohair, dark brown and black glass eyes, webbed paw claws, large shaped feet and slight hump, 21in. tall, 1920s. (Christie's) $645

A Merrythought teddy bear, with rich golden mohair, deep amber and black glass eyes, label stitched to left foot pad, 29in. tall, circa 1932. (Christie's) $849

A blue English teddy bear, with large clear and black glass eyes painted on reverse, cream felt pads and growler, 16in. tall, 1920s.
(Christie's) $1,364

A white Steiff teddy bear with brown and black glass eyes, cream felt pads, hump and button in ear with remains of label, 16in. tall, 1930s.
(Christie's) $3,115

'Edward', a Steiff teddy bear, with golden mohair, black boot button eyes, elongated jointed shaped limbs, felt pads and hump, 17in. tall, circa 1910.
(Christie's) $2,216

A musical teddy bear, with brown curly mohair, deep amber and black glass eyes, concertina musical movement in tummy, 22in. tall, late 1930s, operative.
(Christie's) $254

A Chad Valley teddy bear, with golden mohair, large deep amber and black glass eyes, pronounced clipped snout, black stitched 'button' nose, 24in. tall, 1930s.
(Christie's) $441

A Steiff white plush center-seam teddy bear, German, circa 1908, button removed, with beige stitched snout, black boot button eyes, wide apart pricked ears, 24in.
(Sotheby's) $5,088

A Bing teddy bear, with golden mohair, black boot button eyes, black horizontally stitched nose, large cardboard lined feet and hump, 23in. tall, circa 1908.
(Christie's) $849

A gold plush teddy bear 'purse', probably German, circa 1910, with black stitched snout, black boot button eyes, swivel joints, 9in.
(Sotheby's) $2,180

A Steiff gold plush teddy bear, German, circa 1908, button removed, with black stitched snout, excelsior and kapok stuffed with growler, 17in.
(Sotheby's) $3,089

A Steiff teddy bear, with golden curly mohair, brown and black glass eyes, cream felt pads, growler and button in ear, 16in. tall, circa 1920.
(Christie's) $4,431

A Steiff teddy bear, with golden mohair, black boot button eyes, swivel head, elongated jointed shaped limbs, 16in. tall, circa 1910.
(Christie's) $2,727

A German teddy bear, with dark golden mohair, brown and black glass eyes, pronounced snout, 14in. tall, 1920s, probably Sussenguth.
(Christie's)   **$519**

A Glockenspiel teddy bear by Helvetic Co., with long pink mohair, large ears, large glass eyes, concertina musical movement inside tummy, 16in. tall.
(Christie's) $849

'Thomas', an early English teddy bear, with rich golden mohair, clear and black glass eyes painted on reverse, pronounced snout, 13in. tall, circa 1913.
(Christie's) $340

A white Steiff teddy bear, with black boot button eyes, large spoon shaped feet, hump and button in ear, 20in. tall, circa 1908, dressed in a contemporary sailor's suit.
(Christie's)   **$18,686**

A Steiff gold center-seam teddy bear, German, circa 1927, lacking button, with black stitched snout, black and brown glass eyes, 13in.
(Sotheby's) $1,999

A Steiff gold plush center-seam teddy bear, German, circa 1908, button removed, hump back, swivel joints and excelsior stuffed, 28in.
(Sotheby's) $4,179

'Singapore', a Chiltern teddy bear, with golden mohair, pronounced clipped snout, remains of black stitched nose and claws, 26in. tall, 1920s.
(Christie's)   **$713**

A Danish Jydsk desk telephone with dial and cut-off on side. (Auction Team Köln) $154

A ten-line wooden-cased switchboard, German, for normal local battery traffic. (Auction Team Köln) $770

A desk line telephone 25 C 1/5 by Bosse, Berlin, 1938. (Auction Team Köln) $385

A jubilee-issue candlestick telephone, 1976, (Auction Team Köln) $154

A B Mk V field telephone with handset and buzzer, together with an L M Ericsson mouthpiece, circa 1942. (Auction Team Köln) $169

L M Ericsson wall telephone extension with Bell dual receiver. (Auction Team Köln) $1,039

A small 50 - RFT test board, with instructions, 1952. (Auction Team Köln) $169

A twenty-five piece Siemens & Halske desk telephone, circa 1920. (Auction Team Köln) $1,850

A portable field telephone exchange for 26 lines, with copy usage instructions, circa 1935. (Auction Team Köln) $254

A Kellogg wall telephone with desk, American. (Auction Team Köln)

$181

A German ZB SA 25 'cow-hoof' desk telephone by Merk Telefonbau, Munich, circa 1930. (Auction Team Köln)

$1,540

An L.M. Ericsson skeleton telephone, with plastic flex. (Auction Team Köln)

$1,078

A Norwegian luxury cast iron wall telephone, with tin casing, by the Aktieselskabet Elektrisk Bureau, Kristiania, circa 1895. (Auction Team Köln)

$2,159

An L.M. Ericsson, Stockholm skeleton telephone, with original flex, circa 1910. (Auction Team Köln)

$1,001

A German M-89 wall extension by Krüger, Berlin, with receiver by Siemens & Halske, circa 1890. (Auction Team Köln)

$4,625

A Russian TA-57 bakelite field telephone, circa 1970. (Auction Team Köln)

$154

S & H wooden Bell telephone receiver, circa 1890. (Auction Team Köln)

$1,232

A Mix & Genest switchboard with plugs and metal receiver, 1918. (Auction Team Köln)

$1,386

A Philips bakelite television, 1954.
(Auction Team Köln)　$423

TV Trainer, a didactic television set with pictures and correction buttons, circa 1960.
(Auction Team Köln)　$231

A General Electric television, circa 1948.
(Auction Team Köln)　$122

An RCA Victor 8-TK-29 standard TV receiver, in wooden casing, round tubes.
(Auction Team Köln)　$423

A radiogram television incorporating Baird Televisor with disk and valve in upper two tiers, the base containing speaker, electric turntable and pick-up in drawer, 54in. high.
(Christie's)　$3,500

An Ekcovision TX275, the first portable television, convertible to 12 volt batteries, circa 1955.
(Auction Team Köln)　$65

An English Ekco T.S.C. 48 mirror television, 1948.
(Auction Team Köln)　$524

A Bush 62 bakelite 36-tube television, circa 1953.
(Auction Team Köln)　$214

An HMV Model 900 horizontal mirror television, circa 1937.
(Auction Team Köln)
$3,391

An Italian terracotta bust of a man, with shortly cropped hair, raised on a wooden square plinth, circa 1900, 43cm. high.
(Phillips) $395

A terracotta figure of a gnome, modeled lying to one side, stamped on the underside *J M O*, 28¹/₂in. long.
(Christie's) $1,640

An Etruscan hollow terracotta head of a youth with prominent ears and short hair, the eyes incised, 4th-3rd century B.C., 11in. high.
(Bonhams) $780

A terracotta bust of Tsar Alexander II, signed *Romuald Giedroyc*, circa 1870, wearing the service cap and winter coat of the Chevalier Gardes regiment, 18⁷/₈in. high.
(Christie's) $5,279

A terracotta tile with Daniel in the lions' den, North Africa, 5th-6th century, tooled with the prophet Daniel standing between two sleeping lions, 10¹/₄in. x 7¹/₈in.
(Christie's) $1,055

A white glazed terracotta relief of the Madonna and Child, in the manner of the della Robbia workshop, molded in half-length, 27¹/₄in. high.
(Sotheby's) $2,185

A Continental terracotta bust of General von Steuben, 18th century, wearing a wig tied en queue and with lace cravat, 26¹/₂in. high.
(Sotheby's) $3,450

A circular terracotta antefix with the facing head of Medusa, snakes surround her face, 4th-3rd century B.C., 9in. diameter.
(Bonhams) $1,200

A French terracotta bust probably representing Louis XV, wearing a wig tied en queue, inscribed with date *1739*, 16¹/₄in. high.
(Sotheby's) $1,150

An embroidered woolwork picture of a peacock and a parakeet perched on an urn filled with fruit and flowers, 30 x 28in., mid 19th century.
(Christie's) $329

A woolwork purse, worked in cross stitch, one side with a naval figure, the other with a crown, both within decorative borders, 4¹/₂ x 5in., circa 1850.
(Christie's) $68

18th century framed needlework Mandarin square with k'ossu peacock and sun above curling waves, 12in. square.
(Eldreds) $137

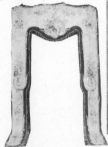

An Aubusson shaped portière woven in shades of red, blue and green wools, the top with roses and other flowers in an urn, 84 x 118in., French, 19th century.
(Christie's) $2,942

Two embellished prints, one depicting Christ meeting the woman of Samaria, the other, Christ blessing little children, 15 x 12in., framed and glazed, late 19th century.
(Christie's) $485

A needlework picture of colored wools with silk thread highlights, depicting a gentleman greeting a lady and her page-boy, 16 x 16½in., early 18th century, possibly American.
(Christie's) $1,040

A crewelwork curtain hanging, embroidered in muted colors with the Tree of Life, with parrots and other birds, 60 x 80in., late 19th/early 20th century.
(Christie's) $640

A circular cover of fine muslin, worked in whitework embroidery to resemble an open fan, with ladies and gentlemen in 18th century dress, circa 1900, 30in. diam.
(Christie's) $485

A silk gauze shawl, the ivory ground printed with a floral border, possibly Towler & Campin, Norwich, 1840s, 66 x 62in.
(Christie's) $346

English needlework dummy board, 18th century, depicting a nattily dressed gentleman, in multicolored stitches.
(Skinner) $2,300

Two of a set of five hand-painted velvet cushions, the cream ground with a large sinuous flower stem in shades of brown and gray, designed by John Fowler, 23in. square, 1950s.
(Christie's) $1,856

A William Morris curtain woven in dark and pale green and ocher with the 'Ispahan' design, 48 x 86in., circa 1888.
(Christie's) $729

A rare canvas-work chimney piece, by schoolgirl Hannah Otis (1732–1801), Boston, circa 1750, executed in wool, silk, metallic threads and beads on linen with a view of Beacon Hill, the 1737 Hancock House, Boston Common, Thomas and Lydia Henchman Hancock and John Hancock, 24½ x 52¼in. (Sotheby's) $1,157,500

Sarouk carpet fragments made into a pillow, West Persia, early 20th century, overall Herati design on the navy blue field, 2ft. 4in. x 2ft. 4in.
(Skinner) $258

A wedding veil, of Carrickmacross guipure, mid 19th century.
(Christie's) $1,012

A 19th century needlework picture, worked with a lady and three children tying a garland of flowers around the neck of a statue of a lion, 15½ x 11in.
(Phillips) $238

A tinned sheet metal candlemold, possibly Pennsylvania, 19th century, the rectangular dished top centering thirty-two cylindrical taper molds.
(Christie's) **$805**

A Directoire scarlet-painted and parcel-gilt toleware serving table, first half 19th century, the oblong octagonal tray with canted gallery, 24½in. long.
(Sotheby's) **$4,887**

A tinned sheet metal and wood squirrel cage, American, 19th century, featuring a punch-decorated house with functional swinging door and sliding tray, 12in. high.
(Christie's) **$1,955**

A tinned sheet metal wrigglework coffee pot, stamped *W. Shade*, working 1842–1866, Pennsylvania, the circular domed hinged lid centering a brass button finial above a molded neck, 11½in. high.
(Christie's) **$36,800**

A rare red-painted tinware cookie box, Pennsylvania, circa 1825, the front painted in yellow and green with paired 'love birds', 8¾in. high.
(Sotheby's) **$23,000**

A black-painted and decorated toleware 'lighthouse' coffeepot, Pennsylvania, 19th century, yellow-painted leaf decoration on a black ground above a flaring cylindrical body, 10¾in. high.
(Christie's) **$5,750**

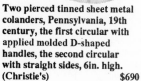

Two pierced tinned sheet metal colanders, Pennsylvania, 19th century, the first circular with applied molded D-shaped handles, the second circular with straight sides, 6in. high.
(Christie's) **$690**

A tinned sheet metal cookie cutter, Pennsylvania, 19th century, in the form of a standing Indian brave, with feather in hair, 9¼in. long.
(Christie's) **$920**

A painted and decorated toleware bread basket, Pennsylvania, 19th century, black-painted interior with symmetric yellow flowers at either side, 12¾in. wide.
(Christie's) **$978**

A black-painted and parcel-gilt tôle jardinière, with pierced gallery and acanthus-wrapped swans' heads above an ovoid-shaped body, 15in. wide.
(Christie's) **$1,671**

A painted and decorated toleware tray, Pennsylvania, 1820–1840, with canted corners centering a comforming crystalline interior surrounded by meandering tulips and leaves, 12¼in. wide.
(Christie's) **$575**

A red-painted and decorated toleware 'lighthouse' coffeepot, Pennsylvania, 19th century, yellow painted leaf decoration on a red ground, 11in. high.
(Christie's) **$9,775**

A tinned sheet metal candlemold, stamped *J. Ketterer*, active circa 1843–1864, Pennsylvania, circa 1860, rectangular rolled top centring eight tapering cylindrical molds, 11¼in. high.
(Christie's) **$4,025**

A wood and tinned sheet metal candlemold, made by I. Walker, Livonia, New York, 19th century, the rectangular open top with applied molding, 12¼in. high.
(Christie's) **$2,760**

A tinned sheet metal circular candlemold, probably Pennsylvania, 19th century, the circular mold centering twelve cylindrical taper molds, all on a conforming base.
(Christie's) **$863**

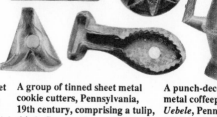

A punch-decorated tinned sheet metal coffeepot, Pennsylvania, 19th century, with circular domed lid centering button finial enclosed by a chased sawtooth surround, 11⅝in. high.
(Christie's) **$748**

A group of tinned sheet metal cookie cutters, Pennsylvania, 19th century, comprising a tulip, thistle-flower, a horse and an eight pointed star, the largest 5¾in. long.
(Christie's) **$748**

A punch-decorated tinned sheet metal coffeepot, stamped *M. Uebele*, Pennsylvania, circa 1848, the body punch-decorated with tulip baskets and geometric forms, 11⅝in. high.
(Christie's) **$5,520**

A Universal E 945 toaster, with large warming rack, circa 1920. (Auction Team Köln) $269

A hand-forged early toaster for an open fire, circa 1830. (Auction Team Köln) $214

A Swedish Volta toaster with original flex and ceramic plugs. (Auction Team Köln) $498

A Gold Seal toaster by the Gold Seal Electric Co., Cleveland, with unusual horizontal side turner, circa 1925. (Auction Team Kiln) $308

A Toastrite Blue Willow luxury American ceramic toaster, prototype, thus without electric connection. (Auction Team Köln) $1,694

An early Hotpoint 114 T 5 two-slice toaster with folding mechanism, by the Edison Electric Appliance Co, New York. (Auction Team Köln) $154

An American Torrid 2-slice toaster with swivel mechanism, 1927. (Auction Team Köln) $130

A General Electric D-12 early porcelain toaster. (Auction Team Köln) $362

A Simplex T-211 very early toaster on enamel base, American, 1909. (Auction Team Köln) $142

A Universal E 9410 push button toaster, circa 1929.
(Auction Team Köln) $616

An unusual, small, Marshmallow one-slice toaster by the Angelus Campfire Bar-B-Q.
(Auction Team Köln) $293

A French Art Deco Elic aluminium toaster, circa 1925.
(Auction Team Köln) $154

An early toaster with unusual heating coil between metal plates, possibly a prototype, circa 1920.
(Auction Team Köln) $577

An American Toastrite ceramic toaster by Pan Electric Mfg. Co., Ohio.
(Auction Team Köln) $1,155

A Universal E 9422 decorative one-slice toaster, by Landers, Frary and Clark, New Britain, CT, chromed brass with bakelite handle.
(Auction Team Köln) $154

An unusual Universal Model E 9950 American toaster.
(Auction Team Köln) $68

An Excelsior Twin Reversible American swivel handle toaster, circa 1920.
(Auction Team Köln) $616

A Saluta No 584 4-slice toaster with turning facility, red feet and handle.
(Auction Team Köln) $121

A French tinplate Vespa motor scooter wind-up toy, by La Hotte, St. Nicholas, 19 cm. long. (Auction Team Köln) $288

A German Bavaria Sepp (KOM) pencil sharpening machine, circa 1955, 10 cm. high. (Auction Team Köln) $308

A lithographed tinplate high-wire cyclist, circa 1905. (Auction Team Köln) $400

A Howdy-Doody Western puppet, Buffalo Bob Smith, with moving mouth, by Goldberger Doll Mfg. Co., Brooklyn, 33cm. high (Auction Team Köln) $38

Japanese battery powered tinplate telephone switchboard by Linemar, with flashing lights as telephonist inserts plug. (Auction Team Köln) $423

A Japanese Ishida Answer-Game calculating machine in the form of a tinplate robot, battery powered, circa 1963. (Auction Team Köln) $1,078

A Zilotone mechanical toy xylophone, playing 'My Old Kentucky Home', American, 1930. (Auction Team Köln) $616

A toy figure of a cow, suede leather covered and wearing a cowbell, the head articulated and 'mooing' when moved, 13in. high, early 20th century. (Neales) $470

The Skating Chef, a wind-up mechanical toy by TPS Toplay, Tokyo, circa 1958, 16 cm. high. (Auction Team Köln) $246

Lehmann performing sealion tinplate toy, circa 1900, 18 cm. long.
(Auction Team Köln) $207

Japanese Monkey on a Motorbike tinplate toy by Asahi Toy Co., Tokyo, with horn, circa 1958, 23 cm. long.
(Auction Team Köln) $308

Gertie The Galloping Goose, an American tinplate wind-up toy which runs and pecks, circa 1930, 23.5 cm. long.
(Auction Team Köln) $184

A monkey in flying suit model by Progressive Art Productions, 1972, 38 cm. high.
(Auction Team Köln) $99

Le Petit Livreur, a Martin tinplate wind-up toy, the spring mechanism driving boy's legs and shoulders and thus turning the trolley wheels, 1911, boxed.
(Auction Team Köln)
                             $2,697

Tinplate carousel toy with turning platform and movable horses, circa 1900, 28 cm. high.
(Auction Team Köln) $577

Japanese tinplate Rock 'n' Roll Monkey, plays guitar, nods head and taps foot, circa 1955, 28 cm. high.
(Auction Team Köln) $462

An English Meccano tinplate signal box, 16.5 x 9 x 16 cm.
(Auction Team Köln) $102

Marx tinplate wind-up toy, Joe Penner and His Duck, walks along, holds out cigar and raises his hat, circa 1935.
(Auction Team Köln) $693

A Bing style tinplate steam powered 'Spider', modern, reservoir and spirit burner to the rear linked to single cylinder below, 9¹/₂in. long.
(Sotheby's)   **$1,817**

A Kosuge 'Action Planet Robot', Japanese, 1960–65, the clockwork toy finished in black with red plastic 'hands', in original box, 9in. high.
(Sotheby's)   **$635**

A Carette tinplate hand-painted clockwork landaulette, German, circa 1910, with one side lamp, one headlamp, opening passenger doors, 15³/₄in. long.
(Sotheby's)   **$15,990**

A Dinky 918 'Ever Ready' Guy van, English, 1955–1958, the 2nd type cab-body finished in blue, with Ever Ready logo and red grooved wheels, boxed.
(Bonhams)   **$249**

A Tipp & Co. tinplate clockwork ladder fire engine, German, circa 1930, lithographed in red with yellow lining, four firemen, bell, overhead extension ladder, 9in. long.
(Sotheby's)   **$945**

A Distler tinplate limousine, German, 1920s, lithographed in orange with green lining and black molded grill, and chauffeur, with wind-up mechanism, 6¹/₂in. long.
(Bonhams)   **$512**

A large display nanny goat, with white and brown plush, dark brown and black plastic eyes set in brown leather eye lids, 42in. tall, 1950s/60s.
(Christie's)   **$143**

A Caremeccanotte tinplate landaulette, German, circa 1910, hand-painted in dark maroon lined orange, with red lined beveled glass windows, 12¹/₂in. long.
(Sotheby's)   **$7,631**

A battery operated Horikawa tinplate 'Gear Robot', Japanese, circa 1960, finished in grey with red tipped antennae, eyes and feet, 12³/₄in. high.
(Sotheby's)   **$654**

A Steiff 'Tige' Boston bull-terrier, with brown rough plush, large black boot button eyes, black stitched nose, button in ear, 13in. long, circa 1912. (Christie's) $322

A rare Dinky 514 'Weetabix' Guy van, English, 1952, the 1st type van finished in yellow with yellow ridged wheels, boxed. (Bonhams) $1,482

A brown and white velvet covered Steiff rabbit, with black bead eyes, original bell and ribbon, 3in. long, circa 1900. (Christie's) $315

A large Steiff Bully on wheels, with black and white mohair, original collar and bell, standing on all fours on four wheels joined by rods, 19in. long, circa 1930. (Christie's) $1,023

A Dinky 923 'Heinz' big Bedford van, English, 1955–1958, finish in red and yellow with Heinz 57 varieties and Baked Bean can logo, boxed. (Bonhams) $343

An Alps 71807 'Cragstan Great Astronaut' robot, Japanese, circa 1960, the battery operated toy lithographed and painted with red body and black arms, 12½in. high. (Sotheby's) $817

A Chad Valley Bonzo, with cream, beige and purple velvet covered body, and plastic dummy, 12in. tall, 1930s, and another, similar, 7in. tall. (Christie's) $1,364

A hand painted tinplate clockwork boy on a rocking horse novelty toy, German, circa 1905, the dappled animal jointed at top of legs, 7in. high. (Sotheby's) $872

'Felix the Cat', with short black mohair, white mohair muzzle, large black velvet button eyes backed on white velvet, 17in. tall, 1920s. (Christie's) $597

An early captive balloon basket, 72 x 36 x 53 cm.
(Auction Team Köln) $276

Crocodile skin suitcase, with six stud feet and solid metal handle.
(Auction Team Köln) $846

A wooden bound sheet iron travel trunk with brass reinforcement, lacking key, circa 1900, 67 x 40 x 48 cm.
(Auction Team Köln) $184

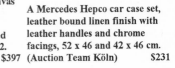

A hat box of brown leather, the lid monogrammed *C.P.*, the interior of the lid lined with quilted green satin, 17 x 10 x 14in., early 20th century.
(Christie's) $135

An Edwardian lady's morocco dressing case with outer canvas cover, the green silk lined interior fitted with silver mounted bright cut engraved accoutrements, London 1912.
(Dreweatt Neate) $397

A Mercedes Hepco car case set, leather bound linen finish with leather handles and chrome facings, 52 x 46 and 42 x 46 cm.
(Auction Team Köln) $231

A Louis Vuitton vanity case, covered in LV fabric and bound in brass, the interior fitted with a strap for holding bottles, 12 x 8¼ x 8in., with keys.
(Christie's) $1,163

Four leather and brass-bound trunks, three in green and one in black, decorated with studs and with side carrying handles, the largest, 36½in. wide.
(Christie's) $2,868

A Louis Vuitton trunk, covered in beige and red striped canvas and bound in leather and brass, circa 1880, 17 x 29½ x 20in.
(Christie's) $4,725

A handbag of brown crocodile leather, lined in brown suede, the interior with pockets and mirror, labeled *THE MARTIN MADE IN ENGLAND*, 14in. base.
(Christie's) $219

A top hat with leather case, circa 1900.
(Auction Team Köln) $130

A small crocodile leather doctor's case with brass locks, with label *Albert Rosenhain, Berlin SW Leipzigerstr. 72.*
(Auction Team Köln) $199

A dressing case of coffee colored leather, with foul weather case, lined in dark brown moiré, fitted with a mirror, stamped *The Goldsmiths & Silversmiths Company Ltd.*, 1930s, 18 x 13 x 6¹/₂in.
(Christie's) $421

A Louis Vuitton vanity case, covered in LV fabric and bound in brass, the interior fitted with straps for holding bottles, 16 x 9 x 8in., with keys.
(Christie's) $1,111

Brexton/Harrods picnic box, plastic dishes with two Thermos flasks, circa 1955.
(Auction Team Köln) $122

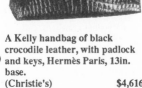

Picnic basket, empty, 45 x 35 x 20 cm.
(Auction Team Köln) $77

A Kelly handbag of black crocodile leather, with padlock and keys, Hermès Paris, 13in. base.
(Christie's) $4,616

An English leather hatbox, by Henry Heath, London, 44 cm. high.
(Auction Team Köln) $85

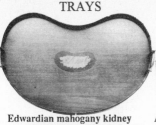

An oak table coaster of rectangular galleried form, the paneled field with gouged borders, English, 18th century.
(Christie's) $2,193

Edwardian mahogany kidney shaped twin handled tray, inlaid conch shell to center and checkered gallery, 22in. long.
(Peter Wilson) $151

An Edwardian oval mahogany and marquetry tea tray well-inlaid with bird at her nest, cast brass handles, 65cm. wide.
(Bristol) $304

Papier mâché two handled tray painted with a landscape of Windermere Lake from Low Wood Inn, 27cm. diameter.
(Peter Wilson) $195

Edwardian brass-mounted mahogany extending tray table, circa 1900–10, 30½in. long, closed.
(Skinner) $2,300

An Edwardian mahogany and inlaid kidney shaped tea tray with raised gallery and two brass handles, 69cm.
(Phillips) $350

A George III mahogany butler's tray, on later mahogany stand with channeled square legs joined by stretchers, 27½in. wide.
(Christie's) $948

A George III mahogany and marquetry tray on later supports, with undulating gallery and crossbanded in kingwood and satinwood, 69cm.
(Phillips) $1,934

A late 19th century chinoiserie decorated papier-mâché tray with scenes of courtiers on terraces, the faces and hands highlighted in 'ivory', 62cm.
(Phillips) $274

A Victorian black and gilt-japanned papier-mâché tray, with scalloped rim decorated around a bird's eye view of Tip Tree Farm, 25½in. wide.
(Christie's) $2,815

French painted tôle tray, mid 19th century, painted with a cupid in an oval reserve, bands of multi-colored floral sprays on the ground, 28½in. long.
(Skinner) $1,035

A yew-wood tray, the rectangular quarter-veneered surface with everted shaped edge with bowed handles, 22¾in. wide.
(Christie's) $1,703

Lula whisk, heavily patinated hardwood, Janus-headed with large topknot, geometric motifs, 9in. high.
(Butterfield & Butterfield)
$1,000

Asmat shield, rectangular form with mirrored meander with hooked ends, 68in. long.
(Butterfield & Butterfield)
$977

Zaramo ritual scepter, glossy brown patina on handle with geometric pattern of dots, metal blade, 19in. long
(Butterfield & Butterfield)
$1,500

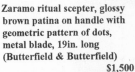

Senufo stringed instrument, Kora, resonator composed of halved gourd and hide diaphragm, rich dark patina from native handling, 29in. long.
(Butterfield & Butterfield)
$4,140

Kuba ceremonial skirt, woven raffia in dark brown and natural wheat color, embroidered motifs associated with the royal court, 16ft. x 2ft.
(Butterfield & Butterfield)
$3,000

Maori feather box, Waka-huia of reddish brown hardwood, body and lid covered with concentric semi-circles bisected by long inter-linked ovals, 18in. long.
(Butterfield & Butterfield)
$1,500

Yoruba Gelede headress, the head supporting a large round container with separately carved lid with arched handle, smiling features, 17in. high.
(Butterfield & Butterfield)
$402

Yoruba single male Ibeji, regional style of Ibadan pronounced buttocks, metal eyes, concentric scarification lines on face, 11½in. high.
(Butterfield & Butterfield)
$350

Ibibio mask, brown color with areas of black and traces of red, two side panels attached by leather thongs, 23in. wide.
(Butterfield & Butterfield)
$4,490

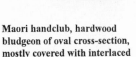

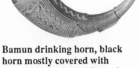

Maori handclub, hardwood bludgeon of oval cross-section, mostly covered with interlaced curvilinear motifs, 19½in. long.
(Butterfield & Butterfield)
$4,312

Bamun drinking horn, black horn mostly covered with geometric, zoomorphic, and anthropomorphic imagery in deep relief carving, 10in. long.
(Butterfield & Butterfield)
$1,955

Bobo mask, horizontal plaque of wings projecting from large face, the so-called 'Butterfly' Bougou Dinde, with concentric eyes, conical mouth, 54in. wide.
(Butterfield & Butterfield)
$12,000

Baule monkey figure, with thick, flaking sacrificial encrustation, standing on flexed knees, brown stain around waist, 21in. high.
(Butterfield & Butterfield)
$1,725

Akan pottery vessel, Abusua kuruwa, the sides ornamented with three half-figures arching backward to grasp rim, 10¹/₂in. high.
(Butterfield & Butterfield)
$1,150

Bangwa figure, standing on flexed legs, protruding abdomen with recessed navel containing magical substance, 34in. high.
(Butterfield & Butterfield)
$1,725

Maniema area face mask, possibly Kumu, brown with traces of red and white, round eyes and grinning mouth pierced with filed teeth, 13¹/₂in. high.
(Butterfield & Butterfield)
$1,610

Nayarit couple, circa 100 B.C.– 250 A.D., matched male and female, each seated and wearing large nose ring, clustered earrings and painted garments, 12in. high.
(Butterfield & Butterfield)
$1,495

Nayarit standing female figure, circa 100 B.C.–250 A.D., firmly positioned on oversized feet, thin arms held to abdomen, jutting jaw with open mouth, 23in. high.
(Butterfield & Butterfield)
$2,300

Veracruz standing figure, beige clay, wearing large bow under chin, headdress and costume of numerous flanges and roundels, 13¹/₂in. high.
(Butterfield & Butterfield)
$1,495

Mayan carved pottery bowl, circa 550–950 A.D., orangeware with red pigment remaining in recessed areas, two glyphic medallions carved in low relief, 5in. high.
(Butterfield & Butterfield)
$1,610

Jalisco pottery warrior with cudgel, circa 100 B.C.–250 A.D., seated, wearing barrel armor with triangular flap hanging down at back, 16in. high.
(Butterfield & Butterfield)
$1,035

Akan pottery effigy, seated male on legless chair with curved back and arms, in erect regal pose, 18in. high.
(Butterfield & Butterfield)
$632

Chinesco seated pottery figure, circa 100B.C.–250 A.D., a shirt or body-painting in red and black covering torso and arms, 18in. high.
(Butterfield & Butterfield)
$3,737

Ethiopian chair, scooped round seat on buttressed tripod legs, rectangular back with openwork triangles, 33in. high.
(Butterfield & Butterfield)
$1,495

Moche portrait head vessel, circa 400–700 A.D., painted red and cream, two large bird heads on one body form with headgear, 9¹/₂in. high.
(Butterfield & Butterfield)
$805

Nayarit couple, circa 100 B.C.– 250 A.D., matching male and female, each seated cross-legged with similar body and head type, wearing thick headband, clustered ear and nose rings, male 19¹/₂in. high.
(Butterfield & Butterfield)
$10,925

Baule Colonial style figure, painted black, playing a guitar, seated on small bench, wearing European style clothing, 14³/₄in. high.
(Butterfield & Butterfield)
$1,380

Nayarit seated female, circa 100 B.C.–250 A.D., legs curled under, wearing wrap-around skirt, holding bowl in left palm, 19¹/₂in. high.
(Butterfield & Butterfield)
$2,185

Colima dog with turtle shell, circa 100 B.C.–250 A.D., redware with black paint in geometric bands on shell, standing on four legs, 7¹/₄in. high.
(Butterfield & Butterfield)
$546

Widekum headcrest, a dark brown color, eyes cut out from tightly stretched hide cover, peg teeth, attached to basketry base, 10¹/₂in. high.
(Butterfield & Butterfield)
$575

A Mignon Model 3 German typecylinder pointer typewriter, 1913.
(Auction Team Köln)
$169

The Graphic, an early German pointer typewriter, with rubber typeplate, in original wooden case, 1895.
(Auction Team Köln)
$6,946

The New American Typewriter No 5 index typewriter, 1890.
(Auction Team Köln)
$1,309

An American Emerson No 3 typewriter with unusual transverse lever arrangement, 1907.
(Auction Team Köln)
$1,463

The first Swedish typewriter, the Sampo, in original tin casing, 1894.
(Auction Team Köln)
$4,625

An Odell No 4 decorative American pointer typewriter, in original wooden case, 1889.
(Auction Team Köln)
$2,157

A rare American Hartford No. 2 upstrike typewriter, with very deep type basket, 1896.
(Auction Team Köln)
$1,927

A decorative American Odell's pointer typewriter, 1889.
(Auction Team Köln)
$1,463

Salter's Standard No 6 lever typewriter with two columns on either side of the type basket, English, 1900.
(Auction Team Köln)
$998

An American Chicago cylinder typewriter with reverse upstrike, 1898. (Auction Team Köln) $1,540

An early American Columbia No 2 typewriter, with large type wheel for upper and lower case, the first machine with proportional type, 1884. (Auction Team Köln) $4,008

American Pittsburgh Visible No 10 lever typewriter, with tin casing, 1902. (Auction Team Köln) $1,078

A Williams No 1 American 3-row keyboard typewriter with independent 'Grasshopper' lever mechanism, in original wooden box, 1891. (Auction Team Köln) $2,158

A French Typo Visible typewriter with French Ideal keyboard and dual upper case mechanism, 1914. (Auction Team Köln) $462

The Fitch Typewriter, with the type bar behind the carriage for legibility, 1891. (Auction Team Köln) $15,402

A rare Densmore No 4 American upstrike machine, circa 1898. (Auction Team Köln) $616

The Liliput child's pointer typewriter, German, 1907. (Auction Team Köln) $4,008

A rare Munson American 3-row type cylinder typewriter, forerunner of the popular 'Chicago', 1890. (Auction Team Köln) $2,582

A molded and silvered zinc prancing horse weathervane, third quarter 19th century, the swell-bodied figure with sheet metal ears, and stylized leaf fitted between, 40½in. long. (Sotheby's)   **$9,200**

A fine molded copper horse and sulky weathervane, stamped *Harris & Co., Boston,* third quarter 19th century, the swell-bodied figure of a running horse pulling the full-bodied figure of a driver in a sulky, 34in. long. (Sotheby's)   **$6,900**

A molded copper and zinc leaping stag weathervane, American, third quarter 19th century, the swell-bodied figure of a stag with a molded cast-zinc head and antlers, 28½in. long. (Sotheby's)   **$6,325**

A molded and gilded copper bull weathervane, American, third quarter 19th century, the full-bodied figure of a bull covered in old weathered gilding, 24½in. long. (Sotheby's)   **$4,887**

Copper and zinc merino ram weathervane, America, 19th century, fine verdigris surface, (repaired bullet holes). (Skinner)   **$6,900**

A molded and gilded copper bull weathervane, American, third quarter 19th century, the swell-bodied figure with lead ears, 32½in. long. (Sotheby's)   **$5,462**

A carved and painted pine running horse weathervane, American, 19th century, the flattened horse with incised mane and tail detail, saddle, reins and hoofs painted black and silver, 37¼in. long.
(Sotheby's) $3,450

A molded and gilded copper and zinc eagle weathervane, attributed to A. L. Jewell & Co., Waltham, Massachusetts, third quarter 19th century, the swell-bodied eagle with outspread sheet-copper rings, 29in. high overall.
(Sotheby's) $12,650

A sheet iron rooster weathervane, Pennsylvania, 19th century, the silhouette form of a rooster with delineated crown and wattles, now on a plinth, 10¾in. high.
(Christie's) $1,955

A molded copper and zinc ram weathervane, American, third quarter 19th century, the swell-bodied figure with scrolled horns and a zinc head, 30in. long.
(Sotheby's) $10,925

Copper cow weathervane, America, early 20th century, (repaired bullet holes),lg. 28in.
(Skinner) $2,875

Gilt copper bull weathervane, America, 19th century, gilt and verdigris surface, 24in. long.
(Skinner) $2,070

Queen Anne, early 20th century, Hill, Thomson & Co. Ltd., Edinburgh, distilled, blended and bottled in Scotland. (Christie's) $383

Old Glen Grant, bottled by Trower & Sons, Glasgow and London, Shipper Since 1780, in original carton. (Christie's) $884

Whyte & MacKay's Special Selected, Double Lion brand Sole Proprietors, Whyte & MacKay, Glasgow. (Christie's) $412

Black & White Choice Old Scotch Whisky, circa 1940, James Buchanan & Co. Limited, Scotch Whisky Distillers, Glasgow and London. (Christie's) $206

Old Vatted Glenlivet Special Reserve, early 20th century, Andrew Usher & Co. London Export Offices, 59 Mark Lane, E.C., two-piece hand made bottle. (Christie's) $2,062

Old Orkney Real Liqueur, early 20th century, McConnell's Distillery Company, Proprietors Stromness Distillery, Orkney, Scotland. (Christie's) $2,356

The Old Blend White Horse, bottled 1952, White Horse Distillers Ltd., Lagavulin Distillery, Island of Islay, screw cap, embossed lead capsule. (Christie's) $177

Hedges & Butler VAT 250, circa 1940, specially vatted to commemorate 250 years establishment of the firm, AD 1667–AD 1917. (Christie's) $383

Long John's Celebrated Dew of Ben Nevis, 1882, Don. P. McDonald, Distiller, Fort William, hand blown bottle, driven cork. (Christie's) $2,062

Buchanan's Red Seal, early 20th century, James Buchanan & Co. Ltd., Distillers, Glasgow and London.
(Christie's) $471

Chivas Regal, 25-year-old, early 20th century, driven cork, lead capsule embossed *Chivas Regal, Aberdeen.*
(Christie's) $3,240

Mackintosh's Ginger Whisky, late 19th century, Mackintosh & Mackintosh, Scotch Whisky Blenders, Stirling.
(Christie's) $412

The Old Blend White Horse, bottled 1955, White Horse Distillers Ltd., Lagavulin Distillery, Island of Islay, screw cap, embossed lead capsule, level: high-fill.
(Christie's) $191

John Begg Liqueur Blended Scotch Whisky, circa 1940, imported by James M. McCunn & Co., Inc., 314 West 14th Street, New York, NY, blended, 86.8°.
(Christie's) $295

Watson's No. 10, circa 1919, James Watson & Co. Ltd., Dundee, strength 30 degrees under proof, maximum price 10/6 per bottle, J. W. & Co., Ltd.
(Christie's) $295

Imperial Federation Scotch Whisky, early 20th century, D. & G. McLaren Ltd., Leith, Sole Proprietors, hand blown bottle, driven cork.
(Christie's) $442

The Victoria Vat, circa 1940, John Dewar & Sons Ltd., Distillers, Perth, Scotland, in original cellophane wrapping and carton.
(Christie's) $265

Ginger Whisky, 20th century, Guaranteed by D. & J. MacEwan & Co. Ltd., Wine Merchants, 40 Port Street, Stirling.
(Christie's) $324

A Spanish gilt and painted wood figure of Saint Dominic, 16th century, with tonsured head and clad in full ecclesiastical garb, 55¹/₂in. wide.
(Sotheby's) $5,175

A pair of Thompson of Kilburn oak four branch five light candelabra, black painted wrought iron dished circular dip pans and scroll branches, fitted for electricity, 29in. high.
(Phillips) $486

Continental carved walnut figural group of a man and boy, 19th century, possibly depicting William Tell and his son, naturally carved, 23in. high.
(Skinner) $1,035

A South Netherlandish or Northern French gilt and painted wood bust of a crowned saint, early 16th century, carved with fancy coif, 17¹/₂in. high.
(Sotheby's) $6,325

Painted and gilt decorated tavern sign, New England, 1845, the molded frame enclosing the date 1845 with gilt eagle on each side, on black background, 43in. high.
(Skinner) $5,750

Carved and painted ship's figure head, America, 19th century, from the ship 'Pocahontas', 51in. high.
(Skinner) $2,300

A Bavarian gilt and painted wood figure of a putto, attributed to Joseph Götsch, circa 1762, the barely draped figure with his right arm upraised, 33¹/₂in. high.
(Sotheby's) $31,625

A pair of Italian gilt and painted wood figures of candlebearing angels, 16th century, each on bended knee and supporting a pricket candlestick in its hands, 24³/₈in. high.
(Sotheby's) $13,800

A Scandinavian burrwood tankard, the domed lid carved with a stylized lion and the date 1817, the scrolling handle surmounted by a recumbent stylized lion, 8½in. high.
(Hy. Duke & Son) $773

A Spanish gilt and painted wood bust of a gentleman, early 17th century, carved with beard and moustache, 17in.
(Sotheby's) $2,300

A pair of Spanish gilt and painted wood figures of angels, 17th century, each carved with curly hair and set with glass eyes, 19⁷/₈in. and 18¹/₄in. high.
(Sotheby's) $5,750

A Scandinavian burl wood tankard, 18th century, the lid carved with crowned lion and turned, 6⁵/₈in. high.
(Sotheby's) $1,265

A Swabian wood figure of a female saint, early 16th century, the crowned, standing figure carved with long hair falling in tresses over her shoulders, 39¹/₂in. high.
(Sotheby's) $4,600

Louis XVI style painted and parcel-gilt boiserie panel, dated *1913*, 40¹/₂ x 40in.
(Skinner) $3,220

Carved and painted bust of a Native American woman, Martha's Vineyard, 19th century, the hair painted black contrasts with the sand finished face and bust, 16in. high.
(Skinner) $1,265

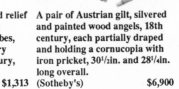

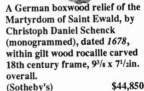

A North German boxwood relief of a kneeling female Saint swathed in diaphanous robes, possibly representing Mary Magdalen, 16th/17th century, 5¹/₄in. high.
(Hy. Duke & Son) $1,313

A pair of Austrian gilt, silvered and painted wood angels, 18th century, each partially draped and holding a cornucopia with iron pricket, 30¹/₂in. and 28¹/₄in. long overall.
(Sotheby's) $6,900

A German boxwood relief of the Martyrdom of Saint Ewald, by Christoph Daniel Schenck (monogrammed), dated *1678*, within gilt wood rocaille carved 18th century frame, 9³/₈ x 7¹/₂in. overall.
(Sotheby's) $44,850

Pair of South German carved walnut wall plaques, 20th century, each depicting dead game on a shaped plaque carved with leaves, 35in. high.
(Skinner) $2,070

Miniature canvas back hen and drake, A. Elmer Crowell (1862–1952), East Harwich, Massachusetts, circular stamp, 2¼ to 3in. high.
(Skinner) $1,150

Grain painted doll's cradle, America, 19th century, 17½in. long.
(Skinner) $230

A carved and painted rooster, attributed to the 'Deco-Tex carver', Southeastern Pennsylvania, late 19th/early 20th century, the full bodied stylized figure with yellow body with green highlights, 7in. high.
(Christie's) $25,300

A rare pair of George III hanging mahogany bird cages, with sliding seed, water and cleaning trays, on ivory bun feet, 26cm. high.
(Bearne's) $6,953

A carved and painted yellow warbler, 'Schtockschnitzler' Simmons, Pennsylvania, 1885–1910, the yellow painted body with olive wings and black highlights, 7½in. high.
(Christie's) $4,600

A South German wood figure of Saint Sebastian, circa 1500, carved with hands tied before him and a perizonium at the waist, 45¾in. high.
(Sotheby's) $1,955

A Georgian mahogany linen press, on turned and square supports surmounted knop finials, 18in. wide.
(Dee, Atkinson & Harrison)
                             $517

A carved and painted stylized rooster, Stephen Polaha, 1920–1977, with incised wings and polychrome decorated tail, 10¼in. high.
(Christie's) $4,600

Stained oak club fender with two upholstered seats divided by 'U' shaped gallery, circa 1900, 56in. wide.
(Peter Wilson) **$196**

An English painted oak relief of a ram, 19th century, perhaps originally a shop sign, 42 x 53in.
(Sotheby's) **$4,312**

A large ship's wheel, brass bound with eight turned spokes, circa 1910, 120 cm. diameter.
(Auction Team Köln) **$254**

A carved and painted yellow goldfinch, 'Schtockschnitzler' Simmons, Berks County, Pennsylvania, 1885–1910, the yellow painted goldfinch with black wings, crown and beak and articulated tail, $4^7/_8$in. high.
(Christie's) **$3,680**

A pair of Tirolean gilt and painted wood figures of angels, late 16th century, each carved with long, curly hair and crowned with a diadem, $16^3/_4$in. high.
(Sotheby's) **$13,800**

A carved and painted grinning tiger, Wilhelm Schimmel, 1817–1890, Carlisle, Cumberland County, Pennsylvania, 1865–1890, the full bodied figure with carved and black-painted details on a white painted ground, 6in. high.
(Christie's) **$55,200**

A carved and painted stylized rooster, Stephen Polaha, Pennsylvania, 1920–1977, with incised wing and tail with polychrome decorated tail, $12^3/_4$in. high.
(Christie's) **$1,725**

A pair of giltwood wall-lights, 20th century, each with circular backplate with central flowerhead, issuing stems of corn and foliage, 23in. high.
(Christie's) **$1,135**

A carved and painted stylized rooster, John Reber, 1857–1938, Pennsylvania, late 19th/early 20th century, with naturalistic feather decoration, red-painted crown and wattle, $7^1/_4$in. high.
(Christie's) **$4,830**

A carved and painted pine pineapple ornament, New England, possibly Rhode Island, early 19th century, carved in the half round, 10^1/$_2$in. high.
(Sotheby's) **$3,737**

A Swabian (Ulm) gilt and painted Lindenwood relief, late 15th century, originally from a predella, with all figures carved in half-length, 18 x 27in.
(Sotheby's) **$29,900**

Early 19th century lignum vitae tobacco jar, tapering cylindrical body with feather-like carving on a stepped ribbed foot.
(Peter Wilson) **$156**

A carved oak heraldic lion, heightened in gilt and red paint, shown crowned standant, on the crown of England, English, 17th century, 15in. high.
(Christie's) **$2,193**

A carved and painted pine American eagle, Wilhelm Schimmel, Cumberland Valley, Pennsylvania, circa 1860, the robust figure carved with spread wings, 22^3/$_4$in. long.
(Sotheby's) **$39,100**

American School, 20th century, Black Head, carved and painted wood, 12^1/$_2$ x 7^3/$_4$ x 7^1/$_4$in.
(Sotheby's) **$690**

A long-billed curlew, H. V. Shourds III, Seaville, New Jersey, the full-carved figure of solid construction with glass eyes, 18^1/$_4$in. long.
(Sotheby's) **$230**

A sycamore platter with single reeded ornament to the rim and depression, straight sided edge, English, possibly 17th century, 8½in. diameter.
(Christie's) **$370**

A French gothic oak framed door, late 15th century, fitted with three leaf-carved uprights above, the lower section fitted with linenfold panels, 72 x 28in.
(Sotheby's) **$2,645**

An artist's figure with an articulated wooden body, late 19th century, 21¼in. high. (Hy. Duke & Son) **$1,468**

A small carved walnut eagle-form finial, American, 19th century, carved in the half-round, 6¾in. high. (Sotheby's) **$632**

German Black Forest carved figural hall stand, late 19th century, 43½in. high. (Skinner) **$1,495**

A chip-carved pine tape loom, New England, late 18th/early 19th century, of arched rectangular form with a tapered neck pierced with a square, 26⅛in. high. (Sotheby's) **$5,750**

A pair of late 18th/early 19th century Italian later decorated blackamoors, crouching with inclined heads supporting scallop shells, 150cm. high. (Phillips) **$25,287**

A 19th century blackamoor stand, modeled as a Venetian gondolier, dressed in elaborate gilt costume and holding an oar, 42½in. high. (Andrew Hartley) **$4,030**

A carved and painted pine dummy board, probably English, late 17th/early 18th century, depicting a young girl seated in a chair, 25½in. high. (Sotheby's) **$9,200**

A painted and gilded pine eagle-form finial, 19th century, carved in the half round with wings spread and head turned to right, 12⅞in. long. (Sotheby's) **$2,587**

A carved and painted pine show figure, attributed to Samuel Robb, New York, third quarter 19th century, the figure holding a cluster of cigars, 23¾in. high. (Sotheby's) **$6,325**

A rosewood roulette wheel, by Harris & Co. of New York, complete with chips, rake and baize, 32in. diameter.
(Christie's) $1,548

A set of three George III mahogany plate-stands, the rectangular plinth with molded edge with sunk turned shafts flanking the rectangular upright, 16in. and 12¼in. high.
(Christie's) $11,287

A parcel-gilt polychrome carved wooden bust of St. John the Evangelist, Italian, 16th century, with a parcel gilt stand, 13½in. high.
(Christie's) $4,777

A parcel-gilt polychrome carved wooden reliquary bust of a male saint, Italian, 18th century, 19½in. high.
(Christie's) $1,592

A pair of polychrome carved wooden putti, South German, late 17th century, 25¾in. and 28½in. high.
(Christie's) $15,925

A pair of George III parcel-gilt rolled paper coasters, one with later glass liner, 5in. diameter.
(Christie's) $1,019

A North Carolina swan, the full-carved figure of solid construction with tack eyes and carved bill detail, 31in. long.
(Sotheby's) $3,450

Carved and painted wood harness maker's model horse, late 19th century, the standing figure spot painted white and gray, 7ft. 2in. high.
(Butterfield & Butterfield)
                               $4,887

A carved wood polychrome bust of a lady, modeled with hair tied, wearing a gilt heightened costume, 19th century, 13in. high overall.
(Christie's) $380